Thomas J. Braga

THE SCHOCKEN BOOK OF MODERN SEPHARDIC LITERATURE

Also by Ilan Stavans

Fiction

The One-Handed Pianist and Other Stories

Nonfiction

On Borrowed Words
Spanglish
The Inveterate Dreamer
Octavio Paz: A Meditation
Bandido
The Riddle of Cantinflas
The Hispanic Condition
Art and Anger
¡Lotería! (*with Teresa Villegas*)

Anthologies

The Scroll and the Cross
The Oxford Book of Jewish Stories
Mutual Impressions
The Oxford Book of Latin American Essays
Tropical Synagogues
Growing Up Latino (*with Harold Augenbraum*)
Wáchale!

Cartoons

Latino USA (*with Lalo López Alcaráz*)

Translation

Sentimental Songs, *by Felipe Alfau*

Editions

The Poetry of Pablo Neruda
The Collected Stories of Calvert Casey
Isaac Bashevis Singer: Collected Stories (*3 volumes*)

General

The Essential Ilan Stavans
Ilan Stavans: Eight Conversations, *by Neal Sokol*

THE SCHOCKEN BOOK OF MODERN SEPHARDIC LITERATURE

Edited and with an introduction by
Ilan Stavans

SCHOCKEN BOOKS, NEW YORK

 Published in the United States by Schocken Books, a division of Random House, Inc., New York, and simultaneously in Canada by Random House of Canada Limited, Toronto. Distributed by Pantheon Books, a division of Random House, Inc., New York.

Library of Congress Cataloging-in-Publication Data

The Schocken book of modern Sephardic literature / edited and with an introduction by Ilan Stavans.

p. cm.

Includes bibliographical references.

ISBN 0-8052-4228-7

1. Sephardic authors—Literary collections. 2. Sephardim—Social life and customs—19th century. 3. Sephardim—Social life and customs—20th century. I. Stavans, Ilan.

PN6067.S35 2005

808.8'9892—dc22 2004052500

www.schocken.com

Book design by Virginia Tan

Printed in the United States of America

First Edition

2 4 6 8 9 7 5 3 1

This volume was made possible, in part, thanks to a generous grant from the Lucius N. Littauer Foundation.

You are not obligated to complete work
but neither are you free to abandon it.

—Rabbi Tarfon

Contents

Preface

OVER THE YEARS I've devoted a substantial amount of energy to the study of Jewish literature in the Hispanic world. This resulted in the publication of several anthologies, such as *Tropical Synagogues, The Scroll and the Cross,* and, to some extent, *The Oxford Book of Jewish Stories,* released between 1994 and 2003. It was also the catalyst for my involvement in the series Jewish Latin America, published by the University of New Mexico Press. My ongoing interest in the subject has pushed me in various directions, the most important of which is unquestionably the polyglot, multinational Sephardic tradition—from the expulsion of the Jewish community from the Iberian Peninsula in 1492 to the present time.

The composite picture, I've come to recognize, is nothing short of astonishing. As a result of a series of historical and demographic forces, contemporary Jewish identity is largely perceived as an Ashkenazic monolith. This monolith is particularly present in the United States and in Israel and has caused an eclipse of Sephardic roots and rituals, at least from mainstream culture. The canonized Jewish literary tradition has eastern Europe as its foundation and Yiddish as its mother tongue, at the expense of the artistic outpouring from Sephardic Jews throughout the world, especially from the former Ottoman Empire. A correction to this imbalance is unlikely to happen overnight, of course, but there are indications that, as a result of immigration and a new emphasis on multiculturalism, Ashkenazic cultural hegemony is starting to weaken.

The Schocken Book of Modern Sephardic Literature is meant to offer a sampling of this rich tradition. The term "modern" is to be understood within the context of the Age of Enlightenment, which began in the late eighteenth century at the onset of the French Revolution, an era that saw the end of the absolute monarchy and the flowering of the rights of the individual. In Jewish historiography, the slow transition from a segregated ghetto existence to the Mendelssohnian concept of "civil participation," in which Jews were permitted to become full-fledged citizens of many western European countries, is known as the *Haskalah*. Ashkenazic and Sephardic paths to modernity might parallel one another but they do not always correspond. In the nineteenth century, the vast majority of Sephardim, located in the Ottoman Empire and North Africa, did not experience dramatic changes in their traditional way of life, but they were nonetheless living in "modern" times.

This anthology doesn't include Medieval and Renaissance authors; nor does it represent the vivid literature produced by *conversos,* Jews who converted to Christianity and no longer identified themselves as Jews. I've left out homiletic and philosophical treatises such as *The Zohar,* the work of Isaac Luria in Safed, and *Me'am Lo'ez.* I've also omitted travel chronicles, such as the works by thirteenth-century Benjamin of Tudela. My genealogy is solely devoted to modern Jewish authors who, although they might be the result of mixed marriages (Jew and Gentile, Ashkenazic and Sephardic), define themselves as Sephardim. I start with the Victorian era in England and the Second Republic in France and end in present-day Israel and the United States. In selecting the material, I sought to be global: More than two dozen authors from some twenty different nations are represented. They write in nine different languages, including Ladino.

Needless to say, *The Schocken Book of Modern Sephardic Literature* is but a modest harvest, an assortment chosen from hundreds of potential candidates. *Ni están todos los que son, ni son todos los que están*—not every one is here. Space and budgetary limitations also shaped the final product. Entries are organized sequentially by the author's date of birth. Each entry is preceded by a headnote placing the author and the work in historic and cultural context and, where relevant, noting the translator's name. This element is crucial, of course: the diasporic existence entails the acquisition of second, third, and fourth languages. But in whatever languages they may have originally been written, these selections come to us in English thanks to translators. To me the translators are as important as the authors themselves. I've carefully chosen the best translation available. Dates for titles listed in the headnotes are of the original publication, followed by the date of the English translation, unless the book or story isn't available in English. In the chronology, the strategy is different: given the historical reach of the section, dates for titles are given only for the original publication.

A word about the appendix: "The Other Jew." In 1994, when I edited *Tropical Synagogues,* I included a similar addendum containing three stories by the philo-Semite Argentine master Jorge Luis Borges. My purpose was to show the other side of the coin: how non-Jews graple with Jewish motifs. This material struck a chord. For a while I contemplated including in this anthology a segment of *The Storyteller,* by the Peruvian novelist Mario Vargas Llosa, about Saul Zuratas, an anthropology student in Lima who is also a Sephardic Jew. Zuratas is presented as somewhat of an allegorical figure: after a long internal struggle, he decides to abandon not only his studies but also his place in Western Civilization to become an integral part of the Machiguengas, an Indian tribe in Peru. Instead, for reasons at once emphatic and geographic, I opted for the Indian writer Salman Rushdie, who has been using Jewish themes in his work since his second novel, *Midnight's Children.* In essays and stories, Rushdie has explored the plight of those who left the Iberian Peninsula at the end of the fifteenth century. "Abraham Zogoiby" is taken from his novel *The Moor's Last Sight.* Readers will find within it echoes from a number of other entries in this anthology. Most of the material presented here is about Sephardim looking out into the world. The inclusion of Rushdie's luscious profile is designed as a mirror image: How does one view the Sephardic Jew, that is, the "other" Jew, from the outside looking in?

Introduction
Unity and Dispersion

"The Sephardic sensibility," states Abraham Joshua Heschel, theologian, existential philosopher, and civil rights activist, in an essay published in Germany in 1946, "is distinguished by a strict, logical orderliness . . . and stress[es] the elements Judaism has in common with the surrounding cultures, frequently overlooking its own specific, peculiar contributions. Often, the thinking is in a foreign pattern, endeavoring to compromise with the theories of the great thinkers; at times even an apologetic note is sounded."

In attempting to understand what makes the Sephardim tick, one often comes across extravagant, Manichaean statements such as these. In Heschel's mind were luminaries, such as Maimonides and Spinoza, stunning assemblers of and commentators on homiletic information, lucid thinkers whose use of the *more geometrico* reduces the universe to algebraic forces. Indeed, the subject of Heschel's doctoral dissertation was Maimonides, in whom he recognizes an extraordinary intellectual reach. But he was also disappointed with "the lack of passion, the absence of angst" in the oeuvre of the author of *Guide for the Perplexed*. Why, he wondered, didn't Maimonides share a bit of the to-be-or-not-to-be that defines Ashkenazic Jewishness?

That Heschel was infatuated, in a somewhat paternalistic fashion, with the people of Ashkenaz (Hebrew for "Germany"), as the Jewish communities in western, central, and eastern Europe have been referred to from the eleventh century to the present day, is no secret. An offspring of the post-Romantic movement and a pupil of the *Wissenschaft des Judentum* (he was born in Berlin in 1907, emigrated to the United States before World War II, taught at the Jewish Theological Seminary, and died in 1972), his infatuation was stoked by his environment. "A unique Jewish person evolved [in Ashkenaz]," Heschel stated, "whose habits and taste are not in accordance with the classical canon of beauty, but who nevertheless possess a specific charm. He is like a page in an open book, static in its own lines and in the proportion of text and margin . . . The charm derives from the [person's] inner richness, from the polarity of reason and feeling, of joy and sorrow."

That polarity, in his view, isn't part of the Sephardic experience. For Heschel the Sephardim are aristocrats. They don't find complete self-fulfillment in their Jewishness. And the fact that they wrote their classic works in languages such as Arabic, intelligible to a minuscule elite, was for him difficult to understand. It is as if Sholem Aleichem had opted for Russian to deliver his masterpiece, *Tevye the Dairyman*. In an essay, published in English several years after his death, Heschel gets into muddier waters when talking about Sephardic literature per se: "[It] is like classical architecture," he stated. Ashkenazic letters, in contrast, are "like a painting by Rembrandt, profound and full of mystery." He adds: "The former prefers the harmony of a system; the latter, the tension of dialectic. The former is sustained by a balanced solemnity; the latter, by impulsive inspiration. Frequently, in Ashkenazic literature, the form is shattered by the overflow of feeling, by passion of thought, and explosive ecstasy. Sephardic literature is like a cultivated park; Ashkenazic, like an ancient forest. The former is like a story with a beginning and an end; the latter has a beginning, but turns frequently into a tale without end. The Sephardim, interested in preserving the spiritual heritage, classify and synthesize the material that has accumulated in the course of the centuries."

Clearly, Heschel's approach to Sephardim is simplistic. It makes use of a hermeneutic technique of argumentation, propagated in the early twentieth century by Karl Popper, known for its use of "negative attributes." The Sephardim are everything that the Ashkenazim are not. The folklore and tradition of the descendants of the Jews expelled from the Iberian Peninsula in 1492 appear to him as unfamiliar, foreign, and bizarre. They are also superficial. Unfortunately, this approach isn't atypical. One stumbles upon manipulative appreciations such as these not only among Ashkenazim but also—frequently and at times even apologetically—among the Sephardim themselves, from the eighteenth century onward.

LET US NOW move away from this Manichaean paradigm and ponder the Sephardic tradition, specifically its literature, on its own terms—not as shadow but as light. The Hebrew term "Sephardim" (singular, "Sephardi") is used for descendants of Jews who lived on the Iberian Peninsula—in Spain and Portugal—before the expulsion. But this term has been misused in a number of ways. For example, the Jews of Djerba, Iraq, Yemen, and Iran, and the Romanoit Jews of Asia Minor are often described as Sephardic but in fact have unique histories of their own. To add to the confusion, as a way of proclaiming the complete absence of Ashkenazic blood in their veins, Sephardim exiled from the Iberian Peninsula began describing themselves as *Sephardi tahor* ("pure Sephardi"). More problematic is the exclusion from contemporary Sephardic history of accounts of Jewish life in Spain prior to the expulsion. Are the Iberian communities from 900 CE to 1492 not part of the same history? Is Sephardic life solely a litany of nostalgia for what has been lost, an impossible quest for *la España perdida,* the land of loss and the lost land?

The Sephardic condition is one of fracture and displacement. Obviously, these ingredients also characterize the last two thousand years of Jewish history as a whole, but the dispersion from the Iberian Peninsula is a particularly dense branch of it, with multiple ramifications. In Mexico, where I was born and came of age in the 1970s, a similar response came from my Sephardic acquaintances: Spain, rather than being *en el corazón*—in the heart, as Pablo Neruda once said—is simply a figment of historical imagination. In *The Pillar of Salt,* Albert Memmi chronicles his upbringing in the 1930s in Tunis in a way that virtually defines the Sephardic condition: "I am ill at ease in my own land and I know of no other," Memmi writes. "My culture is borrowed and I speak my mother tongue haltingly. I have neither religious beliefs nor tradition . . . To try to explain what I am, I would need an intelligent audience and much time. I am a Tunisian, but of French culture . . . I am Tunisian but Jewish, which means that I am politically and socially an outcast. I speak the language of the country with a particular accent and emotionally I have nothing in common with Muslims." To cure his divided heart, Memmi doesn't reach out for Spain as a panacea—the Iberian past is too remote, too severed from his personal experience. Instead, he looks toward French culture as a ticket to salvation.

Spain isn't the only cloudy source of identity among the Sephardim—a myth more than a reality. Historians Esther Benbassa and Aron Rodrigue, authors of *Sephardi Jewry: A History of the Judeo-Spanish Community, 14th to 20th Centuries,* describe the historiography of Sephardim as "so rife with myths that it is tempting to wonder whether they emerged to provide palliatives to the gloomy 'lachrymose' episodes in Jewish history." They continue: "These myths have various origins but end in throwing a halo of shadow around the Sephardim. First, there is the foundation myth that the Jews had a sort of right to the Iberian land . . . Then there is the myth which puts the number of expellees at the astronomical figure of 400,000, whereas recent estimates, erring on the other side, do not exceed 50,000 . . . And what is to be said of the famous myth of the Spanish 'Golden Age,' which certainly pleases everyone?" The expulsion was indeed a traumatic event but it didn't come without warning. In fact, the papal decree that established the Holy Office of the Inquisitions in Aragon was announced in 1238, and increasing anti-Semitic—anti-Jewish and anti-Muslim—outbursts over the next two hundred years certainly signaled what was to come. Forced conversion had been the law of the land during the century that preceded the expulsion. It resulted in a duplicity that marked Sephardic civilization forever: a self at home, another in public. The age of *conversos* was thus established, coinciding with the colonial enterprise. Scores of so-called New Christians traveled across the Atlantic Ocean in search of refuge from the Inquisition, only to find an almost equally oppressive atmosphere on the other side. Some Sephardim did manage to survive in the Caribbean basin, in Brazil, and in other South American countries. A handful eventually moved north, and in the fall of 1654 twenty-three Dutch Sephardic Jews from Brazil arrived in New Amsterdam, thereby founding the Jewish community in what later came to be known as New York.

Sephardic identity, then, is a hall of mirrors. In retrospect, it might be said that the millennial Sephardic journey, from the first settlements on the Iberian Peninsula between 200 BCE and 200 CE, to the expulsion in 1492 and on to five hundred years of wanderings, is marked by a movement toward attrition, which then reverses its course, becoming centrifugal, ultimately exploding in multiple directions. The result is families that within the span of three to four generations found themselves agonizingly disjointed. Edmond Jabès, the Egyptian-born French philosopher, writes in *Return to the Book* of one such family: his own. He discusses the disintegration as a form of death, at once concrete and symbolic. Nowhere is this fragmentation clearer than in the assorted sites where Jabès's relatives are buried. "In the cemetery of Bagneaux, department of the Siene, rests my mother," he writes. "In Old Cairo, in the cemetery of sand, my father. In Milano, in the dead marble city, my sister is buried. In Rome where the dark dug out of the ground to receive him, my brother lies. Four graves. Three countries. Does death know borders? One family. Two continents. Four cities. One language: of nothingness. One pain. Four glances in one. Four lives."

DEMOGRAPHIC NUMBERS might be valuable to the reader at this point. Throughout the Middle Ages and the early Renaissance, the Sephardim comprised the majority of the Jewish people worldwide. According to Jane S. Gerber, author of *The Jews of Spain,* they constituted approximately 90 percent of the total Jewish population by the twelfth century. That percentage changed dramatically after the expulsion, and by 1700 the Jewish people were 50 percent Sephardic and 50 percent Ashkenazic. Sephardic continuity and survival was in peril. As the Ashkenazic community began to grow in Europe, life for the Sephardim in North Africa and in the Levant, as well as in regions where the Inquisition had been established, became extremely difficult. By 1930, of a total of sixteen million Jews worldwide, only 10 percent (some 1.5 million) were Sephardim, the majority of whom were to be found in the Middle East.

In *Sephardi Jewry,* Benbassa and Rodrigue discuss the myth of the golden age of Spanish Jewry, also known as *La Convivencia,* which lasted only from the tenth through the twelfth centuries. Centuries after the Visigoth invasion and extending beyond the splendors of the Andalusian civilization the three religious groups—Christians, Jews, and Muslims—are said to have coexisted in relative harmony under Muslim rule. That is doubtlessly the epoch Heschel invokes in his essay. It was indeed an era of introspection and the quest for an inner life, and it isn't at all surprising that during this time the Iberian Peninsula became the fountainhead of Kabbalah. It was in Spain in the thirteenth century that Moses de León wrote *The Zohar,* the source text for much of the Kabbalah, publishing it as if it had been written by Simeon ben Yohai, a second-century Palestinian rabbi. *The Zohar* gave rise to a series of mystical schools that developed not only in Spain but also in France, Italy, and Palestine. Centuries later, this mystical approach became integral to the philosophy of the Baal Shem Tov, the eastern European founder of Hasidism. It was also in Spain during this period that the great Hebrew poets Samuel ha-Nagid (vizier to the King of Granada), Solomon ibn Gabirol, Judah Halevi, and Moses ibn Ezra, modeling their style on the Arabic *piyyut* (with its Greek root, "poetry"), heralded an age of reflective verse. The magisterial moralistic and philosophical oeuvre of Maimonides (author of *Mishneh Torah, Commentary on the Mishneh,* and *Guide for the Perplexed*) defined the period through solidly argued rational argumentation. Maimonides and other thinkers such as Ibn Gabirol, Nahmanides, Halevi, and Hasdai Crescas paved the way, as Heschel understood, for the seismic philosophical revolution of Baruch Spinoza, who, along with René Descartes, inaugurated modern thought.

But despite common assumptions, *la Convivencia* was far less harmonious than is often acknowledged. It is true that after the conquest of

Granada by the Muslim Almoravids in 1090, the three religious groups engaged in dialogue. Nevertheless, the interruptions were abundant. The reverberations from the First and Second Crusades, which occurred between 1096 and 1147, pushed Spanish Christians into an antagonistic position vis-à-vis the various Muslim factions. The direct impact of the Crusades on Spain was minimal. Still, one reaction was that during the twelfth century the Muslim Almohads intensified their persecution of Jews, Christians, and lax Muslims. And in 1238 the papal Inquisition was established in Aragón, inaugurating an era of fear among the non-Christian population. In 1248, Ferdinand III of Castile captured Seville from the Muslims, which represented a major advance for *La Reconquista,* the "return" of Christian land from Muslim hands, which began in the eleventh century with the recovery of the flatlands of Castile and upper Aragón. Rather than being harmonious, the era is quite discordant. Poetry and philosophy flourished, but so did theological disputations, like the famously acrimonious one in Barcelona in 1263 between Nahmanides and the convert Pablo Christiani.

Then came the expulsion of the Jews from England and France in 1299 and 1309, respectively. By the end of the fourteenth century, Christian mobs attacked Jews in Seville, killing hundreds and forcing many more to convert. (The age of *conversos* officially began in 1391.) Similar riots took place in 1449 in Toledo, which was known as an intellectual center. Less than three decades later, the Catholic monarchs Ferdinand and Isabella established the Holy Office of the Inquisition throughout Spain. Its mission was to cleanse the land of converts who continued to practice Judaism in secret and who were known as *judaizantes,* or Judaizers. The first auto-da-fé, the public execution of *conversos,* occurred in Seville in 1481, approximately thirteen years before the final expulsion.

After the expulsion, Jews, crypto-Jews, and New Christians, *in fugae,* wandered from Portugal to the Netherlands, Italy, and other countries in southern Europe, as well as to the Americas and the territories of what would become, after the Ottoman conquest of Constantinople in 1453, the Ottoman Empire. Thus was created the Sephardic diaspora, which gave rise to a host of issues regarding national and cultural identity. How are Sephardic Jews to be defined henceforth? And under what category do *conversos* fall? Are crypto-Jews to be considered Sephardim? And what about New Christians who maintain their cultural identity even as they embrace a new religion? Are the popular *Dialoghi d'Amore* by Leone Ebreo, grandson of Abraham and son of Isaac Abravanel, and the plays of the Marrano poets of the seventeenth century, Daniel Leví de Barrios and

João Pinto Delgado, dealing with the search of spiritual fulfillment and with the treacherousness of identity, a continuation of the thread? And what to say of *Don Quixote* itself, the first modern novel and, according to some, the story of a soldier with Jewish blood, whose views of the Catholic Church denounce his ancestry, an argument that might be problematic, no doubt, but also denounces a certain *simpatía* for Cervantes as a voice of the oppressed? Not everyone believes in such a flexible definition of the Sephardic experience. In any case, after 1492 family lineage plays an even more important role in both Sephardic and Hispanic civilization, as the debate over *la honradez,* an insidious sense of authenticity, and *la limpieza de sangre,* purity of blood, are exacerbated.

THE *Encyclopaedia Judaica,* first published in the United States in 1971, ambitiously divides Sephardic literature into three categories, using linguistic and authorial tools: first come works written in Hebrew by scholars such as Isaac Abravanel, Joseph Caro, and Menashe ben Israel; then come works in Spanish, Portuguese, and Ladino (an unbalanced mixture of Spanish and Hebrew, also known as Judeo-Spanish and Judezmo, whose vocabulary and grammar are both more than 90 percent Spanish and, depending on location, may include a smattering of Arabic, Greek, Italian, or Bulgarian by writers such as Shem-Tov de Carrión, Samuel Usque, David Nieto, and Isaac Cardozo); and, finally, anonymous Ladino folk literature known collectively as *El Romancero.* The typology is ambitious but flawed. The *EJ* approaches Sephardic literature as that which has been created post-1492, which contradicts Heschel's opinion that works written pre-1492 are also part of the Sephardic experience and thus ought to be included in the canon. Another problem in the typology is the lack of connection between the works published in different languages in the second category: whereas works by Sephardic authors printed in Portuguese and Spanish were meant for a general audience, those in Ladino were exclusively targeted toward a Jewish readership versed in the jargon. This discrepancy is critical. It propelled authors to seek different narrative strategies.

Here a further comment about Ladino literature might be useful. Whereas Yiddish (literally, the word means "Jewish") was the primary—although obviously not the sole—conduit of Ashkenazic angst throughout Europe, Ladino, on occasion referred to as "the other Yiddish" and also as "the Yiddish of the Sephardim," was for the most part only a vehicle of communication for Jews in Spain. After the expulsion, it increased its reach and presence, but only for a while. For a variety of historical and linguistic reasons, Ladino failed to metamorphose itself into a literary language. For one thing, it was never used for intellectual discussion. Coloma Lleal, in a dissertation on Ladino published in 1992, talks about Ladino in *La Convivencia* and offers a mini-anthology of sources that includes this early Mozarabic *jarcha,* a medieval Ladino ballad. It's a lamentation for a beloved one—named Isaac, whose absence brings misery to the female narrator:

Gare, ¿sós debina
e debinas bi-l-haqq?
Garme quánd me bernad
meu habibi Ishac.

Des quand meu çidiello béned
tan bona albixara
como rayo de sol éxed
en Guadalhajara.

Garid bos, ay iermanellas,
com conteneré meu male,
sin el habib non bibreyo,
¿ad ob l' rey demandare?

Béned la Pasca adiún sin elle
lanzando meu corazón por elle.

Bayse meu corazón de mib.
Ya Rab, si se me tornarad.
Tan mal me doled li-l-habib.
Enfermo yed: ¿quánd sanarad?

¿Qué fare, mama?
Meu habib est ad yana.

After the expulsion, Lleal states, Ladino changed substantially as it became exposed to other languages in the diaspora and developed dialectal modalities. Since these variations affect modern Sephardic literature, it is important to discuss them here. Edouard Roditi, the Surrealist author of *Thrice Chosen,* argues in his essay "The Slow Agony of Judeo-

Spanish Literature," published in 1986, that, "as a literary language, Judeo-Spanish . . . has a distinguished past, but it has slowly been dying." Its troublesome present is the result of "a veritable brain drain," which has lasted, according to Roditi, almost a hundred years. He states: "Although publications are nowhere forbidden . . . problems of linguistic assimilation of potential Judeo-Spanish writers to their cultural environment and of the distribution of Judeo-Spanish publications throughout the widely scattered Sephardic diaspora discourage all but the most devotedly nostalgic writers from expressing themselves in this idiom, which seems destined to die out." In particular, there are two varieties and several subdivisions: the so-called Haketiya vernacular of the Spanish-speaking Jews of northern and coastal Morocco, and the Ladino and Judezmo of the Sephardic Jews of the former Ottoman Empire in Turkey, Greece, the Balkans, and other areas of the Near East. "In many ways," Roditi writes, "*Haketiya* remained for several centuries closer to the spoken Spanish of nearby Andalusia, though with more loanwords borrowed from colloquial Moroccan Arabic." On the other hand, the Judezmo spoken in the regions of the former Ottoman Empire gave way to subdialects. The Bosnian variant, for example, reflected a strong Portuguese and Gallegan influence and displayed in its vocabulary a Slavic element of Serbo-Croatian rather than Turkish origin. And then there are the dialects of Salonika and Adrianople, which remained for centuries more purely Spanish, although they incorporated words from Catalán and Portuguese, as well as from Turkish, Greek, Italian, and French. But with the arrival, in the early twentieth century, of French-language schools established by the Alliance Israélite Universelle, a major educational force in Sephardic communities was established. One of the results was that the multiple Judezmos ceased to be used in the written form, and, eventually, they also died out as forms of oral communication.

IN 1819 THE FIRST NOVEL written by an Ashkenazic Jew—Joseph Perl's *Revealer of Secrets*—was published, in Hebrew, in Galicia. This was about thirty years after the French Revolution, and during the time that the German philosopher Moses Mendelsshon, a contemporary of Kant, encouraged European Jews to abandon the ghetto and become full citizens of a society defined, at least on paper, by equality of civil right. The transformation wasn't automatic. For the Jewish communities in Europe, the late eighteenth century and most of the nineteenth century were marked by an incremental tension between rural and urban life and between religion and secularism. More tangibly, the Hasidic revolution, personified by its ecstatic leader, the Ba'al Shem-Tov, and his followers, was fought by the educated *Mitnagdim,* who believed that faith is a form of superstition. As Hasidism was becoming popular among the poorest segments of the Jewish population in eastern Europe, the first products of the *Haskalah* (as the Jewish Enlightenment is known), which demanded a more "scientific" approach to Jewish culture, also began to appear. Joseph Perl and his novel were primary examples. Writers who were part of the Jewish Enlightenment began to influence European Jewry after 1850. Indeed, S. Y. Abramovitch and other masters of Yiddish letters left their stamp as the century came to an end.

But the *Haskalah* was strictly speaking a European phenomenon. Sephardic Jews were only tangentially affected by it. The Ottoman Empire was defeated in World War I, and Turkey emerged as a republic in 1923. It was then that the Sephardic Jews of the Levant were, so to speak, "invited to the banquet of modern times." With various degrees of success Ladino presses sprung up in the mid-eighteenth century in Greece, Turkey, Bulgaria, Mexico, Argentina, and the Middle East. Aside from newspapers and journals, a number of plays, poetic cycles, novellas, and Midrashic narratives were published, at times anonymously or else under pseudonyms. Many authors focused their energy on poetry and fiction, attracting a small yet loyal readership. They include Ysaac Magriso, Yishac ben Micael Badhab, Abraham Galante, Isaac de Botton, Yacov Avraham Yona, Mois Najari, Rachael Castelete, and Clarisse Nicoïdski. But the success of the Ladino press never gave birth to a full-blown aesthetic movement, complete with a cadre of internationally renowned authors. During the 1920s, given the multiplicity of Ladino dialects and the increasing decline in readership, a switch was made from typography that used Hebraic characters to transliterations using Roman letters. In *And the World Stood Silent: Sephardic Poetry of the Holocaust,* a collection edited by Isaac Jack Lévy, virtually all of the selections were translated into English from Ladino originally written in the Roman alphabet.

I found it quite surprising that an important category of Sephardic literature was not discussed in the *Encyclopaedia Judaica.* Where are the scores of works written by Sephardim in languages other than Spanish, Portuguese, and Ladino? Where are the Sephardic authors who write in German, Italian, English, Turkish, Arabic, and Hebrew? Where would the *EJ* fit the poems of Emma Lazarus, the autobiographies of Primo Levi, and the novels by A. B. Yehoshua? A significant literary trend has developed from the mid-nineteenth century to the present day, one defined by its transnational nature and also by its polyglotism. Its practitioners are assimilated, secular Sephardic authors, middle- and upper-middle class Jews whose native tongues are European and Mediterranean languages. This literature is defined by its cosmopolitanism and by the need to explore, for a large audience, the tension between mainstream and minority cultures. As in the case of Ashkenazic novels and stories, this trend is derivative in nature—that is, imitative of Gentile models. One of its early practitioners, for example, is Grace Aguilar, who in 1843 wrote *The Perez Family,* one of the earliest English-Sephardic novels, categorized as such not only by the author's ancestry but by its theme, the depiction of Jewish life in Victorian England. Aguilar dreamt of producing a tale like Sir Walter Scott's *Ivanhoe,* only with a Jewish sensibility. Another founding mother was the American Emma Lazarus, who was affected as much by her country's civil war as by the Russian pogroms in the late nineteenth century. Her poem "The New Colossus" is engraved on a plaque hung on an inner wall of the pedestal at the base of the Statue of Liberty. It was written in 1883 in response to a request to aid in raising funds to create the pedestal. The sonnet was read at a fund-raising auction in December of that year and was engraved on the plaque in 1903. It is included in this anthology.

Lazarus perceived herself as a Sephardic Jew, but she didn't want to isolate herself from the contemporary American literary community. When her friend and mentor Ralph Waldo Emerson failed to include her poems in his anthology *Parnassus* (1874), which included works by prominent and promising national poets, Lazarus wrote him an angry letter. "I cannot resist the impulse of expressing to you my extreme disappointment at finding you have so far modified the enthusiastic estimate you held of my literary labors as to refuse me a place in the large & miscellaneous collection of poems you have just edited," she wrote. And so, she wondered why "I find myself treated with absolute contempt in the very quarter where I had been encouraged to build my fondest hopes." Her letter to Emerson might be read in at least two ways: as a woman's angry response to the "arbitrary" exclusion by a prominent male critic and essayist from "a fair share of immortality"; and as the response by a Jew, as a member of an ethnic and religious minority, who felt that she had been discriminated against.

It is interesting, therefore, to note that Lazarus sought to introduce American readers to figures such as Bar Kokhba, the Jewish soldier who led the final revolt against the Romans in Palestine in 132–35 CE, and to Rashi, the twelfth-century biblical and talmudic commentator from

Troyes, France. She also wrote a poem about the Touro Synagogue, the famous Sephardic house of worship that was established in Newport, Rhode Island, in 1763. In addition to translating into English the poetry of the popular German-Jewish poet Heinrich Heine, Lazarus also translated poems by Ibn Gabirol, Halevi, and Ibn Ezra, thus building a bridge between Sephardic life in the United States and the medieval Hebrew past. The Englishwoman Grace Aguilar was a similar pioneer: her work includes the poems "Song of the Spanish Jews, During Their 'Golden Age' " and "A Vision of Jerusalem, While Listening to a Beautiful Organ in One of the Gentile Shrines," as well as books such as *The Spirit of Judaism, The Women of Israel,* and, posthumously, *Sabbath Thoughts and Sacred Communings.*

Lazarus was one of the first in a long line of Sephardic authors from the Americas—from Argentina to Canada. Indeed, this component of the Sephardic tradition—which includes works published in English, Spanish, French, and Portuguese—is essential. The United States has become a major gravitational center of Sephardic culture. It had auspicious beginnings. In 1790 the Dutch Sephardic Jews of the Touro Synagogue sent a letter of congratulations to the newly elected president George Washington and received from him a reply that included these immortal lines: "The government of the United States . . . gives to bigotry no sanction, to persecution no assistance . . . May the children of the Stock of Abraham who dwell in this land continue to merit and enjoy the good will of the other inhabitants, while everyone shall sit in safety under his own wine and fig tree and there shall be none to make him afraid."

The eighteenth- and early-nineteenth-century Sephardic communities in America were small in number and were quickly overshadowed first by German Jews, who began immigrating to the United States in significant numbers in the 1830s, and then by the Yiddish-speaking immigrants from eastern Europe, who began arriving in the 1880s. The fall of the Ottoman Empire at the end of World War I brought to America Sephardim from Greece, Rhodes, Turkey, Syria, and, eventually, from Egypt—but the numbers were small in comparison to the Ashkenazic waves: between 1899 and 1925, approximately 25,000 Sephardim settled in the United States. They established communities in San Francisco, Seattle, New York, Detroit, Atlanta, and Los Angeles, among other cities.

At the end of the twentieth century there were some 200,000 Sephardic Jews north of the Rio Grande, which amounted to less than 5 percent of the entire American Jewish population. But despite their small numbers, their presence is increasingly felt. This might be explained in a variety of ways: for one thing, the Sephardic community has become more involved in bringing the richness of their culture to the attention of Jews and, indeed, Americans of all backgrounds. But there is also the fact that, in the last quarter of the twentieth century, Ashkenazic Jewry has become less monolithic, more culturally segmented. This has made American Jews more open to cultural experiences outside their own ethnic realm. The growing interest in Sephardic Jewry is, in part, the result of that openness. Who are those "other" Jews whom we have long stereotyped as being less cultured, less accomplished than we are? How has their diaspora experience been different from ours? What experiences do we have in common?

Sephardic American writers are a diverse group. They come from Spanish-speaking countries such as Cuba and Guatemala, from Central Europe, from the Balkans, and from the Middle East. This provides a decidedly multiethnic and international feel to their work. Leon Sciaky, author of the memoir *Farewell to Salonica: City at the Crossroads,* came to the United States as a child with his family in 1915. Stanley Sultan is a professor of English at Clark University who has written acclaimed works on James Joyce, W. B. Yeats, and T. S. Eliot. Ruth Knafo Setton's novel *The Road to Fez,* about a nineteenth-century Moroccan-Jewish martyr, is at once an American and Levantine. André Aciman, author of *Out of Egypt,* and Victor Perera, author of *The Cross and the Pear Tree,* begin their memoirs in the United States, but then take us back to the fifteenth century, when the Sephardim "are offered a choice between conversion, exile and death," as Perera puts it. And thus begins "a story of persecution, escape and renewal" that goes from the Iberian Peninsula to Central Europe and, in the case of Aciman, to the Levant, including the Holy Land, then back to Europe and across the Atlantic. Language plays a role in the shaping of identity in both memoirs: When as a boy Aciman is asked his nationality, he replies "French"; Perera's family settled in Guatemala, and thus his mother tongue was Spanish. But they both chose English to deliver their chronicles—or else, English chose them. The result is a tapestry that is as much about the Sephardic condition as it is, even ruefully, about the American Dream.

Another important Sephardic American writer is the cultural critic Ammiel Alcalay, author of the groundbreaking *After Jews and Arabs: Remaking Levantine Culture,* published in 1993. In it Alcalay redefines the relationships among the mélange of Islamic, Judeo-Arabic, Arabic, Sephardic, Mizrahi, and Mediterranean civilizations, analyzing the cultures of the Levant from an altogether fresh perspective. "Why shouldn't we refer to figures like Maimonides, Ibn 'Arabi or Averroes as Europeans?" he asks. "After all, they were born in Europe, just as I was born in the United States." Why the need to circumscribe them as "others"? The plight of the Sephardic writer is Alcalay's particular concern. In the essay "The Quill's Embroidery: Untangling a Tradition," in *Memories of Our Future,* he suggests that Sephardic writers inhabit "a space of immense human richness, a space that can propose new models for a world rapidly losing sight of the dependence of each part upon every other part."

In Central and South America, the demographics are different. Of the 165,000 Jews in Brazil, some 50,000 are Sephardim. Thirty-five percent of Mexico's 40,000 Jews are Sephardim, but only 10 percent of Argentina's 200,000 Jews are Sephardim. The first Sephardic immigrants to Central and South America were sixteenth-century crypto-Jews fleeing the Inquisition. Luis de Carvajál the Younger, a member of a noted Portuguese *converso* family, attempted to reclaim his Jewish identity in Mexico, was sentenced to exile by the Inquisition, and died in jail. Sephardic Jews who had originally landed in Curaçao migrated to Colombia and Venezuela, including the writers Abraham Zaharia López Penha and Elías David Curiel. Contemporary Sephardic writers in Latin America include Ana María Shua in Argentina, Isaac Chocrón in Venezuela, Ruth Behar in Cuba, Angelina Muñiz-Huberman, and Rosa Nissán in Mexico (the latter the author of *Like a Bride,* which includes portions written in Ladino), and Victor Perera in Guatemala. They write about Jewish life—Sephardic and otherwise—in the modern world. The translingual experience is at the core of the work of contemporary Sephardic authors: those living in the United States write in English, those who have moved to Israel write in Hebrew; those living in Europe write in Spanish, French, and Italian.

With the third largest Jewish population in the world (approximately 700,000 in the year 2000), France provides a crucial chapter in the contemporary Sephardic literary tradition. Albert Cohen, a fervent Zionist born on the island of Corfu but taken to France as a child, dreamt of writing novels in French à la Flaubert and Balzac, but with Jewish protagonists. Cohen is probably the most famous Sephardic writer of the first half of the twentieth century, author of the masterpiece *Belle du Seigneur,* published in French in 1968 and described by the *Times Literary Supplement* as "the greatest love story in modern literature." One of the protagonists is Solal (also one of Cohen's last names, by the way), an idealistic Levantine Jew and the under-secretary general of the League of Nations. His complex portrait in the novel is arguably one of the most inspired moments in modern Sephardic literature. Other contemporary Sephardic authors who write in French are the philosopher-cum-poet Edmond Jabès and the memoirist Albert Memmi, born in Egypt and Tunis respectively. Memmi's *The Pillar of Salt* is an exploration of his North African upbringing and the alienation he felt, as a Jew, from the Muslim world around him. Other French-Sephardic authors include the poet, translator, and art critic Edouard Roditi, the novelist Patrick Modiano (*Trace of Malice, Villa Triste,* and *The Search Warrant*), and the literary critic and novelist Hélène Cixous, a colleague of Michel Foucault and Jacques Derrida at the Commission Nationale des Lettres and the author of studies on James Joyce, Clarice Lispector, Franz Kafka, and Marina Tsvetayeva.

Some of the most notable contemporary Sephardic authors come from Italy. In the novel *The Garden of the Finzi-Continis,* Georgio Bassani explored the impact of the spread of fascism on the Jewish residents of Ferrara. In *Five Stories of Ferrara* Bassani writes about the Jews of northern Italy, an area not noted for anti-Semitism but from which large numbers of Jews were deported during World War II. The novels and essays of Natalia Ginzburg (among them, *The Manzoni Family* and *The Little Virtues*) address both her Sephardic ancestry and her leftist political philosophy. And no listing of Italian Sephardic authors would be complete without Primo Levi, who, along with Elie Wiesel, Imre Kertész, Paul Celan, and Aharon Appelfeld, is one of the most acclaimed chroniclers of the Holocaust. A chemist born into a secular, assimilated family in Turin, Levi is best known for *If This Is a Man,* a straightforward but at the same time heartrending chronicle of his years as a prisoner in Auschwitz, to which he was deported in 1943. When the autobiography was first published in Italian in 1947, it received almost no attention, perhaps because it was too soon after the Holocaust for readers to fully comprehend what had just occurred. But upon its reissue in 1958 under the title *Survival in Auschwitz,* the volume quickly became recognized as a classic of Holocaust literature.

It is a popular misconception that the Nazi destruction of European Jewry had little impact on the Sephardic world. According to Jane S. Gerber, approximately 1.6 million Jews in the Balkans, of whom 10 percent were Sephardim, were deported by the Nazis to concentration camps. This included some 60,000 Greek Jews. Only the Jews of Bulgaria and neutral Turkey—some 150,000 altogether—survived the war more or less intact.

Born in Bulgaria in 1905 and awarded the Nobel Prize for Literature in 1981, Elias Canetti is one of the most important figures in modern

Sephardic literature. He is best known for his novel *Auto-da-Fé* and his nonfiction meditation *Crowds and Power.* Canetti spoke Ladino as a child and moved to London before World War II, but he used German as his vehicle for literary expression. His multivolume *Memoirs* (which consists of *The Tongue Set Free, The Torch in My Ear,* and *The Play of the Eyes*) discusses his Sephardic upbringing as well as his multilingualism. Canetti also examines his status as "an intellectual pariah" in Europe between World War I and II. His memoir is considered one of the most significant works of the twentieth century. Canetti's wife, the Austrian Veza Canetti, was a novelist of mixed Ashkenazic and Sephardic background. Her novel *The Tortoises* tells the story of an Austrian Jewish family in the months leading up to the *Anschluss.* The Serbo-Croatian Danilo Kiš is best known for his collection of stories *A Tomb for Boris Davidovich* and his novel *Hourglass.* Kiš's father was arrested in 1944 and deported to Auschwitz, where he was killed. Kiš's work often includes a shadowy father figure. Turkey is also an important center of Sephardic literature. Turkish-Jewish authors such as Liz Behmoaras, Zeki Ergas, Mario Levi, and Ronnie Margulies have explored in their work the clash between Muslim and Jewish world views within the Ottoman Empire. Moris Farhi's volume of interrelated stories, *Young Turk,* is a lyrical coming-of-age evocation of a multiracial Turkey seeking to divest itself of the Ottoman past and emerge as a modern European nation.

Zionism as an ideological movement is a recurring theme in modern Sephardic literature. Prior to the creation of the State of Israel in 1948, the longing for a promised land figured prominently in the work of poets such as Emma Lazarus and novelists such as Albert Cohen. As early as 1895, Zionist youth organizations were formed in Bulgaria, followed by chapters in Morocco, Tunisia, and Greece. The Alliance Israélite Universelle opposed Zionism, and it influenced a generation of Sephardic schoolchildren and their families. Still, a large percentage of early immigrants to Palestine were of Sephardic descent. Yehuda Burla, the Sephardic founding father of contemporary Hebrew literature, was born in Jerusalem in 1886 into a family that had immigrated from Turkey some three centuries earlier. A passionate admirer of the triumvirate of Yiddish masters, S. Y. Abramovitch, Sholem Aleichem, and I. L. Peretz, Burla nevertheless felt that Palestinian Jewish culture wasn't only too Eurocentric, it was also anti-Sephardic. Works such as the classic *In Darkness Striving,* about relations between Jews and Arabs in Palestine, as well as "Two Sisters," about Sephardic-Ashkenazic relations in Palestine, were his attempt to remedy the situation. Burla's oeuvre represents a significant effort to define Zionist identity in the years prior to Israel's declaration of independence.

After 1948 and with the mass immigration of Jews from neighboring Arab countries, Sephardim quickly became a significant component of Israeli society. But a cultural rift between the Ashkenazim and Sephardim quickly developed, which has persisted to this day. More than a few Sephardic authors in Israel have been published to international acclaim—Sami Michael, A. B. Yehoshua, Shulamit Hareven, and Orly Castel-Bloom spring immediately to mind—and the difficult relations between Sephardim and Ashkenazim in Israel often figures prominently in their work. The Iraqi-born Michael, for example, seeks in his novels to analyze the source of Ashkenazic bias against Sephardim. And in novels such as *Mr. Mani* and *Journey to the End of the Millennium,* Yehoshua (who was born in Israel to Moroccan parents) writes about the Sephardic experience throughout Jewish history as seen from a contemporary Israeli perspective. In the novel *An Alexandrian Summer,* Egyptian-born Yitzhak Gormezano Goren views Israel not as an extension of the shtetl but as part of the Levant. "Yes, Mediterranean," the narrator states. "Really. Maybe it's by right of that same Mediterranean that I sit here unraveling this tale. Here, in the Land of Israel, bordering the shores of the Baltic Sea. Sometimes you find yourself utterly perplexed—is Vilna the Jerusalem of Lithuania or is Jerusalem actually the Vilna of Eretz Israel? It's because of this I wanted so much to tell the story of the Hamdi-Ali family, and the story of the city of Alexandria."

La España perdida, la diáspora ganada . . . This, then, is the landscape of modern Sephardic literature written in "foreign" languages, a fascinating, complex genre that still awaits proper recognition. If in approaching so vast and amorphous a bookshelf one should dare to venture any generalization, it is that the Sephardic cultural sensibility is in a perennial state of fluidity, continually redefining itself. Its purvue spans the world. Nothing is foreign to it: as one door closes, another one opens. The ever-present clash between the local and the universal, between the private and the public, is resolved in different ways, depending on the particular historical circumstance. In the end, though, it is obvious that what matters is the journey itself, the quest and not its ultimate destination. Sephardic authors explore that quest through words in a Babel of tongues. Their watchwords are to be found in *Psalms* 106:35: "They mingled among the nations and learned their ways."

Chronology

It would be futile to attempt in only a handful of pages a complete historical survey of Sephardic culture in general, and its literature in particular. From the outset is the question of definition: Who is Sephardic and when does Sephardic civilization start? Some historians place its birth at the time of the Edict of Expulsion in 1492, while others believe Jewish life on the Iberian Peninsula since the First Temple period in the tenth century BCE should also be included. I hesitate to offer an answer in a literary omnibus whose scope is limited to fairly recent times, from the middle of the nineteenth century to the present day. Still, in order to present a coherent view, I've chosen to list the historical and literary benchmarks as of the second century BCE, which should not be taken as an answer to the question of origins. Dates of titles given are of original publication, and not subsequent translations unless so indicated.

200 BCE–200 CE: Migration of Jews throughout the Roman Empire, including Spain (*aka* Ispania). According to lore, Jews first appeared on the Iberian Peninsula during the reign of King Solomon. There is an ambiguous reference to Spain in Obadiah 1:20.

711: After a period of Visigothic rule, Muslim armies conquer Spain.

Circa 900: Apex of Andalusian civilization, with Córdoba as its capital. The so-called Jewish Golden Age of philosophy, poetry, and science spans the tenth and twelfth centuries.

Circa 940: Hasdai ibn Shaprut becomes a prominent figure in public life.

1013: The Caliphate of Córdoba dissolved. Samuel ha-Nagid (*aka* Samuel ibn Nagrela) is twelve years of age. He will become general of the Granadan army and vizir of Granada, the highest diplomatic position for a Jew at the time.

1085: Toledo falls into Christian hands.

1090: Granada is conquered by the Muslim Almoravids from North Africa.

1096–1147: First and Second Crusades.

1135–1204: Maimonides (*aka* Rabbi Moses ben Maimon), was a noted doctor and the leading scholar and philosopher of Sephardic Jewry. His works include the *Mishneh Torah*, the *Commentary on the Mishneh*, and *Guide for the Perplexed*. Born in Córdoba, he flees the fanatical Almohads for Fez, and later settles in Cairo.

1140: Yehuda Halevi fulfills a lifelong dream and leaves Spain for Palestine. Shortly after his arrival there, he is killed by an Arab horseman. Halevi will write *bon vivant* as well as philosophical poetry, as well as *The Kuzari*.

1148: Persecution by the Muslim Almohads in Spain.

1238: The papal Inquisition is established in Aragón.

1242: An auto-da-fé occurs in Paris under the regime of Louis IX.

1248: Ferdinand III of Castile captures Seville.

1263: The theological disputation of Barcelona takes place between Nahmanides (*aka* Rabbi Moses ben Nachman) and the convert Pablo Christiani.

1299: Expulsion of the Jews from England.

1306: Expulsion of the Jews from France. The edict will have various degrees of success, until 1394, when the Jews are finally expelled from the country.

1378–89: Jews protest anti-Semitic preaching by Dominican monks and other Catholic leaders.

1391: Christian mobs attack Jews in Seville, killing scores and forcibly converting many more. Those who continued to practice Judaism in secret are referred to as *conversos*.

1413–14: Disputation staged in Tortosa results in the conversion of numerous Jews.

1449: Riots in Toledo, Ciudad Real, and elsewhere destroy Jewish districts.

1453: The Ottomans conquer Constantinople.

1462–67: Riots against *conversos* in Seville and Toledo.

1478: The Catholic monarchs Ferdinand and Isabella establish the Holy Office of the Inquisition to root out *conversos*.

1481: First auto-da-fé in Seville.

1482: Tomás de Torquemada is named Chief Inquisitor in Castile.

1492: The Jews of Spain constitute the largest concentration of Jews in the world—perhaps as much as half of the worldwide Jewish population. January: Granada, the last Muslim bastion on the peninsula, surrenders to the Christian army of Ferdinand and Isabella. March: The edict of expulsion orders between 180,000 and 250,000 Jews to leave Spain within four months. Jews establish communities in Portugal, Northern Africa, Italy, and the Ottoman Empire, to which they are welcomed, admitted by Sultan Bayazid II. The Sephardic diaspora is thus established. Antonio de Nebrija, a scholar in Salamanca, publishes the first grammar of the Spanish language. Christopher Columbus sets sail across the Atlantic Ocean, on a journey that will eventually take him to the Caribbean. Groups of both *conversos* and New Christians begin to arrive in the Caribbean and in Central and South America.

1497: Jews who settled in Portugal after the Spanish expulsion are given the choice of conversion or expulsion. Many immigrate to the Ottoman Empire.

1516–17: The Ottomans put an end to Mameluk rule in Egypt and the Holy Land. Sultan Selim I declares himself caliph and receives the key to Mecca. Jacob ibn Habib publishes *Ein Ya'akov* in Salonika. It is a compilation of legends of the Babylonian and Jerusalem Talmuds, with additional commentary.

1553: The Ferrara Bible is translated into Ladino for the benefit of Italy's Sephardim. *Consolation for the Tribulations of Israel,* a polemical treatise by Samuel Usque, circulates in Portuguese in Ferrara.

1558: *The Book of the Zohar,* purportedly written in second-century Palestine by Simeon ben Yohai but actually written in thirteenth-century Spain by Moses de León, is first printed in Italy.

1564–65: The *Shulhan Arukh,* a monumental code of Jewish law compiled by Joseph Caro attempting to bring together the laws and practices that regulated all aspects of Jewish life, is printed in Venice.

1570: The Inquisition is established in Mexico and Peru.

1572: Isaac Luria, a Kabbalist who lived in Safed, dies. His legacy is popularized by his disciples, in particular Hayyim Vital.

1580–1640: Portugal is annexed to Spain. Climax of the Portuguese Inquisition.

1596: Luis de Carvajal the Younger and his family are burnt at the stake by the Holy Office of the Inquisition in Mexico.

1605: Miguel de Cervantes Saavedra, suspected by some historians of having Jewish ancestors, publishes the first of two parts of his novel *Don Quixote of La Mancha*. The second will appear in 1615.

1623: Arrival of the first openly Jewish settlers from Holland and the Iberian Peninsula in Brazil, parts of which were ruled by Holland.

1632: *The Conciliator,* a philosophical treatise on the Bible written by Menashe ben Israel, is published in Spanish, in Holland. His works, eventually translated into Dutch, Hebrew, Latin, and English, influenced Baruch Spinoza, who was born the year *The Conciliator* was first published.

1637: João Pinto Delgado, a crypto-Jewish poet, publishes *Poema de la Reyna Esther.*

1654: Twenty-three Dutch Sephardic Jews, fleeing the Inquisition that had been established in areas of Brazil that were ruled by Portugal, arrive in the Dutch colony of New Amsterdam.

1663: Yehuda Halevi's *Kuzari* is translated into Spanish by Jacob Abendana. He also translated the *Mishneh.*

1665: Miguel Leví de Barrios, also known as Daniel Leví de Barrios, leads a double life—Christian in Brussels, Jewish in Amsterdam. He published the collection of poetry *Flor de Apolo.* His play *Contra la verdad no hay fuerza* appeared in 1666.

1666: Sabbetai Zevi, a Turkish Jew and pseudo-messiah whose charisma and message of messianic restoration of the Holy Land inspired Jews throughout Europe and the Near East to make preparations to move to Palestine, is forced to convert to Islam by the Turkish sultan.

1670: A Portuguese translation of *The Duties of the Heart* by Bahya ibn Paquda, done by Samuel Abbas, is published. It will later appear in a Ladino version.

1677: Baruch Spinoza dies. His oeuvre, which includes *Ethics* and *Tractatus Politicus,* was considered blasphemous by the Amsterdam Jewish community, which excommunicated him.

1679: Isaac Cardozo, born in Portugal but resettled in London, where he reconnected to his Judaism, publishes *Las excelencias y calumnias de los hebreos.* It describes what he calls "the ten privileges" of the Jewish people and "the ten slanders brought against them."

1688: Isaac Aboab da Fonseca publishes the *Pentateuch* in Spanish in Amsterdam.

1714: David Nieto, a rabbi in London's Sephardic community, publishes *Matteh Dan,* which demonstrates the authority of the Oral Law.

1722–25: The last Inquisition trials take place in Spain.

1799: Napoleon Bonaparte invades Egypt.

1810–1823: The Inquisition is gradually abolished in Latin American countries.

1834: The Inquisition is abolished as an institution in Spain.

1840: The Damascus Blood Libel inspires prominent Jews all over the world—and U.S. President Martin van Buren—to protest this overt anti-Semitic attack on Syrian Jews.

1843: Grace Aguilar, a woman of Sephardic ancestry living in England, publishes the novel *The Perez Family.*

1850: France colonizes North Africa, and French culture becomes the model for the Sephardic elites there and in the Ottoman Empire.

1856–64: Reforms and charters are assigned to non-Muslim communities in Turkey.

1860: The Alliance Israélite Universelle is founded in France. The *Haskala* (Enlightenment) spreads from the Ashkenazic world to the Sephardic world, although it commands less influence there. Sephardic *Maskilim,* modern secular intellectuals, such as Yuda Nehama and Barukh Mitrani, establish Ladino newspapers, among them *El Lunar* (Moonlight).

1882: Emma Lazarus, an American poet of Sephardic ancestry who was influenced by Ralph Waldo Emerson, publishes *Songs of a Semite.*

1889–1914: Substanial Jewish immigration from eastern Europe to Latin America. Many of the immigrants are of Sephardic descent.

1892: Portugal affirms freedom of worship.

1897: The World Zionist Organization is founded. Zionism influences and motivates the Jews of the Ottoman Empire, as well as those of eastern Europe.

1900: Jews move to Venezuela from the Dutch colony of Curaçao.

1903: Emma Lazarus's poem "The New Colossus" is engraved on a plaque that is affixed to the base of the Statue of Liberty. Angel Pulido, a non-Jewish Spanish physician and senator, discovers Spanish-speaking Jews in the Balkans and calls for the repatriation of Spanish Jews expelled in 1492. Pulido is the author of *Los israelitas españoles y el idioma castellano* (Spanish Jews and the Spanish Language) and *Españoles sin patria y la raza sefardí* (Spaniards Without a Homeland and the Sephardic Race).

1908: Jews from the Ottoman Empire emigrate to the Americas in significant numbers.

1914–18: World War I. Germany, Austria-Hungary, and the Ottoman Empire are defeated.

1919: Samuel Schwarz discovers a small group of crypto-Jews in Belmonte, Portugal.

1919: A pogrom known as *Semana trágica* takes place in Argentina.

1923: The secular Turkish republic rises from the ashes of the Ottoman Empire.

1924: Restrictive U.S. immigration laws result in increased immigration of European Jews, including *Sephardim,* to Latin America.

1924: The number of Jewish immigrants from the former Ottoman Empire to the United States grows to approximately 20,000.

1927: The Spanish scholar Ramón Menéndez Pidal publishes his study *Catálogo del romancero judío-español.*

1929: The novella *In Darkness Striving* by Yehuda Burla, the first modern Hebrew writer of Sephardic Middle Eastern background, is published in Hebrew, in Palestine.

1934, May–July: Anti-Jewish demonstrations in Çanakkale, Kirklareli, Edirne, and other parts of Turkey force 7,000–8,000 Jews to flee to Istanbul, where they are eventually resettled.

1938: Gershom Scholem, a German-born scholar of Kabbalah, delivers the Hilda Stich Strook Lectures at the Jewish Institute of Religion in New York. In 1946 they will be published as *Major Trends in Jewish Mysticism.* Scholem devotes considerable energy to the study of Sephardic Judaism.

1939: World War II begins.

1940: The Instituto Arias Montano for Sephardic Research is established in Madrid by the fascist government of Francisco Franco.

1942–44: An exorbitant wealth tax is imposed on minorities in Turkey. Those unable to pay are deported to Askale, a labor camp in Eastern Turkey. Scores of Jews die there from exhaustion and exposure.

1939–45: Of the six million Jewish victims in the Holocaust, approximately 10 percent are of Sephardic extraction. (It is estimated that before World War II there were 16.5 million Jews worldwide, of whom 15 million were Ashkenazim and 1.5 million were Sephardim and other non-Ashkenazim.) Communities in Salonika, Ferrara, Florence, Venice, Rhodes, Leghorn, and the Balkan region are substantially decimated. Spain is able to save some Jewish refugees by claiming they are "citizens of greater Spain."

1946: Elias Canetti, a Bulgarian Jew, publishes the novel *Auto-da-Fé.* He will also write the monograph *Crowds and Power* and a three-volume memoir, among other works.

1947: *If This Is a Man,* a memoir by Primo Levi, an Italian chemist who survived the Holocaust, is published in Italy but goes unnoticed. In 1958 it will be published in English as *Survival in Auschwitz* and will become a classic of Holocaust literature.

1948: The State of Israel is created. Approximately 20 percent of the Israeli population is of Sephardic descent. Turkey will be the first Muslim country to recognize the Jewish state.

1953: Albert Memmi, a French author and socialist born in Tunis, publishes his autobiography *The Pillar of Salt.*

1956–58: Jews in North African and Middle Eastern countries are persecuted as a result of the war between Israel and its neighbors known as the Sinai Campaign. This war and the French-Algerian War result in the emigration of large numbers of Jews from these countries to Israel, Europe, and the United States.

1961: *The Collected Works of Yehuda Burla* is published in Israel.

1963: Natalia Ginzburg publishes *Family Sayings* in Italy.

1967: The Six-Day War. Most of the remaining Jews living in North African and Middle Eastern countries are forced to emigrate.

1966: Spanish law guarantees religious freedom.

1968: The Edict of Expulsion of 1492 is revoked by the Spanish government. The first public synagogue opens in Madrid.

1971: The Israeli consul general is kidnapped and subsequently assassinated in Istanbul. The Council of the Sephardic Community in Jerusalem announces plans to establish a Center for the Study of Sephardic Culture at Hebrew University.

1973: The Yom Kippur War.

1974: French-born Edouard Roditi publishes *Thrice Chosen: Poems and Jewish Themes.*

1976: Danilo Kiš, a Yugoslavian Jew, publishes *A Tomb for Boris Davidovich.*

1981: Elias Canetti is awarded the Nobel Prize for Literature.

1986: The first terrorist attack on Synagogue Neve Shalom in Istanbul.

1987: While suffering from deep depression, Primo Levi dies in a fall down a stairwell.

1990: The Israeli A. B. Yehoshua publishes *Mr. Mani,* a multigenerational novel about a transnational Sephardic family.

1992: The quincentennial of Christopher Columbus's first voyage across the Atlantic Ocean is observed worldwide. The expulsion of 1492 and the birth of the Sephardic diaspora are also memorialized in symposia and art festivals.

1994: The A.M.I.A., the Jewish community center in Buenos Aires, is bombed by Middle Eastern terrorists. Dozens of people are killed.

1996: Salman Rushdie publishes *The Moor's Last Sight,* a novel about a Sephardic family from Cochin, India, that can trace its origins to a Jew expelled from Spain in 1492.

2003: Terrorists bomb two synagogues in Istanbul.

THE SCHOCKEN BOOK OF MODERN SEPHARDIC LITERATURE

Grace Aguilar

Grace Aguilar (England, 1816–1847) is considered the first Anglo-Jewish novelist. Her work was a response, in part, to the representation of Jews in Sir Walter Scott's *Ivanhoe* and to Thomas Macaulay's views on Judaism. In her short career—she died in Frankfurt at the age of thirty-one of a spinal ailment affecting her muscles and lungs—she published poetry, fiction, essays, and a history of the Jews in England. Aguilar is the author of the popular novels *Home Influence: A Tale for Mothers and Daughters* (1847), its sequel, *A Mother's Recompense* (1851), and *The Vale of Cedars; or, The Martyr* (1850). Her nonfiction includes *The Spirit of Judaism* (1842), *The Women of Israel* (1845), and *The Jewish Faith* (1846). Her novel *The Perez Family,* released in 1843 by a publishing house dedicated to the edification of working-class Jews and therefore called Cheap Jewish Library, is an insider's depiction of Jewish life in Victorian England. (The most famous slice of that life, Israel Zangwill's *Children of the Ghetto,* would not appear until 1892.) Aguilar's poems, published in journals such as *The Occident,* imagine the affection of Jews for the Spanish soil, and also deal with Jerusalem, the Sabbath, and the Jews in Russia. Her short story "The Escape," published in 1844, is set in Portugal, from which her ancestors fled to escape the Inquisition, finding refuge in England.

The Escape. A Tale of 1755

Dark lowers our fate,
And terrible the storm that gathers o'er us;
But nothing, till that latest agony
Which severs thee from nature, shall unloose
This fixed and sacred hold. In thy dark prison-house;
In the terrific face of armed law;
Yea! on the scaffold, if it needs must be,
I never will forsake thee.

—JOANNA BAILLIE

ABOUT THE MIDDLE of the eighteenth century, the little town of Montes, situated some forty or fifty miles from Lisbon, was thrown into most unusual excitement by the magnificence attending the nuptials of Alvar Rodríguez and Almah Díaz: an excitement which, the extraordinary beauty of the bride, who, though the betrothed of Alvar from her childhood, had never been seen in Montes before, of course not a little increased. The little church of Montes looked gay and glittering for the large sums lavished by Alvar on the officiating priests, and in presents to their patron saints, had occasioned every picture, shrine, and image to blaze in uncovered gold and jewels, and the altar to be fed with the richest incense, and lighted with tapers of the finest wax, to do him honour.

The church was full; for, although the bridal party did not exceed twenty, the village appeared to have emptied itself there; Alvar's munificence to all classes, on all occasions, having rendered him the universal idol, and caused the fame of that day's rejoicing to extend many miles around.

There was nothing remarkable in the behaviour of either bride or bridegroom, except that both were decidedly more calm than such occasions usually warrant. Nay, in the manly countenance of Alvar ever and anon an expression seemed to flit, that in any but so true a son of the church would have been accounted scorn. In such a one, of course it was neither seen nor regarded, except by his bride; for at such times her eyes met his with an earnest and entreating glance, that the peculiar look was changed into a quiet, tender seriousness, which reassured her.

From the church they adjourned to the lordly mansion of Rodríguez, which, in the midst of its flowering orange and citron trees, stood about two miles from the town.

The remainder of the day passed in festivity. The banquet, and dance, and song, both within and around the house, diversified the scene and increased hilarity in all. By sunset, all but the immediate friends and relatives of the newly wedded had departed. Some splendid and novel fireworks from the heights having attracted universal attention, Alvar, with his usual indulgence, gave his servants and retainers permission to join the festive crowds; liberty, to all who wished it, was given the next two hours.

In a very brief interval the house was cleared, with the exception of a young Moor, the secretary or book-keeper of Alvar, and four or five middle-aged domestics of both sexes.

Gradually, and it appeared undesignedly, the bride and her female companions were left alone, and for the first time the beautiful face of Almah was shadowed by emotion.

"Shall I, oh, shall I indeed be his?" she said, half aloud. "There are moments when our dread secret is so terrible; it seems to forebode discovery at the very moment it would be most agonizing to bear."

"Hush, silly one!" was the reply of an older friend; "discovery is not so easily or readily accomplished. The persecuted and the nameless have purchased wisdom and caution at the price of blood—learned to deceive, that they may triumph—to conceal, that they may flourish still. Almah, we are NOT to fall!"

"I know it, Inez. A superhuman agency upholds us; we had been cast off, rooted out, plucked from the very face of the earth long since else. But there are times when human nature will shrink and tremble—when the path of deception and concealment allotted for us to tread seems fraught with danger at every turn. I know it is all folly, yet there is a dim foreboding, shadowing our fair horizon of joy as a hovering thunder-cloud. There has been suspicion, torture, death. Oh, if my Alvar—"

"Nay, Almah; this is childish. It is only because you are too happy, and happiness in its extent is ever pain. In good time comes your venerable guardian, to chide and silence all such foolish fancies. How many weddings have there been, and will there still be, like this? Come, smile, love, while I rearrange your veil."

Almah obeyed, though the smile was faint, as if the soul yet trembled in its joy. On the entrance of Gonzalos, her guardian (she was an orphan and an heiress), he saw her veil was thrown around her, so as completely to envelope face and form. Taking his arm, and followed by all her female companions, she was hastily and silently led to a sort of ante-room or cabinet, opening, by a massive door concealed with tapestry, from the suite of rooms appropriated to the private use of the merchant and his family. There Alvar and his friends awaited her. A canopy, supported by four of the youngest males present, was held over the bride and bride-groom as they stood facing the east. A silver salver lay at their feet, and opposite stood an aged man, with a small, richly bound volume in his hand. It was open, and displayed letters and words of unusual form and sound. Another of Alvar's friends stood near, holding a goblet of sacred wine; and to a third was given a slight and thin Venetian glass. After a brief and solemn pause, the old man read or rather chanted from the book he held, joined in parts by those around; and then he tasted the sacred wine, and passed it to the bride and bridegroom. Almah's veil was upraised, for her to touch the goblet with her lips, now quivering with emotion, and not permitted to fall again. And Alvar, where now was the expression of scorn and contempt that had been stamped on his bold brow and curling lip before? Gone—lost before the powerful emotion which scarcely permitted his lifting the goblet a second time to his lips. Then, taking the Venetian glass, he broke it on the salver at his feet, and the strange rites were concluded.

Yet no words of congratulation came. Drawn together in a closer knot, while Alvar folded the now almost fainting Almah to his bosom, and said, in the deep, low tones of intense feeling, "Mine, mine for ever now—mine in the sight of our God, the God of the exile and the faithful; our fate, whatever it be, henceforth is one"; the old man lifted up his clasped hands, and prayed.

"God of the nameless and homeless," he said, and it was in the same strange yet solemn-sounding language as before, "have mercy on these Thy servants, joined together in Thy Holy name, to share the lot on earth Thy will assigns them, with one heart and mind. Strengthen Thou them to keep the secret of their faith and race—to teach it to their offspring as they received it from their fathers. Pardon Thou them and us the deceit we do to keep holy Thy law and Thine inheritance. In the land of the persecutor, the exterminator, be Thou their shield, and save them for Thy Holy name. But if discovery and its horrible consequences—imprisonment, torture, death—await them, stengthen Thou them for their endurance—to die as they would live for Thee. Father, hear us! homeless and nameless upon earth, we are Thine own!"

"Aye, strengthen me for him, my husband; turn my woman weakness into Thy strength for him, Almighty Father," the voiceless prayer with which Almah lifted up her pale face from her husband's bosom, where it had rested during the whole of that strange and terrible prayer and in the calmness stealing on her throbbing heart, she read her answer.

It was some few minutes ere the excited spirits of the devoted few then present, male or female, master or servant, could subside into their wonted control. But such scenes, such feelings were not of rare occurrence; and ere the domestics of Rodríguez returned, there was nothing either in the mansion or its inmates to denote that anything uncommon had taken place during their absence.

The Portuguese are not fond of society at any time, so that Alvar and his young bride should after one week of festivity, live in comparative retirement, elicited no surprise. The former attended his house of business at Montes as usual; and whoever chanced to visit him at his beautiful estate, returned delighted with his entertainment and his hosts; so that, far and near, the merchant Alvar became noted alike for his munificence and the strict orthodox Catholicism in which he conducted his establishment.

And was Alvar Rodríguez indeed what he seemed? If so, what were those strange mysterious rites with which in secret he celebrated his marriage? For what were those many contrivances in his mansion, secret receptacles even from his own sitting-rooms, into which all kinds of forbidden food were conveyed from his very table, that his soul might not be polluted by disobedience? How did it so happen that one day in every year Alvar gave a general holiday—leave of absence for four and twenty hours, under some well-arranged pretence, to all, save those who entreated permission to remain with him? And that on that day, Alvar, his wife, his Moorish secretary, and all those domestics who had witnessed his marriage, spent in holy fast and prayer—permitting no particle of food or drink to pass their lips from eve unto eve; or if by any chance, the holiday could not be given, their several meals to be laid and served, yet so contriving that, while the food looked as if it had been partaken of not a portion had they touched? That the Saturday should be passed in seeming preparation for the Sunday, in cessation from work of any kind, and frequent prayer, was perhaps of trivial importance; but for the previous mysteries—mysteries known to Alvar, his wife, and five or six of his establishment, yet never by word or sign betrayed; how may we account for them? There may be some to whom the memory of such things, as common to their ancestors, may be yet familiar; but to by far the greater number of English readers, they are, in all probability, as incomprehensible as uncommon.

Alvar Rodríguez was a Jew. One of the many who, in Portugal and Spain, fulfilled the awful prophecy of their great lawgiver Moses, and bowed before the imaged saints and martyrs of the Catholic, to shrine the religion of their fathers yet closer in their hearts and homes. From father to son the secret of their faith and race descended, so early and mysteriously taught that little children imbibed it—not alone the faith, but so effectually to conceal it, as to avert and mystify, all inquisitorial questioning, long before they knew the meaning or necessity of what they learned.

How this was accomplished, how the religion of God was thus preserved in the very midst of persecution and intolerance, must ever remain a mystery, as, happily for Israel, such fearful training is no longer needed. But that it did exist, that Jewish children in the very midst of monastic and convent tuition, yet adhered to the religion of their fathers, never by word or sign betrayed the secret with which they were intrusted; and, in their turn, became husbands and fathers conveying their solemn and dangerous inheritance to their posterity—that such things were, there are those still amongst the Hebrews of England to affirm and recall, claiming among their own ancestry, but one generation removed, those who have thus concealed and thus adhered. It was the power of God, not the power of man. Human strength had been utterly inefficient. Torture and death would long before have annihilated every remnant of Israel's devoted race. But it might not be; for God had spoken. And, as a living miracle, a lasting record of His truth, His justice, aye and mercy, Israel was preserved in the midst of danger, in the very face of death, and will be preserved for ever.

It was no mere rejoicing ceremony, that of marriage, amongst the disguised and hidden Israelites of Portugal and Spain. They were binding themselves to preserve and propagate a persecuted faith. They were no longer its sole repositors. Did the strength of one waver, all was at an end. They were united in the sweet links of love—framing for themselves new ties, new hopes, new blessings in a rising family—all of which, at one blow, might be destroyed. They existed in an atmosphere of death, yet they lived and flourished. But so situated, it was not strange that human emotion, both in Alvar and his bride, should on their wedding-day, have gained ascendancy; and the solemn hour which made them one in the sight of the God they worshipped, should have been fraught with a terror and a shuddering, of which Jewish lovers in free and happy England can have no knowledge.

Alvar Rodríguez was one of those high and noble spirits, on whom the chain of deceit and concealment weighed heavily; and there were times when it had been difficult to suppress and conceal his scorn of those outward observances which his apparent Catholicism compelled. When united to Almah, however, he had a stronger incentive than his own safety: and as time passed on, and he became a father, caution and circumspection, if possible, increased with the deep passionate feelings of tenderness towards the mother and child. As the boy grew and flourished, the first feelings of dread, which the very love he excited called forth at his birth subsided into a kind of tranquil calm, which even Almah's foreboding spirit trusted would last, as the happiness of others of her race.

Though Alvar's business was carried on both at Montes and at Lisbon, the bulk of both his own and his wife's property was, by a strange chance, invested at Badajoz, a frontier town of Spain, and whence he had often intended to remove but had always been prevented. It happened that early the month of June, some affairs calling him to Lisbon, he resolved to delay removing it no longer, smiling at his young wife's half solicitation to let it remain where it was, and playfully accusing her of superstition, a charge she cared not to deny. The night before his intended departure his young Moorish secretary, in other words, an Israelite of Barbary extraction, entered his private closet, with a countenance of entreaty and alarm, earnestly conjuring his master to give up his Lisbon expedition, and retire with his wife and son to Badajoz or Oporto, or some distant city, at least for a while. Anxiously Rodríguez inquired wherefore.

"You remember the Señor Leyva, your worship's guest a week or two ago?"

"Perfectly. What of him?"

"Master, I like him not. If danger befall us it will come through him. I watched him closely, and every hour of his stay shrunk from him the more. He was a stranger?"

"Yes; benighted, and had lost his way. It was impossible to refuse him hospitality. That he stayed longer than he had need, I grant; but there is no cause of alarm in that—he liked his quarters?"

"Master," replied the Moor, earnestly, "I do not believe his tale. He was no casual traveller. I cannot trust him."

"You are not called upon to do so, man," said Alvar, laughing. "What do you believe him to be, that you would inoculate me with your own baseless alarm?"

Hassan ben Ahmed's answer, whatever it might be, for it was whispered fearfully in his master's ear, had the effect of sending every drop of blood from Alvar's face to his very heart. But he shook off the stagnating dread. He combated the prejudices of his follower as unreasonable and unfounded. Hassan's alarm, however, could only be soothed by the fact, that so suddenly to change his plans would but excite suspicion. If Levya were what he feared, his visit must already have been followed by the usual terrific effects.

Alvar promised, however, to settle his affairs at Lisbon as speedily as he could, and return for Almah and his son, and convey them to some place of greater security until the imagined danger was passed.

In spite of his assumed indifference, however, Rodríguez could not bid his wife and child farewell without a pang of dread, which it was difficult to conceal. The step between life and death—security and destruction—was so small, it might be passed unconsciously, and then the strongest nerve might shudder at the dark abyss before him. Again and again he turned to go, and yet again returned; and it with a feeling literally of desperation he at length tore himself away.

A fearful trembling was on Almah's heart as she gazed after him, but she would not listen to its voice.

"It is folly," she said, self-upbraidingly. "My Alvar is ever chiding this too doubting heart. I will not disobey him, by fear and foreboding in his absence. The God of the nameless is with him and me," and she raised her eyes to the blue arch above her, with an expression that needed not voice to mark it prayer.

About a week after Alvar's departure, Almah was sitting by the cradle of her boy, watching his soft and rosy slumbers with a calm sweet thankfulness that such a treasure was her own. The season had been unusually hot and dry, but the apartment in which the young mother sat opened on a pleasant spot, thickly shaded with orange, lemon, and almond trees, and decked with a hundred other richly hued and richly scented plants; in the centre of which a fountain sent up its heavy showers, which fell back on the marble bed, with a splash and coolness peculiarly refreshing, and sparkled in the sun as glittering gems.

A fleet yet heavy step resounded from the garden, which seemed suddenly and forcibly restrained into a less agitated movement. A shadow fell between her and the sunshine, and, starting, Almah looked hastily up. Hassan ben Ahmed stood before her, a paleness on his swarthy cheek, and a compression on his nether lip, betraying strong emotion painfully restrained.

"My husband! Hassan. What news bring you of him? Why are you alone?"

He laid his hand on her arm, and answered in a voice which so quivered that only ears eager as her own could have distinguished his meaning.

"Lady, dear, dear lady, you have a firm and faithful heart. Oh! for the love of Him who calls on you to suffer, awake its strength and firmness. My dear, my honoured lady, sink not, fail not! O God of mercy, support her now!" he added, flinging himself on his knees before her, as Almah one moment sprang up with a smothered shriek, and then next sank back on her seat rigid as marble.

Not another word she needed. Hassan thought to have prepared, gradually to have told, his dread intelligence; but he had said enough. Called upon to suffer, and for Him her God—her doom was revealed in those brief words. One minute of such agonized struggle, that her soul and body seemed about to part beneath it; and the wife and mother roused herself to do. Lip, cheek, and brow vied in their ashen whiteness with her robe; the blue veins rose distended as cords; and the voice—had not Hassan gazed upon her, he had not known it as her own.

She commanded him to tell her briefly all, and even while he spoke, seemed revolving in her own mind the decision which not four and twenty hours after Hassan's intelligence she put into execution.

It was as Ben Ahmed had feared. The known popularity and rumoured riches of Alvar Rodríguez had excited the jealousy of that secret and awful tribunal, the Inquisition, one of whose innumerable spies, under the feigned name of Leyva, had obtained entrance within Alvar's hospitable wall. One unguarded word or movement, the faintest semblance of secrecy or caution, were all sufficient; nay, without these, more than a common share of wealth or felicity was enough for the unconscious victims to be marked, tracked, and seized, without preparation or suspicion of their fate. Alvar had chanced to mention his intended visit to Lisbon; and the better to conceal the agent of his arrest, as also to make it more secure, they waited till his arrival there, watched their opportunity, and seized and conveyed him to those cells whence few returned in life, propagating the charge of relapsed Judaism as the cause of his arrest. It was a charge too common for remark, and the power which interfered too mighty for resistance. The confusion of the arrest soon subsided; but it lasted long enough for the faithful Hassan to escape, and, by dint of very rapid travelling, reached Montes not four hours after his master's seizure. The day was in consequence before them, and he ceased not to conjure his lady to fly at once; the officers of the Inquisition could scarcely be there before nightfall.

"You must take advantage of it, Hassan, and all of you who love me. For my child, my boy," she had clasped to her bosom, and a convulsion contracted her beautiful features as she spoke, "you must take care of him; convey him to Holland or England. Take jewels and gold sufficient; and—and make him love his parents—he may never see either of them more. Hassan, Hassan, swear to protect my child!" she added, with a burst of such sudden and passionate agony it seemed as if life or reason must bend beneath it. Bewildered by her words, as terrified by her emotion, Ben Ahmed removed the trembling child from the fond arms that for the first time failed to support him, gave him hastily to the care of his nurse, who was also a Jewess, said a few words in Hebrew, detailing what had passed, beseeching her to prepare for flight, and then returned to his mistress. The effects of that prostrating agony remained, but she had so far conquered, as to seem outwardly calm; and in answer to his respectful and anxious looks, besought him not to fear for her, nor to dissuade her from her purpose, but to aid her in its accomplishment. She summoned her household around her, detailed what had befallen, and bade them seek their own safety in flight; and when in tears and grief they left her, and but those of her own faith remained, she solemnly committed her child to their care, and informed them of her own determination to proceed directly to Lisbon. In vain Hassan ben Ahmed conjured her to give up the idea; it was little short of madness. How could she aid his master? Why not secure her own safety, that if indeed he should escape, the blessing of her love would be yet preserved him?

"Do not fear for your master, Hassan," was the calm reply; "ask not of my plans, for at this moment they seem but chaos, but of this be assured, we shall live or die together."

More she revealed not; but when the officers of the Inquisition arrived, near nightfall, they found nothing but deserted walls. The magnificent furniture and splendid paintings which alone remained, of course were seized by the Holy Office, by whom Alvar's property was also confiscated. Had his arrest been deferred three months longer, all would have gone—swept off by the same rapacious power, to whom great wealth was ever proof of great guilt—but as it was, the greater part, secured in Spain, remained untouched; a circumstance peculiarly fortunate, as Almah's plans needed the aid of gold.

We have no space to linger on the mother's feelings, as she parted from her boy; gazing on him, perhaps, for the last time. Yet she neither wept nor sighed. There was but one other feeling stronger in that gentle bosom—a wife's devotion—and to that alone she might listen now.

Great was old Gonzalos' terror and astonishment when Almah, attended only by Hassan ben Ahmed, and both attired in the Moorish costume, entered his dwelling and implored his concealment and aid. The arrest of Alvar Rodríguez had, of course, thrown every secret Hebrew into the greatest alarm, though none dared be evinced. Gonzalos' only hope and consolation was that Almah and her child had escaped; and to see her in the very centre of danger, even to listen to her calmly proposed plans, seemed so like madness, that he used every effort to alarm her into their relinquishment. But this could not be; and with the darkest forebodings, the old man at length yielded to the stronger, more devoted spirit, with whom he had to deal.

His mistress once safely under Gonzalos' roof, Ben Ahmed departed, under cover of night, in compliance with her earnest entreaties to rejoin her child, and to convey him and his nurse to England, that blessed land, where the veil of secrecy could be removed.

About a week after the incarceration of Alvar, a young Moor sought and obtained admission to the presence of Juan Pacheco, the secretary of the Inquisition, as informer against Alvar Rodríguez. He stated that he had taken service with him as clerk or secretary, on condition that he would give him baptism and instruction in the holy Catholic faith; that Alvar had not yet done so; that many things in his establishment proclaimed a looseness of orthodox principles, which the Holy Office would do well to notice. Meanwhile he humbly offered a purse containing seventy pieces of gold, to obtain masses for his salvation.

This last argument carried more weight than all the rest. The young Moor, who boldly gave his name as Hassan ben Ahmed (which was confirmation strong of his previous statement, as in Leyva's information of Alvar and his household the Moorish secretary was particularly specified), was listened to with attention and finally received in Pacheco's own household as junior clerk and servant to the Holy Office.

Despite his extreme youthfulness and delicacy of figure, face, and voice, Hassan's activity and zeal to oblige every member of the Holy Office, superiors and inferiors, gradually gained him the favour and goodwill of all. There was no end to his resources for serving others; and thus he had more opportunities of seeing the prisoners in a few weeks, than others of the same rank as himself had had in years. But the prisoner he most longed to see was still unfound, and it was not till summoned before his judges, in the grand of inquisition and of torture, Hassan ben Ahmed gazed once more upon his former master. He had attended Pacheco in his situation of junior clerk, but had seated himself so deeply in the shade that, though every movement in both the face and form of Alvar was distinguishable to him, Hassan himself was invisible.

The trial, if trial such iniquitous proceedings may be called, proceeded; but in nought did Alvar Rodríguez fail in his bearing or defence. Marvellous and superhuman must that power have been which, in such a scene and hour, prevented all betrayal of the true faith the victims bore. Once Judaism confessed, the doom was death; and again and again have the sons of Israel remained in the terrible dungeons of the Inquisition—endured every species of torture during a space of seven, ten, or twelve years, and then been released, because no proof could be brought of their being indeed that cursed thing—a Jew. And then it was that they fled from scenes of such fearful trial to lands of toleration and freedom, and there embraced openly and rejoicingly that blessed faith, for which in secret they had borne so much.

Alvar Rodríguez was one of these—prepared to suffer, but not reveal. They applied the torture, but neither word nor groan was extracted from him. Engrossed with the prisoner, for it was his task to write down whatever disjointed words might escape his lips, Pacheco neither noticed nor even remembered the presence of the young Moor. No unusual paleness could be visible on his embrowned check, but his whole frame felt to himself to have become rigid as stone; a deadly sickness had crept over him, and the terrible conviction of all which rested with him to do alone prevented his sinking senseless on the earth.

The terrible struggle was at length at an end. Alvar was released for the time being, and remanded to his dungeon. Availing himself of the liberty he enjoyed in the little notice now taken of his movements, Hassan reached the prison before either Alvar or his guards. A rapid glance told him its situation, overlooking a retired part of the court, cultivated as a garden. The height of the wall seemed about forty feet, and there were no windows of observation on either side. This was fortunate, the more so as Hassan had before made friends with the old gardener, and pretending excessive love of gardening, had worked just under the window, little dreaming its vicinity to him he sought.

A well-known Hebrew air, with its plaintive Hebrew words, sung tremblingly and softly under his window, first roused Alvar to the sense that a friend was near. He started, almost in superstitious terror, for the voice seemed an echo to that which was ever sounding in his heart. That loved one it could not be, nay, he dared not even wish it; but still the words were Hebrew, and, for the first time, memory flashed back a figure in Moorish garb who had flitted by him on his return to his prison, after his examination.

Hassan, the faithful Hassan! Alvar felt certain it could be none but he; though, in the moment of sudden excitement, the voice had seemed another's. He looked from the window; the Moor was bending over the flowers, but Alvar felt confirmed in his suspicions, and his heart throbbed with the sudden hope of liberty. He whistled, and a movement in the figure below convinced him he was heard.

One point was gained; the next was more fraught with danger, yet it was accomplished. In a bunch of flowers, drawn up by a thin string which Alvar chanced to possess, Ben Ahmed had concealed a file; and as he watched it ascend, and beheld the flowers scattered to the winds, in token that they had done their work, for Alvar dared not retain them in his prison, Hassan felt again the prostration of bodily power which had before assailed him for such a different cause, and it was an almost convulsive effort to retain his faculties; but a merciful Providence watched over him and Alvar making the feeblest and the weakest instruments of his all-sustaining love.

We are not permitted space to linger on the various ingenious methods adopted by Hassan ben Ahmed to forward and mature his plans. Suffice it that all seemed to smile upon him. The termination of the garden wall led, by a concealed door, to a subterranean passage running to the banks of the Tagus. This fact, as also the secret spring of the trap, the old gardener in a moment of unwise conviviality imparted to Ben Ahmed, little imagining the special blessing which such unexpected information secured.

An alcayde and about twenty guards did sometimes patrol the garden within sight of Alvar's window; but this did not occur often, such caution seeming unnecessary.

It had been an evening of unwonted festivity among the soldiers and servants of the Holy Office, which had at length subsided into the heavy slumbers of general intoxication. Hassan had supped with the gardener, and plying him well with wine, soon produced the desired effect. Four months had the Moor spent within the dreaded walls, and the moment had now come when delay need be no more. At midnight all was hushed into profound silence, not a leaf stirred, and the night was so unusually still that the faintest sound would have been distinguished. Hassan stealthily crept round the outposts. Many of the guards were slumbering in various attitudes upon their posts, and others, dependent on his promised watchfulness, were literally deserted. He stood beneath the window. One moment he clasped his hands and bowed his head in one mighty, piercing, though silent prayer, and then dug hastily in the flower-bed at his feet, removing from thence a ladder of ropes, which had lain there some days concealed, and flung a pebble with correct aim against the bars of Alvar's window. The sound, though scarcely loud enough to disturb a bird, reverberated on the trembling heart which heard, as if a thousand cannons had been discharged.

A moment of agonized suspense and Alvar Rodríguez stood at the window, the bar he had removed in his hand. He let down the string, to which Hassan's now trembling hands secured the ladder and drew it to the wall. His descent could not have occupied two minutes, at the extent; but to that solitary watcher what eternity of suffering did they seem! Alvar was at his side, had clasped his hands, had called him "Hassan! Brother!" in tones of intense feeling, but no word replied. He sought to fly, to point to the desired haven, but his feet seemed suddenly rooted to the earth. Alvar threw his arm around him, and drew him forward. A sudden and unnatural strength returned. Noiselessly and fleetly as their feet could go, they sped beneath the shadow of the wall. A hundred yards alone divided them from the secret door. A sudden sound broke the oppressive stillness. It was the tramp of heavy feet and the clash of arms; the light of many torches flashed upon the darkness. They darted forward in the fearful excitement of despair; but the effort was void and vain. A wild shout of challenge—of alarm—and they were surrounded, captured, so suddenly, so rapidly, Alvar's very senses seemed to reel; but frightfully they were recalled. A shriek, so piercing, it seemed to rend the very heavens, burst through the still air. The figure of the Moor rushed from the detaining grasp of the soldiery, regardless of bared steel and pointed guns, and flung himself at the feet of Alvar.

"O God, my husband—I have murdered him!" were the strange appalling words which burst upon his ear, and the lights flashing upon his face, as he sank prostrate and lifeless on the earth, revealed to Alvar's tortured senses the features of his WIFE.

How long that dead faint continued Almah knew not, but when sense returned she found herself in a dark and dismal cell, her upper garment and turban removed, while the plentiful supply of water, which had partially restored life, had removed in a great degree the dye which had given her countenance its Moorish hue. Had she wished to continue concealment, one glance around her would have proved the effort vain. Her sex was already known, and the stern dark countenances near her breathed but ruthlessness and rage. Some brief questions were asked relative to her name, intent, and faith, which she answered calmly.

"In revealing my name," she said, "my intention must also be disclosed. The wife of Alvar Rodríguez had not sought these realms of torture and death, had not undergone all the miseries of disguise and servitude, but for one hope, one intent—the liberty of her husband."

"Thus proving his guilt," was the rejoinder. "Had you known him innocent, you would have waited the justice of the Holy Office to give him freedom."

"Justice," she repeated, bitterly. "Had the innocent never suffered, I might have trusted. But I know accusation was synonymous with death, and therefore came I here. For my faith, mine is my husband's."

"And know you the doom of all who attempt or abet escape? Death—death by burning! And this you have hurled upon him and yourself. It is not the Holy Office, but his wife who has condemned him"; and with gibing laugh they left her, securing with heavy bolt and bar the iron door. She darted forwards, beseeching them, as they hoped for mercy, to take her to her husband, to confine them underground a thousand fathoms deep, so that they might but be together; but only the hollow echo of her own voice replied, and the wretched girl sunk back upon the ground, relieved from present suffering by long hours of utter insensibility.

It was not till brought from their respective prisons to hear pronounced on them the sentence of death, that Alvar Rodríguez and his heroic wife once more gazed upon each other.

They had provided Almah, at her own entreaty, with female habiliments; for, in the bewildering agony of her spirit, she attributed the failure of her scheme for the rescue of her husband to her having disobeyed the positive command of God and adopted a male disguise, which in His eyes was abomination, but which in her wild desire to save Alvar she had completely overlooked, and she now in consequence shrunk from the fatal garb with agony and loathing. Yet despite the haggard look of intense mental and bodily suffering, the loss of her lovely hair, which she had cut close to her head, lest by the merest chance its length and luxuriance should discover her, so exquisite, so touching, was her delicate loveliness, that her very judges, stern, unbending as was their nature, looked on her with an admiration almost softening them to mercy.

And now, for the first time, Alvar's manly composure seemed about to desert him. He, too, had suffered almost as herself, save that her devotedness, her love, appeared to give strength, to endow him with courage, even to look upon her fate, blended as it now was with his own, with calm trust in the merciful God who called him thus early to Himself. Almah could not realise such thoughts. But one image was ever present, seeming to mock her very misery to madness. Her effort had failed; had she not so wildly sought her husband's escape—had she but waited—they might have released him; and now, what was she but his murderess?

Little passed between the prisoners and their judges. Their guilt was all sufficiently proved by their endeavours to escape, which in itself was a crime always visited by death; and for these manifold sins and misdemeanours they were sentenced to be burnt alive, on All Saints' day, in the grand square of the Inquisition, at nine o'clock in the morning, and proclamation commanded to be made throughout Lisbon, that all who sought to witness and assist at the ceremony should receive remission of sins, and be accounted worthy servants of Jesus Christ. The lesser severity of strangling the victims before burning was denied them, as they neither repented nor had trusted to the justice and clemency of the Holy Office, but had attempted to avert a deserved fate by flight.

Not a muscle of Alvar's fine countenance moved during this awful sentence. He stood proudly and loftily erect, regarding those that spake with an eye, bright, stern, unflinching as their own; but a change passed over it as, breaking from the guard around, Almah flung herself on her knees at his feet.

"Alvar! Alvar! I have murdered—my husband, oh, my husband, say you forgive—forgive—"

"Hush, hush, beloved! Mine own heroic Almah, fail not now!" he answered, with a calm and tender seriousness, which to still that crushing agony, strengthened her to bear and raising her, he pressed her to his breast.

"We have but to die as we have lived, my own! True to that God whose chosen and whose first-born we are, have been, and shall be unto death, aye, and *beyond* it. He will protect our poor orphan, for He has promised the fatherless shall be His care. Look up, my beloved, and say you can face death with Alvar, calmly, faithfully, as you sought to live for him. God has chosen for us a better heritage than one of earth."

She raised her head from his bosom; the terror and the agony had passed from that sweet face—it was tranquil as his own.

"It was not my own death I feared," she said, unfalteringly, "it was but the weakness of human love; but it is over now. Love is mightier than death; there is only love in heaven."

"Aye!" answered Alvar, and proudly and sternly he waved back the soldiers who had hurried forward to divide them. "Men of a mistaken and bloody creed, behold how the scorned and persecuted Israelites can love and die. While there was a hope that we could serve our God, the Holy and the only One, better in life than in death, it was our duty to preserve that life, and endure torture for His sake, rather than reveal the precious secret of our sainted faith and heavenly heritage. But now that hope is at an end, now that no human means can save us from the doom pronounced, know ye have judged rightly of our creed. We ARE those chosen children of God by you deemed blasphemous and heretic. Do what you will, men of blood and guile, ye cannot rob us of our faith."

The impassioned tones of natural eloquence awed even the rude crowd around; but more was not permitted. Rudely severed, and committed to their own guards, the prisoners were borne to their respective dungeons. To Almah those earnest words had been as the voice of an angel, hushing every former pang to rest; and in the solitude and darkness of the intervening hours, even the thought of her child could not rob her soul of its calm or prayer of its strength.

The 1st of November 1755 dawned cloudless and lovely as it had been the last forty days. Never had there been a season more gorgeous in its sunny splendour, more brilliant in the intense azure of its arching heaven than the present. Scarcely any rain had fallen for many months, and the heat had at first been intolerable, but within the last six weeks a freshness and coolness had infused the atmosphere and revived the earth.

As it was not a regular auto-da-fé (Alvar and his wife being the only victims), the awful ceremony of burning was to take place in the square, of which the buildings of the Inquisition formed one side. Mass had been performed before daybreak in the chapel of the Inquisition, at which the victims were compelled to be present, and about half past seven the dread procession left the Inquisition gates. The soldiers and minor servitors marched first, forming a hollow square, in the centre of which were the stakes and huge faggots piled around. Then came the sacred cross, covered with a black veil, and its bodyguard of priests. The victims, each surrounded by monks, appeared next, closely followed by the higher officers and inquisitors, and a band of fifty men, in rich dresses of black satin and silver, closed the procession.

We have no space to linger on the ceremonies always attendant on the burning of inquisitorial prisoners. Although, from the more private nature of the rites, these ceremonies were greatly curtailed, it was rather more than half an hour after nine when the victims were bound to their respective stakes, and the executioners approached with their blazing brands.

There was no change in the countenance of either prisoner. Pale they were, yet calm and firm; all of human feeling had been merged in the martyr's courage and the martyr's faith.

One look had been exchanged between them—of love spiritualized to look beyond the grave—of encouragement to endure for their God, even to the end. The sky was still cloudless, the sun still looked down on that scene of horror; and then was a hush—a pause—for so it felt in nature, that stilled the very breathing of those around.

"Hear, O Israel, the Lord our God, the Lord is ONE—the Sole and Holy One; there is no unity like His unity!" were the words which broke that awful pause, in a voice distinct, unfaltering, and musical as its wont; and it was echoed by the sweet tones from woman's lips, so thrilling in their melody, the rudest nature started. It was the signal of their fate. The executioners hastened forward, the brands were applied to the turf of the piles, the flames blazed up beneath their hand—when at that moment there came a shock as if the very earth were cloven asunder, the heavens rent in twain. A crash so loud, yea so fearful, so appalling, as if the whole of Lisbon had been shivered to its foundations, and a shriek, or rather thousands and thousands of human voices, blended in one wild piercing cry of agony and terror, seeming to burst from every quarter at the selfsame instant, and fraught with universal woe. The buildings around shook, as impelled by a mighty whirlwind, though no sound of such was heard. The earth heaved, yawned, closed, and rocked again, as the billows of the ocean were lashed to fury. It was a moment of untold horror. The crowd assembled to witness, the martyrs' death fled, wildly shrieking, on every side. Scattered to the heaving ground, the blazing piles lay powerless to injure; their bonds were shivered, their guards were fled. One bound brought Alvar to his wife, and he clasped her in his arms. "God, God of mercy, save us yet again! Be with us to the end!" he exclaimed, and faith winged the prayer. On, on he sped; up, up, in direction of the heights, where he knew comparative safety lay; but ere he reached them, the innumerable sights and sounds of horror that yawned upon his way! Every street, and square, and avenue was choked with shattered ruins, rent from top to bottom; houses, convents, and churches presented the most fearful aspect of ruin; while every second minute a new impetus seemed to be given to the convulsed earth, causing those that remained still perfect to rock and rend. Huge stones, falling from every crack, were crushing the miserable fugitives as they rushed on, seeking safety they knew not where. The rafters of every roof, wrenched from their fastenings, stood upright a brief while, and then fell in hundreds together, with a crash perfectly appalling. The very ties of nature were severed in the wild search for safety. Individual life alone appeared worth preserving. None dared seek the fate of friends—none dared ask, "Who lives?" in that one scene of universal death.

On, on sped Alvar and his precious burden, on over the piles of ruins; on, unhurt amidst the showers of stones which, hurled in the air as easily as a ball cast from an infant's hand, fell back again laden with a hundred deaths; on, amid the rocking and yawning earth, beholding thousands swallowed up, crushed and maimed, worse than death itself, for they were left to a lingering torture—to die a thousand deaths in anticipating one; on over the disfigured heaps of dead, and the unrecognised masses of what had once been magnificent and gorgeous buildings. His eye was well-nigh blinded with the shaking and tottering movement of all things animate and inanimate before him; and his path obscured by the sudden and awful darkness, which had changed that bright glowing hue of the sunny sky into a pall of dense and terrible blackness, becoming thicker and denser with every succeeding minute, till a darkness which might be felt, enveloped that devoted city as with the grim shadow of death. His ear was deafened by the appalling sounds of human agony and Nature's wrath; for now, sounds as of a hundred waterspouts, the dull continued roar of subterranean thunder, becoming at times loud as the discharge of a thousand cannons; at others, resembling the sharp grating sound of hundreds and hundreds of chariots driving full speed over the stones; and this, mingled with the piercing shrieks of women, the hoarser cries and shouts of men, the deep terrible groans of mental agony, and the shriller screams of instantaneous death, had usurped the place of the previous awful stillness, till every sense of those who yet survived seemed distorted and maddened. And Nature herself, convulsed and freed from restraining bonds, appeared about to return to that chaos whence she had leaped at the word of God.

Still, still Alvar rushed forwards, preserved amidst it all, as if the arm of a merciful Providence was indeed around him and his Almah, marking them for life in the very midst of death. Making his rapid way across the ruins of St. Paul's, which magnificent church had fallen in the first shock, crushing the vast congregation assembled within its walls, Alvar paused one moment, undecided whether to seek the banks of the river or still to make for the western heights. There was a moment's hush and pause in the convulsion of nature, but Alvar dared not hope for its continuance. Ever and anon the earth still heaved, and houses opened from base to roof and closed without further damage. With a brief fervid cry for continued guidance and protection, scarcely conscious which way in reality he took, and still folding Almah to his bosom—so supernaturally strengthened that the weakness of humanity seemed far from him—Rodríguez, hurried on, taking the most open path to the Estrella Hill. An open space was gained, half-way to the summit, commanding a view of the banks of the river, and the ruins around. Panting, almost breathless, yet still struggling with his own exhaustion to encourage Almah, Alvar an instant rested, ere he plunged anew into the narrower streets. A shock, violent, destructive, convulsive as the first, flung them prostrate; while the renewed and increased sounds of wailing, the tremendous and repeated crashes on every side, the disappearance of the towers, steeples, and turrets which yet remained, revealed the further destructiveness which had befallen. A new and terrible cry added to the universal horror.

"The sea! the sea!" Alvar sprung to his feet and, clasped in each other's arms, he and Almah gazed beneath. Not a breath of wind stirred, yet the river (which being at that point four miles wide appeared like the element they had termed it) tossed and heaved as if impelled by a mighty storm—and on it came, roaring, foaming, tumbling, as every bound were loosed; on, over the land to the very heart of the devoted city, sweeping off hundreds in its course, and retiring with such velocity, and so far beyond its natural banks, that vessels were left dry which had five minutes before ridden in water seven fathoms deep. Again and again this phenomenon took place; the vessels in the river, at the same instant, whirled round and round with frightful rapidity, and smaller boats dashed upwards, falling back to disappear beneath the booming waters. As if chained to the spot where they stood, fascinated by this very horror, Alvar and his wife yet gazed; their glance fixed on the new marble quay, where thousands and thousands of the fugitives had congregated, fixed, as if unconsciously foreboding what was to befall. Again the tide rushed in—on, on, over the massive ruins, heaving, raging, swelling, as a living thing; and at the same instant the quay and its vast burden of humanity sunk within an abyss of boiling waters, into which the innumerable boats around were alike impelled, leaving not a trace, even when the angry waters returned to their channel, suddenly as they had left it, to mark what had been.

" 'Twas the voice of God impelled me hither, rather than pausing beside those fated banks. Almah, my best beloved, bear up yet a brief while more—He will spare and save us as he hath done now. Merciful Providence! Behold another wrathful element threatens to swallow up all of life and property which yet remains. Great God, this is terrible!"

And terrible it was: from three parts of the ruined city huge fires suddenly blazed up, hissing, crackling, ascending as clear columns of liquid flame; up against the pitchy darkness, infusing it with tenfold horror—spreading on every side—consuming all of wood and wall which the earth and water had left unscathed; wreathing its serpent-like folds in and out the ruins, forming strange and terribly beautiful shapes of glowing colouring; fascinating the eye with admiration, yet bidding the blood chill and the flesh creep. Fresh cries and shouts had marked its rise and progress; but, aghast and stupefied, those who yet survived made no effort to check its way, and on every side it spread, forming lanes and squares of glowing red, flinging its lurid glare so vividly around, that even those on the distant heights could see to read by it; and fearful was the scene that awful light revealed. Now, for the first time could Alvar trace the full extent of destruction which had befallen. That glorious city, which a few brief hours previous lay reposing in its gorgeous sunlight—mighty in its palaces and towers—in its churches, convents, theatres, magazines, and dwellings—rich in its numberless artizans and stores—lay perished and prostrate as the grim spectre of long ages past, save that the fearful groups yet passing to and fro, or huddled in kneeling and standing masses, some bathed in the red glare of the increasing fires, others black and shapeless—save when a sudden flame flashed on them, disclosing what they were—revealed a strange and horrible PRESENT, yet lingering amid what seemed the shadows of a fearful PAST. Nor was the convulsion of nature yet at an end;—the earth still rocked and heaved at intervals, often impelling the hissing flames more strongly and devouringly forward, and by tossing the masses of burning ruin to and fro, gave them the semblance of a sea of flame. The ocean itself, too, yet rose and sunk, and rose again; vessels were torn from their cables, anchors wrenched from their soundings and hurled in the air—while the warring waters, the muttering thunders, the crackling flames, formed a combination of sounds which, even without their dread adjuncts of human agony and terror, were all-sufficient to freeze the very life-blood, and banish every sense and feeling, save that of stupefying dread.

But human love, and superhuman faith, saved from the stagnating horror. The conviction that the God of his fathers was present with him, and would save him and Almah to the end, never left him for an instant, but urged him to exertions which, had he not had this all-supporting faith, he would himself have deemed impossible. And his faith spake truth. The God of infinite mercy, who had stretched out His own right hand to save, and marked the impotence of the wrath and cruelty of man, was with him still, and, despite the horrors yet lingering round them, despite the varied trials, fatigues, and privations attendant on their rapid flight, led them to life and joy, and bade them stand forth the witnesses and proclaimers of His unfailing love, His everlasting providence!

With the great earthquake of Lisbon, the commencement of which our preceding pages have faintly endeavoured to portray, and its terrible effects on four millions of square miles, our tale has no further connection. The third day brought our poor fugitives to Badajoz, where Alvar's property had been secured. They tarried there only long enough to learn the blessed tidings of Hassan ben Ahmed's safe arrival in England with their child; that his faithfulness, in conjunction with that of their agent in Spain, had already safely transmitted the bulk of their property to English funds; and to obtain Ben Ahmed's address, forward tidings of their providential escape to him, and proceed on their journey.

An anxious but not a prolonged interval enabled them to accomplish it safely, and once more did the doubly rescued press their precious boy to their yearning hearts and feel that conjugal and parental love burnt, if it could be, the dearer, brighter, more unspeakably precious, from the dangers they had passed; and not human love alone. The veil of secrecy was removed, they were in a land whose merciful and liberal government granted to the exile and the wanderer a home of peace and rest, where they might worship the God of Israel according to the law he gave; and in hearts like those of Alvar and his Almah, prosperity could have no power to extinguish or deaden the religion of love and faith which adversity had engendered.

The appearance of old Gonzalos and his family in England, a short time after Alvah's arrival there, removed their last remaining anxiety, and gave them increased cause for thankfulness. Not a member of the merchant's family, and more wonderful still, not a portion of his property, had been lost amidst the universal ruin; and to this very day, his descendants recall his providential preservation by giving, on every returning anniversary of that awful day, certain articles of clothing to a limited number of male and female poor.

Emma Lazarus

Emma Lazarus (USA, 1849–1887) is regarded as the most significant Jewish-American author of the nineteenth century. Writing during a period of intense productivity in American letters—her contemporaries included Walt Whitman, Herman Melville, Nathaniel Hawthorne, Edgar Allan Poe, and her friend and mentor Ralph Waldo Emerson—she published poetry and translated works by Heinrich Heine. Her translations of the works of the medieval Hebrew poets Solomon ibn Gabirol, Yehuda Halevi, and Moses ibn Ezra were themselves based on the German translations of Michael Sachs and Abraham Geiger. Lazarus was German-Jewish on her mother's side and Sephardic on her father's. She was deeply moved by the moral and humanitarian tragedy that resulted from the Civil War and by the draft riots of 1863 in her native New York City. Lazarus published her first book, *Poems and Translations* (1867), when she was only seventeen years old. Other collections of her poetry include *Admetus and Other Poems* (1871) and *Songs of a Semite: The Dance to Death, and Other Poems* (1882). She also wrote a novel, *Alide* (1874), and the drama *The Spagnoletto,* published in 1876, the American centennial year. The news of the anti-Jewish riots in Russia in the 1880s turned Lazarus into an advocate for Jewish causes. Toward the end of her life she became a supporter of a Jewish state in Palestine for Jews fleeing pogroms. A number of her poems deal with Jewish and proto-Zionist themes: "In the Jewish Synagogue at Newport" is included in *Admetus and Other Poems,* and "The Banner of the Jew" is from *Songs of a Semite.* She also wrote poems about Rashi, the noted biblical and talmudic commentator from Troyes (1040–1105), and about Bar Kokhba, who led the Jews in their unsuccessful revolt against the Romans in Palestine in 132–35 CE. But she is, of course, best remembered for her sonnet "The New Colossus," which she composed in 1883 to aid in the fund-raising effort to complete the pedestal of the Statue of Liberty. In 1903 the poem was engraved onto a plaque that was affixed to the inner walls of the statue's pedestal.

In the Jewish Synagogue at Newport

Here, where the noises of the busy town,
    The ocean's plunge and roar can enter not,
We stand and gaze around with tearful awe,
    And muse upon the consecrated spot.

No signs of life are here: the very prayers
    Inscribed around are in a language dead;
The light of the "perpetual lamp" is spent
    That an undying radiance was to shed.

What prayers were in this temple offered up,
    Wrung from sad hearts that knew no joy on earth,
By these lone exiles of a thousand years,
    From the fair sunrise land that gave them birth!

Now as we gaze, in this new world of light,
    Upon this relic of the days of old,
The present vanishes, and tropic bloom
    And Eastern towns and temples we behold.

Again we see the patriarch with his flocks,
    The purple seas, the hot blue sky o'erhead,
The slaves of Egypt,—omens, mysteries,—
    Dark fleeing hosts by flaming angels led.

A wondrous light upon a sky-kissed mount,
    A man who reads Jehovah's written law,
'Midst blinding glory and effulgence rare,
    Unto a people prone with reverent awe.

The pride of luxury's barbaric pomp,
    In the rich court of royal Solomon—

Alas! we wake: one scene alone remains,—
    The exiles by the streams of Babylon.

Our softened voices send us back again
    But mournful echoes through the empty hall;
Our footsteps have a strange unnatural sound,
    And with unwonted gentleness they fall.

The weary ones, the sad, the suffering,
    All found their comfort in the holy place,
And children's gladness and men's gratitude
    Took voice and mingled in the chant of praise.

The funeral and the marriage, now, alas!
    We know not which is sadder to recall;
For youth and happiness have followed age,
    And green grass lieth gently over all.

Nathless the sacred shrine is holy yet,
    With its lone floors where reverent feet once trod.
Take off your shoes as by the burning bush,
    Before the mystery of death and God.

The New Colossus

Not like the brazen giant of Greek fame,
With conquering limbs astride from land to land;
Here at our sea-washed, sunset gates shall stand
A mighty woman with a torch, whose flame
Is the imprisoned lightning, and her name
Mother of Exiles. From her beacon-hand
Glows world-wide welcome; her mild eyes command
The air-bridged harbor that twin cities frame.

"Keep, ancient lands, your storied pomp!" cries she
With silent lips. "Give me your tired, your poor,
Your huddled masses yearning to breathe free,
The wretched refuse of your teeming shore.
Send these, the homeless, tempest-tost to me,
I lift my lamp beside the golden door!"

The Banner of the Jew

Wake, Israel, wake! Recall to-day
The glorious Maccabean rage,
The sire heroic, hoary-gray,
His five-fold lion-lineage:
The Wise, the Elect, the Help-of-God,
The Burst-of-Spring, the Avenging Rod.

From Mizpeh's mountain-ridge they saw
Jerusalem's empty streets, her shrine
Laid waste where Greeks profaned the Law,
With idol and with pagan sign.
Mourners in tattered black were there,
With ashes sprinkled on their hair.

Then from the stony peak there rang
A blast to ope the graves: down poured
The Maccabean clan, who sang
Their battle-anthem to the Lord.
Five heroes lead, and following, see,
Ten thousand rush to victory!

Oh for Jerusalem's trumpet now,
To blow a blast of shattering power,
To wake the sleepers high and low,

And rouse them to the urgent hour!
No hand for vengeance—but to save,
A million naked swords should wave.

Oh deem not dead that martial fire,
Say not the mystic flame is spent!
With Moses' law and David's lyre,
Your ancient strength remains unbent.
Let but an Ezra rise anew,
To lift the *Banner of the Jew*!

A rag, a mock at first—erelong,
When men have bled and women wept,
To guard its precious folds from wrong,
Even they who shrunk, even they who slept,
Shall leap to bless it, and to save.
Strike! for the brave revere the brave!

Yehuda Burla

Yehuda Burla (Israel, 1886–1969) is the first Hebrew novelist of Sephardic (i.e., Middle Eastern) background. Born in Jerusalem, he studied yeshivot and served in the Turkish army during World War I. He directed Hebrew schools in Damascus, Syria, and also taught in Haifa and Tel-Aviv. Burla headed the Arab Department of the Histadrut, was an envoy of Keren-Hayesod to Latin America in 1946, and directed the Arab Affairs section of the Ministry of Minorities in 1948. He was also president of Israel's Authors' Association. Strongly influenced by the three masters of Yiddish literature—S. Y. Abramovitch, Sholem Aleichem, and I. L. Peretz—he nevertheless was unhappy about the fact that only Ashkenazim appeared in Jewish fiction. Burla's writings are filled with Sephardic characters. His first published work, "Lunah," is a love story set in Old Jerusalem among Sephardim. The same milieu and cast of characters appear in Burla's later work. He is also the author of the novels *In Darkness Striving* (1929; English, 1968) and *The Adventures of Akavyah* (1939), and of two historical narratives: *The Journey of Judah Halevi* (1959), about the medieval Hebrew poet and a proto-Zionist, and *On the Horizon* (1943), a three-part depiction of Rabbi Judah Hai Akalai, an early nineteenth-century Sephardic rabbi who advocated the resettlement of Jews in Palestine without waiting for divine intervention. Burla's *Collected Works* appeared in Hebrew in 1961. His story "Two Sisters," translated by Richard Jacobson, was first published in English in *Jewish Frontier* (October 1964).

Two Sisters

I

The Old People of Jerusalem

IN EVERY ONE of the many courtyards of Jerusalem you might have run into them, old men and women in the twilight of their lives, immigrants from all the countries of the world, living, alone or in company, in cave-like rooms, in dim alcoves, like monks in some great monastery. But the look on their faces was different from that of quiet ascetics. On the contrary, they were full of quiet—and joy. On the faces of many of them the light of purity would rest; security and the pleasure of a great certainty shone forth from all their actions, the pleasure of a peace that comes after one does away with all the accounts and labors, all the worries of the great way, the way of man's life.

And along their twisting way, gently bent on their sticks, among the narrow alleys, in the midst of dark archways and twisting streets, their appearance shone from a double light, a light breaking forth from within and without, from within them and from around them. For they were in Jerusalem, long inscribed in their hearts, longed for by generations, dear above the dearest, and She was now their portion, the joy of their salvation. She would daily light them with the light of holiness and glory. If their way would still go hither and yon, if their eye would sometimes rest on this or that, their heart was addressed yonder, beyond the horizon; thence would they direct their step, and for that would they prepare themselves. They looked upon themselves as eternal wanderers who had passed days upon days, journeys without number, and at their end—their feet now stand before their destination.

And as the number of the dispersions of Israel, so could be seen in Jerusalem all the different types among these old folk, who kept in their mouths the language of their country of origin, who cleaved to their customs, their dress, and way of life. Near Sephardim from Anatolia, who walked always the way of nobility, careful in their fine clothes as in the majesty of the Commandments, would be seen those who had come from Babylon and Yemen, Bukhara and Persia, those who had left Russia and Poland, Germany and Hungary and the rest of the countries of the world—every group with the sign of its birthplace in its speech and manner, and every one silently demonstrating the strength of the love and the eternal bond that is in the hearts of the Exiles of Israel towards the rock of their origin—Jerusalem.

But perhaps the eye would be drawn more after the sight of the old women, the solitary ones, those who had left behind them a full world: the warmth of family, support in life, the love of children and grandchildren. They lived alone here, in small rooms and in poverty—for the love of Jerusalem was stronger in their hearts than the love of all life's treasures.

And they looked as though they had thrown off all life's burden with its tumult and confusion, its joy and sorrow.

II

The Two Sisters

THEY WEREN'T VERY OLD when they first came from Rhodes to Jerusalem. The first-born, Busa Rivka, was about fifty-five, and the younger, Malka, was younger by seven or eight years. It was a long time before any one in Jerusalem knew they were sisters. They dwelt far from each other, one at one end of the Jewish quarter, and one at the other. And when it was finally made known, years after their arrival, that they were sisters, the matter awoke a certain suspicion among men. What was responsible for this alienation? What was the secret between these two? Something was sealed within, but no one knew just what.

When it was first discovered that they were sisters, people suddenly looked back and realized that there was indeed something strange about the manner of these two women. The very fact of their being sisters seemed doubtful. Sisters—but they did not resemble one another at all, neither in physical appearance nor in the character of the soul. The older, Busa Rivka, was short, red-faced, with a full figure, and her glance, since she wore spectacles, was always sent on high, as if she walked always on mountaintops, and her face was turned to heaven. And the younger, Malka, was tall, thin and pale. The older was involved with people, curious, and given to an extra measure of speech. At every opportunity she would tell anyone—whether he were listening or not—almost anything, and more than anything else she would speak of her wealth and the glory of her past in Rhodes. Indeed, all her hearers knew, to her credit, that it was not in complaint that she spoke of the past, that not the quietest whisper of rebellion was in her mouth. On the contrary, she always spoke kindly, with security and satisfaction, and she would never wait for her guest to begin speaking. No, it always was she who began, following the saying, "Before they call me, I answer." And thus would she answer her questioner even if he had not asked: "Blessed be He every day. I—like a queen in my castle. Have I need for anything? And if so, what could it be? As if a dweller in Jerusalem might lack for anything! 'If thou hast merited Jerusalem, what more needest thou?' No, brother, now that I am here, I need wish for nothing more."

And about her "castle," her narrow room, she would say: "It is good for me; better my narrow room than all the comfort of my estate in Rhodes. So I will arrive at the last day with the Truth of Truths in my mouth. Is there any palace that can compare in glory to Jerusalem? For one need just look at 'The House of God' [the Cabbalistic synagogue] or at 'The Great Congregation' [the synagogue dedicated to Rabbi Johanan ben-Zakkai], or even at the Wailing Wall—and his heart will be full of joy and light. How can the palaces of kings compare to the sanctity of Jerusalem? If only the 'Great Father' will deal well with me, to gather me up in peace on my last day! I will never tire of thanking 'His Blessed Name.' "

And when she went out every day to the houses of near or distant neighbors, her mouth would be full of words of thanksgiving, and her hands would turn to some task of knitting or spinning. Wherever she went she would put her hand to help in the housework, and in return she asked for nothing. But if she were invited to eat bread in the morning, afternoon, or any time—she would not refuse.

But the other sister used to stay at home, quieter than most, and closed up within herself. From morning until evening she worked at her hand sewing-machine; knees touching, she would move her hand about the machine without stopping, sewing simple clothes for the Arab villagers at a meager wage.

On rare occasions she would go outside. As she walked her way, modestly and simply, she would straighten her step without turning her eye, right or left—as if she feared some chance meeting on the street might stop her. Her whole manner justified what they said: that this woman is given over to something, body and soul.

So the days passed, all in all several years, until it became known that they were sisters.

How did their sisterhood become known, and who found it out?

Students of the wise, masters of the Torah—they first discovered it.

The students of the wise in Jerusalem used to lie in wait for the old women like hunters after game. Well-to-do women, owners of property, used to buy themselves a "padrino," that is, a proper young student who agreed to be at the right hand of the lady all the days alloted to her on earth. He might, for example, read her "Creed" (Maimonides' Thirteen Principles) in Ladino every Eve of the New Month, with the lady repeating it word by word, and he might visit her from time to time. After her death he served as a son to his mother—for Kaddish, for the study of the Mishnah in her name, and for all the needs of the deceased in the World of Truth. In return for this—on her last day the "padrino" would inherit all she had. Many lucky students found such a "madrona," so that it was worth their while to wait, even if she tarried.

But old women whose purses weren't large enough to buy a "padrino" "managed" with the Kolel (the central community organization): they turned over to it in their lifetime all they had, and received a monthly allowance until their last day. But from then on the Kolel had no obligation to them.

These old women who could not afford an "heir" were in despair all their days in this world.

The "sages" who looked after the possessions of these two women found out, though not from the women themselves, that they were sisters. And those who knocked on their doors realized that the sisters were penniless: they "got along" with the Kolel. But their allowances were much too meager to afford them sustenance. Therefore they had to toil, ceaselessly, each one her own way, to make up what was needed for their poor existence.

But even so, the feeling of mystery about the sisters didn't subside. If they were so poor and needy, whence this peace, this security about their ends? And how could these women find satisfaction in this world, while their "world to come" was not at all in order?

And thus an added mystery in the images of these two sisters.

III

The Happy Pair

YEARS WENT BY. Year after year the days went along their path. Many old men and women came to shelter in the shade of Zion, and many went to their reward in the twenty years that passed, but no change took place in the way of life of the two sisters, although a great change took place in their own selves: the seal of age became stamped on their looks. And even the curious among men, those who generally don't stop talking about something until they find out all the details, even they gave up trying to understand the sisters. The regularity of their lives overcame curiosity. With quietude and the diligence of ants the sisters made their way, until the time came for their secret to be revealed. And this was with the arrival of a new couple from Rhodes, an old man and woman of seventy years or more.

The couple lived in a room in the courtyard of Rabbi Jacob Meshullam, a treasurer of the Great Synagogue in the city. And very quickly did the nature of this pair become known—especially the nature of the old man—and they were called, "the Happy Pair." The "good life" (domestic peace) they led was full of the charm of affection, the peace of truth and goodness of heart, so that the viewer came to look on the pair as an example of the excellence to which mankind could aspire.

The old man was expert in his humor, which never left his speech. But his jokes never hurt, and were never directed against others. All his many words flowed about one subject—"the wife of his youth." Like many old couples, the two of them were always together, and would not let themselves be separated even for a scant hour; because of this the old man called his wife his "in-the-nose" (the breath of his life), and it was clear that he could not live without her for a moment. But behind her back—so to speak—he would tell his hearers with a whisper and a sigh: really he could never trust her, "the Righteous knows." At this age—he would say—a man must tread cautiously . . . it is precisely this age which is dangerous . . . that if, God forbid, she should raise her eyes towards some man, or some man should be attracted to her, "where do I go?" Before, he never would worry if she should follow the fancy of her heart; on the contrary, let her go. Why worry? Hasn't he still strength in his loins? And couldn't he always "draw" favors from her? But now—she can adjust herself easily to anyone. Her power of adjustment is—fantastic! The Righteous knows . . . and he, at his age, is bound up only with her—not from great love, but from the force of habit. All in all, he would say, it is fifty years that we are together (we were twenty when we married), and the first twenty years were experimental, and he could let her get away with anything—even burning the food and casting her eyes on other men. So, in the second twenty years he realized that she wasn't fit for him, but he remained with her—from pity, pity more for himself than for her—and in these twenty years, he found that there is no good in her for him . . . so powerful is habit . . . but she—her ability to adjust is terrifying . . . therefore, he is worried. He doesn't sleep securely in his bed. Every day he must look upon her as if she were newly in his house.

In all the housework—in cooking, cleaning, and even in washing the floor—he took part. With sleeves rolled up, wrapped in a white apron, he busied himself in the work with joy, while she sat at the window and sewed.

And, occasionally, when people came to visit them, he attended to the guests, prepared the coffee and served cakes. And whether the guests noticed or not, he stood engaged in whatever work was at hand, and explained the "upside down" world of his house: not from great love for her does he bear this yoke but from a calculation . . . that is, from *her* calculations . . . many are her schemes. To the eye, she is merely an innocent dove, a sweet raisin, but no one knows the fire pent up within her.

And all the while he spun stories like these about her scheming, she would sit among the visitors, a smile made all of love and goodness on her lips, and pretended to be angered by his joking. "And what are my calculations? What did I say to him? When did I say a word? He won't even let me slip a word in . . ."

"'This also I need, that she should raise her voice. . . . Certainly I don't let her speak . . . because . . . because I know just what she thinks. Before she opens her mouth, I know what she's thinking—fifty years! One can know . . . I know, just like this she thinks: in old age the husband is obliged to do everything, all the housework, and she, the wife—her place is sewing in the corner. For in her youth the woman is much more weary than the man: nine months of pregnancy, the pangs of birth, teaching the children, sleepless nights, and so forth and so on . . . and multiply these—she says to herself—five times (for God has blessed us with three sons and two daughters, may they live long lives!). And you see, this is just a part of the weariness she suffers while the husband still spends his days and nights in comfort. And when will the husband make up the difference? In old age . . . that's her calculation. And what can I answer her? She's more right than I. And it's in my nature to love the right. And besides that, I'm full of worries—at this age . . . I can't trust her . . . You don't know what this pretty one can do . . . And for the sake of the 'good life' in my old age—I'm ready to bear her yoke. . . . Let her burden me with what she will—I've learnt how to take it . . . fifty years!"

And as it sometimes happened that he would arrive home and not find her (because she'd gone over to one of the neighbors or the store), he would go after her from neighbor to neighbor and ask worriedly: "Have you seen her? Perhaps you heard something? With whom did she go? Perhaps he's rich? What did he promise her? I'm worried . . . all my days I worry that she might go after someone richer than I . . ."

And he would go from neighbor to neighbor, spinning his humor, and all the inhabitants of the neighborhood would answer him with a pleased smile, grateful to him for the light and pleasing air he imparted to his surroundings.

IV

Two Torah Scrolls

Rabbi Jacob Meshullam, the treasurer of the synagogue, was universally respected for his reverence and knowledge.

In those days, after Passover, an elderly woman asked to speak with the Rabbi, and she was brought into his study. The woman, thin of body and pale of face, spoke humbly to the Rabbi. "Señor Haham, I wish to contribute a scroll of the Torah in your Honor's synagogue. I have with me thirty gold *napoleones*. I have been told that these thirty will suffice to buy a Torah and a cover with lines of silver, and also to cover the expenses of the celebration on Shavuot, when it will be brought from here to the synagogue."

And she added that she didn't ask anything from the Honorable Rabbi save two things. First, that on the cover of the holy scroll it will say that it has been contributed by Malka, the daughter of Gentil, to atone for her sins upon earth. And second, that his Honor the Rabbi will say Kaddish for her, every year on the anniversary of her death, for she has neither relative nor kinsman. She has already arranged for burial and a shroud; all the expenses of her last day are in order with the Kolel; the Rabbi need not trouble himself except to say Kaddish. She is very embarrassed that she cannot give anything to the Rabbi himself for his trouble but she no longer has anything, and the *napoleones* she earned with much sweat and untold labor. *Pruta* upon *pruta* she saved it up in the last fifteen years—from the time of her arrival in Jerusalem.

The Rabbi answered her with words of encouragement and comfort, as was his way; and praised her work, for there is none like it in greatness. He promised to follow her will, and to add "honor" to her memory, after many days, in a way fitting for a woman so righteous.

A few days afterwards, another elderly lady came to the Rabbi's house, and entered his study. She told him her request in the midst of much begging for forgiveness and apology. The essence of what she said was like that of the woman who had preceded her a few days before, and even her conditions and requests were almost exactly like those of the other woman. When. the Rabbi heard that her name was Rivka, the daughter of Gentil, and that she also came from Rhodes, he asked carefully: "Doesn't your mother have a sister here in Jerusalem?"

"Sister?" She seemed surprised. "Yes," but what is the connection of her sister with her own matter?

"Certainly, it is not our concern now," agreed the Rabbi, but he simply wanted to know, for he knew of another lady, also from Rhodes, whose mother was also named Gentil.

And how did the Rabbi come to know this?

The Rabbi told her the whole story—that she also brought money and that she wanted the same thing as the lady now before him.

"So. Good for her. She too saved her pennies. And she worked harder than I. I worked for twenty years to fulfill this mitzvah, and she only fifteen. My sister is more righteous than I."

"Ah, good Mother, but is it not better that two scrolls will go forth on the Festival of Shavuot from this house to the synagogue? Just as the good deed is doubled, so will the joy be doubled. The gift of two sisters—this will bring a manifold joy."

The woman looked away, full of confusion and doubt, but after she had thought a while, she said quietly, "I agree, but we must know: if she accepts."

The Rabbi agreed to ask the sister, and after he had spoken with her he received her consent.

Rabbi Jacob now became quite curious about the mystery of the sisters. He tried asking the neighbors, the Happy Pair, who had also come from Rhodes. When the two of them heard the details from the Rabbi, about the buying of the scrolls and that the two women had consented to celebrate the mitzvah together, they exchanged secretive glances. The old man said hurriedly, "Yes, Señor Rabbi, we know them because they are from Rhodes. But we don't know the first little thing about them."

And on the day of the Festival, the Rabbi's house was noisy with the tumult of many guests. Two scrolls of the Torah stood on a high platform, upright and sparkling with their silver ornaments, and on these were additional adornments—silk cloths embroidered with gold. These were like angels come down from heaven to bestow a higher holiness on those assembled, whose eyes cleaved unto them, and were never full of seeing them.

And next to the platform sat the two old women, dressed in striped dresses, according to the fashion of Rhodes, and because of the light of the two brothers—the two scrolls—there was a light of sanctity on their faces and limitless joy in their souls.

Students of the wise and the principal men of the community danced before the scrolls, and sang holy psalms.

In the midst of the tumult, the neighbors entered, the Happy Pair, Gelibon and his wife Saraji, and when they approached the two women, they arose, full of emotion, and fell each one upon the neck of Busa Saraji, and each held one of her arms, as their eyes streamed tears without end. But from their faces, which shone with joy, it was seen that their weeping was from gladness. And he, Señor Gelibon, stood bowing, full of respect for the elder sister, Busa Rivka—until the time came to bring the scrolls of the Torah to the synagogue, and they all went with songs of praise.

V

The Explanation

A FEW DAYS after Shavuot, some of the neighbors were sitting in the courtyard at twilight. The Happy Pair were among them. At that time Rabbi Jacob also came in and sat in his usual corner. The mistress of the house, the Rabbi's wife, was chiding Señor Gelibon and Saraji, for they had been asked several times to explain the mystery of the sisters, and they had refused.

But now the Rabbi himself joined with the request of his wife and said that it was indeed proper for them to answer people's requests. "It would be well simply to inform us of the truth of the matter."

"If the Rabbi asks we can't refuse," said Saraji. "You tell them Gelibon, for you're the better speaker."

"No, dear. You speak very well."

"I will tell the truth: I would gladly tell you the story, only I don't know where to begin and end. I think that if I tell it all just as it happened, it would take many days. So many days of anger, worry and heartbreak, so many tears were poured out in those days—I don't have the strength to tell of these things as they were."

"Let Saraji tell the important parts, without the details, just a summary of the thing," suggested the Rabbi.

"All right, for the sake of his Honor I can't refuse. I remember both of them from the time when I was a girl. Their father, Señor Nissim, was a proper Jew, a simple merchant in a small store. And even though the girls were quite mature when he married them off—marry them off he did, before he died, peace upon him.

"In the beginning nothing passed between them, no insult, to be sure, but not much love. At first, as I said, they had a common fate: they were barren. Malka finally gave birth, first to a girl, and later to a boy, but—far be it from us!—she buried them both.

"But Busa Rivka's husband, Joseph Ruse, who was in his youth handsome, smart and sober, became a man of substance. Success marched before him; whatever he touched turned to gold. Before long everyone called him Señor Joseph Ruso, with a full measure of respect. And after ten years he was already wealthy. Two big stores, a two-story house, two servants, pleasure trips—in short, wealth. Nothing was lacking. Lacking only was a child. Both their souls cried out for a child. But—He knoweth His ways—they had no child.

"Now, Malka's husband, Rafael Capilote, had only black luck. Whatever he touched—withered. He was also a merchant, and tried his luck in many different enterprises, but he always seemed to go backwards rather than forwards. I remember—twice he went bankrupt. And all his life he was gloomy and needy. His brother-in-law, Señor Joseph, set him on his feet more than once, helped him both with money and advice, but in vain. As the saying goes, 'If a man is born luckless, even treasures cannot save him.' In the meantime, Malka gave birth, rather late, as I already said, to the first son. It was no surprise the Señor Joseph loved the child, and used to give the parents anything the child might need. And from the goodness of his heart—and really from his despair, as well—he loved the child, and used to go every day to see him and play with him, but secretly, for he feared that Busa Rivka might become more unhappy if she knew.

People talked, as they always will, and said, he came to visit the child's mother. So he would send whatever the child needed, some of it openly, but much more in secret. But the eye of woman is sharper than the eye of the eagle. Then thorns began to grow between the two families. May He guard us from jealousy which devours the heart. Every day anger and sorrow, argument and dejection, gossip and slander. And Buis Rivka's hate for her sister reached such a height that once, towards evening, she came suddenly to Malka's house—for she knew her husband was there—with anger in her eyes, and bitterness in her heart, and would have poured out her fire and brimstone on the heads of her husband and her sister. But when she saw him, her husband, holding the child in his arms with such laughter and joy—she was struck dumb; then she screamed one long and bitter scream, and fell down and fainted.

"From that time on, Señor Joseph stopped going to his sister-in-law's house. Busa Rivka showed the strength of a lioness in refusing to let him give them anything. Then the evil between the two sisters grew, and the hate became a flame—be it never upon us!—that licked at all around it. Jealousy became—far be it from us!—black bitterness. Some insanity seized her and she didn't take her eyes off her husband for a moment. Even when he went to his business, she made sure of his whereabouts. And when once he secretly sent something to his nephew, it was immediately reported to her by 'evil angels'—and she arranged her own hell for her husband.

"Of course, her sister, Malka, did not keep her tongue cloven to the roof of her mouth. She hated her sister with a lasting hatred. But she, the poor one, with what could she pain her rich sister? What is the power of a needy one against a wealthy one? This only she did: at every opportunity she called her sister not by her name, but *La Haruva Seca* ("the dry carob"). And there are always evil angels, who are ready to add fat to the fire. So Rivka heard each day's gossip, and hated Malka the more for her mouth, and her epithet. The reproaches and insults burned like embers.

"AND THEN it was announced: Busa Rivka was pregnant. Finally God came to see her suffering. For she was then about thirty-five. Many rejoiced in honest gladness. Praise be to God—may He be blessed! said everyone who heard the news—now will the Lady be comforted and silent. The voices will stop, and the envious ones will be quiet—and an end will come to these evil days!

"The news came during the summer, while the rich family was staying at its villa in the mountains. It is hardly necessary to tell with what care they watched over the Lady. The doctors gave instructions that she was not to go about until after the sixth month. They found the mountain air better for her—so she must stay there until after the birth. And so it was. At the end of the sixth month she used to go down to the village for short walks.

"And now the evil angels came to rub salt into the wounds of Malka's heart. They came time after time and told her of the greatness and the glory of the Lady during her pregnancy. When she went down for her walks in the village or the meadow, there were always a pair of servants with her; they would guard her from every light collision, and they seemed almost to count the number of her steps, and await her orders.

"Malka heard all these things—and they were like bites of scorpions to her heart. Her eyes brought forth only tears. And her heart was torn to pieces. Why did God do so? Why did He bring her down to the dust? Is it not—she said, profaning her lips—that God is also on the side of the rich?

"But—to shorten the story—at the end of nine months came the great news: she gave birth to a boy. A fine and healthy one. A mouth would tire to tell of the joy: parties, feasts, charity for the poor, and singing and singing—and the gladness of the day the child entered the Covenant was endless. They called his name Nathan—for they said that the Creator 'had given' him to Rivka.

"But one who looked with a discerning eye at Señor Joseph saw that some hidden thing clouded his eye: something stood between him and all that rejoicing. Sometimes his glance seemed to freeze suddenly—and then awaken and return. But all the parties and all the money he spent and all he spoke—he did it all with gladness.

"And after the days of feasting, life returned to its path. The Lady went out with the infant, in the company of a wet-nurse and a servant girl. Sometimes she went to the city to the homes of relatives, and sometimes she received guests in her own house—and life went its accustomed path.

"Anyone who saw the Lady going out with the child, saw how great is the pleasure which wealth can impart to its possessors. The Lady's face was always shining and happy. And why not? Would she be tired from lack of sleep, or from carrying the child in her arms? All that work was given to the child's nurse, and not to the Lady.

"Indeed, the nurse also never lacked for a thing. The saying is true: the servants of the King also lived in the royal palace. And when the child was weaned, and they returned to the city, they took the nurse with them, and she and her family lived with them.

"The child grew, and if he was not the handsomest, at least his clothes and his bearing gave him a certain charm.

"But let's go back and see what happened to Malka, the other sister, in that period of five or six years. No changes took place in her house. What changes with the poor? Yesterday was like the day before. But one change took place in her own self: she was visited by a black depression, which never left her. She sat alone and angry in her house. And when once in a while she had someone to talk to, she always began with words of complaint and bitterness against her Maker, for He had embittered her life. He had gladdened her enemies and reduced her to the dust.

"It once happened that she saw the child, Nathan, in the house of relatives. From the moment she sent her eyes on the boy, she seemed to be sticking pins in him.

"Then, she spoke neither good nor evil, but some days later—a month or two—there were no bounds to what she said. Like a stream of water of flood-time that will pass over anything it meets, so did her words overflow every house and conversation among the great and among the small, in every street of the city of Rhodes. Many were those whose eyes filled with tears to hear her words. But she, Malka—may He guard us!—was like a drunkard when she lifted the veil and revealed the secret. She revealed to everyone that the Lady hadn't been pregnant at all, that she hadn't given birth, and had not merited fruit of the womb. Rivka was the same dry carob she had always been."

"How?" asked all the listeners together.

Rabbi Jacob, who had listened carefully to her words, asked, "Busa Saraji, didn't you tell us that the Lady was pregnant while she was in the village, and that she gave birth there?"

"Yes, yes," panted Busa Saraji, and she said, "She, Malka, revealed the secret that the son was really the son of the nurse that lived in the village near the villa. The Lady had been in the village, and when she discovered that the nurse was early in pregnancy, she poured out her heart with tears and begging before the woman, telling her of sorrow and the torture of her soul because of her sister. The nurse and her husband were very touched, for they were good people, and also very poor, and they already had three children, so they agreed to the Lady's wish, and to everything which she arranged in secret, with much discretion and good sense. It was signed and sealed on paper that it would be announced that the Lady was pregnant during the nurse's term of pregnancy. The Lady would let it be known that she had been blessed with conception. She was to go out once or twice with a swollen belly, and she did, the poor thing—she tied a small pillow around her stomach and went out, and while the nurse was giving birth, the Lady's labor would be announced. Rivka arranged it all very cleverly, and as soon as the child was born, it would be brought to her. The child was to be raised as a prince in the Lady's house. The nurse's child would be mourned as a still birth—may such things never come about!

"And so it was. The nurse was a wet-nurse as far as the people were concerned, and a mother to her son. There was this further condition between them: when the child reached eighteen years, both families would go to Jerusalem. There the parents of the child could do with him as they wished, either leave him in the house of the Lady, as heir to Señor Joseph, or take him away.

"And Malka revealed it all out of envy. How did she find out the secret? No one knows. No one ever found out how the 'paper' with the conditions got to her. But many people, both strangers and friends, cursed the sister—for her heart was made of stone; she knew neither a sister's compassion nor human sympathy.

"And Malka's evil was repaid from Heaven. Her first son did not last the year. We remember that very Sabbath when the child fell off the roof and died on the spot. A year or two later the girl sickened and died, and they were left bereaved of both.

"From all her many trials and tribulations the Lady was sick for many days, until they said her mind was deranged, and when she recovered—though she never recovered completely, if you judged by the way she looked afterwards—then Señor Joseph became sick. For some years he lived on, broken and sick at heart. Much of his money melted away in these evil days—they certainly lasted ten years—until he was left nearly penniless. As the saying goes, 'To spend and not to earn—until you sink.' And when he died, he left tremendous debts. The Lady was left with nothing but crumbs.

"Many days hadn't passed before she decided to go to the Land of Israel. She gathered the little she had and came to Jerusalem. And when Malka's husband also died, she too came to Jersualem.

"This then is the story, though I told it only in part, as it came to me, but how happy we are that God has seen fit to let us see them alive here—with Jerusalem sheltering them with her peace. The grace of Jerusalem has done this, and with the grace of the Torah certainly the sins of one sister against the other have been forgiven."

The Rabbi, who had been silent, wondering at the works of God and the destinies of man, praised Busa Saraji, who had indeed spoken very well, as if she were an eyewitness to all these things. Perhaps she was a relation of the sisters?

"No. There is no blood relationship. Maybe . . . something more."

"More? How can that be?"

The old woman bowed her head and said quietly, "I was the nurse."

Albert Cohen

Albert Cohen (Greece-France, 1895–1981) was born in Corfu. His family emigrated to France in 1900, ultimately settling in Marseilles, but he held a Turkish passport until he became a Swiss citizen in 1919. He early on chose French as his literary medium. Cohen studied literature and jurisprudence. In the 1920s he edited the short-lived *La Revue Juive.* He worked for the International Labor Office in Geneva from 1926 to 1930. A fervent Zionist, he was Chaim Weizmann's personal representative in Paris in 1939. In 1940, as World War II raged, Cohen fled to London, where he served as official advisor to the Jewish Agency for Palestine and then as legal advisor to the Intergovernmental Committee on Refugees. After the war he returned to Switzerland, where he worked at the United Nations headquarters of the International Refugee Organization. Cohen is the author of a sequence of novels called *Solal of the Solals.* It is considered one of the most accomplished fiction cycles of the twentieth century. In the first installment, *Solal* (1930; English, 1933), the tragic protagonist from humble origins is undone by hubris. He achieves high political office and the love of women but hides his Jewish roots, which, when revealed, force him to sacrifice everything. He commits suicide but is resurrected in order to confront his defeat. *Nailcruncher* (1938; English, 1940) is also part of the cycle, but the most ambitious installment is Cohen's masterpiece, *Belle du Seigneur* (1968; English, 1995), where Solal attempts to redeem the world from fascism but succumbs again to a love that proves to be illusory. The novel, consisting of a million and a half words, became an international bestseller. *The Valiant of France* (1969) concludes the narrative cycle. Cohen's early poetry is compiled in *Jewish Words* (1921). He also wrote a play, *Ezéchiel* (1930), and, while in London, an homage entitled "Churchill d'Angleterre." A personal essay written in 1943 upon the death of his mother was revised and expanded into *Book of My Mother* (1954; English, 1997). It was translated into English by his daughter, Bella Cohen. I have excerpted four sample chapters.

From *Book of My Mother*

I

Every man is alone and no one cares a rap for anyone and our sorrows are a desert island. Yet why should I not seek comfort tonight as the sounds of the street fade away, seek comfort tonight in words? Oh, poor lost creature who sits at his table seeking comfort in words, at his table with the phone off the hook for he fears the outside, and at night with the phone off the hook he feels like a king, safe from the spiteful outside, so soon spiteful, gratuitously spiteful.

What a strange little joy, sad and limping yet sweet as a sin or a drink on the sly. What a joy even so to be writing just now, alone in my kingdom and far from the swine. Who are the swine? Do not expect me to tell you. I want no trouble with those from outside. I do not want them to come and disturb my would-be peace and prevent me writing pages by the dozen or the hundred as this heart of mine, my destiny, may dictate. I have resolved to tell all painters they are geniuses, otherwise they bite. And in general I tell everyone that everybody is charming. Such are my daytime manners. But in my nights and my dawns my thoughts are not constrained.

Sumptuous, O my golden pen, roam over the page, roam at random while I yet have some youth; wend your slow, erratic way, hesitant as in a dream, faltering but controlled. Roam on, pen, I love you, my sole consolation; roam through the pages which give me dismal delight and in whose squinting eye I gloomily revel. Yes, words are my homeland, words console and avenge. But words will not bring back my mother. Brimful though they be of the vibrant past drumming at my temples and distilling its fragrance, the words I write will not bring back my dead mother. That subject is banned in the night. Begone, vision of my mother living when I saw her for the last time in France. Begone, maternal wraith.

Suddenly, because all is tidy on the table where I write, and because I have a cup of hot coffee and a cigarette just lit and a lighter that works and a pen that writes well, and because I am by the fire with my cat at my side, I feel a surge of delight so intense that I am moved—moved to pity for myself, pity for that childish capacity for boundless joy which bodes no good, pity for the pleasure I find in a pen that writes well, pity for this poor devil of a heart that would suffer no more and clutch at some reason for loving in order to live. For just a few minutes I bask like a bourgeois in a little oasis of comfort and order. But a sorrow lurks below, unremitting, unforgettable. Yes, it is grand to be a bourgeois like them for a while. We love to be what we are not. There is no greater artist than a genuine middle-class lady drooling over a poem or going into a trance and frothing at the mouth at the sight of a Cézanne and pontificating as she jabbers in some jargon she has scrounged here and there with no inkling of what it means and nattering about mass and volume and proclaiming that red is so sensual. Sensual my foot! I have lost my thread. Well, let's make a little doodle in the margin to conjure up ideas—a consolation doodle, a doleful little doodle, a dawdling doodle to be packed with decisions and plans, a dinky little doodle, a curious isle and a land of the soul, a sad oasis for thoughts that follow its curves, a wee-bit-crazy little doodle, neat, childish, docile and filial. Hush, do not awaken her, daughters of Jerusalem. Do not awaken her while she sleeps.

"Who sleeps?" enquires my pen. Who but my mother—eternally. Who but my mother—that is my grief. Do not awaken her, daughters of Jerusalem. Do not awaken my grief that lies buried in the graveyard of a town whose name I may not speak, for that name means my mother deep down in earth. Come, pen, flow free once more, be resolute, sober and sensible, take up anew your task of enlightenment, steep yourself in willpower and do not make such long commas: that is not a bright idea. Soul, O my pen, be valiant and diligent, leave the dark land, cease to be wild, near-mad and possessed, morbidly stilted. And you, my sole friend, you whom I face in my mirror, hold back your dry sobs and, since you would so dare, tell of your dead mother with a fake heart of bronze, tell of her calmly, pretend to be calm, it may be—who knows?—no more than a habit which can be acquired. Tell of your mother in their serene manner, whistle softly to imagine things are not all that bad, and above all smile—never forget to smile. Smile to cheat your despair, smile to go on living, smile in your mirror and at people and even at this page. Smile with your bereavement which pants faster than fear. Smile to make yourself believe nothing matters, smile to make yourself simulate living, smile with the sword of your mother's death hanging over you, smile all your life till you can bear it no more, smile till you die of that perpetual smile.

II

On Friday afternoon, which for Jews marks the beginning of the holy Sabbath day, she would make herself beautiful and wear her adornments. She would put on her solemn black silk dress and such jewels as were left to her. For I was open-handed in my light-hearted adolescence and gave banknotes to beggars if they were old and long-bearded. And if a friend liked my cigarette case, the gold case was his. In Geneva, when I was a student with wild black locks exalting my head and a heart that was ardent and sometimes crazy though tender, she had sold her finest jewels. She was so proud of them, poor darling; they were essential to her simple dignity as the daughter of notables of a bygone age. How often—and the jeweller always swindled her—had she sold some of her jewels for me, unbeknown to my father, whose sternness, which we feared, fed our complicity. I can see her now, leaving that jeweller's shop in Geneva, so proud of the small large sum she had got for me, happy, heart-stirring in her joy, happy and her pearls, which were her caste marks, her honour as a lady of the Orient. So happy, my darling, walking with difficulty even then, already dogged by death. So happy to despoil herself for me, to ply me with banknotes which would flame and vanish in but a few days in my nimble young hands, quick to give them away. I took, wild that I was and wreathed in sunlight and not much concerned about my mother, for I had fine dazzling teeth and I was the loved though loving lover of this pretty girl and that fair lass and so on without end, infinite reflections in the mirrors of the castle of love. O curious pallor of my loves long dead! I took the banknotes, and I did not know, for I was a son, that those meagre large sums were a sacrifice offered up by my mother on the altar of motherhood. O priestess of the cult of her son, O majesty too long unacknowledged! Too late now.

Every Sabbath in Marseilles, where I went from Geneva to spend my leaves, my mother would wait for my father and me to return from synagogue with myrtle sprigs in our hands. When she had finished adorning her modest flat for the Sabbath, the flat that was her Jewish realm and her piteous homeland, she would sit all alone at the ceremonial Sabbath table, and ceremoniously would she wait for her son and her husband. Sitting perfectly still so as not to rumple her Sabbath best, excited and stiff in her corseted dignity—excited because she was smart and respectable and about to find favour with those she loved, her husband and son, whose momentous tread would soon be heard on the stairs; excited because her hair was well-combed and gleaming with age-old sweet-almond oil, for she knew little of the arts of titivation; excited as a little girl at a prizegiving—my ageing mother would wait for her two aims in life, her son and her husband.

Seated under her altar, a portrait of me at fifteen, a frightful portrait which she thought admirable, seated at the Sabbath table where three candles glowed, at the festive table, first fragment of the realm of the Messiah, my mother sighed contentedly but a trifle wistfully, for soon they would arrive, her two men, the lights of her life. Oh yes, she thought happily, they would find the flat spotless and sumptuous on this Sabbath day, they would commend her for its sparkling trimness, and they would compliment her on the elegance of her dress. Her son, who never seemed to be looking but whom nothing escaped, would cast a quick glance at her brand-new lace collar and cuffs and, yes, they would surely receive his all-important approval. And she would be proud beforehand, would prepare in advance what to say to them, perhaps with some guileless exaggeration of the speed and skill of her domestic accomplishments. And they would see what a capable woman she was, what a queen of the household. Such were the ambitions of my mother.

She would sit there, brimming over with love for those near and dear to her, telling them in her mind of all she had cooked and cleaned and tidied. From time to time she would go into the kitchen, and her little hand with its gravely glinting wedding ring would give a few graceful, artistic but quite unnecessary pats with the wooden spoon to the meatballs simmering in garnet-red tomato sauce. She had plump little hands sheathed in smoothest skin, which I would admire with a touch of hypocrisy and a wealth of love, for her naïve pleasure delighted me. She was such an excellent cook, yet so deficient in all other skills. But, once in her kitchen, that spruce little old lady was also a fine, resolute captain. Unnecessary patting of my mother in her kitchen, the caress of spoon on meatballs, O rites, wise, tender and dainty caresses, absurd and ineffectual caresses, caresses so expressive of love and contentment which showed that her mind was at rest for all was well and the meatballs were perfect and her two men, so hard to please, would approve them. O shrewd and simple patting that has gone for ever, the tapping and patting of my mother smiling faintly all alone in her kitchen, clumsy and majestic grace: majesty of my mother.

Back from the kitchen she would sit down again, demure in her priestly role as custodian of the home, content with her poor little respectable lot, which was solitude lightened only by the presence of her husband and son, whose servant and guardian she was. This woman who once had been young and pretty was a daughter of the Law of Moses, of the moral Law which meant more to her than God. So there were no sentimental love affairs, no Anna Karenina capers. There were a husband and son to be guided and served with humble majesty. She had not married for love. A husband had been found for her and she had meekly accepted. And biblical love had been born, so far removed from my Western passions. The sacred love of my mother had been bred in marriage, grown with the birth of the baby I had been, and bloomed in an alliance forged with her dear husband against the harshness of life. There are whirling sunlit passions. But there is no greater love.

On a Sabbath which now comes to mind she was sitting there waiting, exuding contentment, for all was in order and her son had looked very well that morning. She was concocting a plan to make him almond paste on Sunday. "I'll let it cook a little longer than last time," she said to herself. And on Monday, yes on Monday, she would make him a maize cake with masses of currants. Fine. Suddenly glancing at the clock and seeing that it was already eight, she was seized with panic and showed it too dramatically, for she lacked the self-control which is the property of peoples certain of what tomorrow will bring, who are accustomed to happiness. They had said they would be back at seven. An accident? Run over? Damp-browed, she went to check the time on the clock in the bedroom. Only ten to seven. A smile in the mirror and a murmur of thanks to the God of Abraham, of Isaac and of Jacob. But as she closed the door of the bedroom her hand brushed the tip of a nail. Tetanus! Quick, the iodine! Jews are a little too fond of life. She was suddenly afraid of dying and thought of the nightdress she had worn on her wedding night and which they would put on her again on the day of her death, the awesome nightdress locked up in the bottom drawer of her wardrobe, a terrifying drawer which she never opened. Despite her religion, she had scant faith in everlasting life. But suddenly the joy of living returned, for she had just heard the thrilling tread of her loved ones at the foot of the stairs.

A final glance in the mirror to remove the last traces of the powder which she put on in secret with a strong sense of sin on that festal day, a simple white powder made by Roger et Gallet which I believe was called "Vera Violetta." She ran to open the door, which was secured by a safety chain, for one never knew and memories of pogroms die hard. Quick, make way for the entry of the two beloved. Such was the love life of my holy mother. Not much like Hollywood, as you can see. The compliments of her husband and son and their happiness were all that she asked of life.

She would open the door before they had time to knock. The father and son were not surprised when the door opened as if by magic. That was always the way, and they knew that their loving watchman kept a constant lookout. Yes, so much so that her gaze, ever probing my health and my worries, sometimes irked me. For some obscure reason I resented the fact that she scrutinized too closely and guessed too much. O holy sentinel lost for ever! Standing by the open door, she would smile excitedly, dignified yet almost flirtatious. How clearly I can see her when now I dare to look: how living are the dead! "Welcome," she would say shyly, proper and formal, eager to please, thrilled at being nobly arrayed for the Sabbath. "Welcome. Peace unto you this Sabbath day," she would say. And with her hands uplifted and spread out like sunbeams she would bestow on me a priestlike blessing. Then she would give me an almost animal look, vigilant as a lioness, to see if I was still in good health, or a human look to see if I was sad or worried. But all was well on that particular day and she breathed in the scent of the traditional myrtle we had brought her. She rubbed the sprigs between her little hands and inhaled their scent rather theatrically, as becomes the people of our Oriental tribe. She was so pretty then, my aged Maman who walked with difficulty, my Maman.

XIX

In the streets I am obsessed by my dead mother, and gloomily I watch the bustling crowds of people who do not know that they will die and that the wood of their coffin already exists in some sawmill or forest; vaguely I watch the young made-up women who are tomorrow's corpses laughing and displaying the teeth which are the sign and beginning of their skeleton, displaying their thirty-two little bits of skeleton and splitting their sides as though they shall never die. In the streets I am as sad as an oil lamp alight in bright sunshine, pale, useless and dismal as a lamp alight on a fine summer day, pitiful in the streets, those rivers which nurture the lone soul that I am, slowly wandering and absent-minded, absent-minded in streets teeming with useless old women and not one is my mother though all of them look like her. I am a sweating nightmare in the streets, where incessantly I think of my living mother just before the instant of her dying. Should I go up to that passer-by and tell him that I have lost my mother and that we must exchange a kiss of fellowship, a fervent kiss of communion in a misfortune which he himself has known or is destined to know? No—he would report me to the police.

Today I am driven crazy by death, death is everywhere, and those roses which on my table exhale their fragrance as I write, horribly alive, are pre-corpses forced to simulate life three days longer in water, and people enjoy watching that, watching death-throes, and they buy flower corpses and girls feast their eyes on them. Begone, dead roses! I have just thrown them out of the window on to a beribboned old lady with a shopping-bag. Old—we well know what that forebodes. All the same, she at least is alive this morning. The old lady looked at me reproachfully. "Such beautiful flowers," she thought, "it's not right throwing them out of the window like that." She does not know that the helpless child that I am wanted to seize death by the throat and kill it.

I must find a little pastime here and now. Anything will do. Yes, I shall make up absurd little ditties to the tune of that old French song about the church cock or something similar. I shall amuse myself listlessly all alone by inventing cows which do strange things with a something air, the something being a word that ends in -ive. A cow in night attire Sings in the church choir With a suggestive air. A cow consumed with passion Dances in wifely fashion With a restive air. A cow ill at ease Swings on a trapeze With a pensive air. A cow in fine fettle Puts on the kettle With a dubitative air. A cow on a dune Smiles at the moon With a passive air A cow pale and gaunt Flirts in a low haunt With a plaintive air. A lily-white cow Prances on a bough With an expressive air. A cow in the sun Gobbles a cream bun With an impulsive air. A small Jewish cow Fans her sweating brow With a fugitive air. A cow in a stole Dances round a maypole With a vindictive air. A cow with a sheen Munches a tureen With a contemplative air. A cow black as night Flies a huge kite With a ruminative air. A cow with a feller Waltzes in the cellar With a festive air. A cow clad in yellow Strums on a cello With a sensitive air. A cow with rheumatics Performs acrobatics With a tentative air. A cow of small girth Splits her sides with mirth With an aggressive air. A cow in despair Sighs on her chair With a naïve air. A cow on a scooter Keeps blowing her hooter With a furtive air. A cow drunk on claret Skips in a garret With a massive air. A cow above reproach Sucks mints in a coach With an active air. There. Grief is not always expressed in noble words: it can also find an outlet in sad little jokes, little old ladies making faces at the dead windows of my eyes. Anyway, my cows didn't do the trick.

What about trying mixed-up proverbs? Here we go. A stitch in time is worth two in the bush. A rolling drone blows nobody any good. Too many crooks have a silver lining. Birds of a feather repent at leisure. Virtue is the root of all evil. I do not feel any brighter. I have this obsessive thought that I can see my mother's gaze in the attentive eyes of my cat. What about trying God? God—that reminds me of something. I have had a few set-backs in that department. Anyway, when He has a free moment He can let me know.

Poets who have sung of grief which uplifts and enriches have never known grief. Lukewarm souls and stunted hearts, they have never known grief, even though they start a new line and see genius in creating blank spaces sprinkled with words, idlers who in their impotence make a virtue of necessity. Their feelings are short-lived, and that is why they start a new line. Little fusspots, pretentious dwarfs perched on high heels and brandishing the rattle of their rhymes, so utterly wearisome, making a song and dance about each word they excrete, terribly proud of their adjectival torments, enraptured when they have produced fourteen lines, spewing over their desk miserable little words in which they see countless wonders and which they suck and force you to suck with them, informing all and sundry of the rare words which have emerged, padding their skinny shoulders with colossal impertinence, wily managers of their constipated genius, so convinced of the importance of their poems. Had they known grief which harps and sweats with a gaping mouth, these self-satisfied poseurs, who never paid for anything with their blood, would not sing of its beauty, nor would they tell us that nothing uplifts as much as a great sorrow. I know what grief is, and I know that it neither uplifts nor enriches, but that it shrivels you till you are reduced to size like the boiled shrunken head of a Peruvian warrior, and I know that poets who suffer as they search for rhymes and sing of the honour of suffering, refined midgets strutting on stilts, have never known grief which makes of you a man who once was.

XX

LET'S FACE IT, I too am but one of the living, a sinner like all the living. My beloved lies buried in earth, rotting all alone in the silence of the dead, in the terrifying solitude of the dead, and I am outside and I go on living and my hand is moving selfishly just now. And if my hand traces words which tell of my grief, it is a movement of life, that is of joy after all, which stirs that hand. And tomorrow I shall reread these pages and add more words and that will give me a kind of pleasure. Sin of living. I shall correct the proofs, and that too will be a sin of living.

My mother is dead, but I gaze at the beauty of women. My mother lies abandoned in earth, where horrible things go on, but I love the sunshine and the tittle-tattle of tiny birds. Sin of living. When I was telling of a mother's departure and a son's remorse for having gone to see a Diane that same evening, I described that Diane with too much pleasure. Sin of living. My mother is dead, but on the radio ceaselessly burbling beside me as I write the "Blue Danube" has only to start to flow and I cannot resist its corny charm and despite my filial grief I fall immediately under the spell of those slender, gently twirling Viennese maidens.

The sin of living is everywhere. If the sister of the consumptive wife is young and healthy, may God take pity on the husband and the sister who together nurse the sick woman they sincerely love. They are alive and well, and when the consumptive wife is asleep, drugged with morphine and smiling with a rattle in her throat, they walk together in the garden steeped in night. They are sad, but they savour the sweetness of the fragrant garden, the sweetness of being together, and that is almost an act of adultery. Or take the widow who, sincere in her grief, has nonetheless put on silk stockings to go to the funeral and powdered her face. Sin of living. Tomorrow she will wear a dress which she has no wish to be unflattering and which will set off her beauty. Sin of living. And beneath the grief of this lover sobbing in despair at the graveside there lurks perhaps an awful involuntary joy, a sinful joy at being still alive, an unconscious joy, an organic joy which is beyond his control, an involuntary joy at the contrast between the dead woman and the living man giving vent to grief which nevertheless is sincere. To feel grief is to live, to be one of the living, to be still of this world.

My mother is dead but I am hungry, and soon, despite my grief, I shall eat. Sin of living. To eat is to consider oneself, to love living. My dark-ringed eyes are in mourning for my mother, but I want to live. Thank God, they who sin by living soon become the dead whom the living offend.

What is more, we very soon forget our dead. Poor dead, how forsaken you are in your earth and how deeply I pity you, poignant in your everlasting solitude. Dead, my darlings, how terribly alone you are. In five years or less I shall be more willing to accept the idea that a mother is something ended. In five years I shall have forgotten some of her gestures. If I were to live a thousand years, perhaps in my thousandth year I would no longer remember her.

Veza Canetti

Veza Canetti (Austria, 1897–1963) was born Venetiana Taubner-Calderón in Vienna into a mixed Ashkenazic and Sephardic family. She worked as a translator and a private schoolteacher. In 1924 she met her future husband, Elias Canetti, whom she married in 1934. In 1932 and 1933 she published stories in *Arbeiter-Zeitung.* Some of her characters come from underprivileged homes and must struggle twice as hard as their educated, wealthy counterparts. With the rise of Nazism in Austria, Canetti found it impossible to continue publishing her work. At times she used pseudonyms, such as Veza Magd ("maid") and Veronika Knecht ("servant"), in order to circumvent the restrictions placed on Jewish authors. The Canettis moved to Paris in 1938 and to London in 1939. Veza Canetti appears prominently in *The Memoirs of Elias Canetti* (1999). Her four works of fiction were all published posthumously. They include *Yellow Street: A Novel in Five Scenes* (1990; English, also 1990) and *The Tortoises* (1999; English, 2001). The latter is about a Jewish family in Austria in the months before the *Anschluss.* It includes "Yom Kippur, the Day of Atonement," translated by Ian Mitchell. Canetti also wrote a play, *The Ogre* (1991). In 1956, out of frustration with her lack of literary success, she destroyed most of her unpublished work. Not until the 1990s did Veza Canetti begin to receive the recognition she deserves.

Yom Kippur, the Day of Atonement

Felberbaum was sitting at the table he had set. The distinguished couple occupied the places of honor at the top, while he perched on the edge of his chair, since he was busy passing round the platters, with cold cuts, slices of bread (which he spread for the lady), topping up the teacups, and feeling awkward because he was an outsider, not participating, embarrassed on account of his custom of observing the day of fasting, an utterly ridiculous custom, incomprehensible to such educated people, and, on top of that, an unhealthy thing at his age. He was altogether ridiculous, he well knew, but in the end he laughed up his sleeve at himself, grinned to himself, a feeble but happy grin.

For it turned out that these new friends were not looking down on him, the two, that is, who mattered. If anything, they were delighted by his zeal, it did them good, that was very clear, and even his comical remarks cheered them up, he knew.

And the lady was smiling.

The unhappy man, sitting at the farthest corner of the table, couldn't control himself. He poured scorn on the feast day, the well-laid table, the tablecloth and, naturally, on Felberbaum, who was fasting. Wood, he said. To cover wood with a tablecloth, wood that would one day turn to stone, was crass. Just as crass as a man, who looked like a fat sack of flour, fasting. Fasting was right and proper for the monk with stony features and not for fat flesh.

At this, his brother countered with the name of Luther, but Werner paid no heed to the objection and went on grumbling. You had to have a fair amount of sawdust between your ears to call a day a holiday with the streets swarming with brownshirts, arrests coming thick and fast, and cattle trucks rolling through the streets loaded with people beaten to a pulp.

Here, the lady heaved a deep sigh which cut Felberbaum to the quick, and he pulled himself together. Arrest wasn't the worst thing, and he wasn't just talking off the top of his head, but from experience, he had that behind him; and besides, did anyone believe that people were being arrested only here in this country? He himself had been arrested in Cairo, and why? Because of an old rag wrapped round a filthy piece of wood, because of a mere nothing, because of a bit of rubbish. How interesting, the guests said and begged him to be more specific, and so Felberbaum told the tale of how he came to be arrested in Cairo.

One day, a stall-keeper came running after him, carrying a mummy, the mummy of a small child. That is to say, at first he saw before him a few filthy rags of faded dressing material wrapped round some wood, and he waved it away. When the man demanded twelve pounds for the filthy object, it began to interest him—what it might contain—and, back home, he looked up in his lexicon what it could possibly be that cost so much.

The next day, the trader scurried after him again. Herr Felberbaum now knew roughly what this bundle represented, and ran a curious eye over it. The world is quite mad, he thought, and has no interest in anything other than digging up corpses and stuffing them. Then these would be sold at a high price and sold on again. The dealer had noticed his searching look and refused to leave his side. By the time they arrived at the great Sphinx, the price of the mummy stood at no more than two pounds. Then the man, who was in a state of great desperation, asked for only one pound. Felberbaum bought the mummy for a pound.

So now he looked forward to enjoying his purchase and to discovering the true value of his find, because he knew from his lexicon that a mummy was worth much more than a pound. Therefore, with the mummy in his arms, he set off for the museum and searched through the rooms for mummies. At last he found the mummy of a child, which suffered by comparison with his own; it was closely similar, which pleased him greatly, but his seemed far better preserved. He carried it in both arms, very carefully, as one carries a newborn infant, into a second room, the one with the large mummies. He was standing in front of them, scrutinizing and comparing, when suddenly he found himself being roughly grabbed and, in short, being arrested by two museum guards. Ignoring his wild protests, they took him to the director's office, where a severe-looking gentleman stared coldly at him. Terrified and bathed in sweat, he started to tell his story, convinced that he was being arrested because of some theft from the museum someone else had committed, or at best because of his questionable purchase. Then, all of a sudden, the director smiled, laughed even, dismissing the two guards with a haughty gesture and a reproachful glance, and revealed to Herr Felberbaum that the scraps of cloth wrapped round the mummy dating back thousands of years probably came from the very factory which Herr Felberbaum represented in the area.

This tale produced the effect of a sack of gold thrown into a beggar's house. There was indeed a city called Cairo, there were mummies, dead bodies preserved by people of culture—just how would they protect the living, the prisoners? We are protected elsewhere, abroad, that is obvious, here they keep an eye on us, who are deprived of all rights, the newspapers pose a threat to peace and tranquillity—you could never set eyes on these newspapers, without hearing the grinding, the gnashing of teeth of the helpless, yes, the helpless out there. Let them carry on their wanton vandalism here as much as they liked. This was the only solace, the only protection for anyone in a land where the leaders encouraged murder, in which the custodians carried out robbery as a profession: here they were, in Cairo, in Egypt, far from this town in which no god struck down the sinners with the ten plagues. They were here, in this peaceful room, safeguarded by the hearty laughter of Herr Felberbaum from the Handelskai.

Still, Werner raged on. It was significant, he said, and absolutely typical of certain people that they should go after mummies instead of going to feel the Sphinx, to touch it with their finger-tips, millions of years that one could breathe in, overwhelming forms and materials, called diorites, porphyries, basalts, granites, the Sphinx divulges its secret, and this fool bought a mummy.

His brother steered the conversation away, believing that Herr Felberbaum had found the happy solution: it was more stimulating and more appropriate to the holiday if each of them would tell a story. He himself was prepared to take it from there and, since imprisonment and arrest seemed the order of the day, he would tell a tale of imprisonment. The man arrested was—a writer, who lived alone and isolated in a small village. He was very well liked in that village, as he had been for a long time. He was pretty well established, settled there, he left the place only seldom and briefly, liked living there, worked away, brought honor to the village, was something of a showpiece, a rare part of the place. He would greet the natives as friends, join them in the inn and pay for the whole company's wine.

When, therefore, the new regime issued the decree that arrests were to be made, there was embarrassment in the village. The only people who lived there were the villagers themselves, and it seemed impossible to arrest any of them, since they were like one big family, intermarried, related by marriage or by blood, each one sticking by the other. In their awkward situation, the police hit upon the idea of locking up the one and only outsider in the place. It was no pleasant task, there were no real grounds, but orders from above were reason enough. The warden of the jail himself was delegated the task, for he was the hardest man in the village, as was only fitting for his difficult office.

Early in the morning, he knocked at the door of the learned gentleman, who immediately showed him in. When the hardest man in the village found himself face-to-face with the distinguished gentleman, who was always giving his little daughter cherries, or whatever fruit happened to be in season, he stood twisting his hat in his hands, embarrassed. After all, talking was not his strong point, he talked with his fists. Fortunately, a policeman had come along with him, who was good at reeling off stock phrases, especially where transients causing a public nuisance with their cars were concerned, and so this policeman said, "No offence, Herr Doktor, but we have to place you under arrest."

"Arrest me? And why?"

At this, the warden gave a shrug, while the policeman, quick-witted as his profession demanded, searched for a response and found one.

"There's a warrant for your arrest."

The poet was deeply shocked; he could think of so many things that could give this new regime reasons for committing him to prison that he had no idea what was to become of him. He cast a despairing glance at the writings piled on his desk, which might provide evidence for practically anything frowned upon these days. It could be his pacifism; his friendship with a cardinal; his latest essay on modern art; his membership card from the party which had still been the government in power only a few months before; the sketches by a world-famous caricaturist: all these amounted to so much that the rest of his life (which was already half behind him) would not suffice to atone for all these sins, from that other, and as he hoped, better, more noble half. With bowed head, he walked off between the warden and the policeman in the direction of the jail.

Now this jail was nothing more than a room in the warden's house, because it was not worth the trouble of setting up a separate prison for the extremely rare occasions when crimes were committed in the little village; any robbers and murderers were hauled off to the capital in the green van, and that happened but once every ten years. Petty thieves were simply locked up, in short order, in the warden's house where he had them at his finger-tips and this saved space.

Since, in this case, there was no charge of theft, fraud, fencing, tax-evasion, smuggling, drunken excess, vagrancy or anything whatsoever—to tell the truth, there was nothing at all against him—the warden left the door to his living room open, so that the warmth from his cheery fire could spread through to the cell. In addition, since they were dealing with a refined gentleman who was to be lodging here, the warden's wife had freshly made up the bed with her best linen, had lent her own eider-downs and placed pots of pelargoniums in the window. Then she also immediately set about preparing a hearty meal of the sort reserved only for festivals and holidays.

So now the writer was sitting in this small room, which was hardly different from his own at home, gazing out of the sweet little window at the wonderful mountains, which, after a shower of rain, looked close enough to touch. Altogether, this wasn't so bad at all. What was bad, though, was the desk he had left behind, with all that material or, to put it in technical terms, with all those incriminating documents, those pieces of writing, his own and others', those letters and signed papers from authorities who were now all of a sudden being termed murderers, subhumans, traitors to their country, turncoats and Jews.

Undoubtedly, his wisest course of action was to try to do something about it, and when the warden's wife came in, the gentleman got to his feet and approached her as she was stuffing a thick duvet into a crisp white linen cover. He fixed his blue, infinitely clear, infinitely gentle, eyes on her and said:

"I'm afraid I have been interrupted in the middle of an important piece of work. Would it be too much to ask, for me to be given my papers? They are lying on the right-hand side of my desk, among many other ones. I might as well be working here as sitting about idly."

The wife went into the living room, where the warden was sitting by the stove with a very long pipe, staring into the fire. Because that was *his job,* to sit there wearing a rather important expression, ready to clench his fists should the delinquent behave improperly. He listened to his wife's message, drew on his pipe, gave the matter some consideration and hit on the bright idea that it would be better if a prisoner kept himself occupied rather than snooping on his jailer's movements and thinking evil thoughts. So he deputed his wife to go and fetch the papers at once. The woman was delighted to bring this news to the gentleman in his room. After all, because of him, a festive mood reigned in the house. And no one wanted it to look for a moment as if this gentleman, who wore a silk shirt, was here to serve a sentence. Far from it: he added something festive to the place and such a fine fragrance radiated from him, such a warmth, his eyes rested so seriously on her, so steady, so strange. Only on one unforgettable occasion had she seen their like, when, two years before, the Herr Chancellor had passed through the village and fixed his gaze upon her. What they had here was another of those inconceivably refined, boundless human beings whose radiance lit the way to somewhere where one could only be afraid, where one sank down, deep down, out of awe and fear and reverence.

It was probably the case that the prisoner had some idea of the effect he had on the wife, because suddenly he raised his head, and looking her steadily in the eye, said, succinctly, that it would be best if she were to empty the suitcase in his room and pack into it all the writings and booklets and papers lying on his desk, otherwise she might pick up the wrong bundle, or mix some things up, all very delicate documents, and anyway there was such a mess there that he himself was unable to remember whether his work was lying on the right or on the left side of his desk. It would also be good if she could bring him some fresh laundry, at least six shirts, as well as his shaving things and toiletries, which were lying on the washstand.

The woman obeyed him to the letter and returned very soon. She opened the suitcase, and in it she had packed everything, every single printed and handwritten item that had been in the house. Yes, even an old newspaper that had been lying around. The laundry had been meticulously wrapped separately in brown paper.

The writer had thus, as it were, localized the possible conflagration, yet the fire was still glowing, and all that was needed was the appearance of some malevolent official for the carefully guarded fire to blaze up more fearfully than ever. So he now began sorting through the papers, laying the harmless ones in a conspicuous place and tearing up the "evidence against him" into tiny scraps, all of which he stuffed into the coal-scuttle; he piled it full to overflowing and then sat back, greatly relieved. But now there arose a new problem. Where was he to put this enormous mountain of "evidence" now staring everyone in the face?

He peered through to the next room. The fire was crackling invitingly, the warden had nodded off in front of it; his long pipe, which had fallen from his hand, was standing erect like a walking stick. The writer took up a mountain of paper in both arms and carried it towards the fire.

But suddenly he stopped in his tracks. The warden's child, the little cherry-lover, who had been asleep in the laundry basket, woke up, caught sight of him and broke out into a happy yell, hungrily opening her little mouth wide. The writer retreated, because his guard was opening his eyes.

This was risky. If he were brazenly to set about burning the papers, arousing the suspicions of these guileless people, all would be lost.

In the prison cell, intended for miscreants and hidden behind a gray, stained curtain, there was a privy. So, with both arms full, the prisoner carried the shreds of paper over and stuffed them down it. He pulled the chain, the water came only in a trickle and flowed over the scraps, turning them gray and making the ink run, and the writer himself turned gray with the effort of trying to make them all disappear. He looked across to the huge pile that still had to be disposed of and then despairingly back to the old-fashioned toilet—then he jumped in alarm. Before him stood the warden. The forebearing man's features were going red with rage. "City folk just don't have an ounce of sense in their heads," he said, wagging his pipe menacingly. "Over there, there's a roaring fire burning, and here you're choking everything. Now, sir, if you don't mind, you just take all your trash over there where it belongs. That sort of stuff belongs in the fire."

The writer immediately picked up the whole box-full, and carried it over as fast as he could manage. With relief, he watched one pile after another of the evidence against him crumbling into ashes.

A few weeks later, he was released.

Herr Felberbaum thought the story was marvelous, and wonderfully told. A great talent. It all came out in the person of the teller, in the tale and in the language. Beside himself with happiness, he looked across to the lady, whose turn it was now.

"I'm not so good at storytelling," said Eva. "And certainly not a story from my own experience. But this one was told to me, in fact several times."

A Jewish woman took refuge in a park belonging to Prince Sch—. She had been chased in there, pursued in the process of a manhunt; she had that pallid, death-stricken complexion typical of prisoners facing execution. Here, too, a brownshirt spots her and barks at her to leave the gardens. This catches the attention of the old groundskeeper, a man with a reputation for being a wrathful watchdog: young people in particular preferred to give him a wide berth.

"My master, the prince," says he with the loftiest possible air of dignity (as is well known, servants love to play the part of their lords and masters, for their masters cannot be bothered), "my master, the prince, regards all visitors to this park as his guests and does not wish them to be harassed." His expression becomes so impenetrable that the SA-man goes on his way.

"A prince of a servant."

"And what happened to the woman, if I may be permitted to ask?"

"She remained in the gardens, Herr Felberbaum, while the grounds-keeper looked out on all sides to see if anyone was lying in wait for her. Only then did he let her leave."

"Nice, very nice. It could well have turned out differently. By heaven yes, my dear lady. Altogether differently. I always say, we are all human beings together, and that being, created by God in His own image, is not facing extinction. A corrupt species may be trying to push its way to the forefront, but, God willing, it will not succeed. Another example of humanity in its purest form. It remains the victor in an unequal struggle."

"That's what I want to tell my story about," began Werner. "For many years now I have been working at our institute with a number of colleagues. They are Aryans, every last one of them. Quite a few of them are in sympathy with the new regime, some are dissatisfied, but all of them agree that the work being done there is valuable work, that it must be preserved at all costs, even if there is no prospect of carrying on any further. The rooms have been confiscated, the Hitler Youth is going to hold its meetings there, and a date has been set for vacating the premises. And another thing my colleagues agree about is that the valuable collection of rock samples must be saved. We decided unanimously to hand them over to the Natural History Museum, to which I have also donated my own private collection. An appointment was made for a museum attendant to come at twelve o'clock. At eleven in the morning, on that same day," said Werner, a deep flush spreading over his face, "at eleven in the morning"—he was gasping for breath and Kain was looking at him anxiously—"the brownshirts arrived, those pillagers and desecrators of culture dressed up as clowns, and took away all the material—the valuable collection of stones, along with the institute's inventory—off to the garbage dump. . . ." He was panting, unable to go on, but then, all at once, he slammed his fist down on the table and shouted, "There on the trash heap out in the yard at the back lay our stones, our priceless stones!" Kain had leapt to his feet and dipped his napkin in a glass of water to cool his brow. The unhappy man thrust him away.

Then the bell rang, jarringly.

They all caught their breath. Even Werner had gone quite still, and it was as if this ringing had ripped the curtain of a fateful rage. It seemed as if it had brought him to his senses. Without further resistance he allowed his brother to place the compress on his fevered brow.

Eva hurried to open the door.

Felberbaum rubbed his hands with pleasure. Doubtless, this would be a most welcome visitor. Perhaps his friend, the precentor in the synagogue. He had already prayed, had eaten well in anticipation of the day of fasting, had prayed again; and he didn't usually make any visits on the eve of Yom Kippur, but then this was a state of emergency. Now he'd be coming to see how Felberbaum was doing, whether everything was in order, no arrests carried out and no new restrictions imposed. And no doubt he would have something interesting to relate.

Or it could be his mother-in-law, that was even quite likely, the solemn festival day gave good reason for hope. His mother-in-law would be bringing a letter from his wife in England, along with the visa. Very probably he was about to get his visa. Most of all, he would love to give it up in favor of this wonderful couple here, if such a thing were possible. For they had been waiting even longer than he, and they needed it more urgently. They had had to sign a paper that they would leave, and couldn't get away. The deadline had arrived and the danger for the two of them was great, greater than Felberbaum would admit to them. The danger that they would be arrested, locked up—all that simply because they cannot get away. Terrible times indeed.—No, it couldn't be his visa, nor a visitor for him either, it was too quiet outside for that and the lady was away too long. It would be that beautiful girl, that Hilde, a friend of this dignified couple.

The door swung open. As it opened, it seemed to Werner as if there were no one standing within its frame. As if a black, menacing emptiness were yawning there.

The door closed again. Eva was standing in the room. How had she come in? Was that Eva? What had happened? She was trembling.

"Hadn't you better sit down?" asked Werner.

"What's the matter, Eva?" Kain, startled, rushed towards her.

"Is there someone outside?" Felberbaum inquired.

"You ought not to talk of the devil, Werner, or he's sure to appear. He was here a moment ago. One of those robbers dressed up as clowns, as you call them."

"An SA-man? Here?" Felberbaum's eyes widened with fear.

"Did he harm you, Eva?" Kain stroked her head.

She turned away from him and moved over to the window.

"So what happened, Eva?"

"We have to leave the country. All of us. All four."

"Leave the country?"

"And vacate the apartment within twelve hours."

"Who says so?"

"A man from the local administration was here."

"Did they also tell you how we are supposed to go about it?"

She shrugged.

"Didn't you give him the answer they deserve?"

She said nothing.

"And what will happen if we don't leave the country?" cried Felberbaum. "What can they do to us? We're willing, all too willing. But no one will let us in anywhere. All the paths are barred!"

She propped her cold hands against the window frame.

Her tongue was cleaving to her mouth. She was unable to bring the words out. She could never have allowed past her lips, never have brought herself to repeat, the answer she had had to listen to. Never would she utter what that person had spoken through cold lips. And no god made a move, no avenger appeared, the ceiling did not fall in upon them all.

She had replied to him that, yes, they intended to leave. They themselves were desperate because it was not working out. And so what would happen if they were not after all able to leave?

"Then," he had said, "you will be shot."

Yehuda Haim Aaron ha-Cohen Perahia

THEODOR ADORNO CLAIMED that poetry is impossible after the Holocaust. Yehuda Haim Aaron ha-Cohen Perahia proves him wrong. A businessman and author of both poetry and prose, he is practically unknown in the English-language world. His poem "After the Catastrophe in Salonika," translated by Isaac Jack Lévy, is included in *And the World Stood Silent: Sephardic Poetry of the Holocaust* (2000), edited by Lévy, who writes of Perahia's life and career: "The representative of a tobacco company with headquarters in Xanthi, [Perahia], with the assistance of his maid, spent the World War II years in hiding in Athens. His devotion to Judaism, his religious background, and his fervor for the political future of the Jews were the main inspiration of his prose and poetry. Among his writings are the novels *Bimba* and *El ultimo enforso,* the monograph *La famille Perahia a Thessaloniki,* a book of poetry entitled *Poemas,* as well as lectures and commentaries on his family and on Judaism in and around Salonika. (Perahia continually copied all his works by hand, often making orthographic changes and commenting on previous statements.) His genealogy dates back to Josephus and the early arrival of the Jews in Spain. The Spanish Inquisition forced a move to Italy, where his family became famous in the rabbinate and in the sciences, especially after they came under the protection of the Sultan in Salonika. After his death, Perahia left his nephew Moise Pessah of Kavalla in charge of his library."

After the Catastrophe in Salonika

How into rusted iron pure gold has been transmuted!
How our character has been changed into a foreign one!
How, in this great city called Yr Vaem beisrael
Everything became alien and one no longer hears the name Asael!

I walked along the streets of this blessed city.
In spite of the sun it all seems dark.
My face appears to be happy, but my eyes shed tears.
My soul, more than sad, yearns to see a Jew.

On the contrary, from my lips, dry and trembling,
Surge curses and passionate words, hardly comforting
To a person who suffers the misfortunes of his people,
Of this people, of all the Earth's nations the most innocent.

And without wanting to, I murmured, my eyes lifted toward God.
Thus Job began his dirge for himself and for Israel:
"Would that the day on which I was born had utterly vanished
As well as the night in which it was said, 'Of a male she is pregnant'!

"Would that this night had been dark and been taken away by Death,
And, because of its evil fate, would that God in Heaven had not
summoned it,
And would that neither light nor hope had dawned on it;
Would that darkness had encircled it and no human had seen it!"

I stopped. I saw Professor Michael Molho stop.
He shook my hand. "We are safe Zehout Avoth," he told me again and
again.
I kept silent. The sob caught in my throat
And prevented me from uttering even one clear and holy word.

I mourned the catastrophe. I saw that it spread with all haste.
Who is going to mourn now the disappearance of these Jews?
Who is going to proclaim the colossal and great loss,
The total extinction that God inflicted upon us?

And I slowly walk away, beaten, my head bowed.
I want to walk firmly and have my soul resigned.
I do not want to cry. I want to be indifferent, but I cannot—
The misfortunes of my people are many and touch me deeply!

I see corteges of human beings, en masse, herded into wagons
Of animals, frozen, closed, and sealed like melons,
Brought to the funereal and cursed places of execution,
The aged and sick condemned on the spot.

Afterward also the young, sent to the baths to wash,
Asphyxiated all together, unable ever to rise again,
Then thrown, pushed into the sinister and dreadful crematoria;
There vanished from my people a great number of Jews!

A tragedy such as this has never happened before in the world!
At the thought of this, my vision darkens at once.
My tears fall; my cry is that of a decent man.
I run away quickly, hiding my pain within myself.

Salonika 29 Av 5705
8 August 1945—Wednesday
To Professor Michael Molho

Shlomo Reuven

Like Yehuda Haim Aaron ha-Cohen Perahia, Shlomo Reuven (Greece-Israel), left a poetic testimony of his odyssey through the Holocaust. In *And the World Stood Silent: Sephardic Poetry of the Holocaust,* Isaac Jack Lévy states: "Born in Salonika, Chelomo Reuven received his primary education in French and while still a student began to publish poetry and prose articles in Judeo-Spanish and French, by demand, in the most prestigious newspapers, including *La Action, El Messagero,* and *La Verdad.* He also published poems in French using the pseudonym Le Reveur Solitaire. Upon finishing his studies, Reuven took an active part in the Zionist movement as the director of the Bethar, a youth organization, and was the editor of the Zionist papers *La Nasyon* and *La Boz Sionista.* He is the author of a musical, *Esther,* and a play, *Amor por la tierra;* his literary accomplishments include a novel, *Bacho el sielo blu de oriente encantador* [Under the Blue Sky of the Enchanted Levant], and a study entitled *La calomnia de la sangre a traverse la estoria* [Blood Libels through History]. In 1935 he moved to Israel, where he continued writing and lecturing on national themes and on the Holocaust, becoming one of the leaders of the Greek community and president of the Association de Amistad Israël-Hellas. 'The Holocaust was the cause of the death of my mother, my sister and two brothers and their eight children' [he told Lévy]. 'Sixty thousand Jews of Salonika and other Greek cities also perished.' This tragic chapter in the Diaspora continued to influence this journalist and poet, who dedicated all his efforts to the Centre de Recherches sur le Judaïsme de Salonika." The poem "Yom Hachoa," translated by Lévy, was published in Ladino newspapers in Israel.

Yom Hachoa

To the memory of my mother and all
my dear ones who disappeared in Auschwitz.

. . . And the years pass, and the hair turns gray,
and the eyes dim, and we tremble when we walk;
we can never forget that heavy pain
of seeing an entire nation condemned to the slaughter.

Incurable is the wound because great is the tragedy;
the tears have dried and the pain does not cease.
The day passes, the night comes, and a new day dawns
without suppressing my moans, without my accepting my misfortune.

They come to visit me in my sleep every night:
men, women, children, all guided by the top boots
of beasts armed to the teeth . . . and an atrocious scream
emerges from my breast and breaks the silence.

Living skeletons, among whom are my dear ones, can be seen,
mother, brothers with their children, sister, walking in the tranquility
of a vast necropolis, sacrifices offered
to an unknown Moloch, bathing in his cruelty.

They carry on their shoulders the weight of their bondage;
their faces are lifeless and their breathing weak.
They sense that these camps will be a vast cemetery
where soon will reign a profound desolation.

Auschwitz, Treblinka, Maidanek, unknown places
that became overnight symbols of bestiality,
that uprooted millions of souls from their warm homes
and changed into empty words culture and humanity.

For abundance operated the crematoria,
vast trenches were covered with cadavers and lime,
and the Jewish blood ran, warm and gushing,
emptied by an assassin nation that will never be equaled.

And men, women, and children continue to walk
toward their sad destiny, toward the gas chambers.
They sense in advance the horrible tortures
that await them, and their breathing goes out of perception.

In but a few moments . . . and from the ovens rises a heavy cloud,
gray, in flame, and spreads a strong odor,
and earth does not tremble, nature is not moved,
and the Heavens do not quiver at a just rage.

Thus vanished six million brethren.
The thousand-armed hydra swallowed them pitilessly:
the assassin did his work and the German people,
as if they were not guilty, today enjoy their freedom.

The whole world participated in the macabre spectacle
without trying to save, to help, to punish,
without being moved by a whole nation dead,
without giving signs of repentance or even denial.

But over the death camps and from that gray cloud
grew the delicate flower of our liberation;
and over the beloved bones and mountains of ash,
at the cost of new blood, our nation was restored.

Rest, beloved souls, from your last sleep.
You have fallen. With your death, evil seemed to have conquered,
but with your last breath, you have given life to our genius
and our lips murmur: "Yitgadal veyitkadash."

ELIAS CANETTI

ELIAS CANETTI (Bulgaria-Germany-England, 1905–1994) won the Nobel Prize for Literature in 1981. He was born into a Ladino-speaking Sephardic family in Ruschuk, Bulgaria, and was taken as a child to Manchester in 1911. He pursued his studies in England, Austria, Switzerland, and Germany. He received a Ph.D. in chemistry from the University of Vienna. Canetti is the author of a number of important works, among them the socioanthropological study *Crowds and Power* (1960; English, 1962), a groundbreaking reflection on the disappearance of individuality in masses. The book is written in a nonacademic style at once engaging and abstruse. Canetti also wrote *Kafka's Other Trial: The Letters to Felice* (1969; English, 1974), as well as *The Memoirs of Elias Canetti,* published in English in a single volume in 1999. Canetti's Sephardic identity is thoroughly explored in its pages, in the context of European intellectual history. The memoir was originally published in English in three separate volumes: *The Tongue Set Free: Remembrance of a European Childhood,* translated by Joachim Neugroschel (1977; English, 1979), from which the excerpts that follow are taken; *The Torch in My Ear,* translated by Joachim Neugroschel as well (1980; English, 1982); and *The Play of the Eyes,* translated by Ralph Manheim (1985; English, 1986). Canetti's feelings about his Jewish identity and his empathy toward the Muslim community are evident in *The Voices of Marrakesh: A Record of a Visit* (1967; English, 1978), an account of a trip he made in 1954. Known primarily as an essayist, Canetti published fiction, too. His novel *Die Blendung* (1936), a macabre meditation on literature and society, was banned in Adolf Hitler's Germany. It was published in English as *Auto-da-Fé* in the United Kingdom (1946) and as *The Tower of Babel* in the United States (1947) and is regarded as his masterwork. He also translated into German three books by Upton Sinclair: *Leidweg der Liebe, Das Geld schreibt,* and *Alkohol.* He died in Zürich.

From *The Tongue Set Free*

Family Pride

RUSCHUK, on the lower Danube, where I came into the world, was a marvelous city for a child, and if I say that Ruschuk is in Bulgaria, then I am giving an inadequate picture of it. For people of the most varied backgrounds lived there, on any one day you could hear seven or eight languages. Aside from the Bulgarians, who often came from the countryside, there were many Turks, who lived in their own neighborhood, and next to it was the neighborhood of the Sephardim, the Spanish Jews—our neighborhood. There were Greeks, Albanians, Armenians, Gypsies. From the opposite side of the Danube came Rumanians; my wet nurse, whom I no longer remember, was Rumanian. There were also Russians here and there.

As a child, I had no real grasp of this variety, but I never stopped feeling its effects. Some people have stuck in my memory only because they belonged to a particular ethnic group and wore a different costume from the others. Among the servants that we had in our home during the course of six years, there was once a Circassian and later on an Armenian. My mother's best friend was Olga, a Russian woman. Once every week, Gypsies came into our courtyard, so many that they seemed like an entire nation; the terrors they struck in me will be discussed below.

Ruschuk was an old port on the Danube, which made it fairly significant. As a port, it had attracted people from all over, and the Danube was a constant topic of discussion. There were stories about the extraordinary years when the Danube froze over; about sleigh rides all the way across the ice to Rumania; about starving wolves at the heels of the sleigh horses.

Wolves were the first wild animals I heard about. In the fairy tales that the Bulgarian peasant girls told me, there were werewolves, and one night, my father terrorized me with a wolf mask on his face.

It would be hard to give a full picture of the colorful time of those early years in Ruschuk, the passions and the terrors. Anything I subsequently experienced had already happened in Ruschuk. There, the rest of the world was known as "Europe," and if someone sailed up the Danube to Vienna, people said he was going to Europe. Europe began where the Turkish Empire had once ended. Most of the Sephardim were still Turkish subjects. Life had always been good for them under the Turks, better than for the Christian Slavs in the Balkans. But since many Sephardim were well-to-do merchants, the new Bulgarian regime maintained good relations with them, and King Ferdinand, who ruled for a long time, was said to be a friend of the Jews.

The loyalties of the Sephardim were fairly complicated. They were pious Jews, for whom the life of their religious community was rather important. But they considered themselves a special brand of Jews, and that was because of their Spanish background. Through the centuries since their expulsion from Spain, the Spanish they spoke with one another had changed little. A few Turkish words had been absorbed, but they were recognizable as Turkish, and there were nearly always Spanish words for them. The first children's songs I heard were Spanish, I heard old Spanish *romances;* but the thing that was most powerful, and irresistible for a child, was a Spanish attitude. With naive arrogance, the Sephardim looked down on other Jews; a word always charged with scorn was *Todesco,* meaning a German or Ashkenazi Jew. It would have been unthinkable to marry a *Todesca,* a Jewish woman of that background, and among the many families that I heard about or knew as a child in Ruschuk, I cannot recall a single case of such a mixed marriage. I wasn't even six years old when my grandfather warned me against such a misalliance in the future. But this general discrimination wasn't all. Among the Sephardim themselves, there were the "good families," which meant the ones that had been rich since way back. The proudest words one could hear about a person were: "*Es de buena famiglia*—he's from a good family." How often and ad nauseam did I hear that from my mother. When she enthused about the Viennese *Burgtheater* and read Shakespeare with me, even later on, when she spoke about Strindberg, who became her favorite author, she had no scruples whatsoever about telling that she came from a good family, there was no better family around. Although the literatures of the civilized languages she knew became the true substance of her life, she never felt any contradiction between this passionate universality and the haughty family pride that she never stopped nourishing.

Even back in the period when I was utterly in her thrall (she opened all the doors of the intellect for me, and I followed her, blind and enthusiastic), I nevertheless noticed this contradiction, which tormented and bewildered me, and in countless conversations during that time of my adolescence I discussed the matter with her and reproached her, but it didn't make the slightest impression. Her pride had found its channels at an early point, moving through them steadfastly; but while I was still quite young, that narrowmindedness, which I never understood in her, biased me against any arrogance of background. I cannot take people seriously if they have any sort of caste pride, I regard them as exotic but rather ludicrous animals. I catch myself having reverse prejudices against people who plume themselves on their lofty origin. The few times that I was friendly with aristocrats, I had to overlook their talking about it, and had they sensed what efforts this cost me, they would have forgone my friendship. All prejudices are caused by other prejudices, and the most frequent are those deriving from their opposites.

Furthermore, the caste in which my mother ranked herself was a caste of Spanish descent and also of money. In my family, and especially in hers, I saw what money does to people. I felt that those who were most willingly devoted to money were the worst. I got to know all the shades, from money-grubbing to paranoia. I saw brothers whose greed had led them to destroy one another in years of litigation, and who kept on litigating when there was no money left. They came from the same "good" family that my mother was so proud of. She witnessed all those things too, we often spoke about it. Her mind was penetrating; her knowledge of human nature had been schooled in the great works of world literature as well as in the experiences of her own life. She recognized the motives of the lunatic self-butchery her family was involved in; she could easily have penned a novel about it; but her pride in this same family remained unshaken. Had it been love, I could have readily understood it. But she didn't even love many of the protagonists, she was indignant at some, she had scorn for others, yet for the family as a whole, she felt nothing but pride.

Much later, I came to realize that I, translated to the greater dimensions of mankind, am exactly as she was. I have spent the best part of my life figuring out the wiles of man as he appears in the historical civilizations. I have examined and analyzed power as ruthlessly as my mother her family's litigations. There is almost nothing bad that I couldn't say about humans and humankind. And yet my pride in them is so great that there is only one thing I really hate: their enemy, death.

Kako la Gallinica

Wolves and Werewolves

AN EAGER AND YET TENDER word that I often heard was *la butica.* That was what they called the store, the business, where my grandfather and his sons usually spent the day. I was rarely taken there because I was too little. The store was located on a steep road running from the height of the wealthier districts of Ruschuk straight down to the harbor. All the major stores were on this street; my grandfather's *butica* was in a three-story building that struck me as high and stately because the residential houses up on the rise had only one story. The *butica* dealt in wholesale groceries, it was a roomy place and it smelled wonderful. Huge, open sacks stood on the floor, containing various kinds of cereals, there was millet, barley, and rice. If my hands were clean, I was allowed to reach into the sacks and touch the grains. That was a pleasant sensation, I filled my hand, lifted it up, smelled the grains, and let them slowly run back down again; I did this often, and though there were many other strange things in the store, I liked doing that best, and it was hard to get me away from the sacks. There was tea and coffee and especially chocolate. There were huge quantities of everything, and it was always beautifully packed, it wasn't sold in small amounts as in ordinary shops. I also especially liked the open sacks on the floor because they weren't too high for me and because when I reached in, I could feel the many grains, which meant so much to me.

Most of the things in the store were edible, but not all. There were matches, soaps, and candles. There were also knives, scissors, whetstones, sickles, and scythes. The peasants who came from the villages to shop used to stand in front of the instruments for a long time, testing the keenness with their fingers. I watched them, curious and a bit fearful; I was not allowed to touch the blades. Once, a peasant, who was probably amused by my face, took hold of my thumb, put it next to his, and showed me how hard his skin was. But I never received a gift of chocolate; my grandfather, who sat in an office in the back, ruled with an iron hand, and everything was wholesale. At home, he showed me his love because I had his full name, even his first name. But he didn't much care to see me in the store, and I wasn't allowed to stay long. When he gave an order, the employee who got the order dashed off, and sometimes an employee would leave the *butica* with packages. My favorite was a skinny, poorly dressed, middle-aged man, who always smiled absently. He had indefinite movements and jumped when my grandfather said anything. He appeared to be dreaming and was altogether different from the other people I saw in the store. He always had a friendly word for me; he spoke so vaguely that I could never understand him, but I sensed that he was well disposed towards me. His name was Chelebon, and since he was a poor and hopelessly incapable relative, my grandfather hired him out of pity. My grandfather always called to Chelebon as if he were a servant; that was how I remembered him, and I found out only much later that he was a brother of my grandfather's.

THE STREET RUNNING PAST the huge gate of our courtyard was dusty and drowsy. If it rained hard, the street turned into mud, and the droshkies left deep tracks. I wasn't allowed to play in the street, there was more than enough room in our big courtyard, and it was safe. But sometimes I heard a violent clucking from outside, it would get louder and louder and more excited. Then, before long, a man in black, tattered clothes, clucking and trembling in fear, would burst through the gate, fleeing the street children. They were all after him, shouting *"Kako! Kako!"* and clucking like hens. He was afraid of chickens, and that was why they harrassed him. He was a few steps ahead of them and, right before my eyes, he changed into a hen. He clucked violently, but in desperate fear, and made fluttering motions with his arms. He breathlessly dashed up the steps to my grandfather's house, but never dared to enter; he jumped down on the other side and remained lying motionless. The children halted at the gate, clucking, they weren't allowed into the courtyard. When he lay there as if dead, they were a bit scared and ran away. But then they promptly launched into their victory chant: *"Kako la gallinica! Kako la gallinica!*—Kako the chicken! Kako the chicken!" No sooner were they out of earshot than he got to his feet, felt himself all over, peered about cautiously, listened anxiously for a while, and then stole out of the courtyard, hunched, but utterly silent. Now he was no longer a chicken, he didn't flutter or cluck, and he was once again the exhausted neighborhood idiot.

Sometimes, if the children were lurking not too far away in the street, the sinister game started all over again. Usually, it moved to another street, and I couldn't see anything more. Maybe I felt sorry for Kako, I was always scared when he jumped, but what I couldn't get enough of, what I always watched in the same excitement, was his metamorphosis into a gigantic black hen. I couldn't understand why the children ran after him, and when he lay motionless on the ground after his leap, I was afraid he would never get up again and turn into a chicken again.

The Danube is very wide in its Bulgarian lower reaches. Giurgiu, the city on the other bank, was Rumanian. From there, I was told, my wet nurse came, my wet nurse, who fed me her milk. She had supposedly been a strong, healthy peasant woman and also nursed her own baby, whom she brought along. I always heard her praises, and even though I can't remember her, the word "Rumanian" has always had a warm sound for me because of her.

In rare winters, the Danube froze over, and people told exciting stories about it. In her youth, Mother had often ridden a sleigh all the way over to Rumania, she showed me the warm furs she had been bundled in. When it was very cold, wolves came down from the mountains and ravenously pounced on the horses in front of the sleighs. The coachman tried to drive them away with his whip, but it was useless, and someone had to fire at them. Once, during such a sleigh ride, it turned out that they hadn't taken anything to shoot with. An armed Circassian, who lived in the house as a servant, was supposed to come along, but he had been gone, and the coachman had started without him. They had a terrible time keeping the wolves at bay and were in great danger. If a sleigh with two men hadn't happened to come along from the opposite direction, things might have ended very badly, but the two men shot and killed one wolf and drove the others away. My mother had been terribly afraid; she described the red tongues of the wolves, which had come so close that she still dreamt about them in later years.

I often begged her to tell me this story, and she enjoyed telling it to me. Thus wolves became the first wild beasts to fill my imagination. My terror of them was nourished by the fairy tales I heard from the Bulgarian peasant girls. Five or six of them always lived in our home. They were quite young, perhaps ten or twelve years old, and had been brought by their families from the villages to the city, where they were hired out as serving maids in middle-class homes. They ran around barefoot in the house and were always in a high mettle; they didn't have much to do, they did everything together, and they became my earliest playmates.

In the evening, when my parents went out, I stayed at home with the girls. Low Turkish divans ran all the way along the walls of the huge living room. Aside from the carpets everywhere and a few small tables, they were the only constant furnishing that I can remember in that room. When it grew dark, the girls got scared. We all huddled together on one of the divans, right by the window; they took me into their midst, and now they began their stories about werewolves and vampires. No sooner was one story finished than they began the next; it was scary, and yet, squeezing against the girls on all sides, I felt good. We were so frightened that no one dared to stand up, and when my parents came home, they found us all wobbling in a heap.

Of the fairy tales I heard, only the ones about werewolves and vampires have lodged in my memory. Perhaps no other kinds were told. I can't pick up a book of Balkan fairy tales without instantly recognizing some of them. Every detail of them is present to my mind, but not in the language I heard them in. I heard them in Bulgarian, but I know them in German; this mysterious translation is perhaps the oddest thing that I have to tell about my youth, and since the language history of most children runs differently, perhaps I ought to say more about it.

To each other, my parents spoke German, which I was not allowed to understand. To us children and to all relatives and friends, they spoke Ladino. That was the true vernacular, albeit an ancient Spanish, I often heard it later on and I've never forgotten it. The peasant girls at home knew only Bulgarian, and I must have learned it with them. But since I never went to a Bulgarian school, leaving Ruschuk at six years of age, I very soon forgot Bulgarian completely. All events of those first few years were in Ladino or Bulgarian. It wasn't until much later that most of them were rendered into German within me. Only especially dramatic events, murder and manslaughter so to speak, and the worst terrors have been retained by me in their Ladino wording, and very precisely and indestructibly at that. Everything else, that is, most things, and especially anything Bulgarian, like the fairy tales, I carry around in German.

I cannot say exactly how this happened. I don't know at what point in time, on what occasion, this or that translated itself. I never probed into the matter; perhaps I was afraid to destroy my most precious memories with a methodical examination based on rigorous principles. I can say only one thing with certainty: The events of those years are present to my mind in all their strength and freshness (I've fed on them for over sixty years), but the vast majority are tied to words that I did not know at that time. It seems natural to me to write them down now; I don't have the feeling that I am changing or warping anything. It is not like the literary translation of a book from one language to another, it is a translation that happened of its own accord in my unconscious, and since I ordinarily avoid this word like the plague, a word that has become meaningless from overuse, I apologize for employing it in this one and only case.

Purim; The Comet

THE HOLIDAY THAT WE children felt most strongly, even though, being very small, we couldn't take part in it, was Purim. It was a joyous festival, commemorating the salvation of the Jews from Hamán, the wicked persecutor. Hamán was a well-known figure, and his name had entered the language. Before I ever found out that he was a man who had once lived and concocted horrible things, I knew his name as an insult. If I tormented adults with too many questions or didn't want to go to bed or refused to do something they wanted me to do, there would be a deep sigh: *"Hamán!"* Then I knew that they were in no mood for jokes, that I had played out. *"Hamán"* was the final word, a deep sigh, but also a vituperation. I was utterly amazed when I was told later on that Hamán had been a wicked man who wanted to kill all the Jews. But thanks to Mordecai and Queen Esther, he failed, and, to show their joy, the Jews celebrated Purim.

The adults disguised themselves and went out, there was noise in the street, masks appeared in the house, I didn't know who they were, it was like a fairy tale; my parents stayed out till late at night. The general excitement affected us children; I lay awake in my crib and listened. Sometimes our parents would show up in masks, which they then took off; that was great fun, but I preferred not knowing it was they.

One night, when I had dozed off, I was awakened by a giant wolf leaning over my bed. A long, red tongue dangled from his mouth, and he snarled fearfully. I screamed as loud as I could: "A wolf! A wolf!" No one heard me, no one came; I shrieked and yelled louder and louder and cried. Then a hand slipped out, grabbed the wolf's ears, and pulled his head down. My father was behind it, laughing. I kept shouting: "A wolf! A wolf!" I wanted my father to drive it away. He showed me the wolf mask in his hand; I didn't believe him, he kept saying: "Don't you see? It was me, that was no real wolf." But I wouldn't calm down, I kept sobbing and crying.

The story of the werewolf had thus come true. My father couldn't have known what the little girls always told me when we huddled together in the dark. Mother reproached herself for her sleigh story but scolded him for his uncontrollable pleasure in masquerading. There was nothing he liked better than play-acting. When he had gone to school in Vienna, he only wanted to be an actor. But in Ruschuk, he was mercilessly thrust into his father's business. The town did have an amateur theater, where he performed with Mother, but what was it measured by his earlier dreams in Vienna? He was truly unleashed, said Mother, during the Purim festival: He would change his masks several times in a row, surprising and terrifying all their friends with the most bizarre scenes.

My wolf panic held on for a long time; night after night I had bad dreams, very often waking my parents, in whose room I slept. Father tried to calm me down until I fell asleep again, but then the wolf reappeared in my dreams; we didn't get rid of him all that soon. From that time on, I was considered a jeapordized child whose imagination must not be overstimulated, and the result was that for many months I heard only dull stories, all of which I've forgotten.

The next event was the big comet, and since I have never thought about one event without the other, there must be some connection between them. I believe that the appearance of the comet freed me from the wolf; my childhood terror merged into the universal terror of those days, for I have never seen people so excited as during the time of the comet. Also, both of them, the wolf and the comet, appeared at night, one more reason why they came together in my memory.

Everyone talked about the comet before I saw it, and I heard that the end of the world was at hand. I couldn't picture what that was, but I did notice that people changed and started whispering whenever I came near, and they gazed at me full of pity. The Bulgarian girls didn't whisper, they said it straight out in their unabashed way: The end of the world had come. It was the general belief in town, and it must have prevailed for quite a while since it left such a deep stamp on me without my fearing anything specific. I can't say to what extent my parents, as educated people, were infected with that belief. But I'm sure they didn't oppose the general view. Otherwise, after our earlier experience, they would have done something to enlighten me, only they didn't.

One night, people said the comet was now here and would now fall upon the earth. I was not sent to bed; I heard someone say it made no sense, the children ought to come into the garden too. A lot of people were standing around in the courtyard. I had never seen so many there; all the children from our houses and the neighboring houses were among them, and everyone, adults and children, kept staring up at the sky, where the comet loomed gigantic and radiant. I can see it spreading across half the heavens. I still feel the tension in the back of my neck as I tried to view its entire length. Maybe it got longer in my memory, maybe it didn't occupy half, but only a smaller part of the sky. I must leave the answer to that question to others, who were grown up then and not afraid. But it was bright outdoors, almost like during the day, and I knew very well that it actually ought to be night, for that was the first time I hadn't been put to bed at that hour, and that was the real event for me. Everyone stood in the garden, peering at the heavens and waiting. The grownups scarcely walked back and forth; it was oddly quiet, voices were low, at most the children moved, but the grownups barely heeded them. In this expectation, I must have felt something of the anxiety filling everyone else, for in order to relieve me, somebody gave me a twig of cherries. I had put one cherry into my mouth and was craning my neck, trying to follow the gigantic comet with my eyes, and the strain, and perhaps also the wondrous beauty of the comet made me forget the cherry, so that I swallowed the pit.

It took a long time; no one grew tired of it, and people kept standing around in a dense throng. I can't see Father or Mother among them, I can't see any of the individual people who made up my life. I only see them all together, and if I hadn't used the word so frequently later on, I would say that I see them as a mass, a crowd: a stagnating crowd of expectation.

The Magic Language

The Fire

The biggest cleaning in the house came before *Pesakh,* Passover. Everything was moved topsy-turvy, nothing stayed in the same place, and since the cleaning began early—lasting about two weeks, I believe—this was the period of the greatest disorder. Nobody had time for you, you were always underfoot and were pushed aside or sent away, and as for the kitchen, where the most interesting things were being prepared, you could at best sneak a glance inside. Most of all, I loved the brown eggs, which were boiled in coffee for days and days.

On the seder evening, the long table was put up and set in the dining room; and perhaps the room had to be so long, for on this occasion the table had to seat very many guests. The whole family gathered for the seder, which was celebrated in our home. It was customary to pull in two or three strangers off the street; they were seated at the feast and participated in everything.

Grandfather sat at the head of the table, reading the Haggadah, the story of the exodus of the Jews from Egypt. It was his proudest moment: Not only was he placed above his sons and sons-in-law, who honored him and followed all his directions, but he, the eldest, with his sharp face like a bird of prey, was also the most fiery of all; nothing eluded him. As he chanted in singsong, he noticed the least motion, the slightest occurrence at the table, and his glance or a light movement of his hand would set it aright. Everything was very warm and close, the atmosphere of an ancient tale in which everything was precisely marked out and had its place. On seder evenings, I greatly admired my grandfather; and even his sons, who didn't have an easy time with him, seemed elevated and cheerful.

As the youngest male, I had my own, not unimportant function; I had to ask the *Ma-nishtanah*. The story of the exodus is presented as a series of questions and answers about the reasons for the holiday. The youngest of the participants asks right at the start what all these preparations signify: the unleavened bread, the bitter herbs, and the other unusual things on the table. The narrator, in this case my grandfather, replies with the detailed story of the exodus from Egypt. Without my question, which I recited by heart, holding the book and pretending to read, the story could not begin. The details were familiar to me, they had been explained often enough; but throughout the reading I never lost the sense that my grandfather was answering me personally. So it was a great evening for me too, I felt important, downright indispensable; I was lucky there was no younger cousin to usurp my place.

But although following every word and every gesture of my grandfather's, I looked forward to the end throughout the narrative. For then came the nicest part: The men suddenly all stood up and jigged around a little, singing together as they danced: *"Had gadya, had gadya!"*—"A kid! A kid!" It was a merry song, and I was already quite familiar with it, but it was part of the ritual for an uncle to call me over when it was done and to translate every line of it into Ladino.

WHEN MY FATHER CAME home from the store, he would instantly speak to my mother. They were very much in love at that time and had their own language, which I didn't understand; they spoke German, the language of their happy schooldays in Vienna. Most of all, they talked about the *Burgtheater;* before ever meeting, they had seen the same plays and the same actors there and they never exhausted their memories of it. Later I found out that they had fallen in love during such conversations, and while neither of them had managed to make their dream of the theater come true—both had passionately wanted to act—they did succeed in getting married despite a great deal of opposition.

Grandfather Arditti, from one of the oldest and most prosperous Sephardic families in Bulgaria, was against letting his youngest, and favorite, daughter marry the son of an upstart from Adrianople. Grandfather Canetti had pulled himself up by his bootstraps; an orphan, cheated, turned out of doors while young, he had worked his way up to prosperity; but in the eyes of the other grandfather, he remained a play-actor and a liar. "*Es mentiroso* (He's a liar)," I heard Grandfather Arditti once say when he didn't realize I was listening. Grandfather Canetti, however, was indignant about the pride of the Ardittis, who looked down on him. His son could marry any girl, and it struck him as a superfluous humiliation that he wanted to marry the daughter of that Arditti of all people. So my parents at first kept their love a secret, and it was only gradually, very tenaciously, and with the active help of their older brothers and sisters and well-disposed relatives, that they succeeded in getting closer to making their wish come true. At last, both fathers gave in, but a tension always remained between them, and they couldn't stand each other. In the secret period, the two young people had fed their love incessantly with German conversations, and one can imagine how many loving couples of the stage played their part here.

So I had good reason to feel excluded when my parents began their conversations. They became very lively and merry, and I associated this transformation, which I noted keenly, with the sound of the German language. I would listen with utter intensity and then ask them what this or that meant. They laughed, saying it was too early for me, those were things I would understand only later. It was already a great deal for them to give in on the word "Vienna," the only one they revealed to me. I believed they were talking about wondrous things that could be spoken of only in that language. After begging and begging to no avail, I ran away angrily into another room, which was seldom used, and I repeated to myself the sentences I had heard from them, in their precise intonation, like magic formulas; I practiced them often to myself, and as soon as I was alone, I reeled off all the sentences or individual words I had practiced—reeled them off so rapidly that no one could possibly have understood me. But I made sure never to let my parents notice, responding to their secrecy with my own.

I found out that my father had a name for my mother which he used only when they spoke German. Her name was Mathilde, and he called her Mädi. Once, when I was in the garden, I concealed my voice as well as I could, and called loudly into the house: "Mädi! Mädi!" That was how my father called to her from the courtyard whenever he came home. Then I dashed off around the house and appeared only after a while with an innocent mien. My mother stood there perplexed and asked me whether I had seen Father. It was a triumph for me that she had mistaken my voice for his, and I had the strength to keep my secret, while she told him about the incomprehensible event as soon as he came home.

It never dawned on them to suspect me, but among the many intense wishes of that period, the most intense was my desire to understand their secret language. I cannot explain why I didn't really hold it against my father. I did nurture a deep resentment towards my mother, and it vanished only years later, after his death, when she herself began teaching me German.

One day, the courtyard was filled with smoke; a few of our girls ran out into the street and promptly came back with the excited news that a neighborhood house was on fire. It was already all in flames and about to burn up. Instantly, the three houses around our courtyard emptied, and except for my grandmother, who never rose from her divan, all the tenants ran out towards the blaze. It happened so fast that they forgot all about me. I was a little scared to be all alone like that; also I felt like going out, perhaps to the fire, perhaps even more in the direction I saw them all running in. So I ran through the open courtyard gate out into the street, which I was not allowed to do, and I wound up in the racing torrent of people. Luckily, I soon caught sight of two of our older girls, and since they wouldn't have changed directions for anything in the world, they thrust me between themselves and hastily pulled me along. They halted at some distance from the conflagration, perhaps so as not to endanger me, and thus, for the first time in my life, I saw a burning house. It was already far gone; beams were collapsing and sparks were flying. The evening was gathering, it slowly became dark, and the fire shone brighter and brighter. But what made an even greater impact on me than the blazing house was the people moving around it. They looked small and dark from that distance; there were very many of them, and they were scrambling all over the place. Some remained near the house, some moved off, and the latter were all carrying something on their backs. "Thieves!" said the girls, "Those are thieves! They're carrying things away from the house before anyone can catch them!" They were no less excited about the thieves than about the fire, and as they kept shouting "Thieves!" their excitement infected me. They were indefatigable, those tiny black figures, deeply bowed, they fanned out in all directions. Some had flung bundles on their shoulders, others ran stooped under the burden of angular objects, which I couldn't recognize, and when I asked what they were carrying, the girls merely kept repeating: "Thieves! They're thieves!"

This scene, which has remained unforgettable for me, later merged into the works of a painter, so that I no longer could say what was original and what was added by those paintings. I was nineteen, in Vienna, when I stood before Brueghel's pictures. I instantly recognized the many little people of that fire in my childhood. The pictures were as familiar to me as if I had always moved among them. I felt a tremendous attraction to them and came over every day. That part of my life which had commenced with the fire continued immediately in these paintings, as though fifteen years had not gone by in between. Brueghel became the most important painter for me; but I did not absorb him, as so many later things, by contemplation and reflection. I found him present within me as though, certain that I would have to come to him, he had been awaiting me for a long time.

Edouard Roditi

Edouard Roditi (France-USA, 1910–1992), a leading Surrealist poet, translator, and art critic, was educated in France, England, Germany, and, in the United States, at the University of Chicago and the University of California at Berkeley. He began publishing poetry in 1928 in *transition,* the expatriate Paris periodical to which James Joyce, Gertrude Stein, and Hart Crane also contributed. In 1934, T. S. Eliot published some of his poems in *The Criterion.* He served as an interpreter at the Nuremberg war crimes tribunal. After World War II, Roditi published his own work in French and German, and translated works from French, German, Spanish, and Turkish. He translated Albert Memmi's *The Pillar of Salt* into English and Fernando Pessoa's *Selected Poems* into German. Roditi's own books include *Poems 1928–1948* (1949); *Oscar Wilde,* a critical study of his writings (1967); *The Delights of Turkey: Twenty Tales* (1974); and *Dialogues on Art* (1960). He is also the author of a biography, *Magellan of the Pacific* (1972), as well as two other books of poetry: *Emperor of Midnight* and *Thrice Chosen* (both 1974). "The Complaint of Joshua Abravanel," about the Italian philosopher, Leone Ebero, is from *Thrice Chosen.* Roditi stated in a memoir: "Three of my grandparents were Jews, but the forth, my maternal grandmother, was a Flemish Catholic, so that neither my mother nor I were born Jews according to traditional Jewish law. I chose, however, to be one of the Chosen People, a choice that already implies a kind of double election. Since the most remote antiquity, it has moreover been generally believed by most people that those who are subject to certain seizures are also elect in a way, since they are believed to be visited, when their fits occur, by visions that transcend the understanding of other mortals. From birth, I have been prone to such seizures, which have often appeared to me to be veritable experiences of death and of an afterlife from which I return painfully but gratefully to what others believe to be the only reality."

The Complaint of Jehuda Abravanel

I

This is already the twentieth year
That my chariots and my horses have not rested.
In my travels through Europe,
A myriad of mercies have been shown me,

Shielding me from accident, from the swift stroke
Of collision at crossroads.
My drivers have been careful and my horses
Have miraculously dodged disaster.

In my studies, my unerring thought
Made me the lion of my tribe;
Refuting the wise of the nations, I taught
Foreigners and my people throughout the world.

On foundations of my father's wisdom,
Out of my labors I have built
A great house; now, an old man
Stops as he climbs the winding stair.

For the mind grows weary of its duty of discerning
Between the being and no-being of things,
Weary in the springtime, yearning
For the endless winter when at last the mind may rest.

I, Leo, exiled in Genoa,
When the spring breeze blows beyond the closed gate,
Remember the flowers on the open Spanish hills
And the rose-laurels by the river and my boy.

I, the lion, unrivalled in thought,
Faint before the phantom of this lamb

Playing among the rose-laurels, then lost
In a strange land and faith, under a strange name.

I, the doctor who have healed so many sick,
Am sick in turn, of a wound that never heals.
Always, my scrupulous diagnosis of symptoms,
After hour-long hesitation, brings me back

To this son begot within a pair of minutes,
Fruit of a long-forgotten joy
Whose taste lingers on, surviving the fruit,
With a flavor in each formless memory.

Why does one ponder, wearying the brain,
In order that one may know and make known
And that it become known,
In order that the hidden word may be revealed,

The mystery of the Beginning and the Throne,
Of that which can be whispered only to the wise
In secret academies, or read in dusty libraries
While the grass grows and the birds sing outside?

Why have I borne this honey and milk
Sweet beneath my tongue, if it must turn bitter
Because I have no son to whom I can birdlike
Feed my words placed in his beloved mouth?

Why study the spirit in this exile of flesh
If no flesh of my flesh can rule what I conquered,
Seated on the throne which once I won
By my wisdom, over my people and the nations?

My wisdom must be lost and my words spoken
To the weevil and bat and the slowly crumbling stones
Of the palace that I built but can no longer keep
When time leaves me an old man seated among ruins.

II

In order that the hidden word
Be open, the unspoken word
Spoken, known from open lips,
That the known word be open, spoken,

I have lived righteous, limited by law,
Remembering the covenant, submitting
My determinations to its disposings,
My practice to its providence, bearing its badge

On my body, my heart, my mouth and my mind.
Year by year, a great rock, this promise
Has embedded itself deeper in my being,
Ballasting me with faith in storms of doubt.

Pondering over the sacred problem
Of the gift, the action and the design,
I have sought to follow the Architect's plan
Building a palace for the promised prince,

Raising this ark around my hopes,
This walled garden where I walked,
Trimming the trees which another had planted,
Waiting for the prince to redeem, each leaf.

The foundations of my faith have fallen.
The prince of my ruined tower has died,
Strangled by his chains as he strained
Like a hound to break loose on the world.

To my father, to my mother's father
And to their fathers before them,
Always was it foretold that a prince
Among their sons would release the word.

Each father has lived within the law,
Each father's father before him:

Fathers were born, their sons were born,
Till my son was born who now is lost.

My son was this prince or father to this prince,
Born in due time, of the seed of his loins.
But the seed is lost, the prince is lost,
In spite of the law and the promise.

My son was my spring. All flowers, all light
And foliage within his one body were bound.
Each spring rings like false prophecy:
Why promise fruit and branches to the half-dead trunk?

Why taunt me, the arrowless, the broken bow,
Exiled, uprooted, maimed of my child,
With this promise of a prince like an arrow to be shot
At the noontide sun, to hold perfection fixed?

My prince, who lay in prison, died.
His palace has waited in vain.
The bats flit through its ruined roof,
The empty moonlight shines on his empty throne.

Let not the nations know of this loss,
Lest they laugh at an aged father,
Taunting me: "Where is this prince, this promise?
How are the wise mistaken!"

I no longer know the hour of dawn-rising
Nor that of night-retiring. Wine brings no joy
To my dead palate, salt has lost its savor.
I have lost my savior and he was my salt.

III

In spring, the sap, roused from its sleep,
Surges from withered roots
To winter-numbed limbs; old wounds
Now bleed afresh, old pains revive.

The exile remembers the loved landscape
And crosses the frontier, in spite of police;
Is caught, shot. The spy in foreign parts
Throws caution to the winds, sings his native songs.

I, topmost branch of my race's tree,
Bleed where my son was lopped off
By fate; no further can I cleave
The stormy years towards sheer light.

Fate, with its wiles, annuls my spring,
Cancels the infant buds, the sap
Rising to feed the leaves. Fate's frost
Withholds me in winter, blights my hopes.

He who, I hoped, would win where I
Had failed, climb where I stopped
Panting at the foot of the last
Flight, find light in my dark, strength in my weakness,

Remembering my errors, profiting by my
Successes, firm with my creditors, just
With my debtors, defeating all those who would cheat
An old father, my son, can never read

The words, signs of the hidden word,
The books where I set down
All that I sought and found, still sought
Or left for my son or my son's son to find.

My individual entity, that mask
Is so torn asunder, I can no longer
Suffer, nor feel, when memory's knife
Cuts to the quick my age-numbed mind.

On evenings when friendship no longer
Suffices, nor the disputations
Of doctors, when the air is thick
With the day's dust, the mind with its talk,

The last sunray falls across the open book
And the mind finds no meaning in the written word,
Weary of too much study, too much
Seeking after cause in a world of effect.

Desire, like this last sunray, falls
Across the dim book of memory,
Casts light on one word, gives a clue to the text,
Offers my son as the key to my life.

For the mind is a mirror reflecting the thing,
Loving that which it has known, desiring
That which it knows: there is
No love of a thing unknown, unremembered.

Nor may I ever forget my loved son
Who can no longer be made twain
From his loving father. Each spring, the dry crumbs
Of that which, last year, had leavened my thoughts

Are swept out of my mind. New bread is baked.
But the memory, intent on the old,
Swerves away from the new, can never forget.
I see my son walking towards me in each street.

IV

In spring, when each tree sees its leaves reborn
And I, maimed of my son, have lost
Little by little the life-blood of sleep,
I know that the end of my endless vigils

Is death or madness. When I'm mad,
I'm brave, see my son in every street
Walking towards me, found my faith
On dreams and desires, love things not known

Through the five fingers of physical sense
That shape the potential world's fresh clay.

Then the unknown, unremembered, is loved,
Remembered and known: that the same is God,

Maker and Creator, who made in six days,
Limited by law of numbers, six numbers
Chosen according to the hidden word
Which must not be spoken, must not escape

Through the scorched lips of fire-speaking babes
Lest the world shake on its broad base, hearing
The word misspoken by lisping lips
Of those who know not the discernible world.

Their fingers are numb, their senses have not
Yet grasped the world's meaning. How can
The word, light of the first day, shine
Without strife in dark minds that set no fixed

Police of evening and dawn to keep
Firm watch at the frontiers, where strife is most likely?
How can a man whose mind has never ordered,
Like an army, the fingers of unruly sense,

Who has no knowledge of tactics and plans,
Know the plan of creation, the pattern whereby
The foundations of unfinished Zion
Were laid in six days by the Architect?

How can the Architect know our worth
Till the city be finished, the plan worked out?
The prince must approve the builder's work,
Then live in the palace. The word of the first

Day is hidden, is handed down
In secret academies from father to son,
Teacher to disciple, expounding the plan.
The prince must approve the finished city

And hold high court in the palace built
With that wisdom, financed by those talents
Left on trust to his chosen race
By contract of the word sealed in our flesh.

Fate has twisted this race like a turban
About her mad head. My house was destroyed,
My family scattered, my one son lost;
But the word still lives in the world, the hidden

Word which must rise like a bubble of fire
Through the shapeless mire of the unshaped world
Till the world is shaped, New Jerusalem built
And the word released, when the prince returns

Clothed in white light, releasing godhead
From each stone he touches, approving the city
Planned in the first day of light, fulfilling
The contract sealed in our flesh with a word.

V

It is now time that I
Should lay aside this dim
Understanding men miscall
Knowledge. For my mind

Has seen the infinite light
Of inactual no-being
Straining, imprisoned prince,
To become actual being.

For my mind has seen
Itself as thin barrier
Between dim being, known,
And bright no-being, unknown;

Beelike, out of the breeding world,
Building its comb of consciousness,
Shaping the unknown into the known,
Sealing the gift with its own design;

Diluting, in dim secret honey
Of wisdom, the pure radiance
Of the lost sunlight, thwarting
Trees as it trims their twigs.

In the evening of life, the last sunray
Falls on the open book of the world,
Casts light on one point, reveals the whole truth:
The last heaven is built and the world made complete.

For the mind finds new truths in the open book
Of the world, new letters in the word;
Studying, builds new heavens of thought
Till the whole word is spelled, the whole world built.

Then that which lay hidden since the beginning,
The plan concealed in the Architect's mind,
Though known as no-being to the unknowing,
Is shaped into being, made open and known

By the shaping mind, crowned prince of the world.
Though this prince grow weary of his duty of discerning
Between extremes, of seeing himself
Judge of the strife of rival worlds,

Torn by himself, by his strife with himself,
Between stress and strain, being and becoming,
Striving to rise to his promised throne;
Still the unfinished world must strain

At its chains to release the thriving word
From the womb where the seed of the promise
Has lain, since the beginning of being,
And gathered strength to unite the world.

And even if my one son is lost,
Out of the darkness into realms of light
Others arise to win their place
In the actual world that can no longer change.

I see them arise towards the city
Of finished crystal as they leave
Dim slums, their flowerlike faces drawn
To freedom and light where Zion is built

According to plan, the whole word spelled
And spoken aloud, though by foreign lips,
And the contract fulfilled that was sealed in my flesh
With an unspoken word that I could never speak.

Edmond Jabès

Edmond Jabès (Egypt-France, 1912–1991) was a prolific *philosophe* and poet born in Cairo into a Jewish family of Italian origin. French was his mother tongue. He studied at College Saint-Jean Baptiste de la Salle, the Lycée français, and the Sorbonne. Jabès lived in Palestine during World War II, writing poetry while he worked for the British. He then returned to Egypt, but was among those Jews who were expelled following the Suez War in 1956. He immigrated to France in 1957 and became a French citizen in 1967. In Paris he began to study the Talmud and Kabbalah, and from then on rabbis, appearing as transient, disembodied voices, begin to figure in his work. This device, Jabès argued, echoed Talmudic debates. Exile and the love of books are favorite themes. They are approached as metaphysical conditions: exile dates back to the act of divine creation, and the Book (with capital *B*) is a palliative to the fracture and sadness brought along by exile. Jabès is the author of the seven-volume *The Book of Questions* (1963–1983; English, 1976–1984), *The Book of Margins* (1975; English, 1993), *The Book of Resemblances* (1976; English, 1990), *The Book of Dialogue* (1984; English, 1986), and *The Book of Shares* (1987; English, 1989). *The Sand: Complete Poems, 1943–1988* was published in French in 1990. Jabès also wrote meditations on Paul Eluard and Paul Celan and a series of conversations called *From the Desert to the Book: Conversations with Marcel Cohen* (1980; English, 1990). The excerpts that follow are from *The Book of Questions,* translated by Rosmarie Waldrop. They are representative of Jabès's poetic prose style.

From *The Book of Questions*

I

("What is light?" one of his disciples asked Reb Abbani.

"In the book," replied Reb Abbani, "there are unsuspected large blank spaces. Words go there in couples, with one single exception: the name of the Lord. Light is in these lovers' strength of desire.

"Consider the marvelous feat of the storyteller, to bring them from so far away to give our eyes a chance."

And Reb Hati: "The pages of the book are doors. Words go through them, driven by their impatience to regroup, to reach the end of the work, to be again transparent.

"Ink fixes the memory of words to the paper.

"Light is in their absence, which you read.")

DO I KNOW, at this hour when men lift their eyes up to the sky, when knowledge claims a richer, more beautiful part of the imagination (all the secrets of the universe are buds of fire soon to open), do I know, in my exile, what has driven me back through tears and time, back to the wells of the desert where my ancestors had ventured? There is nothing at the threshold of the open page, it seems, but this wound of a race born of the book, whose order and disorder are roads of suffering. Nothing but this pain, whose past and whose permanence is also that of writing.

The word is bound to the word, never to man, and the Jew to his Jewish world. The word carries the weight of each of its letters, as the Israelite has, from the first dawn, carried that of his image.

Water marks the boundaries of oases. Between one tree and another, there is all the thirst of the earth.

"I am the word. And you claim to know me by my face," said Reb Josué, one day, to a rabbi come to meet him, indignant that the inspired man should be known by his features.

A town at night is a shopwindow emptied of things.

A few graffiti on a wall were enough for the dormant memories in my hand to take over my pen, for my fingers to determine what I see.

The story of Sarah and Yukel is the account, through various dialogues and meditations attributed to imaginary rabbis, of a love destroyed by men and by words. It has the dimensions of the book and the bitter stubbornness of a wandering question.

("The soul is a moment of light, which the first word can touch off. Then we are like the universe with thousands of heavenly bodies on our skin. You know them apart by the intensity of their radiance, as you tell a star by the clarity of its avowal."

—REB ABER

"Distance is light, as long as you keep in mind that there are no limits. "We are distance."

—REB MIRSHAK)

. . . .

3

"You dream of having a place in the book and, right away, you become a word shared by eyes and lips."

—REB SENI

"Signs and wrinkles are questions and answers of the same ink."

—JE BÂTIS MA DEMEURE

"You chose," said Reb Eloda. "Now you are at the mercy of your choice.

"But did you choose to be Jewish?"

And Reb Ildé: "What is the difference between choosing and being chosen, since we cannot help submitting to choice?"

"You are silent: I was. You speak: I am."

—REB MOLINE

. . . .

5

("If we have been created to endure the same suffering, to be doomed to the same prearranged death: why give us lips, why eyes and voices, why souls and languages all different?"

—Reb Midrash

To be in the book. To figure in the book of questions, to be part of it. To be responsible for a word or a sentence, a stanza or chapter.

To be able to say: "I am in the book. The book is my world, my country, my roof, and my riddle. The book is my breath and my rest."

I get up with the page that is turned. I lie down with the page put down. To be able to reply: "I belong to the race of words, which homes are built with"—when I know full well that this answer is still another question, that this home is constantly threatened.

I will evoke the book and provoke the questions.

If God is, it is because He is in the book. If sages, saints, and prophets exist, if scholars and poets, men and insects exist, it is because their names are found in the book. The world exists because the book does. For existing means growing with your name.

The book is the work of the book. It is the sun, which gives birth to the sea. It is the sea, which reveals the earth. It is the earth, which shapes man. Otherwise, sun, sea, earth, and man would be focused light without object, water moving without going or coming, wealth of sand without presence, a waiting of flesh and spirit without touch, having nothing that corresponds to it, having neither doubles nor opposites.

Eternity ticks off the instant with the word.

The book multiplies the book.

Yukel, you have never felt at ease in your skin. You have never been *here,* but always *elsewhere,* ahead of yourself or behind like winter in the eyes of autumn or summer in the eyes of spring, in the past or in the future like those syllables whose passage from night to day is so much like lightning that it merges with the movement of the pen.

The present is, for you, this passage too rapid to be seized. What is left of the passage of the pen is the word, with its branches and leaves green or already dead. The word hurled into the future in order to translate it.

You read the future. You give us the future to read. Yet yesterday, you were not. And tomorrow, you will no longer be.

And yet you have tried to incrust yourself in the present, to be that unique moment when the pen holds the word which will survive.

You have tried.

You cannot say what your steps want, where they lead you. One never knows very well where the adventure begins and where it ends. And yet it begins in a certain place and ends some place farther off, at a precise point.

At a certain hour. On a certain day.

Yukel, you have gone through dreams and through time. For those who see you (but they do not see you—I see you) you are a shape moving in the fog.

Who were you, Yukel?

Who are you, Yukel?

Who will you be?

"You" means, sometimes, "I."

I say "I," and I am not "I." "I" means you, and you are going to die. You are drained.

From now on, I will be alone.

(Have you ever seen blind legs, arms, a blind neck?

Have you ever seen blind lips? Like those of the man taking a walk this evening, this last evening

at the end of his life.

Yukel, have I been the sight you lack, the sight of your foot on the tile, of your arms in the embrace, of your neck in thirst? The sight of your lips kissing and speaking?

"I" means you. You are going to die. And I will be alone.)

You are walking toward death. It has spared you till now, so that you should go towards it of your own accord. You are walking on all the deaths which belong to you and your race, on the obscure sense and the lack of sense of all these deaths.

And it is I who force you to walk. I sow your steps.

And I think, I speak for you. I choose and cadence.

For I am writing

and you are the wound.

Have I betrayed you, Yukel?

I have certainly betrayed you.

Between earth and sky, I have kept nothing but the childish opening of your pain. You are one of the grains of the collective scream which the sun paints golden.

I have given your name and Sarah's to this stubborn scream,
to this scream wedded to its breath and older than any of us,
to this everlasting scream
older than the seed.

Forgive me, Yukel. I have substituted my inspired sentences for yours. You are the toneless utterance among anecdotal lies. An utterance like a star engulfed among stars. In the evening, only my stars will be seen, only their warm and wonderful sparkle. But just for the time of your brief vanishing. Returning, you will take your place again. Silent.

How could you have expressed yourself, when you open your mouth only to prolong the scream? How could you have the desire and the patience to explain your steps,
when you are without desire or patience?

Who are you, Sarah, in Yukel's springtime?

(Where the blood of the earth is rounder than the earth, where dawn, to clothe her, weaves the flax,

where she is,

where water endlessly drips from her toes: can we know what happens to a woman pulled out of the water,

separated from the simple life of her hands, from the joys of the waves?

They have cut her to pieces.

She is prey to their ropes.)

Who are you, Yukel, in Sarah's springtime?

(Do you ask your shadow what became of it during the night?

Or ask the night about your shadow?)

You were the night. And you walk towards the night. You miss it because you know how gentle it is, how cooling its palm on your eyes. Day was all pain for you, night, recreation. And nevertheless you dream of light, of fields, of horizons of light.

"Is it true," the innocent Maimoun asked Reb Nati, one day, "is it true I was born with the first man?"

"You were born with the first divine wish," replied Reb Nati. "And this wish was that you should be a man."

"Is it true," the innocent Maimoun asked again, "that loving God means loving Him in men?"

"Loving God," answered Reb Nati, "means making your own His love of men.

"God is an unobtrusive wick, which will be light through you. It waits under glass for the gesture of fire which makes it your lamp."

"In this case, I have lost my God," groaned the innocent Maimoun. "I do not love the men who killed my father. And since then, I have lived in the dark."

Who are you, Sarah, in Yukel's winter?

(Doe tracked down in the maze of asphalt and lead, which I am walking through tonight. Doe caught alive to be burned (you escaped the fire of men, but not your own), led off by the hunters of your country to be given up to the receivers of your stolen freedom, the butchers of your light step, your open arms.

Sarah, all white,
like the wall the graffiti nail you to,
like the sea, which turns into words of love wherever you go,
Sarah of wandering.)

Who are you, Yukel, in Sarah's winter?

You are my companion with your invisible crown of thorns. You are no hero and not quite a citizen. Kept in the background by your kind. I accompanied you through your school books, where your lot was traced in pencil, through your later note books, illegible with erasures.

One after the other, I retrieved all the sentences I could not read. (But did you write them? Did you say them? Did you only think them?)

I let ink run into the body of every letter I guessed, so that it should live and die of its own sap,

which is yours, Yukel, in the book,

in what the book approaches and conceals.

"Whosoever does not believe in the book," said Reb Gandour, "has lost faith in man and in the kingdom of man."

Is there, brother, a word dreamier and more alert, more miserable and more fraternal than the one you incarnate?

6

"Our ties to beings and things are so fragile they often break without us noticing."

"A breath, a glance, a sign, and sometimes just confiding a shadow: such is, roughly, the original nature of our ties."

"If our ties are eternal, it is because they are divine."

"You try to be free through writing. How wrong. Every word unveils another tie."

—Reb Léca

"I name you. You were."

—Reb Vita

You have a name you did not ask for. All your life, this name will prey on you.

But at which moment do you become aware of it?

(If your name has only one letter, you are at the threshold of your name.
If your name has two letters, two doors open your name.
If your name has three letters, three masts carry off your name.
If your name has four letters, four horizons drown your name.
If your name has five letters, five books blow the leaves off your name.
If your name has six letters, six sages interpret your name.
If your name has seven letters, seven branches burn your name.)

You have the void for face.

"Child, the letters of your name are so far apart that you are a bonfire in the starry night.

"In time, you will feel the dimensions of your name, the anguish of the nothing you answer to."

—Reb Amiel

You have the void for voyage.

"Once you have taken possession of your name, the alphabet is yours. But soon you will be the slave of your riches."

—Reb Teris

"You take on yourself the sin of the book."

—Reb Levi

7

The Commentaries of the Rabbis Ab, Ten, Zam, Elar, Daber, Elati, and Yukel's Second Speech

"Do not neglect the echo. You live by echoes."

—Reb Prato

The commentary of Reb Ab:

"A writer's life takes its sense through what he says, what he writes, what can be handed down from generation to generation.

"What is remembered is sometimes only one phrase, one line.

"There is the truth.

"But what truth?

"If a phrase or line survives the work, it is not the author who gave it this special chance (at the expense of the others): it is the reader.

"There is the lie.

"The writer steps aside for the work, and the work depends on the reader.

"So truth is, in time, the absurd and fertile quest of lies, which we pay with tears and blood."

("You, who think I exist,
how can I tell you what I know
with words which mean
more than one thing,

with words like me, which change
when looked at,
words with an alien voice?
How can I say
that I am not,
yet in every word
I see,
I hear,
I understand myself?
How say all this to you
whose new reality
is that of the light
by which
the world
knows the world
while losing you?
And yet you answer
to a borrowed
name?
How can I show what I create,
outside myself,
page after page,
when doubt
erases
every trace of my passage?
Who ever saw
the images I give?
Last of all, I claim my due.
But how prove my innocence
when the eagle rose from my hand
to conquer the sky
which hugs me?
I die of pride
at the end of my strength.
What I await is always farther.
How could I make you part
of my adventure,
when it is the avowal of
my loneliness
and of the road?")

The commentary of Reb Ten:

> "My road had its hours of greatness,
> its blows, its pain.
> My road has its crest and its groundswell,
> its sand and its sky.
> My road. Yours."

("I do not know
if you were taught
that the earth is round
like thirst.
And that,
when lovers' shadows move
at the approach of dawn,
the poet's tongue,
the tongue of wells and centuries,
is dry,
is rough and dry.
It has done so much service
and disservice,
has been so long exposed to the air,
to the noise,
to its own words,
that it has hardened,
glazed,
and crumbled.
After the road,
and before the road,
there are stones
and ashes on scattered stones.
The book
rises out of the fire
of the prophetic rose,
from the scream of the sacrificed petals.
Smoke.
Smoke
for all who see only fire,
who smell only
dawn

and death.
But the order of summits,
the order or ruins,
is wedding gladness.")

The commentary of Reb Zam:

"You enter the night,
as a thread enters the needle,
through an opening
propitious or bloody,
through the most luminous breach.
Being both thread and needle,
you enter the night
as you enter yourself."

—*The commentary of Reb Elar:*

"From one word to another,
possible void,
far,
irresistible.
Dream the instalment,
the small,
the first one down.

You can retrace a road in your mind
or your veins.

You can dig a road in men's eyes.
The child is the master of roads.

Descend.
Melt and melt into
the fall,
oblivion,
which is falling of things
and beings.
With the weight
that has found its weight
for dying."

Yukel, how many pages to live, to die, are between you and yourself, between the book and leaving the book?

And Yukel speaks:

I look for you.
The world where I look for you is a world without trees.
Nothing but empty streets,
naked streets.
The world where I look for you is a world open to other worlds without name,
a world where you are not, where I look for you.
There are your steps,
steps which I follow and wait for.
I followed the slow road of your steps without shadow,
unaware who I was,
unaware where I went.
One day, you will be there.
Here, elsewhere, it will be
a day like all the days when you are there.
Perhaps tomorrow.
To find you, I followed yet other bitter roads
where salt broke salt.
To find you, I followed other hours, other banks.
Night gives its hand to him who follows the night.
At night, all the roads fall.
There had to be this night when I took your hand, when we were alone.
There had to be this night, as there had to be this road.
In the world where I look for you, you are both grass and ore.
You are the scream lost where I lose my way.
You are also, where nothing wakes, oblivion with ashes of mirror.

The commentary of Reb Daber:

"The road which leads me to you is safe even when it runs into oceans."

"How can I know if I write verse or prose," Reb Elati remarked. "I am rhythm."

And elsewhere: "Without rhythm, you would not see the sun every morning.

"You could not.

"Rhythm is internal. It is the rhythm of fate.

"No matter how you tried, you could neither go faster nor more slowly.

"You could not but move in harmony with your blood, with your mind, with your heart.

"In harmony.

"You could not be fast or slow.

"You could not.

"Is it conceivable for the moon to come after the moon?

"I went to God, because God was my fate.

"I went to the word of God, because the word of God was my fate.

"I went to the word

"to make it my gesture.

"I went.

"And I am going."

Giorgio Bassani

Giorgio Bassani (Italy, 1916–2000) was born in Bologna into a bourgeois Sephardic family that was able to trace its roots back to the Iberian Peninsula. He was imprisoned during World War II and joined the Italian resistance in 1943. Bassani lived in the northern Italian city of Ferrara until 1943, when he moved to Rome. He worked as a screenwriter and a film dubbing editor and, from 1958 to 1964, at the publishing house Feltrinelli. He eventually became vice president of the media corporation Radiotelevisione Italiana. Bassani's most famous work is *The Garden of the Finzi-Continis* (1962; English, 1965), which was made into an Academy Award–winning film that was directed by Vittorio De Sica. The novel is about the promulgation of anti-Jewish legislation in Italy in 1938 and its impact on an assimilated Jewish family not unlike Bassani's. It uses the garden as a provocative metaphor that invokes both Paradise and the self-enclosed Jewish ghetto. Other semiautobiographical works by Bassani include *Five Stories of Ferrara* (1956; English, 1962 and 1971); *Behind the Door* (1964; English, 1972); *The Heron* (1968; English, 1970); and *The Smell of Hay* (1972; English, 1975). Bassani's work focuses in particular on the impact of fascism and anti-Semitism on Italy's Jews. "A Plaque on Via Mazzini," translated by William Weaver and included in *Five Stories of Ferrara,* tells of the return of one Geo Josz to Ferrara after World War II. Of 183 Jews deported by the Nazis, Geo is the only one who survives. His return opens the door to reconciliation with the past, but the embarrassment of memory looms large.

A Plaque on Via Mazzini

Et j'ai vu quelquefois ce que
l'homme a cru voir.

—Rimbaud

I

In August 1945, when Geo Josz reappeared in Ferrara, sole survivor of the hundred and eighty-three members of the Jewish Community whom the Germans had deported in the autumn of '43 and whom most people not without reason considered long since exterminated in the gas chambers, at first nobody in the city recognized him.

They didn't remember who he was, to tell the truth. Unless, some added in a dubious tone, unless he could be a son of that Angelo Josz, well-known cloth wholesaler, who though exempted for patriotic reasons (these were the terms of the decree of '39; and after all it had been only human, on the part of the late Consul Bolognesi, at that time already the Fascist Party Secretary of Ferrara and always a good friend of old Josz, to adopt, in memory of their common enterprises with the Fascist squads of their youth, a language that was so generic) had been unable, despite this distinction, to keep himself and his family out of the great roundup of Jews in '43.

Yes, one of those withdrawn young people, they began to recall, pursing their lips and frowning, no more than ten in all, who after '38 had perforce broken off all relations with their former schoolmates and had also, in consequence, stopped visiting their homes, and had been seen about only rarely, growing up with strange faces, frightened, wild, contemptuous, so that when people saw them every now and then, rushing off, bent over the handlebars of a bicycle, speeding along Corso Giovecca or Corso Roma, they became upset and preferred to forget about them.

But apart from that: in this man of indefinable age, so fat he seemed swollen, with an old lambskin hat on his shaven head, wearing a kind of sampler of all the known and unknown uniforms of the time, who could have recognized the frail boy of seven years ago, or the nervous, thin, shy adolescent of four years later? And if a Geo Josz had ever been born and had existed, if he too, as he asserted, had belonged to that band of a hundred and eighty-three shadows devoured by Buchenwald, Auschwitz, Mauthausen, Dachau, etc.; was it possible that he, only he, should come back from there now, and present himself, oddly dressed, true, but very much alive, to tell about himself and about the others who hadn't come back and would never, surely, come back again? After all this time, after so much suffering which all had more or less shared, without distinction of political belief, social position, religion or race, what did he want, Geo, at this moment? Even Signor Cohen the engineer, the President of the Jewish Community, who had insisted on dedicating, the moment he got back from Switzerland, in memory of the victims, a large marble plaque which now stood out, rigid, enormous, brand-new, on the red brick façade of the Temple (and then the plaque had to be done over, naturally, to the satisfaction of those who had reproached Signor Cohen for his commemorative haste, since dirty linen—as love of Fatherland teaches us—can always be washed without causing scandal), even he, at first, had raised a host of objections; in short, he wanted nothing to do with it.

But we must proceed in an orderly fashion; and before going any further, we must linger for a moment on the episode of the plaque set in the façade of the Temple thanks to Signor Cohen's rash initiative: an episode which is, properly speaking, the beginning of the story of Geo Josz's return to Ferrara.

To tell it now, the scene might appear scarcely credible. And, to doubt it, you have only to picture it taking place against the background—so normal, so familiar to us—of Via Mazzini (not even the war touched the street: as if to signify that nothing, ever, can happen there!): the street, that is, which from Piazza delle Erbe, flanking the old ghetto—with the Oratorio of San Maurelio at the beginning, the narrow fissure of Via Vittoria at the halfway point, the red brick façade of the Temple a bit farther on, and the double line of its hundred warehouses and shops, each harboring, in the semidarkness steeped in odors, a cautious little soul, imbued with mercantile skepticism and irony—connects the winding, decrepit little streets of Ferrara's medieval core with the splendid Renaissance avenues, so damaged by bombardments, and the modern section of the city.

Immersed in the glare and silence of the August afternoon, a silence interrupted at long intervals by the echoes of distant shooting, Via Mazzini lay empty, deserted, intact. And so it had appeared also to the young workman wearing a paper hat, who at half past one, climbing onto a little scaffold, had started working on the marble slab that they had given him to put in place; six feet from the ground, against the dusty bricks of the synagogue. His presence there, a peasant forced to the city by the war and obliged to turn himself into a mason (he was slowly filled by the sense of his own solitude and by a vague fear, because this was a commemorative plaque, surely; but he had taken good care not to read what was written on it!), had been erased from the beginning by the light, and he was unable to cancel the deserted quality of the place and the hour. Nor had it been canceled, this emptiness, by the little group of passers-by who, gathering later, apparently without his being aware of them, had come gradually to cover, in their various attitudes and colors, a good part of the cobbled pavement behind his back.

The first to stop were two youths: two bearded, bespectacled partisans, with knee-length shorts, red kerchiefs tied around their throats, automatic rifles slung over their shoulders: students, young gentlemen of the city, the young mason-peasant had thought, hearing them speak and turning slightly just to glance at them. A little later they were joined by a priest, unperturbed despite the heat, wearing his black cassock, but with its sleeves rolled up—he had a strange, battlelike manner, as if defiant—over his hairy white forearms. And then, afterward, a civilian, a man of sixty with a grizzled beard, an excited manner, his shirt open over his scrawny chest and his bobbing Adam's apple: this man, after beginning to read in a low voice what was presumably written on the plaque (and this was names and names; but not all Italian, or so it seemed), had broken off at a certain point to cry, emphatically: "A hundred and eighty-three out of four hundred!" as if he too, Aristide Podetti of Bosco Mesola, by chance in Ferrara, where he had no intention of staying longer than strictly necessary, a man who stuck to his work and nothing else, could be stirred by those names and those numbers to unknown memories, as if they aroused unknown emotions in him. What did it matter, to him, whose names those were and why they had been carved in marble? The remarks of the people who had instead been attracted precisely by them, and who were becoming more and more numerous, made a tiresome buzzing in the mason's ears. Jews, yes, all right, a hundred and eighty-three out of four hundred. A hundred and eighty-three out of the four hundred who lived in Ferrara before the war. But what were they, after all, these Jews? What did they mean, they and the *others,* the Fascists, by that word? Ah, the Fascists! From his very village, in the Po plain, which in the winter of '44 they had made a kind of headquarters, they had sown terror through the countryside for months and months. The people called them *tupín*, mice, because of the color of their shirts; and exactly like mice, when the time had come for settling scores, they quickly found holes to hide in. They stayed hidden, now. But who could guarantee they wouldn't come back? Who could swear they weren't still walking around the streets, also wearing red kerchiefs at their throats, waiting for the moment of revenge? At the right moment, as quickly as they had hidden, they would jump out again with their black shirts, their death's-heads; and then, the less a man knew, the better off he was.

And he, the poor boy, was so determined not to know anything, because all he needed was work, nothing else interested him; so unaware and distrustful of everything and everybody, as, locked in his rough dialect of the Po delta, he turned his stubborn back to the sun, that when, all of a sudden, he felt a light touch on his ankle ("Geo Josz?" a mocking voice said at the same time) he wheeled around promptly with a nasty look.

A short, square man, with a strange fur hat on his head, stood before him. Raising his arm, the man pointed to the plaque behind the boy's shoulders. How fat he was! He seemed swollen with water, like a drowned man. And there was nothing to be afraid of; because he was laughing, surely to make himself agreeable.

"Geo Josz?" the man repeated, still pointing to the plaque, but now serious.

He laughed again. But at once, as if repentant, and dotting his words. frequently with "please" like the Germans (he spoke with the polish of a gifted salon conversationalist; and Aristide Podetti, since he was the one being addressed, listened open-mouthed), he declared that he was sorry, "believe me," to spoil everything with his interruption, which, as he was ready to admit, bore all the earmarks of a faux pas. Ah, yes, he sighed, the plaque would have to be done over again, since that Geo Josz, to whom it was partly dedicated, was none other than himself, in person. Unless (and, saying this, his pale blue eyes looked around, as if to seize an image of the Via Mazzini from which the little crowd, surrounding him, holding its breath, was excluded; not a head, meanwhile, had peered out of the many shops nearby), unless the Committee which sponsored the commemoration, accepting this event as a hint from fate, were to give up entirely the idea of the memorial plaque: which, he sneered, though it offered the unquestionable advantage of being set in that place where there was so much traffic that it had to be read almost perforce ("You aren't bearing in mind the dust, however, my dear friend; in a few years no one will notice it any more!"), had also the serious defect of unsuitably altering the straightforward, homely façade of "our dear old Temple": one of the few things, including also Via Mazzini—which the war, thank God, had spared completely, and which had remained exactly as "before"—the few things on which (". . . yes, dear friend, I mean this for you also, though I imagine you are not Jewish . . .") one could still count.

"It's a bit as if you—for example—were obliged with that face, with those hands, to put on a dinner jacket."

And, at the same time, he displayed his own hands, callused beyond all belief, but with white backs where a registration number, tattooed a bit above the right wrist in the skin so flabby it seemed boiled, could be read distinctly, all five numbers, preceded by the letter *J*.

II

AND SO, with a look that was not menacing but rather ironic and amused (his eyes, a watery blue, peered up coldly from below, as if he were emerging, pale and swollen as he was, from the depths of the sea), Geo Josz reappeared in Ferrara, among us.

He came from afar, from much farther than the place he actually had come from! And to find himself again suddenly here, in the city where he had been born . . .

Things had gone more or less like this:

The military truck, on which he had been able to travel in a few hours from the Brenner Pass to the Po Valley, after driving off the ferry at Pontelagoscuro had slowly climbed up the right bank of the river. And then, having reached the top, after a final, almost reluctant jolt, it offered to his gaze the immense, forgotten plain of his childhood and adolescence. Down there, a bit to the left, should lie Ferrara. But was Ferrara, he had asked himself, and had asked, also, the driver sitting at his side—was Ferrara that dark polygon of dusty stone, reduced, except for the Castle's four towers which rose airy and unreal in the center, to a kind of lugubrious flatiron which weighed, heavy, on the fields? Where were the green, luminous, ancient trees that once rose along the crest of the maimed walls? The truck was rapidly approaching the city, as if, gradually accelerating along the intact asphalt of the straight highway, it were going to plunge on Ferrara from above; and through the wide breaches here and there in the bastions, he could already see the streets, once so familiar, now made unrecognizable by the bombings. Less than two years had gone by since he was taken away. But they were two years that counted for twenty, or two hundred.

He had come back when no one expected him any longer. What did he want, now?

To answer calmly a question like this—with the calm necessary to understand and sympathize with what, at first, had probably been only a simple, if unexpressed, desire to live—perhaps other times, perhaps another city was required.

It required, in any case, people a bit less frightened by those certain gentlemen who set the norm, again as always, for the city's public opinion (there were, in that group, along with some big merchants and landowners, several of the most authoritative professional men of Ferrara: the sinew, in short; of what had been, before the war, our so-called leading class): the people who, having been forced to "support," more or less in a body, the defunct Fascist Social Republic, and who couldn't resign themselves to step down even for a short while, now saw traps, enemies, and even political rivals on all sides. They had accepted Party cards, the infamous card, true. But out of pure civic duty. And, in any case, not before that fatal December 15th of 1943, when fully eleven fellow citizens had been shot at once, the date which had marked the beginning, in Italy, of the never sufficiently deplored "fratricidal struggle." Riddled with bullets across the street from the portico of the Caffè della Borsa, they had lain for a whole day, guarded by troops with guns at the ready; and the others had seen them, with their own eyes, the bodies of those "poor wretches," flung in the filthy snow like so many bundles! And so, continuing in this tone, all caught up as they were in their effort to convince others and themselves that, though they may have erred, they had erred more from generosity than fear (for this reason, having removed all other badges, they began to appear with every possible military decoration stuck in the buttonhole of their jacket), they surely couldn't be considered the ideal sort to recognize in others that simplicity and normality of intentions, that famous "purity" of action and ideas which, in themselves, they were unable to give up. As for the specific case of the man in the old fur hat: even assuming he was Geo Josz—and they weren't entirely convinced of that, however—assuming he was, he still could not be trusted. That fat of his, all that fat made them suspicious. Oh yes, starvation edema! But who besides Geo could have started such a story circulating, in a clumsy attempt to justify a corpulence in singular contradiction to what was said about German concentration camps? Starvation edema didn't exist, it was an outright invention. And Geo's fat meant two things: either in those *Lagers* one didn't suffer the great hunger that propaganda insisted on, or else Geo had enjoyed conditions of special favor there. One thing was sure: under that fur hat, behind that lip curled in a perpetual smile, there was room, they would have sworn, only for hostile thoughts and plans.

And what of the others—a minority, to tell the truth—who remained shut up in their houses, ears alert to the slightest noise from outside, the very image of fear and hate?

Among the latter there was the man who had offered to preside, a tricolor-sash across his chest, at the public auction of the Jewish Community's confiscated possessions, including the silver chandeliers of the Temple and the ancient vellum Scriptures; and those who, pulling black caps with the Brigade's death's-head over their white hair, had been members of the special tribunal responsible for various executions: almost always respectable people, for that matter, who perhaps before then had never shown any sign of being interested in politics, and who, in the majority of cases, had led a largely retired life, devoted to the family, to their profession, their studies. . . . But they feared greatly for themselves, these people; they had, on their own account, such a fear of dying that even if Geo Josz had wanted only to live (and this was the least, really, that he could want)—well, even in such a simple and elementary request, they would have found some personal threat. The thought that one of them, any night of the week, could be seized quietly by the "reds" and carried off to be slaughtered in some unknown place in the country: this terrifying thought returned, constantly, to drive them mad with anxiety. To live, to stay alive, no matter how! It was a violent demand, exclusive, desperate.

If at least that man in the fur hat, "that wreck," would make up his mind to leave Ferrara!

Unconcerned that the partisans, having taken over the command post of the Black Brigade, were using the house on Via Campofranco, his father's property, as their barracks and prison, he was clearly content, on the other hand, to carry around that obsessive, ill-omened face of his: surely to add new fuel to the wrath of those who would make it their business to avenge him and all his people. The greatest scandal, in any case, was that the new authorities put up with such a state of things. It was no good appealing to the Prefect, Doctor Herzen, installed in office just after the "so-called" Liberation, by the same National Committee of Liberation of which, after the events of December '43, he had been the underground President, if it was true, and it was, that they compiled black lists every evening in his office, in the Castle. Ah yes, they knew him well, they did, that character who in '39 had allowed his property to be confiscated, almost smiling at the loss of the big shoe factory he owned at the gates of the city, and whose possession now, if Allied bombers hadn't reduced it to rubble, he would surely demand again! A man of about forty, bald, tortoise-shell spectacles, he had the typically peaceful and inoffensive look (except for the "Jewish" name, Herzen, and the stiff, inflexible back which seemed fastened to the seat of his inseparable bicycle) of all those who are seriously to be feared. What about the Archbishopric? And the English military government? Was it, unfortunately, a sign of the times that even from these offices no better answer came than a sigh of desolate solidarity or, worse, a mocking grin?

There's no reasoning with fear and hate. For if they had wanted, getting back to Geo Josz himself, to understand something of what was really going on in his spirit, they had only to begin, after all, with his extraordinary reappearance in Ferrara; and specially with the sequel of that singular scene which, just by the entrance to the Temple on Via Mazzini, at a certain point had led him to extend his hands, not without sarcasm, to a young mason's stunned examination.

Perhaps the man of sixty, with the sparse grizzled beard, will recall it, he who was among the first to stop before the marble slab, the memorial plaque desired by Signor Cohen, the man who at a given moment had raised his shrill voice ("A hundred and eighty-three out of four hundred!" he had shouted proudly) to remark on its content.

Well, after silently following with the others what happened in the next minutes, when he pushed his way awkwardly through the little crowd and fell on the neck of the man in the fur hat, kissing him noisily on the cheeks and showing that, first of all, he had recognized in him Geo Josz, the latter, his hands still outstretched, remarked coldly: "With that ridiculous beard, dear Uncle Daniele, I hardly knew you"—a remark that was truly revealing, not only of the kinship between him and one of the city's surviving representatives of the Josz family (a brother of his father's, to be precise, who having miraculously eluded the great roundup of November '43 had returned to the city the end of last April), but also of the deep, sharp intolerance that he, Geo, felt for any sign that spoke to him, in Ferrara, of the passage of time and of the changes, even the tiny ones, that it had wrought in things.

And so he asked: "Why the beard? Do you think perhaps that beard is becoming?"

It honestly seemed he could think of nothing but observing, with critical eye, all the beards of various form and shape that the war, and the notorious forged papers, had caused to become common usage; and this was his way, since he could hardly be called a talkative type, of expressing his disagreement.

In what had been before the war the Josz house, where uncle and nephew appeared that same afternoon, there were, naturally, plenty of beards; and the little, low, red-stone building surmounted by a slender Ghibelline tower, so long that it covered almost a whole side of the brief and secluded Via Campofranco, assumed a military, feudal air, perhaps suitable for evoking the ancient lords of the palace, the Marquesses Del Sale, from whom Angelo Josz had bought it in 1910 for a few thousand lire, but it hardly evoked Angelo, the Jewish cloth wholesaler who had vanished with his wife and children in the ovens of Buchenwald.

The main door was wide open. Outside, seated on the steps of the entrance with guns between their bare legs, or lying on the seats of a jeep pulled up by the high wall that, opposite, separated Via Campofranco from a vast private garden, about a dozen partisans were loafing. But others, in greater numbers, some with voluminous files under their arms, and all with faces marked by energy and resolution, came and went constantly despite the sultry air of the late afternoon. And so, between the street half in shadow and half in the sun and the breached door of the old aristocratic palazzo, there was an intense bustle, lively, gay, in perfect harmony with the cries of the swallows that dipped low, grazing the cobbles, and with the typewriters' clicking that came steadily through the enormous seventeenth-century grilles of the ground floor.

The strange couple—one tall, thin, perky, the other fat, slow, sweating—came in the door then, and immediately attracted the attention of those present: mostly armed men, generally with long hair and flowing beards, sitting, waiting on the rough benches set along the walls. They gathered around; and Daniele Josz, who evidently wanted to demonstrate to his nephew his own familiarity with this environment, was already willingly answering their questions, for himself and for his companion.

But he, Geo, examined, one by one, those tanned, flushed faces that pressed around him, as if through the beards he wanted to investigate some secret, some hidden corruption.

Ah, you can't fool me! his smile said.

He seemed reassured only for a moment, discovering that beyond the gate of the portico, right in the center of the bare little garden that stretched beyond, there still shone, dark and flourishing, a large magnolia. But not sufficiently reassured to prevent him, a little later, upstairs, in the office of the young Provincial Secretary of the Partisans Association (the same man who two years later was to become the most brilliant Communist member of the Italian Parliament, so polite, reserved, and reassuring that he made not a few of our most worthy *mères de famille* sigh with regret, since he also belonged to one of the finest middle-class families of Ferrara, the Bottecchiaris, and, what's more, was a bachelor) from repeating his now time-worn remark:

"That beard isn't at all becoming to you, do you know that?"

So, in the frozen embarrassment that fell immediately on what until then, thanks entirely to Uncle Daniele, had been a fairly cordial conversation, in the course of which the future Deputy had acted as if he didn't notice the formal *Lei* which Geo on his part had maintained, while the other man insisted on the affectionate *tu* used among those of the same age and the same Party, it was suddenly clear what Geo Josz really wanted, the reason why he was there (and if only those who, on the contrary, were so afraid of him could have been present!). That house where *they,* like the *others,* the blacks, had made their headquarters before them, was his, didn't they remember that? By what right had they taken possession of it? He looked threateningly at the typist, who jumped and suddenly left off striking the keys, as if he meant to tell even her, especially her, that he wouldn't be at all satisfied with a single room, even if it were this one, so handsome and sunny—once a salon for receiving, of course, even if the parquet had been torn from the floor probably for firewood—which was nice and comfortable, wasn't it, from dawn to dusk, and perhaps even after dusk, working with the young partisan commander who seemed so determined, out of the goodness of his heart, to remake the world.

Down in the street they were singing:

> The wind is whistling, the tempest screams,
> Our shoes have holes, and yet we must march on . . .

and the song, impetuous and absurd, came through the window, open to the sky, which was a tender, very gentle pink.

But the house was his, they should have no illusions. Sooner or later he would take it back, all of it.

III

THIS WAS TO HAPPEN, in fact, though obviously not at once.

For the moment, Geo seemed to be satisfied with only one room—and it wasn't, of course, the office of Nino Bottecchiari! Instead, it was a kind of attic at the very top of the tower that dominated the house, and to reach it he had to climb at least a hundred steps, then, at the end, some worm-eaten little wooden stairs which led directly from a space below once used as a storeroom. It was Geo himself, in the disgusted tone of one resigned to the worst, who first spoke of this "makeshift." As to the storeroom below, that too, he added, would be rather useful, since he could put, as he meant to, his Uncle Daniele there. . . .

But it was soon clear that Geo could follow from that height, through a wide glass window, whatever happened in the garden, on one side, and in Via Campofranco, on the other. And since he hardly ever left the house, presumably spending a great part of his day looking at the vast landscape of dark tiles, gardens, and green countryside that stretched out below him (an immense view, now that the leafy trees of the city wall were no longer there to cut it off!), for the occupants of the lower floors, his constant presence soon became a troublesome, nagging thought. The cellars of the Josz house, which all opened onto the garden, since the time of the Black Brigade had been transformed into secret prisons, about which many sinister stories had been told in the city even after the Liberation. But now, subjected to the probable, untrustworthy control of the guest in the tower, they no longer served, naturally, those purposes of summary and clandestine justice for which they had been set up. Now, with Geo Josz installed in that sort of observatory, there was no being sure even for a moment, since the kerosene lamp he kept burning all night long—and you could see its faint glow through the panes, up there, until dawn—led everyone to suppose he was always alert, he never slept. It must have been two or three in the morning after the evening Geo first appeared on Via Campofranco, when Nino Bottecchiari, who had stayed working in his office until that hour and was finally about to allow himself some rest, stepping out into the street, happened to raise his eyes to the tower. "Watch yourself!" Geo's lamp warned, suspended in the starry sky. And the young future Deputy was bitterly reproaching himself for guilty carelessness and his acquiescence—but at the same time, as a good politician, preparing to take the new circumstances into account—as he decided, with a sigh, to climb into the jeep.

But it was also possible for him to turn up at any hour of the day, as he soon began to do, from one moment to the next, on the stairs or down in the entrance: passing before the eyes of the partisans permanently gathered there, dressed in his impeccable civilian suit of olive gabardine which had almost immediately replaced the fur hat, the leather jacket, and the tight trousers of his arrival in Ferrara. He walked among the mute partisans without greeting anyone, elegant, perfectly shaven, with the brim of his brown felt turned down at one side of his brow, over a cold, icy eye; and in the vague uneasiness that followed each of his apparitions, he was from the beginning the authoritative landlord of the house: too polite to quarrel, but strong in his right, he needs only to show himself to the vandal tenant in arrears, who has to leave. The tenant grumbles, pretends not to notice the silent, insistent protest of the owner of the building, who for the present is saying nothing though, at the right moment, will surely ask for an accounting of the ruined floors, the stained walls; so, from month to month, the situation worsens, becomes more and more embarrassing and precarious. It was late, after the elections of '48, when so many things in Ferrara had by then changed, or rather had gone back to their prewar state (but meanwhile young Bottecchiari's candidacy for Parliament had had time to be crowned with the most complete success)—it was then that the Partisans Association decided to move its headquarters elsewhere, specifically to three rooms in the former Casa del Fascio on Viale Cavour, where in 1945 the Provincial Labor Council had established its offices. It is true, all the same, that the silent, implacable action of Geo Josz made that move seem long overdue.

He hardly ever left the house, then, as if he wanted them not to forget him there, not even for a moment. But this didn't prevent him from showing up every so often on Via Mazzini, where in September he had arranged for his father's storehouse, in which the Community had collected all it could recover of the possessions confiscated from the Jews during the period of the Fascist Republic, to be cleared out in view of the "more than necessary"—as he said to Signor Cohen in person—"work of restoration and reopening of the business"; or, more rarely, along Corso Giovecca, with the uncertain tread of one advancing in prohibited territory, his spirit torn between the fear of unpleasant encounters and the sharp, conflicting desire for them, joining the evening promenade that had already begun once more, animated and lively as always; or at the apéritif hour, sitting abruptly at a little table—because he arrived each time breathless, dripping sweat—at the Caffè della Borsa on Corso Roma, which had remained the political center of the city. Nor did the ironic, contemptuous attitude habitual with him, which had persuaded even the expansive Uncle Daniele, so electrified by the early postwar atmosphere, to renounce quickly all conversation through the trapdoor above his head, show any signs of being disarmed by the show of cordial welcome, the affectionate cries of "Good to have you back!" which now, after the uncertainty of the first moment, began to be addressed to him from every direction.

People came from the shops near the one that had been his father's and was now his, with the outstretched hand of those offering help and advice or even promising, in a hyperbole of generosity, honest competition forever; or they crossed the Giovecca on purpose, broad as it was, with excessive enthusiasm, made even more hysterical by the fact that, as a rule, they knew him only by name, and they flung their arms around his neck; or else they left the counter of the bar, still immersed in that turbulent darkness where, in the past, every day at 1 p.m. the radio's announcements of defeat had come (announcements that could just reach, as it passed, the fleeting bicycle of the young Geo), to come and sit beside him, under the yellow awning that offered such slight protection from the blinding sun and the dust of the rubble. He had been in Buchenwald and had come back from there, the only one, after having undergone God only knows what physical and moral torments, after having witnessed unknown horrors. And they were there, at his disposal, all ears, ready to listen. He should tell them; and they would never grow tired, prepared to sacrifice, for him, even the dinner to which the Castle clock, with two strokes, was already summoning them. In general these seemed so many pathetic apologies for having delayed recognizing him, for having tried to reject him, to exclude him once again. It was as if, in chorus, they said: "You've changed, you know? A full-grown man, by God, and then, you've put on so much weight! But, you see, we've changed too, time's gone by for us as well . . ."; and as if to testify to their sincerity, supporting the development, they displayed their trousers of rough canvas, their rolled-up sleeves, the military bush jackets, the collars without ties, the sandals without socks, as well as, naturally, their beards, since nobody was without one now. . . . And they were sincere in submitting themselves, each time, to Geo's examination and judgment, and sincere, afterward, in lamenting his inflexible repulsion: just as, in their way, just about everybody in the city after April of '45—including those who had most to fear from the present and to distrust of the future—was sincere in the conviction that, for better or worse, a new period was about to begin, better in any event than the other, which, like a long slumber filled with atrocious nightmares, was ending in bloodshed.

As for Uncle Daniele, who for three months had been living hand-to-mouth and without a fixed address, the stifling storeroom in the tower had immediately appeared, in his incurable optimism, a marvelous acquisition, and nobody was more convinced than he that, with the end of the war, the happy age of democracy and of universal brotherhood had begun.

"At last we can breathe freely!" he had ventured to say, the first night he had taken possession of his stairwell—and he spoke, lying supine on his straw mattress, his hands clasped behind his head.

"Aah, at last we can breathe freely," he repeated, in a louder voice. And then:

"Don't you feel, too, Geo, that the air in the city is different from what it was before? Things have changed, believe me: inside, in people's bones, not just on the outside. These are the miracles of liberty. For myself, I am profoundly convinced . . ."

What had profoundly convinced Daniele Josz must have seemed of quite dubious interest to Geo, since the only reply he ever let fall from the aperture towards which the wooden ladder and his uncle's impassioned exclamations rose was an occasional "Hmm!" or a "Really?" which didn't encourage the other man to continue. What can he be doing? the old man would ask himself then, falling silent, as his eyes went to the ceiling, scraped back and forth by a pair of tireless slippers; and he didn't know what to think.

To him, it seemed impossible that Geo didn't share his enthusiasm.

After fleeing Ferrara in the days of the armistice, he had spent almost two years as the guest of some peasants, hidden in a remote village of the Tuscan-Emilian Apennines. And up there, after the death of his wife, who, poor thing, devout as she was, had to be buried under a false name in consecrated ground, he had joined a partisan brigade as political commissar. He had been among the first, tanned and bearded on top of a truck, to enter liberated Ferrara. What unforgettable days! To find the city half destroyed, true, almost unrecognizable, but completely clear of Fascists, of those from *before* and the last-ditch Salò ones—all those faces, in short, many of which Geo should also recall: this, for him, had been such a complete, such an extraordinary joy! To sit calmly at the Caffè della Borsa, which, as soon as he returned, he immediately made the base of his operations in his old, modest activity as an insurance agent, where no frowning eye ordered him to leave but, on the contrary, where he felt the center of universal affection; now, after the fulfillment of such a wish, he was ready even to die. But Geo? Was it possible Geo felt none of all this? Was it possible that, after having descended into hell, and having miraculously risen from it, there was no impulse in him except the desire to evoke the static past, as was demonstrated somehow by the ghastly array of photographs of his dead family (poor Angelo, poor Luce, and little Pietruccio born ten years after Geo, when nobody in the family was expecting him, born to know only violence and anguish and to end at Buchenwald!): the photographs which, one day when he had secretly climbed into the room above, his nephew's room, he had found papering all four walls? Was it possible, finally, that the only beard in the whole city to which Geo had raised no objection was the beard of that old Fascist Geremia Tabet, poor Angelo's brother-in-law, who even after 1938, despite the racial laws and the consequent ostracism imposed against Jews everywhere, had still been able to frequent the Merchants Club for the afternoon bridge, though not officially? The very evening of Geo's return, he, Daniele Josz, had had reluctantly to accompany his nephew to the Tabet house on Via Roversella, where he had never set foot since his return to the city. Well, wasn't it inconceivable, the former political commissar kept repeating to himself, the sixty-year-old ex-partisan, as his nephew, in the room above, never stopped pacing heavily up and down—wasn't it inconceivable that, the minute the Fascist uncle peered out of a second-floor window, Geo should let out a shrill cry, ridiculously, hysterically passionate, almost savage? Why that shout? What did it mean? Did it mean perhaps that the boy, despite Buchenwald and the massacre of all his family, had grown up like his father Angelo, who in his ingenuousness had been to the last, perhaps even to the door of the gas chamber, a "patriot," as he had heard Angelo proclaim himself so many times with foolish pride?

"Who is it?" a worried voice asked, from above.

"It's me, Uncle Geremia; it's Geo!"

They were down below, outside the closed front door of the Tabet house. It was ten o'clock by then, and at the end of the narrow street you couldn't see more than a foot ahead. Geo's cry, Daniele Josz recalled, had made him start with surprise. It had been a kind of strange howl, choked by the most violent and inexplicable emotion. Surprise and embarrassment: impossible to say anything. In silence, bumping into each other, stumbling over the steps, they had groped their way, in the most total darkness, up two steep flights of stairs.

Finally, at the top of the stairs, half in and half out of the door, the lawyer Geremia Tabet, wearing his pajamas, had appeared, in person. In his right hand he was holding a little dish, with a candle erect in it, whose wavering light cast vague, greenish glints over the natural pallor of his face, framed by the beard which hadn't even become very gray. As soon as he saw him, he, Daniele Josz, stopped short. It was the first time he had seen him since the end of the war; and if he was there now, on the point of visiting him, he had been induced into it only to please Geo, who, on the contrary, after his examination of the house on Via Campofranco a few hours earlier, seemed to have thoughts only for "Uncle Geremia." Setting the candle on the floor, Lawyer Tabet clasped his nephew to his bosom, in a long embrace; and this sufficed to make the outsider, who had remained on the lower landing to observe the scene, forgotten down there like a stranger, feel once more the poor relation that all of them—his brother Angelo agreeing, in this, with the Tabets—had always avoided and scorned for his "subversive" ideas. He should go away. Go away without a word of good-by. Never set foot in that house again. What a pity he had resisted that temptation! Actually, he had been stopped by a hope, an absurd hope. After all, he had thought, poor Luce, Geo's mother, was a Tabet, Geremia's sister. Perhaps it was only his mother's memory which, at first, kept Geo from behaving toward his maternal uncle with the coldness the old Fascist deserved. . . .

But he had been mistaken, unfortunately, and for the rest of the evening, indeed until late in the night, as Geo seemed never to make up his mind to leave, Daniele had to sit in a corner of the dining room and witness displays of affection and intimacy which were little short of disgusting.

It was as if a kind of instinctive understanding had been established between the two, and with equally immediate promptness the other members of the family had fallen in with it: Tania Tabet, so aged and worn, and hanging always, with those dazed eyes, from her husband's lips; and also the three children, Alda, Gilberta, and Romano, though, like their mother, they soon went off to bed. The pact was this: Geo would not refer, not even indirectly, to his uncle's political past, and his uncle, for his part, would avoid asking his nephew to tell about what he had seen and undergone in Germany, where he too, for that matter—and this should have been recalled also by those who wanted to throw some of his little youthful errors in his face, some only human mistakes in political choices—had lost a sister, a brother-in-law, and a nephew whom he loved very much. What a misfortune, to be sure, what a calamity! But a sense of proportion and discretion (the past was past, no use digging it up again!)

should now prevail over every other impulse. It was better to look ahead, to the future. And in fact, while they were on the subject of the future, what—Geremia Tabet asked at one point, assuming the serious but kindly tones of the head of the family, who looks ahead and can deal with many things—what were Geo's plans? He was surely thinking of reopening his father's shop: a very noble ambition, which his uncle could only approve, since the storehouse, *at least,* was still there. But to make a success of it, he would need money, a lot of money; he would have to have the backing of some bank. Could he help him, in this last matter? He hoped he could, he really did. But if, in the meanwhile, in any case, seeing that the Via Campofranco house had been occupied by "the reds," he would like to come and live temporarily with them, a cot, if not a proper bed, could always be found!

It was exactly at this point, Daniele Josz recalled, that he, looking up with more lively attention, had tried once more, though in vain, to understand.

Sweating profusely, even in his pajamas, old Tabet sat with his elbows propped on the great black "refectory" table in the center of which the candle was guttering, about to die; and at the same time, puzzled, Geremia twisted with his fingertips the little gray beard, the classical Fascist goatee which, alone among the old Fascists of Ferrara, he had had the courage, or the effrontery, or—who knows?—perhaps the cleverness not to cut off. As for Geo, while he shook his head and, smiling, declined the invitation, that now-graying goatee and the pudgy hand toying with it were the object of his attention, from the other side of the table, as his pale-blue eyes looked at them with a stubborn, fanatical stare.

IV

The autumn ended. Winter came, the long, cold winter of our region. Then spring returned. And slowly, with the spring, but still as if only Geo's examining gaze were evoking it, the past also returned.

Strange, isn't it? And yet time was arranging things in such a way that between Geo and Ferrara—between Geo and us—you might say a kind of secret dynamic relationship seemed to exist. It's hard, I know, to explain clearly. On the one hand, there was the progressive reabsorption by Geo's body of those unhealthy humors, that fat which, at his first appearance on Via Mazzini in August of the previous year, had given rise to so much argument and perplexity. On the other hand, there was the simultaneous reappearance, first timid, then more and more evident and determined, of an image of Ferrara and of ourselves, moral and physical, which no one, in his heart, had ever wanted, at a certain point, to forget. Slowly Geo grew thinner, as the months went by; he regained, except for his sparse hair prematurely gray at the temples, a face whose glabrous cheeks made it even more youthful. But also the city, after the highest piles of rubble were removed, and an initial rage for superficial changes had died down, also the city was slowly settling into its sleepy, decrepit lines, which centuries of clerical decadence, suddenly at history's malicious decree, following the remote and ferocious and glorious times of the Ghibelline Seigniory, had by now fixed for any possible future in an unchangeable mask. Everything in Geo spoke of his desire, or rather of his determination, to be a boy again, the boy he had been, yes, but also, plunged as he was into the timeless hell of Buchenwald, the boy he had never been able to be. And so we too, his fellow citizens, who had been the witnesses of his childhood and adolescence, and yet recalled him as a boy only vaguely (but he recalled us, to be sure, so different from what we were today!), we became what we had once been, our prewar selves, our selves of forever. Why resist? If *he* wanted us like that, and if, especially, that's how we were, why not satisfy him? We thought with sudden indulgence and weariness. But our will, one could feel clearly, had little or nothing to do with it. We had the impression that we were all involved, Geo Josz on one side and the rest of us on the other, in a vast, slow, fatal motion, which it was impossible to evade. A motion so slow—synchronized, like that of little connected wheels, gears operated by a single, invisible pivot—that only the growing of the little plane trees replanted along the city's bastions as early as the summer of '45, or the gradual accumulation of dust on the big commemorative plaque on Via Mazzini, could have furnished an adequate measurement of it.

We came to May.

So that was the reason! we said to ourselves, smiling. So it was only in order that an absurd nostalgia wouldn't seem so absurd, so that *his* illusion could be perfect, that, at the beginning of the month, along the Via Mazzini, their bicycles' handlebars spilling wild flowers, flocks of pretty girls, their arms enlaced, came pedaling by, returning from excursions to the nearby countryside and heading for the center of the city. And it was, moreover, for the same reason that, at the same time, coming from God knows what hiding place and resting his back against the marble shaft that for centuries had supported one of the three gates of the ghetto, there appeared again down at the corner, unchanged, like a little stone idol, a symbol for all of us, without exception, of the truly blissful *entre deux guerres*, the enigmatic little figure of the notorious Count Scocca. ("Look, the old madman's back again!" people muttered, spontaneously, as soon as they recognized in the distance the unmistakable yellowish boater tilted over one ear, the toothpick clenched between thin lips, the fat sensual nose raised to sniff the odor of the hemp-macerating vats that the little evening breeze carried with it.)

And since, in the meanwhile, Ferrara's latest generation of beautiful girls, inspiring open exclamations of praise from the narrow sidewalks, and more secret glances of admiration from the darkness of the shops beyond, had almost finished, one of those evenings, their lazy ride back down Via Mazzini and, indeed, was about to debouch in Piazza delle Erbe and go by, laughing: thus, facing the spectacle of life eternally renewing itself, and yet always the same, and indifferent to the problems and passions of mankind, no grudge, no matter how stubborn, could at this point continue to put up resistance. The little stage of Via Mazzini displayed, to the left, emerging against the sun from the end of the street, the close and radiant ranks of the cycling girls; and to the right, motionless and gray against the wall where he was leaning, Count Lionello Scocca. How could you help but smile at such a spectacle, and at the light that enfolded it, as if of posterity? How could you not be moved at the sight of that kind of wise allegory that suddenly reconciled everything: the anguished, atrocious yesterday, with the today so much more serene and rich in promises? Certainly, on seeing the aged, penniless nobleman openly resume his former observation post, where a man with sharp eyesight and keen hearing, like his, could observe the whole extent of Via Mazzini and, at the same time, the adjacent Piazza delle Erbe, you suddenly lost the heart to reproach him for having been a paid informer of the Secret Police for years or for having directed, from 1939 to 1943, the local bureau of the Italo-German Cultural Institute. He had allowed that little Hitler mustache to grow for the occasion, and he kept it still; now didn't it lead you to considerations tinged with fondness, and even—why not?—even with gratitude?

It seemed scandalous therefore that, with Count Scocca—a harmless eccentric, after all—Geo Josz, on the contrary, behaved in a way that not only showed no fondness or gratitude, but had to be considered lacking in even the most elementary humanity and discretion. And the surprise was all the greater because for some time it had become customary to smile benevolently, understandably at him and his own oddities, including his dislike of the so-called "war beards." To speak of Geo and his famous whims ("He's against beards! Well, if that's all it amounts to . . .") and to assume the resigned air of one, harassed, who prepares to give in "just to make him happy," above all "to please him": this was the custom and this was, also, the profound truth. Though at the same time the city's beards fell one by one beneath the barber's scissors and, for this, much of the credit was his—since, I repeat, everything was done "to let him have his way," above all "to make him happy"—as so many gentlemen's faces dared finally reappear, naked, in the naked light of the sun. And it was true, entirely true, on this score, that Geremia Tabet, Lawyer Tabet, Geo's maternal uncle, hadn't yet cut off his beard, nor in all likelihood would he ever cut it off. But his case might have represented a valid exception only for those who couldn't mentally associate that poor little white goatee with the black wool tunic, the shiny black boots, the black fez, in which every Sunday morning, until the late summer of '38, to the very end of the "good old days," Geremia had gloriously displayed himself, between noon and one o'clock, at the Caffè della Borsa.

At first the incident seemed unlikely. Nobody believed it. It was positively impossible to picture the scene: Geo, coming without surprise, with his languid walk, into the eyeshot of Count Scocca, leaning against the wall; Geo, striking the old, resuscitated spy's parchment cheeks, with two sharp, peremptory slaps, "like a real Fascist bully." The event, however, actually did take place: dozens of people saw it. But, on the other hand, wasn't it fairly strange that various, even contradictory, versions immediately started circulating, about the course events had taken? One was almost tempted to doubt not only the authenticity of each version, but even the true, objective reality of that double slap, itself, *smack-smack,* so full and resounding, according to the general report, that it had been heard for a good part of Via Mazzini: from the Oratorio di San Maurelio, a few yards from where the Count was standing, all the way to the Temple and even beyond.

For many people Geo's act remained unmotivated, without any possible explanation. A few moments before he had been seen walking slowly in the same direction as the bicycling girls, letting them pass him. He never turned his face from the center of the street; and nothing in his face, where a mixed emotion of joy and amazement was legible, could have led anybody to imagine what was to happen a moment later. So when he came up to Count Scocca, and looked away from a trio of girls about to turn from Via Mazzini into Piazza delle Erbe, Geo, all of a sudden, stopped abruptly, as if the Count's presence, at that spot and at that hour, seemed, to say the least, inconceivable to him. His hesitation, in any case, had been minimal. Just long enough for him to frown, purse his lips, clench his fists convulsively, mutter some broken, incoherent words. After which, as if operated by a spring, he had literally flown at the poor Count, who, for his part, had until then shown no sign of having noticed him.

Is that all? And yet there was a reason, there had to be, others insisted, pulling down their lips, dubiously. Count Scocca hadn't noticed Geo's arrival; and that, though in itself might seem strange, found all more or less in agreement. But how could one think that Geo became aware of the Count at the very moment when the three girls, at whom his eyes were greedily staring, were about to disappear on their bicycles into the golden mist of Piazza delle Erbe?

According to those others, the Count, instead of standing motionless and silent to watch the passers-by, concerned only with remaining absolutely identical to the image that he and the city, in a united emotion of fondness, both wanted, was doing something. And this something, which nobody who went by at a distance greater than two yards could have noticed—also because his lips, in spite of everything, persisted in shifting the toothpick from one side of his mouth to the other—this something was a soft whistling, so faint that it seemed not so much timid as accidental: a lazy, random little whistle, which would certainly have remained unobserved if the tune he was indicating had been something other than "Lili Marlene." (But wasn't this, after all, the final, the really toothsome detail, for which one should be most grateful to the old informer?)

Underneath the lamplight, by the barracks gate . . .

Count Scocca whistled, softly but distinctly, his eyes also lost, despite his seventy-odd years, in pursuit of the cycling girls. Perhaps he too, breaking off his whistling for an instant, had briefly joined his voice to the unanimous chorus of praise that rose from the sidewalks of Via Mazzini, murmuring in dialect, following the goodhearted, sensual custom of the Emilian province: "Blessed by God!" or "Blessed are you and the mothers that bore you!" But as bad luck would have it, that idle, peaceful, innocent whistling—innocent to anyone, that is, except Geo—came at once to his lips. Needless to say, from this point on, the second version of the incident coincided with the first.

There was, nevertheless, a third version: and this, like the first made no mention of "Lili Marlene" nor of any other whistling, innocent or not, provocative or not.

If this last report was to be believed, it was the Count himself who stopped Geo. "Hey there!" he exclaimed, seeing him go by. Abruptly Geo stopped. And then the Count immediately started speaking to him, starting right off with his full name ("Why, look here, you aren't by chance Geo Josz, son of my friend Angiolino?"), because he, Lionello Scocca, knew everything about everybody, and the years he had been forced to spend in hiding, God knows how or where, hadn't in the least befuddled his memory or diminished his ability to recognize a face among thousands—even when it was a face like Geo's, which at Buchenwald, not in Ferrara, had become the face of a man! And so, long before Geo flung himself on the old spy and, heedless of his age and of everything else, slapped him violently, for a few minutes the two had gone on talking between themselves with great affability, Count Scocca questioning Geo about the end of Angelo Josz, of whom, he said, he had *always* been so fond, inquiring closely into the fate that had befallen the other members of the family, including Pietruccio, deploring those "horrible excesses" and at the same time congratulating him, Geo, on his return; and Geo, answering, with a certain embarrassed reluctance, true, but answering all the same: to look at, they were not unlike a normal couple of citizens, stopping on a sidewalk to talk of this and that, waiting for night to fall. What had driven Geo, then, suddenly to attack the Count, whom it was logical to credit with having said nothing to offend or in any way hurt his interlocutor, and, in particular, with not having hinted at even the slightest whistle: all the oddness of Geo's character lay there, in the opinion of those who told such things, it all lay in this "enigma"; and the gossip and the suppositions on the subject were to continue for a long while still.

V

No matter what really took place, one thing is sure: after that May evening many things changed. If anybody chose to understand, he understood. The others, the majority, were allowed at least to know that a turning point had been reached, that something serious had happened, something irreparable.

It was on the very next day, for example, that people could really become aware of how much weight Geo had lost.

Absurd as a scarecrow, to the wonder, the uneasiness and alarm of all, he reappeared, wearing the same clothes he had been wearing when he came back from Germany, in August of '45, fur hat and leather jerkin included. They were so loose on him, now—and, obviously, he had done nothing to make them fit better—that they seemed to droop from a clothes hanger. People saw him coming along Corso Giovecca, in the morning sun that shone happily and peacefully on his rags, and they could hardly believe their own eyes. So, during those months he had done nothing but grow thin, dry himself out! Slowly, he had shrunk to the rind! But nobody managed to laugh. Seeing him cross the Corso at the Teatro Communale, and then take Corso Roma (he crossed, looking out for the cars and the bicycles, with an old man's caution), there were very few who, in their hearts, didn't feel a shudder.

And so, from that morning on, never changing his dress, Geo installed himself, so to speak, permanently at the Caffè della Borsa, on Corso Roma, where, one by one, excepting the recent torturers and slaughterers of the Black Brigade, who were still kept hidden, distant, by sentences already "out of date," the old Fascist bullies showed up again, the remote dispensers of castor oil of '22 and '24, whom the last war had scattered and swept into oblivion. Covered with rags, he, from his little table, stared at the groups of them with a manner that lay between defiance and supplication. And his attitude contrasted, entirely to his own disadvantage, of course, with the shyness, the wish not to be too noticeable, that every gesture of the former tyrants betrayed. Old now, harmless, with the ruinous marks that the years of misfortune had multiplied on their faces and their bodies; and yet reserved, polite, well dressed: these men appeared far more human, more moving and deserving of pity than the other, than Geo. What did he want, this Geo Josz? many began to ask themselves once again. But the time of uncertainty and puzzlement, the time—which now seemed almost heroic!—when, before making the slightest decision, one paused and, as they say, split hairs: that time full of romanticism just after the war, so suited to moral questions and examinations of conscience, unfortunately, could not be called back. What did he want, Geo Josz? It was the old question, yes, but uttered without secret trembling, with the impatient brutality that life, eager to assert its rights, now forced one to adopt.

For this reason, except for Uncle Daniele, in whom the presence at those same tables, "so in the public eye," of some of the leading members of the local Fascist bands, former Consuls of the Militia, former Provincial Secretaries, former Mayors, etc., always aroused indignation and an argumentative streak (but his loyalty was too natural, too obvious: who could feel it was a real exception, a true consolation?)—for this reason, I say, the frequenters of the Caffè della Borsa still able to make the effort to rise from their wicker chairs, cover the few necessary yards, and finally sit down beside Geo had become few.

There were some, in any case, more unwilling than the others to surrender to their inner repugnance. But the embarrassment they brought back each time from those voluntary corvées was always the same. It was impossible, they would cry, to converse with a man in costume! And, on the other hand, if they let him do the talking, he immediately started telling about Fòssoli, about Germany, Buchenwald, the end of all his relatives; and he went on like that for whole hours, until you didn't know how to get away from him. There, at the café, under the yellow awning which, whipped obliquely by the sirocco, had a devilishly hard time protecting the little tables and the chairs from the fury of the noonday sun, there was nothing to do, while Geo narrated, but follow with one eye the movements of the workman opposite, busy filling with plaster the holes made in the parapet of the Castle's moat by the shooting of December 15, 1943. (By the way, the new Acting Prefect, sent from Rome after Doctor Herzen's sudden flight abroad, must have issued precise instructions in this matter!) And meanwhile Geo repeated the words that his father had murmured in a whisper, before dropping exhausted in the path from the *Lager* to the salt mine where they worked together; and then, still not satisfied, he imitated with his hand the little gesture of farewell his mother had made to him, at the grim station of their arrival, in the midst of the forest, as she was pushed aside with the other women; and then, going on, he told about Pietruccio, his little brother, seated beside him, in the dark, in the truck transporting them from the station through the fir trees to the huts of the camp, and how all of a sudden he vanished, like that, without a cry, without a moan, and nobody could find out anything more about him, then or ever. . . . Horrible, of course, heart-rending. But in all this there was something excessive, everyone declared, in agreement, returning from those too-long and depressing sessions, not without frank amazement, it's only fair to say, at their own coldness—there was something false, forced. It's the fault of all this propaganda, perhaps, they added, excusing themselves. It's true that countless stories of that sort had been heard, *at the proper time,* and to hear them thrust on one now, when the Castle's clock was probably striking the hour of dinner or supper, one simply couldn't fend off, honestly, a certain feeling of boredom and incredulity. As if, after all, to make people listen with greater attention, it was enough to put on a leather jerkin and stick a fur hat on your head!

During the rest of '46, all of '47, and a good part of '48, the more and more tattered and desolate figure of Geo Josz never stopped appearing before our eyes. In the streets, in the squares, at the movies, in the theaters, by the playing fields, at public ceremonies: you would look around and there he would be, tireless, always with that hint of saddened wonder in his gaze, as if he asked only to start a conversation. But all avoided him like the plague. Nobody understood. Nobody wanted to understand.

When he was just back from Buchenwald, his soul still tortured by dread and anguish, it was completely understandable, everyone admitted, that he would preferably stay in his house, or, on coming out, instead of streets like Corso Giovecca, so broad and open that at times it made even the most normal people feel a bit dizzy, he would instinctively turn to the winding alleys of the old city, the narrow and dark little streets of the ghetto. But afterward, removing the gabardine suit that Squarcia, the best tailor in the city, had made to order for him, and taking out again his lugubrious deportee's uniform, if he planned to turn up wherever there were people with a desire to enjoy themselves or, simply, a healthy wish to emerge from the shoals of that dirty postwar period, to go forward somehow, to "reconstruct," what excuse could be found for such outlandish and offensive conduct? And what should he care, he, who one August evening in '46 had had the bad taste to appear, in this guise, and extinguish the laughter on all lips, what should he care, for God's sake, if more than a year after the war's end they had decided to open a new outdoor dance hall, the one just beyond Porta San Benedetto, in fact, in the bend of the Doro? It wasn't one of the usual places, after all! As anyone had to admit, it was a very modern establishment, in the American style, with magnificent neon lighting, a fine bar and restaurant permanently open, kitchen always ready, which could provoke no more serious criticism (according to the article in the *Gazzetta del Po* written by that poor dreamer, the young Bottecchiari) than that it was located less than a hundred yards from the place where, in '44, five leaders of the underground National Liberation Committee had been shot in reprisal. Well, apart from the fact that the dance hall, in the bend of the Doro was, as the crow flies, not a hundred, but at least two hundred yards from the little marble column commemorating the execution, only a maniac, a hater of life, could think of venting his wrath on such a pleasant and jolly place. What harm was there? The first months everyone went there, more or less, coming out of the movies after midnight, with the idea of a late snack. But often people ended by having supper there; and then they danced to the radio, perhaps, among transient groups of truck drivers, making merry and enjoying the good company until dawn. It was only natural. Society, shattered by the war, was trying to pick up again. Life was resuming. And when it does, of course, it pays no attention to anyone.

Suddenly, faces, bitterly interrogatory until a moment before, without a ray of hope, brightened with malicious certitude. And what if Geo's disguise and self-exhibition, so insistent and irritating, had a political aim? What—and they winked—if he were a Communist?

That evening at the dance hall, for example, when he started displaying left and right the photographs of his relatives who had died in Buchenwald, he reached such an excess of arrogance that he tried to grasp the lapels of some young people who wanted only, at that moment—since the orchestra, meanwhile, had started playing again—to fling themselves, embracing, onto the dance floor. These weren't tales, hundreds of people saw him. And then, what could he be getting at, with those gestures, those honeyed grins, those imploring—ironically imploring!—grimaces, that bizarre and macabre pantomime of his, in short, unless he and Nino Bottecchiari, having recently come to an agreement about the house on Via Campofranco, were now, *also in other matters and namely Communism,* hand in glove? And if that's how things stood, if he was only a useful idiot, wasn't it right, after all, that the Friends of America Club, where in the chaos and enthusiasm of the immediate postwar period somebody had officially signed up Geo also, should now arrange to drop him, as a measure of obvious prudence, from its list of members? Probably no one, to tell the truth, at least for the moment, dreamed of thinking about him, about Geo Josz. But he *wanted* a scandal, that was clear: on that notorious evening when he had forcibly demanded entrance to the Club (it was in '47, in February), the waiters had seen appear before them not a decently dressed gentleman, but a strange character in the condition of a beggar, with a shaved neck like a prisoner—something, considering also the filth and the stink, very similar to Tugnín, the poor city beggar—who, from the vestibule full of overcoats and furs hanging in full view from the racks, had started proclaiming in a loud voice that he, being, as then proved quite correct, a regularly inscribed member of the Club, could visit it when he liked. And on what grounds, anyway, could the Club itself seriously be criticized, for having made such a radical decision toward Geo, when in the autumn of the preceding year the assembly of members had expressed a unanimous desire for the organization to return as soon as possible to its former, glorious name, the Circolo dei Concordi, again restricting the membership to the aristocracy—the Costabili, Del Sale, Maffei, Scroffa, Scocca families, and others of the sort—and to the most select members of the bourgeoisie? If the Friends of America, *pro temporum calamitatibus,* had been wise to accept anybody at all without fuss, the Circolo dei Concordi had certain standards, certain long-established customs, certain natural exclusions—and politics had nothing to do with this—and, really, there was no reason to fear restoring them. Why? What was odd about it? Even old Maria, Maria Ludargnani, who in that same winter of '46–'47 had reopened her house of ill-fame in Via Arianuova (it had remained the only place, after all, where people could foregather, without political opinions cropping up to spoil friendly relations; and evenings were spent there as in the old days, mostly limited to gossip or to playing rummy with the girls . . .)—even she would have nothing to do with Geo, that night he came to knock at her door; she wouldn't let him in, nor would she move away from the peephole, her eye glued to it observing him for a long time, until she saw him go off in the fog. In short, if on that occasion nobody thought for a moment that Geo had been deprived of some right; then all the more reason to recognize that the Circolo dei Concordi had behaved toward him in the most correct and sensible fashion. Democracy, if the word had a meaning, had to safeguard *all* citizens: the lower ranks, of course, but also the upper ones!

It was only in '48, after the elections of April 18th, after the Provincial Office of the Partisans Association was forced to move into three rooms of the former Casa del Fascio on Viale Cavour (and this proved, belatedly, that the rumors about the owner of the house on Via Campofranco and his Communism were purely imaginary), it was only in the summer of that year that Geo Josz decided to leave the city. He disappeared suddenly, leaving not the slightest trace after him, like a character in a novel; and immediately some people said he had emigrated to Palestine, following the example of Doctor Herzen; others said to South America; others, to an unknown country "behind the curtain."

They went on talking about him for a few months more: at the Caffè della Borsa, at the Doro, in Maria Ludargnani's house, and in many other places. Daniele Josz was able to hold forth publicly on the subject many times. Geremia Tabet, the lawyer, stepped in as administrator of the disappeared man's not inconsiderable possessions. And meanwhile:

"What a madman!" one heard repeated on all sides.

They would shake their heads good-naturedly, purse their lips, silently raise their eyes to heaven.

"If he had only been a bit more patient!" they would add, with a sigh; and they were again sincere, now, sincerely grieved.

They said time, which adjusts all things in this world, and thanks to which also Ferrara, luckily, was rising, identical, from its ruins, time would finally have calmed even him, would have helped him to return to the fold, fit in once more, in short—because, when you got down to it, this was his problem. But no. He had preferred to go away. Vanish. Act the tragic hero. Just when, by renting properly the now empty palazzo on Via Campofranco, and giving a good push to his father's business, he could have lived comfortably, like a gentleman, and, among other things, devoted himself to building a family again. Marrying, naturally; since there wouldn't have been a young lady in Ferrara, of the class to which he belonged, who, in the event, would have bothered about the religious difference (the years, on this score, had not passed in vain; in these matters people everywhere were much less strict than in the past!), no one would have considered it an insuperable obstacle. Odd as he was, he couldn't know that; but, with a 99 per cent probability, this is how things would have gone. Time would have settled everything, as if absolutely nothing had ever happened. To be sure, you had to wait. You had to be able to control your nerves. But, instead, had a more illogical way of behaving ever been seen? A more inscrutable character? Ah, but to realize the sort of person he was, the kind of living enigma who had turned up in their midst, the Count Scocca episode, without waiting for all the rest, was really more than enough. . . .

VI

An enigma, yes.

Still, on closer examination, when, lacking surer clues, we fell back on that sense of the absurd and, at once, of revealed truth, which at the approach of the evening any encounter can arouse in us, that very episode with Count Scocca revealed nothing enigmatic, nothing that couldn't be understood by a slightly sympathetic heart.

Oh, it is really true! Daylight is boredom, the deaf sleep of the spirit, "boring hilarity!" as the poet says. But let, finally, the twilight hour descend, the hour equally steeped in shadow and in light, a calm May dusk; and then things and people who a moment before seemed utterly normal, indifferent, can suddenly show themselves for what they truly are, they can suddenly speak to you—and at that point it is as if you've been struck by lightning—for the first time of themselves and of you.

"What am I doing here, I, with this man? Who is he? And I, who answer his questions, and at the same time lend myself to his game, who am I?"

The two slaps, after a few moments of mute wonder, answered like lightning the insistent though polite questions of Lionello Scocca. But those questions could also have been answered by a furious, inhuman scream: so loud that the whole city, as much as was still contained beyond the intact, deceitful scenery of Via Mazzini to the distant, breached walls, would have heard it with horror.

Natalia Ginzburg

Natalia Ginzburg (Italy, 1916–1991) was born Natalia Levi in Palermo and was descended from a dynasty of Sephardic bankers from Trieste. Her father was a Jewish professor of anatomy at Turin University, and her mother was Catholic. In 1938 she married Leone Ginzburg, a Russian expatriate writer and activist. In 1943, with the fall of Mussolini and the Nazi occupation, Ginzburg went into hiding, first in Rome and then in Florence. Her husband died in 1944, while a political prisoner. After the war, Ginzburg returned to Rome, where she worked at the publishing house Einaudi and married Gabriele Baldini. In 1983 she was elected to the lower house of the Italian Parliament. Family relationships are at the heart of her work. She is the author of *All Our Yesterdays* (1952; English, 1956, 1957, and 1985), *Family: Family and Borghesia, Two Novellas* (1983; English, 1987), *The Manzoni Family* (1983; English, 1987), and *The City and the House* (1984; English, 1987). Her nonfiction works include *The Little Virtues* (1962; English, 1985), in which she explores her Jewish identity, and *A Place to Live and Other Selected Essays* (2002). In her essays she discusses how Jews instinctively recognize each other beyond words, through *quid* (air of home). Ginzburg also wrote plays, including *The Advertisement* (1968; English, 1969). She translated into Italian *Swann's Way* by Marcel Proust and *Madame Bovary* by Gustave Flaubert. "He and I," translated into English by Dick Davis, is an astonishingly moving personal essay. Human empathy and nonverbal communication between men and women are its principal concerns but, as critics have suggested, it might also be read as a meditation on Jewishness. It is excerpted from *The Little Virtues*. Ginzburg's *Complete Works* were published in Italian in two volumes in 1986–87.

He and I

He always feels hot, I always feel cold. In the summer when it really is hot he does nothing but complain about how hot he feels. He is irritated if he sees me put a jumper on in the evening.

He speaks several languages well; I do not speak any well. He manages—in his own way—to speak even the languages that he doesn't know.

He has an excellent sense of direction, I have none at all. After one day in a foreign city he can move about in it as thoughtlessly as a butterfly. I get lost in my own city; I have to ask directions so that I can get back home again. He hates asking directions; when we go by car to a town we don't know he doesn't want to ask directions and tells me to look at the map. I don't know how to read maps and I get confused by all the little red circles and he loses his temper.

He loves the theatre, painting, music, especially music. I do not understand music at all, painting doesn't mean much to me and I get bored at the theatre. I love and understand one thing in the world and that is poetry.

He loves museums, and I will go if I am forced to but with an unpleasant sense of effort and duty. He loves libraries and I hate them.

He loves travelling, unfamiliar foreign cities, restaurants. I would like to stay at home all the time and never move.

All the same I follow him on his many journeys. I follow him to museums, to churches, to the opera. I even follow him to concerts, where I fall asleep.

Because he knows the conductors and the singers, after the performance is over he likes to go and congratulate them. I follow him down long corridors lined with the singers' dressing-rooms and listen to him talking to people dressed as cardinals and kings.

He is not shy; I am shy. Occasionally however I have seen him be shy. With the police when they come over to the car armed with a notebook and pencil. Then he is shy, thinking he is in the wrong.

And even when he doesn't think he is in the wrong. I think he has a respect for established authority. I am afraid of established authority, but he isn't. He respects it. There is a difference. When I see a policeman coming to fine me I immediately think he is going to haul me off to prison. He doesn't think about prison; but, out of respect, he becomes shy and polite.

During the Montesi trial, because of his respect for established authority, we had very violent arguments.

He likes tagliatelle, lamb, cherries, red wine. I like minestrone, bread soup, omelettes, green vegetables.

He often says I don't understand anything about food, that I am like a great strong fat friar—one of those friars who devour soup made from greens in the darkness of their monasteries; but he, oh he is refined and has a sensitive palate. In restaurants he makes long inquiries about the wines; he has them bring two or three bottles then looks at them and considers the matter, and slowly strokes his beard.

There are certain restaurants in England where the waiter goes through a little ritual: he pours some wine into a glass so that the customer can test whether he likes it or not. He used to hate this ritual and always prevented the waiter from carrying it out by taking the bottle from him. I used to argue with him about this and say that you should let people carry out their prescribed tasks.

And in the same way he never lets the usherette at the cinema direct him to his seat. He immediately gives her a tip but dashes off to a completely different place from the one she shows him with her torch.

At the cinema he likes to sit very close to the screen. If we go with friends and they look for seats a long way from the screen, as most people do, he sits by himself in the front row. I can see well whether I am close to the screen or far away from it, but when we are with friends I stay with them out of politeness; all the same it upsets me because I could be next to him two inches from the screen, and when I don't sit next to him he gets annoyed with me.

We both love the cinema, and we are ready to see almost any kind of film at almost any time of day. But he knows the history of the cinema in great detail; he remembers old directors and actors who have disappeared and been forgotten long ago, and he is ready to travel miles into the most distant suburbs in search of some ancient silent film in which an actor appears—perhaps just for a few seconds—whom he affectionately associates with memories of his early childhood. I remember one Sunday afternoon in London; somewhere in the distant suburbs on the edge of the countryside they were showing a film from the 1930s, about the French Revolution, which he had seen as a child, and in which a famous actress of that time appeared for a moment or two. We set off by car in search of the street, which was a very long way off; it was raining, there was a fog, and we drove for hour after hour through identical suburbs, between rows of little grey houses, gutters and railings; I had the map on my knees and I couldn't read it and he lost his temper; at last, we found the cinema and sat in the completely deserted auditorium. But after a quarter of an hour, immediately after the brief appearance of the actress who was so important to him, he already wanted to go; I on the other hand, after seeing so many streets, wanted to see how the film finished. I don't remember whether we did what he wanted or what I wanted; probably what he wanted, so that we left after a quarter of an hour, also because it was late—though we had set off early in the afternoon it was already time for dinner. But when I begged him to tell me how the film ended I didn't get a very satisfactory answer; because, he said, the story wasn't at all important, the only thing that mattered was those few moments, that actress's curls, gestures, profile.

I never remember actors' names, and as I am not good at remembering faces it is often difficult for me to recognize even the most famous of them. This infuriates him; his scorn increases as I ask him whether it was this one or that one; "You don't mean to tell me," he says, "you don't mean to tell me that you didn't recognize William Holden!"

And in fact I didn't recognize William Holden. All the same, I love the cinema too; but although I have been seeing films for years I haven't been able to provide myself with any sort of cinematic education. But he has made an education of it for himself and he does this with whatever attracts his curiosity; I don't know how to make myself an education out of anything, even those things that I love best in life; they stay with me as scattered images, nourishing my life with memories and emotions but without filling the void, the desert of my education.

He tells me I have no curiosity, but this is not true. I am curious about a few, a very few, things. And when I have got to know them I retain scattered impressions of them, or the cadence of phrase, or a word. But my world, in which these completely unrelated (unless in some secret fashion unbeknown to me) impressions and cadences rise to the surface, is a sad, barren place. His world, on the other hand, is green and populous and richly cultivated; it is a fertile, well-watered countryside in which woods, meadows, orchards and villages flourish.

Everything I do is done laboriously, with great difficulty and uncertainty. I am very lazy, and if I want to finish anything it is absolutely essential that I spend hours stretched out on the sofa. He is never idle, and is always doing something; when he goes to lie down in the afternoons he takes proofs to correct or a book full of notes; he wants us to go to the cinema, then to a reception, then to the theatre—all on the same day. In one day he succeeds in doing, and in making me do, a mass of different things, and in meeting extremely diverse kinds of people. If I am alone and try to act as he does I get nothing at all done, because I get stuck all afternoon somewhere I had meant to stay for half an hour, or because I get lost and cannot find the right street, or because the most boring person and the one I least wanted to meet drags me off to the place I least wanted to go to.

If I tell him how my afternoon has turned out he says it is a completely wasted afternoon and is amused and makes fun of me and loses his temper; and he says that without him I am good for nothing.

I don't know how to manage my time; he does.

He likes receptions. He dresses casually, when everyone is dressed formally; the idea of changing his clothes in order to go to a reception never enters his head. He even goes in his old raincoat and crumpled hat; a woollen hat which he bought in London and which he wears pulled down over his eyes. He only stays for half an hour; he enjoys chatting with a glass in his hand for half an hour; he eats lots of hors d'oeuvres, and I eat almost none because when I see him eating so many I feel that I at least must be well-mannered and show some self-control and not eat too much; after half an hour, just as I am beginning to feel at ease and to enjoy myself, he gets impatient and drags me away.

I don't know how to dance and he does.

I don't know how to type and he does.

I don't know how to drive. If I suggest that I should get a licence too he disagrees. He says I would never manage it. I think he likes me to be dependent on him for some things.

I don't know how to sing and he does. He is a baritone. Perhaps he would have been a famous singer if he had studied singing.

Perhaps he would have been a conductor if he had studied music. When he listens to records he conducts the orchestra with a pencil. And he types and answers the telephone at the same time. He is a man who is able to do many things at once.

He is a professor and I think he is a good one.

He could have been many things. But he has no regrets about those professions he did not take up. I could only ever have followed one profession—the one I chose and which I have followed almost since childhood. And I don't have any regrets either about the professions I did not take up, but then *I* couldn't have succeeded at any of them.

I write stories, and for many years I have worked for a publishing house.

I don't work badly, or particularly well. All the same I am well aware of the fact that I would have been unable to work anywhere else. I get on well with my colleagues and my boss. I think that if I did not have the support of their friendship I would soon have become worn out and unable to work any longer.

For a long time I thought that one day I would be able to write screenplays for the cinema. But I never had the opportunity, or I did not know how to find it. Now I have lost all hope of writing screenplays. He wrote screenplays for a while, when he was younger. And he has worked in a publishing house. He has written stories. He has done all the things that I have done and many others too.

He is a good mimic, and does an old countess especially well. Perhaps he could also have been an actor.

Once, in London, he sang in a theatre. He was Job. He had to hire evening clothes; and there he was, in his evening clothes, in front of a kind of lectern; and he sang. He sang the words of Job; the piece called for something between speaking and singing. And I, in my box, was dying of fright. I was afraid he would get flustered, or that the trousers of his evening clothes would fall down.

He was surrounded by men in evening clothes and women in long dresses, who were the angels and devils and other characters in Job.

It was a great success, and they said that he was very good.

If I loved music I would love it passionately. But I don't understand it, and when he persuades me to go to concerts with him my mind wanders off and I think of my own affairs. Or I fall sound asleep.

I like to sing. I don't know how to sing and I sing completely out of tune; but I sing all the same—occasionally, very quietly, when I am alone. I know that I sing out of tune because others have told me so; my voice must be like the yowling of a cat. But I am not—in myself—aware of this, and singing gives me real pleasure. If he hears me he mimics me; he says that my singing is something quite separate from music, something invented by me.

When I was a child I used to yowl tunes I had made up. It was a long wailing kind of melody that brought tears to my eyes.

It doesn't matter to me that I don't understand painting or the figurative arts, but it hurts me that I don't love music, and I feel that my mind suffers from the absence of this love. But there is nothing I can do about it, I will never understand or love music. If I occasionally hear a piece of music that I like I don't know how to remember it; and how can I love something that I can't remember?

It is the words of a song that I remember. I can repeat words that I love over and over again. I repeat the tune that accompanies them too, in my own yowling fashion, and I experience a kind of happiness as I yowl.

When I am writing it seems to me that I follow a musical cadence or rhythm. Perhaps music was very close to my world, and my world could not, for whatever reason, make contact with it.

In our house there is music all day long. He keeps the radio on all day. Or plays records. Every now and again I protest a little and ask for a little silence in which to work; but he says that such beautiful music is certainly conducive to any kind of work.

He has bought an incredible number of records. He says that he owns one of the finest collections in the world.

In the morning when he is still in his dressing gown and dripping water from his bath, he turns the radio on, sits down at the typewriter and begins his strenuous, noisy, stormy day. He is superabundant in everything; he fills the bath to overflowing, and the same with the teapot and his cup of tea. He has an enormous number of shirts and ties. On the other hand he rarely buys shoes.

His mother says that as a child he was a model of order and precision; apparently once, on a rainy day, he was wearing white boots and white clothes and had to cross some muddy streams in the country—at the end of his walk he was immaculate and his clothes and boots had not one spot of mud on them. There is no trace in him of that former immaculate little boy. His clothes are always covered in stains. He has become extremely untidy.

But he scrupulously keeps all the gas bills. In drawers I find old gas bills, which he refuses to throw away, from houses we left long ago.

I also find old, shrivelled Tuscan cigars, and cigarette holders made from cherry wood.

I smoke a brand of king-size, filterless cigarettes called Stop, and he smokes his Tuscan cigars.

I am very untidy. But as I have got older I have come to miss tidiness, and I sometimes furiously tidy up all the cupboards. I think this is because I remember my mother's tidiness. I rearrange the linen and blanket cupboards and in the summer I reline every drawer with strips of white cloth. I rarely rearrange my papers because my mother didn't write and had no papers. My tidiness and untidiness are full of complicated feelings of regret and sadness. His untidiness is triumphant. He has decided that it is proper and legitimate for a studious person like himself to have an untidy desk.

He does not help me get over my indecisiveness, or the way I hesitate before doing anything, or my sense of guilt. He tends to make fun of every tiny thing I do. If I go shopping in the market he follows me and spies on me. He makes fun of the way I shop, of the way I weigh the oranges in my hand unerringly choosing, he says, the worst in the whole market; he ridicules me for spending an hour over the shopping, buying onions at one stall, celery at another and fruit at another. Sometimes he does the shopping to show me how quickly he can do it; he unhesitatingly buys everything from one stall and then manages to get the basket delivered to the house. He doesn't buy celery because he cannot abide it.

And so—more than ever—I feel I do everything inadequately or mistakenly. But if I once find out that he has made a mistake I tell him so over and over again until he is exasperated. I can be very annoying at times.

His rages are unpredictable, and bubble over like the head on beer. My rages are unpredictable too, but his quickly disappear whereas mine leave a noisy nagging trail behind them which must be very annoying—like the complaining yowl of a cat.

Sometimes in the midst of his rage I start to cry, and instead of quietening him down and making him feel sorry for me this infuriates him all the more. He says my tears are just play-acting, and perhaps he is right. Because in the middle of my tears and his rage I am completely calm.

I never cry when I am really unhappy.

There was a time when I used to hurl plates and crockery on the floor during my rages. But not any more. Perhaps because I am older and my rages are less violent, and also because I dare not lay a finger on our plates now; we bought them one day in London, in the Portobello Road, and I am very fond of them.

The price of those plates, and of many other things we have bought, immediately underwent a substantial reduction in his memory. He likes to think he did not spend very much and that he got a bargain. I know the price of that dinner service—it was £16, but he says £12. And it is the same with the picture of King Lear that is in our dining room, and which he also bought in the Portobello Road (and then cleaned with onions and potatoes); now he says he paid a certain sum for it, but I remember that it was much more than that.

Some years ago he bought twelve bedside mats in a department store. He bought them because they were cheap, and he thought he ought to buy them; and he bought them as an argument against me because he considered me to be incapable of buying things for the house. They were made of mud-coloured matting and they quickly became very unattractive; they took on a corpse-like rigidity and were hung from a wire line on the kitchen balcony, and I hated them. I used to remind him of them, as an example of bad shopping; but he would say that they had cost very little indeed, almost nothing. It was a long time before I could bring myself to throw them out—because there were so many of them, and because just as I was about to get rid of them it occurred to me that I could use them for rags. He and I both find throwing things away difficult; it must be a kind of Jewish caution in me, and the result of my extreme indecisiveness; in him it must be a defence against his impulsiveness and open-handedness.

He buys enormous quantities of bicarbonate of soda and aspirins.

Now and again he is ill with some mysterious ailment of his own; he can't explain what he feels and stays in bed for a day completely wrapped up in the sheets; nothing is visible except his beard and the tip of his red nose. Then he takes bicarbonate of soda and aspirins in doses suitable for a horse, and says that I cannot understand because I am always well, I am like those great fat strong friars who go out in the wind and in all weathers and come to no harm; he on the other hand is sensitive and delicate and suffers from mysterious ailments. Then in the evening he is better and goes into the kitchen and cooks himself tagliatelle.

When he was a young man he was slim, handsome and finely built; he did not have a beard but long, soft moustaches instead, and he looked like the actor Robert Donat. He was like that about twenty years ago when I first knew him, and I remember that he used to wear an elegant kind of Scottish flannel shirt. I remember that one evening he walked me back to the *pensione* where I was living; we walked together along the Via Nazionale. I already felt that I was very old and had been through a great deal and had made many mistakes, and he seemed a boy to me, light years away from me. I don't remember what we talked about on that evening walking along the Via Nazionale; nothing important, I suppose, and the idea that we would become husband and wife was light years away from me. Then we lost sight of each other, and when we met again he no longer looked like Robert Donat, but more like Balzac. When we met again he still wore his Scottish shirts but on him now they looked like garments for a polar expedition; now he had his beard and on his head he wore his ridiculous crumpled woollen hat; everything about him put you in mind of an imminent departure for the North Pole. Because, although he always feels hot, he has the habit of dressing as if he were surrounded by snow, ice and polar bears; or he dresses like a Brazilian coffee-planter, but he always dresses differently from everyone else.

If I remind him of that walk along the Via Nazionale he says he remembers it, but I know he is lying and that he remembers nothing; and I sometimes ask myself if it was us, these two people, almost twenty years ago on the Via Nazionale; two people who conversed so politely, so urbanely, as the sun was setting; who chatted a little about everything perhaps and about nothing; two friends talking, two young intellectuals out for a walk; so young, so educated, so uninvolved, so ready to judge one another with kind impartiality; so ready to say goodbye to one another for ever, as the sun set, at the corner of the street.

Primo Levi

Primo Levi (Italy, 1919–1987), a chemist by profession, was born in Turin into a secular, assimilated Sephardic family. His interest in science was matched by his interest in the humanities. Levi was deported to Auschwitz in 1944, where he became a slave laborer. He survived the camp, as he himself put it, thanks to luck, a rudimentary knowledge of German, and the help of a selfless Italian worker who smuggled food into the camp for Levi and other prisoners. Levi's experience in Auschwitz is chronicled in *If This Is a Man* (1947), which received little notice upon its initial publication in Italy but, when published more than a decade later in English became a bestseller and is now considered a classic of Holocaust literature, along with the works of Anne Frank, Elie Wiesel, and Imre Kertész. Stuart Woolf's English translation was published in 1959 and it changed the title in 1961 to *Survival in Auschwitz: The Nazi Assault on Humanity.* After World War II, Levi returned to Turin, worked as a chemist, and eventually managed a varnish factory until his retirement, at which point he devoted himself to writing. His return to Turin is chronicled in a picaresque novel, *The Truce* (1963; English, 1965), also known in English as *The Reawakening.* Levi is also the author of *The Periodic Table* (1975; English, 1984), *Moments of Reprieve* (1981), in which "Story of a Coin," translated by Ruth Feldman, appears along with *If Not Now, When?* (1982; English, 1985). Three biographies of Levi are available in English: *Primo Levi: Tragedy of an Optimist* (1998), by Myriam Anissimov; *The Double Bond: Primo Levi, a Biography* (2002), by Carole Angier; and *Primo Levi: A Life* (2002), by Ian Thompson. Also available in English is *The Voice of Memory: Interviews 1961–1987* (2001), edited by Marco Belpoliti and Robert Gordon. Levi's *Collected Poems,* in which "Shemà" appears, was published in English in 1988. Having spent years suffering from deep depression, Levi died in a fall down a stairwell in his home in 1987.

Shemà

You who live secure
In your warm houses,
Who return at evening to find
Hot food and friendly faces:

Consider whether this is a man,
Who labors in the mud
Who knows no peace
Who fights for a crust of bread
Who dies at a yes or a no.
Consider whether this is a woman,
Without hair or name
With no more strength to remember
Eyes empty and womb cold
As a frog in winter.

Consider that this has been:
I commend these words to you.
Engrave them on your hearts
When you are in your house, when you walk on your way,
When you go to bed, when you rise.
Repeat them to your children.
Or may your house crumble,
Disease render you powerless,
Your offspring avert their faces from you.

10 January 1946

Story of a Coin

When I returned from Auschwitz, I found in my pocket a strange coin of a lightweight metal alloy. It is scratched and corroded, and on one face has the Jewish star (the "Shield of David"), the date 1943, and the word *"getto,"* which in German is pronounced "ghetto." On the other face are the inscriptions *"Quittung über 10 Mark"* and *"Der Aelteste der Juden in Litzmannstadt,"* that is, respectively, "Receipt against 10 marks" and "The Elder of the Jews in Litzmannstadt." For many years I didn't pay any attention to it; for some time I carried it in my change purse, perhaps inadvertently attributing to it the value of a good luck charm, then left it in the bottom of a drawer. Recently, information which I gathered from various sources has made it possible for me to reconstruct, at least in part, its history, and it is unusual, fascinating, and sinister.

On modern atlases there is no city named Litzmannstadt, but a General Litzmann was and is renowned in Germany for having in 1914 broken through the Russian front near Lodz in Poland. In Nazi times, in honor of this general, Lodz was rechristened Litzmannstadt. During the last months of 1944, the last survivors of the Lodz ghetto were deported to Auschwitz. I must have found that coin on the ground at Auschwitz immediately after the liberation, certainly not before, because nothing I had on me up till then could have been kept.

In 1939 Lodz had approximately 750,000 inhabitants, and was the most industrialized, most "modern," and ugliest of Polish cities. It was a city that, like Manchester and Biella, lived on its textile industry, its situation determined by the presence of numerous large and small mills, mostly antiquated even then, and for the greater part they had been established several decades earlier by German and Jewish industrialists. As in all the cities of a certain importance in occupied Eastern Europe, in Lodz the Nazis were quick to set up a ghetto, reviving the conditions (harshened by modern ferocity) of the ghettos of the Middle Ages and the Counter Reformation. The Lodz ghetto, already open by February 1940, was the first in order of time and the second in number of inhabitants after the Warsaw ghetto: it reached a population of more than 160,000 Jews and was closed down only in the autumn of 1944. Hence it was also the most long-lived of Nazi ghettos and this must be attributed to two reasons: its economic importance for the Germans, and the disturbing personality of its president.

His name was Chaim Rumkowski, formerly co-owner of a velvet factory in Lodz. He had gone bankrupt and made several trips to England, perhaps to negotiate with his creditors; he had then settled in Russia, where somehow he had again become wealthy; ruined by the revolution in 1917 he had returned to Lodz. By 1940 he was almost sixty, was twice widowed, and had no children. He was known as the director of Jewish charitable institutions, and as an energetic, uneducated, and authoritarian man. The office of president (or elder) of a ghetto was intrinsically dreadful, but it was an office; it represented recognition, a step up on the social ladder, and it conferred authority. Now Rumkowski loved authority. How he managed to obtain the investiture is not known: perhaps thanks to a joke or hoax in the sinister Nazi style (Rumkowski was or appeared to be a fool with a very respectable air; in short, an ideal puppet), perhaps he himself intrigued in order to obtain it, so strong in him must have been the will to power.

It has been proved that the four years of his presidency, or better, his dictatorship, were an amazing tangled megalomaniacal dream of barbaric vitality and real diplomatic and organizational ability. He soon came to see himself in the role of absolute but enlightened monk arch, and certainly he was encouraged on this path by his German bosses, who, true enough, played with him but appreciated his talents as a good administrator and man of order. From them he obtained the authorization to mint money, both metal (that coin of mine) and paper—on watermarked paper which was officially issued to him: this was the money used to pay the enfeebled ghetto workers, and they could spend it in the commissaries to buy their food rations, which on the average amounted to 800 calories per day.

Since he had at his disposal a famished army of excellent artists and artisans, anxious at his slightest gesture to jump to do his bidding for a quarter-loaf of bread, Rumkowski had them design and print stamps bearing his portrait, his hair and beard snow-white and gleaming in the light of Hope and Faith. He had a coach drawn by a skeletal nag, and in it rode about his minuscule kingdom, through the streets swarming with beggars and petitioners. He wore a regal cloak, and surrounded himself with a court of flatterers, lackeys, and cutthroats; he had his poet-courtiers compose hymns celebrating his "firm and powerful hand" and the peace and order which thanks to him reigned in the ghetto; he ordered that the children in the nefarious schools, constantly decimated by death from hunger and the Germans' roundups, be assigned essays extolling and praising "our beloved and provident President." Like all autocrats, he hastened to organize an efficient police force, supposedly to maintain order but in fact to protect his person and enforce his control: it was composed of six hundred policemen armed with clubs, and an indefinite number of informers. He delivered many speeches, which in part have come down to us, and whose style is unmistakable. He had adopted (deliberately? knowingly? or did he unconsciously identify with the man of providence, the "necessary hero," who at that time ruled over Europe?) Mussolini's and Hitler's oratorical techniques—that inspired performance, that pseudo-exchange with the crowd, the creation of consensus through moral plunder and plaudits.

And yet this personage was more complex than what appears so far. Rumkowski was not only a renegade and an accomplice. In some measure, besides making people believe it, he himself must have become progressively convinced that he was a *mashiach,* a Messiah, a savior of his people, whose good he must, at least intermittently, have desired. Paradoxically, his identification with the oppressor is flanked by, or perhaps alternates with, an identification with the oppressed because man, as Thomas Mann says, is a confused creature. And he becomes even more confused, we may add, when he is subjected to extreme tensions: he then eludes our judgment, the way a compass needle goes wild at the magnetic pole.

Although despised, derided, and sometimes beaten by the Germans, Rumkowski probably thought of himself not as a servant but as a lord. He must have believed in his authority: when the Gestapo, without advance notice, seized "his" councillors, he courageously rushed to their aid, exposing himself to the Nazis' mockery and blows, which he endured with dignity. Also on other occasions, he tried to bargain with the Germans, who demanded ever more cloth from his slaves at the looms and ever-increasing contingents of useless mouths (old people, sick people, children) to send to the gas chambers. The harshness with which he hastened to suppress outbreaks of insubordination by his subjects (there existed at Lodz, as in other ghettos, nuclei of obstinate and foolhardy political resistance of Zionist or Communist origin) did not spring so much from servility toward the Germans as from *lèse majesté,* from indignation at the offense inflicted on his royal person.

In September 1944, since the Russian front was approaching the area, the Nazis began the liquidation of the Lodz ghetto. Tens of thousands of men and women who until then had been able to withstand hunger, exhausting labor, and illness, were deported to Auschwitz, *anus mundi,* ultimate drainage point of the German universe, and almost all of them died there in the gas chambers. In the ghetto about a thousand men were left to dismantle and take down the precious machinery and to erase traces of the massacre. They were liberated shortly after by the Red Army, and to them is owed the greater part of the information reported here.

About Chaim Rumkowski's final fate there exist two versions, as though the ambiguity under whose sign he had lived had extended to envelop his death. According to the first version, during the liquidation of the ghetto he tried to oppose the deportation of his brother, from whom he did not want to be separated; a German officer then proposed that he should leave voluntarily with this brother, and Rumkowski supposedly accepted. According to another version, Rumkowski's rescue from death at the hands of the Germans was attempted by Hans Biebow, another personage surrounded by a cloud of duplicity. This shady German industrialist was the official responsible for the ghetto's administration and at the same time was its contractor. His was an important and delicate position because the ghetto factories worked for the German army. Biebow was not a wild animal: he was not interested in causing suffering or punishing the Jews for their sin of being Jewish, but in making money on his contracts. The torment in the ghetto touched him only indirectly; he wanted the slave-workers to work and therefore he did not want them to die of hunger; his moral sense stopped there. Actually *he* was the true boss of the ghetto and was tied to Rumkowski by a supplier/purchaser relationship that often leads to a rough friendship. Biebow, that little jackal, too cynical to take racial demonology seriously, would have liked to postpone the closing down of the ghetto, which for him was excellent business, and to protect Rumkowski, his friend and partner, from deportation: which goes to show how quite often a realist is better than a theoretician. But the SS theoreticians held a contrary opinion and they were the stronger. They were *gründlich,* radicals: get rid of the ghetto and get rid of Rumkowski.

Unable to arrange matters otherwise, Biebow, who enjoyed good connections, supplied Rumkowski with a sealed letter addressed to the commander of the Camp he was being sent to, assured him that it would protect him, and guaranteed that he would receive special consideration. Apparently Rumkowski requested and got from Biebow travel arrangements all the way to Auschwitz with the propriety befitting his rank, that is, in a special coach hooked on to the end of the convoy of freight cars jammed with deportees without privileges; but the fate of Jews in German hands was just one, whether they were cowards or heroes, humble or proud. Neither the letter nor the special coach saved Chaim Rumkowski, the King of the Jews, from the gas of Auschwitz.

A story like this goes beyond itself: it is pregnant, asks more questions than it answers, and leaves us in suspense; it cries out and demands to be interpreted because in it we discern a symbol, as in dreams and signs from heaven, but it is not easy to interpret.

Who is Rumkowski? He's not a monster, but he isn't like other men either; he is like many, like the many frustrated men who taste power and are intoxicated by it. In many of its aspects, power is like drugs: the need for the one and for the other is unknown to those who have not experienced them, but after the initiation, which may be accidental, addiction is born, dependency, and the need for ever larger doses; also born is the rejection of reality and return to infantile dreams of omnipotence. If the hypothesis of a Rumkowski intoxicated with power is valid, it must be admitted that the intoxication arose not because of but despite the ghetto environment, that indeed it is so powerful as to prevail even under conditions that would appear to be likely to extinguish all individual will. In fact, the well-known syndrome of protracted and unchallenged power was only too visible in him: the distorted vision of the world, dogmatic arrogance, convulsive clinging to the levers of command, regarding oneself as above the law.

All this does not exonerate Rumkowski from his responsibility. That a Rumkowski did exist pains and rankles; it is likely that, had he survived his tragedy and the tragedy of the ghetto which he polluted by super imposing on it his histrionic figure, no tribunal would have absolved him, nor certainly can we absolve him on the moral plane. There are, however, some extenuating circumstances. An infernal order such as Nazism exercises a dreadful power of seduction, which it is difficult to guard against. Instead of sanctifying its victims, it degrades and corrupts them, makes them similar to itself, surrounds itself with great and small complicities. In order to resist, one needs a very solid moral framework, and the one available to Chaim Rumkowski, the merchant of Lodz, and to all his generation, was fragile. His is the regrettable and disquieting story of the Kapos, the smalltime officials in the rear of the army, the functionaries who sign everything, those who shake their heads in denial but consent, those who say "if I didn't do this, somebody worse than I would."

It is typical of regimes in which all power rains down from above and no criticism can rise from below, to weaken and confound people's capacity for judgment, to create a vast zone of gray consciences that stands between the great men of evil and the pure victims. This is the zone in which Rumkowski must be placed. Whether higher or lower, it's hard to say; he alone could clarify it if he could speak before us, even lying, as he perhaps always lied; he would help us understand him, as every defendant helps his judge, and helps him even if he doesn't want to, even if he lies, because man's ability to play a role has its limits.

But all of this is not enough to explain the sense of urgency and threat emanating from this story. Perhaps its meaning is different and vaster: we are all mirrored in Rumkowski, his ambiguity is ours, that of hybrids kneaded from clay and spirit; his fever is ours, that of our Western civilization which "descends to hell with trumpets and drums," and his miserable tinsel trappings the distorted image of our symbols of social prestige. His folly is that of the presumptuous and mortal Man as Isabella in *Measure for Measure* describes him, Man who

> "Dressed in a little brief authority,
> Most ignorant of what he's most assured,
> His glassy essence, like an angry ape
> Plays such fantastic tricks before high heaven
> As makes the angels weep . . ."

Like Rumkowski, we too are so dazzled by power and money as to forget our essential fragility, forget that all of us are in the ghetto, that the ghetto is fenced in, that beyond the fence stand the lords of death, and not far away the train is waiting.

Albert Memmi

Albert Memmi (Tunis-France, 1920–) is a novelist, sociologist, and cultural critic. He fought with the Free French during World War II, completed his studies in Tunis, and directed a psychological institute. In 1959 he moved to Paris in order to join the Centre National de la Recherche Scientifique and eventually became a teacher at the École Pratique des Hautes Études, where he was appointed professor in 1966. He advocated an end to colonialism in North Africa, even though he understood that it would result in the exodus of the Jewish communities from those countries. Memmi is the author of the novel *Strangers* (1955; English, 1958), about the divided self of a Tunisian Jew who is at home neither among the French nor among the Arabs. He became a theoretician of the social consequences of oppression and colonization. His books on the subject include *The Colonizer and the Colonized* (1957; English, 1965), *Dominated Man: Notes Toward a Portrait* (1968; English, also 1968), and *Dependence: A Sketch for a Portrait of the Dependent* (1979; English, 1984). These concerns also made Memmi an outspoken advocate for Jewish causes, but his depiction of the Jew is controversial: he perceives his people as "shadow figures" that are caught between two worlds, assimilation and distinctiveness. Memmi's other fiction includes *The Scorpion, or, The Imaginary Confession* (1969; English, 1971) and *Le Pharaoh* (1988). He continued his reflections on the nature of Jewishness in *Portrait of a Jew* (2 vols., 1962; English, 1962) and *Jews and Arabs* (1974; English, 1975). Memmi is a champion of Israel, which he sees as "our only solution, our one trump card, our last historical opportunity." The excerpt that follows is from *The Pillar of Salt* (1953; English, 1955), which brought him worldwide acclaim. This autobiographical novel discusses his protagonist's education in Tunis within the confines of the insular Jewish community, his embrace of French civilization, and his ultimate disappointment with Western values. It was translated by Edouard Roditi.

From *The Pillar of Salt*

Chosen Out of Many

I WAS EXPECTED to attend the lycée, the French high school, at the beginning of the school year that followed my *bar mitzvah.* This extraordinary happening was the consequence of an unexpected piece of luck. The road was straight and easy for sons of the middle class: first junior high school, then senior high school, then the university or their father's business. If they branched off somewhere along the line, it was because they wanted to. But I knew nothing of my own future beyond the school certificate. Not that I had no exact dreams or ambitions but, beyond this certificate, all was still shrouded in darkness.

I wanted very much to become a physician, after having been to the free dispensary at the hospital where we had waited for hours before being admitted finally into the presence of a doctor as distant and sure of his own authority as God Himself. I had been impressed by the prestige of the nurses, the humility of the poor patients. At home, in our eyes, the "Doctor" remained a magician, still inheriting much of the wonder inspired by a sorcerer and having all of the latter's assurance. Often, with a hairpin, I gave imaginary injections to Kalla and Poupeia, the neighbors' daughters, and then bound them up with a handkerchief. When they objected, I gravely reduced them to silence by invoking their inevitable recovery from illness.

But all this was imaginary play. In due time I would realize how impossible it was for me to pursue my studies, and I would probably, like the other boys of my sort, have to bow before the inevitable, without any chance to revolt. After that, as an errand boy or an apprentice in a workshop, all my childhood ambitions would be forgotten.

To encourage us all the better to study, one of my instructors later compared the school system to a series of sieves. In the first, with its coarser-grained holes, a first selection took place; in the second, and finer sieve, a second sorting, and so on. Only the very finest and best elements thus survived the whole screening process. The comparison was good, but unfortunately explains too little. To compete successfully, one needed, in addition to intelligence and the ability to work hard, some financial stability too. But a larger income was required at each test, for it had to make up for the student's lack of any earnings, to counteract the jealousies of relatives, the nagging criticisms of his family, the low morale of the student who grows weary of having too many problems and is soon tempted by the first steady earnings of his former classmates. Nor should one forget school fees, schoolbooks, and clothes. Such, at least, is the problem that arises for students of my social background.

The number of obstacles that ill luck made me contend with was really very considerable. But fate's first gift to me was to open the doors of high school.

I was eleven years old when I was ready to take the examinations for my school certificate, an exceptional age for grade school, which was usually completed at thirteen. Foolishly, we made jokes about the ignorance of the high-school kids who were taking the same examination, but we overlooked the fact that they were much younger than we. Besides, the certificate was not required for them, and whatever backwardness they revealed at the examination was made up for in the course of their seven high-school years. They then came up for their baccalaureate exam at the age of sixteen, whereas the former grade-school pupils could not achieve this before the age of eighteen or nineteen. But I had not yet begun to look so far ahead. I was merely proud of getting into the last year of grade school and of being the youngest in my class. Still, it meant no advantages for me, as the lowest age for admission as a candidate was twelve. Everything was indeed very well worked out. If one of us managed to overcome all these handicaps, it proved that he was really much better than all the sons of middle-class parents. When our instructor, Monsieur Marzouk, drew up the list of official candidates, he was sorry to have to warn me that I had to wait until the next year. For a brief moment, the whole class concentrated its attention on me and I was more proud of it all than disappointed. Nor did I even dream that there was such a thing as an entrance examination for admission to the lowest high-school grade, which one could take at any age and that made the school certificate unnecessary. Who could have informed me? My father, who had attended only a year or two of school, or my mother, who has never learned to read or write any language? Our tribe, too busy with the daily preoccupations of its difficult life, had no knowledge of the passionate discussions of middle-class families concerning the future or their children. My immediate future, in school, was always far too uncertain to allow any long-term planning. So I quietly made the most of this honor of having to mark time for a full year and completed a second year of the same grade, winning all the prizes. These easy prizes indeed had more influence on my future, perhaps, than any precocious success at the school certificate might have had.

Toward the end of my second year, Graziani, our Italian school porter, came into the classroom one day and said to Monsieur Marzouk that the school principal wanted to speak to me. To speak to *me*? Me, of all people? The principal? The school principal was in our eyes a very important person, so majestic and distant that he was almost a legend. His orders were abstract commands, impersonal, communicated to us by signs like the orders of a divinity. But why to me? I could see no connection. On one or two occasions a pupil had had some contact with the principal, but always as the result of a catastrophe or some grave misdeed. The principal had, for instance, broken the news to Nataf Pipo, in the fifth year, of his mother's death, which had occurred suddenly at ten in the morning. And Brami Pinhas, in the third year, had also been summoned to the principal's office, because he had thrown an inkwell against the wall; he had then been expelled and subsequently became insane. My heart beat so violently I could feel it thump beneath my ribs.

The orders of the principal required immediate execution, so I stood up at once and left the room, my knees already weak. I walked across the yard that was strangely empty at this hour, though intensely alive with the concealed presence of a thousand silent children. This magic silence, the unbelievable concentrate of a thousand shouts, was ready, I felt, to explode in all directions as soon as Graziani's bell should ring. But all the demons were still safely bottled up, and only I was free to walk between the two rows of giant eucalyptus trees. A freedom that went to my head, magical, with the whole universe obeying me at that moment; the freedom of the first few days of vacation, or of an adventurer taking off and abandoning his country to its rhythm of everyday life, the office workers at their desk jobs, the workers in their plants, the children in their schools. As I crossed the yard that I had never seen so silent and went by the windows of the classrooms where all my classmates watched me with envy, their arms crossed, I felt privileged indeed, with a great adventure beginning ahead of me.

For the first time in my life, I opened the glass-paneled door of the principal's office and saw him writing at his desk. I was now within the sacred precincts and all my gestures were therefore slow and studied, as if for a ritual. I was careful to close the door and progressed slowly across three platforms or stages, end to end. The desk of Monsieur Louzel was placed at the end of the third, at the far end of the room, against the wall.

Three black cabinets, some framed reproductions in black and white, and black curtains. Behind Monsieur Louzel, a bay window revealed a tiny garden that seemed full with a single green banana tree and one aloe tree that somehow tempered the school-like severity, so solemn and cold, of this room.

With a gesture of his hand, the principal invited me to be seated, then he got up to fetch my file from one of the cabinets. I stole a glance at him, full of admiration. His hair was spotlessly white, of a fine silky white, and gave him a distinguished air. He was, I feel, a bit histrionic, but with sincerity, out of an awareness of his function and his importance in our eyes. He always impressed us because of his perfect diction and polished manners that represented, for us, the real Frenchman from metropolitan France whose prestige remains undiminished.

My various instructors and he too, the principal informed me, had noted my uninterrupted successes and had decided to reward them. So I had been proposed as candidate for the annual school scholarship. It is wrong to think that a child of twelve cannot grasp the importance of a decisive moment in his own life. I remained speechless, so deeply moved that I was overwhelmed. A mass of vague projects, all wonderful, suddenly ceased to be merely imaginary and gained some probability. The prestige of the doctor's white smock at the hospital, the respect that the nurses felt for him, all this exquisite but serious play, the money earned. . . . It would now become true, and I would be a physician. I could hear the word repeated rhythmically in my head: physician, physician, physician. . . . Monsieur Louzel understood my emotion and my absent-mindedness. He was kind enough to pretend not to notice it, and set about explaining to me the ingenious institution of which I was a beneficiary. Each year the school brought to the attention of the community a brilliant student who needed help. The community then entrusted him to the care of one of its own former scholars who now, in turn, paid for the new scholar's studies. Later, once his studies were completed and his position assured, the new scholar was expected to assume some day the responsibility for a younger scholar's studies. I found this idea of a chain that went on forever quite wonderful, and looked upon the men who had invented it as benefactors of mankind.

The principal then paused, with some solemnity. He still had to ask me my opinion, whether I was prepared to continue my studies. The Jewish community of Tunis, on the recommendation of the Alliance Israélite Universelle, would undertake to finance my studies, at first my high-school years, then the university too. What had I to say? The principal was already asking me what I had to say! Here I was, already acquiring importance. Did I want to study? Good God, did I want to continue my studies. . . . "Well," the principal concluded by himself, "you've agreed. Of course, we first had to get the approval of your father, and it has meant his accepting a heavy sacrifice and agreeing to carry on without any help from you until you have received your final diplomas." The principal thus revealed to me that my father had already been consulted several days earlier, and that nothing had then been said to me, to avoid any possible disappointment. Only that same morning had my father at last given a favorable answer. So, my father had accepted! How could he possibly have said no! I was utterly aghast, full of revolt against the mere possibility of my father's objecting. Obscurely, I imagined an argument with my father, but he never would have been able to prevent me from choosing the path toward glory.

Monsieur Louzel continued to speak in his dictatorial tone, and I continued to remain silent. Still, I had an answer for every question, repartee came spontaneously to my lips, I was bubbling over with promises, gratitude, and dreams. I reacted to every one of his sentences with gestures that were born of my whole body, approving, denying, committing me. There had been some hesitation, Monsieur Louzel confided in me, between choosing Lévy, the son of the widow, and myself. His financial status deserved more consideration, but I was the better student. I nodded, with an expression that wished to convey deep sympathy for Lévy Isidro; but my joy was too great to allow any qualification, except that of retrospective anguish.

"Well, you have deserved your luck," concluded the principal. "Now you must go back to your classroom to fetch your things and go at once to see Monsieur Bismuth, who has been appointed your sponsor. He wants to see you at once, as he has to leave town this afternoon. So, you had better go. . . . But wait, I haven't told you anything about Monsieur Bismuth."

We were already going ahead with the application of our plans and biting into the future. I assumed an attentive and preoccupied look, ready to rush wherever he would send me. Monsieur Bismuth, the well-known druggist, was going to be, it seemed, my paying sponsor. Yes, I knew his drugstore well, though I had never met Monsieur Bismuth: a modern storefront, spacious display windows, with neon lighting at night. A stout thread of gold now bound me to the city. The principal began to speak to me in detail about my sponsor; a sponsor of poor parents, who had been a courageous and hard worker, with the community scholarship coming to bring recognition to his merits, and here he was a wealthy man, an honored member of the community, the owner of the finest drugstore in our part of the country.

"Let him be your inspiration," concluded Monsieur Louzel. "Your destinies have much in common, and I hope, for you, that they'll continue to have as much in common."

Abandoning his histrionic manner to become almost paternal, the principal then asked me:

"What do you want to be?"

"A physician," I answered, without any hesitation.

"Well, if you continue to study as hard as you have been, we'll make a physician of you."

He then dismissed me, and I went again across the three stages, opened the glass-paneled door, closed it carefully. To me, it seemed as if I were awakening from a dream. But unlike those awakenings when one is seized with the irresistible desire to check on the real existence of one's treasure, my own gold was here with me: magically, my dream had acquired a body. The school principal, Monsieur Bismuth, the influential druggist, the Alliance Israélite Universelle, the whole of the Jewish community of Tunis had decided that it must come true.

This was no time for self-satisfied jubilation. My destiny pushed me ahead: I was expected. So I hurried across the yard, without paying any attention to the benevolent eucalyptus trees, to the big bronze bell that waited there, patient and almost motherly, to the sidelong glances of all my classmates indoors. I climbed the old wooden staircase four steps at a time. As I feverishly gathered my things together, I felt on me the gaze of all my classmates. They were perhaps astonished to see me summoned like this by the principal; perhaps Monsieur Marzouk had announced to them my new and sudden glory. But I was sure that they all stared at me. So as not to have to compete against this general lack of concentration in the class, Monsieur Marzouk interrupted his teaching. In the silence that ensued, my heart beat cheerfully, with big, heavy beats, as if it were dancing.

My father's store was not far from my sponsor's office, so I went first to see my father. I showed him, almost without any self-consciousness, how deeply I was moved. He told me all about his talk with the principal that same morning; he had come back from it very proud and convinced that I should continue my studies. The principal had been very complimentary indeed, and this had confirmed my father in his faith in his own intelligence and in that of his offspring. Then I went to the drugstore.

Monsieur Bismuth was no longer there, but his clerk reassured me: Monsieur Bismuth had expected me, but now asked me to come back in two weeks. So the various threads were indeed all tied together.

The city's siren that announced noon now rang. I rushed into the street, at last aware of my own appetite, but also because I felt a need to run. I wanted to sing, to announce my unbelievable adventure to everyone, to make polite remarks to utter strangers in the street. Some Moslem laborers were repairing the streetcar tracks, and the sun was glistening on the metal. I shouted out to them:

"May God be with you!"

This is how we greet, in the countryside, laborers whom we do not necessarily know, but merely to reaffirm, in the face of loneliness, the solidarity of all mankind. Now, these men were surprised, because such conventions are generally respected only among believers in their faith; still, they answered me:

"The blessing of Allah be upon you!"

This feeling of communion with all of mankind made me happy. I gave a couple of coins to a Bedouin beggar, now that I would henceforth be so wealthy! An old idea that disappointments had caused to wilt now blossomed again, binding my adolescence that was beginning more closely to my childhood that was gone: I had been chosen among many, ahead of Lévy, who could not be surpassed in mathematics, ahead of Spinoza, who was Monsieur Marzouk's favorite! I was surely better than all my classmates, all the students in the school, perhaps all the students in all the Alliance schools! Surely, I would go far and be very powerful. True, I couldn't yet foresee the nature of this power, but it was a kind of broad movement toward the future, a lunging that was almost muscular.

Following the advice of my father, who was more aware of such necessities, my mother began inspecting my wardrobe.

"You know," he explained to her, "only rich men's sons attend high school, and our boy must be decently dressed, too."

In their eyes, as in my own, my entering high school acquired the importance of an introduction into society, which it actually turned out to be, even more than I had guessed. Our alley and the Alliance School belonged to one society, but the European sections of town and the high school to another. Above all, I was now setting forth on the adventure that leads to knowledge. I sometimes think back now, with horror, on the darkness in which I might have been forced to live, and I then consider the many aspects of the universe that I might never have come to know. I would not even have dreamed of their existence, like some deep-sea fish that remain ignorant of the very existence of light.

Knowledge was the very origin, perhaps, of all the rifts and frustrations that have become apparent in my life. I might have been happier as a Jew of the ghetto, still believing confidently in his God and the Sacred Books, devoting his Sabbaths to the fun of *pilpul* distinctions of Talmudic right and wrong, flouting tiny details of the sacred edifice of the Law but never going beyond the approved limits of the game. But I could only see, in those days, the element of new adventure, and I approached it violently and full of confidence, sure that I had everything to gain. All my family difficulties, from now on, took on the appearance of unworthy worries. I had the whole world to conquer.

A month later, I successfully passed the scholarship examinations that relieved me of almost all the school fees, much to Monsieur Bismuth's satisfaction. The city high school isn't free, which of course reduces one's chances of being admitted to it. I was less brilliant in the exams for the school certificate than had been expected: I was too confident and, carried away by the impetus of my enthusiasm, had already embarked, in my mind at least, on my high school career.

Sami Michael

Sami Michael (Iraq-Israel, 1926–) was born in Baghdad and attended Jewish schools there. In response to the Iraqi government's support for Nazi Germany, Michael joined Iraq's Communist underground. Forced to flee Iraq in 1948, he went first to Iran and then, in 1949, to Israel. He studied Arabic literature and psychology at Haifa University and worked for Haifa's Arabic newspaper, *Al-Ittibad*. Michael's place in Israeli literature is unique in that he identifies himself as an Arab Jew, and his use of Hebrew is strongly influenced by Middle Eastern elements. The discrimination that non-Ashkenazic Jews experience in Israel is a recurring theme in Michael's work. He is the author of the acclaimed novel *Refuge* (1977; English, 1988), which was translated from the Hebrew by Edward Grossman. Set in the early days of the Yom Kippur War, *Refuge* tells the story of Arab Jews who decide to become Communists as a response to the discrimination they experience in Israeli society. Another subject that appears in Michael's work is the Israeli-Palestinian situation. His other books include the international bestseller *Victoria* (1993; English, 1995), which chronicles the lives of Iraqi Jews in the twentieth century and whose title character is based in part on Michael's mother, and *A Trumpet in the Wadi* (1987; English, 2003), about the intersecting lives of Christian Arabs, Muslims, and Russian Jews in the Arab quarter of Haifa. Michael has also written plays and books for young adults. He adapted *Refuge* for the stage in 1980 and *A Trumpet in the Wadi* in 1988. He also published *These Are the Tribes of Israel* (1984), a series of twelve interviews with Knesset members, journalists, and other Israeli personalities.

From *Refuge*

Marduch was in the bathroom, and his voice was muffled behind a towel as he asked, "If Israel is wiped out, what will future generations remember about it?"

Shula, who was dressing obstinate, helpless Ido, mumbled something.

"Only two things." Her husband answered his own question. "Fantastic desert agriculture, and the royal screwing the Arabs got. And I've got nothing to do with either."

Shula and Marduch both belonged to the Party, and thus stood disgraced in Jewish society. But Shula balked silently at wearing the yoke of ideological discipline the Party imposed on its members, whereas Marduch questioned everything and everybody. Now, as she held out his shorts for him, Shula's son thrust his head forward. "Children your age can dress themselves," she scolded him. Ido stared at her stupidly with his beautiful eyes.

"What did you say?" Marduch asked from the bathroom.

"You can always change jobs. You're not married to the stationery company. You could sell tractors just as well."

"Right. I'm not married to anything."

Shula knew this trait, this mark of transience, impermanence. As if Marduch went about with a knapsack on his back, prepared at the first sign to set off again on his wanderings. Ido, the retarded child, was his only anchor. Her husband loved but did not trust her—trusted no one. Ten years they had been married, and it still seemed as if he were expecting her to make some important announcement. As a result, Shula felt, deep in her heart, that she was still in love with Rami.

She struggled with her son's rigid, twisting feet. "I can't fasten your sandals for you this way. Relax. Come on. Relax."

"What?" Marduch said.

"They won't wipe out Israel!" Shula called.

"How do you know?"

She gave Ido a pat on the knee and shrugged. How? Because Rami's a lieutenant colonel. Because he's standing up on the Golan Heights like the mast on a ship. Because the end of Israel would be the end of Rami. Because they won't get by him so easily. Aloud she said, "Because!"

Marduch laughed his flat, intellectual, jailhouse laugh. "Glorious empires have collapsed before," he said. And added, without connection, "When they hauled me off to the desert, I saw a buffalo run amuck and destroy an entire village. Left not a single mud hut standing. Killed ten Lords of the Creation. A dumb buffalo, who can't drive a car or row a boat, killed ten human beings like the ones who sent a rocket to the moon. Can you imagine?"

Shula pulled Ido to his feet and held his limbs, slack now, between her knees. She combed his hair, so like her own. "You just don't know these people," she said, but what she meant was, "You don't know Rami." She was thinking of Rami this morning because last month she'd heard that he was divorced and last night she had dreamt about him. In her dream it's spring, she wears a springtime dress and a smile on her lips, and they're on their way to a gallery to see an exhibition of paintings. They go from room to room, and there are flowers, nothing but flowers, and the walls shimmer like transparent screens projecting light, and they don't even look for the paintings, which aren't there anyway. The light speckles Rami's eyes, and he walks without touching her, striding along in his army boots, and he's big and strong and she's a little girl from Kiryat Haim. Twice she called him "Daddy," but he didn't hear.

Her own father had always been an old man.

Marduch, too, is a father of sorts. Maybe he has more of the qualities of a mother than of a father. He's dark-skinned, but he's not an Arab, and he had knocked Rami out of the running. Shula's mother, lying on her single bed, separated by a wide space from her husband's, had spent many sleepless nights. She and Haim the Technician student and Mahmoud the teacher had made a pact against Rami. Yet it was precisely when Shula's ties with Rami dissolved that her mother was seized with panic—she feared that Shula might take revenge on her by bringing an Arab home. She would sit in the company of some of the women comrades from the fifties, who had buried their husbands in the forties, airing her worries until the others got fed up and silenced her with the pious reproach: "You're a chauvinist!"

Most of these comrades didn't have children, and not a single one had a daughter. These blighted old women abhorred male flesh and for the objects of their Platonic love chose none other than the Arab leaders of the Party. In those crucial months when Shula and Rami were separating, Marduch seemed heaven sent. An airplane had brought him from Iraq, straight from jail after he had served a sentence of thirteen years' hard labor. The hearts of the women comrades went out to him. Only once in a great while would he straighten up to his full height. He seemed still to dread that cudgel raised to strike him in the back. He preferred tête-à-tête conversations—otherwise he listened passively. But he was all the rage. He'd been arrested at the age of seventeen, the women comrades said, taking pains to be precise—really just a child. He had been brought to Israel against his will. Released from prison in the desert, he was dispatched by registered air mail to the Jewish State. For a while, the Arab members of the Party had bided their time, but when they realized that he preferred not to speak of the atrocities that had taken place back there, they offered him their sincere friendship. His smile was as bashful as an adolescent boy's. He shunned loud noises and bright lights. He couldn't dance and he garbled foreign names. When Shula took up with him, her mother accepted it; she even resigned herself to people cracking pumpkin seeds in the living room and relieving themselves in the courtyard.

She kept a sharp eye on Shula's belly. "What, already?" she cried. That same month she withdrew her savings and bought a spacious apartment for them, up on the slopes of Mount Carmel. Four bedrooms for the flock to come. Mother tried to teach daughter the principles of prudent married life, but the only method that she knew was abstinence. Her talks with Shula veered off course and went in circles, leaving the mother blushing and the daughter bewildered.

To the mother's growing astonishment, the deluge of children failed to materialize. Two rooms stood empty and unused. Ido was the obstacle. Six years passed, and Tova, the mother, asked Shula, the daughter, "Well?"

Shula shook her head.

"It was just chance," said Tova. "It doesn't mean anything."

"It's an omen," Shula replied.

"You're giving up!" Tova cried, as she did during question time at Party meetings.

"He doesn't want to."

"What?" Tova could not understand. She herself had been obliged to employ some curious stratagems to wean her Zalman from his beastly habits. From time to time the English had helped by jailing him for considerable periods. And Zalman was a mild-mannered fellow, a bookworm. Marduch's a solid hunk of a man, and besides, he comes from there, from Iraq, from an Arab country. "But how? How can it be?" Tova asked, her voice trembling noticeably. Secretly, she hoped that Shula would let her in on her clever little tricks. "Just like that, for no reason? He just doesn't want to . . . ?"

Shula exploded. "It's disgusting! Your generation finished sex off, but you're still nosey about it."

As far as Tova was concerned, her daughter might have been speaking in Sanskrit. She heard her out and then said, "So tell me . . . tell me about it." She blushed. "I don't have to teach you how."

"He's afraid, Mother."

Tova suppressed a smile. She'd never heard of fear holding a man back. "Afraid? Of you?"

"Of another Ido."

This she could understand, and it made her furious. It was a clear evasion of duty. Here is a man refusing to ram his head against a wall, just because he doesn't believe he can break through. "Listen, child." Tova adopted her Party-meeting tone. "Do you know how many brothers and sisters we were in our family? Seven." She raised seven fingers, stained yellow with nicotine. "The first was buried the same day he was born. The second came along and he was just fine." She folded two fingers and dropped one hand to her angular knee. "The third was so-so. We cried when he laughed and we laughed when he cried. He grew up but he stayed a baby. One day he went to have a look at the mob that was looting the shops in town, and we never saw him again." Her thumb pressed flat in the palm of her hand. "The rest of us? Look at us now. . . . No problems!"

Shula shook her head. Hatred flashed briefly in her gray eyes and then was snuffed out.

"Tell your husband he's making a mistake. He's from back there in Iraq, and when it comes to complicated matters like this, he obviously doesn't know the first thing."

NOW THAT SHE had dressed Ido, Shula was weak and irritable. Marduch was in the other room. "Have you invited them already?" she asked him.

"No. Anyhow, Shoshana's going to be here soon, and you can tell her."

"And you'll sit around the whole evening reciting Arabic poetry?"

She remembered that Rami detested poetry. When they were young, he had refused even to pretend for her sake. He said that poetry readings smelled like the slogans that she and her parents spouted. Only the simple-minded believed that human thought could be expressed in a couple of words, contained in rhyme and meter. By its very nature, poetry, like propaganda, negates doubt. And doubt is what sets man apart from the beasts. So go to the university and philosophize there, she challenged him; stop hiding in a tank. You can meditate in a tank, too, he answered. She told him that that sounded like a line of poetry, and he said that it was just a fact.

Haim the student and Mahmoud the teacher told her that after reprisal raids, Rami dismembered the Arab corpses, arranged the arms and legs like so many sausages, and then photographed them.

She confronted him with this and he said that if she believed that, she must be sick.

"Shula," Ido said, "I want to go to Daddy."

"So go. He's in the kitchen."

"Daddy! Daddy!" His shout was like that of a ten-year-old, his lurching walk a three-year-old's. "Shula says I can eat with you."

"Okay. How about a kiss?" And a moment later, "I think the kid's running a temperature."

"I'll tell Shoshana not to take him out."

Another smacking kiss.

The sound drove her to the bathroom, where she stood facing her reflection in the mirror, thinking of Rami again. Her thoughts gravitated to him, though not out of desire. She got no erotic thrill thinking of him. She didn't consider him a missed opportunity. She loved Marduch—loved him as a woman loves her husband after eleven years of marriage. Yet her womb cried out for Rami. She tried to persuade herself, with her own special brand of logic, that with Rami she wouldn't have conceived Ido. And even if Ido had come along, Rami would have tried again: He's a soldier, and if the first assault fails, he doesn't give up.

Marduch is stamped with the caution, the excessive caution, of a man who's been in the underground.

Once and only once in his life he had blundered, and he paid for it back there with his whole youth. Once he had quoted a saying to her from the folk wisdom of another people: "A wise man doesn't fall into the same hole twice."

He keeps the contraceptives under a heap of towels in the closet. Eight months ago, while he was away, she climbed up on a chair and found the packets. She took a pin and poked. When she drew the pin out, she saw the fine rubber sealing over the hole she had made. Although she was alone in the house, she glanced over her shoulder; then she bit into the rubber, its taste vapid on the tip of her tongue.

For three weeks she concealed a sly smile behind her gray eyes. When she opened her mouth, laughter would roll out. She hugged the children at the kindergarten, embraced the jars of sugar and jam in the kitchen, and spread her arms around the azure bay visible through the windows of the apartment. She walked on tiptoe, as if dancing. Her whole being was focused on the sweet tick-tock of her body's inner clock. Marduch suspected nothing, but her radiant face aroused his feelings. Within a week he had used up all the packets under the towels and bought more, and she welcomed him, giggling shyly, like an Eskimo girl.

This charade ended in a crimson nightmare. The clock was turned back and started ticking away again toward the next month, hopelessly.

From the bathroom she asked, "Do we have to invite Fatkhi, that poet of yours?"

Ido caught up the word *poet*. "Poet, doet, shoet, Shula's crazy!"

"Fatkhi's okay," Marduch said.

"That's what you think."

"When we're out working in Tel Aviv, all the girls devour him with their eyes. I have to pinch myself to prove that I'm there, too."

"You're silly," she said with genuine affection.

"I'm not blind," he said.

"Are you jealous of him?"

"Sometimes."

"No kidding." She laughed. Suddenly the clouds inside her dispersed, her spirits glowed. A ray of light, a sudden surging moment of happiness. "You're more of a man than he is. My girlfriends . . ."

He gagged on his coffee—he wasn't used to compliments from a woman. "Well, then," he asked, "is it yes or no?"

"If that's what you want, it doesn't matter to me. But it'll be just too bad for both of you if you sit around reciting Arabic poetry all night."

"Okay, okay. I promise. Shalom, Shula. I have to run."

Ido panicked. "Daddy!" he cried.

"Son, tomorrow's a holiday, we'll spend the whole day together."

"What holiday?"

"Tomorrow's Yom Kippur. That's why you're not going to school today. Shalom, Ido."

He opened the door in that cautious way of his and, although he was late, he took the stairs down to the street slowly and deliberately. After all these years, he still had not rid himself of the habit of checking every corner along the way.

"Marduch," Shula called after him, giving voice to the happiness that was surging in her—but her husband was gone. With an urgency that she herself couldn't understand, she hurried out to the balcony, hoping to see him emerge from the staircase and get into the car. But he was already in the car. The exhaust pipe coughed transparent fumes, Marduch drove off, and she didn't see him. She leaned on the railing and gazed at the smoke of the refineries and tried to recall when she had last seen his face. She stood consoling herself: People who live together rarely look one another in the face. When she was depressed she didn't see people, and this morning she was very depressed. She hadn't caught a glimpse of that hard face, marked by the blind assurance of a man who can cross the desert alone, who learned from childhood to master loneliness. Suddenly she realized that she was sucking her finger, and she took it out of her mouth and turned this way and that to see if anyone had caught her red-handed, and blushed even though no one was there. You're crazy, she scolded herself. He went to work. He'll come back. This is his home. You are his wife.

Sometimes it seemed to her that Marduch wasn't as sure about this as he might be. On several occasions she had discovered him propped up on his elbows, gazing at her face in the uncertain, deceptive light of dawn. His dark eyes were keen and penetrating, and she imagined that his eyes alone had awakened her. The first time this happened, she snuggled up to him and murmured, "Can't you sleep?" And dozed off again without waiting for an answer. Once she started up out of her sleep and laughed to conceal what she felt. "What's the matter, Marduch?"

His smile then was odd, very odd. "You're still here." He paused, raised his arm and pointed east. "Back there, everything vanished with the dawn."

His face, she saw, was glistening with sweat. The tufts of hair trembled on his bare chest with every breath he took. "You're sick," she said. She wiped the sweat from his brow and kissed him on the temple.

He shook his head, frightened still. "How long?" There was a kind of wonder in his voice.

She hadn't understood, and tried to soothe him. "It'll pass, all this will pass away. It won't last long."

He shivered. "No, no," he cried. "It will pass, sure, but don't say so. That's terrible."

"Are you scared?" She couldn't believe it.

"When I was back there, I imagined what you'd be like. Gray eyes, a nose just like this . . ." Dreamily he started to unbutton her nightgown. "Two big dark crowns on your tits." He threw the blanket from her. "Legs . . . even all these different colors. Have you got any idea how many colors your body has? Black, gray, white, pink, brown . . ."

"Enough!"

His pupils were wide open. "Even your voice."

"My voice is as ordinary as can be."

He was hurt—she had struck a blow at his fantasy. "What are you saying? It's a voice that comes from deep in the garden. It carries the scent of water. It's a woman's voice."

"You see what that Arabic poetry does to you?" she said.

"And every morning you'd fly away, you'd escape from the coughing and the TB and the rattling of our chains. I never held that against you, Shula."

She put a finger out to his face, touching him. "Did they put you in chains?"

He drew back, laughed uneasily. "Oh, it was nothing, nothing . . ."

"Tell me. I'm your wife."

"You're spoiling the fantasy," he said and bent to kiss her. "What is there to tell?" he asked, evading the question like a child.

She moved away from him, angrily. "Tell me!"

He shook his head.

"You told me you got the scars on your wrists and ankles when you were a child. But it's not true. You lied to me."

Again he shook his head.

"Look!" she pulled at the blanket, wrestled with him and touched the pale, purplish, dried-up skin. "They took a little boy, chained him, and threw him into the desert."

"I wasn't a little boy then," he said defensively, as if guilty.

"And all this time you haven't said a word."

"It doesn't hurt any more."

Her eyes flashed. "You were afraid of embarrassing the comrades, weren't you?"

"Oh, come on! Really, you're ripping the fantasy to shreds."

She flopped down onto her back and said, in a dry voice that was unfamiliar to him, "What kind of fantasy could you have had back there?"

"You see? You're asking completely senseless questions. Fantasies flourish back there. Once we called a strike. They surrounded the prison with armored cars and cut off the water. We dug a hole with our fingers in the courtyard until we reached damp mud. The leaders of the secret Party cells were talking of manifestoes and petitions, but all I was thinking was that thanks to the strike, I could lie in bed longer in the morning, and you wouldn't run off."

She relented. "Baby."

"And then . . ."

"Tell me, go on. Why stop?"

"It's not important."

She embraced him, her nose touching his cheek. "And then?"

He pushed her away gently, and gazed at the ceiling. "Then . . ."

"Is it so hard for you?" she asked.

He nodded.

"Then don't tell me," she said, frightened, as if she were standing on the brink of some dark abyss.

"And then they took him away."

"Took who?"

"My brother. Next day, at dawn, they displayed his body in the square. He was as shy as a girl. Ours was a rough man's world. And he was so gentle. They had to pick him, his body, to show off to the women and children, hanging from a rope." Marduch rubbed his face in his powerful hands. He came back to his senses.

"Enough," he said. "Let's get up."

Shula stayed where she was. "And you're still afraid."

"Because of you."

"Because of me," she said modestly.

"You might slip away again."

"I'm here. I'll always be here."

He was on his feet now. "Everything slips away. The only thing that's sure is what's already been. As for tomorrow, I'm no prophet."

"If I leave," Shula said, "you'll find someone better than me."

He threw her a reproachful look. "That's not funny."

It never occurred to him that this same fear, multiplied and magnified, was settling into her own heart. She could never be certain that he had stopped wandering and really intended to settle down. He came from back there. She didn't know anyone from his family. He was tied up in knots that he had yet to reveal to her. She wanted to know about his past. About every day of his life. Only after reliving his life would she know whether he'd stopped roaming.

Ido had been quiet too long, so now Shula left the balcony and found him in the bathtub, rolling in soapy, milk-white water. His shirt and pants stuck to his skin and the dirty water spilled from the corners of his mouth like saliva. "Ido, what are you doing?"

Occasionally words meant nothing to him, tones of voice made no impression. But he was always sensitive to faces. He looked at Shula. He tried to get out at once but slipped. "I wanted to clean the tub," he wailed.

The doorbell rang, and Shula called, "It's open!"

Shoshana came in and pushed Shula to one side. She attended to the child, saying in a comforting voice, "They can really drive you up the wall."

Shula wept silently and didn't respond.

"It's no disaster," Shoshana added. "I'll dress him in a minute and take him for a walk."

"He's a bit feverish."

"Then we'll stay in."

"Shoshana."

"Don't cry," she scolded. "At least he's not unhappy."

"But what could be worse than this?"

"When your son's got an I.Q. of one hundred and forty and his father's an Arab and his mother's a Jewish whore, that's what."

"How's your back?"

"They took a beautiful X-ray. There are three screwed-up vertebrae."

"Don't you dare do any housework," her friend warned her. "Put the child to bed and rest a while."

Shoshana was Shula's age, but she looked like a horse that had been let out to pasture. Only her sense of humor remained from her carefree youth, and in the meantime even that had become embittered. "Your mother's paying me good kosher money."

"Is your conscience bothering you?"

"Conscience? What conscience?"

"Then rest a while."

"Spare me the rest. Rest is all I need to go crazy."

"Shoshana, I'm going to fire my helper at the kindergarten. You want the job?"

"Do you think that's more respectable than taking care of Ido?"

"You're awful."

"We need the money."

"Well?"

"Amir and Naim and Victor stuff themselves with humus and jam. Your mother's money is good money."

"It's not nice for me."

"You're crazy. Just think how many meals I turn this money into."

"Marduch wants to invite you and Fuad and that poet Fatkhi over for tomorrow night."

"Then he should get the American cigarettes ready for Fuad."

"Call up Fuad."

"Okay. So go already."

Shoshana got Ido dressed and played with him a while and then put him to bed. Then she swept the spacious apartment. She stood in her bra and panties facing the mirror and spat into it. Then she wiped it off with a newspaper, cursing it and her mother and her brother and the Arabs and the Chosen People. She poured a cup of coffee and sat herself down next to the telephone. The editor-in-chief's obscene, measured voice sounded in her ear. "Good morning, Shoshana. How are you?"

She sensed the restrained anger in his jovial voice.

"Let me speak to Fuad."

"He's in an editorial meeting. It's Friday."

"Editorial meeting! All you do there is screw each other."

"What do you expect us to do? There aren't any women here."

"Go get Fuad."

"Is it an emergency?"

"No. I just wanted to tell him that he forgot to comb his hair with brilliantine this morning."

"Fuad, the woman's on the line."

"What?" her husband shouted.

"Fuad . . ." And she stopped short, hearing two voices shouting at each other and the screams of a third rising above them. "Fuad, can you hear me?"

"In this madhouse? Comrades, a little quiet please. Hamdan, control yourself. Keep your antics for home. What we're telling you is that your writing is shit, so face it: It stinks. One of these days you'll land us all in the soup. . . . Yes, that's my opinion and I'm sticking to it. You're a member of the editorial board here, here in fucked-up Israel. You're not the P.L.O.'s foreign correspondent. If you want to write . . . No! Listen to me. If you want to write just to please them, then go do like Fakhri did and go to Beirut. Here you've got to consider public stinking opinion." Fuad remembered his wife. "So what do you want?" he said to her.

"Marduch and Shula have invited us over to their place tomorrow night. Pass the invitation on to Fatkhi."

"The females in Tel Aviv have turned his head. He took today off, and he's taking tomorrow, too. . . . Your Jewish Yom Kippur."

"So what should I say?"

"You want to go?"

"Only if we haven't got any other place to hang out."

"You know very well that I like Marduch. Hamdan! I piss on your innuendoes. I'm weak-kneed, am I?"

"I'm hanging up."

"Listen, woman. Hamdan, as far as I'm concerned, you're still a child. It's not fear, I tell you. You won't find a single Jew who'll swallow the P.L.O.'s program whole."

"I'm listening," his wife reminded him.

"There's no paycheck today."

"It's already the fifth of the month."

"The treasurer's broke."

"Get a loan from somebody else at the office, then."

"They're all *tafranim* [paupers]. The only reason we're winding up the meeting is we've run out of cigarettes."

"There's nothing at home, Fuad."

"What can I do, woman?" he burst out. "I can't carry the whole world on my shoulders. Didn't you get some cash from Shula?"

"She doesn't touch it. Her mother handles the money."

"So ask her."

"I won't go to Kiryat Haim to beg."

"Okay, so we'll drink air and chew water. So long, woman."

"So long, Fuad."

Victor Perera

Victor Haim Perera (Guatemala-USA, 1934–2003) was born in Guatemala City. His parents were Sephardim from Jerusalem who resettled in Guatemala in the 1920s and then moved to New York when Perera was twelve. Perera graduated from Brooklyn College and received an M.A. from the University of Michigan. He taught journalism and creative writing at the University of California at Santa Cruz and then taught journalism at the Graduate School at UC Berkeley. "To be a Sephardi, I discovered, is to see the world as mystery, so that even ordinary events are infused with the sense of otherness," Perera wrote in the late 1990s. "Sephardim are prone to be polyglot and multicultural from infancy, as they crisscross religious and ethnic boundaries with deceptive ease." His first novel, *The Conversion* (1970), is about modern Sephardim in Spain. Perera is also the author of the memoir *Rites: A Guatemalan Boyhood* (1985) and of *Unfinished Conquest: The Guatemalan Tragedy* (1993). The excerpt that follows is from *The Cross and the Pear Tree: A Sephardic Journey* (1995), in which Perera unravels his family's labyrinthine Sephardic past, going all the way back to 1492 and uncovering in the process both Christian and Muslim ancestors. (He was convinced he was related to Yehuda Burla.) Perera's great-grandfather, Rabbi Yitzhak Moshe Perera of Jerusalem, had warned his sons and grandsons never to leave the Holy Land without his consent "from now to eternity," and the Perera family believes that the various tragedies that have befallen family members are directly traceable to the violation of this admonition. In 1988, Perera suffered a stroke from which he never fully recovered.

Israel

What was, what is, the aim of the Alliance? . . . In the first place, to cast a ray of the Occident into communities degenerated by centuries of oppression and ignorance; next, to help them find work more secure and less disparaged than peddling by providing the children with the rudiments of an elementary and rational instruction; finally, by opening spirits to Western ideas, to destroy certain outdated prejudices and superstitions which were paralyzing the life and development of the communities.

—Declaration, Alliance Israélite Universelle, 1860

I

"When we lived in Montefiore, in Jerusalem, we were poor, but we had no *espanto,* no fears like we do today. We bought our fruits and vegetables from the Arabs, and they bought from us the fruit jams my parents prepared. We moved in and out of the Old City walls like they were our backyard—and in fact that's what they were. Those were the days before the Arabs wanted to push us into the sea."

My aunt Rachel, youngest of my father's four sisters, has invited me to her apartment in Jolon, a suburb of Tel Aviv, to reminisce about the old days. In her mid-seventies, she is a grudging memoirist, and has waited until the eve of my departure to confide some of her stories. Her reluctance is fed by an unbending conviction that her four brothers and an older sister committed a fatal misstep when they emigrated to the New World. In the mid-1920s my father and two of his brothers opened a department store in Guatemala City, where I was born. Aunt Rachel regards their departure as the source of the calamities that befell the family during the next half century. Of the five émigrés, only one is still alive, her youngest brother, Moshe, who to this day runs a shoe store in Guatemala City.

The sad truth is that Aunt Rachel's own fortunes have not been that much better, for all her adherence to family tradition and the patriarch's injunctions to remain in the Holy Land. Her husband died of a coronary while still in his forties, and her firstborn son met the same fate at about the same age. On top of that, her two daughters have been unable to hold on to a husband; their success as career women cannot remove the compounded stigma of childlessness and divorce.

Today, in her tidy, pincushion-size apartment, Aunt Rachel seems almost voluble. She recalls that in 1935, when she was in her teens, her eldest brother, Alberto, brought from America the first gramophone ever seen in the Holy Land. (They called it a "patiphone.") Uncle Alberto played Caruso and Toscanini on his scratchy 78s, to the rapt wonderment of his mother and younger sisters.

"The truth is," Aunt Rachel confesses, "we were poor and terribly provincial, and could hardly afford a decent meal, much less luxuries like a patiphone. When your grandfather Aharon Haim gave me a piastra for a sweet on my birthday, it was an event. But we lived in peace with our Arab neighbors, and we observed our Sephardic traditions. After my father died in Alexandria, Alberto came to take my mother and the rest of us back to America. But when she overheard him bragging that they conducted business on the Sabbath and no longer kept kosher, my mother put her foot down and refused to leave. My older sister Reina, who was already married with children, Simha, my little brother Moshe and I all stayed behind as well."

I have learned enough family history to ask questions that unlock memories. In 1980 I was invited to a two-month residence at Mishkenot Sha'ananim in the Yemin Moshe quarter of Jerusalem, which my aunt still calls by the name of its founder, Montefiore. After Yemin Moshe was reclaimed from Jordan as a result of Israel's victory in the 1967 war, Jerusalem's mayor Teddy Kollek renovated the decayed buildings of Mishkenot and converted them into a sumptuous residence for visiting artists and scholars. During my stay there I discovered that I was two short blocks from the house where my father and his seven brothers and sisters had been born. My paternal grandfather, Aharon Haim, and his wife, Esther, had moved there in the 1890s from the Old City, where Aharon Haim's father, Yitzhak Moshe, lived until his death.

With the meteoric rise in property values during the past decades, Yemin Moshe has become gentrified, and now only the most successful artists can afford to live side by side with wealthy Jewish lawyers and businessmen, among them my cousin Avshalom Levy.

"Aunt Rachel," I prod her, "how was it when you were a girl? Can you describe a typical day in your life?"

"I already told you," she says testily. "We were poor but contented.

The Turks and the Arabs left us alone. The problems began with the British Mandate. I remember, whenever my mother baked bread I would take two loaves to my great-aunt Rivka, who lived alone inside the Old City. I was eight years old, but I walked in and out of the Old City gates without fear. The Arab vendors liked me, and sometimes gave me an orange or a sliver of *halwah.*" She shuts her eyes and sighs. "Today that time seems like a dream from another life."

"You say you were poor. How did you survive?"

Aunt Rachel turns on me her sharp-eyed look of reprimand. Her aquiline features and stern brown eyes convey a haughtiness that is only skin-deep. "You think because we had no fancy cars, no mansions and servants like you had in America, that we lived in misery? You think we had no pride? Your grandfather was a *shohet.* Don't you forget it. He butchered livestock and poultry according to the laws of *kashrut,* and he was paid well for it. In the winter he and my mother prepared jams and conserves from figs and other fruits, which they sold in the *shuk.* Our neighbors kept after my mother for her recipe, because their jams were thin and not as sweet as ours. Mother's secret was two spoonfuls of flour she mixed in with the fruit before she sealed the jar; she confided in no one, and the neighbors never suspected.

"My father was highly respected in the community, even by the Arabs. His grandfather, also named Aharon Haim, had been the Sephardic rabbi of Hebron. When we lived in Montefiore, my father held services in the Old City. And then he took it into his head to travel, ignoring his father's admonition not to leave Jerusalem. Before the First World War, Father had traveled to Bukhara, a Russian province in Central Asia, as a religious envoy, and stayed so long his congregation asked him to take a second wife. But he turned them down after his father sent him a stern telegram. In 1922, when I was a small girl, Father sailed to Alexandria, and from there he never returned. He developed a canker sore—they call it 'rose of Jericho'—and as he had no one to look after him there, the canker festered and got worse until it killed him."

"And you think his death was connected to his father's admonition?"

"Only God knows. Your father and uncles also flouted the prohibition by traveling abroad. My grandfather's testament was pinned to the wall, but no one heeded it." In 1973 Aunt Rachel and her two older sisters Reina and Simha showed me a framed document bequeathed by my great-grandfather Rabbi Yitzhak Moshe Perera of Jerusalem. In a flowing, prophetic Hebrew he exhorted his sons and grandchildren never to leave the Holy Land without his consent, "from now to eternity": "If ye have need to go abroad on a religious mission then ye shall go alone, and in no circumstances stay away from thine house for more than six months. . . . If ye heed my command not to live abroad from now to eternity, ye shall earn all the blessings of the Torah." Three blessings are enumerated: wealth, honor and a long life. The testament ends: "If ye comply with the above conditions then I, Yitzhak Moshe Perera, Servant of God, forgive thee. . . ."

In the center of the document is the three-letter Hebrew word *Nahash,* or "Snake." In 1992 I learned from an Israeli specialist in such documents that "Nahash" is an acronym for *Nidui, Herem,* and *Shamta,* which represent three degrees of excommunication. Evidently my great-grandfather meant business.

"Your grandfather Aharon Haim Perera was the first to break the pledge when he traveled to Bukhara and Egypt," Aunt Rachel reminded me. "He stayed only a few months in Alexandria, and then he died. After that your father and his brothers went to live in America, which my grandfather called 'the land of idolatry.' And look how they ended up."

In 1980 I traveled to Alexandria to retrace my grandfather's footsteps. In the Eliyahu Hanavi Synagogue I found a ledger recording the death of Aharon Haim Perera on January 22, 1923. But none of the surviving elders of the Jewish community remembered him, and I was unable to find his gravestone in the Jewish cemetery. Three years later, Aunt Rachel and one of her daughters traveled to Alexandria, but they had no better luck locating the grave than I had. She concluded that a lonely death and burial in a pauper's grave had been Aharon Haim's punishment for disregarding his father's commandment.

"Aunt Rachel, what was my great-grandfather Yitzhak like?"

"I don't remember. I was too little when he died. But my sister Reina remembers he was tall, had eyes like an eagle and a thick white beard, and always dressed in white. He never smiled."

"Where was he from?"

"I don't remember. I think it was Salonika. Or perhaps that was his father. At that time Salonika belonged to Turkey." I made a quick calculation. Twenty-three years after my great-grandfather Yitzhak Moshe wrote down his testament, the first trainloads of Jews left Salonika for Auschwitz.

Aunt Rachel turns toward me. "I just remembered something about your grandfather Haim." For the first time in my several meetings with her, her eyes appear to soften a little. Aunt Rachel's childhood years are the only ones in which she remembers having known happiness.

"The best time was the New Year, Rosh Hashanah. That's when he had the most work. On the eve of Yom Kippur neighbors brought him their poultry, and he performed a *kapara* [sacrificial ceremony]. He raised the chicken or goose by both feet and swung it over its owner's head, reciting a *berachah* [blessing]. Afterward they gave him part of the slaughtered chicken—the liver or breast, or a whole drumstick. The next day we broke the fast with our richest meal of the year.

"Of the older generation, the one I remember best was my maternal grandmother, Rachel, who married David Pizanty. She had named me herself, and so I was her favorite." The color rises to Aunt Rachel's cheeks. The hard lines dissolve. She is a small girl once again. "When I was little, she used to sit me beside her and smile naughtily. Although nearly ninety, she was a large, handsome woman with long silver hair that she combed every evening before she went to bed.

" 'We were *maderas*—"sticks"—when we were young,' she would say in Ladino. 'We knew nothing of the world, nothing. I was promised to your grandfather when I was twelve, and I knew nothing, nothing at all. But he was a handsome boy of fifteen, a little pale from too much study. His father was as strict as your grandfather Yitzhak, and he went to prayers every day. I learned his hours, and knew exactly when he would pass in front of our garden on his way to the synagogue. I would climb on the swing in time for the wind to lift my skirts just as he walked by, so he would look in and catch a glimpse of my white britches. That way, he would arrive at prayers with his cheeks aflame, and I knew he was mine.' "

Aunt Rachel dissolves into laughter, her cheeks flushed by the memory as her grandfather's had been by the sight of her grandmother's britches more than a century and a half ago.

II

IN DECEMBER 1989 I arrive in Israel to look after my eighty-six-year-old mother, who is dying of old age. This is my fifth visit with her since she and my father moved back to the Holy Land in 1960. Two years earlier, my father had sold his share of the department store in Guatemala City to his younger brother, Isidoro, known to his sisters as Nissim. Father died of a heart attack at age sixty-three, four months after returning to his place of birth. My aunts and cousins tell me that he died at peace, reconciled with the patriarch Yitzhak Moshe and his harsh posthumous judgment on his male descendants.

The discovery of my great-grandfather's testament had struck me with the force of revelation, just as my aunts had intended. Among other things, that parchment helped me begin to understand the tangled motives behind the sacrificial rites that Father had performed on himself and on me, starting with the day of my birth. Upon his arrival in the New World, Father turned his back on the religious observances of his forefathers. He resolved to slough off his inheritance and become a man of the world—a conversion, I was to discover, that has ample precedent in my family. Nearly all the Pereras (or Pereiras) in my ancestry have been either rabbis and Talmudic scholars or successful men of business, with a high percentage of crossovers. But that is for later.

When I was born in Guatemala City, Father ignored the standard practice in the Jewish community of sending for a *mohel* from Mexico; instead he had me circumcised by a gentile doctor who cut my foreskin with a book open at his side. When an Istanbuli rabbi was hired by the community five years later, he learned of my unclean circumcision and persuaded my father that I should undergo a proper *brit,* which the rabbi would perform himself. I have described that second circumcision—and my father's role in it—in a memoir that I began long before I had any inkling of my great-grandfather's testament.

Father, a lifelong Zionist, had studied and taught the Talmud in Jerusalem. In hindsight, I can only surmise that he somehow hoped to atone for his dereliction by putting an end to the Perera male line, embodied in myself. But the symbolic castration, although it scarred me psychologically, failed to achieve its purpose. When I reached maturity, I came to the conclusion that I had been the victim of double jeopardy. As the first-born son of a descendant of Yitzhak Moshe Perera, I was condemned to excommunication by virtue of having been sired by my father in the land of idolatry. By being born in Guatemala, I was redefining original sin.

On the other hand, civil law in a democratic society states that you cannot be punished twice for the same offense and so, rather than confirm me as a Jew, that second circumcision gave me license to renegotiate my forefathers' covenant with Yahweh. As I delved into my roots, I conceived an affinity with Pere(i)ras who had converted to Christianity to escape the Inquisition, only to reconfront their Jewishness after they fled from Spain and Portugal.

In later years I took an ironic revenge on Father by saving his life on two separate occasions: The first time was when he suffered a stroke; the second followed his first coronary. My pious aunt Simha, who worshipped Father, firmly believed I became an instrument of God's design to fetch him back in one piece to the Holy Land and assure him proper burial in the sacred ground of his ancestors.

Whenever I questioned Mother about my second circumcision, she invariably placed all the blame on Father. "I pleaded with him to send for a *mohel* when you were born, but he was intent on adopting modern ways. The second time, I entreated him day and night not to scar you again; but he was immovable, like stone. Rabbi Musan lectured him on Talmudic law, which he had sworn to uphold. He said you were a heathen, and only a proper *brit* could make you a Jew. My tears and supplications were in vain."

From my earliest awareness I had a sense of my mother as an unstable, egotistical woman who used me as a foil for her romantic fantasies. I did not believe in her tears and supplications to prevent my second branding. But following Father's death another side of Mother's personality surfaced unexpectedly. I would discover that she possessed a more sturdy, expansive self—a second bloom—that had lain dormant during her unhappy bondage in Guatemala.

Like Father, to whom she was a blood relation, Mother had been nurtured in a patriarchal religious tradition. Her father, Shmuel Nissim, had been a Jerusalem rabbi and a *shohet,* and a rival to Aharon Haim Perera. In 1973 my cousin Malka, eldest daughter of my mother's elder brother Jacob, took me inside the four underground Sephardic synagogues of Ben Zakkai, in the Old City. She pointed to the restored *bimah,* or raised altar, of the Istanbuli synagogue, the largest of the four, where our grandfather Shmuel Nissim had held prayer services. My paternal grandfather, Aharon Haim, and *his* father, Yitzhak Moshe, had led Shabbat services in the adjacent and far smaller Middle Synagogue. Like his cousin Aharon Haim, Shmuel Nissim was restless and ambitious, and traveled to Russia as a religious emissary. He arrived in Samarkand, where he was warmly received by the city's thriving Sephardic congregation, which invited him to become its head rabbi. Rabbi Nissim summoned his family to Samarkand, where Mother, her two sisters and older brother spent their early years. Around 1913, when Mother was seven, he sent them all back to Jerusalem, with the promise that he would soon follow. But World War I and Lenin intervened, and my grandfather could not get out. His congregation persuaded him to take a second wife, with the approval of the Beit Din, or rabbinical court of Samarkand; the Beit Din ruled that the marriage would be annulled the moment he was free to return to his first family in Jerusalem.

Grandfather was as good as his word. At war's end he left his second wife and two children behind and set out for the Holy Land. He traveled in a train crammed with Russian soldiers in the middle of a cholera epidemic. Grandfather caught the plague and died in a remote village in the Ukraine. He was buried in a common grave with hundreds of Russian soldiers who never came home from the front. Mother's brother Jacob traveled to the Ukraine to say Kaddish over Grandfather Shmuel's remains and to collect his prayer books and prayer shawl from the custodian of the cemetery. Like Aunt Rachel and her younger brother Moshe, Mother would grow up without the guidance and solace of a father.

Grandfather Shmuel's death when Mother was a young girl left her with a profound grievance against the world, an ineradicable sense of bright expectations forever dashed. "If my father had lived, I would have had a proper dowry, and another rooster would crow for me," she used to tell me, unmindful that if she had married another suitor, I would never have been born.

Following Father's death, Mother at last appeared to come to terms with her life. Her thirty years in the Americas gradually receded from her memory. She all but forgot her Guatemalan vernacular and went back to conversing in the Ladino she had known as a girl. She moved into a small apartment in Ramat Gan, two blocks from the flat of her widowed older sister Rebecca, who had been the rival beauty in the family. At fifty-three Mother was still a vivacious, attractive woman. But although she was not too old to remarry, she remained single, indulging in occasional flirtations with widowers and older married men.

WHEN I STAYED with Mother in the aftermath of the October 1973 war, she spent much of her time watching television and baking the Sephardic Middle Eastern dishes she loved: cheese and spinach *burrecas,* carp in gelatin, ground-meat *kubes* and her favorite almond marzipan and other sweets. After the late news on TV she sat in the dark for a long time, sighing heavily.

"This war has had a bad effect on me," she would say, staring at her gnarled hands. "Morally."

Her grandnephew Oded, the firstborn son of her firstborn brother Jacob's firstborn son Moshe, had been killed in action in the Suez. Oded, of whom great things had been expected, was the first member of our family to be killed in one of Israel's wars. He would not be the last.

In the afternoons Mother visited her sister. Aunt Rebecca had spent her youth and middle years in Egypt, and returned to Israel with her husband and two sons after the establishment of the state. She had been a widow for nearly twenty years.

"How did you like Golda last night?" Mother would ask at the door, and they proceeded to discuss the prime minister's latest speech in the Knesset, the color of her dress, the type of handbag she carried.

"It was green, the size of a shopping bag," Aunt Rebecca remembered, although she could not be certain because the image on her TV screen kept jumping.

"She's going shopping in the Knesset," Mother said, laughing aloud. "What a brave old lady," she added, shaking her head in admiration. "She flies around the world, telling everybody off, and she's already seventy-five. I'm only sixty-seven, and look what it costs me to cross the street." She showed Aunt Rebecca her swollen ankles.

Golda Meir was the only Ashkenazic Jew my mother and Aunt Rebecca wholly approved of.

Afterward they talked of their children and grandchildren, the latest movies on TV, the dishes they had planned for the week. When they got around to the war and Oded, they began to sway and moan softly.

"Qué negradea, qué negradea," my aunt said. "What a blackness. I knew him as a baby. He lived in my house a whole year when he was two." She wiped her eyes and pressed her chest to calm her heart.

"And poor Moshe," Mother said. "Alone in the family without his first-born. It is all on his shoulders now." They did not speak of Nehama, Oded's mother, whom they regarded as proud and headstrong, a regrettable mistake. "With all the attractive Sephardic girls in Israel," Mother remarked when I first arrived, "Moshe had to go and marry a stuck-up German intellectual. She gives him no peace."

Aunt Rebecca brought us tea and sweets.

"No, no tea for me today," Mother said. "When I am in a state like this, tea swells my intestines."

Aunt Rebecca nodded sympathetically and drew her shawl tight. "I can't have tea either. My heart pounds all night. It has been black, black like my star—*como la estrella mía*—since the news of Oded." In hard times Aunt Rebecca's thoughts invariably returned to Alexandria.

"We were so happy there," she says, as her eyes roll toward the ceiling and her face lights up. "We had live-in servants, a wonderful old villa, the best French schools for my two sons, and the oranges—ah, the oranges were large and golden, like the sun. . . ."

I stayed on with Aunt Rebecca when my mother went shopping. She poured more tea and watched me eat her clover-shaped marzipan. When

I finished she smiled girlishly and rubbed her hands. "Better than your mother's, no?"

The following day I escorted my mother and Aunt Rebecca to the home of their grandnephew Oded. Moshe, his wife, Nehama, and their fourteen-year-old son, Ofer, live in a spacious home in Ramat Hasharon, a fashionable Tel Aviv suburb. Moshe is a communications expert in the Israeli Army and makes several times the salary of his postal-worker father, Jacob. I had last seen them in New York City, where Moshe was on a tour of duty. In Flushing I had attended the bar mitzvah of Oded, who was a rail-thin, intense youngster with extraordinary black eyes. After his high-school graduation, Oded had returned to Israel to enlist in the army. He was one of the firstborn sons in our extended family who kept faith with the patriarch's commandment.

Nehama, a sabra of German and Lithuanian parents, has light skin and blue eyes. She looks more beautiful—and prouder—than I remember. She greets me with a smile and a firm handshake. "Forgive me," she says. "I do not yet know how to show grief. I will learn." She holds her head high as she sits Mother and Aunt Rebecca in the far sofa, and immediately begins to speak of Oded.

Oded, she says, died in a commando operation south of the Bar-Lev line on the fifth day of battle. He was a captain in the reserves, having served his regular army duty two years earlier. Still, he had volunteered for four missions and insisted on going on the fifth, a diversionary maneuver that would be the most dangerous.

She brings out photographs and a newspaper account of the battle, which is officially named "Battle of the Shades." Oded's intense black eyes look out from every photo.

Aunt Rebecca begins to sway and moan softly, but she is stopped by a sharp look from Nehama.

"Oded had to be first, always," Nehama says, addressing me. "He had always a very strong drive to excel. The day after he died, a scorecard arrived from the university, where he had studied engineering." She pauses, fighting back tears. "He had scored a perfect ten. . . .

"His strong competitiveness is partly my fault, I suppose," she says in a softer voice. "I have always been very strongly competitive, and I'm afraid I transferred much of it to my sons. I wanted Oded to be perfect. Not just good or very good, but perfect."

I look once more at the photos of Oded and feel drawn irresistibly into the myth-making process. I sense that the soul of all Israel is in this house.

I am still looking at photos when Moshe returns from the synagogue, where he has been saying Kaddish for Oded. The moment he walks in, Aunt Rebecca and Mother give vent to their grief.

"Qué negradea, qué negradea," they wail antiphonally, swaying from side to side. "It is not worth the pain to raise children and grandchildren," Aunt Rebecca says, "only to have them killed in the wars."

As we embrace, I feel on Moshe's shoulders the accumulated weight of our rabbinical ancestors. Haggard and stooped, he slumps into a chair and begins to speak of the war, slowly, in a thin voice. "In this war we have lost the flower of Israel's youth; a whole generation has been maimed and killed. We have paid a terrible price for our unpreparedness. It was not American pressure that kept us from protecting our borders; it was our arrogant assumption that the Arabs would not dare attack us again after '67."

He raises his voice. "It is written that the guardians of Israel cannot sleep, day or night. The Maccabees knew this, and the Zealots on Masada knew it also when they fought the Romans and destroyed themselves rather than be taken as slaves. Israel has always known war. The longest peace in this land lasted seventeen years, between the death of David and the later years of Solomon's reign."

"They are all our enemies now," interjects Nehama. "Everyone is against Israel. Look at Africa, where we invested so much money and technical assistance. We helped to bring them into the twentieth century, and they repay us by breaking relations with us. Well, let them go, let them all go. I say good riddance to them and all other fair-weather friends. Israel will survive without them."

"The Jews are always alone," Moshe says. "When they forget their traditions, tragedy results. This war is a punishment on Israel for its unpreparedness, for its excessive confidence and for the greed and materialism that were growing among our people. When Jews leave the path and forget their prophetic destiny, they find ways to bring about their own destruction."

Nehama agrees about the greed and materialism, but recasts it in her own terms. She is a disillusioned supporter of Golda Meir's Labor party. "This war has come in the middle of a wave of tremendous corruption," she says. "Everyone has gotten rich almost overnight, but they want more, always more. There is no more real parliament in this country. The Knesset has been taken over by power-mad, corruptible old men. Right now the young still do not have a voice in Israel's government. After peace is made this will be the main thrust of reform. The young soldiers who fought for this country will demand to be represented. When this happens, then Oded's death will begin to have some meaning for me."

Moshe looks at Nehama in silence as she gives in to tears at last. I feel the close bond of love between them, and also the rivalry—a competition between two ways of grieving, two ways of seeing the world, Sephardic and Ashkenazic. I look down once more at the extraordinary black eyes, the fine light-brown skin and firm set of the jaw in all the photos of Oded, and I see in them the two forces that shaped modern Israel.

Moshe gets up to pace the floor. "What is it about this piece of earth?" he asks, absorbed in Old Testament language and imagery. "What is it that made these young men burn and fight, burn and fight again? Where did they get the courage? I love my Oded, but I know he is no different from 99 percent of the young men of Israel's army. They all want peace. They don't like to fight, but if their country is endangered they will not hesitate to die in its defense. Oded—" he says, sitting down. "My son Oded went to his death as if it were an important appointment." He buries his head in his hands.

III

When I next visit Mother in 1980 I find her calmer than she was on my previous visit, although her morale has still not recovered from the October war and its aftershocks. She has become obsessed with the Ayatollah Khomeini.

The night of my arrival she sets before me a heaping plate of boiled lamb and rice. "See? I serve you meat," she announces proudly, as if we were back in the Palestine of her girlhood, when meat was a luxury.

Mother spends most of her days and her flagging energies preparing for hard times, though she has inherited a nest egg of hard-earned dollars from my father. In the evenings she rehearses her old age, sitting for hours in her cozy chair, bemoaning her faded beauty, the price of milk and eggs, her aching bones and her unlucky star. *"Como la estrella mía,"* has become her yardstick for the world's calamities. She watches both Arabic and Hebrew newscasts, so she can sigh *"Dios mío"* twice over and click her tongue. Her favorite is the weekly Ladino radio newscast, whose soft-voiced announcer consoles her by treating *"Las locuras de Khomeini"* ("the antics of Khomeini") as the aberrations of a demented distant relative who will sooner or later be put to rights. The down-to-earth Ladino idiom creates an illusion of continuity ("this too will pass") by reducing global crises to the dimensions of Mother's living room.

In 1980 Mother rarely visited Aunt Rebecca, who was seventy-six and in failing health. Mother lived for her grandson, Daniel, my sister's only child, who was seventeen and had grown up in Kibbutz Beit Oren, outside Haifa. Daniel would soon be subject to the Israeli military draft, although he was born in the States and has retained his U.S. citizenship. Before long he would have to decide whether to join the army or return to California, where his mother lives. My sister has spent the past fifteen years in a halfway house in Santa Cruz, recovering in slow stages from a severe mental illness that struck her down in her youth. When Daniel was three Mother brought him to Israel because my sister was no longer able to care for him.

"Take Danny with you," Mother urged me every morning. "I don't want him killed in the next war, like Oded."

By evening she had changed her mind. "No, Danny belongs here with me. He is an Israeli now, and America would spoil his sweet temper. Why, he can hardly even speak English."

Which was true. Daniel, a tall, strapping young man who loves riding the kibbutz horses and is a long-distance runner, seems in many ways more a sabra than his sabra cousins. He is a nurturer who cut his eyeteeth on caring and cooperating rather than on competing. I could picture him one day as a first-rate veterinarian. On the other hand, when I tried to envision him in the Israeli Army, in another war, my mind drew a blank. The fate of Oded was too vivid.

Mother's return to her origins has honed her storytelling skills. For the first time, she speaks of the hard times in the Holy Land during World War I. "The happiest years were before the war, here and in Russia with my father. When I was small I had two grandmothers to pamper me; my grandfather Jacob's first wife, Rivka, was barren, and under Jewish law he was permitted to take a second wife to bear his children. Rivka was the kindest person in our family. Having no children of her own, she spoiled all of us with affection and frequent small gifts. Your great-uncle Yehuda Burla, who became a famous writer, wrote of my grandfather and his two wives in his story "Two Women." At that time I thought our happiness would last forever. Although we were not rich by any means, we got by well enough. In Russia we were well treated by the Jews of Samarkand, who held my father in high esteem. Then the war came, my father stayed behind and died in Russia, and nothing has ever been the same again."

I ask her how they managed to survive during the war.

"The post office. My brother Jacob landed a job in the post office at Mount Tabor, and when I was sixteen they hired me as a mail sorter. The postmaster was a tall, kindly Britisher who complimented me on my excellent English. At sixteen, I already spoke seven languages, including Russian and Arabic. Jacob was married with two children and had mouths of his own to feed, so my small salary went for feeding my mother and sisters as well as myself. At an age when I should have been enjoying life, entertaining beaux and preparing my trousseau, I was the family's provider."

She showed me a photograph of the family taken after the war. The two beauties, Mother and Aunt Rebecca, stand erect and tall at opposite ends. Rebecca's right hand rests on the shoulder of her older brother. Uncle Jacob, who was to die in his sixties, looks care-worn and middle-aged, although he was not yet thirty. Mother's tresses nearly reach her waist. Their mother, Rachel, seated below, gazes sadly into the distance, her dignity intact. Between Mother and Aunt Rebecca stands Aunt Leah, not yet twenty, with steel-rimmed glasses and long black hair combed back behind her ears like a spinster's. My aunt Leah, who never married, would die of cancer in her early thirties. Mother seldom spoke of Leah, who lacked the cameo beauty of her older sisters and dressed in mourning black for most of her adult life.

"Leah became a victim of that terrible time," Mother acknowledges matter-of-factly. "We had so little to eat, a few crusts of bread and a fistful of potatoes or green beans. Mother boiled them with lots of salt to deceive our palates. But our stomachs were not deceived, and we went to bed hungry." Mother gazes at the ceiling, sorting out the images flickering before her eyes.

"Even after I started sorting mail at the post office we never had enough to eat. Mother and Leah were unaggressive, but Rebecca and I always got our share. If there were only two crusts of bread, Rebecca and I divided them between us." She reaches a thin, bony hand across the table and snatches at an invisible crust of bread. "Leah died of cancer brought on by vitamin deficiency. She had no iron in her blood. My mother also died years before her time. She was undernourished, but it was the sorrow that killed her."

Mother sighs, hunched low over the table by the dowager's hump that would twist her body within a few years into the gnarled shape of a Gethsemane olive tree. "In the end we did not get enough iron either, Rebecca and I, and that is why our bones are so brittle." ("Iron, animal!" Mother would scream in Guatemala, shoving a forkful of spinach into my mouth. "It's full of iron!")

The early deaths of her mother and younger sister were not the only shadows cast over Mother's years in the Americas. She told me of another brother, Natan, who was born two years before her and died long before the family picture was taken.

"Of malnutrition?" I asked in consternation.

"No, of the *ayin hara*. He was a very pretty boy, and the neighbors cast the evil eye on him."

IV

IN 1973 and again in 1980 I met with Dr. Eliyahu Eliachar, cofounder and vice president of the prestigious World Sephardic Federation and president for years of Jerusalem's Sephardic Council. Dr. Eliachar, a tall, aristocratic octogenarian whose family has lived in Jerusalem for eighteen generations, at first reacted skeptically to my proposal to write a chronicle of the Pere(i)ras. At the time I had only begun to probe the family tree, and the patriarchal legacy that had haunted the lives of my father and his brothers.

"You are evidently an educated, intelligent person," Dr. Eliachar remarked acerbically, "but in terms of understanding your ancestry, you are still in swaddling clothes. You come from a distinguished family with deep roots in Jerusalem, and you know next to nothing about them."

Having put me smartly in my place, Dr. Eliachar went on to expound in his elegant English on the erosion of the Sephardic communities in Israel and throughout the world. "The fate of the Sephardim may well be decided in Israel within your lifetime. The problem is most acute here, for we comprise well over fifty percent of Israel's population. The tragic reality is that we are losing not only our religion but our cultural cohesiveness, and to a large extent we have only ourselves to blame. We have permitted ourselves to be exploited by unprincipled Ashkenazic leaders who turn us against one another by playing on our feelings of inferiority."

Dr. Eliachar denounced the efforts of Israel's first prime minister, David Ben-Gurion, to prevent what he called the "levantinization" of Israel by segregating the North African and Oriental Jews from the Eastern Europeans and the established Sephardic families. "Most of the Iraqis and the Moroccans never lived in the Iberian Peninsula, and they do not speak Ladino," Dr. Eliachar conceded, "but they are our blood brothers all the same. The sad truth is that we too have our 'Uncle Toms'—Sephardim who give lip service to solidarity with the North African and Oriental Jews but have sold their souls to the state. Unfortunately, your great-uncles Yehuda Buda and Nissim Ohanna, who was chief Sephardic rabbi of Haifa, fall into this category. They became leading spokesmen for the state's discriminatory policies. The Ashkenazim have come to me as well, offering me laurels, pensions and whatnot. I tell them, 'I don't need your honors. I distribute them.'

"Our present decadence," Dr. Eliachar continued, with his silken inflection, "began a hundred and twenty years ago when the Alliance Israélite Universelle, an international Jewish body based in Paris, began to erect elementary schools—lycées—all over the world. They were established with the best of intentions, to help raise the standard of living in poor Sephardic communities. Under the guise of eliminating centuries of Oriental superstition and backwardness, however, the Alliance did irreparable damage to our Sephardic traditions and customs. Throughout the Middle East and North Africa, lycées began to supersede and replace the yeshivas, which had provided not only excellent religious training but a sound secondary education. These yeshivas were the backbone of our Sephardic identity. Many of our brighter young men, who formerly would have gone on to rabbinical studies, contented themselves with elementary schooling in these lycées and then went on to white-collar occupations to earn money for their families. This, in essence, is what befell your father's and mother's generation in Jerusalem."

His introductory lecture over, Dr. Eliachar pulled from his bookshelf a biographical dictionary of illustrious Jerusalemites and thumbed through it, picking out Pereras and Pereiras who had made their mark in the Holy Land over the centuries. There were Kabbalistic rabbis, noted scholars, and Abraham Israel Pereira, a Dutch Marrano businessman and author who had founded yeshivas in Jerusalem and Hebron in the seventeenth century without ever setting foot in the Holy Land.

"These are only the tip of the iceberg," Dr. Eliachar assured me. "To get the full story you will have to dig into the Inquisition archives of Portugal, Spain, Holland, and the New World. Your great-great-grandfather came here from Salonika, whose Sephardic community, as you know, was all but exterminated by Hitler. But your roots here go back much farther. To find them, you will have to go back to the beginning and work your way to the present. In the process, you may be able to find the link connecting the Dutch Pereiras, who were Marranos, or secret Jews, with the Portuguese Pereiras who are your direct ancestors. I suspect you will find ancestors who played a role in the Sephardic Golden Age in Spain. You will also have to discover your ancestral Jewish name before the Inquisition foisted on your family the name Pereira, and engraved the pear tree on our family escutcheon. Once you have dug up your original Jewish name, you can trace your origins prior to the Iberian Peninsula, possibly all the way back to the Twelve Tribes. It should be an interesting journey, and one full of surprises. I wish you the best, and do keep me posted on your progress." Dr. Eliachar rose stiffly to shake my hand, signaling an end to our interview.

As he showed me to the door, I presented him with a photocopy of Yitzhak Moshe Perera's testament. Dr. Eliachar's impeccable composure faltered, and his face paled. "I have written a similar document for my sons," he said.

Eliyahu Eliachar died two years later. His widow, Hava, a stately Russian Jew imbued with Dr. Eliachar's patrician dignity as well as his dry humor, is carrying on her husband's life work. At our first meeting she offered to make his extensive library available to me. And then she voiced regret that their two sons had emigrated to America, and showed little interest in family history. Dr. Eliachar's sons had, it seems, disdained their father's testament as resoundingly as my grandfather had evidently ignored his father's.

V

Aunt Rebecca, who lived with her elder son Morris, died of cervical cancer in 1987. Two years later my mother moved to a state nursing home in the heart of Ramat Gan. Her sister's death deepened Mother's despondency, which never left her after the death of Oded. Israel's invasion of Lebanon in 1982 had soured Mother on Menachem Begin, who had been favored by most Sephardim. She switched her loyalties to David Levy, Begin's Sephardic housing minister, who later became foreign minister under Yitzhak Shamir, although he speaks hardly a word of English.

In 1989 a second tragedy struck an enlisted young man in our family, this time on my father's side. Eighteen-year-old Boaz, a tall, gangly grandson of Aunt Simha, was killed in a car crash during a weekend leave from his army posting on the West Bank. The story made all the papers after his seventeen-year-old girlfriend, who announced that she had no desire to live without Boaz, was killed a week later in an automobile accident in

Eilat. Boaz, a Peace Now supporter, had been a prison guard in the Gaza camp of Jebaliyah, a bitter experience that had poisoned his sympathy for the Palestinians.

"All the best of our young men are dying," Mother remarked when I informed her of the death of Boaz. Mother had been close to Aunt Simha and her children, the only family members on Father's side who continued to show an interest in her.

At the nursing home Mother declared, "I have grown old *en un dos por tres,*" a Ladino phrase that roughly translates as "in a trice." Arteriosclerosis was clouding Mother's memory, and her dowager's hump had caused her frame to shrink several inches. During her last year of life, she weighed less than she had as a twelve-year-old girl, and stood no taller. Still, her spirits rallied whenever Daniel or I came to visit, and although she was by no means the youngest, she was by all accounts the liveliest resident of the home.

When Daniel and I were both abroad, her most frequent visitor was her nephew Morris, a sixty-year-old bachelor who had transferred his nurturing vocation from Rebecca, his mother, to his last living aunt.

"She is the last of her generation," Morris reminds me without reproach as he presents Mother with *burrecas* and her favorite sweets. Mother returns his favors by calling him a prince and "my salvation." She made a point of complimenting Morris whenever Daniel and I were in the room. And she invariably greeted me with the rebuke, "Why can't you be more like your cousin Morris?"

Childhood stories poured from my mother with the least encouragement. The color rose in her emaciated cheeks, and her hands moved with a life of their own. Although her eyes were clouded with rheum, she could still peer into space to snatch at a memory and render it marvelously whole. Her favorite childhood recollection was the voyage to Samarkand, when she stayed on deck for hours on end. *"Bailaba y bailaba sin pena ni verguenza,"* she would say ("I danced and danced without guilt or shame"). The ship's captain, as Mother tells it, was so smitten by her that he wanted to buy her, and actually quoted her mother a price.

Toward the end of her second year in the nursing home, Mother's sclerosis worsened, and her spirits declined markedly. She complained constantly of bad food and of surly nurses who stole her dentures. When someone in the ward screamed, Mother invariably remarked, *"está pariendo"* ("she's giving birth") even if the scream came from a man. Mother prayed to God to deliver her from old age as she had once prayed to be delivered from Guatemala. "Why doesn't He take me? I have no teeth, my eyes are gone, and I have to be wiped clean like an infant. I am ready for the rabbi to give me the blessing."

One morning she accused an Arab orderly of having raped the nine-year-old granddaughter of her roommate, a senile Polish woman who spoke no Hebrew. And yet the Palestinian was the only male nurse she would allow near her after dark to change her underclothes and tuck her into bed. Mother's ambivalence toward Arabs is a family trait. She loved to watch Egyptian films on Jordanian TV, and she fondly recalled her childhood expeditions to Ein Kerem, outside Jerusalem, where the Arab residents invited her to pick oranges from their trees.

On the evening news Mother learned of Saddam Hussein, and he soon replaced Khomeini as her favorite monster. Mother assured the Iraqi nurse who served her dinner that Saddam was a new Hitler who would never rest until he had destroyed Israel. "He has no pity," she said aloud to anyone who would listen, "no pity at all." It would have amused her to know that President George Bush—among others—might have considered her a prophet.

Toward the end, Mother found kind words even for Father, whom she had often criticized for not having given her more children. "He was the only one of the Perera brothers with any brains," she said in one of her typical snap judgments. "The others were *calabazas*" (pumpkins).

Crouched in her wheelchair, Mother glances up to reproach me for not having married and given her more grandchildren. When I remind her that I had been married for twelve years to an East Indian woman she never approved of, she attempts, after thirty years of adamant silence on the subject, to make amends.

"I had nothing personal against your Hindu bride, but you have to understand I was brought up in a religious family. My father was a *shohet.*"

My hopes rise that we might yet make peace of a kind before her death. But on my next visit she gives me a sidelong glance and says, "You're waiting for me to die, aren't you, so you can remarry your little Hindu?"

The closest Mother and I came to reconciliation was during one of my last visits to the home, before she lapsed into incoherence. She concluded one of her oft repeated reminiscences with a Ladino phrase she had not used before: *"Agora ya kaparates mi storia."* ("Now you know my story.") And then, as if to emphasize that the gift of her life story did not come without strings, she added, *"Dices las vedrades, tienes que pagar."* ("You tell truths, you must pay.")

An old friend of Mother's who had known her in Guatemala advised me: "At bottom, your mother wished the best for you and your sister. And naturally she wished the best for herself. She could not always tell the difference." I have come to regard this syllogism as Mother's epitaph.

MOTHER DIED IN June 1990 and was buried in a new cemetery in a Tel Aviv suburb. The state, which takes responsibility for its citizens when they are born, when they apply for marriage and after they die, turned down her request for a grave site next to her sister Rebecca, on the mistaken ground that it was already taken. As the next of kin, I was invited into the morgue to identify Mother's body, and I noted that her face was contorted in a grimace, as though she had died in struggle. The coarse shroud that covered her body was labeled *isha* (woman); only the men are buried in their prayer shawls. She was laid in the ground, enclosed by four slabs of concrete.

A Sephardic prayer maker recited the Kaddish at her funeral. The prayer maker, who mispronounced her name "Ferrera," as though she were Italian, snipped the top of my worn T-shirt with his scissors as a token of bereavement and extended his hand for payment before I had finished my recitation. The summer sun was pitilessly hot and bleached the sky of all color. There were no trees in view—not even the obligatory cypresses—only sand dunes and rows upon rows of incised granite or marble tombstones from Hebron. Despite her seven languages, her brief career in the post office, her thirty years abroad and her irrepressibly alert, lively mind, Mother lived her eighty-six years unable to conceive of a life lived outside the traditions of her forefathers. What would she have made of the startling hypothesis that the original Five Books of Moses were composed by a woman?

Seven months after her death, one of Saddam Hussein's Scud missiles landed in Ramat Gan, a few short blocks from Mother's nursing home. Two elderly people, the first casualties of Hussein's attacks on Israel, died of heart attacks. They could have been Mother and Aunt Rebecca, had their lives been prolonged by an iron-rich diet when they were young.

Moris Farhi

Moris Farhi (Turkey-England, 1935–) was born in Ankara, Turkey. Several relatives of his Salonika-born mother died in Auschwitz. He attended Istanbul American College and then went to London to study drama. Farhi became a British citizen in 1964. In the 1960s he acted with various English repertory companies. His novels include the thriller *The Pleasure of Your Death* (1972) and *The Last of Days* (1983), which is set in Israel after the Yom Kippur War and has a Jewish protagonist from Salonika. The epic *Journey through the Wilderness* (1989) is set in an unidentified South American country. Its central character is a Jew whose father died in Auschwitz and who has embarked on a mission to find the man who murdered him. Farhi's fourth book, *Children of the Rainbow* (1999), deals with an often forgotten group victimized during the Holocaust—the Roma (Gypsies). Farhi was a screenwriter for BBC Television and Independent Television from 1960 to 1983. His film credits include *The Primitives* (1960). He wrote *From the Ashes to Thebes,* a play in verse, in 1969. Farhi is also the author of a volume of interconnected stories, *Young Turk* (2004), which includes "A Tale of Two Cities," originally published in the journal *Hopscotch: A Cultural Review.* He is on both the Executive Committee and the Writers in Prison Committee of the English PEN and is a vice president of International PEN. In 2001, Farhi was appointed a Member of the British Empire for "services to literature."

A Tale of Two Cities

This July of 1942, the people of Istanbul were insisting, "was the hottest in living memory. Around Sultan Ahmet Square, where the Blue Mosque and the Byzantine monuments faced each other in historical debate, the traditional *çayhanes* had appropriated every patch of shade. The patrons of these tea-houses blamed the heat on *Şeytan:* the land was fragrant with the verses and compositions of the young bards, and the Arch-demon, jealous of the Turk's ability to turn all matter into poetry or music, was venting his resentment. The narghile-smokers, mostly pious men revered as guardians of the faith, disagreed: such temperatures occurred only when sainted imams lamented the profanation of Koranic law and, under this heathen administration called a "republic," had much to lament, not least the growing number of women who were securing employment—as well as equal status with men—in all walks of life. But down the hill, along the seaside *mayhanes,* where the solemn imbibing of raki engendered enlightenment far superior to that of tea or opium, the elders, veterans of the First World War, offered a more cogent reason. Pointing at the dried blood from Europe's latest battlefields settling as dust on this city, which Allah had created as a pleasure garden for every race and creed, they affirmed that man, that worshipper of desolation, was once again broiling the atmosphere with guns.

We believed the drinkers. Well, we either had just reached our teens or, like Bilâl, were at the threshold and knew, with the wisdom of that age, that old soldiers, particularly those who open their tongues with alcohol, never lie. Besides, Bilâl—actually, his mother, Ester—had kept us apprised, with first-hand information, of the carnage devastating Europe. In Greece, where she had been born, Death was reaping a bumper harvest. Letters from Fortuna, Ester's sister in Salonica, were chronicling the atrocities. Though these accounts often verged on hysteria—and tended to be dismissed as exaggerated, even by some Jews—they were corroborated, in prosaic detail, by the family's lawyer. When, about fifteen years before, Ester had left Greece to get married in Turkey, this gentleman, Sotirios Kasapoglou by name, had promised to report regularly on her family's situation.

It was in the wake of this lawyer's latest missive that Bilâl, Naim and

Can, another gang member, approached me. You may have guessed, from my references to Ester's concern for her relatives, that Bilâl—and, indeed, Naim and Can—were Jewish; and you may be intrigued by their Muslim names. There is a simple explanation: Atatürk, determined to distance the new republic from the iniquities of the Ottoman empire, had sought to instill in the people pride in their Turkishness. Consequently, by law, all minorities were obliged to give their children a Turkish name in addition to an ethnic one. Thus Benjamin had acquired Bilâl; Nehemiah, Naim; and Jacob, Can.

I remember the exact date of their visit: Monday 27 July 1942. I was with my parents in sleepy Florya, a resort some fifty kilometres west of Istanbul, on the European coast of the Sea of Marmara where, during the summer months, the British embassy maintained a spacious villa for its staff. We had just heard that the RAF had bombed Hamburg and, somehow, this news had raised the morale of the diplomatic corps much more than the month's significantly greater achievements such as holding the line at El Alamein and bombing the U-boat yards in Danzig. Suddenly the whole British legation felt convinced that we would win the war and my father, Duncan Stevenson, had seen fit to offer me my first dram of *uisge beatha*, the water of life. Though, at the time, I had already perfected the art of downing leftover drinks, these had mainly been sherry; consequently, my first taste of whisky proved a revelation—which may well be the real reason I remember the date.

My father must have come up to Istanbul for an "appearance." His outfit, the British-American Coordination Committee, set up to entice a still-neutral Turkey to join the Allies by providing its army with vital supplies, was headquartered in the capital, Ankara. To shield his activities from enemy agents, his official position had been listed as vice-consul in Istanbul. To safeguard this cover, he had to be seen living there. Thus we became prominent residents of the cosmopolitan suburb, Nişantaşi. It was there that Bilâl, Naim and Can found me drifting aimlessly in parks and playing fields. And when they discovered that I could kick a football like a budding William Shankly, they made me their friend for life.

We had changed into our bathing suits with unusual decorum. I attributed my friends' subdued spirits to the Gorgon's presence. For, throughout the time we undressed, even when we turned our backs to her to prevent our willies from turning to stone under her serpent's eyes—when normally, like most boys celebrating puberty, we would have been comparing sizes—Mrs. Meredith, the housekeeper, had not shifted her chilling scrutiny from us. This martinet, who aspired to discipline even the daisies on the lawn (the epithet "Gorgon" had originated, some years back, from one of our senior diplomats), had a particular fetish for the parquet flooring which contributed so much to the villa's elegance; no one, certainly not four strapping boys, could shuffle or, heaven forbid, run on it without forfeiting their lives.

We reached the villa's private beach. My friends remained subdued. They should have been bubbly: this was a day stolen for fun. Normally, during the week, they helped in their fathers' shops; moreover, except for the Johnson horde, who were a jolly bunch, the beach was deserted and we could run riot. I became concerned. "What's up?"

Bilâl, distracted by the Johnsons waving at us, spoke quietly. "It's grim!"

Thinking that he was referring to yet another crisis with the girl who lived across the road from him and whom he audaciously worshipped from his window, I offered a sympathetic smile. "Selma's ignoring you?"

"No. She returns my gaze. Smiles even."

"Well then?"

"Salonica . . ."

The Johnson children had risen from their chairs and were coming towards us.

I stared at Bilâl. "What?"

Can, always the soft voice that calmed us down, whispered, "His cousins. Difficult times for them."

Naim, the oldest among us and hence our leader, spoke gravely. "We must do something."

I stared at them. Children talking like adults. "What can we do?"

Bilâl muttered, "We can save them. If you help us . . ."

"Me? What can I do?"

Can, mindful of the Johnson brood who were almost upon us, whispered, "Passports—we need passports."

"What for?"

"For the family. To get them out."

"Yes, get them out! Let's have a look!" This from Dorothy, the Johnsons' oldest. A miniature Mae West since she started growing a couple of tangerines on her chest. But a tease: she wouldn't let any boy touch her.

"We're having man-talk, Dorothy! Go away!"

She hissed. "Men, Robbie? Where?" Then she smiled. She could be blade and balm in the same breath. "Dad says: come and join us. Someone's sent a hamper of goodies: *lokum*, figs, halva . . ."

I noted my friends' reluctance, but we couldn't refuse; it wouldn't have been, in my father's parlance, diplomatic. Why do junior staff always feel obliged to pamper youngsters? Still, Dorothy had said figs and Turkish figs were worth an empire: "Don't mind if we do, thank you."

We followed her.

I nudged Naim. "We'll talk later."

Naim didn't respond. He was studying Dorothy's widening hips. Wide hips are childbearing hips, he had once told us, quoting old Kokona, our neighbourhood know-all, as an authority. Well, that formidable Greek matriarch would have known; she had given birth to fourteen children and, by all accounts, it would have taken her husband a good few minutes to run a caressing hand from one buttock to the other.

In time, both Naim and Can developed a healthy preference for wide hips. I never did. Like most northerners, I ended up thinking that ample flesh and carnal living were joys that led to immoderation. These days I ask: what's wrong with immoderation?

FIGS AND THE OTHER treats were followed by a chess game between Mr. Johnson and Can, spectacularly won by the latter who, had he not set his mind on medicine, would have become a grand master. Then a bout of jousting in the sea during which Naim had the bliss of carrying Dorothy on his shoulders—his mouth barely centimetres away from her freckled thighs—while she repeatedly unseated her four brothers despite the valiant efforts of Bilâl and Mrs. Johnson, who served as their mounts. Then a couple of hours of serious swimming, an activity at which I excelled. Finally a succulent lunch, courtesy of Emine, the cook, who, except for special requests, never repeated her menus.

Thus privacy eluded us until the obligatory siesta. Because of my father's privileged status, I had managed to secure, as my retreat, the big room in the attic, which served as a dump for the villa's oddments. That's where we secreted ourselves, much to the displeasure of the Gorgon, who could not keep an eye on us in there.

Bilâl brought out the letter his mother had received from the family lawyer and translated it. His Greek was perfect. Since Ester claimed to have taught the language to Bilâl's father, Pepo, in the early years of their marriage (not true, actually; Pepo had known Greek before he met Ester, had even acted as an interpreter during the War of Independence) we used to tease Bilâl that he had learned it by listening to his parents' pre- and post-coital cooing. (A crass banter that we instantly abandoned after Bilâl confided in us that all was not well between his mum and dad.)

Much of the letter was devoted to an incident that had taken place on 11 July. On that day, a Sabbath, the *Wehrmacht* commander of northern Greece had decreed that all male Jewish citizens of Salonica between the ages of eighteen and forty-five must gather at 8 a.m. in Plateia Eleftherias, "Freedom Square," to register for civilian labour. Some 10,000 men, Ester's elderly father Salvador among them, had duly reported in the hope of securing work cards. The Germans had chosen to humiliate the assemblage by keeping them standing in the blistering heat, without hats, until late afternoon. Those who had collapsed from sunstroke had been hosed down with cold water and beaten up; others, ordered to perform arduous exercises until they, too, had passed out, had received similar treatment. These horrific and arbitrary abuses, the lawyer admitted with mortification, had been witnessed, mostly with indifference, sometimes with glee, by a large number of the city's inhabitants—people who, no doubt, considered themselves good Christians. Worse still, the following day, the newspapers, brandishing photographs supplied by the German army, had praised this attitude. Perhaps even more invidious was the fact that not a single professional organization, nor any members of one, had spoken up on behalf of a Jewish colleague or in protest against the Jews' maltreatment. But what was even worse was that in Salonica—and nowhere else in the country—there had been many denunciations of Jewish neighbours by the citizens. These denunciations had much to do with Greek nationalism, which still resented the fact that throughout the centuries when Salonica had been an Ottoman city, Jews and Turks had had very harmonious relations. But it must be remembered, the lawyer bitterly lamented, that every institution in Salonica, not to say every citizen, had also worked and maintained close ties with Jews for generations. How could that tradition be forgotten? After all, history had produced only one constant in the Balkans: the Jew's word as his bond.

To date, the Germans had dispatched most of the men who had assembled on that Saturday to build roads and airfields. What the future held for other Jews, the lawyer dared not imagine. Reports from eastern Thrace and Macedonia augured the worst. The Germans had delegated the administration of these territories to their ally, the Bulgarians; but since the latter kept prevaricating on the matter of surrendering their own Jews, the Germans had decided to deal with the Jews of Thrace and Macedonia themselves. Lately there had been rumours that these unfortunates would be deported en masse to Occupied Poland. All of this made the lawyer look back regretfully to the time when the Italians had been the occupying power. The Italians had been humane, often in defiance of Mussolini's edicts. Throughout their occupation, they had persistently warned the Jews of the Nazis' racist policies and urged them to leave the country; on many occasions they had even granted Italian passports to those who heeded their advice. Ester might remember one Moiz Hananel, a distant cousin from Rhodes: he was now safe in Chile. But, alas, Ester's father, Salvador, disinclined to liquidate his considerable investments, had procrastinated. Now the Italians had gone and Salvador's wealth had evaporated.

There the lawyer's letter ended.

Then Bilâl brought out another letter, the latest from Ester's sister, Fortuna. It was written in French, the lingua franca of the educated Sephardim, and he read it out loud. As might be expected of my Scottish lineage—the antithesis of the insular, monolingual English—I was quite cosmopolitan and spoke several languages fluently.

Fortuna's letter was like that of a dying person, without a trace of the billowing fury with which she normally faced adversity, Her husband, Zaharya, one of those impressed for road construction, had suffered a heart attack and died. Viktorya and Süzan, her daughters, aged eight and ten, had become the family's breadwinners. Every morning before dawn, they would leave home—which, these days, was a corner in a disused warehouse—and climb to the lower slopes of Mount Hortiatis where they would collect wildflowers. They would then run back, at breakneck speed, to reach the city by noon and sell the flowers, often in competition with equally destitute Gypsy children, to German officers relaxing at the waterfront tavernas.

Every morning, as they left, Fortuna felt sure she would never see her daughters again. Her son, David—who, like Bilâl, was nearly thirteen—fared worse. His daily task was to scour the city for scraps of food. In doing so, he had to avoid the German patrols for whom the humiliation of rabbis, women and the elderly, the beating of children and the random shooting of "die-hard communists"—a euphemism for semitic-looking people—had become favourite pastimes.

Salvador, a man who, in his time, had never backed down from a fight, was now a ghost. Since the expropriation of his villa by the *Wehrmacht,* a few days after 11 July, he had ensconced himself in a shack, near the Eptapyrgio fortress, that terrible prison on the crest of the old upper city. Vowing that he would never again be maltreated and calling for his wife, mercifully dead for many years, to come and take him away, he had not left the shack since. Viktorya and Süzan took him food, but how long could they go on doing that?

All of this had persuaded Fortuna that she would have to learn the ways of this new world, become cunning and predatory and, abandoning all notions of decency, survive any way she could. She was still young and attractive. Greek men, everybody knew, had a fondness for Jewish flesh. The Germans, too, it was said, had a secret passion for it.

BILÂL'S RELATIVES HAD to be saved. They were, to all intents and purposes, our kindred too. Bilâl, who had met them when he and his parents had visited Salonica in the summer of 1939, just before the war, had praised them to us so highly that we had adopted them unreservedly as family. Viktorya and Süzan, adorable little girls threatened by every peril under the sun, were the little sisters we all wished we had. (Naim's older sister Gül had died two years earlier.) David was our age and, on the evidence of photographs, looked like Bilâl's twin; therefore he was our twin. In Fortuna's, case, the prevailing moral view that prostitution was a fate worse than death plunged us into gruesome fantasies. Thus, though we secretly felt aroused by the thought of a woman who gave herself to any man, we could not let her face perdition in a thousand and one horrific ways. We had our reservations about Salvador—he had been a veritable tyrant all his life—but we decided that abandoning him would be heinous.

Given our eventual course of action, it might be assumed that we deliberated on the matter for days. We didn't. Our decision was instant and unanimous. Such considerations as to how we would solve any problems that arose could be dealt with, we decided, in due course. We were young; and according to Plato, who had captured our imagination in those days, we were wiser than our elders. We could make the world a better place. Eradicate wars. Establish universal justice and human rights. Stop the sacrifice of millions at the altar of monomaniacs.

Bilâl presented an "if only" scenario that had become his mother's lament. If only we could procure five Turkish passports and deliver them to Fortuna . . .

He had investigated the possibilities.

As anybody who went around Istanbul with eyes and ears open knew, the black-market trade in passports was a thriving business. Those of neutral countries, like Sweden and Switzerland, or from regions outside the theatres of war, like Latin America, were worth a fortune. There were some exceptions: Turkey was neutral, yet because it was feared that Germany, seeking to destroy Soviet oilfields and refineries east of the Black

Sea, would invade the country, Turkish passports were not much in demand. Basically, the market value of a passport was governed by the vagaries of war. On occasion, even passports from war-battered countries could prove a gold-mine—British passports, for instance, though they had the same modest status as Turkish ones, would fetch a fortune from Jewish refugees seeking to settle in Palestine.

In the main, Bilâl instructed us, the black market in passports was dominated by the Levantines, that tiny minority of Europeans who, enamoured of the Orient, had settled in the Ottoman empire and intermarried with its many peoples. Immensely proud of their mixed ethnicity, the Levantines had evolved, in eastern Mediterranean eyes, into "lovable rogues." In the new Turkey, they had perfected the highly specialized métier of *iş bitirici*, "job-accomplisher." It was said that once they accepted a commission, only death would prevent them from completing it to the client's satisfaction.

Here, Bilâl declared, luck favoured us. Naim had a perfect entrée into this community. His classmate, Tomaso (Turkish name, Turgut), was the son of "Neptune," owner of the famous restaurant in the Golden Horn, which served the best fish in the world. Neptune was a scion of the Adriatiko, an elite strain of Levantines who were the descendants of Venetian sailors taken prisoner in the sea battles of the sixteenth and seventeenth centuries, then used as galley-slaves in Ottoman men-of-war and, eventually, set free and allowed to settle in the empire. Neptune had a horde of "cousins" who, in pursuit of their smuggling activities, covered Turkey's four seas with a fleet of trawlers; not surprisingly, they had ended up dominating the fishing trade—which explained the excellence of his restaurant.

So, if we could get hold of five British passports, Bilâl concluded, we could approach the Adriatiko and arrange a barter for Turkish ones. The latter, he reminded us, were worth about the same but had the advantage of being bona fide for the German occupation forces because Turkey was not only a neighbouring country but also neutral. They offered the only chance of escape for Ester's family.

And this is where I came in. I was a member of the British diplomatic community. Perfectly placed to lay my hands on new passports. Fate had brought me to Istanbul for that very purpose.

WE WOVE an ingenious plan.

During the rest of the holidays I would be especially friendly with the

Johnsons, particularly Mr. Johnson, who was His Majesty's Consul. And I would find out, by asking the sort of casual questions that might occur to any curious youngster, how the consulate issued passports and where it stored them. Then, on my father's next trip to Istanbul, I would visit him at the consulate on some pretext and, while everybody went on with their work, slip into whichever storeroom contained the passports and pinch the five we needed. If the passports were kept under lock and key, the boys would provide me with a passe-partout. Obtaining such an item from a locksmith would be easy; having worked the markets with their fathers, they knew countless tradesmen.

Once we had the passports, Naim would prevail on Tomaso to introduce us to the Adriatiko for the exchange with Turkish ones.

The next phase, slipping into Greece, should be equally simple, we convinced ourselves. We could engineer a good excuse to leave town for a few days. Our district boy scout troop had a progressive programme of fitness and culture that included excursions to famous archaeological sites. Since our parents approved of these activities—to date we had explored several digs in Anatolia—we would "invent" such a jaunt to, say, the Royal Hittie Archives in Boğazköy.

For entering Greece, we had two options. We could either waft into eastern Thrace by crossing the Meriç river, which ran along the Turkish-Greek frontier, or sail directly, in a hired boat, to a deserted cove.

We discounted the first as dangerous. To do that we would have to evade two armies, the German and the Bulgarian occupation forces. Moreover, despite Germany's assurances that it would not invade Turkey, the Turkish government, remembering that similar pledges had been given to the Soviets, remained alert. Consequently, the border was assiduously patrolled by a third military outfit, the Turkish army.

Naim felt sure that his friend Tomaso could be as helpful on this matter as with the passports by enabling us to hire a boat from one of his father's "cousins" for the short hop over to Greece.

The journey to Salonica—by bus, we surmised—would be uneventful thanks to Bilâl's impeccable Greek. Once there, we would intercept Viktorya and Süzan as they went to sell flowers and would be taken to the rest of the family.

We would have a fair amount of money; we all had some savings. Moreover, because of the war, the exchange rate between the Greek drachma and the Turkish lira greatly favoured the latter. However, to be on the safe side, the best-off among us—me—would sell his bicycle and tell his parents that it had been stolen.

The journey back, we believed, would be just as easy. We would sneak back into our boat at night and reach Turkey before dawn.

Bilâl's relatives, now equipped with Turkish passports, would execute the formalities for exit visas and travel to Istanbul either by rail—directly or via Sofia—or by steamer, if services were still operational.

THE FIRST PHASE WENT perfectly smoothly.

It took me only a few days to become Mr. Johnson's favourite youngster. I did so rather cunningly, by undertaking to give daily math lessons to his oldest son, Ernest—not the brightest of boys—who had to retake an exam in September. The fact that snooty Dorothy, after an initial bout of cold-shouldering, began to take an interest in me and contrived invitations to some of their family outings also helped. So did my mother's condition: reduced, in the space of a year, from a jolly, athletic woman to a listless, tumbledown person by the death of her younger brother in action with the Royal Navy, she had ceased engaging with the world. The Johnsons, dear people, were determined to compensate for her neglect of me by lavishing treats on me.

One such treat was a standing invitation to the consulate which, Mr. Johnson must have assumed, would impress me with His Majesty's Government's delicate work and thus further justify my pride in being British. Indeed, I found the activities there—comprising, in the main, preparatory work for my father's committee—fascinating. And I discovered, to my surprise, that the passport office was seldom manned; it had never occurred to us that, in the midst of war, there would not be many travellers. As for the passports, they were stacked in neat piles, together with the consulate's stationery, in a large metal locker behind the front desk. The locker had a key, but it was always left hanging from the handle for the benefit of those who needed stationery.

I decided to take my chance straightaway and arranged another visit to the consulate, this time with Ernest and Dorothy, after having taken them to the cinema. At a convenient moment, pretending to go to the lavatory, I slipped away, stole into the passport office, filched the five passports and stuffed them in my satchel. I had brought my satchel to borrow books from the consulate library and, as might be expected of a bookworm, had made a habit of taking it with me everywhere, even to the toilet. To make sure that the numbers would not be consecutive, I picked each passport from a different pile. That was an inspired move, worthy of a seasoned agent. I am proud of it even today.

. . .

Naim, too, had an easy time.

His friend Tomaso, envious of the adventure we had planned, went to work diligently. Arranging an exchange of passports, he told us, should be child's play. But when it came to getting in and out of Greece, he dissuaded us from approaching the old-timers. Since Germany's invasion of the Balkans, these veterans had abandoned their legendary braggadocio. They had even stopped smuggling. These swastika-Huns, they told everybody, were not like the Germans who had fought in the Great War; they were rabid dogs, just like their Führer.

However, the new generation, the *delikanli*—those with "crazy blood," to use that graphic Turkish expression—were itching to prove their mettle; they were particularly keen to match wits with the "master race." And none more so than Marko, Tomaso's mother's kid brother, not yet twenty-five, but already extolled as a Sinbad.

The exchange of passports did turn out to be child's play. Tomaso, pretending that he had undertaken a job—his first—for a Greek friend, sought advice from his father on how to arrange the exchange. Neptune, proud of the boy's initiative, supervised the transaction himself. In the true tradition of the fixer, he asked no questions. But he made sure to turn a profit of seventy-five liras.

Tomaso then introduced us to Marko.

Even today, Marko is imprinted on my mind as the manliest man I've ever met: a blend of film star, athlete and Olympian god with the thick, perfectly groomed regulation moustache of a Casanova; serene as if he had perfected the art of being a loner, yet a man always living at the peak of his spirits. We fell under his spell immediately. Even Naim, who at first perceived him as puzzlingly ingenuous, ended up mesmerized by his irrepressible confidence. But then, Marko had every reason to be confident. Since embarking on his career, he had undertaken all sorts of perilous assignments and had accomplished every one with panache, an unprecedented achievement in a very precarious profession. Moreover, he had so souped up his boat, the *Yasemin,* that he could outrun any patrol craft in the Aegean.

Marko readily agreed to help us. But he would not hire out his boat. He pointed out that we not only knew nothing about the vagaries of the Aegean Sea, but also were totally unfamiliar with the Thracian coastline. If we were chased by Turkish or German patrol boats, we would not be able to give them the slip and would either get captured or blown out of the sea.

There was only one way we could succeed: he would smuggle us in and out of Greece personally. He was an experienced sailor who knew the region like the back of his hand. He could put us ashore very close to Salonica, for instance at Acte, the easternmost promontory of the three-tongued Khalkhidiki peninsula where the monasteries of Mount Athos were situated. In fact, operating near the monasteries would be wise; in case of mishaps, the monks could be expected to provide us with food and shelter. Last but not least, he, Marko, was an irrepressible romantic who believed that saving people was a sacred duty; consequently, he would do the job for a pittance, say, a month's supply of raki.

His evaluation made good sense; his enthusiasm lifted our spirits. We could finally leave the realm of "if only" and enter the world of action. So we agreed.

We set the date for Sunday 6 September. We would return, we calculated, a week later, on the thirteenth.

"ACCOUNTS MADE AT HOME never tally in the market," say the Turks. True enough. In no time at all, everything went wrong.

Our request to go on a week's camping with the boy scouts elicited little enthusiasm from our fathers. Naim and Can's, desperately trying to keep their businesses afloat, needed their sons for odd jobs and refused them permission outright. My father, stuck in Ankara and loath to leave my mother alone with her depression, insisted that I stay by her side. Only Bilâl's parents acquiesced—with indecent haste, according to Bilâl. Their marriage, as everybody could see, had turned sour; they welcomed the opportunity to give their son a respite from their bickering.

Two days later Marko had second thoughts. An operation that entailed the rescue of five people of different ages, he reasoned, was beyond the capabilities of youngsters, no matter how bright or brave. Moreover, we were too many—almost a crowd. We would be conspicuous. We would get caught and would probably be executed on the spot. (We hadn't told him that only Bilâl had permission to go away; we still hoped that we might prevail upon our parents to change their minds.)

Marko suggested a new plan. He would go on his own. Like every Levantine, he spoke fluent Greek. And he knew his way around Salonica: before the war, he had had a wild time there with the lusty *koritzia*. Ah, those girls—Aphrodites, all of them! Just hand over the passports and he'd be in and out in a flash. He wouldn't even ask for additional payment.

We were devastated. We asked for a day or so to reconsider. Our first thought—certainly mine—was that, all along, Marko's sole interest in our project had been the passports. I could picture him selling them to the highest bidder, making hay for a while and eventually reappearing with a cock-and-bull story about how he had very nearly succeeded but had suddenly, tragically, been struck by misfortune. But since, except for Bilâl, we had been reduced to non-participants, what counter-arguments could we offer?

At the next meeting, Bilâl confronted Marko with a sang-froid that surprised us all. "You're right. All of us would be too many. So we'll be just two. You and I."

Marko chuckled and ruffled Bilâl's hair. "My little brother. Fellow spirit. Lovely boy. No." He sipped his raki and chased it with mineral water. "I must be alone. Only way. In and out. Finished in no time." He flexed his biceps. "Marko can do it. Word of honour."

Bilâl, half-teasing Marko, flexed his own muscles. "You and I."

Marko stared at Bilâl's thin arms and roared with laughter. "Oh, little brother . . ."

Bilâl poured more raki into Marko's glass, then proffered his hand. "Deal?"

Marko pushed Bilâl's hand away angrily. "No!" He gulped down the drink, then leaned menacingly across. "You don't trust Marko, little brother? Even when he gives his word of honour?"

"I do. But they won't."

Marko turned to us, even more menacingly. His thick, perfectly groomed moustache bristled. "You won't?"

Bilâl punched him on the shoulder. "Not them, Marko. My family in Salonica."

Marko chuckled. "Don't worry, little brother. They will trust me. Instantly—they will love me. They will kiss my hands. They will kiss me everywhere."

At moments like these I felt that Marko, beneath all his manliness, was a simpleton.

"They are Jews, Marko. They have to be introduced before they can kiss."

Marko stared at him. "You're joking . . . ?"

Bilâl nodded. "Yes. But it's also true. My relatives don't know you. They won't trust a stranger. Not after what's been happening to them."

Marko shook his head mournfully. "But I can save them, little brother! I am ready to save them!"

"They know me. They will trust me. I'm family. Then they'll kiss your hands. Kiss you everywhere."

Marko became ebullient. "They will?"

"Especially the women."

Marko looked up suspiciously. "Only one woman, little brother. Your aunt. The girls are too young."

Bilâl smiled. "Fine! The girls can kiss me!"

Marko grinned and clasped Bilâl's hand. "Right! You and I then!"

THEY LEFT ON Sunday 6 September, as scheduled, from Beşiktaş, at the mouth of the Bosporus, where Marko normally berthed his boat. Naim, Can and I sailed with them as far as Florya. We arranged to meet a week later at the same place. Did any of us believe Marko and Bilâl would succeed? I don't know. I have suppressed a great deal since then. I would say Marko, ingenuous as ever, did believe. The rest of us, I imagine, pretended.

THE DAY OF their return, 13 September, came and went. We waited on the beach, at our rendezvous, until dawn the next day. We smoked countless cigarettes and slunk into dark corners to weep. Finally we admitted that we would never see them again. We were inconsolable.

Later all hell broke loose.

Ester, distraught at her son's failure to return home, contacted the boy scouts and was told that Bilâl could not have joined an excursion since, due to lack of funds, none had been organized.

She and Pepo then contacted our parents, who duly summoned us to an inquisition. My father managed to extricate himself from Ankara and rushed over. My mother, too distressed—she had been very fond of Bilâl—confined herself to her room.

We saw no point in hedging. Desperate to save Bilâl, if this were still possible, we told them everything.

Much to our surprise and despite harshly reprimanding us for being so immature and foolhardy, they understood us, even sympathized. Bilâl's parents, in particular, for once equable, muttered praises, in between sobs, for our compassion and courage. I believe my father, too, felt proud of me even as he told me that I must not expect him to intercede on my behalf when the legation put me on trial for stealing the passports.

Several decisions were taken. The consulate would approach the Turkish immigration authorities and ask them whether there had been entry records for the five Turkish passports—fortunately, we had noted their numbers. If, by some miracle, Ester's relatives had reached Turkey or were being held in custody at a border post, then my father, with the ambassador's blessing, would prevail on the Turkish government to grant them asylum. The parents of Naim and Can would, in turn, make inquiries in the Levantine community about Marko's fate.

ON SATURDAY 19 SEPTEMBER Tomaso came up with some news. His father had had reports that Marko's boat, the *Yasemin,* had been seized by German patrol cutters in a cove in the bay of Kassándra, in the Khalkhidiki peninsula, on 12 September, the day before he and Bilâl were due back in Istanbul. The seizure itself, the sources insisted, was due to bad luck: a plank nailed over the *Yasemin*'s name and port of registration, Gelibolu, had worked loose and a sharp-eyed German official, intrigued at finding a vessel with Roman lettering instead of Greek, had gone to investigate.

As far as the sources could ascertain, there had been no arrests. That suggested that the boat was empty when the Germans discovered it.

It was likely, therefore, that Marko and Bilâl were lying low, conceivably with Ester's relatives—Salonica was no more than fifty kilometres from the bay of Kassándra—or somewhere on the peninsula.

We held on to this hope.

Four days later, we heard about Marko's death. He had appeared, the previous evening, inside Bulgaria, near the Svilengrad rail-bridge close to the Turkish border. He had acquired a mule and was galloping towards the Meriç river.

He had been spotted by German and Bulgarian motorcycle patrols, who had given chase. When he started scampering across the river, the Bulgarians, respecting the neutrality of no-man's-land, had stopped chasing. Not the Germans—they had opened fire. Turkish border guards, appearing on the scene, had asked the Germans to stop firing and threatened to fire back. An argument had ensued. Meanwhile, Marko had reached the bank. The Turkish soldiers, rushing to help, had found him mortally wounded. He had died shortly after, delirious and repeatedly asking after Bilâl.

. . .

WEEKS PASSED.

We visited Bilâl's parents every day. We told them we were mourners, too, that Bilâl's loss was equally unbearable for us because he was our brother in every sense of the word, except by parentage. I imagine we were insufferably insensitive. Yet Bilâl's parents, particularly Pepo, clung to our company gratefully. As if wanting to know their son all over again, they asked endless questions about him. They laughed and cried at all the crazy, boyish things he had done and begged us to repeat his more outlandish capers. We recounted as best we could, often exaggerating details, invariably glorifying the deeds. They listened avidly. They no longer quarrelled; they even held hands dumbly. As Naim bitterly commented on one occasion, Bilâl had had to sacrifice his life to reconcile his parents.

During these weeks, my father—and the Turkish authorities—continued to investigate Bilâl's fate through various channels. But all these efforts led to dead ends.

Then it was mid-November. And we, the British, were cock-a-hoop. Military analyses confirmed that, after El Alamein, Germany was no longer a threat in North Africa. The end of the Third Reich was near.

As if this were the news she had been waiting for, Ester started avoiding us. Did she, with her Jewish imagination, think that a wounded Germany would be even more ruthless towards its victims? Whenever we went to see her and Pepo, she decided either to go shopping or to drop in on a friend. Pepo, who had to receive us on his own, looked increasingly tense and apologetic.

Soon we started hearing that Ester was not going shopping or calling on friends, but was roaming through Istanbul. Sometimes she would undertake these rambles methodically, district by district, at other times, she would move about aimlessly. Inevitably, this mysterious behaviour spawned all sorts of rumours. Some said that she had a lover, others that she had several; still others, that she could no longer bear Pepo's company; one or two implied that he was losing her mind. The grief of losing her son, the guilt from having lost him because he had tried to save his parents' marriage by rescuing her family, would be unbearable for any person, they said.

Pepo sold his business to pay the *Varlik Vergisi,* or Wealth Tax. He went to work as a caretaker in a textile factory, a job that kept him away from home at nights and much of the day. This appeared to satisfy Ester. She stopped roaming. However, she still avoided us.

Pepo continued to see us, almost daily, but in the afternoons, after school.

. . .

The year 1943 arrived.

Churchill, seeking to lure Turkey into the ranks of the Allies, met with President İnönü.

February brought news of the Red Army's victory, after months of heroic resistance, at Stalingrad. Confronted by the Soviet counter-offensive and the merciless Russian winter, the Germans now faced a cataclysm similar to that suffered by Napoleon.

The economic situation deteriorated. Naim and Can, increasingly required to help their fathers, began to miss some of our meetings with Pepo. I strongly objected to their truancies, even accused them of betraying Bilâl's memory.

Pepo explained the prevailing situation. Anti-semitism had finally seeped into Turkey. Some senior politicians, still nostalgic for the Turco-German alliance of the First World War, believed that a new alliance with Germany would repair history and restore the old Ottoman glory. So they had been easily captivated by Nazi ideology. Consequently, aided and abetted by lackeys and opportunists in important government departments, they were blaming the Jews for Turkey's economic problems. Unscrupulous journalists were competing with each other to revive the hackneyed Christian lies about the Jews' time-honoured pursuits of usury, speculation, exploitation and the conspiracy for world dominion. Cartoons inspired by that Nazi publication, *Der Stürmer,* and depicting the Jews as monstrously obese, long-nosed profiteers, counterpointed these slanders. As a result, since last November, the Turkish National Assembly had levied a discriminatory tax on all Jews—and, for good measure, on certain other minorities. Known as the *Varlik Vergisi,* this tax was so inflated that few Jews could pay it. The penalties for non-payment were extremely severe. Consequently countless Jews were not only having all their possessions seized but were also being deported to labour camps where they would "work off their debts." Pepo, who had sold his business in order to pay the tax, thought that sooner or later he, too, would be sent to a camp.

Then it was 12 February, Bilâl's birthday. This year it was also to be his bar mitzvah, the day he would have joined his community as an adult.

We had arranged to meet Pepo in our usual *çayhane.* Instead, unexpectedly, Ester summoned us to their home.

She greeted us warmly, almost as affectionately as in the old days. But there was a strangeness to her. Despite her thick make-up, she had a neglected air. Her hair, which normally shone like ebony—and which Bilâl had inherited—had lost its lustre. And she was in an unstable mood: very excited one moment, in a trance the next. I remember feeling uneasy and looking at Pepo for reassurance. He seemed to be in a reverie, eyes fixed on his folded hands.

Hurriedly, Ester served tea and cakes. For a while, brandishing a fixed smile, she watched us eat. Then, suddenly, with a flourish, she took out a letter from her handbag and waved it at us. "Bilâl is alive!"

I jumped up. We all did. We fired questions at her. Naim wept. Somehow Ester calmed us down. She kept on waving her letter. "From my sister. He saved them. Bilâl saved them." Then she placed the letter on the table. "You can read it yourselves . . ."

This time we responded more coherently. One of us, noting that the letter had been written in Hellenic script, said we couldn't read Greek. Someone else urged her to tell us what had happened. I kept asking, "Where is he? Where is he?" And wondering why Pepo kept silent.

She related the events impersonally: "Bilâl found my sister. Gave her the passports. They're in Macedonia now. My father. Fortuna. The children. In Skopje. Safe there . . ."

I shouted. We all did. Skopje had a large Turkish minority. Turkey and Germany were not at war. So Turkish subjects were indeed safe. "Is Bilâl with them? In Skopje?"

She stared at us, at first distractedly, then with an amiable smile. "Oh, no, no, no. He and Marko were coming back. Well, you know: Marko's boat was spotted. So they had to separate. Bilâl was wise. He didn't run to the border. He decided to hide. In a monastery. On Mount Athos."

After a very long silence, one of us managed to ask, "How do you know?"

"Bilâl sent word with a priest. To Fortuna." She pointed at the letter. "It's all in there. Read it!"

WE SAW VERY LITTLE of Ester after that—just occasionally, in the street. She never acknowledged us. We felt that having told us about Bilâl she had decided that she had discharged her last obligation to his friends and could now expunge us from her life.

Oblivious to Pepo's pain and embarrassment, we continued to pester him with the cruelest question: had Ester told us the truth?

He always gave the same answer: "You saw the letter . . ."

Then the Wealth Tax claimed Pepo. He was sent to Aşkale, an infamous labour camp in eastern Turkey, where, we later learned, some twenty middle-aged inmates, unable to withstand the heavy work and the atrocious conditions, died of heart attacks.

Pepo survived and returned to Istanbul in March 1944 after the Turkish government, finally acknowledging the iniquity of the Wealth Tax, had abolished it and pardoned all the defaulters. By then I had returned to Britain. But my last moment with him, as we embraced at Haydarpaşa railway station before he was herded on to the train to Aşkale, both of us trying to ignore the stench rising from the tattered soldier's fatigue he had been issued, will stay with me for ever.

The sixth of June saw D-Day.

My father was transferred to European Command for the big push to Berlin. My mother, having been coaxed by a friend into helping out in a rehabilitation centre for disabled servicemen, started to return to a purposeful life. I went to Scotland, to my father's old school, to continue my studies.

Like every Briton, I lived through the last years of the war vacillating between grief and joy, anguish and hope. But every day I sojourned, sometimes briefly, sometimes at length, in my adopted Turkey, in the company of Naim, Can and Bilâl, my soul mates.

And so, no sooner had we celebrated VE-Day than I began to seek ways of tracing Bilâl.

It was a horrendous time. Every day brought further monstrous details of the extent of Nazi atrocities committed against European Jewry. People began to use a leaden word, *genocide*, oratorically, as if they had just coined it. But I think they all felt—I am sure everybody did—that they lacked the imagination to conceive of what it really meant.

Months passed.

I kept drawing blanks.

Naim and Can, with whom I was in regular contact, fared no better with their inquiries in Turkey.

Ester bombarded with petitions the various authorities who dealt with Jewish survivors and displaced people. But none of her family had been traced. It seemed probable that if Fortuna and the rest had really found asylum in Skopje, they would have been deported to extermination camps despite their Turkish passports.

Given this grim prediction, all we could do was hope that Bilâl had found sanctuary at Mount Athos. But of course we knew, deep down, that, like Ester, we were indulging in make-believe.

Eventually, we decided to direct our inquiries to Greece. But that was easier said than done. The resistance groups, the communist-backed EAM-ELAS and the centrist-royalist EDES which, since the early forties, had carried out a guerrilla war against the Germans, had now turned against each other. And although British troops were trying to establish some sort of peace, chaos ruled.

Inevitably, we turned to my father for help. Since he had been very fond of Bilâl and, indeed, had admired his bravery, he promised to pull some strings.

MONTHS LATER, we received a comprehensive report.

According to unimpeachable sources in Greece, Bilâl and Marko had succeeded in contacting Fortuna. But they had been observed by an informer, who had duly alerted the Germans. When the Gestapo had arrived, Fortuna and her family had created a distraction to help Marko and Bilâl escape.

Marko, as we knew, had made it as far as the Turkish border.

Fortuna and her family had been arrested and deported to Auschwitz in March 1943 in one of the early transports. (There had been nineteen from Salonica, carrying almost the entire Jewish population of the city.)

Of Bilâl's fate, there were conflicting versions. One report stated that he had been shot while running away; another, that he had been taken into custody and had either died under interrogation or been deported. But deportation could not be verified. Though the transport lists were usually compiled meticulously and included all the names of the deportees, there had been occasions when persons, either too ill or too badly tortured, were added without anybody bothering to amend the register. A third version mentioned that a youngster who fitted Bilâl's description had been spotted jumping off a precipice—the old town had numerous such drops—and had never been seen again. Curiously, the youngster's body had never been recovered. But since in those days hungry dogs scavenged like hyenas, this had not been considered unusual.

HEART-BROKEN, I relayed this report to Naim, Can and Pepo.

Three days later, Naim and Can telephoned to tell me that Ester had killed herself. As if re-enacting the defiance of the boy who had jumped off the precipice, she had thrown herself from Galata Tower, the Genoese edifice that dominated Istanbul and served as a fire-watch station.

A week later, I received a parcel from Pepo. It contained the copy of a text of some sixty pages written by Bilâl. Pepo and Ester had found it in Bilâl's room while clearing it out after my news about the boy who had jumped off the precipice. It was addressed to his parents and written as a valediction in case he didn't come back. He had finished writing it the day before he and Marko had left for Greece.

I read it, then immediately telephoned Pepo. One of the people he worked with told me he had left his job as well as his flat.

Alarmed, I telephoned Naim and Can. They told me they, too, had received copies of Bilâl's text and were trying to find Pepo's whereabouts. But he had disappeared.

We have never been able to trace him.

I HAVE A recurring dream. I meet Pepo in our regular *çayhane* in the shadow of the Blue Mosque. He tells me Bilâl is alive. Has to be. Or there is no meaning to life.

Danilo Kiš

Danilo Kiš (Yugoslavia, 1935–1989), a poet, translator, essayist, and novelist, was born in Subotica, Serbia. In 1942, after the massacre of Serbs and Jews in Novi Sad, Kiš and his family escaped to the Yugoslav-Hungarian border. Kiš's mother was an Orthodox Christian from Montenegro, and he and his sister were given Orthodox baptisms in 1939. His father, a Sephardic Jew from Hungary, was arrested in 1944, deported, and died in Auschwitz. Kiš's novel *Hourglass* (1972; English, 1990) chronicles the horrors endured by a Serbo-Croatian railway clerk in the months leading up to his deportation by the Nazis to a slave-labor camp. His first published story, "Judas," appeared in a youth newspaper in 1953. He studied comparative literature at the University of Belgrade. He moved to Paris in 1979 and remained there until his death. Strongly influenced by Bruno Schulz and Jorge Luis Borges, Kiš wrote four novels, including *Garden, Ashes* (1965), translated into English from the Serbo-Croatian by William J. Hannaher in 1975. It is a novel obsessed with childhood memories. The protagonist is loosely based on Kiš's father and is presented as a messianic figure and as a Wandering Jew. "[My father] became mythical to me," Kiš said, "when I realized that he had an exceptional destiny and that my own destiny was marked by his Jewishness." His stories are compiled in five volumes, including *Early Sorrows: For Children and Sensitive Readers* (1970; English, 1998), *A Tomb for Boris Davidovich* (1976; English, 1978), which contains a gallery of fictitious anti-Stalinist characters, and *The Encyclopedia of the Dead* (1983; English, 1989). A collection of essays and interviews, *Homo Poeticus* (1983; English, 1995), was edited by Susan Sontag. Kiš's *Collected Works* were published in Belgrade in ten volumes in 1983.

From *Garden, Ashes*

Late in the morning on summer days, my mother would come into the room softly, carrying that tray of hers. The tray was beginning to lose its thin nickelized glaze. Along the edges where its level surface bent upward slightly to form a raised rim, traces of its former splendor were still present in flaky patches of nickel that looked like tin foil pressed out under the fingernails. The narrow, flat rim ended in an oval trough that bent downward and was banged in and misshapen. Tiny decorative protuberances—a whole chain of little metallic grapes—had been impressed on the upper edge of the rim. Anyone holding the tray (usually my mother) was bound to feel at least three or four of these semicylindrical protuberances, like Braille letters, under the flesh of the thumb. Right there, around those grapes, ringlike layers of grease had collected, barely visible, like shadows cast by little cupolas. These small rings, the color of dirt under fingernails, were remnants of coffee grounds, cod-liver oil, honey, sherbet. Thin crescents on the smooth, shiny surface of the tray showed where glasses had just been removed. Without opening my eyes, I knew from the crystal tinkling of teaspoons against glasses that my mother had set down the tray for a moment and was moving toward the window, the picture of determination, to push the dark curtain aside. Then the room would come aglow in the dazzling light of the morning, and I would shut my eyes tightly as the spectrum alternated from yellow to blue to red. On her tray, with her jar of honey and her bottle of cod-liver oil, my mother carried to us the amber hues of sunny days, thick concentrates full of intoxicating aromas. The little jars and glasses were just samples, specimens of the new lands at which the foolish barge of our days would be putting ashore on those summer mornings. Fresh water glistened in the glass, and we would drink it down expertly, in tiny sips, clucking like experienced tasters. We would sometimes express dissatisfaction by grimacing and coughing: the water was tasteless, greasy like rainwater, and full of autumnal sediment, while the honey had lost its color and turned thick and turbid, showing the first signs of crystallization. On rainy days, cloudy and gloomy, our fingerprints would stay on the teaspoon handle. Then, sad and disappointed, hating to get up, we would get back under the covers to sleep through a day that had started out badly.

THE BRANCHES OF the wild chestnut trees on our street reached out to touch each other. Vaults overgrown with ivylike leafage thrust in between these tall arcades. On ordinary windless days, this whole architectural structure would stand motionless, solid in its daring. From time to time the sun would hurtle its futile rays through the dense leafage. Once they had penetrated the slanting, intertwined branches, these rays would quiver for a while before melting and dripping onto the Turkish cobblestones like liquid silver. We pass underneath these solemn arches, grave and deserted, and hurry down the arteries of the city. Silence is everywhere, the dignified solemnity of a holiday morning. The postmen and salesclerks are still asleep behind the closed, dusty shutters. As we move along past the low one-story houses, we glance at each other and smile, filled with respect: the wheezings of the last sleepers are audible through the dark swaying curtains and accordion shutters. The great ships of sleep are sailing the dark Styx. At times it seems as though the engines will run down, that we are on the verge of a catastrophic failure. One engine starts to rattle, to lose its cadence, to falter, as if the ship has run aground on some underwater reef. But the damage has apparently been repaired, or possibly there had never been any damage at all. We are sailing downstream, at thirty knots. Alongside the panting sleepers stand large metal alarm clocks, propped up on their hind legs like roosters, pecking away at the fine seeds of the minutes, and then—charged to the point of an explosion, stuffed, enraged—they strain their legs against the marble surface of the night table just before beginning to crow triumphantly, to crow in swaying, bloody crests.

LUGGING HER CARDBOARD BOXES, Fräulein Weiss shows up on the street corner facing the caserne. Thin, gnarled legs in orange socks peer out from underneath her ragged clothing. Fräulein Weiss, an elderly German woman, sells sugar candies. As she sways along, bent under her burden, sheltered by her boxes and tied to them by a cord made of paper, only her head peeps out, as though she were carrying her own head in a box under her arm. Age and illness have transformed her face into a dark puddle. Wrinkles have spread radically from her mouth, which, like the wound in Christ's palm, has shifted to the center of her face. All the channels of her wrinkles flow, starlike, into that one place, that huge old wound. You see, children, this heap of eroded bones, this shuffling, this rattling—is a whole brilliant, kitschy novel, the last chapter in a threadbare volume, replete with splendor, festivities, defeats. One of the survivors of the spectacular sinking of the *Titanic,* Fraülein Weiss had once attempted suicide. Imitating some famous actress, she had filled up her hotel room with roses. All day the bellhops and elevator boys were delivering bouquets of the most fragrant flowers, like cherubs. The elevators that day turned into great hanging gardens, into greenhouses that carried the burden of their fragrances up into heaven and then came back down again at a dizzying pace, their orientation all gone. Thousands of pink carnations, hyacinths, lilacs, irises, hundreds of white lilies, all had to be sacrificed. But her soul, lulled by the fragrances and intermixed with them, would soar up somewhere, hovering above, relieved of one life, on into the rose gardens of paradise, or would turn into a flower, into an iris. . . . The next day, she was found unconscious amidst the murderous flowers. Subsequently, as the victim of the vengeance of the flower gods, she fell beneath automobiles and streetcars. Peasant carts and swift fiacres ran over her. Yet every time she emerged from under the wheels hurt but alive. Thus, in her passionate brush with death, she had come to know the secret of everlasting life. Groaning and emitting painful sounds from her depths, like a child crying, she passes by us like the filthy, yellowed pages of some worn novel. . . . *Gut'n Morgen, Fräulein Weiss, küss die Hand!*

A little further on, local Germans wearing lederhosen and carrying knapsacks on their backs are starting out on a weekend excursion. Golden mallets quiver on their muscular legs. Inside their belts, they carry magnificent scouting knives with rosewood handles. They are playing harmonicas, mimicking crickets. In front of the pastry shop at the corner, they pop open bottles of pink soda that smells like eau de cologne. Then they return the harmonicas to their fishy mouths and bite down, dividing their instruments into three parts with single thrusts of their powerful jaws. Small streetcars, blue, yellow, and green, are racing to catch up with each other in their senseless cruising through the deserted holiday streets, sounding melodious tunes on their lyres and tinkling their bells gently.

We arrive shortly at a small red train which transports swimmers in the summertime and which in the off season dashes about the woods and fields entirely according to its own mood and disposition. The miniature train, with its pretty little locomotive, looks like a rope chain of red bugs. The cars of the train shove and smash against each other, an outsize raspberry-colored accordion playing dance tunes. Then this dragonfly, this carnival enticement, begins to fly away, buzzing and puffing along, and the poppies in the grainfields beside the track draw long unbroken lines as though inscribed with a red pencil.

My dizziness grows more and more unbearable, and my mother takes me by the hand. By the time we reach the castle, I am squinting. All I can remember is the fireworks display flaring up in front of my tightly closed eyes. I move forward blindly, guided by my mother's hand, my shoulders occasionally grazing against a tree trunk.

We stand by the castle fence, pushing our hands through the bars. First a doe and then a stag, with their great dark eyes. Springing from the dense underbrush, from hidden, enigmatic corners of the Count's forest, they come out of their dignified captivity, proud in their bearing and gait, a bit on the blasé side. On their supple legs, with dark moist spots on their noses, they approach the fence to take sugar cubes from my mother's hands.

Borne along by the inertia of our days and by habit, we continued to visit the castle all through that summer. Since the castle had obviously been abandoned, we appropriated it for ourselves without benefit of the law. My mother would not only say "our deer" but "our castle," even though we had never passed beyond the fence to encroach on the castle's solitude and dignity. We simply believed, and I completely agree with my mother on this point, that we had every right to consider an abandoned castle—offering the beauty of its ruins to the inquisitive eye—to be part of our own resources, that we could lay claim to it accordingly, just as we laid claim to the golden hull of that sun-filled day. Presuming this discovery to be due at least in part to our own merits, we decided to keep it a secret, to tell no one where we were spending our weekends.

Then came the last days of summer, a half season, half summer and half autumn. In the morning the air allowed the assumption that summer was still in its prime and that the blush on the leaves was the consequence of a long heat wave. The chestnut trees in front of the house, long since deprived of their fruits, were shedding in their lazy way. The leaves, yellow and smelling like tobacco, had started to fall indecisively from the branches. My mother decided that we should have confidence in the color of the sky—various shades of aquamarine—and in the promise of the morning sun. While we were standing on the bridge my mother had a peculiar presentiment about the advent of autumn. Indeed, the waters of the Danube were strangely altered, a muddy green, full of some dubious sediment that meant showers somewhere in Switzerland. The hints in the air of rain made us head straight for the red train, even though there was not a cloud in the sky. Our decision was a wise one, no doubt about it. We climbed aboard the last train of the summer season, decorated for the occasion with strips of crepe paper and wild flowers. A gentleman wearing a bowler, presumably representing the provincial government, gave a speech that my mother considered amusing and affecting. "Gentlemen," he intoned, "in honor of this last train of the summer season, and to the greater glory of our town's traditions, the red train today—on its last trip of the season—is going to take all passengers . . . all passengers . . ." Applause and shouts of "Long live the orator," along with the happy yells of children, drowned out his concluding words, since the word had been going around town that the traditional ceremony would be canceled due to certain events in the realm of foreign policy that favored economy and caution in daily affairs.

My mother's suspicions had proved correct. We had just reached the castle when darkness, looming over the hills of Fruška Gora, began to spread toward us. We did not even have time to coax the doe and stag over to us. The dark cloud was upon us, and rain began to patter down.

To protect ourselves from the rain, we took a short cut through the woods. We emerged completely soaked and intoxicated with ozone. All at once, we realized that we were lost. In vain did my mother attempt to hide the fact from us. The rain had totally altered the appearance of the area. . . .

My mother crossed herself, stopping abruptly. A herd of black buffalo charged out of the woods, thundering like a regiment of cavalry, veiled in mist, suicidally resolved to resist the onslaught of the water, to silence the ironic chorus of the frogs. In close formation, horns in attack position, the buffalo were leaping out of the woods, marching fearlessly with a Prussian step toward the swamps. At that very instant, the rain stopped, and we succeeded—at the last moment—in reaching the main road. From where we stood we could see the buffalo vanishing into the muddy quicksand, a cleverly prepared trap. They sank helplessly and fast.

My mother, affected by the gruesome sight and aware of the danger we had eluded, crossed herself once more. . . .

When we returned to town, signs of autumn's offensive were everywhere. Huge yellow posters called for order and compliance on the part of the citizenry, and an airplane was dropping leaflets—yellow and red—speaking in the arrogant language of the victor about the forthcoming reprisal.

"Your uncle is dead," my mother said. The tinkling of silver teaspoon against crystal was louder, betraying the trembling of her hands, and I opened my eyes to check my suspicion. She looked pale in the glare of the sunlight, as if her face were powdered. Her eyes were framed by pink circles. Sensing my confusion, she whispered, without looking at me, "You didn't know him." She seemed surprised and touched by the fact that this sudden death had frustrated an acquaintance full of promise. Following the train of her own thoughts, or perhaps mine, she added, "And now you will never see him." The word "death," the divine seed that my mother sowed in my curiosity that morning, began to soak up all the fluids coursing through my consciousness. The consequences of this premature gestation turned palpable all too fast: dizziness and nausea. My mother's words, while entirely obscure, suggested to me that some dangerous idea lurked behind them. With my mother's approval, I set out, with head bowed, to get a breath of fresh air. Actually it was just an attempt to escape. I went out in front of the house and leaned against a wall. I looked at the sky through the bare branches of the wild chestnut tree. The day was ordinary, routine. And then, all of a sudden, I sensed some strange anxiety in my intestines, some torment and agitation hitherto unknown to me, as though castor oil were rampaging around my stomach. I was looking through half-open eyes at the sky, like the first man, and thinking about how—there you are—my uncle had died, about how they would now be burying him, about how I would never meet him. I stood petrified, thinking that one day I too would die. At the same time I was horror-stricken to realize that my mother would also die. All of this came rushing upon me in a flash of a peculiar violet color, in a twinkling, and the sudden activity in my intestines and in my heart told me that what had seemed at first just a foreboding was indeed the truth. This experience made me realize, without any circumlocution, that I would die one day, and so would my mother, and my sister Anna. I couldn't imagine how one day my hand would die, how my eyes would die. Looking over my hand, I caught this thought on my palm, connected to my body, indivisible from it. Astonished and frightened, I had suddenly come to understand that I was a boy by the name of Andreas Scham, called Andi by my mother, that I was the only one with that particular name, with that nose, with that taste of honey and cod-liver oil in his mouth, the only one in the world whose uncle had died of tuberculosis the previous day, the only boy who had a sister named Anna and a father named Eduard Scham, the only one in the world who was thinking at that particular moment that he was the only boy named Andreas Scham, whom his mother called by the pet name Andi. The flow of my thoughts reminded me of a tube of toothpaste that my sister had bought a few days earlier, on which there was a picture of a young lady smiling and holding a tube on which a young lady was smiling and holding a tube. . . . The mirror game tormented and exhausted me, because it did not let my thoughts come to a halt on their own—on the contrary, it crumbled them still more, turning them into a fine powder that hung in the air, in which there was a picture of a young lady smiling and holding in her hand a tube on which . . . a young lady, oh yes, a young lady . . .

At first it was easier for me to bear the thought of my own death—in which I simply did not wish to believe—than the thought of my mother's. At the same time, I became aware that I would not be in attendance at my own death, just as I was not in attendance at my dreaming, and that calmed me down a bit. Moreover, I started to believe in my own immortality. I thought that since I already knew the secret of death, that is to say, since I was aware of the existence of death (I called it "the secret of death" in my own mind), I had thereby discovered the secret of immortality. With this belief in hand, this illusion of my own omnipotence, I succeeded in calming myself down, and I no longer felt the fear of dying so much as some kind of tearful melancholy over the death of my mother. Despite everything, I was not so irrational as to believe that I would succeed in sparing her and my other relatives from death. I kept this right for myself alone, not out of selfishness but out of an awareness that I would not be in a position to come up with so much trickery as that—there would scarcely be room for myself.

I couldn't fall asleep that night. This was the start of the nightmare that tormented me all through my childhood. Since the thought of death particularly obsessed me in the evening, just before bedtime, I began to fear going to bed: I was afraid of being alone in the room. My mother, realizing from the raving and screaming I did in my sleep that I was overcome by some childish fright, gave in and let me be lulled to sleep by the velvety voice of the epileptic Miss Edith. I was to start school the following year, so everyone made fun of me for my attachment to my mother, and so did Miss Edith, who, by her own admission, was in love with me. But my mother was pleased by my devotion and always took my side, saying that I was excessively sensitive, which she liked, since it proved that I would not be selfish like my father, although at the same time it made her worry a lot about my future. By the time the guests departed, I had long since fallen asleep, having forgotten for a moment to think about my mission, about how I was going to outwit death, about how I would one day have to be in attendance at my mother's death. She would be lying in a bed of flowers, just as Madame Melanie had the previous year, and I would uselessly call out her name and kiss her. Afterward, they would take her away to the cemetery and bury her under beds of roses. . . . Though I tried very hard, I was never able to bring this thought to its conclusion. And yet my nightmares were an effort to avoid bringing this thought to its conclusion. When I thought of death, and I thought of it as soon as darkness enveloped the room, the thought unwound itself, like a roll of black silk thrown from a fourth-floor window. No matter how hard I tried, the thought inexorably unwound to the end, borne along by its own weight. . . .

First I knelt down in my blue pajamas next to my sister Anna and whispered a prayer to God, staring up at a painting of an angel watching over children as they cross a bridge. It was a cheap lithograph in color, in a narrow gilt frame, that my mother had received when Anna was born. A little girl with a bouquet of wild flowers in her hand is crossing the bridge, along with a little boy in short pants. The bridge is rotting; planks have fallen off. Under the bridge, down below in the abyss, a foaming stream rumbles away. Evening is descending, a thunderstorm looms on the horizon. The little girl is holding on to her straw hat, while the little boy hangs on to the twisted railing of the bridge. And above them, above their insecure steps, above the violet gloom, hovers the guardian angel with its wings extended, the nymph of children's dreams, butterfly-woman, *Chrysidia Bellona*. Only the toes of its divine feet show underneath its pink tunic, while the arc of its wings ends in a tip of fiery brilliance. My mother used to say that my sister and I were that little girl and boy, and for a long time I believed that we truly were, fixed at a moment when we were wandering through that area and our guardian angel was not on the alert. So I was looking, then, at the painting of the angel hanging over our bed and was praying quietly. But once I had finished the "Our Father" and another prayer that my mother had carefully composed, which I no longer remember, I would lie down and pull the blanket all the way over my head and begin praying for a long life for my mother and my nearest relatives. Then, since this prayer amounted essentially to thinking of death, I would begin to shudder from fear and from the strain of trying not to think about it, because fatigue would overcome me gradually. I would begin counting to keep the black silk from falling abruptly, to avoid thinking, to prevent my own thought from unwinding to the end. One night, when I was weakened by fatigue, however, a diabolical idea came to me. I had counted up to sixty (I knew how to count to two hundred) when that number ceased to figure in my consciousness as just a prime number devoid of any sense other than a part of a child's telling his beads to lull himself to sleep—we may similarly pronounce a given word countless times, over and over again, straining to discern through the name the word's meaning, the object denominated by the word, yet then at one instant it is exactly the substance of the word that is spilled out like a liquid, leaving only the word's empty crystal dish. Instead, through a contrary process, one of the numbers had become a beaker. At the bottom of the beaker, the dark sediment of meaning was sloshing about. One of the numbers had become at that instant *a number of years,* and thereby all the remaining numbers had taken on the same significance: the number of years left in my mother's life. What sort of a lifetime is that, two hundred years, for the mother of a boy who is resolved to elude death's grasp, not like a lizard but as a person who has, who will have, a sure plan (no room for chance or improvising there), a plan to be conceived and developed through a whole human lifetime? So I counted to two hundred, and back again. My awareness that you could count all your life and never come to the final number, as Anna said, since the last number would always be followed by the next one, only brought the nearness and certainty of my mother's death closer to my eyes. The numbers were years, and I knew—by a rough mathematical reckoning that same night—that my mother could not live more than another seventy or eighty years, since she was over thirty-five, and the oldest of old people, somewhere in Russia (so said Mr. Gavanski), lived barely one hundred and twenty years. Tormented by this counting, I suddenly got lost in eternity's abyss, and the last consolation that I would not founder down below against some underwater reef was the hand of my mother, whose presence I verified with the last atom of my tortured consciousness. . . .

A. B. Yehoshua

Abraham B. Yehoshua (Israel, 1936–) was born in Jerusalem, to a fifth-generation Israeli and a Moroccan immigrant. He attended Hebrew University and served in the Israeli army from 1954 to 1957. He lived in Paris in the mid-1960s and has been a professor of literature at Haifa University since 1972. He has also taught at Harvard, the University of Chicago, and Stanford. Yehoshua's novels include *Three Days and a Child* (1969; English, 1970), *The Lover* (1977; English, 1978), *A Late Divorce* (1982; English, 1994), *Open Heart* (1994; English, 1996), *A Journey to the End of the Millennium* (1997; English, 2000), and *The Liberated Bride* (2001; English, 2003). Described by the *New York Times* as "a kind of Israeli Faulkner," Yehoshua explores both personal and communal complexities and anxieties in the lives of his characters. Yehoshua has also written plays, including *A Night in May* (1969; English, 1974) and *Last Treatment* (1973; English, 1974). He wrote the screenplays for *Three Days and a Child* (1967) and *The Lover* (1986). His short fiction is anthologized in *The Continuing Silence of a Poet: The Collected Stories of A. B. Yehoshua* (1988). His nonfiction includes *Between Right and Right* (1980; English, 1981). This fragment from "The Partners," translated by Hillel Halkin, comes from the novel *Mr. Mani* (1990; English, 1992), which traces, in reverse chronology, the history of a transnational Sephardic family. And another novel in which Yehoshua explores Sephardic identity is *Five Seasons* (1987; English, 1989), in which a Sephardic Israeli comes to terms with the death of his German-Jewish wife in the so-called post-Zionist age.

From *Mr. Mani*

AVRAHAM MANI, forty-nine years old, born in 1799 in Salonika, then part of Turkey, to his father Yosef Mani.

Avraham's grandfather, Eliyahu Mani, was a supplier of fodder to the horses of the Turkish Janissaries and followed behind the Turkish army with five large wagons that housed his large family, which included two wives and two young rabbis who tutored his sons. A shrewd merchant, he sensed immediately upon hearing of the outbreak of the French Revolution that Europe was in for a period of upheavals in which his services as a cavalry supplier would be in great demand. With this in mind, he began to move his activities westward. In 1793, as news reached him of the execution of Louis XVI, Eliyahu Mani crossed the Bosporus and proceeded as far as Salonika, where he found a flourishing Jewish community. And indeed, his gamble paid off and the political and military instability of the times proved a boon for his business. He was able to marry off his children to wealthy and prominent families, and these ties in turn enabled him to expand his affairs even more.

Eliyahu Mani dearly loved his eldest grandson Avraham, who was born at the very end of the eighteenth century. He did not, however, have many years of pleasure from the boy, because soon after the Treaty of Tilsit in 1807, he himself passed away. His concern was taken over by his son Yosef, who was born in 1776 in the Persian town of Ushniyya near Lake Shahi, then part of the Ottoman Empire too. Despite the many reversals suffered by the empire during the first decade of the nineteenth century, Yosef ran the business enterprisingly and did especially well during Napoleon's campaigns in Eastern Europe. At the same time, he did not neglect his children's education and sent his eldest son Avraham to study in Constantinople with one of the most profound and original rabbinical minds of the times, Shabbetai Hananiah Haddaya. Avraham Mani developed a great liking for this rabbi, who was wifeless and childless despite his over fifty years. Rabbi Haddaya, for his part, was fond of Avraham and decided to sponsor him for rabbinical ordination even though he was not a particularly keen student.

In 1815, however, Yosef Mani's business suddenly collapsed in the wake of both the Congress of Vienna peace agreements and the first signs of Greek war of independence against the Turks, which endangered transport and commercial shipments. In 1819 his son Avraham was summoned back to Salonika to help his father, who had lost everything and was reduced to eking out a living from a small spice shop in the port. Before long the brokenhearted man died, leaving the shop in Avraham's possession.

His forced separation from his rabbi weighed on Avraham greatly. Even though the war with the Greeks made travel perilous, whenever he was able to free himself of his business obligations he would take a week or two off and cross the Bosporus to visit Rabbi Haddaya. Although Avraham never received his ordination, the rabbi presented him with a certificate authorizing him to serve on a nonpaying basis as the spiritual leader of a small synagogue in the port that was frequented mainly by Jewish stevedores and sailors.

Despite his mother's urging him to marry, Avraham did not take a wife until 1825, when he wed the daughter of a petty merchant named Alfasi. The couple had a son and daughter: Yosef, born in 1826, and Tamar, born in 1829. In 1832, Avraham Mani's wife died of an unknown illness that was apparently transmitted by a sailor whom the Manis had put up in their home.

As Avraham's business began to prosper, he was able to travel to Constantinople more often. However, he did not always find his old teacher there, because Rabbi Haddaya, who had traveled widely as a young man, was again smitten by wanderlust and was often away on some journey. Generally, his trips took him south and east, and he once even spent a few months in Jerusalem. There he met a woman who several months later came to Salonika and became, to everyone's surprise, the wife of his old age.

After his son Yosef's bar-mitzvah, which took place in 1839, Avraham, who was still a widower with two children, decided to bring the boy to Rabbi Haddaya's school in Constantinople just as his father had brought him. In doing so, he wished both to obtain vicariously the ordination denied to himself and to strengthen his ties with his old rabbi, for whom his admiration had only grown with the years. Before setting out with Yosef, he even taught himself a few words of French, the mother tongue of the rabbi's wife, in order to help create a bond with her.

Rabbi Haddaya's wife, Flora Molkho, took a great liking to Yosef, a vivacious and imaginative youngster who was more intellectually gifted than his father. Having no children of her own, she treated him as her own son and made him her closest companion, since her husband was often away on his travels to the various Jewish communities that invited him to arbitrate legal disputes too knotty for others to unravel.

And so, even though young Yosef did not study with Rabbi Haddaya himself but rather in a school where his education was so laxly supervised that he spent much of the time roaming the streets of Constantinople, all were in favor of his remaining at the rabbi's house: his father because of the connection this gave him with his revered teacher; the rabbi's wife because the boy helped occupy her solitude; and the rabbi himself because he regarded the youth highly, even if the reason for this was none too clear to him.

Early in 1844 the news reached Doña Flora that her younger sister's daughter, Tamara Valero, whom she had not seen since Tamara was little, was planning to travel to Beirut with her stepmother Veducha in order to attend the wedding of Veducha's brother, Tamara's step-uncle Meir Halfon. Doña Flora asked and received her husband's permission to travel to Beirut and meet her niece there—and since he himself was unable to accompany her, it was decided that Yosef Mani, who was by now already a young man, should go with her. Avraham Mani raised no objections, and Yosef and Doña Flora sailed to Beirut. They remained there longer than expected and returned with the announcement that—subject of course to the consent of the two fathers and Rabbi Haddaya—Yosef and Tamara were betrothed.

And indeed, when Tamara returned to Jerusalem, her father gave his approval. But although it was agreed that she would come to Constantinople for the wedding, which was to be presided over by her renowned uncle, the revered Rabbi Haddaya, she failed to arrive—and in the end, unable to restrain himself, Yosef set out by himself for Jerusalem in the winter of 1846 with the intention of bringing his bride back with him. Instead, however, as the families in Constantinople and Salonika later found out, the two were married in a modest ceremony in Jerusalem, where Yosef Mani found work in the British consulate that had opened there in 1838.

Avraham Mani and Flora Haddaya were both greatly disappointed, since they had looked forward to a grand wedding in the rabbi's home in Constantinople and to the young couple's being close to them. Apparently, however, young Mani felt sufficiently drawn to Jerusalem to wish to remain there. In any event, since the mails between Jerusalem and Constantinople were highly irregular and a long while went by without any word from the newlyweds, Avraham Mani decided to travel to Jerusalem in the hope of persuading them to settle in Salonika, or at least, in Constantinople.

Avraham entrusted his shop to his son-in-law, took with him several bags of his favorite rare spices in the hope of finding a market for them in Jerusalem, and sailed for Palestine, arriving there in the late summer of 1847. Although he had expected to be back within a few months, he remained there for over a year, during which nearly all contact with him was lost. Meanwhile, a mysterious rumor that reached Constantinople in December 1847 told of Yosef Mani's being killed in a brawl. And indeed, in February 1848, a rabbi from Jerusalem who arrived in Constantinople on a fund-raising mission confirmed this story, to which he added that Avraham Mani had remained in Jerusalem with his son's wife Tamara in order to be present at the birth of the child she was expecting.

Throughout the first half of 1848, the elderly Rabbi Haddaya and his wife Flora were greatly upset at being out of touch with Jerusalem, especially since they did not even know when the birth was supposed to take place. The infrequent greetings or bits of news that arrived from Avraham Mani were vaguely worded and confused. And then, unexpectedly, on the first night of Hanukkah, Avraham Mani arrived at the inn in Athens where Rabbi Haddaya had been lying ill for several weeks.

Flora Molkho-Haddaya was born in Jerusalem in 1800 to her father Ya'akov Molkho, who had moved there several years previously from Egypt. In 1819 her younger and only sister married a man named Refa'el Valero, and soon after a son was born to them. Flora Molkho herself, however, remained unmarried, for there was a dearth of eligible young men in Jerusalem and her attachment to her sister and her little nephew made her spurn all suggestions to travel to her father's family in Egypt, or to her mother's family in Salonika, in the hope of finding a match. When Rabbi Shabbetai Haddaya visited Jerusalem in 1827, he stayed with the Valeros and met Flora Molkho, whose refusal to leave the city in search of a husband intrigued him. Indeed, Flora's adamance was now greater than ever, because her sister, having gone through two difficult miscarriages after the birth of her son, was well into another pregnancy.

Soon, however, all this changed, because shortly after Rabbi Haddaya's departure a devastating cholera epidemic broke out in Jerusalem that took the life of Flora's beloved nephew. Her sister, who meanwhile had given birth to a daughter, sank into a depression that led to her death in 1829. Flora Molkho, fearing that her widowed brother-in-law Refa'el Valero would feel obligated to propose marriage to her, hastened to leave Jerusalem for her mother's family in Salonika. Rabbi Haddaya followed her arrival there with interest and even sought, in 1833, to arrange a match between her and his protégé Avraham Mani, whose wife had recently died. Avraham Mani was keen on the idea, but Flora, although already a woman of thirty-three, refused. Her unmarried state troubled Rabbi Haddaya so greatly that he tried proposing other husbands for her, every one of whom she turned down, until he offered in his despair to marry her himself. Despite being forty years younger than he was, she did not reject his offer. The two were wed within a year and in 1835 Flora Molkho took up residence in Constantinople.

Although the rabbi and his wife had no children and he was away on his travels for weeks on end, the two appeared to get along well. As for Avraham Mani, he quickly recovered from his hurt at being spurned by Flora in favor of his elderly teacher, resumed his ties with the rabbi more intensely than ever, and in 1838 brought him his son Yosef to be his pupil. The rabbi's wife received the youngster with open arms and—quite taken by his charms, his keen intelligence, and his many interests—chose to have him keep her company. Whenever Rabbi Haddaya went away, he asked his wife to take young Yosef into their home because the latter was an independent and adventurous boy who took advantage of the rabbi's absence to enjoy the freedom of the city and needed to have an eye kept on him. And indeed, Flora Molkho-Haddaya watched Yosef closely. He helped her around the house and sometimes, when the rabbi was gone, even slept beside her in his bed.

In 1844, Doña Flora was informed that her niece Tamara was planning to travel to Beirut with her stepmother Veducha for a family wedding. At once she had the inspiration of arranging a match between Tamara and Yosef in order to formally link her young favorite with her family. She received permission for Yosef to escort her to Beirut from both the rabbi and Avraham Mani, who was thrilled by the prospect of a marriage bond with his revered master. Although Tamara, for some reason, seemed doubtful about the match, the firm inducements of Doña Flora, coupled with Avraham Mani's encouragements from afar, resulted in a hasty betrothal in 1845. Tamara returned to Jerusalem to prepare for the wedding, which was to be held in Constantinople. She did not, however, set out, and the rather vague letters that arrived from Jerusalem implied that the groom was expected to come there first in order to meet the bride's family and make the acquaintance of her native city. Finally, in 1846, Yosef

Mani complied, and eventually word reached Constantinople that he and Tamara had been married in Jerusalem and that he was working for the British consul there.

In 1847, Flora Haddaya and Avraham Mani, doubly distressed by the wedding's not having been held in Constantinople and by their separation from the newlyweds, decided to travel to Jerusalem themselves in order to visit their relatives there and persuade Avraham and Tamara to move back to Constantinople. Since Rabbi Haddaya, however, did not consent to his wife's making the trip alone with Avraham Mani, the latter had to go by himself. Once there, not only did he fail to bring his son and daughter-in-law back with him, he disappeared unaccountably for a long time himself until it became known that his son had been killed and that he was attending the birth of his daughter-in-law's child.

In 1848, Rabbi Haddaya, who was now over eighty, set out for Jerusalem and Avraham Mani, but on the way he suffered a stroke and lost the power of speech. He now had to be constantly cared for by his wife, who served as the link between him and an outside world that still looked to him for answers that it could no longer understand.

RABBI SHABBETAI HANANIAHA HADDAYA did not know the exact date of his birth. His rapid walk and young, energetic exterior often misled people as to his age. He himself did not take the question seriously, and since he had no family, there was no way of ascertaining the truth. In any event, he was in all likelihood born no later than 1766. His birth was known to have occurred aboard a ship that had set sail from the eastern Mediterranean, and it was jokingly said that he had been born straight from the sea, since both his parents died without reaching land from an outbreak of plague that swept through the vessel on its way from Syria to Marseilles. In France the little baby made the rounds of several charitable institutions until, inasmuch as it was circumcised, it was given for adoption to a Jewish family. Its foster parents were a childless old couple named Haddaya; according to one version, the infant was named Shabbetai for the false messiah Shabbetai Tsvi, who had lived in the previous century but whose remaining followers the Haddayas were connected with. The child did not remain with them for long, however. He was soon transferred to a Jewish orphanage, where he was raised and educated and given the additional name of Hananiah. Before long his intellectual capacities became apparent to his teachers, who arranged a special curriculum whereby he could advance in his studies.

Eventually, Shabbetai Hananiah was accepted into the talmudical academy of Rabbi Yosef Kardo, a descendant of a family of Marranos that had returned to Judaism in the early 1700s. So greatly did he excel in his studies that he was chosen headmaster after Rabbi Kardo's death, even though he was often away on his travels to various Jewish communities, which was something he had a passion for. He was thought highly of by his fellow French rabbis and in 1806 was even invited to Napoleon's famous convocation of Jewish leaders in the Tuilleries Palace in Paris, which met to debate the civil and national status of the Jewish people in the postrevolutionary era. His experience there, and in the discussions that took place in 1807 concerning the possible reconstitution of the Sanhedrin, was a deeply disturbing one for him. Unlike most of his colleagues, who basked in the honor accorded them and believed they were acting to ameliorate the Jewish condition, Rabbi Haddaya was seized by a strange pessimism. In 1808 he decided to leave the academy in Marseilles. After parting from his pupils, he sailed eastward to Sardinia and from there to southern Italy, from which he proceeded to Venice, where he resided for a considerable period. Subsequently, he moved on to Greece, wandered among its islands, reached as far as Crete, returned to Athens, and worked his way up along the Aegean coast until he arrived in Constantinople. Wherever he found himself, he offered his services as a preacher and a rabbinical judge. Although he kept up his legal erudition, theoretical studies did not greatly interest him and he preferred the active life of sermonizing and sitting on courts.

Not the least remarkable thing about Rabbi Haddaya was his bachelorhood, which seemed particularly inexplicable in light of his fondness for arranging matches and raising doweries for brides. Sometimes he even traveled great distances for the sole purpose of presiding at some wedding. And yet he himself declined to take a wife, a refusal that he justified by claiming that a childhood injury had left him unable to have children.

When Rabbi Haddaya first came to Salonika in 1812, he stayed at the home of Yosef Mani, Avraham Mani's father, and made a great impression on him and his family, especially by virtue of his observations about Napoleon, who was then in the midst of his Russian campaign. After spending several months in Salonika, the rabbi continued on to Constantinople, where he finally appeared to settle down. He ceased his wandering and opened a small school in the Haidar Pasha quarter along the Asiatic coast, and soon after Avraham Mani arrived to study there. Although the boy was not a particularly good student, Rabbi Haddaya appreciated his good qualities, among which was a great capacity for loyalty.

Young Avraham Mani sought the closeness of the old rabbi and grew so dependent on him that Rabbi Shabbetai sometimes referred to him in private as "that little *pisgado*." Nevertheless, he was sad to see the boy go when he had to return to Salonika after the failure of his father's business. Indeed, the emotion that he felt on that occasion quite surprised him. Soon after, his old wanderlust returned. Once again he began to travel all over the Ottoman Empire, particularly to Mesopotamia and Persia, although he also journeyed southward to Jerusalem, where he stayed at the home of Refa'el Valero and became acquainted with Refa'el's wife and his sister-in-law Flora, whose unmarried state was a cause of great wonderment to him.

Upon his return to Constantinople in the early 1830s, Rabbi Haddaya resumed his ties with ex-pupil Avraham Mani, who crossed the Bosporus from time to time to visit his former teacher. Rabbi Haddaya even tried to arrange a match between Avraham, whose wife died in 1832, and Flora Molkho, who had in the meantime moved from Jerusalem to Salonika after her sister's death. When Flora Molkho showed no interest in such a marriage, the rabbi invited her to Constantinople in the hope of changing her mind, and when this proved impossible, he suggested several other possibilities, all of which she rejected too. Finally, in a surprising and perhaps even despairing step, he proposed to her himself and was astonished when she accepted. The betrothal took place secretly in order to avoid hurting his dear disciple Avraham Mani; similarly, not wanting tongues to wag over his marriage to a woman forty years his junior, Rabbi Haddaya wed Flora in a ceremony conducted by himself in a remote town in Mesopotamia, for which he was barely able to round up the ten Jews needed for the occasion.

Despite the age difference between them, the couple's marriage worked out well. Rabbi Haddaya continued to travel widely, and his wife Flora was accustomed to being alone. When Avraham Mani sent him his son Yosef, the rabbi was pleased by the gesture of conciliation and took the boy in, even though he himself hardly taught anymore due to his frequent absences. Although Yosef proved to be a highly imaginative child who at times seemed out of touch with reality, he was able to charm whomever he met, and above all, the rabbi's wife, whose childlessness had left her increasingly isolated. Thus, he grew up in the Haddaya household, the excitable child of two elderly "parents."

Rabbi Haddaya did not play an active role in the betrothal of his wife's niece Tamara Valero to Avraham Mani in Beirut. For a while, he even seemed opposed to it. However, after the newlyweds settled in Jerusalem and Avraham Mani disappeared there too, and especially, after hearing of Yosef Mani's death from the rabbinical fund-raiser Gavriel ben-Yehoshua, Rabbi Haddaya grew so distraught that his health was affected. He decided to set out for Jerusalem to find out what had happened, and since travel by land was unsafe, he resolved to sail from Salonika on a ship manned largely by Jews. In the late spring of 1848, more than thirty years after last having set foot in Europe, he crossed the Bosporus westward.

Rabbi Haddaya was received in Salonika with great pomp and ceremony and seen off at his ship by Rabbis Gaon, Arditi, and Luverani. Yet his own excitement must have been even greater than theirs, because the robust though slender old man had hardly been at sea for a day when he suffered a stroke, a thrombosis in the left hemisphere of his brain that caused him to lose the power of speech and all control over the right side of his body. Although able to understand everything said to him, he could no longer answer, and when he tried writing, the letters came out backward in an illegible scrawl. Since it was impossible to sail on in such circumstances, the captain changed course for the port of Piraeus, from which the paralyzed man was brought to a Jewish inn in Athens. There he lay, often smiling, nodding, and making sounds like "tu tu tu."

News of the revered rabbi's illness spread quickly and Jews gathered from near and far to help Doña Flora minister to him. In no time an entire support system sprang up that was most ably directed by her. The Greek governor of Athens stationed a permanent guard by the entrance to the inn, and Rabbi Haddaya, who sat covered by a silk blanket in a special wheelchair brought from Salonika, seemed almost to be enjoying his new situation, which spared him the need at last to express his opinions and left him free to listen to the Jews who came to see him while smiling at them and occasionally nodding or shaking his head. Nevertheless, his wife, who discerned a slow but gradual deterioration in his condition, did everything she could to avoid exciting him.

Thus, when the "vanished" Avraham Mani turned up unexpectedly one winter day at the inn in a state of great agitation, Doña Flora granted him permission to see his old rabbi "for a brief while and only for a single conversation."

Doña Flora's half of the conversation is missing.

. . .

—In truth, Doña Flora, for a brief while only, for one short conversation. I am compelled to, for the love of God! Please do not deny me that. Am I not, after all, besides a member of the family, also the eldest of his pupils?

. . . .

—Indeed it did. The infant was delivered on the night after the Day of Atonement.

—A boy child, señores, a boy child born in Jerusalem—and you, madame, will be his grandmother. Your poor sister of blessed memory did not live to be one, and you must be one for her.

—Yes, I too, it would seem . . . that is . . . well, yes . . . I too, with the help of God . . .

—Both mother and infant are well. I bring you greetings from them all: a greeting of peace from Jerusalem—from Refa'el Valero—from the rabbis of the city—from its streets and houses—from the Street of the Armenians and the Hurva Synagogue—from the cisterns and the marketplaces—even from your room, Doña Flora, your little alcove by the arched window—yes, even from your bed, the bed of your maidenhood, in which you slept so many a night. Wrapped in your quilt, I thought of your youth and of mine . . .

—In your very bed . . . and with great pleasure. Your brother-in-law Refa'el assigned the bed of your parents, may they rest in peace, to our young couple, and that was where the unfortunates slept, while I was put up in the little room nearby, between those two most wondrus looking-glasses that you hung on the walls, which played the very devil with my mind. It is not to be marveled at, Doña Flora, that you never looked for a husband in Jerusalem, because in such a room one feels sure that there is already someone with one, hee hee hee . . .

—I named him Moshe Hayyim in the hope of a fresh start.

—No, he was not named after his father. It is enough that I am accursedly boxed in by the same name before me and after me. I am weary of the names of dead patriarchs commemorating downfalls and defeats; I had my fill of Genesis and went on to Exodus, from which I took the name of Moses in all simplicity. May his great merit stand us in good stead . . . for there was a miracle here . . . before death could drain away the vital fluids, life saved a few precious last drops . . . look, Doña, how wonderfully he smiles again. Does he approve of the name Moshe?

—He is nodding. He understands! God be praised. I promise you,

Doña Flora, that the rabbi's salvation is nigh and that in a twinkling of the eye he will preach again . . . 'tis but an interval . . .

—With moderation . . . of course . . . without compulsion . . .

—With much travail, Doña Flora, although through clenched teeth . . .

—Her father Refa'el so feared the birth that he ran off to the synagogue to say psalms, leaving me standing there for ten hours in my robe and shoes like one of the Sultan's honor guard, ministering with hot water and compresses.

—No, madame. It was in your old bed, which had become my bed and now became Tamara's. You may rejoice in the thought that the infant was born in your bed.

—At the very last minute Tamara was stricken with fear and refused to give birth in her bridal bed and had belonged to her parents. She beseeched the help of heaven, and so we moved her to the old bed of her beloved aunt, which conducted the efflux of her uncle's great merit . . . and in truth, it was only his merit—does Your Grace hear me?—that stood by us in that difficult birth.

—Ten hours, one labor pain after another . . .

—There were two midwives. One the wife of Zurnaga, and the other a nunlike Englishwoman called Miss Stewart, a lady as tall and thin as a plank, but most proficient. She was sent by the British consul in Jerusalem, who has not yet ceased mourning our Yosef.

—'Twas at night, Doña Flora, before the first cockcrow, that we heard the long-awaited cry. And if I may say so without fear of misunderstanding, the two of us, the mother and I, so longed for you, madame, at that moment that our very souls were faint with desire for you in that great solitude . . .

—No, I will not cry . . .

—No, there will be no more tears . . . *señor* . . . *maestro mío* . . . he is listening . . . I feel the lump of his silence in my throat . . .

—Your niece kept calling your name while racked by her pains. She was pining for you—she gave birth for you, madame—and in the times between one labor pain and the next, while I sat in the next room and watched her face dissolve toward me in the small mirror, I could not help but imagine you as a young woman in Jerusalem, lying in your bed in the year of Creation 5848 or '49 and giving birth too. We were too much surrounded by the shades of the dead, Doña Flora . . . we needed to think of the living to give us strength . . .

—Most truly.

—Again you say I "vanished." But where did I vanish to?

—In Jerusalem, only in Jerusalem. I walked back and forth between those stony walls with their four gates, thinking, "It was here that little madame toddled about forty years ago, among the stones and the churches, from the Jaffa Gate to the Lions' Gate, skipping over the piles of rubbish in the fields between the mosques, glared on by the red sun and in the shadow of sickness and plague."

—In truth, Doña Flora. I took upon myself all your longing for Jerusalem, and all the memories of His Grace too, my master and teacher, who honored our sacred city with a visit in the year 5587. There are men there who still recall sheltering in his presence. Who knows but that that poor city throbs on in his heart if not in his mind. Ah! . . .

—Is he listening?

—The Lord be praised.

—But how was I silent? And again, Doña Flora: why was the silent one me? All last winter I prayed for some word from you. The lad was already dead and buried, and our own lives were as dark as the grave, because at the time, madame, his seed alone knew that it had been sown in time. And since I knew that the news would travel via Beirut to Constantinople on the dusty black robe of that itinerant almsman, Rabbi Gavriel ben-Yehoshua. I hoped for a sign that it had reached you. I even entertained the thought that the two of you would hasten to Jerusalem with tidings of strength and good cheer, for I knew that the lad had been dear to you. You took him under your wing . . . you indulged him and foresaw great things for him . . . you lay him beside you, madame, in His Grace's big bed . . .

. . . .

—Of course she is nursing, although not without some assistance. Her left teat went dry within a few days and left her without enough milk, and the consul made haste to send her an Armenian wet nurse who comes every evening with a supplement, for he heard say that the milk of the Armenians is the most fortified . . .

—In truth, he is a good angel, the consul. He has not withheld his kindness from us, and how could we have managed without him? We have been ever in his thoughts since that black and bitter day. He remains consoled for the loss of our Yosef, on whom he pinned great hopes. *Baby Moses* he calls the infant in English, and he has already issued him a writ of protectorship as if he were an English subject. Should he ever wish to leave Jerusalem for England, he may do so without encumbrance . . .

—Little Moshe.

—In the Rabbi Yohanan ben-Zakkai Synagogue. Tamara dressed *baby Moses* in a handsome blue velvet jersey with a red *taquaiqua* on his head, and Rabbi Vidal Zurnaga said the blessings and performed the circumcision. The cantors sang, and we let the English consul hold and console the child for his pain, and Valero and his wife Veducha handed out candies and dough rings—here, I have brought you in this handkerchief a few dried chick-peas that I carried around with me for weeks so that you might bless them and eat them and feel that you were there . . . may it please you, madame . . . the consul and his wife blessed and ate them too . . .

—And here is one for him too, my master and teacher . . . a little pea . . . just for the blessing . . .

—No, he will not choke on it . . . 'tis a very little pea . . .

—Ah! He is eating . . . His Grace understands . . . he remembers how he used to bring me "blessings" from weddings, how he woke me from my sleep to teach me them . . . now I will say it for him! Blessed be Thou, O Lord our God, King of the Universe, Who createth all kinds of food.

—Amen.

—He cannot even say the amen for himself . . . ah, Master of the Universe, what a blow!

—No, I will cry no more. I have given my word.

—Of course, madame. God forbid that my tears should lead to his. But what can I do, Doña Flora, when I know that no matter how dry-eyed I stand before him, he—even as he is now—can read my soul! The great Rabbi Haddaya understands my sorrow. I have always, always been an open book to him . . . "like the clay in the hands of the potter" . . . ah, Your Grace . . .

—Slowly but surely . . . for I am not yet over my departure from your Jerusalem, madame, which is a most obdurate city—hard to swallow and hard to spew out. And hard too was my parting from the young bride, my son's widow and your most exquisite ward. But most impossible of all, Doña Flora, was parting from the infant Moshe, who is so sweet that he breaks every heart. If only madame could see him . . . if only His Grace, my teacher and master, could have seen *baby Moses* in his circumcision suit, his blue blouse and red *taquaiqua,* peacefully stretching his limbs without a sound, without a cry, sucking his thumb, meditating for hours on end . . . did I say hours? For whole days at a time, in a basket on the back of a horse . . .

—Amost excellent consular horse, madame, which bore him and his mother from Jerusalem to Jaffa.

—I should bite my tongue!

—'Twere better left unsaid.

—In truth, on a horse. But not a hair of his was harmed, madame. He reached Jaffa in perfect condition.

—What winter? There was no sign even of autumn. I see you have forgotten your native land, Doña Flora, where "summer's end is harsher than summer" . . .

—Even if there was a touch of chill in the mountains, it did him no harm. He was wrapped in my robe, my fox fur that I brought from Salonika, and well padded in the basket, most comfortably and securely . . .

—Indeed, a tiny thing, but flawless. We miscalculated, she and I. Our parting was difficult, and so we longingly prolonged it until obstinacy led to folly . . .

—No, there was no guile in it; 'twas in all innocence. When we reached the Jaffa Gate and she saw me standing there, endlessly dejected, amid the camel and donkey train that was bound for Jaffa, she said to me, "Wait, it is not meet that you leave Jerusalem in sorrow, you will be loathe to return"—and she went to the consul's house and borrowed a horse to ride with me as far as Lifta. By the time she had tied the basket to the horse and wrapped the infant, the caravan had set out. We made haste to overtake it, and soon we were descending in the arroyo of Lifta—and the way, which at first seemed gloomy and desolate, quickly grew pleasant and attractive, because there were vineyards and olive groves, fig trees and apricots, on either side of it. When we reached the stone bridge of Colonia, there was a pleasant sweetness in the air. Jerusalem and its dejection were behind us, and perhaps we should have parted there—but then she insisted on continuing with me to Mount Castel. She thought she might catch a glimpse of the sea from there, for she remembered being taken as a child to a place from where she had glimpsed it. And so we began to climb the narrow path up that high hill. In the distance we spied my caravan, lithely snaking its way above us, and there was a great clarity of air, and the voice of the muezzin from the mosque at Nebi Samwil seemed to call to us, and we cried back to it. But we had no idea that the ascent would take so long or that the approach of darkness was so near, and by the time we reached the top of the hill there was not a ray of twilight left, so that whatever sea was on the horizon could not be seen but only thought. My caravan was slowly disappearing down the slope that led to Karyat-el-Anab, and all we could hear from afar were the hooves of the animals scuffing an occasional stone. What was I to do, Doña Flora? Say adieu there? I did not want to return with her to Jerusalem, because I knew that I then would have no choice but to become an Ashkenazi, and I had no wish to be one . . .

—Because I was down to my last centavo and all out of the spices I had brought from Salonika, and had I returned to Jerusalem as a pauper, I would have had to join the roster of Ashkenazim to qualify for the dole they give only to their own. And that, Your Grace, *señor y maestro mío,* I was not about to do—would His Grace have wanted me to Ashkenazify myself?

. . . .

—In truth, I clutch at my memories as one clutches at a lifeline, for I can picture nothing that happened without welling up with compassion. Thus it began—with a father riding behind his son in the Holy Land, rather chagrined and bewildered, regarding the wasteland around him, although 'twas not always waste.

—Well said, madame, that is so. Suddenly you see a fine grain field, or an orchard, or some date palms and fruit trees by a water course, or a peasant's hut, or a group of children playing by a well—and then there is wasteland again and the remnants of a most ancient devastation. At sunset we reached a large khan and found it deserted, because the caravan had already moved on to pass the night in Ramleh. Fresh straw was scattered for us in a corner of the hall, beside a blackened wall, and our pallets were made there. I stepped outside and looked at the vast and most exceedingly dark plain in which there shone not a single light. Smoke curled up from an oven where bread was being baked for our supper. Yosef went to see to our horses. I watched him, a handsome, erect young man, stride over to a hedgerow of prickly pears and hang the feedbags on the horse's necks while patting their heads and talking to them, his head nestled in the mane of your mare. Perhaps he was whispering some consolation to her for her mistress's failure to arrive! An Ishmaelite standing nearby made some remark to him and he listened with friendly attention—and once again I was struck by how the soft, pampered youth who went shopping with you in the bazaar of Kapele Carse, carrying your dresses and perfumes, had turned into a young man beneath whose newly grown mustache there was already something quite secretive. He resembled my father as a young man, before his bankruptcy, and I suddenly felt such a bitterness of spirit, señores, that I longed to return to the sea I had come from no more than a few hours before, which had played with me and tossed me on its waves. I thought of my parents of blessed memory, and all at once I felt a great desire to say the kaddish for them in the Holy Land and to pray for their souls. And so I asked my son if there might be a village nearby with enough Jews in it for a prayer group. At first he was as startled as if I had asked him to pluck a star from the sky. *"Jews? Here?"* "And is there anywhere without them?" I marveled. He cocked his head and stared at me, and then he smiled a bit—and I wonder, Your Grace, whether it was then that the frightful idea was born in him, or whether it had been there all along—and after mulling it over for a moment he said softly, "Right away, *Papá,* right away." He ducked through a gap in the prickly pear hedge and stepped into some mud huts, from which he pulled out one shadowy form after another and brought them to me. I looked about me and saw these dark-faced, bare-legged Ishmaelites, some with battered fezes on their heads and some with black keffiyehs, most silent and docile, as if they had just been torn out of their first sleep, madame. "Here, *Papá,*" says Yosef, "here is your *minyan.*" He frightened me. "But who are these men, son?" I asked him. And he, standing there in the still of evening, *señor y maestro mío,* he said, *mí amiga* Doña Flora, as if he were *loco* in the head, "But these are Jews, *Papá,* they just don't know it yet . . ."

—Yes, madame, those were his words. "These are Jews who will understand that they are Jews," he said. "These are Jews who will remember that they are Jews." Before I could even stammer an answer, he was chiding them in his friendly manner and making them face east toward Jerusalem, where there was nothing but a black sky full of stars, after which he began to chant the evening prayer in a new melody I never had heard. From time to time he went down on his knees and bowed like a Muslim so that the Ishma elites would understand and bow too . . . and I, Your Grace—señor—Rabbi Haddaya—my master and teacher—allowed myself to go along with it . . . sinful man that I was, I could not resist saying the kaddish and profaning the blessed Name of the Lord. I said it from beginning to end in memory of my parents and of my poor wife . . . madame, the blanket . . . it is falling off . . .

—Here, let me, Doña Flora, I'll do it. I . . . he is shaking . . . something is bothering him . . . perhaps . . .

—I . . .

—But what means that, madame? "Tu-tu-tu"? What would he say?

—But what wishes he to say, for the love of God?

—But the blanket is wet, Doña Flora. It is most wet. Perhaps we should make a fire and dry it over the stove, and meanwhile I can change His Grace . . .

—No. Why?

—Why a servant? Why a Greek? I am at your complete service, madame, with all my heart . . . let the good deed be mine . . . he was like a father to me, Doña Flora . . . I beg you . . .

—No. He is listening. His eyes are following me. Rabbi Shabbetai knows my mind . . . he remembers what I said . . . that every idea has a pocket and in that pocket is another idea . . . "There is no man without his hour nor any thing without its use" . . . but what means he by "tu-tu-tu"? What would he say? He seems most agitated . . .

—Well, then, in a word, in a word, Doña Flora, so my visit began, on that route leading from Jaffa to Jerusalem, seeking to catch up with a caravan of pilgrims that kept a day ahead of us. For three whole days we shadowed and smelled its trail, trampling the grasses it had trampled, coming upon the embers of its campfires, treading on the dung of its animals. The two of us rode, and your mare, madame, which was now just an extra mouth to feed, trotted along between us. Sometimes, in the twilight, it even seemed that we could see your silhouette astride her . . . My son tried being a good guide to his father. He pointed out to him the threshers in Emmaus, and the winnowers in Dir Ayub, and had him dismount to smell the wild sweet basil and the green geranium, and to chew the stems of shrubs and grasses from which perhaps some new spice might be concocted. The next evening too, by a stone fence belonging to Kafr Saris, he disappeared for a while among some rocks and olive trees and returned with a new group of wraiths, more *Jews who did not know that they were Jews*—which is to say, another band of drowsy peasants and shepherds who were rousted from their first sleep. This time he gave them all a quarter of a bishlik for their pains—and all this, señores, was entirely for my sake, to enable the touring father to satisfy his craving to chant the kaddish, not only for the souls of his parents, but also for those of his grand-, and great-grand-, and even greater grand-grandparents than that, until the first father of us all must have heard in heaven that Avraham Mani had arrived in the Land of Israel and was about to enter Jerusalem.

—Ah! That afternoon we finally caught up with the Russian pilgrims—who, now that Jerusalem was just around the corner, had taken off their fur hats and were walking on their knees from sheer devoutness, following the narrow road up and down in long, crawling columns from the Big Oak Tree to the Little Oak Tree and from there to the Monastery of the Cross, which was bathed by red flowers in its lovely valley. And then suddenly, there was Jerusalem: a wall with turrets and domes, a clear, austere verse written on the horizon. Soon I was walking through its narrow streets by myself, led by the consular mace-bearer.

—Because Yosef could not wait and went to return the horses to the consulate and tell the consul about his trip while I was packed off with my bundles behind the mace-bearer, who struck the cobblestones with his staff and led me along a street and up some steps to a door that did not need to be pushed open because it already was. I stood hesitantly in the entrance, staring in the looking-glass that faced me at the unkempt form of a sun-ravaged, sunken-eyed traveler. And just then, Rabbi Shabbetai, who should step out of the other room but Doña Flora herself, but thirty years younger! It was as if she had flown through the air above my ship and arrived there before me! A most wondrous apparition, señores—here, then, was the secret that explained Beirut and that had, so it seemed, quite swept Yosef off his feet! One passage through life had not been enough for so charming a visage, and so it had come back a second time . . . I was so exhausted from the trip and from the sun, and so excited to be in Jerusalem and its winding lanes—I already felt, *mi amiga,* that I had arrived in a city of bottomless recesses—that I whispered like a sleepwalker: "Madame Flora, is it truly you? Has the rabbi then relented?" Hee hee hee hee . . .

—That is how muddled I was.

—No, wait . . . I beg you . . .

—But wait, madame . . . You have no idea of the wondrous resemblance between you, which is perhaps what lured you to Beirut in the first place in order to meet your own double and give my poor departed son . . . I mean, tacitly . . . eh?

—We knew nothing. What did we know?

—The betrothal was carried out in haste . . . the rabbi too was notified after the fact . . .

—Yes. A tremendous resemblance.

—Yes. Even now—are you listening, *señor y maestro mío*?—when I look at the *rubissa,* I see as in a vision Tamara thirty years from now. The very spit and image . . . in charm as well as beauty . . .

—At first she was alarmed. She turned very red but kissed my hand and let me bless her, and then took my bundle and laid it gently and with great respect on your childhood bed beneath the large, arched window, madame, in which henceforward I slept, in hot weather and in cold. She set the table for me and warmed water for me to wash my hands and feet, and then stood over me to serve me as the sun was setting outside. I noticed that she seemed not at all surprised that Yosef was taking so long at the consul's instead of hurrying home, even though he had been away for a week; it was as if she were used to the consul's coming before her. When I was all washed and cleaned and full of food, she summoned her father Valero to make my acquaintance and take me with him to the synagogue for the evening prayer, after which we chatted a bit about Jerusalem and its plagues and then lit candles against the darkness of the night. It was only then that Yosef came home at last. He was carrying a lantern and was still disarrayed from his journey, which for him had only now ended. He greeted his wife and the rest of us with a polite nod, but he was so tired that he confused a bag of his clothes with a packet of some documents from the consulate and even began to speak to us in English until he realized his mistake. It was then that I first understood, *chère* madame and señor, that he was in the grips of a notion more important to him than his own marriage—of an *idée fixe,* as the French say, that mattered to him more than having seed.

—His own, madame.

—Of course . . .

—I will get to that shortly.

—As brief as I can make it.

—What will His Grace eat?

—But why should a little porridge disturb us?

—Of course . . .

—Perhaps, Your Grace, it was Doña Flora who first fired his imagination and put such mettle into him. The stories you told the lad about Jerusalem, madame, on those nights when he lay by your side in the bed of the *hacham,* were what filled his head with grand thoughts . . . what made him think you could roll the world around like an egg without cracking or spilling any of it . . . although all he had to roll it on were the *pensamientos pequeños* gathered from those that Rabbi Shabbetai had discarded. Because before many days had gone by, it was clear to me that he had not merely been humoring me by dragging sleepy peasants out of their huts for a quarter of a bishlik apiece. You see, ever since he had come to Jerusalem to fetch Tamara to her wedding and stayed on there because she would not leave, he had resolved that if stay he must, he would stay among Jews, even if they did not know yet that they were Jews or had completely forgotten it. That was why he treated them with such warm sympathy. Their forgetfulness pained him, and he feared the shock of remembrance that would befall them, so that, together with the British consul, he did all he could to soften it in advance.

—Yes, *muy estimada* madame. Is my master and teacher listening? Such was the thought that possessed my son's mind, the *idée fixe* rammed home as forcefully by the consul as if it were an iron rod driven into his brain.

—There was no knowing which of them was the bellwether and which prevailed upon which, because the consul, like all Englishmen, looked upon us Jews not as creatures of flesh and blood but as purely literary heroes who had stepped out of the pages of the Old Testament and would step back into those of the New at the Last Judgment, and who meanwhile must be kept from entering another story by mistake—which made me realize at once that I must be on guard to protect my only son's marriage.

—Of course. The next morning the mace-bearer came to invite us to high tea with the consul and his wife. I bought myself a new fez by the Lions' Gate, Tamara cleaned and ironed my robe, and off the three of us went to present me to the consul at that time of day when Jerusalem is ruled by a cinnamon light.

—The consulate is near the Church of the Holy Sepulchre. You cut across to it from the Via Dolorosa.

—By way of the Street of the Mughrabites, via Bechar's courtyard and Navon's stairs. 'Tis behind Geneo's wine shop, on Halfon's side of it.

—No, the other Halfon. The little one who married Rabbi Arditi's daughter.

—The Ashkenazim are a bit further down.

—'Tis all built up there now, madame, all built up. There are no empty lots there any more.

—It is built up behind the Hurva Synagogue too. The Ashkenazim are spreading all over.

—For the moment, no. But they will build there too, never fear. There is nothing to be done about it, madame. You have greatly come up in the world since leaving the Holy City, but although Time remained behind there, it has not stood still either.

—As brief as I can make it. Nevertheless, Doña Flora, I must let the story unfold out of me in its entirety, with all its joys and its sorrows, its tangs and its tastes—and for the moment I was still in Jerusalem as an esteemed visitor, a *passer-through* and not a *stayer-on*. The consul and his wife received us most lovingly, and the consul even spoke a bit of Hebrew to me . . . Madame?

—Yes, madame, a rather Prophetic Hebrew. Yosef circulated about the house as if it were his own, and once again it struck me how adept the lad was at making himself liked and finding himself a father or a mother when he needed one. Meanwhile, more guests arrived: an old sheikh who had been fetched from the village of Silwan to provide me with company, and his son, an excellent young man who was a clerk at the consulate; some newly arrived French pilgrims; several English ladies who drank tea, puffed hookahs, and seemed quite startled by their own utterances; a German spy in a dark suit who had in tow a baptized Austrian Jew; and so on and so forth. But I, madame—I, my master and teacher—I, señores—did not forget the mission I had entrusted myself with, so that even as I listened to everyone with enthusiasm as a good guest should—"Who is honored? He who honors his fellow man"—I kept one eye, madame, on Tamara, who was sitting there silent but glowing among the Englishwomen, squeezed in between them like a baby lamb in a team of bony old nags and sipping her tea while nibbling a dry English scone in that clear, winy light. She was smiling absently to herself and considering the air, and I could see at once that her absence was due not to plenitude but vacuity. It was as if she were still not over her betrothal and had not yet been properly wed . . . and at that moment, I thanked God for having sent me to Jerusalem . . .

—I am referring to matters of the womb.

—No. Not even a miscarriage. Nothing.

—In a word, nothing, madame. And to make a long story short, it was from that nothing that I commenced my mission, that is to say, that I made it my business to see that that marriage bore seed and not only *idées fixes* that were bound to lead to some fiasco. By the time we guests of the consul returned home that night, each of us carrying his or her lantern *à la* Jerusalem and weaving through the narrow streets behind the macebearer, who kept rapping the cobblestones with his staff to warn the inhabitants of the underworld of our approach, I had made up my mind to become a *stayer-on*—that is, to settle as deeply as I could into the young couple's home, and into my bed in your little alcove, from which I could quietly carry out my designs. And that, señores, was the meaning of my *desaparición* that you were so worried about. Does Your Grace hear me? How charmingly he nods!

—No, I do not wish to weary him. But if I do not unfold my story to the end, how will he pass his silent verdict on it? Because that same night, Your Grace, I was already having my first second thoughts as I lay secretly plotting in bed not far from the two of them. Their door was slightly ajar; moonlight bathed the bottom of their blanket; a ray of it strayed back and forth between the looking-glasses; and as I listened to their breathing—to the sounds they made as they stirred or murmured in their dreams—to their laughter and their sighs—I tried reckoning how to tell the wheat from the chaff and how to read the signs, that is, to understand where the fault or impediment lay, and if it did not perhaps involve some flight or falling-off, some inversion or infirmity, that must needs be remedied if the seed was to be conjoined by the potency of its yearning with Constantinople and with what I held most dear there, namely, *señor y maestro mío,* with Your Grace. And so I was up the next day before dawn, with the crowing of the first cock, which I encountered strutting in our little street as I groped my way in the dim light to the Wailing Wall, brimming with the lusts and life of Jerusalem, to weep for the destruction of our Temple and say the morning prayer. I licked the dew from the stones of the wall and asked God to prosper my way, and then I turned and ascended the Harat Bab-el-Silsileh to the silent souk and bought some dough rings, hard-boiled eggs, and oregano from the Arabs there. I took these back to my young couple, who were still luxuriating in sleep, brewed them a big pot of strong coffee, brought it all to their bed, and woke them, saying: "I am not merely your father, I am also your two mothers who died in the prime of their lives, and so it is only meet that I pamper you a bit—but in return, as Rachel says to Jacob, "Give me sons or I shall die." The two of them blushed and smiled a bit, glanced anxiously at each other, pulled the blanket tight around themselves, and turned over in bed. Meanwhile, the muezzin had begun calling the faithful to prayer in the great mosque. Yosef listened carefully to the long wailing chant that was making my head spin and suddenly sat up and said, "That chant, *Papá,* is what we must work our way into until the truth that has been forgotten comes to light, because if we do not, what will become of us?" And with that he threw off his blanket, shook out of it the *idée fixe* that he had spent the night with, clapped it in his fez, and went off to wash and finish waking up.

—'Twas a jest, Doña Flora . . . a fantastical remark . . . a mere parable . . .

—I will not do it again. It was only to explain why I now changed from a passer-through to a stayer-on and began to establish myself in Jerusalem, which was rapidly exchanging the soft breezes of spring for a fierce summer heat that its inhabitants, Your Grace, call the *hamseen,* though so still is the air that I call it the *unseen.* Before a day or two had gone by I had a staff of my own to rap the cobblestones with and a lantern to make me visible in the dark, and within a week I was conferring the pleasure of my voice on the worshipers in the Stambouli Synagogue, who let me read from the Torah every Monday and Thursday. By now I was shopping in the market too, and helping Tamara peel vegetables and clean fish, and after another week or two I rented half a stand from an Ishmaelite in the Souk-el-Kattanin and set out on it the spices I had brought from overseas, to which I added some raisins, almonds, and nuts that I sold for a modest profit. I was becoming a true Jerusalemite, rushing up and down the narrow streets for no good reason, unless it were that God was about to speak somewhere and I was afraid to miss it.

—And sleeping all the while in your bed, madame, in the little alcove beneath the arched window, where I hung a new looking-glass of my own across from your old one to keep it company and to bring me news of the rest of the house, so that I might work my secret will. And though my big beard kept getting in all the mirrors, the youngsters seemed to be fond of me; not only did I not feel a burden to them, I felt I was breathing new life into a house that I had found dreamy, disorderly, and impecunious, because Yosef was paid more respect than money at the consulate, the consul being a dreamer himself who seemed to think he was not a consul but a government and who was already quite bankrupt from the prodigal sums he spent, partly on the pilgrims whose lord protector he sought to be even though most were not English, and partly on the Jews, whom he considered his wards and the keys to the future. No touring lady could visit Jerusalem from abroad without being royally put up in his home and having Yosef to guide her to the churches of Bethlehem and the mosques of Hebron, down to Absalom's Tomb and hence to the Spring of Shiloah and from there to the Mount of Olives, first putting everything in its proper perspective and then passionately, by the end of the day, scrambling it all up again, expertly stirring faiths, languages, peoples, and races together and pitilessly baking them in the desert sun until they turned into the special Jerusalem soufflé that was his favorite dish . . .

—A guide, madame, if you wish; also a dragoman for roadside conversation; plus a courier for light documents; and a scribe for secret correspondence; and sometimes too, a brewer of little cups of coffee; and when the spirit moved him, the chairman of the disputatious literary soirees of the Jerusalem Bibliophile Society. In a word, a man for all times and seasons, particularly those after dark, for so accustomed was he to coming home at all hours that I had developed the habit of waking up in the middle of the night and going to see if he was in his bed yet, and of becoming frantically, heartstrickenly worried if he was not, as if the very life were being crushed out of him at that moment. And since I was afraid to step out into the silent street, I would ascend to the roof to peer through the moonlit darkness at the ramparts of the city, and then down into the bowels of the streets, hardly breathing while I waited to espy, bobbing as it approached from the Muslim or Christian Quarter, a small flame that I knew from its motion to be his. At once, madame, I slipped down from the roof and ran to the gate to admit him into his own house, as if it were he who was the honored guest from afar whose every wish must be indulged, even more than you indulged it when he was a boy, madame. I took off the fez that was stuck to his sweaty hair, helped him out of his shoes, opened his belt to let him out of his *idée fixe,* brought water to wash his face and feet, and warmed him something to eat, because whole days would go by without his taking anything but coffee. At last, relaxed and with his guard down, the color back in his cheeks, he would tell me about his day: whom he had met, and whose guide he had been, and where he had taken them, and what the consul had said about this or his wife about that, and what was written about them in the English press, and their latest protest to the Turkish governor—and I would listen most attentively and ask questions, and every question received its answer, until finally I teased him about his *idée fixe* that was lying unguardedly in the open and inquired, "Well, son, and what of your Jews who don't know that they are Jews yet?" At first my mockery made him angry. But after a while the anger would pass and he would say with a twinkle in his eyes, "Slowly but surely, *Papá*. They've only forgotten, and in the end they'll remember by themselves. And if they insist on being stubborn, I'll be stubborn too, and if they still don't want to remember . . ." Here his eyes would slowly shut, trapping the twinkle inside them until it grew almost cruel. "If they insist," he would say, weighing my own insistence, "we shall sorely chastise them until they see the error of their ways."

—Yes. He definitely said "chastise," although without explaining himself, as if all chastisement were one and the same and there was no need to spell it out chast by chast.

—Your Grace, *señor y maestro mío,* are you listening?

—Ah! And so, Your Grace, we joked a bit at the expense of his *idée fixe* until Yosef fell softly asleep and I helped him to his feet with the lantern still in his hand and led him off to bed—where, madame, his wife, silently opened the same beautiful, bright eyes with which you are staring at me right now . . .

—God forbid, Doña Flora! Not coerced but gently assisted.

—No further.

—My silent support, madame . . . my fondest encouragement . . .

—No further.

—I had to know.

—I was looking for a definite sign, madame.

—The looking-glass showed only shadows . . .

—Someone is knocking, madame . . . who can it be?

—Is it time for his dinner? Praise God . . .

—But how in the way? Not at all!

—God forbid! I am not going anywhere. I am most eager, *mía amiga* Doña Flora, to see how the rabbi is fed . . .

—I will sit quietly in this corner.

—So this is what Rabbi Shabbetai eats! It is, madame, a dish as pure as snow.

—So it is . . .

—Soft porridge . . . so it is . . .

—So it is. The poor man! Your Grace always hated mushy food . . .

—Of course. There is no choice. It is the wise thing to do, madame. Nothing else would go down as easily, filling the belly while soothing the soul. And who, may I ask, was the servant who brought it?

—A fine-looking young man. Would it not be best, though, for the holy rabbi to be waited on by one of our own?

—Well, a fine-looking young man.

—God forbid! Nothing to excite him, madame. Nothing to spoil his appetite. Why don't you rest and let me feed Rabbi Shabbetai myself? It would be a great pleasure and a privilege.

—Well, then, perhaps later.

—His bib? Where is it?

—One minute . . . in truth, he seems most hungry . . .

—Master of the Universe! Lord have mercy! Why, 'tis a perfect infant . . . a perfect infant . . .

—What, Your Grace?

—In a word . . . in a word . . . in the briefest of words, Doña Flora, but with much fear and trembling, because despite the cloudless summer—that is, we were now in the midst of a fiery, cloudless summer—there had even been a mild outbreak of some sort of plague, the exact name of which no one was quite sure of—I already had, Doña Flora, from all those dreams, nighttime walks, and—whoever was the bellwether—fantasies of that Hebrew-speaking English consul, a sense of impending disaster. Sometimes, when I lost patience standing on the roof, I went back down and took the lantern and waited for my son Yosef on the corner, by Calderon's barred window. I stood beneath the moon and prayed to see that crookedly bobbing little flame, which sometimes appeared from the south, with a herd of black goats coming home late from their distant pasture in the Valley of the Cross, and sometimes from the west, with a band of pilgrims returning from midnight mass in the Holy Sepulchre, to whom my son had attached himself in the darkness as an unnoticed guide to penetrate a place that Jews were barred from . . .

—Of course, madame. A most flagrant provocation. The Christians themselves are divided into mutually suspicious sects that ambush each other in the naves of the church and brawl over every key and lock, and they certainly did not need an uninvited Jew peeking into God's tomb and reminding them of what they did not believe they had forgotten and had no intention of remembering. And as if that were not enough, he sometimes proceeded from there to the Gate of the Mughrabites, from where steps lead up to the great mosque, in order to bid a fond good night to its two Mohammedan watchmen before heading home for the one place that he feared most of all—namely, his own bed.

—That is only in a manner of speaking, of course, Doña Flora . . . most hyperbolically. But see how Rabbi Shabbetai looks at me as he eats! Perhaps my story will take my master's mind off his mush, hee hee hee . . .

—No, no, madame. I did not mean the bed itself. Just the idea of it . . .

—I mean—

—God forbid! 'Twas always with the most friendly respect and affection . . .

—Of . . . why, in all simplicity, of the sleep awaiting him there . . . that was what troubled him so, madame . . .

—That he might awake to discover that the world had changed while he slept . . . that something had happened in it without his knowing or being a party to it . . . that his *idée fixe,* whose sole reliable consular representative he considered himself to be, had burst like a bubble before he had time to bring it back to life . . .

—So he felt, madame. "The day is short and the labor is great." And perhaps—who knows, *maestro y señor mío*—he already sensed his approaching death in that much-provoked Jerusalem of his.

—Tamara, Doña Flora, said nothing.

—That is, she heard and saw everything. And waited . . .

—She was not unreceptive to his views, provided that something came of them . . .

—At night she slept. I kept an eye on her in the looking-glass I had hung on the wall, which was reflected in your old glass, madame, which in turn was reflected in the glass hanging over their bed, and I saw that she slumbered peacefully . . . But look, Doña Flora, he is getting food all over his mouth and chin . . .

—Here . . .

—Perhaps we need a fresh towel.

—As you wish, madame. I am at your service. Perhaps that handsome young Greek made the porridge a bit too mushy . . .

—God forbid, madame! I am not interfering in anything. It was just a thought, and I have already taken it back.

—Of course, madame. Briefly and to the point. Which is that I found your niece an admirable housewife who baked and cooked quite unvaryingly excellent food. She simply forgot at times to make enough of it, so that I had to—

—*Mahshi, kusa,* and *calabaza,* and certain days of the week a *shakshuka* . . .

—Fridays she put up a Sabbath stew with *haminados.*

—Sometimes it had meat in it, and sometimes it had the smell of meat . . .

—Of course. She did all her own cleaning and laundering. The house, Doña Flora, was as spic and span as the big looking-glass. And she also helped her father Valero and his young wife, and took her little stepsister and stepbrother to the Sultan's Pool every afternoon to enjoy the cool water and play with the Atias children among the Ishmaelite tombstones . . .

—The Atias who married Franco's youngest daughter.

—'Tis on the tip of my tongue, *rubissa,* and will soon come to me. Meanwhile, *maestro y señor mío,* permit me to sketch the picture for you. Is he still listening? I was, you see, in Jerusalem to shore up a marriage that needed consolidating, for it had yet to outgrow its hasty Beirut betrothal; and so I did my best to keep the young bride from sinking into too much housework, and from time to time I took her with me to my spice-and-sundries stand in the Souk-el-Kattanin, where she could sit and catch the notice of the passersby with her winning mien, so that—after walking on and stopping short and doubling back for a better look and possibly even a word with her—they might interest themselves in a spice or two. And meanwhile, the air around her began to shoot sparks—one of which, I hoped, would fly all the way to her young husband, who was busy escorting the consul's guests to Bethlehem and Hebron. It would do him no harm, I thought, to wonder why his wife was attracting such looks . . .

—God forbid! God forbid! 'Twas done most honorably. And each day when the sun began to glow redly in my jars of rosemary, cinnamon, and thyme, and to tint my raisins with gold, I put away my goods and folded my stand and brought her to the woman's gallery of the synagogue of Rabbi Yohanan ben-Zakkai to listen to the Mishnah lesson and be seen among the widows and old women by the men arriving from the souk for the afternoon prayer. Sometimes Yosef came too, all in a great dither, his *idée fixe* sticking out of his pocket; and while he said his prayers devoutly enough, he kept running his eyes over us ordinary Jews who *could not forget that we were Jews* and so had nothing to remember, nothing to do but say the same old prayers in the same old chants. Now and then he glanced up at the women's gallery, squinting as if into the distance at his petite wife—who, like himself, though a year had gone by since their Beirut betrothal, still was daubed with its honey-gold coat that had to be patiently, pleasurably, licked away. And I, Rabbi Shabbetai, began to lick . . . slowly but surely, madame . . .

—A parable, of course, madame, never fear . . . *à la fantastique,* as the French would say . . . 'twas merely to bring them together . . . to conclude the good deed started in Beirut, Your Grace. And thus the two of us, madame, the motherless bride and myself, wandered through a Jerusalem summer that burned with a clear, bright light I first caught a glimpse of in your own wondering eyes, Doña Flora, the first time we met in Salonika. I was determined to see this marriage through, and I began taking my daughter-in-law with me everywhere . . . to the courtyard of the consulate, for example, where we sat in the shade of a tree by the cistern and watched the builders lay the foundations for a new house of prayer that is to be called Christ's Church, for the greater glory of England. The air shot sparks; the builders put down their tools and turned to look, for nothing disarms more than beauty; men walking down the lane slackened stride, even backtracked a bit, as if the sight of her made them unsure whether they suddenly had lost or found something. A gentle commotion commenced all around us, until the consul's wife had to step outside and invite us in for a hookah and some English tea with milk while sending a servant to pry Yosef loose from one of the inner rooms. At first he was alarmed to see us there; yet as soon as he saw that all were smiling and in good spirits, he inclined his head with loving resignation and took us under his wing. In this manner I was occasionally able to get him to come home for lunch with us, to have a bite to eat and cool off in his bed with his wife, whom the eyes of Jerusalem were beginning to make him most appreciative of. I did not remain to peer into the looking-glass. I went outside and left them by themselves, locking the door behind me, because by now I had an *idée fixe* of my own, a much smaller and more modest one than his, to be sure, but every bit as powerful . . . and with it, señores, with my craving for seed, I kept after them for all I was worth. And in those hot afternoons, at that most still and torrid hour when the air is dry and without a hint of a breeze, which is the best time for olfaction, I strode through the Lions' Gate and down to the house of the sheikh of Silwan village, where I was shown little fagots of weeds and grasses, roots and flowers that the Ishmaelites had gathered at the old man's behest from the mountains of Judea and Samaria, from the shores of the Dead Sea to the coast of our Mediterranean, for me to sniff and perhaps find some new species or plant from which to concoct the spice of the century . . .

—In truth, madame, one sniff was all I needed. And thus, sniff by sniff and weed by weed, I smelled my way through our Promised Land . . .

—A spice more aromatic and tangy than any of those I had brought from Salonika, which I had begun to run out of by that summer's end that was harsher than summer itself . . .

—In truth, madame, they were running low, and even though this drove up my prices, it did not drive the buyers away. They snatched whatever I had, be it thyme or basil or saffron or rosemary or marjoram or nutmeg or oregano, because it was the month of the great Mohammedan fast, which they broke every night with spicy meals that kept them smacking their lips throughout the next day until the boom of the cannon at sunset announced they could eat once again . . . and that, *su merced*, Rabbi Shabbetai Hananiah, was the sound that sent a shiver through my son Yosef one evening, when I found him sitting by himself in the half-light by his bed, straight as a knife blade and wrapped in a sheet, striped by a sun that was in its last throes above the Jaffa Gate. He had finished the siesta I made him take every day and had already smuggled his wife out through the kitchen window into the Zurnagas' backyard, from where she could proceed to her father's to take the children to the pool, and was now waiting for me to return from my *olfateo* in Silwan to open the locked door for him . . .

—Yes, he was waiting, madame, wrapped with thoughtful patience in a sheet. I took some fragrant herbs and roots from my robe and scattered them on the bed to dispel the mournful ambience of struggle and sorrow in the odor of seed that hung over it and its pale homunculi, sad-faced gossamer ghosts who were none other than the less fortunate brothers and sisters of our future *baby Moses,* demon children spilled like pollen in that room that still shook from the blast of the cannon, which now fired again, Your Grace, into our holy hills . . .

—Madame?

—God forbid, *muy distinguida rubissa*!

—God forbid, Doña Flora, with all due respect . . .

—God forbid! With all due respect, but also, madame, in all truth . . .

—But how am I disgusting? Surely not to him!

—No, our Yosef would not be angry. He would not even be upset. He would understand how justified my little *idée fixe* was . . . Why, in my honor he even had his own *idée fixe* devour it, so that now the two of them thrashed about together in his soul, which yearned to join the throng of believers gathered before the great mosque—forgetful Jews who soon, with God's help, would remember and bow, not southward to faraway Mecca, but inwardly to themselves, happy to be where they were, beneath the sky above them . . .

—In truth, madame . . .

—How was it possible, you ask? Oh, but it was!

—More than once. In the mosque and in the Dome of the Rock too.

—In truth, *mi amiga,* a frightful provocation . . .

—Yes. To them too. Not just to the Christians.

—A double provocation, the entire justification of which lay in its doubleness, and therefore, in its peaceful intentions, since according to him, once all remembered their true nature, they would make peace among themselves.

—He felt too much compassion to fed fear, Doña Flora. You see, he had already racked his brain for all the chastisements he would chastise them with for their obduracy, for all the pain and sorrow he would inflict on them and their offspring, and he was now so full of compassion that he never dreamed that before he would have time to pity them all they would seize and massacre him . . .

—But how, madame, do you restrain a thought?

—The consul? But that was the very root of the evil—that boundlessly audacious English consular enthusiasm that made him think that the entire British fleet was at anchor just over the hills, somewhere between Ramallah and el-Bireh, covering his every movement . . .

—How, Doña Flora? How? Time was already running out!

—Because I had begun to despair of his accursed *idée fixe,* which devoured every other *idée* that it encountered as if it were simply grist for the mill, like that which madame is now spooning into His Grace. I was persuaded more than ever that the marriage must be made to bring forth a child, which alone could do battle—yes, from its cradle!—with the unnatural thoughts of a father by means of a simple cry or laugh, or of the riddle of its own future; and thus, Doña Flora, thus, Your Worship, began the race between my son's death and the birth of his son. It was the month of Elul, whose penitential prayers broke the silence of the night, that time of year when—perhaps you remember, madame—wondrous breezes are born that get their odors and tastes from all over, taking a pinch of the warmth of the standing water in the Pool of Hezekiah, adding a touch of dryness from the scorched thistles in the fields between the houses of the Armenians, mixing in the bitterness of the cracked, furrowed graves on the Mount of Olives, whipping up a flying incense that whirls from street to street. Only now do I realize, *señor y maestro mío,* that the true spice, the spice of the future, will not come from any root, leaf, berry, or pollen, but from the shapeless, formless wind, for which I shall uncork all my vials and bottles to let it blend with their contents and infuse them with strength for the Days of Awe, awful in every sense of the word . . .

—No, Doña Flora, no, *su merced, I* made sure he did not miss the services. The consul and his wife had gone to 8135.5 Jaffa on consular business, and the air was tremulous in that subtle way it is in Jerusalem on Yom Kippur, as if the Merciful One, the chief judge Himself, had secretly returned to the city from His travels and was hiding in one of its small dwellings, in which He planned to spend the holy fast day with us, the signed list of men's fates—"Who by fire and who by water, who in due time and who before his time"—already in His pocket, although He was afraid to take it out and read it. Yosef seemed more at peace with the world too, full of an inner mirth that took the edge off even his *idée fixe,* while Tamara had been busy cooking her delicious holiday dishes, her eyes, which were inflamed with dust all summer, now clear and wide—indeed, Rabbi Shabbetai, they were so like madame's that are looking at us right now that the growing resemblance between Constantinople and Jerusalem sent a shiver down my spine. And so I awoke him before dawn, and took him to the synagogue, and stood with him not far from the cantor, so that we could be quick to snatch the tidbits thrown to the worshipers from time to time—a verse from "God the King Who Sitteth on His Mercy Seat," a word from "O Answer Us," or even a whole section of "Lord of Forgiveness"—and raise our voices on high in token of our piety and in hope that the Master of the Universe would hear us and let us have our way for once . .

—What say you, Doña Flora? I never knew!

—Old Tarabulus? Who does not remember him? Why, he would bring tears to our eyes every Sabbath eve in the Great Synagogue with his "Come, My Love" !

—Truly?

—O my son!

—Yes, that old prayer shawl that was black with age . . . of course I do . . . it was already that color when I was a child . . . I always felt drawn to it too, but I never dared touch it . . .

—Truly? Oh, the poor boy . . . my poor son . . .

—O my poor son . . . you speak of him with such love . . .

—No, I will not cry.

—Oh, madame, oh, Your Grace, what sweet sorrow I feel at the thought of my boy standing wrapped in that grimy prayer shawl by the hearth of your salon in Constantinople, pretending to be the great Tarabulus . . .

—Of course . . . "This Day Hath the World Conceived" . . . the Rosh Hashanah prayer . . . "Be We Thy Sons or Slaves" . . .

—No, I will not sing now . . . ah, the poor lad . . . my poor son . . . because you see, even though I knew that all things were decided in heaven, I knew too that "If I am not for myself, who will be for me?" . . . and so I kept after him . . . because to whom could I pass on what consumed me if I let go of it? Your most agreeable brother-in-law Refa'el Valero had little children of his own, and his Veducha was pregnant again, and they certainly did not need another child, not even if it was only a grandchild . . . and so, because if I was not for myself who would be for me, and if not now, when, I began to pursue him through courtyards and down alleyways on his visits to Jews and to Gentiles. I never let him out of my sight, until I acquired a most infernal knowledge of Jerusalem myself, of the city of your tender youth, Doña Flora.

—Why, I was able to pop up anywhere, like a wise old snake . . .

—Because—and this I learned from Yosef—it is a city in which all places are connected and there is a way around every obstacle. You can traverse the whole of it by going from house to house without once stepping out into the street . . .

—For example, for example, by climbing Arditi's stairs you can get to Bechar and Geneo's roof, and then through their kitchen to the courtyard of the Greek patriarch, from where, if you cut straight through the chapel, you need only open a little gate to find yourself in She'altiel's salon. If She'altiel is home, you may have a cup of coffee with him and ask his leave to proceed, but if he is not, or if he is sleeping, you need not turn back. Just tiptoe down his little hallway without peeking into the bedroom and you will come to five steps belonging to the staircase of an old building destroyed by the accursed Crusaders, which lead directly to the storeroom of Franco's greengrocery. Once there, you need only move some watermelons and sacks aside and stoop a bit to enter the little synagogue of the Ribliners, where you will find yourself behind the Holy Ark. If they happen to be praying, you can join them, even if they are Ashkenazim, and if they are in the middle of a Mishnah class, you can ask to go to their washroom, which is shared by the guard of the Muslim wakf—who, no matter how sleepy he seems, will be happy to take half a mejidi to lead you across the large hall of the Koran scholars and back out into the street, where you will look up in amazement to espy the house of your parents, may they rest in paradise, the very house of your childhood, madame . . .

—From the rear? Why from the rear?

—But it is all built up there, madame . . . the buildings are now conjoined . . . that empty space is no more . . .

—Never once, Doña Flora. I myself was amazed that I was not once lost . . . because in Constantinople—does Your Grace remember?—does he?—that happened to me all the time, not just as a boy but as a young man too, and without the slightest effort, hee hee . . . For example, *rubissa,* if I was sent to fetch something for Rabbi Shabbetai, some tobacco, or coffee, or a sesame cake, or cheese, I would end up wandering from bazaar to bazaar, past the rug dealers, past the fabric stalls, past all the colorful, good-smelling dresses, across the Golden Horn without even noticing, passing from Asia to Europe—and there, madame, I would get so hopelessly confused that I could no longer find my way back, so that evening would come—does Your Grace remember?—and Rabbi Shabbetai would see that there was no tobacco, no coffee, no sesame cake, no cheese, and no Mani, and he would have to leave his books, go downstairs, find some horseman or soldier from the Sultan's Guard, and give him a bishlik to go to Galata and bring me back home to Asia, frightened and white as a sheet . . . hee hee hee . . . he remembers . . . by God, he is smiling! Even after so many years, that Constantinople of yours is a maze for me . . . your crooked Stamboul, which to this day I cannot get straight in my head . . . whereas Jerusalem, madame, could not only be gotten straight, it was getting too straight for comfort . . . night by night I felt it tighten around me . . .

—Because at night, Doña Flora—in those nights that grew longer and longer now that we had seen the last of the last holiday, and on which the sun set sooner and sooner—the *idée fixe* that I thought had faded with summer's end now raised its head again with winter's start and was soon raging out of control, like an illness that had gone to sleep not because it had run its course but in order to wake up stronger than ever. And by now I was mortally afraid for my own soul . . .

—Of his *idée fixe* infecting me too, Doña Flora, so that I would start seeing the world through his eyes. Because there was more strength in his silence, in the calm way he shut his eyes while quietly listening to me, than there was in all my warnings and rebukes, which he crossed out with a single thin-lipped smile before donning a large, odd cloak that he had found in the market in Hebron and setting out on his nighttime excursions. It did not even help to hide his lantern, because his pockets were full of little candles, which he stuffed them with in case he had to light one and declare himself to the Turkish watch. The spirit moved him with the fall of night, so that while the two of us, Tamara and I, were preparing for bed, he slipped out of the house without his lantern despite the danger of it and—in the same roundabout way he had of going from Jewish house to Jewish house—went to call on his *Jews who did not know yet they were Jews,* most boldly walking in and out of their homes, without once stepping into the street, in his eagerness to find some sign or testimony that would prove them wrong . . .

—For example, madame, a scrap of parchment, a piece of cloth, a potsherd, a stone, some old ritual object—and when he despaired of all these, he would strain to catch some word murmured in their dreams and to seize it as if it were the handle of a coal scoop burning in the fire of forgetfulness, which he must snatch from the embers to let its contents cool until they regained, like soft white gold, their elemental form. And thus, Rabbi Shabbetai, thus, Doña Flora, he entered the houses of his forgetful Jews as they were turning in for the night, which was young enough for their doors to be still open, passing through hallways, up and down stairways, and in and out of dwellings whose inhabitants, soft with sleep, were getting ready for bed and having a last cup of tea while their new cuckoo clocks—for German salesmen had been to Jerusalem too—cooed away in the corners. He conversed with them gently, with that slight inclination of his head, most amiably and politely; gave them regards from one another; asked them for news of themselves; and listened to what they had to say. Not that they had the least idea of who he was or what he wanted from them—but his good nature was infectious and they welcomed him so warmly that they hardly even noticed that he was already in their bedrooms, bending down to look at something, pulling back a blanket, reaching out to touch a baby or to turn over one of the many children who lay wrapped in their little bed smocks, sound asleep as only youngsters can be who are busy growing in their slumber and not merely resting in it, their eyes sealed by the thin yellow crust still left over from the summer's trachoma. And then, thinking of the chastisements he must bring upon them for their obduracy, my poor son felt his resolve weaken, swallowed the lump in his throat, and ran his hands over the walls as if looking for a dark opening that memory might burst forth from. And thus, madame, thus, Your Grace, the autumn came and went with the winter on its heels. Freezing rains lashed the walls of the holy city, to which the Russian pilgrims were still crawling on their knees, bundled in their heavy fur coats, their reddish beards and mustaches making them look like so many giant silkworms with their heads in the air. They packed the square of the Church of the Holy Sepulchre and the streets all around, waiting in puddles of rain and mud for the birth of their god, their hate for the Jew greater than ever, because not only he had killed their Christ, he had done it in the remotest and most forsaken of places instead of in Mother Russia . . .

—Because they were already mourning their approaching departure from that lavish sepulcher, which they were growing fonder of by the minute, and were quite distraught at not being able to tear it out of the earth in one piece and carry it back to their native land with them. And so, madame, it was hardly surprising that they should have been looking in their most pious ardor for a substitute corpse, preferably a young Jew's . . . and in truth, it was given them . . .

—*He* was given them.

—He gave himself . . . he let himself be passed from hand to hand . . .

—In parable . . . *à la fantastique* . . . Your Grace understands . . .

—Again? But have I not made you shudder enough, madame? I have already brought tears to your eyes . . .

—Again? I cannot.

—I saw nothing . . . I only know what I was told . . .

—I have already told you all I know.

—They slit his throat.

—There, you are shaking again, madame. And Rabbi Haddaya has stopped eating . . .

—He was passed from hand to hand.

—In truth, he stole into that pilgrim crowd, and on the night of the holy fire . . .

—I suppose his *idée fixe* had swallowed all his fears and made a fine grist of them.

—'Tis no wonder, madame. Even the Mohammedans are afraid to approach on such a night . . .

—Perhaps he expected to convert them too . . . who knows?

—I am saying that I do not know what my son really thought, or what he thought that he should have thought. Insofar as he had decided that everyone in Jerusalem was connected, not even the wildest or strangest of pilgrims could fail to arouse his insatiable curiosity, which was forever looking for ways to link strangers together and do battle with what he deemed their self-immurement . . .

—At first, perhaps, the motherless bride you found for him, madame . . . and possibly, he considered me too to be such a case of self-inflicted isolation . . .

—No, God forbid—he loved her, madame! He loved and honored her greatly, and always spoke to her with much tact and circumspection, as if they were still in the midst of their betrothal and he must not encumber her—which is why he went off each evening and left her to her own devices. And once he realized that I would stay with her, he grew more unbridled than ever . . .

—Followed him at night too, madame?

—At first I tried. But the nights grew colder and colder, the pilgrims having managed to their great satisfaction to bring their Russian snow and hail with them, and his *idée fixe* could no longer hold in check my own dreadful fright. And so I begged his friend from the consulate, the son of the sheikh from Silwan, to do all he could to save him from himself while I sat home by the coal-burning stove and sang Tía Loja's *conacero* to that little drop of fluid, which I knew by the first candle of Hanukkah, madame, to be safely deposited where it belonged . . . Here, this is how I sang it, Doña Flora—

—Because I saw no sign of menstrual blood.

—I always noticed, although don't ask me how. And I was so happy that I sang like this—

—I have a pleasant voice. Come, listen, madame . . . 'tis but a short *conacero*. . .

—No, he is. He knows the song . . .

—No, I will not!

—It was his favorite of all Tía Loja's *conaceros.* I beg you . . . I desire to sing it for him!

—No, he is looking at me. He is pleased. I will not sing much . . . soon I will be gone, madame . . . the best hope of man is the maggot . . .

—No. 'Tis not I but you who needs rest, Doña Flora. Your face is so pale that the light passes right through it. And the worst times are still to come . . .

—I will stay here . . . I will watch over him . . . I will take it on myself . . .

—I will not be a burden to him . . . I will lullaby him to sleep . . .

—Most pleasantly . . . until he falls asleep. Does Your Grace remember? Go now, madame. Adieu, madame. I am only lullabying him . . . go, madame . . . adieu, madame . . .

When all go to the kehillá,
I go to your house,
Istraiqua, apple of my eye.
When all kiss the mezuzá,
I kiss your own face,
Istraiqua, apple of my eye.

To the graveyard has your mother gone
For my death to pray,
That I may take you as my bride not.
To the graveyard have your sisters gone
For my death to pray,
That I may take you as my bride not.

She is finally gone, then, the woman! And you and I, my master and teacher, are alone again as once when we were young. She is most wondrous, Doña Flora! "A woman of valor who can find? For her price is far above pearls; the heart of her husband doth safely trust in her, so that he shall have no need of spoil." But will she have the strength? In the port in Salonika we had a saying, "What good is gold when the husband is old?" And suppose he is sick too? Once it seemed to me, Rabbi Shabbetai, that I envied Your Grace for his marriage, but today I understand that my envy was of her, for taking Your Grace away from me. Will she prove equal to the task, though? 'Tis the hand of God that has brought me, Your Grace's oldest and most trusty disciple, back to him. Now that the two of us are alone, I would be most grateful if Your Grace would kindly whisper a word to me. I am all silent anticipation. What can be the meaning of this great silence of yours?

Is it in truth silence, then? Is señor's muteness decreed? Perhaps the lute has indeed popped a string. Is it that, then: that there is no longer a voice to give utterance? Even the "tu tu tu" that Your Grace sounded before would be most welcome. "Rabbi Elazar ben Hisma says, 'Cryptic portents are but the crumbs of wisdom.' " But I would make something whole even of Your Grace's crumbs, for I am well versed in Your Grace's manner and have been for ages. Your Grace need not fear me . . . Ai, will you cling to your silence forever, then, or is this but an interval? Can it be that you will leave us without breaking it? Who would have thought it, señor, who would have imagined it! Not that I did not know that the day would come when His Grace would grow weary of us, but I somehow had never foreseen it as silence, only as a vanishing, a *desparición* like all your others: one day the rabbi would set out again to preach and hold court in some far place, and while we were still thinking that he was there, or elsewhere, he would be already nowhere, quite simply gone and no more. So I imagined your departure: your tobacco on the table, your little nargileh next to it, the quill and inkwell in their usual place, an open book lying beside them, your cloak flapping near the looking-glass by the doorway—and Your Grace *gone.* I would go look for him in a place that I knew he always had yearned for, in Mesopotamia, señor, or Babylonia, where your furthest, your first father is buried. And I already pictured myself, Rabbi Haddaya, following in Your Grace's tracks and entering a most ancient synagogue at the time of the afternoon prayer, a synagogue rosy with age, in which a sole Jew sat on a divan saying his vigils and asking him about Your Grace—and without ceasing to recite from his book, he would point to the open window with a gesture that meant, "You have a long, long way to go, for he was here and moved on; he has crossed the purple fields in the bounteous light of a tawny, dry Eden and is gone . . ." *He is gone:* eastward into the great interior, into the land of primeval ruins, into the last light of the shattered blocks of giant idols, headless, buttockless . . . eastward . . . so I imagined it . . . and now, this silence. Is that all, then? Silence? Not a word to clutch at—not even a tiny pearl of wisdom—just this dark little room in a Europe that Your Grace swore never to set foot in again, in an inn run by Greek rebels against the Porte, bound to a bed on wheels? And what is this that I see out the window? A chapel for their dead saints, may their bones rot! Your Grace breaks my heart with his little eyes that are so full of pain and sorrow. See, here I am, *maestro y señor mío,* come from the Land of Israel, in dire need of a word, of a verdict—ah, *su merced* Rabbi Shabbetai, I am in need of a judgment from you! I demand that you convene a rabbinical court, right here and now . . .

. . . .

I AM WHISPERING, because perhaps Doña Flora is listening in the next room. *Her* I wish to spare sorrow, because even though she is a most clever woman, it is inconceivable that she has already understood what Your Grace—I could tell by the gleam in his eyes—understood in silence. For in truth, there was no seed, nor could there have been any, so that the seed could not yet know that it was seed but could only hope to be the seed that it longed to be. That is, it was the seed of longing, the seed of yearning to be seed—seed on the doorknob, seed on the parched earth, seed of shroud and sepulcher, "seed of evil-doers, children of corruption . . ."

. . . .

IS THAT BETTER? Here, let me rub your back a bit too, to help the lazy blood circulate. Does Your Grace remember how he taught me as a boy to scratch his back? There, that's better. The *muy distinguida doña* swaddled you too much. Her worry made her overdo it, the poor thing. The ties need to be loosened some more. There was a time, señor, I won't deny it, when I thought of madame as a kind of trust that Your Grace was safekeeping for me, for she had held out against marriage and had no father to impose his will, and I thought that Your Grace was merely trying to tame her. And indeed, I added a son to tame her even more—until little by little it dawned on me that the trust was not meant for me. And yet even when Your Grace forbade her to join me on my journey to Jerusalem, I still supposed that this was only because he wished us not to jump to any hasty conclusions. It was not until I saw my son's anguish in the port in Jaffa as I stepped out of the ship by myself, and watched him producing Jews who did not know yet they were Jews on our way to Jerusalem, that my understanding began to grow by leaps and bounds—and each leap and each bound leaped and bounded still more when I entered their little house and saw madame's motherless niece for the first time, the Jerusalem damsel who had been betrothed in Beirut. Did Your

Grace have any idea of the fascinating, the frightening resemblance between them? Why, she is the very image of Doña Flora, just thirty years younger and fresher, a thing of beauty!

. . . .

. . . ASSUMING, THAT IS, that it were possible, that the resemblance were not already perfect, that it could have been even greater—because I have already told you, señor, that we both were innocents when we failed to look more deeply into that betrothal in Beirut and to take the necessary precautions . . . But be that as it may, the evening prayer was concluded, and I bitterly sobbed the kaddish one last time, and the comforters wept along with me, and I saw Refa'el Valero rise to go, and his wife Veducha put a towel over the tray of food she had brought, the *mahshi, kusa,* and *burekas,* and went to join him, leaving Tamara with me—for such is the custom in Jerusalem, that once a mourner has eaten of the never-ending egg, he or she does not leave the house they are in. It was getting dark, and one by one everyone left, *even that murderer,* who rose and said good night as sweetly as you please. No one stayed behind but old Carso, who was assigned to chaperone us; he sank down between us, warming himself by the stove, his mouth open as if to gulp its heat. And all along I felt Tamara's eyes on me, as if she wished to tell me what my soul was too frightened to ask. The night dropped slowly. The snowflakes drifted outside, red in the moonlight. Old Carso fell asleep by the stove, taking what heat it gave all for himself. Until, *señor y maestro mío,* I woke him and sent him respectfully home. And even though I knew it was a sin for a man and a woman to be left alone by themselves, I did not lose my presence of mind, for had I lost my presence of mind over a little sin like that, how could I ever have gone on to a much greater one . . .

THE FACT IS, Shabbetai Hananiah, that your silence suits me and that I find it most profound. I only wish that I could be as mute as you—that I could declare: I have said all I have to say, señores, and now you can make what you like of it . . . although since no one ever particularly listened to me anyway, no one would notice my silence either. But still, my master and teacher, I pray you not to cast me yet out of your thoughts. All I am asking from you is a nod or a shake of your head, a yes or a no, in accordance with your sentence. I already know the verdict. 'Tis but the sentence I require.

Well, señor, the stove went out early, because the coals brought by the consul's men were damp and would not catch. It grew colder and colder. I watched her keep going to the closet and take out more and more clothes to put on, but although by now she looked like a big puffball, she could not stop shivering. She even would have put on her husband's Hebron cloak, knife holes and all, had I not made haste to offer her my fox-fur robe, which she took without hesitation and draped over herself. And still the cold grew worse. I too kept donning layer after layer, and finally I wrapped myself in the bloody cloak and looked like a big ball myself. We went from room to room and bed to bed, two dark balls reflected by the moonlight from the looking-glasses, in which you could not tell which of us was which. Jerusalem had shut its gates for the night: no one came, no one went. It was as silent outside as if we were the last two people on earth, alone in the last vestigial shelter, each in his or her room, each on his or her bed, each looking at the other in the looking-glass. The candle was burning down in my hand, and before it went out altogether I blurted, "My daughter, I wish to comfort myself with the child that you will bear, and so I will stay here until the birth, that I may know that I am not the world's last Mani." And she, in my fox robe, a furry ball on her big bed, answered as clear as a bell: "You are the last. Do not stay, because there is nothing, and will be nothing, and was nothing, and could have been nothing, since I differ in nothing from the woman I was, as you have guessed since you entered Jerusalem. We never were man and wife, for we could not get past the fear and pain. Not even my father knows. I am still a virgin." At that, Rabbi Shabbetai, my heart froze. I was so frightened by her words that I quickly blew out my candle lest I see even her shadow . . .

. . . .

So you see, this then was the meaning of the *idée fixe.* (I am whispering lest madame be listening impatiently on the other side of the door, for she has been most suspicious of me since the moment I arrived at this inn.) This then was its meaning—for why else would he insist on his surreptitious visits to those unwashed Ishmaelites just as they were dropping off to sleep—why would he think them forgetful Jews, or Jews who would remember that they were Jews—if he had not, *señor y maestro mío,* already upon arriving in the wasteland between Jaffa and Jerusalem, been quite simply overwhelmed by his loneliness—a loneliness that only grew greater when he first glimpsed the ramparts and cloistering gates of that obstinate desert city of stone, in which he was awaited by his motherless Beirut fiancée, the look-alike of his adored madame? That was what made him decide to see a former Jew in every Ishmaelite! And yet, señor, or so I often asked myself, this fit of loneliness—was it only, because he had been so pampered by you in Constantinople? Everyone knew how shamelessly your madame spoiled him there—why, he would barely appear in the morning at your academy long enough to propose some unheard-of answer to some Talmudic question and already he was off, and away to the bazaars, across the Golden Horn to the bright carpets, the burnished copper plates, the fragrant silk dresses fluttering above the charcoal grills and the roast lambs, adored and smiled at by everyone, so that it was perhaps this very coddling that later made him afraid of the solitude that possessed him. Or could it be that he was only coddled in the first place because even then his manliness was in doubt, which was why he so amiably—so mildly—so casually—sought to enlist those drowsy Ishmaelites in the procreation that he himself could not affect from within himself? Are you listening to me, Shabbetai Hananiah? You must listen, for soon I will be gone. The best hope of man is the maggot, says Rabbi Levitas of Yavneh . . .

And yet why should he have doubted his manly powers already then, as he was wending his way through the savage wasteland between Jaffa and Jerusalem with the slow caravan, or as he glimpsed from the Little Oak Tree the ramparts and spires of the city written like a sentence in letters whose language was no longer known to men? Why did he not rejoice to see his bride, who had come in all innocence with her kinfolk to a family wedding in Beirut and been trapped there by her aunt's love, if not for his fear of hurting the look-alike of the one woman he ever loved, half a mother and half an older sister, to whose very scent he had been bound since the days he tumbled in your giant bed, Rabbi Haddaya, a thousand times forbidden though it was?

It was then, my master and teacher, it was only then, sitting wrapped like a ball on the bed in that freezing room while seeking in the little looking-glass to make contact again with her shadow, which was traced with exquisite delicacy by the moonlight in its own furry ball, that I felt how my sorrow and pity for my dead son, who was lying naked beneath snow and earth on the Mount of Olives, were deranging my mind, and I wished I were dead. Because, knowingly or not, we had gulled him with a paradox that compelled him to produce his *idée* as a consolation in his solitude. I could feel it, that solitude, clutching me in its deadly grip, and I wished to atone for it, even though I knew that to be worthy of such atonement I first would have to die with him, would have to lie naked beneath snow and earth too and let myself be slaughtered like he was. And so, Rabbi Haddaya, layer by layer I began to strip off my clothes, until I was standing naked in that frozen room, in that locked, vestigial house, facing a looking-glass that was facing a looking-glass, thinking back to the night I sent him forth out of myself and preparing to take him back again. He was turning among the old graves on the Mount of Olives, he was icy and shredding, his blood was ebbing from him, his flesh was ebbing and being eaten away, and as I drew him back into myself his seed flew through the darkness like a snowflake and was swallowed inside me until we were one again, I was he and he was me—and then, by solemn virtue of his betrothal in Beirut and of his holy matrimony in Jerusalem, he rose, and went into the next room, and unballed the ball, and possessed his bride to beget his grandson, and died once more.

And died once more, Rabbi Shabbetai, do you hear me?

And so I too roundaboutly, along an arc bridging the two ends of Asia Minor, entered your bed, señor, a bed I had never dared climb into even as a lonely boy running down your long hallway in my *blouson,* scared to death of the cannons firing over the Bosporus. Now, in Jerusalem, I slipped between your sheets and lay with your Doña Flora, thirty years younger, in her native city, in her childhood home, in her parents' bed, smelling your strong tobacco in the distance, giving and getting love that sweetened a great commandment carried out by a great transgression. At dawn, when old Carso knocked on the door to take me with him to the Middle Synagogue for the morning service and the mourner's prayer, he scarcely could have imagined that the bereaved father he had left the night before was now a sinful grandfather.

If we undo this knot and that button over there, *señor y maestro mío,* and loosen the ties, perhaps we can calm the growl in your sore tummy with a little massage, so that the rice gruel cooked for you by that fine-looking young Greek can arrive at its proper destination. I hear little steps behind the door. Perhaps the Jews gathered outside the inn are afraid I am absconding with Your Grace's last words and are so jealous of our ancient ties that soon they will demand to be admitted too. And yet I have not come to amuse myself with Your Grace but to ask for judgment. Because when I returned from the synagogue, I was certain that Tamara would already have fled back to her father Valero's home, so that I wondered greatly to find her not only still wrapped in her mourner's shawl and blowing on the wet coals to make me breakfast, but looking taller and lighter on her feet, with no sign of the infection in her eyes that had clouded them all summer. The beds were made like plain, respectable beds; the floor was sparkling clean; the looking-glasses were covered with sheets as they were supposed to be. I ate, took off my shoes, and sat down in my mourner's corner to study a chapter of Mishnah. She followed me in her slippers and sat down not far from me. And when she peered in my eyes, it was not as a sinner or a victim, but as a fearless judge who wished to determine whether I was made for love.

I said love, *señor y maestro mío,* and even though, Rabbi Shabbetai Hananiah, your eyes are shut and your breathing is inaudible, I can feel your flesh tautly listening beneath my massaging hands. I beg you in your loving kindness, be with me now, for I still do not know what the judgment is on such love, which began to blossom that winter. Does it mitigate my sentence or compound it? For it was not something that I sought for myself, and had she risen that morning and gone back to her father's home, I would have said nothing. But she remained with me, and all of Jerusalem was so frightened of the great snow brought by the Russian pilgrims that we would have been totally forgotten had not old Carso come every morning to take me to the Middle Synagogue, or to the synagogue of Yohanan ben-Zakkai, and had not Valero and his wife Veducha, along with Alkali, and the Abayos, and a few other acquaintances, come late each afternoon with their pots and trays for the prayer and to talk about the marvels of the snow. And in the evening the consul and his wife would come too, and sometimes they brought the Ishmaelite murderer with them, and they talked about my dead son and his sufferings into the night, until all sighed and lit their lanterns and went home. And then I sent old Carso home too, and spent the night getting deeper into love. And when the week of mourning was over, on a clear, sparkling day, we climbed the Mount of Olives to say farewell to him for the last time, surrounded by a great crowd of family, rabbis, consular attendants, and my son's Ishmaelite friends, and I saw that a little piece of white ice had remained at the head of the grave like a stubborn casting of the dead man's seed upward through the earth, and my spirit rebelled and I cast her out of me, falling faint among the gravestones for all to see that I too craved such a death. What says Your Grace to that?

BUT EVEN IF you persist in your silence, my master and teacher, measuring me with narrowing eyes, you must know, Rabbi Shabbetai, that I could not die then, for first I fell ill and ran a high fever and was cared for by the motherless widow of a bride, who looked after me with wondrous composure, with great patience and aplomb. She refused to put me in the hospital of the Italian nuns and insisted on keeping me at home with the help of the consul, who came every day with all the produce of the market. He would look in on me in my room too, and ask how I was in the few Hebrew words that he knew, which were all quite sublime and Prophetic, and whose British accent so alarmed me that it made my fever worse each time. Tamara, though, had the good sense to keep him from me, and by the first month-day of the death, Rabbi Haddaya, I was able to hobble with a cane to the graveyard and consecrate the tombstone that had been erected. And when the "Lord, Full of Mercy" was sung opposite the yellow walls of that dreary city while a raw winter wind cut to the bone, I felt most certain, Rabbi Haddaya, that I had succeeded in preventing any future disgrace. That is, if that month of mourning had been started by the two of us, it was now being ended by us three.

. . .

THE WORLD WOULD have its Manis after all.

AND THUS, my master and teacher, the months of child-carrying began. The days flowed slowly in Jerusalem, which was battling the winter winds that fell on it from the coast and from the desert. By now the whole city was pining for summer, even if no one knew what plague the summer would bring first. And meanwhile, all of Jerusalem went about feeling sorry for my Yosef, who would never see his own son, and most appreciative of his foresight in taking care to have one. No one wondered that Tamara and I were constantly together, because everyone knew that we were linked by the approaching birth, which was outlined for all to see and approve of by the lovely little belly she paraded in front of us. The consul, especially, took a great interest in it and allotted it a modest consular stipend of one gold napoleon payable on the first of each month. And indeed, without it we might not have made ends meet, even though

I did my best to keep up my business, mixing my spices from Salonika, which were strong enough to retain their special flavor, with local ingredients and selling them in the hours before the afternoon prayer in the Souk-el-Lammamin or the Souk-el-Mattarin while Tamara sat by my side. Against her black clothes, her large eyes shone so brightly that passers-by hurrying down the lane sometimes thought that two lanterns had been suddenly beamed at them and turned around to ascertain the reason. And though I did what I could, *señor y maestro mío,* to persuade her to stay home and spare the little embryo the noise and tumult of the street, she insisted on coming with me everywhere, most gracefully bearing herself and her belly in the afternoon breeze. She showed not the least sign of illness or fatigue, and even her eye infection was late in arriving that year; as if the child in her womb were shielding her from all harm. "Dr. Mani," I called him in jest, regretful that I could not carry him too as a cure for whatever ailed me. And when spring came, and even the ancient olive trees along the Bethlehem Road broke into bloom, I could not keep from thinking, *señor y maestro mío,* that if my motherless little widow of a bride, the look-alike of her renowned aunt, was following me around everywhere, this could only be because she had been brazen and thoughtless enough to fall ever so slightly in love with me, thus atoning, though no doubt unwittingly, for my unrequited love in Salonika in the year of Creation 5552.

But Your Grace must listen to me, he must listen and not sleep! Here, let me rub your weary bones a bit with some of this oil. Not that I have any reason to doubt the excellent intentions of Doña Flora and her attendants, Jewish or not, but I do believe, señor, that they are afraid that you will come apart in their hands, which is why they wrapped you like a mummy, swaddling band by swaddling band, until, God forbid, you were hardly able to breathe. Let us then, my master and teacher, remove the last of these ties without a qualm, because only a trusty old disciple like myself who has known your most unphlegmatic body for ages will not fear to hurt you in order to make you feel better. There . . . that does it . . . a bit more . . . and now, Rabbi Haddaya, lie back and listen to how the *passer-through* who became a *stayer-on* was now a *beloved-of* in a Jerusalem that was being built from day to day, not always by us, to be sure, but always, with God's help, for our benefit—and there were times, I must say, when the love of that motherless widow both astonished and frightened me, because what could possibly come of it? "Why, I am a dead man, my child," I would say to her every evening when we sat down to our dinner of radishes, tomatoes, and pita bread dipped in olive oil while the sun set outside the window and the muezzin sounded his mournful call. "I will go to Rabbi Haddaya in Constantinople and get leave to strangle myself like Saul son of Kish." She would listen and say nothing, her big, bright eyes wide with tears, her little hands trembling on her belly, as if above all she wished to assure young señorito Mati that he need not fear the grandfather who had skipped a generation to sow him and was now threatening to miss the harvest. Then she would rise, go to wash the bowls at the cistern, and come back to make the beds, trim the candles, and take up the red blouse and *taquaiqua* that she was knitting for little Mani, never taking her eyes off me, as if I were already preparing the rope to hang myself. Now and then she glanced in the mirror over her bed to see what I was up to in the mirror over my bed. And thus, *señor y maestro mío,* from mirror to mirror I was so encircled by anxiety and love that I lost all my strength and began to flicker out like a candle. I went up to the roof to say good night to the last breeze of the day, which was winging its way to the Dead Sea above the last lanterns bobbing in the narrow streets, and when I came down again, I found her still awake, sitting up in bed. Unable to hold it back any longer, she burst out all at once into a great, bitter cry that I had to make haste to calm, swearing to her that I would not abandon her before the birth. And although, my master and teacher, she was firm in her belief that the final truth bound us together, even she did not know that behind that truth too yet another truth was hiding . . .

. . .

There, they are starting to bang on the door, Rabbi Shabbetai, they want me out of here. But I am not leaving until I have been given a clear judgment, even though "His son Rabbi Yishmael used to say"—is not that what you taught me, rabbi?—" 'he who judges not has no enemies.' " And he used to say: "Whoever is born, is born to die, and whoever dies, dies to live again, and whoever lives again, lives to be judged, to know, to make known, and to be made known." Well, let us stir the fire a bit to warm this room, and raise the curtain for a look at the sky dropping low over their chapel of graven images, may they all rot in hell, and tell at last and in truth the final, the one and only story, the story of sweet perdition that recurs in every generation.

Quickly, quickly, though, because the banging on the door is growing louder, and soon, *señor y maestro mío,* Doña Flora and her men will come bursting in here. It is time, Rabbi Haddaya, *betabsir, vite-*

vite, to come forth with the story that I have kept for last, the story of a murderer—because I have already told you, *señor y maestro mío,* that there was a bit of a murderer here—or, *si quiere, su merced,* a *man*slaughterer, a *shohet-uvodek*—to whom, ever since that first night, one felt drawn again and again in the crowded lanes of Jerusalem—in the souks, by the cisterns, gazing out from the gates of the city—by a lightning-like glitter of a glance—a wordless nod—an imperceptible bow—a casting-down of the eyes—a sudden shudder. Ah, how drawn—on the chalky hillside of Silwan, among the olives on the road to Bethlehem—so powerfully that sometimes one's feet stole of an evening to the consulate, to one of its literary soirées, to listen to some Englishwoman praise some British romance that no one ever had read or ever would read, for the sole purpose of staring wordlessly at the silent shade standing in the doorway and bearing the memory of my poor son—oh, rotting! oh, beloved in his grave! Yosef, my only one—who on that accursed night of snow and blood . . . But who could restrain himself, Rabbi Shabbetai Hananiah, from running after him through the streets in an attempt to forestall an assault that was in truth a retreat, a provocation that was in truth a flight from the pain and punishment that he imagined twirling over his bed like an angry, patient carving knife? And it was thus that slaughterer joined slaughterer by the light of the torches of the Russian pilgrims, who were bellowing their piety on the stone floor of the Holy Sepulchre—thus that the two of them, the frantic father and the Ishmaelite friend, the aristocratic, mustachioed sheikh's son—linked forces to catch in time the *idée fixe* that in its passionate pride was about to turn on its own self and become the very prototype that it was searching for of the *Jew forgetful of being a Jew,* an example and provocation for all recalcitrants. For as he elbowed his way into the crowd of pilgrims that was excitedly tramping through the mud and snow, wary of being recognized by some excitable Christian who might inform on him to the Turkish soldiers surrounding the square, he was seeking, or so I felt, Rabbi Shabbetai, to forget us all—Salonika, Constantinople, myself, yourself—as if he had been conceived and born from the very floor of the church, rising up from the cisterns and the souk as *a new Ishmaelite* who had discovered that he was a forgetful Jew who might remember . . . only *what*?

In truth, Your Grace has good reason to hold his breath and shut his eyes, fearful in thought and spirit for the story's end . . . and no less fearfully, although ever so gently and clandestinely, did the two of us, the murderer and myself, plan to pluck my son from that crowd of celebrants and lead him back home to his bed. But when we stepped up and seized his lantern so as to make him follow us, he took fright and started to flee—and seeing us run after him, the celebrants at once joined in the pursuit. He ran down the long, deserted street of the Tarik Bab-el-Silseleh with his cloak flapping behind him like a big black bird—or so, from that moment, I began to think of him, an odd bird that must be pinioned before it flew away above our heads. He ran and ran through the cover of snow that made all of Jerusalem look like a single interconnected house, but instead of heading for home, for the quarter of the Jews, and then doubling back through the Middle Synagogue or the synagogue of Yohanan ben-Zakkai, he kept going straight ahead, turning neither left nor right until he came to the Bab, the Gate of the Chain leading up to the great mosque. He shook it a bit until he realized that it was locked, and then, without giving it any thought, as if trusting in the snow to protect him, turned left and proceeded in the same easy, flying, unconcerned lope to the second gate, the Bal-el-Matra, from which he entered the great, deserted square in front of the golden dome, which the snow had covered with a fresh head of white hair. The echoes of his footsteps were still ringing out when he was seized by two sleepy Mohammedan guards. Perhaps they too thought that he was some kind of black bird that had fallen from on high and soon would fly back there, because why else would they have hurried to bind him with long strips of cloth and lay him on the stairs amid the columns, where his squirming shape now made an imprint in the snow?

My master and teacher. Rabbi Shabbetai. My master and teacher. Your Grace. Rabbi Haddaya. *Señor y maestro mío.* Shabbetai Hananiah. Hananiah Shabbetai. *Su merced* . . . can it be?

In no time he was surrounded, because the news spread quickly from gate to gate across that huge deserted square, from the golden dome to the silver dome, so that soon more sleepy guards appeared, although this time there was no telling what time of sleep my son had roused them from. They crowded about him and bent over him to read in his eyes the mad chastisements that he planned for them and that he was begging them to inflict now on himself so that he might demonstrate how he was the first to awaken and recollect his true nature. And although the guards could see for themselves that the man in the cloak spread out in the snow on the steps was an infirm soul, they did not, simple beings that they were, give credence to this soul's suffering but rather suspected it of taking pleasure in itself and its delusions and sought to share that pleasure with it, so that they began to make sport of it and roll it in the snow, a glitter marking the passage of a half-concealed knife from hand to hand. And I, my master and teacher, was outside the gate, I was watching from afar while listening to the distant bell of a lost flock, silently, wretchedly waiting for the worst of the night to wear itself out and the morning star to appear in the east, faint and longed-for, so that I might go to him, to the far pole of his terror and sorrow, whether as his slaughterer or whether as the slaughterer's inspector, and release him from his earthly bonds, because I was certain that he had already deposited his seed . . .

YOU HAVE BECOME, *señor y maestro mío,* most silent. Can it be that you are already gone?

WAIT! I WANT to come too, Rabbi Shabbetai Hananiah . . . Why don't you answer me? . . . For the love of God, answer me . . .

'TWOULD TAKE but a nod . . .

'TIS NOT AS IF I need words to understand . . .

IN TRUTH . . .

IS IT SELF-MURDER, then?

YES? . . . NO? . . .

Angelina Muñiz-Huberman

Angelina Muñiz-Huberman (France-Mexico, 1936–) was born in France into a family of refugees from the Spanish Civil War. She grew up Catholic until, as an adult, she discovered her Sephardic roots and began to read Kabbalah and other Jewish texts. Her work is influenced by the stories and essays of Jorge Luis Borges and by the culture of Spain's "Golden Age," in particular, by the works of Cervantes, Francisco de Quevedo and Luis de Góngora. Muñiz-Huberman is a professor of comparative literature at Universidad Nacional Autónoma de México. Her novels include *Internal Abode* (1972), *Inland* (1977), *Enclosed Garden* (1985; English, 1988), a collection of mystical, almost hallucinatory stories translated into English by Lois Parkinson Zamora that includes "The Most Precious Offering," and *The Confidants* (1997). Muñiz-Huberman is the editor of *The Florid Tongue* (1989), an anthology, in Spanish, of Sephardic literature that extends from the pre-expulsion era to the present. Her nonfiction works include *The Roots and the Branches: Sources and Derivations of Judeo-Hispanic Kabbalah* (1993). Her novel *The Merchant of Tudela* (1998) is a palimpsest based on the adventures of the twelfth-century traveler Benjamin of Tudela. In 2001, Muñiz-Huberman published *Windmills: Pseudo-Autobiography,* in which she recounts her life as if it were fiction.

The Most Precious Offering

Am I my brother's keeper?
GENESIS 4:9

IN SOME BOOK it was written, in a thick, dense book which contained the whole history of man, a book which traced every destiny and taught which roads to take, a book which besides shouting God's word sang to strong men and weak, powerful and impotent, to men who love and loathe. In some book, perhaps that one, my deed was also written. Most men worry about leaving their fleeting shadow on the slippery surface of history, but I knew that my life had already been lived and that I only repeated an ancient and unjust tale. Knowing it did not spare me from suffering. So from childhood, from the day that you were born, I began to hate you.

Why did your birth excite such praise? Why the gifts and the predictions, the words, the wishes, and the joy? I felt none of this. Your presence displeased me: there you were, small, shapeless. Incapable of doing anything. Impossible to love. You had taken my place without effort, without even allowing me to resist, the place which I had painstakingly created for myself, which belonged to me and was respected by everyone till you arrived.

Where did you come from and why did you displace me so easily and cruelly? Our blood was not the same: mine boiled with hatred and passion; yours, sweet and peaceful, engendered love.

I slipped into solitude and oblivion. No one asked about me, no one remembered that I was the first born. And worse, to hear words that before were meant for me alone, now spoken to you alone. What did you possess, newborn, shapeless, inept, that made a curse fall upon me?

Because I had been cursed. For some reason unknown to me, I had fallen from favor with the others. Nothing I did was appreciated; my tears, my screams, my games offended them. It was for me a reign of silence and perpetual boredom.

No, I could never love you, and they even dared to ask me if I did. How could I love you if it was forbidden? How could I play with you if they would not permit it?

. . .

Time passed and the moment came when the first fruits were to be picked, when some offering was to be made, in view of everyone, by both of us. You had grown and were strong and handsome; I was always in your shadow, with no light of my own and no one to discover me. You were a young man now, and your beauty was calm and certain and peaceful, like a landscape of pines and high meadows. You possessed an aura of sanctity: those who fell in love with you did not dare to tell you. Your name was often spoken, a word magical and round. The murmur of running water accompanied your steps and a glow lit up the faces that beheld you. Your walk, measured and graceful, reflected the perfect proportion of your limbs and the soft weight of your sex. You were not aware of this, and your innocence gave you yet another halo.

The day of our offering approached and I thought of something beautiful and grand, something unattainable, perfect, precise. You, on the other hand, did not think of anything, because you knew that whatever you gave would seem magnificent. I hated your serenity, your certainty of triumph, your sense of the sublime, and an idea began to grow in me, inchoate, surreptitious, insinuating itself in my mind with only the slightest warning. That obscure idea slowly became a stabbing pain which made my heart beat. And these stabs began to acquaint me with the idea, and the idea began to form, grow, shine, glow. Until it reached maturity and I recognized its integrity and its radiance.

The day of the offering, everyone would know the perfection and plenitude of the form I was seeking, a form which would draw the center of the universe to me. At the moment of its revelation, no one would love me, as no one loves me now; everyone would hate me, but I would exist for them, I would be more than the vague shadow that they had made me, and my life would be worthwhile.

Now I am in his room. I wait naked in his bed. When he came in and saw me, he said nothing: slowly he began to undress, and our smooth bodies knew the caresses of love for the first time. Ecstasy enveloped our senses in waves: we forgot everything and drowned ourselves in a distant and swelling sea. Only when we had begun our return to the lost shore, but before our complete release, did I stab him.

Despite his astonishment and pain, his image of perfection was not destroyed. He smiled slightly and his limbs relaxed sweetly: his head rests on my shoulder, and his naked body, stretched upon mine, bleeds warmly. I no longer hate him; I feel an immense love for him: he is utterly mine, and I will love him eternally.

TOMORROW, WHEN THEY open the door, they will discover my offering.

Hélène Cixous

Hélène Cixous (Algeria-France, 1937–) was born in Oran, Algeria, into a mixed German-Ashkenazic and North African Sephardic family. She moved to Paris in 1955, where she studied English literature and did a doctoral dissertation on James Joyce. With Tzvetan Todorov and Gérard Genette, she cofounded the structuralist magazine *Journal poétique.* A noted feminist theorist, in 1974 she became director of Centre de Recherche en Études Féminines at University of Paris VII, St. Vincennes. She created the first Commission Nationale des Lettres with Michel Foucault and Jacques Derrida. Cixous is the author of *The Exile of James Joyce* (1968; English, 1972) and *"Coming to Writing" and Other Essays* (English, 1991), translated by Sarah Cornell, Deborah Jenson, Ann Liddle, and Susan Sellers. She has published studies on Clarice Lispector, Franz Kafka, and Marina Tsvetayeva. Her fiction includes *The Newly Born Woman* (1975; English, 1986), *The Book of Promethea* (1983; English, 1991), *Manna: For the Mandelstams for the Mandelas* (1988; English, 1994), and *First Days of the Year* (1990; English, 1998). Cixious is also a poet and a playwright. Her plays include *The Terrible but Unfinished Story of Norodom Sihanouk, King of Cambodia* (1985; English, 1994). *The Hélène Cixous Reader,* edited by Susan Sellers, was published in 1994. Cixous's view is that we are "born inside language" and that language itself is our world. Her Jewish identity is explored through labyrinthine meditations on the value of texts in life and vice versa.

From *Coming to Writing*

IN THE BEGINNING, I adored. What I adored was human. Not persons; not totalities, not defined and named beings. But signs. Flashes of being that glanced off me, kindling me. Lightning-like bursts that came to me: Look! I blazed up. And the sign withdrew. Vanished. While I burned on and consumed myself wholly. What had reached me, so powerfully cast from a human body, was Beauty: there was a face, with all the mysteries inscribed and preserved on it; I was before it, I sensed that there was a beyond, to which I did not have access, an unlimited place. The look incited me and also forbade me to enter; I was outside, in a state of animal watchfulness. A desire was seeking its home. I was that desire. I was the question. The question with this strange destiny: to seek, to pursue the answers that will appease it, that will annul it. What prompts it, animates it, makes it want to be asked, is the feeling that the other is there, so close, exists, so far away; the feeling that somewhere, in some part of the world, once it is through the door, there is the face that promises, the answer for which one continues to move onward, because of which one can never rest, for the love of which one holds back from renouncing, from giving in—to death. Yet what misfortune if the question should happen to meet *its* answer! Its end!

I adored the Face. The smile. The countenance of my day and night. The smile awed me, filled me with ecstasy. With terror. The world constructed, illuminated, annihilated by a quiver of this face. This face is not a metaphor. Face, space, structure. Scene of all the faces that give births to me, contain my lives. I read the face, I saw and contemplated it to the point of losing myself in it. How many faces to the face? More than one. Three, four, but always the only one, and the only one always more than one.

I *read* it: the face signified. And each sign pointed out a new path. To follow, in order to come closer to its meaning. The face, whispered something to me, it spoke and called on me to speak, to uncode all the names surrounding it, evoking it, touching on it, making it appear. It made things visible and legible, as if it were understood that even if the light were to fade away, the things it had illuminated would not disappear, what it had fallen on would stay, not cease to be here, to glow, to offer itself up to the act of naming again.

The moment I came into life (I remember with undiminishing pain), I trembled: from the fear of separation, the dread of death. I saw death at work and guessed its constancy, the jealousy that wouldn't let anything escape it alive. I watched it wound, disfigure, paralyze, and massacre from the moment my eyes opened to seeing. I discovered that the Face was mortal, and that I would have to snatch it back at every moment from Nothingness. I didn't adore that-which-is-going-to-disappear; love isn't bound up for me in the condition of mortality. No. I loved. I was afraid. I am afraid. Because of my fear I reinforced love, I alerted all the forces of life, I armed love, with soul and words, to keep death from winning. Loving: keeping alive: naming.

The primitive face was my mother's. At will her face could give me sight, life, or take them away from me. In my passion for the first face, I had long awaited death in that corner. With the ferocity of a beast, I kept my mother within my sight. Bad move. On the chessboard, I brooded over the queen; and it was the king who was taken.

Writing: a way of leaving no space for death, of pushing back forgetfulness, of never letting oneself be surprised by the abyss. Of never becoming resigned, consoled; never turning over in bed to face the wall and drift asleep again as if nothing had happened; as if nothing could happen.

Maybe I've always written for no other reason than to win grace from this countenance. Because of disappearance. To confront perpetually the mystery of the there-not-there. The visible and the invisible. To fight against the law that says, "Thou shalt not make unto thee any graven image, nor any likeness of any thing that is in Heaven above or that is in the earth beneath, or that is in the water under the earth." Against the decree of blindness. I have often lost my sight; and I will never finish fashioning the graven image for myself. My writing watches. Eyes closed.

You want to have. You want everything. But having is forbidden to human beings. Having everything. And for woman, it's even forbidden to hope to have everything a human being can have. There are so many boundaries, and so many walls, and inside the walls, more walls. Bastions in which, one morning, I wake up condemned. Cities where I am isolated, quarantines, cages, "rest" homes. How often I've been there, my tombs, my corporeal dungeons, the earth abounds with places for my confinement. Body in solitary, soul in silence. My prison times: when I'm there, the sentence is of a really unforeseeable type and duration. But I feel, after all, "at home." What you can't have, what you can't touch, smell, caress, you should at least try to see. I want to see: everything. No Promised Land I won't reach someday. Seeing what you will (n)ever have. Maybe I have written to see; to have what I never would have had; so that having would be the privilege not of the hand that takes and encloses, of the gullet, of the gut; but of the hand that points out, of fingers that see, that design, from the tips of the fingers that transcribe by the sweet dictates of vision. From the point of view of the soul's eye: the eye of a womansoul. From the point of view of the Absolute, in the proper sense of the word: separation.

Writing to touch with letters, with lips, with breath, to caress with the tongue, to lick with the soul, to taste the blood of the beloved body, of life in its remoteness; to saturate the distance with desire; in order to keep it from reading you.

Having? A having without limits, without restriction; but without any "deposit," a having that doesn't withhold or possess, a having-love that sustains itself with loving, in the blood-rapport. In this way, give yourself what you would want God-if-he-existed to give you.

Who can define what "having" means; where living happens; where pleasure is assured?

It's all there: where separation doesn't separate; where absence is animated, taken back from silence and stillness. In the assault of love on nothingness. My voice repels death; my death; your death; my voice is my other. I write and you are not dead. The other is safe if I write.

Writing is good: it's what never ends. The simplest, most secure other circulates inside me. Like blood: there's no lack of it. It can become impoverished. But you manufacture it and replenish it. In me is the word of blood, which will not cease before my end.

At first I really wrote to bar death. Because of a death. The cruelest kind, the kind that doesn't spare anything, the irreparable. It goes like this: you die in my absence. While Isolde is not there, Tristan turns to the wall and dies. What happens between that body and that wall, what doesn't happen, pierces me with pain and makes me write. Need for the Face: to get past the wall, to tear up the black sail. To see my loss with my own eyes; to look loss in the eye. I want to see the disappearance with my own eyes. What's intolerable is that death might not take place, that I may be robbed of it. That I may not be able to live it, take it in my arms, savor a last breath on its lips.

I write the encore. Still here, I write life. Life: what borders on death; right up against which I write my

Letters from the Life-Watch: Who Goes There?

STATING, TO LESSEN IT, the fragility of life and the trembling of the thought that dares hope to grasp it; circling around the trap set out by life each time you ask the question death whispers to you, the diabolical question: "Why live? Why me?" As if it were a matter of death trying to understand life. This is the most dangerous question, as it threatens to arise, like a tombstone, only at the moment you have no "reason" to live. Living, being-alive, or rather not being open to death, means not finding yourself in the situation where this question becomes imminent. More specifically: we always live *without* reason; and living is just that, it's living without-reason, for nothing, at the mercy of time. This is nonreason, true madness, if you think about it. But we don't think about it. Once "thought" is introduced, once "reason" is brought into proximity with life, you have the makings of madness.

Writing prevents the question that attacks life from coming up. Don't ask yourself, "Why . . . ?" Everything trembles when the question of meaning strikes.

You are born; you live; everyone does it, with an animal force of blindness. Woe unto you if you want the human gaze, if you want to know what's happening to you.

Madwomen: the ones who are compelled to redo acts of birth every day. I think, "Nothing is a given for me." I wasn't born for once and for all. Writing, dreaming, delivering; being my own daughter of each day. The affirmation of an internal force that is capable of looking at life without dying of fear, and above all of looking at itself, as if you were simultaneously the other—indispensable to love—and nothing more nor less than me.

I'M AFRAID: that life will become foreign. That it will no longer be this nothing that makes immediate sense in my body, but instead, outside me, will surround me and beset me with Its question; that it will become the enigma, the irrational, the roll of the die; the final blow.

Terror: life arrest, death sentence: every child's Terror. Perhaps being adult means no longer asking yourself where you come from, where you're going, who to be. Discarding the past, warding off the future? Putting history in place of yourself? Perhaps. But who is the woman spared by questioning? Don't you, you too, ask yourself: who am I, who will I have been, why-me, why-not-me? Don't you tremble with uncertainty? Aren't you, like me, constantly struggling not to fall into the trap? Which means you're in the trap already, because the fear of doubting is already the doubt that you fear. And why can't the question of why-am-I just leave me in peace? Why does it throw me off balance? What does it have to do with my woman-being? It's the social scene, I think, that constrains you to it; history that condemns you to it. If you want to grow, progress, stretch your soul, take infinite pleasure in your bodies, your goods, how will you position yourself to do so? You are, you too, a Jewoman, trifling, diminutive, mouse among the mouse people, assigned to the fear of the big bad cat. To the diaspora of your desires; to the intimate deserts. And if you grow, your desert likewise grows. If you come out of the hole, the world lets you know that there is no place for your kind in its nations.

"Why did you put me in the world if only for me to be lost in it?"

Determining whom to put this question to is beyond you.

Sometimes I think I began writing in order to make room for the wandering question that haunts my soul and hacks and saws at my body; to give it a place and time; to turn its sharp edge away from my flesh; to give, seek, touch, call, bring into the world a new being who won't restrain me, who won't drive me away, won't perish from very narrowness.

Because of the following dream:

My rejection of sickness as a weapon. There is a self that horrifies me. Isn't she dead yet? Done for. I fear her death. There, on that great bed. Sad, horribly so. Her sickness: cancer. A diseased hand. She herself is the sickness. Will you save her by cutting off the hand? Overcome the atrocious, anguishing disgust, not at death but at the condemnation, the work of sickness. My whole being is convulsed. Tell her what must be said: "You have two hands. If one hand can't live, cut it off. You have twomorrow. When one hand doesn't work, replace it with the other hand. Act. Respond. You've lost the hand that writes? Learn to write with the other hand." And with it-her-self-me-her-hand, I begin to trace on the paper. And now at once there unfurls a perfect calligraphy, as if she had always had this writing in that other hand. If you die, live.

With one hand, suffering, living, putting your finger on pain, loss. But there is the other hand: the one that writes.

A Girl Is Being Killed

In the beginning, I desired.

"What is it she wants?"

"To live. Just to live. And to hear myself say the name."

"Horrors! Cut out her tongue!"

"What's wrong with her?"

"She can't keep herself from flying!"

"In that case, we have special cages."

Who is the Superuncle who hasn't prevented a girl from flying, the flight of the thief, who has not bound her, not bandaged the feet of his little darling, so that they might be exquisitely petite, who hasn't mummified her into prettiness?

How Would I Have Written?

Wouldn't you first have needed the "right reasons" to write? The reasons, mysterious to me, that give you the "right" to write? But I didn't know them. I had only the "wrong" reason; it wasn't a reason, it was a passion, something shameful—and disturbing; one of those violent characteristics with which I was afflicted. I didn't "want" to write. How could I have "wanted" to? I hadn't strayed to the point of losing all measure of things. A mouse is not a prophet. I wouldn't have had the cheek to go claim my book from God on Mount Sinai, even if, as a mouse, I had found the energy to scamper up the mountain. No reasons at all. But there was madness. Writing was in the air around me. Always close, intoxicating, invisible, inaccessible. I undergo writing! It came to me abruptly. One day I was tracked down, besieged, taken. It captured me. I was seized. From where? I knew nothing about it. I've never known anything about it. From some bodily region. I don't know where. "Writing" seized me, gripped me, around the diaphragm, between the stomach and the chest, a blast dilated my lungs and I stopped breathing.

Suddenly I was filled with a turbulence that knocked the wind out of me and inspired me to wild acts. "Write." When I say "writing" seized me, it wasn't a sentence that had managed to seduce me, there was absolutely nothing written, not a letter, not a line. But in the depths of the flesh, the attack. Pushed. Not penetrated. Invested. Set in motion. The attack was imperious: "Write!" Even though I was only a meager anonymous mouse, I knew vividly the awful jolt that galvanizes the prophet, wakened in mid-life by an order from above. It's a force to make you cross oceans. Me, write? But I wasn't a prophet. An urge shook my body, changed my rhythms, tossed madly in my chest, made time unlivable for me. I was stormy. "Burst!" "You may speak!" And besides, whose voice is that? The Urge had the violence of a thunderclap. Who's striking me? Who's attacking me from behind? And in my body the breath of a giant, but no sentences at all. Who's pushing me? Who's invading? Who's changing me into a monster? Into a mouse wanting to swell to the size of a prophet?

A joyful force. Not a god; it doesn't come from above. But from an inconceivable region, deep down inside me but unknown, as if there might exist somewhere in my body (which, from the outside, and from the point of view of a naturalist, is highly elastic, nervous, lively, thin, not without charm, firm muscles, pointed nose always quivering and damp, vibrating paws) another space, limitless; and there, in those zones which inhabit me and which I don't know how to live in, I feel them, I don't live them, they live me, gushing from the wellsprings of my souls, I don't see them but I feel them, it's incomprehensible but that's how it is. There are sources. That's the enigma. One morning, it all explodes. My body experiences, deep down inside, one of its panicky cosmic adventures. I have volcanoes on my lands. But no lava: what wants to flow is breath. And not just any old way. The breath "wants" a form. "Write me!" One day it begs me, another day it threatens. "Are you going to write me or not?" It could have said: "Paint me." I tried. But the nature of its fury demanded the form that stops the least, that encloses the least, the body without a frame, without skin, without walls, the flesh that doesn't dry, doesn't stiffen, doesn't clot the wild blood that wants to stream through it—forever. "Let me through, or everything goes!"

What blackmail could have made me give in to this breath? Write? Me? Because it was so strong and furious, I loved and feared this breath. To be lifted up one morning, snatched off the ground, swung in the air. To be taken by surprise. To find in myself the possibility of the unexpected. To fall asleep a mouse and wake up an eagle! What delight! What terror. And I had nothing to do with it, I couldn't help it. And worse, each time the breathing seized me, the same misery was repeated: what began, in spite of myself, in exultation, proceeded, because of myself, in combat, and ended in downfall and desolation. Barely off the ground: "Hey! What are you doing up there? Is that any place for a mouse? For shame!" Shame overcame me. There is no lack on earth, so there was no lack in my personal spaces, of guardians of the law, their pockets filled with the "first stone" to hurl at flying mice. As for my internal guardian—whom I didn't call superego at the time—he was more rapid and accurate than all the others: he threw the stone at me before all the other-relatives, masters, prudent contemporaries, compliant and orderly peers—all the noncrazy and antimouse forces—had the chance to let fire. I was the "fastest gun." Fortunately! My shame settled, the score without scandal. I was "saved."

Write? I didn't think of it. I dreamed of it constantly, but with the chagrin and the humility, the resignation and the innocence, of the poor. Writing is God. But it is not your God. Like the Revelation of a cathedral: I was born in a country where culture had returned to nature—had become flesh once again. Ruins that are not ruins, but hymns of luminous memory, Africa sung by the sea night and day. The past wasn't past. Just curled up like the prophet in the bosom of time. At the age of eighteen, I discovered "culture." The monument, its splendor, its menace, its *discourse.* "Admire me. I am the spirit of Christianity. Down on your knees, offspring of the bad race. Transient. I was erected for my followers. Out, little Jewess. Quick, before I baptize you." "Glory": what a word! A name for armies or cathedrals or lofty victories; it wasn't a word for Jewoman. Glory, stained-glass windows, flags, domes, constructions, masterpieces—how to avoid recognizing your beauty, keep it from reminding me of my foreignness?

One summer I get thrown out of the cathedral of Cologne. It's true that I had bare arms; or was it a bare head? A priest kicks me out. Naked. I felt naked for being Jewish, Jewish for being naked, naked for being a woman, Jewish for being flesh and joyful!—So I'll take all your books. But the cathedrals I'll leave behind. Their stone is sad and male.

The texts I ate, sucked, suckled, kissed. I am the innumerable child of their masses.

But write? With what right? After all, I read them without any right, without permission, without their knowledge.

The way I might have prayed in a cathedral, sending their God an impostor-message.

Write? I was dying of desire for it, of love, dying to give writing what it had given to me. What ambition! What impossible happiness. To nourish my own mother. Give her, in turn, my milk? Wild imprudence.

No need for a severe superego to prevent me from writing: nothing in me made such an act plausible or conceiveable. How many workers' children dream of becoming Mozart or Shakespeare?

Everything in me joined forces to forbid me to write: History, my story, my origin, my sex. Everything that constituted my social and cultural self. To begin with the necessary, which I lacked, the material that writing is formed of and extracted from: language. You want—to Write? In what language? Property, rights, had always policed me: I learned to speak French in a garden from which I was on the verge of expulsion for being a Jew. I was of the race of Paradise-losers. Write French? With what right? Show us your credentials! What's the password? Cross yourself! Put out your hands, let's see those paws! What kind of nose is that?

I said "write French." One writes *in*. Penetration. Door. Knock before entering. Strictly forbidden.

"You are not from here. You are not at home here. Usurper!"

"It's true. No right. Only love."

Write? Taking pleasure as the gods who created the books take pleasure and give pleasure, *endlessly;* their bodies of paper and blood; their letters of flesh and tears; they put an end to the end. The human gods, who don't know what they've done; what their visions, their words, do to us. How could I have not wanted to write? When books took me, transported me, pierced me to the entrails, allowed me to feel their disinterested power; when I felt loved by a text that didn't address itself to me, or to you, but to the other; when I felt pierced through by life itself, which doesn't judge, or choose, which touches without designating; when I was agitated, torn out of myself, by love? When my being was populated, my body traversed and fertilized, how could I have closed myself up in silence? Come to me, I will come to you. When love makes love to you, how can you keep from murmuring, saying its names, giving thanks for its caresses?

You can desire. You can read, adore, be invaded. But writing is not granted to you. Writing is reserved for the chosen. It surely took place in a realm inaccessible to the small, to the humble, to women. In the intimacy of the sacred. Writing spoke to its prophets from a burning bush. But it must have been decided that bushes wouldn't dialogue with women.

Didn't experience prove it? I thought it addressed itself not to ordinary men, however, but only to the righteous, to beings fashioned out of separation, for solitude. It asked everything of them, took everything from them, it was merciless and tender, it dispossessed them entirely of all riches, all bonds, it lightened them, stripped them bare; then it granted them passage: toward the most distant, the nameless, the endless. It gave them leave—this was a right and a necessity. They would never arrive. They would never be found by the limit. It would be with them, in the future, like no one.

Thus, for this elite, the gorgeous journey without horizon, beyond everything, the appalling but intoxicating excursion toward the never-yet-said.

But for you, the tales announce a destiny of restriction and oblivion; the brevity, the lightness of a life that steps out of mother's house only to make three little detours that lead you back dazed to the house of your grandmother, for whom you'll amount to no more than a mouthful. For you, little girl, little jug of milk, little pot of honey, little basket, experience reveals it, history promises you this minute alimentary journey that brings you back quickly indeed to the bed of the jealous Wolf, your ever-insatiable grandmother, as if the law ordained that the mother should be constrained to sacrifice her daughter, to expiate the audacity of having relished the good things in life in the form of her pretty red offspring. Vocation of the swallowed up, voyage of the scybalum.

So for the sons of the Book: research, the desert, inexhaustible space, encouraging, discouraging, the march straight ahead. For the daughters of the housewife: the straying into the forest. Deceived, disappointed, but brimming with curiosity. Instead of the great enigmatic duel with the Sphinx, the dangerous questioning addressed to the body of the Wolf: What is the body for? Myths end up having our hides. Logos opens its great maw, and swallows us whole.

SPEAKING (CRYING OUT, yelling, tearing the air, rage drove me to this endlessly) doesn't leave traces: you can speak—it evaporates, ears are made for not hearing, voices get lost. But writing! Establishing a contract with time. Noting! Making yourself noticed!!!

"Now *that* is forbidden."

All the reasons I had for believing I didn't have the right to write, the good, the less good, and the really wrong reasons: I had no grounds from which to write. No legitimate place, no land, no fatherland, no history of my own.

Nothing falls to me by right—or rather everything does, and no more so to me than to any other.

"I have no roots: from what sources could I take in enough to nourish a text? Diaspora effect.

"I have no legitimate tongue. In German I sing; in English I disguise myself; in French I fly, I thieve. On what would I base a text?

"I am already so much the inscription of a divergence that a further divergence is impossible. They teach me the following lesson: you, outsider, fit in. Take the nationality of the country that tolerates you. Be good, return to the ranks, to the ordinary, the imperceptible, the domestic."

Here are your laws: you will not kill, you will be killed, you will not steal, you will not be a bad recruit, you will not be sick or crazy (this would be a lack of consideration for your hosts), you will not zigzag. You will not write. You will learn to calculate. You will not touch. In whose name would I write?

You, write? But who do you think you are? Could I say: "It's not me, it's the breath!"? "No one." And this was true: I didn't think I was anyone.

This was in fact what most obscurely worried me and pained me: being no one. Everyone was someone, I felt, except me. I was no one. "Being" was reserved for those full, well-defined, scornful people who occupied the world with their assurance, took their places without hesitation, were at home everywhere where I "was"-n't except as an infraction, intruder, little scrap from elsewhere, always on the alert. The untroubled ones. "To be?" What self-confidence! I thought to myself: "I could have not been." And: "I will be." But to say "I am"? I who? Everything that designated me publicly, that I made use of—you don't turn down an oar when you're drifting—was misleading and false. I didn't deceive myself, but, objectively, I deceived the world. My true identification papers were false. I wasn't even a little girl, I was a fearful and wild animal, and I was ferocious (although they may have suspected this). Nationality? "French." Not my fault! *They* put me in the position of imposture. Even now, I sometimes feel pushed to explain myself, to excuse myself, to rectify, like an old reflex. For at least I believed, if not in the truth of being, in a rigor, a purity of language. If a given word turned to the practice of lying, it was because it was being mistreated. Twisted, abused, used idiotically.

"I am": who would dare to speak like God? Not I . . . *What* I was, if that could be described, was a whirlwind of tensions, a series of fires, ten thousand scenes of violence (history had nourished me on this: I had the "luck" to take my first steps in the blazing hotbed between two holocausts, in the midst, in the very bosom of racism, to be three years old in 1940, to be Jewish, one part of me in the concentration camps, one part of me in the "colonies").

So all my lives are divided between two principal lives, my life up above and my life down below. Down below I claw, I am lacerated, I sob. Up above I pleasure. Down below, carnage, limbs, quarterings, tortured bodies, noises, engines, harrow. Up above, face, mouth, aura; torrent of the silence of the heart.

Infantasies

("She first awakens at the touch of love; before this time she is a dream. Two stages, however, can be distinguished in this dream existence: in the first stage love dreams about her, in the second, she dreams about love.")

André Aciman

André Aciman (Egypt-USA, 1951–) was born in Alexandria, Egypt, into a Sephardic family that had arrived there in 1905 from Italy via Turkey. He and his family left the country when he was fourteen, after anti-Semitic harassment intensified in the wake of the 1948 and 1956 wars between Israel and her Arab neighbors. They first traveled to Rome, then to Paris, and finally settled in New York. As a result of this odyssey, exile has been the major motif in Aciman's work. For him place "means something only if it is tied to its own displacement" and he speaks of "firming up the present by experiencing it as a memory, by experiencing it from the future as a moment in the past." Aciman is the author of *Out of Egypt: A Memoir* (1994), in which he describes the various journeys of his flamboyantly eccentric family members, including his great uncle Vili, who managed to be both an Italian Fascist sympathizer and a spy for Great Britain during World War II. Of his own literary apprenticeship, Aciman said in an interview: "My *bildung* is totally European, even if it was always a derivative form of European culture. This was true in Egypt; it is still true in the United States. I was twenty when I read my first American novel, Saul Bellow's *Seize the Day,* and I couldn't feel a thing in common with it, or with the sensibility of most other American-Jewish writers. On the other hand, Sephardic writers such as Albert Cohen and Elias Canetti left me cold too . . . The only Sephardic author who influenced me—in part—was Natalia Ginzburg. It is because of the zany capers in her family that I finally realized that my own family was not the only warped one, and that I shouldn't write about it with a hand tied behind my back. And then, of course, there is Marcel Proust, but he was only half a Jew." Aciman also published *False Papers* (2000), a collection of autobiographical essays, and edited *Letters of Transit: Reflections on Exile, Identity, Language and Loss* (2000), which includes essays by Eva Hoffman, Edward Said, and Charles Simic. Aciman lives in New York City, where he teaches at the CUNY Graduate Center. "The Last Seder" is excerpted from *Out of Egypt.*

The Last Seder

When my father put down the receiver, he looked at us in the dining room and said, "It's started." No one needed to be told what he meant. It was common knowledge that *these* telephone calls came at all hours of the night—threatening, obscene, abusive calls in which an unidentified voice claiming to represent a government office asked all sorts of questions about our whereabouts, our guests, our habits, reminded us that we were nothing, that we had no rights and would soon be driven out, like the French and the British before us.

Until then, we had been spared these calls. Now, in the fall of 1964, they started. The voice seemed to know all about us. Indeed, it knew all our relatives abroad, read all our mail, named many of my friends and teachers at the American School, which I had been attending since leaving VC four years earlier. It knew everything. It even knew about the incident of the stone that day. "And I bet you're enjoying quail tonight," it said. "*Bon appétit.*" "A bad omen," said my grandmother.

Aunt Elsa said she hated Wednesdays. Bad things always came on Wednesdays.

My father said he, too, had had premonitions, but what had the voice meant about the incident of the stone?

At which point Aunt Flora decided to tell him. Earlier that day we had joined the crowd that lined the Corniche, waiting to get a look at President Nasser, standing for hours in the sun, cheering and waving each time anything resembling a motorcade came around the bend of Montaza Palace. Then we saw him, perched in his Cadillac, waving with a flat, open palm, looking exactly as he did in the pictures. People began to cheer, men and women jumping and clapping, waving small paper flags. A girl in a wheelchair, perched at the edge of the sidewalk almost touching the curb, had been holding a rolled-up sheet of paper tied with a green ribbon. Now the president had passed and she was still holding it, looking disheartened and crying. She had failed to drop her written message into his car. Abdou, who had come with us, had noticed her earlier and said she probably wanted the Raïs to pay for an operation or a new wheelchair. Her older brother, equally distraught—and probably blaming himself for failing to maneuver her close enough to the motorcade—was busy telling her it didn't matter, they would try the next time. "I don't want to live like this," she wailed, covering her face with shame as he wheeled her away toward a part of Mandara we did not know.

On our way home a stone hit Aunt Flora on the leg. "Foreigners out!" someone yelled in Arabic. We never saw precisely who had thrown it, but as soon as she shouted, a group of youths immediately began to disperse. The stone had hit her on the ankle, but it didn't break the skin, there wasn't any blood. "As long as I can walk—" she kept saying, rubbing her shin with her hand. Then, remembering the bottle of cologne in her bag, she applied some liberally over the bruise, occasionally massaging her leg as she limped along.

No sooner had we reached home that afternoon than we came upon another commotion, this time in our garden, where everyone was screaming, including al-Nunu who, on hearing the sudden noise, had come out of his hut armed with his machete. Al-Nunu was yelling the most, followed by Mohammed and my mother, everyone racing about in the garden, even my grandmother, who was now yelling at the top of her lungs. I asked Gomaa, al-Nunu's helper and catamite, what was the matter. Out of breath, Gomaa shouted, *"Kwalia!"*

Quail!

Every autumn, quail would descend on Egypt from as far away as Siberia and, as soon as they caught sight of land, would literally drop from the sky, exhausted. That afternoon a bird had fallen in our garden right next to where my grandmother was having tea with Arlette Joanides and her daughter, who were leaving Egypt and had come to say farewell. Instinctively my grandmother had taken the elaborate needlepoint canvas on which she had been working for over a year and thrown it over the exhausted quail. The bird, though it was faster than the old woman, was too tired to fly away. It kept hopping about our garden until it was joined by two more birds that must have fallen earlier, unbeknownst to my grandmother. This was far better than anything she could have dreamed of, and the old woman began to yell. Everyone came rushing to her rescue until they saw the birds, and then they joined the trapping party.

From adjoining gardens as far back as Rue Mordo we could hear similar screams as everyone at home or on the street dropped whatever they were doing to catch this exquisite manna that tumbled from the heavens each year.

And yet, despite the great joy they brought that day—to Abdou, although he would have to start dinner all over again; to Aunt Flora, who had almost forgotten her wound and was resolved to keep it from my father; and to my grandmother, for whom grail season coincided with the making of fruit preserves—still, the sight of this peerless Egyptian delicacy struggling for life as it tried to elude our frenetic grasp never failed to announce the arrival of autumn and the end of our summer in Mandara.

No one stayed on in Mandara after quail season. By early October, the streets were deserted, with only a few Egyptians, mostly Bedouins, remaining where they lived all year round. Packs of stray dogs—some young enough to have been adopted by summer residents who then left them behind at the end of the season—would come out from everywhere, scrounging for food, sometimes landing at our door, always barking, especially at night. By then, the beaches were completely empty, the Coca-Cola shacks were all closed, and, at night when we drove back from the movies, ours was the only light on our street, a faint, forty-watt flare beckoning from our kitchen, where Abdou would wait up for us, listening to Arab songs on the radio. Sometimes, though, he would have gone back to the city at night, and then there was no light awaiting our return, and Mandara would become a ghost town, and all one heard when my father turned off the car radio, and then the engine, was the sound of our movements in the car, the sound of our steps along the pebble path leading to our door, and, behind the house, down by the bend near al-Nunu's shack, the sound of waves.

Once in the house, my first impulse was always to turn on the lights in the entry and rush down the oppressive corridor and light up one room after the other—the veranda, the kitchen, the living room, even the radio in my bedroom, hoping to liven the entire house and give myself and my parents the illusion that there were still summer guests in the house who would presently come out of their rooms. One could even nurse the illusion of guests to come.

At midnight our anonymous caller asked whether we had been to the theater. My father told him the name of the film we saw.

We stayed at Mandara very late into the fall that year. We always stayed too long. It was my mother's way of refusing to admit summer was over. But there was another reason for delaying this year. After Mandara, we had decided not to return to Cleopatra but to move instead to Sporting, so that everyone in the family might be together. My mother was put in charge of selling all the furniture at Cleopatra.

I saw the apartment at Cleopatra for the last time a few weeks later, when my mother asked me to go up with her to set aside clothes for Abdou and Aziza. All of our furniture was now covered in sheets, and the window shutters were closed tight, lending our apartment, usually so sunny in October, a gloomy, sepulchral air, while the old sheets, which I could remember Abdou hastily throwing over sofas and armchairs at the very last minute before leaving for Mandara early that June, looked like tired, old, deflated phantoms. "All of it will be sold," said my mother with a pert, busy air that could easily be mistaken for anger but which was her way of showing enthusiasm. She loved novelty and change and was as excited now as she had been on moving here five years earlier.

I never met the man who bought all of our furniture, nor did I witness the transaction nor the actual lining up of our bedroom and dining room furniture on our sidewalk at Cleopatra. Aziza said Abdou was the only one who wept. I came back one day after school to find the place empty. "Maybe we shouldn't have moved," said my father. His voice sounded different now that the rugs and the furniture were gone.

I asked him if he was going to throw away all those books on the floor. No, he replied. We would take them to Sporting. Meanwhile, he was leafing through what looked like twenty to thirty thick green notebooks, tearing out occasional sheets that he intended to save. I asked him what he was doing. "These are notebooks I kept when I was a young man." Was he going to throw them away? "Not all, but there are things here I would rather disappeared." "Did you write anything against the government back then?" I asked. "No, nothing political. Other things," he said, unable to conceal a tenuous smile. "Some day you'll understand." I tried to tell him I was old enough to understand. But I knew what he'd say: "You think you are." He said he could still remember witnessing his parents' emptied home thirty years before on the day they had left Constantinople. As had his father seen his own father's home. And our ancestors before that as well. And so would I, too, one day, though he didn't wish it on me—"But everything repeats itself." I tried to protest, saying I hated this sort of fatalism, that I was free from Sephardi superstitions. "You think you are," he said.

I looked at the apartment, incredulous at how much larger it was without furniture.

I tried to remember the first time I had seen it, five years earlier. My grandmother and I had gotten lost in it, mistaking our way through doors and corridors, watching the workers sanding the floors and putting up a wall to create an additional room for someone called Madame Marie. I remembered the kitchen talk in the month of Ramadan, the smell of fresh paint and of newly restained furniture and of Mother's jasmine, and the window she threatened to throw herself from each time she thought she'd lose my father. I remembered Mimi and Madame Salama. They had moved to Israel. Monsieur Pharès lived in Florida; Abdel Hamid was paralyzed from the waist down; and Madame Nicole's husband had converted to Islam and finally repudiated her for behavior unbecoming a wife. Fawziah worked for an Egyptian family who treated her poorly. Monsieur al-Malek was now a second-tier schoolteacher in Marseilles waiting for a pension. And Abdou's son, Ahmed, so full of kindness, was shipped back from Yemen after a guerrilla patrol had captured and beheaded him.

Then, without warning, Aunt Flora, too, received a telephone call. In her case, the voice informed her that she had two weeks to leave Egypt. She left, as did other family friends, in the fall of that year, just a few days after we moved to Sporting. We knew our turn would come.

AUNT ELSA USED TO say that when bad things happen they come in threes. If you broke two plates, no one was really surprised when a third fell from your hands. If you cut yourself twice, you knew that a third cut was already hovering, waiting for the perfect alignment of sharp object and skin. If you got scolded twice, if you failed two tests, or lost two bets, you simply cowered for a few days and tried not to look too dismayed when the third blow came. When it did come, however, you would never say it was the last of the three. You had to pretend that a fourth might follow or that perhaps you had counted wrong or that this millennial rule had just been changed to confound you. That was called tact. It meant you were not presumptuous and would never dare trifle with the inscrutable machinations of fate.

Of course, we always sensed that our midnight caller knew exactly how we thought about these things. He would call twice and then not call again that night, knowing we would not go to bed until his third call came. Or he would call three times, let us sigh in relief and then, just as everyone was getting ready to retire, call again. "Is he there?" the voice would ask, meaning my father. "No, we don't want to speak with him. Just checking." "Who were your guests tonight?" "What did you buy today?" "Where did you go?" And so on.

Harassment calls began to punctuate all our evenings—by their absence as much as by their presence—reminding us that what were agreeable family evenings could easily deteriorate into bitter feuds as soon as grandmother hung up the telephone. "But why did you have to answer. Didn't I tell you not to?" my father would complain. "And why couldn't you tell him where I was?" he would add. "Because I don't think it's his business," his mother would reply. "But why do you persist in being rude to them? Why provoke them?" he would shout back at her. "Because this is what I felt like doing. Next time you answer."

Part of the late-night caller's ploy lay in calling when he knew my father was not home. Then, sometimes, thinking it was my father or even a friend calling late in the evening, I would pick up the receiver, and the stranger's voice, seemingly so harmless, even obsequious, would begin saying things I knew I should know nothing about. At other times, it was a rough street vendor's voice barking questions whose purpose I couldn't fathom, much less know how to answer. He would always end with the same words: "Tell him we'll call again tomorrow."

A day would pass. Then another. Sometimes three. Then two phone calls in succession. No one would pick up. "Maybe it's your father," my grandmother would say. It wasn't. Then no calls for another week.

Perhaps, the law of *jamais deux sans trois* didn't hold after all. But then, just when you were on the verge of giving up on it, it showed signs of renewed regularity—just long enough, that is, to trick you again.

Now, it so happened that Aunt Elsa had had strange forebodings the week before the Egyptian government nationalized all of my father's assets. *Une étrange angoisse,* a strange anxiety, right here, she kept repeating, pointing to her chest. "Here, and here, sometimes even here," she would say, hesitantly, as though her inability to locate the peculiar sensation in her chest made it more credible. "Something always happens when I have these feelings." She had had them on the eve of President Kennedy's assassination. And back in 1914. And of course in 1939. Madame Ephrikian, warned by Aunt Elsa to leave Smyrna in 1922, still called her *une voyante,* a seer. "Seer my eye!" exclaimed my grandmother behind her back.

"She's swallowed a cheap barometer, and it rattles inside her old rib cage. Whatever is itching her there, you can be sure it's just her conscience."

My grandmother was alluding to a quarrel the sisters had had over who would get Uncle Vili's prized nineteenth-century barometer following his sudden escape from Egypt. Uncle Vili liked to hunt duck, so, naturally, the sisters quarreled over who would inherit his rifles as well. One day, the rifles, the barometer, and his golf clubs disappeared. *"Les domestiques,"* alleged Aunt Elsa. *"Les domestiques* my eye!" replied my grandmother. "She swallowed them, just as she'll swallow everything we own one day." "We don't have to worry about that now," interjected my father, "the Egyptian government has already thought of it."

The news that my father had lost everything arrived at dawn one Saturday in early spring 1965. The bearer was Kassem, now the factory's night foreman. He rang our bell, and it was my father who opened the door. Seeing his boss look so crushed on guessing the reason for his untimely visit, the young foreman immediately burst into a fit of hysterical crying. "Did they take her, then?" asked my father, meaning the factory. "They took her." "When?" "Last night. They wouldn't let me call you, so I had to come." Both men stood quietly in the vestibule and then moved into the kitchen while my father tried to improvise something by way of tea. They sat at the kitchen table, urging one another not to lose heart, until both men broke down and began sobbing in each other's arms. "I found them crying like little children," was Aunt Elsa's refrain that day. "Like little children."

The crying had also awakened my grandmother, who, despite protestations that she never slept at night on account of the "troubles," was a very sound sleeper. She shuffled all the way into the kitchen to find that Abdou, who had just come in through the service entrance, had also joined in the tears. "This is no good," she snapped, "you'll wake Nessim. What's happened now?" "They took her." "Took whom?" "But the factory, signora, what else?" he said using the pidgin word for factory, *al-fabbrica.*

My grandmother never sobbed. She got angry, stamped, kicked, and grew flushed. Aunt Elsa was right when she claimed that her sister cried out of rage—like Bismarck, the Iron Chancellor—and not out of sorrow. Her eyelids would swell and grow red, and with the corner of her handkerchief she would blot away her tears with flustered and persistent poking motions, as though, in her fury, she was determined to inflict more pain on herself. This was the ninth time she had seen the men in her life lose everything; first her grandfather, then her father, her husband, five brothers, and now her son.

A moment of silence elapsed. "Here," she said, mixing sugar in a glass of water and handing it to my father. It was reputed to calm one's nerves. "I'm having tea, thank you," he said. But Abdou, who was still sobbing, said he could use it. Meanwhile, Aunt Elsa kept repeating, "See? I knew it, I knew it. Didn't I tell you? Didn't I?" "Do you want to shut up!" shouted her sister, suddenly shoving a large bowl containing last night's homemade yogurt along the kitchen countertop with such force that it exploded against the wall. "Who cares?" she shouted, anticipating her sister's reproach. "Who cares at a time like this, who?" She began to pick up the shards while Abdou, still sobbing, begged her not to bother, he would pick them up himself.

It was the noise of this quarrel that finally woke me that Saturday morning. I could tell something was amiss. As happened each time someone died, everyone's instinct was always to keep the bad news from me. Either the names of the deceased were scrupulously withheld from everyday conversation, or, when the names were mentioned, those present would heave a sigh signifying something nebulous and clearly beyond my scope, adding the adjectival *pauvre,* poor, to the name of the afflicted like a ceremonial epithet conferred on the occasion of one's death. *Pauvre* was used for the departed, the defeated, and the betrayed. "*Pauvre* Albert," my deceased grandfather; "*pauvre* Lotte," my deceased aunt; "*pauvre* Angleterre," who had lost all of her colonies; "*pauvres nous,*" said everyone! "*Pauvre moi,*" said my mother about my father. "*Pauvre fabrique*" was on everyone's lips that day. The last time they had used that expression was when the factory's main boiler exploded, severely damaging the building and almost ruining my father.

I found my father sitting in the living room with Kassem and Hassan, whispering instructions to them. When he saw me, he nodded somewhat absentmindedly, a sign that he did not want to be disturbed. I picked up the newspaper—a grown-up habit I was trying to acquire—and sat by myself in the dining room. I had heard at the American School that all young men in America read the newspaper first thing in the morning with their coffee. Coffee, too, was on my list. One sipped and thought of things to do that day and then remembered to go on reading one's newspaper. No yogurt this morning. Instead, the smell of eggs and bacon and of butter melting on toast wafted from the kitchen. I had seen American breakfasts in movies and at school and had instructed Abdou I wanted eggs with bacon every Saturday.

The early-spring sun beamed on the brown table in the dining room, spilling sweeps of light down the backs of the chairs and onto the faded red rug. My grandmother was like me; we liked bright rooms whose shutters were kept open all night and day, liked the clean, wholesome smell of sun-dried sheets or of sun-washed rooms and balconies on windy summer days; liked the insidious, stubborn eloquence of sunlight flooding under the door of a shuttered room on unbearable summer days; even the slight migraines that came from too much sun we liked. Through the window, as always on clear Saturday mornings, sat patches of unstirring turquoise in the distance, rousing the thirst for seawater which all schoolboys in Alexandria knew, and which seduced you into thinking of long hot hours on the summer beaches. Two more months, I thought.

When my grandmother walked into the dining room, she tried to hide that she had been crying. "Nothing," she replied to my unasked question. "Nothing at all. Here is your orange juice." She shuffled toward me on her ever-grieving bunions, kissing me on the back of the head, and then pinching my nape. *"Mon pauvre,"* she said, passing her fingers through my hair. "Couldn't this have waited a while longer, couldn't it?" she kept muttering, nodding to herself. Then, sensing I was about to renew my question, she said, "Nothing, nothing," and drifted out of the dining room. I ate my eggs in silence. Then my mother walked in and sat across from me. She, too, looked upset. Nobody was eating. So they had quarreled. But I hadn't heard her shouting.

"Look," she said, "they took everything."

It was like hearing that someone had died, a sinking feeling in my diaphragm and a tickling at the back of my ears. I pushed my plate away. My mother, whom I had not seen get up, was stirring sugar into a glass of water, saying, "Drink it all up now." It meant I had had my nerves shaken. I was a man, then.

Even so, I did not fully understand what was so frightful about losing one's fortune. A few of those we knew who had lost theirs went about living normal, everyday lives, with the same number of houses, cars, and servants. Their sons and daughters went to the same restaurants, saw the same number of movies, and spent as much money as they always had. On them, however, loomed the stigma—even the shame—of the fallen, the ousted, and it came with a strange odor that infallibly gave them away: it was the smell of leather. "Did you smell the abattoir," was my father's word for it, whispered maliciously after visiting friends about to leave the country. Every family that had lost everything knew it was destined to leave Egypt sooner or later, and, in one room, usually locked and hidden from guests, sat thirty to forty leather suitcases in which mothers and aunts kept packing their family's belongings at a slow, meticulous pace, always hoping that things might right themselves in the end. Until the very end, they hoped—and each of their husbands always swore he knew someone in high places who could be bribed when the time came. My father began to boast of the same contacts.

And then it dawned on me. When people came to visit us, they, too, would sniff out that funny leather smell and whisper *abattoir* behind our backs as they nosed about our home, wondering where on earth we had tucked all of our suitcases. The *abattoir* phase was bound to start soon, and with it an accelerated dose of family squabbles. Which store sold which suitcases cheaper? The question would tear our family apart. What articles should we buy for Europe? Gloves, socks, blankets, shoes? No, raincoats. No, hats. More fights. What would we leave behind? Aunt Elsa wanted to take everything. It figures, said my grandmother, who wanted to leave it all behind. Should we tell anyone? No. Yes. Why? More screaming. And finally, the one question bound to send everyone flying into a rage: Where would we settle? "But we don't even know the language they speak over there." "Why, did you know Arabic before coming here?" "No." "So?" "But it's so cold there." "And here it was too hot. You've said so yourself."

Meanwhile, we were given a reprieve, and like a baffled prisoner whose sentence has been temporarily commuted, or a stranded traveler whose return trip is inexplicably delayed, we were allowed to move about freely and do as we pleased, our lives suspended, taken over by unreal pursuits. It was well known that the fallen spent more and worried less. Some even started to enjoy Egypt, especially now that they could splurge, knowing they couldn't take abroad what the government was determined to seize from them. Others took advantage of the respite and did nothing all day save roam about aimlessly and hang around cafés, affecting, they thought, the unruffled dignity of condemned aristocrats.

When finally I spoke with my father that morning, he said it had come as no surprise. He had gone to bed knowing what awaited him in the morning and had told no one, not even Mother. Then I mustered the courage and asked what would happen now. They still needed him at the factory, he said. But that would pass, and then the inevitable would arrive. What? They would ask us to leave. Everything would have to be left behind. Meanwhile, there were some savings tucked away here and there, though technically we owned nothing. They might let us sell the furniture. But the cars were no longer ours. My father would recall old debts. Bound to be ugly, that. I wanted to know who owed him money. He told me their names. I was surprised. Their son was always having new shoes made. "How long, do you think?" I finally asked, like a patient imploring his doctor to say things aren't so hopeless after all. He shrugged his shoulders. "A few weeks, maybe a month." Then, pausing, he added, "At any rate, for us it's finished."

It meant our everyday lives, an era, the first uncertain visit to Egypt in 1905 by a young man named Isaac, our friends, the beaches, everything I had known, Om Ramadan, Roxane, Abdou, guavas, the loud tap of backgammon chips slapped vindictively upon the bar, fried eggplants on late-summer mornings, the voice of Radio Israel on rainy weekday evenings, and the languor of Alexandrian Sundays when all you did was go from movie to movie, picking up more and more friends along the way until a gang was formed and, from wandering the streets, someone would always suggest hopping on the tram and riding upstairs in second class all the way past San Stefano to Victoria and back. Now *it* all seemed unreal and transitory, as if we had lived a lie and suddenly had been found out.

"What should I do in the meantime?" I asked, emphasizing distress in my voice, because I could not see pretending that life would go on as usual. "Do? Do whatever you want—" my father started to say, letting me already savor the thought of dropping out of school and spending every day that spring going to the museum in the morning and then wandering through the bustling streets of downtown Alexandria, stalking my every whim. But my grandmother interrupted: "Never, no," she said with growing agitation. "He has to go to school. I won't accept it." "We'll see," said my father, "we'll see." She was about to go on, when he said, "Don't raise your voice, now of all times, not now." As she walked out of the room, I heard the tail end of her sentence, "—telling his son to become a degenerate, of all things. Who's ever seen such a thing? Who? Who? Who?"

At that point a click was heard at the front door and Uncle Nessim walked in. He had recently abandoned his habit of leaving the house at the crack of dawn and taking long walks along the Corniche, and seeing him now, everyone was dumbstruck. All morning we had been whispering because we were sure he was sleeping in his room. We had never even discussed whether to keep the bad news from him.

The truth is that, at the age of ninety-two, Uncle Nessim was dying of stomach cancer. He would spend hours in bed, crouched in a semifetal position which he said was the least painful—and thus, folded in two, hugging himself, he would sometimes fall asleep. Only once had I caught him in that position. They were tidying his room, and as I passed by his open door, I spied him lying in bed, wearing striped pajamas, holding his chest as if it were the dearest thing he owned. He looked sallow and small. The previous Friday evening, while reading the Sabbath prayers, he seemed absent and exhausted. He did not smile when my father said, as he always did before prayers, "*Falla breve,* Nessim, make it short." He ate nothing. His sisters had prepared a special pinkish jelly pudding for him, and it stood staring at him in a glass goblet while he kept reading. He cut the prayer short. But when it was time to eat, he dipped his spoon into the wobbly pudding, played with it, tasted it, and then, sensing we were all staring at him, said he couldn't. It was then I realized that beneath his dark smoking jacket and the glistening purple ascot peeped the faded, blue-striped outline of his pajamas. He wanted to go to bed. There was no one to take over the prayer. Neither my father nor I knew Hebrew, and both of us refused to have anything to do with prayers, even in French. "This is very sad," said Aunt Elsa. "There was a time when this room was full of people, full of candles, too. The table didn't even have enough leaves to seat everyone. The house is too big now. And Nessim is not well."

I remembered the room on those crowded *taffi al-nur* evenings, generations piled together, the oldest and the youngest separated by a century—so many of us. Now no one was left. They had stowed away the good china and gaudy silverware; dinner was served in one course; someone was always listening to the radio during the meal; and, because Aunt Elsa was put in charge of family expenses, even the wattage of the dining room lamp had been dimmed, so that a weak, pale-orange glow was cast over our faces and our meals, the shade of our last year in Egypt. My mother compared the once-resplendent dining room chandelier to a dying man's night-light.

The old furniture looked older, drabber, and there were entire sections of the apartment that had probably never been touched since the Isotta-Fraschini days. The service stairway had become so dirty that I never ventured near it. Almost all the furniture was in disrepair, much of it patched together or put aside, waiting for a heaven-sent visitor who, with the patience, know-how, and devotion of a carpenter's son, might finally remove the gummed paper that held so many caned chairs together in our dining room and perform the long-awaited miracle. "Sand always wins in the end," Aunt Elsa said, quoting her brother Vili as she ran her finger through the dust that had accumulated on the brown furniture after a particularly fierce *hamsin* that year. No one cleaned much of anything any longer. The apartment smelled of cloves, not just because they used it in cakes all the time, but because the three remaining siblings used it on their aching teeth.

Nessim was scheduled for surgery two weeks before Passover. As a precautionary measure, he was persuaded to transfer all of his assets to Aunt Elsa. "You watch," said my grandmother, peeved they had considered her unfit to handle the responsibility because she had suffered a mild stroke a few summers before. "Mark my words," she said and proceeded to make gestures mimicking the passage of food from the mouth down the esophagus and into the stomach. "She'll swallow all of it." In fact, Nessim's money was never seen or heard of again.

Strangely, Uncle Nessim had suddenly felt better during the night and had decided to go out for his usual walk at dawn. Everyone was so surprised to see him up and about, that instead of chiding him for taking a walk in his condition they began to pester him with questions. "But nothing's the matter with me," he kept saying, "I feel perfectly fine." "But you could have fallen, or gotten sick. Something might have happened." "Then I would have died and that would have been the end of that." When you get old, he used to tell me, you don't care about death. You aren't even ashamed of dying.

He proceeded to light a cigarette and asked for a cup of coffee. Dazzled by his spectacular recovery, Aunt Elsa kept fretting. "I knew it was a *kapparah.*" *Kapparah,* in Jewish lore, was the necessary catastrophe that precedes an unforeseen windfall. You do badly at school, but that same afternoon someone you love narrowly escapes being hit by a car; you lose a precious jewel, but then you run into a very old acquaintance you thought had entirely disappeared. *Kapparah* allowed you to experience bad luck, but with the understanding—and it had to be a vague, uncertain understanding, not a clear-cut *deal*—that for each blow you received, you averted a significantly worse one.

No sooner had my grandmother heard the word than she shot her sister a venomous stare. "Look at her, the pernicious viper that she is," she whispered to me, "look how she's dying to tell him about the factory. She's going to keep dropping hint after hint until he finds out." "Not at all," protested Elsa in whispers. "Can't one be happy without having one's motives questioned every time? Living with you is like being in jail sometimes."

As soon as coffee was brought in, Nessim took his cup and motioned to my father and me to follow him into the living room, then shut the frosted glass door behind him. "They took her, didn't they?" he asked. My father nodded. "How did you know?" "What am I, stupid?" he interjected. "All I had to do was take a look at all your dour faces." Then, smiling, "This *kapparah* is costing you quite a bit, isn't it?" he said. "But don't worry, I'm not really better. I just wanted to see the Corniche for the last time." Then, still smiling, he pointed to the door where the crouched outlines of both sisters could be seen glued to the glass. They moved away as soon as he neared the door.

A week later Nessim died. During the night following his operation, the sutures tore open and blood began to seep into his mattress, soaking the floor beneath. When Aunt Elsa, who was spending the night with him in his hospital room, awoke from a slumber, he was already gone.

"I wonder what the third blow will be," said my grandmother a few days afterward. "We don't need many hints to guess that," was my father's reply.

On the morning when the news of Nessim's death arrived, I awoke to a strange, persistent, owl-like hooting coming from the other end of the apartment. It had probably been going on for hours. I remembered trying to dispel it in my dreams. Finally, I slipped out of bed to see what it was. There were two nurses in the foyer, and with them Aunt Elsa, sobbing. She was seated on the sofa, still wearing her hat and clasping her handbag. She must have slumped down on the sofa as soon as she entered the apartment. Before her was an empty glass of what had undoubtedly been sugar-water. I tried to comfort her by caressing her arm. She didn't seem to feel it, but when I stopped, she whimpered something inaudible that sounded like a plea. "Stay, stay," she repeated, but I did not know whether she meant me or her brother. Then the hooting started again and she began saying things in Ladino, always repeating the same five or six words in a ritual intonation which I could not understand. Abdou was trying to make her drink some more; she kept refusing, turning to him and repeating the same words she had been saying to me. He answered her in Ladino, saying the señora was right, she was right, of course he had had plenty of life left in him, but fate willed otherwise, and who could question Allah. I shot him a quizzical look, wondering what she had been saying, and on our way back to the kitchen he explained, in Arabic, "She keeps saying he was only ninety-two, only ninety-two," whereupon both of us burst out laughing, repeating "only ninety-two" as if it were the funniest *mot de caractère* in Molière. The joke spread to Zeinab, across the service entrance, who passed it on to the servants upstairs, and downstairs, down to the porter, to the grocer across the street, and who knew where else.

My grandmother's reaction was no better. Upon seeing her sister seated half-dazed on the sofa, she immediately threw a tantrum. The two sisters hugged each other, and Aunt Elsa, whose tears had subsided by then, once again began to sob. "See what you've made me do," she kept repeating, "I didn't want to cry again, I didn't want to cry."

The sight was so moving, that I, too, would have sobbed along with them had I not bit my tongue and forced myself to think of other things, of funny things, anything. But as though guided by a perverse logic, my thoughts, however farfetched and bizarre, seemed determined to lead me back to poor Uncle Nessim, who, until two weeks ago, would sit in the family room busily refreshing his knowledge of spoken Hebrew because he wanted to die in Israel. There was nowhere to turn to forget. I tried to read in my room but could not. No one wanted to speak. Even the servants were unusually quiet. I would go to the kitchen and sit with Abdou and try to squeeze yet one more droplet of humor out of *only ninety-two.* But even that seemed stale now.

Uncle Nessim had lent me a nineteenth-century edition of Lord Chesterfield's letters. He thought I should read them; all young men should, he said. A few days later, Aunt Elsa knocked at my door and asked for the book. It would be put together with his other things, she said. I don't know how she found out I had it. But a few evenings later, when she was not home, I unlocked her bedroom door and rifled through her possessions, determined to rob her. Not only did I take back the Chesterfield, but I relieved her stamp collection of some of its rarest items. Many years later, while visiting her in Paris, I was helping her arrange her stamps in a new album when it finally occurred to her that she was missing her most valuable specimen. "These Arabs fleeced me well," she complained, while I threw a complicit look at my grandmother, who, at the time, had found out about my expedition into her sister's bedroom. This time, however, my grandmother returned an empty gaze. She had forgotten.

THAT EVENING, I slipped into Uncle Nessim's bedroom. I sat on his bed, looking out the window, catching the flicker of city lights, remembering how he spoke of London and Paris, how he said that all gentlemen, of whom he fancied himself one, would have a glass of scotch whiskey every evening. "It will kill me one day," he prophesied, "but I do love to sit here and watch the city and think about things for a while before dinnertime." And now, I, too, would do the same, think about *things,* as he put it, think about leaving, and about all the people I would never see again, and about this city, so inseparable from who I was at that very instant, and how it would slip into time and become stranger than dreamland. That, too, would be like dying. To be dead meant that others could come into your room and sit and think about you. It meant that others could come into your room and never know it had once been yours. Little by little they would remove all traces of you. Even your smell would go. Then they'd even forget you had died.

I opened the window to let in the city noise. It came—though distant and untouched, like the laughter of passersby who don't know someone's ill upstairs. The only way to shake off this lifeless gloom was to go out again, or find a secluded corner somewhere and read Cousin Arnaut's dirty books.

That night we all went to see the late-night showing of the new French film *Thérèse Desqueyroux*. It was the first time I had been to the theater at that hour, and I was immediately dazzled by this unfamiliar adult world, by its glamour and mystery, the whispered undertones during intermission, the spiffed-up young men two to three years older than I sitting with girls in the back rows, and the strange legend of perfume, mink, and cigarettes, that hovered about women like an elusive presage of love and laughter in crowded living rooms where they sat and talked with the men who loved them, as men and women talked in my parents' living room when there was company and I had gone to bed.

Later we went to an expensive restaurant in the city, and when I asked whether we could afford it, my father looked amused and said something like, "Don't worry, it isn't as bad as all that." We were with friends, and my grandmother and Aunt Elsa had come, and no one spoke of Nessim, and we ate with hearty appetites, and afterward, as was sometimes our habit, we drove along the Corniche, no one saying a word as we listened to the French broadcast until we stopped the car and got out to take a good whiff of the sea, listening to the bronchial wheezing of the waves as their advancing lines of spray clashed against the seawall.

That night the midnight caller called. Was everyone home? Yes, everyone was home. Where had we been? We're in mourning, please, leave us alone. Where did you go, he insisted. "May a curse fall on the orifice that spawned you and your mother's religion," said my father and hung up.

THE FOLLOWING DAY, returning from tennis, I was greeted by loud howling from the kitchen. My mother and my grandmother were quarreling at the top of their lungs, and Abdou, who normally took Sunday afternoons off, was busily trying to appease them both.

"Here are your damned prunes," shouted my mother. "Damn yourself, damned ingrate," retorted my grandmother, her voice cracking with emotion. "Who did you think I was trying to cook it for? For me?" The rest was sputtered in random fragments of Turkish, Ladino, and Greek.

Fearing for her sister, and despite her desire to remain impartial, Aunt Elsa tried to calm my grandmother and whispered something in Ladino, which sent my mother flying into a greater rage. "Always whispering, you two, with your cunning, beady, shifty, Jewish eyes, whispering your furtive little Ladino secrets like two ferrets from the ghetto of Constantinople, always siding with each other, the way she"—indicating my grandmother—"sided with you against her husband until she killed him like a dog, like a dog he died, wouldn't even let her visit him in his hospital room when he died." "What do you know, what? You good-for-nothing seamstress from Aleppo," shouted Elsa now, openly joining the fray. "Aren't you ashamed to speak like this while Nessim's body is still warm with life?" "Nessim this, Nessim that," tittered my mother. "He is well rid of you both. If you knew how he loathed you. Turned him into an alcoholic in his own bedroom, you did. Ha, don't make me say any more. You killed him, both of you, just as you killed your husbands. Whose turn is it now? Mine, do you think?"

It was then that I saw my grandmother, who clearly could not tolerate much more of this, do something I had never seen done in our family: she slapped herself on the face. "*This* for allowing my son to marry her. And this"—she slapped her other cheek, harder—"for begging, begging him to remain faithful to her." "Don't do that," shouted my mother, "don't do that." She grabbed both of her arms. A quick look at Abdou signified, "Get her a chair."

Things immediately began to subside. "Do you want to have a stroke, so he'll be able to blame me for the rest of my life? Enough like this!" Meanwhile, my grandmother had slumped on the chair next to the telephone in the corridor, holding her head in her hands. "I can't go on like this, can't go on like this. I don't want to live, let me die." "Die?" exclaimed my mother, "she'll outlive all of us. Sit down. Abdou, bring some water for the signora."

Finally Abdou and I separated the trio, and I discovered how the quarrel had started. Mother and daughter-in-law had disagreed on the recipe for *haroset,* the thick preserve made from fruits and wine that is eaten at Passover. My mother wanted raisins and dates, because *her* mother used raisins and dates, but my grandmother wanted oranges, raisins, and prunes, because this had been her family's recipe for as far back as she could remember. "*Maudite pesah!* Cursed Passover!" cried my grandmother. Sugared water was promptly distributed to all three in their respective rooms. "Your mother should be put away, this is not a life," said Elsa. When I went to see how my mother was doing, I made the mistake of telling her what Aunt Elsa had said, whereupon she got up and stomped into Elsa's room, ready to start another row. "But I didn't mean anything by it," she pleaded, beginning to sob. "Ach, there is no end to this. Poor Nessim, poor Nessim," she lamented, then changing her mind, "lucky Nessim, lucky Nessim."

At that moment the doorbell rang. I was convinced it was one of the neighbors coming to complain about the noise. Instead, standing at our door were two Egyptian gentlemen wearing three-piece suits. "May we come in?" one asked. "Who are you?" "We are from the police." "One moment," I said, "I will have to tell them inside," and, without apologizing, shut the door in their faces. Immediately I rushed inside and told my grandmother, who told Aunt Elsa, who told Abdou to tell the gentlemen to wait outside; she would be with them presently. Aunt Elsa locked her bedroom door, then went to wash her face before walking calmly into the vestibule. "May we come in?" they repeated. "I am a German citizen," she declaimed as if she had been practicing these lines with a third-rate vocalist for many, many months, "and will not allow you into this house." "We want to speak to the head of the household." "He is not here," she replied. "Where is he?" "I do not know." "Who is *he*?" asked one of the two, pointing at me. "He is a child. He doesn't know anything," said Aunt Elsa who, only a few days before, had said I was quite a *jeune petit monsieur.*

Although she had just sprinkled her face after crying, Aunt Elsa's glasses were smeared by a white film, probably dried tears, which made her look tattered and poor and certainly not the *grande dame* she was trying to affect at the moment. "*Cierra la puerta,* shut the door," Aunt Elsa told me in Ladino, referring to the door leading to the rest of the apartment. This was the first time she had ever spoken to me in Ladino, and I pretended not to hear and stood there gaping at the two policemen, while my grandmother, who didn't want to interfere with her sister's handling of the men, kept shuffling up and down the long corridor, peeking furtively into the vestibule, only to turn around and walk back along the corridor, pinching her cheeks—a gesture of anxiety in our family—as she repeated to herself "*Guay de mí, guay de mí,* woe is me, woe is me."

Meanwhile, at the other end of the apartment, my mother, who was not even aware of the policemen's visit, was weeping out loud, and Elsa, who could not understand spoken Arabic very well, kept straining her ears, apologizing for the noise within. "She is crazy," she said to one of the policemen, referring to my mother. "*Toc-toc,*" she smiled, rotating her index finger next to her skull, "*toc-toc.*" The policemen departed, leaving a warrant for my father. "I made them go away," she said.

Another disaster occurred no more than an hour later. Abdou had left, taking whatever remained of his day off. My mother had gone to wash her face, and, after leaving the bathroom, went directly to her room and slammed the door behind her. My grandmother, who hated sudden noises, winced but said nothing. A while later, on my way to the living room, where I planned to read by myself, I felt something damp about my feet. It was water. Mother, as I immediately realized, had once again forgotten to turn off the faucet and had flooded the bathroom, kitchen, and corridor areas. I rushed to tell her of this latest mishap, and as we were coming out of her room, I saw my grandmother standing in the dark corridor, looking at the ceiling, trying to determine where all this water had come from.

My mother rushed to the kitchen, took as many burlap rags as she could find and immediately threw them on the floor, asking me to help her roll the carpets away from the flood. She then brought a large pail, and kneeling on all fours, was attempting to soak up the water with the rags, wringing and unwringing swatches of cloth that bore the pungent odor of Abdou's floor wax. "I forgot to turn off the faucet," she lamented, starting to weep again. "Because I am deaf and because I am crazy, deaf and crazy, deaf and crazy," she repeated to the rhythm of her sobs. My grandmother, who was also on all fours by now, was busily wringing old towels into the pail, soiling her forearms with the grayish liquid that kept dribbling from the cloth. "It doesn't matter, you didn't hear the water, it doesn't matter," she kept saying, breaking down as well, finally exclaiming, "*Quel malheur, quel malheur,* what wretchedness," looking up as she wrung the towels, referring to the flood, to Egypt, to deafness, to having to squat on the floor like a little housemaid at the age of ninety because we no longer had servants on Sunday.

Early that evening, the caller rang. "Why were you not at home this afternoon?" asked the voice. "May you rot in sixty hells," replied my father.

"I WANT YOU to sit down and be a big boy now," said my father that night after reading the warrant. "Listen carefully." I wanted to cry. He noticed, stared at me awhile, and then, holding my hand, said, "Cry." I felt a tremor race through my lower lip, down my chin. I struggled with it, bit my tongue, then shook my head to signal that I wasn't going to cry. "It's not easy, I know. But this is what I want you to do. Since it's clear they'll arrest me tomorrow," he said, "the most important thing is to help your mother sell everything, have everyone pack as much as they can, and purchase tickets for all of us. It's easier than you think. But in case I am detained, I want you to leave anyway. I'll follow later. You must pass one message to Uncle Vili and another to Uncle Isaac in Europe." I said I would remember them. "Yes, but I also want each message encoded, in case you forget. It will take an hour, no more." He asked me to bring him a book I would want to take to Europe and might read on the ship. There were two: *The Idiot* and Kitto's *The Greeks*. "Bring Kitto," he said, "and we'll pretend to underline all the difficult words, so that if customs officials decide to inspect the book, they will think you've underlined them for vocabulary reasons." He pored over the first page of the book and underlined *Thracian, luxurious, barbaroi, Scythians, Ecclesiastes*. "But I already know what they all mean." "Doesn't matter what *you* know. What's important is what *they* think. *Ecclesiastes* is a good word. Always use the fifth letter of the fifth word you've underlined—in this case, *e*, and discard the rest. It's a code in the Lydian mode, do you see?" That evening he also taught me to forge his signature. Then, as they did in the movies, we burned the page on which I had practiced it.

By two o'clock in the morning, we had written five sentences. Everybody had gone to bed already. Someone had dimmed the lamp in the hallway and turned off all the lights in the house. Father offered me a cigarette. He drew the curtains that had been shut so that no one outside might see what we were doing and flung open the window. Then, after letting a spring breeze heave through the dining room, he stood by the window, facing the night, his chin propped on the palms of his hands, with his elbows resting on the window ledge. "It's a small city, but I hate to lose her," he finally said. "Where else can you see the stars like this?" Then, after a few seconds of silence, "Are you ready for tomorrow?" I nodded. I looked at his face and thought to myself: They might torture him, and I may never see him again. I forced myself to believe it—maybe that would bring him good luck.

"Good night, then." "Good night," I said. I asked him if he was going to go to bed as well. "No, not yet. You go. I'll sit here and think awhile." He had said the same thing years before, when we visited his father's tomb and, silently, he had propped his chin on one hand, his elbow resting on the large marble slab. I had been asking him questions about the cemetery, about death, about what the dead did when we were not thinking of them. Patiently, he had answered each one, saying death was like a quiet sleep, but very long, with long, peaceful dreams. When I began to feel restless and asked whether we could go, he answered, "No, not yet. I'll stand here and think awhile." Before leaving, we both leaned down and kissed the slab.

THE NEXT MORNING, I awoke at six. My list of errands was long. First the travel agency, then the consulate, then the telegrams to everyone around the world, then the agent in charge of bribing all the customs people, then a few words with Signor Rosenthal, the jeweler whose brother-in-law lived in Geneva. "Don't worry if he pretends not to understand you," my father had said. After that, I was to see our lawyer and await further instructions.

My father had left the house at dawn, I was told. Mother had been put in charge of buying suitcases. My grandmother took a look at me and grumbled something about my clothes, especially those "long blue trousers with copper snaps all over them." "What snaps?" I asked. "These," she said, pointing to my blue jeans. I barely had time to gulp down her orange juice before rushing out of the house and hopping on the tram, headed downtown—something I had never done before, as the American School was in the opposite direction. Suddenly, I was a grown-up going to work, and the novelty thrilled me.

Alexandria on that spring weekday morning had its customary dappled sky. Brisk and brackish scents blew in from the coast, and the tumult of trade on the main thoroughfares spilled over into narrow side-lanes where throngs and stands and jostling trinket men cluttered the bazaars under awnings striped yellow and green. Then, as always at a certain moment, just before the sunlight began to pound the flagstones, things quieted down for a while, a cool breeze swept through the streets, and something like a distilled, airy light spread over the city, bright but without glare, light you could stare into.

The wait to renew the passports at the consulate was brief: the man at the counter knew my mother. As for the travel agent, he already seemed apprised of our plans. His question was: "Do you want to go to Naples or to Bari? From Bari you can go to Greece; from Naples to Marseilles." The image of an abandoned Greek temple overlooking the Aegean popped into my head. "Naples," I said, "but do not put the date yet." "I understand," he said discreetly. I told him that if he called a certain number, funds would be made available to him. In fact, I had the money in my pocket but had been instructed not to use it unless absolutely necessary.

The telegrams took forever. The telegraph building was old, dark, and dirty, a remnant of colonial grandeur fading into a wizened piece of masonry. The clerk at the booth complained that there were too many telegrams going to too many countries on too many continents. He eyed me suspiciously and told me to go away. I insisted. He threatened to hit me. I mustered the courage and told the clerk we were friends of So-and-so, whose name was in the news. Immediately he extended that inimitably unctuous grace that passes for deference in the Middle East.

By half past ten I was indeed proud of myself. One more errand was left, and then Signor Rosenthal. Franco Molkho, the agent in charge of bribing customs officials, was himself a notorious crook who took advantage of everyone precisely by protesting that he was not cunning enough to do so. "I'm always up front about what I do, madame." He was rude and gruff, and if he saw something in your home that struck his fancy, he would grab and pocket it in front of you. If you took it away from him and placed it back where it belonged—which is what my mother did—then he would steal it later at the customs shed, again before your very eyes. Franco Molkho lived in a kind of disemboweled garage, with a makeshift cot, a tattered sink, and a litter of grimy gearboxes strewn about the floor. He wanted to negotiate. I did not know how to negotiate. I told him my father's instructions. "You Jews," he snickered, "it's impossible to beat you at this game." I blushed. Once outside, I wanted to spit out the tea he had offered me.

Still, I thought of myself as the rescuer of my entire family. Intricate scenarios raced through my mind, scenarios in which I pounded the desk of the chief of police and threatened all sorts of abominable reprisals unless my father was released instantly. "Instantly! Now! Immediately!" I yelled, slapping my palm on the inspector's desk. According to Aunt Elsa, the more you treated such people like your servants, the more they behaved accordingly. "And bring me a glass of water, I'm hot." I was busily scheming all sorts of arcane missions when I heard someone call my name. It was my father.

He was returning from the barber and was ambling at a leisurely pace, headed for his favorite café near the stock exchange building. "Why aren't you in jail?" I asked, scarcely concealing my disappointment. "Jail!" he exclaimed, as if to say, "Whoever gave you such a silly notion?" "All they wanted was to ask me a few questions. Denunciations, always these false denunciations. Did you do everything I told you?" "All except Signor Rosenthal." "Very good. Leave the rest to me. By the way, did Molkho agree?" I told him he did. "Wonderful." Then he remembered. "Do you have the money?" "Yes." "Come, then. I'll buy you coffee. You do drink coffee, don't you? Remember to give it to me under the table." A young woman passed in front of us and father turned. "See? Those are what I call perfect ankles."

At the café, my father introduced me to everyone. They were all businessmen, bankers, and industrialists who would meet at around eleven in the morning. All of them had either lost everything they owned or were about to. "He's even read all of *Plutarch's Lives,*" boasted my father. "Wonderful," said one of them, who, by his accent, was Greek. "Then surely you remember Themistocles." "Of course he does," said my father, seeing I was blushing. "Let me explain to you, then, how Themistocles won the battle at Salamis, because that, my dear, they won't teach you in school." Monsieur Panos took out a Parker pen and proceeded to draw naval formations on the corner of his newspaper. "And do you know who taught me all this?" he asked, with a self-satisfied glint flickering in his glazed eyes, his hand pawing my hair all the while. "Do you know who? Me," he said, "I did, all by myself. Because I wanted to be an admiral in the Greek navy. Then I discovered there was no Greek navy, so I joined the Red Cross at Alamein."

Everyone burst out laughing, and Monsieur Panos, who probably did not understand why, joined them. "I still have the Luger a dying German soldier gave me. It had three bullets left, and now I know who they're for: one for President Nasser. One for my wife, because, God knows, she deserves it. And one for me. *Jamais deux sanstrois.*" Again a burst of laughter. "Not so loud," the Greek interrupted. But I continued to laugh heartily. While I was wiping my eyes, I caught one of the men nudging my father's arm. I was not supposed to see the gesture, but I watched as my father turned and looked uneasily at a table behind him. It was the woman with the beautiful ankles. "Weren't you going to tell me something?" asked my father, tapping me on the knee under the table. "Only about going to the swimming pool this morning." "By all means," he said, taking the money I was secretly passing to him. "Why don't you go now?"

TWO DAYS LATER the third blow fell.

My father telephoned in the morning. "They don't want us anymore," he said in English. I didn't understand him. "They don't want us in Egypt." But we had always known that, I thought. Then he blurted it out: we had been officially expelled and had a week to get our things together. "Abattoir?" I asked. "Abattoir," he replied.

The first thing one did when *abattoir* came was to get vaccinated. No country would allow us across its border without papers certifying we had been properly immunized against a slew of Third World diseases.

My father had asked me to take my grandmother to the government vaccine office. The office was near the harbor. She hated the thought of being vaccinated by an Egyptian orderly—"Not even a doctor," she said. I told her we would stop and have tea and pastries afterward at Athinéos. "Don't hurt me," she told the balding woman who held her arm. "But I'm not hurting you," protested the woman in Arabic. "You're not hurting me? You *are* hurting me!" The woman ordered her to keep still. Then came my turn. She reminded me of Miss Badawi when she scraped my scalp with her fingernails looking for lice. Would they really ask us to undress at the customs desk when the time came and search us to our shame?

After the ordeal, my grandmother was still grumbling as we came down the stairs of the government building, her voice echoing loudly as I tried to hush her. She said she wanted to buy me ties.

Outside the building, I immediately hailed a hansom, helped my grandmother up, and then heard her give an obscure address on Place Mohammed Ali. As soon as we were seated, she removed a small vial of alcohol and, like her Marrano ancestors who wiped off all traces of baptismal water as soon as they had left the church, she sprinkled the alcohol on the site of the injection—to *kill* the vaccine, she said, and all the germs that came with it!

It was a glorious day, and as we rode along my grandmother suddenly tapped me on the leg as she had done years earlier on our way to Rouchdy and said, "Definitely a beach day." I took off my sweater and began to feel that uncomfortable, palling touch of wool flannel against my thighs. Time for shorts. The mere thought of light cotton made the wool unbearable. We cut through a dark street, then a square, got on the Corniche, and, in less than ten minutes, came face-to-face with the statue of Mohammed Ali, the Albanian founder of Egypt's last ruling dynasty.

We proceeded past a series of old, decrepit stores that looked like improvised warehouses and workshops until we reached one tiny, extremely cluttered shop. "Sidi Daoud," shouted my grandmother. No answer. She took out a coin and used it to knock on the glass door several times. "Sidi Daoud is here," a tired figure finally uttered, emerging from the dark. He recognized her immediately, calling her his "favorite *mazmazelle.*"

Sidi Daoud was a one-eyed, portly Egyptian who dressed in traditional garb—a white *galabiya* and on top of it a grossly oversized, gray, double-breasted jacket. My grandmother, speaking to him in Arabic, said she wanted to buy me some good ties. "Ties? I have ties," he said, pointing to a huge old closet whose doors had been completely removed; it was stuffed with paper bags and dirty cardboard boxes. "What sort of ties?" "Show me," she said. "Show me, she says," he muttered as he paced about, "so I'll show her."

He brought a stool, climbed up with a series of groans and cringes, reached up to the top of the closet, and brought down a cardboard box whose corners were reinforced with rusted metal. "These are the best," he said as he took out tie after tie. "You'll never find these for sale anywhere in the city, or in Cairo, or anywhere else in Egypt." He removed a tie from a long sheath. It was dark blue with intricate light-blue and pale-orange patterns. He took it in his hands and brought it close to the entrance of the store that I might see it better in the sunlight, holding it out to me with both hands the way a cook might display a poached fish on a salver before serving it. "Let me see," said my grandmother as though she were about to lift and examine its gills. I recognized the tie immediately: it had the sheen of Signor Ugo's ties.

This was a stupendous piece of work. My grandmother looked at the loop and the brand name on the rear apron and remarked that it was not a bad make. "I'll show you another," he said, not even waiting for me to pass judgment on the first. The second was a light-burgundy, bearing an identical pattern to the first. "Take it to the door," he told me, "I'm too old to come and go all day." This one was lovelier than the first, I thought, as I studied both together. A moment later, my grandmother joined me at the door and held the burgundy one in her hands and examined it, tilting her head left and right, as though looking for concealed blemishes which she was almost sure to catch if she looked hard enough. Then, placing the fabric between thumb and forefinger, she rubbed them together to test the quality of the silk, peeving the salesman. "Show me better." "Better than this?" he replied. "*Mafish,* there isn't!" He showed us other ties, but none compared to the first. I said I was happy with the dark-blue one; it would go with my new blazer. "Don't match your clothes like a pauper," said my grandmother. The Egyptian unsheathed two more ties from a different box. One with a green background, the other light blue. "Do you like them?" she asked. I liked them all, I said. "He likes them all," she repeated with indulgent irony in her voice.

"This is the black market," she said to me as soon as we left the store, the precious package clutched in my hand, as I squinted in the sunlight, scanning the crowded Place Mohammed Ali for another horse-drawn carriage. We had spent half an hour in Sidi Daoud's store and had probably looked at a hundred ties before choosing these four. No shop I ever saw, before or since—not even the shop in the Faubourg Saint Honoré where my grandmother took me years later—had as many ties as Sidi Daoud's little hovel. I spotted an empty hansom and shouted to the driver from across the square. The *arbaghi,* who heard me and immediately stood up in the driver's box, signaled he would have to turn around the square, motioning us to wait for him.

Fifteen minutes later, we arrived at Athinéos. The old Spaniard was gone. Instead, a surly Greek doing a weak impersonation of a well-mannered waiter took our order. We were seated in a very quiet corner, next to a window with thick white linen drapes, and spoke about the French plays due to open in a few days. "Such a pity," she said. "Things are beginning to improve just when we are leaving." The Comédie Française had finally returned to Egypt after an absence of at least ten years. La Scala was also due to come again and open in Cairo's old opera house with a production of *Otello.* Madame Darwish, our seamstress, had told my grandmother of a young actor from the Comédie who had knocked at her door saying this was where he had lived as a boy; she let him in, offered him coffee, and the young man burst out crying, then said good-bye. "Could all this talk of expulsion be mere bluffing?" my grandmother mused aloud, only to respond, "I don't think so."

After a second round of mango ice cream, she said, "And now we'll buy you a good book and then we might stop a while at the museum." By "good book" she meant either difficult to come by or one she approved of. It was to be my fourteenth-birthday present. We left the restaurant and were about to hail another carriage when my grandmother told me to make a quick left turn. "We'll pretend we're going to eat a pastry at Flückiger's." I didn't realize why we were *pretending* until much later in the day when I heard my father yell at my grandmother. "We could all go to jail for what you did, thinking you're so clever!" Indeed, she had succeeded in losing the man who had been tailing us after—and probably before—we entered Athinéos. I knew nothing about it until we were inside the secondhand bookstore. On one of the stacks I had found exactly what I wanted. "Are you sure you're going to read all this?" she asked.

She paid for the books absentmindedly and did not return the salesman's greeting. She had suddenly realized that a second agent might have been following us all along. "Let's leave now," she said, trying to be polite. "Why?" "Because." We hopped in a taxi and told the driver to take us to

Ramleh station. On our way we passed a series of familiar shops and restaurants, a stretch of saplings leaning against a sunny wall, and, beyond the buildings, an angular view of the afternoon sea.

As soon as we arrived at Sporting, I told my grandmother I was going straight to the Corniche. "No, you're coming home with me." I was about to argue. "Do as I tell you, please. There could be trouble." Standing on the platform was our familiar tail. As soon as I heard the word *trouble,* I must have frozen on the spot, because she immediately added, "Now don't go about looking so frightened!"

My grandmother, it turned out, had been smuggling money out of the country for years and had done so on that very day. I will never know whether her contact was Sidi Daoud, or the owner of the secondhand bookstore, or maybe one of the many coachmen we hired that day. When I asked her in Paris many years later, all she volunteered was, "One needed nerves of steel."

DESPITE THE FRANTIC PACKING and last-minute sale of all the furniture, my mother, my grandmother, and Aunt Elsa had decided we should hold a Passover seder on the eve of our departure. For this occasion, two giant candelabra would be brought in from the living room, and it was decided that the old sculptured candles should be used as well. No point in giving them away. Aunt Elsa wanted to clean house, to remove all traces of bread, as Jews traditionally do in preparation for Passover. But with the suitcases all over the place and upside down, nobody was eager to undertake such a task, and the idea was abandoned. "Then why have a seder?" she asked with embittered sarcasm. "Be glad we're having one at all," replied my father. I watched her fume. "If that's going to be your attitude, let's *not* have one, see if I care." "Now don't get all worked up over a silly seder, Elsa. Please!"

My mother and my grandmother began pleading with him, and for a good portion of the afternoon, busy embassies shuttled back and forth between Aunt Elsa's room and my father's study. Finally, he said he had to go out but would be back for dinner. That was his way of conceding. Abdou, who knew exactly what to prepare for the seder, needed no further inducements and immediately began boiling the eggs and preparing the cheese-and-potato *buñuelos.*

Meanwhile, Aunt Elsa began imploring me to help read the Haggadah that evening. Each time I refused, she would remind me that it was the last time this dining room would ever see a seder and that I should read in memory of Uncle Nessim. "His seat will stay empty unless somebody reads." Again I refused. "Are you ashamed of being Jewish? Is that it? What kind of Jews are we, then?" she kept asking. "The kind who don't celebrate leaving Egypt when it's the last thing they want to do," I said. "But that's so childish. We've never not had a seder. Your mother will be crushed. Is that what you want?" "What I want is to have no part of it. I don't want to cross the Red Sea. And I don't want to be in Jerusalem next year. As far as I'm concerned, all of this is just worship of repetition and nothing more." And I stormed out of the room, extremely pleased with my *bon mot*. "But it's our last evening in Egypt," she said, as though that would change my mind.

For all my resistance, however, I decided to wear one of my new ties, a blazer, and a newly made pair of pointed black shoes. My mother, who joined me in the living room around half past seven, was wearing a dark-blue dress and her favorite jewelry. In the next room, I could hear the two sisters putting the final touches to the table, stowing away the unused silverware, which Abdou had just polished. Then my grandmother came in, making a face that meant Aunt Elsa was truly impossible. "It's always what she wants, never what others want." She sat down, inspected her skirt absentmindedly, spreading its pleats, then began searching through the bowl of peanuts until she found a roasted almond. We looked outside and in the window caught our own reflections. Three more characters, I thought, and we'll be ready for Pirandello.

Aunt Elsa walked in, dressed in purple lace that dated back at least three generations. She seemed to notice that I had decided to wear a tie. "Much better than those trousers with the snaps on them," she said, throwing her sister a significant glance. We decided to have vermouth, and Aunt Elsa said she would smoke. My mother also smoked. Then, gradually, as always happened during such gatherings, the sisters began to reminisce. Aunt Elsa told us about the little icon shop she had kept in Lourdes before the Second World War. She had sold such large quantities of religious objects to Christian pilgrims that no one would have guessed she was Jewish. But then, at Passover, not knowing where to buy unleavened bread, she had gone to a local baker and inquired about the various qualities of flour he used in his shop, claiming her husband had a terrible ulcer and needed special bread. The man said he did not understand what she wanted, and Elsa, distraught, continued to ask about a very light type of bread, maybe even unleavened bread, if such a thing existed. The man replied that surely there was an epidemic spreading around Lourdes, for many were suffering from similar gastric disorders and had been coming to his shop for the past few days asking the same question. "Many?" she asked. "Many, many," he replied, smiling, then whispered, "*Bonne pâque,* happy Passover," and sold her the unleavened bread.

"*Se non è vero, è ben trovato,* if it isn't true, you've made it up well," said my father, who had just walked in. "So, are we all ready?" "Yes, we were waiting for you," said my mother, "did you want some scotch?" "No, already had some."

Then, as we made toward the dining room, I saw that my father's right cheek was covered with pink, livid streaks, like nail scratches. My grandmother immediately pinched her cheek when she saw his face but said nothing. My mother, too, cast stealthy glances in his direction but was silent.

"So what exactly is it you want us to do now?" he asked Aunt Elsa, mildly scoffing at the ceremonial air she adopted on these occasions.

"I want you to read," she said, indicating Uncle Nessim's seat. My mother stood up and showed him where to start, pained and shaking her head silently the more she looked at his face. He began to recite in French, without irony, without flourishes, even meekly. But as soon as he began to feel comfortable with the text, he started to fumble, reading the instructions out loud, then correcting himself, or skipping lines unintentionally only to find himself reading the same line twice. At one point, wishing to facilitate his task, my grandmother said, "Skip that portion." He read some more and she interrupted again. "Skip that, too."

"No," said Elsa, "either we read everything or nothing at all." An argument was about to erupt. "Where is Nessim now that we need him," said Elsa with that doleful tone in her voice that explained her success at Lourdes. "As far away from you as he can be," muttered my father under his breath, which immediately made me giggle. My mother, catching my attempt to stifle a laugh, began to smile; she knew exactly what my father had said though she had not heard it. My father, too, was infected by the giggling, which he smothered as best as he could, until my grandmother caught sight of him, which sent her laughing uncontrollably. No one had any idea what to do, what to read, or when to stop. "Some Jews we are," said Aunt Elsa, who had also started to laugh and whose eyes were tearing. "Shall we eat, then?" asked my father. "Good idea," I said. "But we've only just begun," protested Aunt Elsa, recovering her composure. "It's the very last time. How could you? We'll never be together again, I can just feel it." She was on the verge of tears, but my grandmother warned her that she, too, would start crying if we kept on like this. "This is the last year," said Elsa, reaching out and touching my hand. "It's just that I can remember so many seders held in this very room, for fifty years, year after year after year. And I'll tell you something," she said, turning to my father. "Had I known fifty years ago that it would end like this, had I known I'd be among the last in this room, with everyone buried or gone away, it would have been better to die, better to have died back then than to be left alone like this." "Calm yourself, Elsica," said my father, "otherwise we'll all be in mourning here."

At that point, Abdou walked in and, approaching my father, said there was someone on the telephone asking for him. "Tell them we are praying," said my father. "But sir—" He seemed troubled and began to speak softly. "So?" "She said she wanted to apologize." No one said anything. "Tell her not now." "Very well."

We heard the hurried patter of Abdou's steps up the corridor, heard him pick up the receiver and mumble something. Then, with relief, we heard him hang up and go back into the kitchen. It meant she had not insisted or argued. It meant he would be with us tonight. "Shall we eat, then?" said my mother. "Good idea," I repeated. "Yes, I'm starving," said Aunt Elsa. "An angel you married," murmured my grandmother to my father.

After dinner, everyone moved into the smaller living room, and, as was her habit on special gatherings, Aunt Elsa asked my father to play the record she loved so much. It was a very old recording by the Busch Quartet, and Aunt Elsa always kept it in her room, fearing someone might ruin it. I had noticed it earlier in the day lying next to the radio. It meant she had been planning the music all along. "Here," she said, gingerly removing the warped record from its blanched dust jacket with her arthritic fingers. It was Beethoven's "Song of Thanksgiving." Everyone sat down, and the adagio started.

The old 78 hissed, the static louder than the music, though no one seemed to notice, for my grandmother began humming, softly, with a plangent, faraway whine in her voice, and my father shut his eyes, and Aunt Elsa began shaking her head in rapt wonder, as she did sometimes when tasting Swiss chocolate purchased on the black market, as if to say, "How could anyone have created such beauty?"

And there, I thought, was my entire world: the two old ones writhing in a silent stupor, my father probably wishing he was elsewhere, and my mother, whose thoughts, as she leafed through a French fashion magazine, were everywhere and nowhere, but mostly on her husband, who knew that she would say nothing that evening and would probably let the matter pass quietly and never speak of it again.

I motioned to my mother that I was going out for a walk. She nodded. Without saying anything, my father put his hand in his pocket and slipped me a few bills.

Outside, Rue Delta was brimming with people. It was the first night of Ramadan and the guns marking the end of the fast had gone off three hours earlier. There was unusual bustle and clamor, with people gathered in groups, standing in the way of traffic, making things noisier and livelier still, the scent of holiday pastries and fried treats filling the air. I looked up at our building: on our floor, all the lights were out except for Abdou's and those in the living room. Such weak lights, and so scant in comparison to the gaudy, colored bulbs that hung from all the lampposts and trees—as if the electricity in our home were being sapped and might die out at any moment. It was an Old World, old-people's light.

As I neared the seafront, the night air grew cooler, saltier, freed from the din of lights and the milling crowd. Traffic became sparse, and whenever cars stopped for the traffic signal, everything grew still: then, only the waves could be heard, thudding in the dark, spraying the air along the darkened Corniche with a thin mist that hung upon the night, dousing the streetlights and the signposts and the distant floodlights by the guns of Petrou, spreading a light clammy film upon the pebbled stone wall overlooking the city's coastline. Quietly, an empty bus splashed along the road, trailing murky stains of light on the gleaming pavement. From somewhere, in scattered snatches, came the faint lilt of music, perhaps from one of those dance halls where students used to flock at night. Or maybe just a muted radio somewhere on the beach nearby, where abandoned nets gave off a pungent smell of seaweed and fish.

At the corner of the street, from a sidewalk stall, came the smell of fresh dough and of angel-hair being fried on top of a large copper stand—a common sight throughout the city every Ramadan. People would fold the pancakes and stuff them with almonds, syrup, and raisins. The vendor caught me eyeing the cakes that were neatly spread on a black tray. He smiled and said, "*Etfaddal,* help yourself."

I thought of Aunt Elsa's chiding eyes. "But it's Pesah," I imagined her saying. My grandmother would disapprove, too—eating food fried by Arabs on the street, unconscionable. The Egyptian didn't want any money. "It's for you," he said, handing me the delicacy on a torn sheet of newspaper.

I wished him a good evening and took the soggy pancake out onto the seafront. There, heaving myself up on the stone wall, I sat with my back to the city, facing the sea, holding the delicacy I was about to devour. Abdou would have called this a real *mazag,* accompanying the word, as all Egyptians do, with a gesture of the hand—a flattened palm brought to the side of the head—signifying blissful plenitude and the prolonged, cultivated consumption of everyday pleasures.

Facing the night, I looked out at the stars and thought to myself, over there is Spain, then France, to the right Italy, and, straight ahead, the land of Solon and Pericles. The world is timeless and boundless, and I thought of all the shipwrecked, homeless mariners who had strayed to this very land and for years had tinkered away at their damaged boats, praying for a wind, only to grow soft and reluctant when their time came.

I stared at the flicker of little fishing boats far out in the offing, always there at night, and watched a group of children scampering about on the beach below, waving little Ramadan lanterns, the girls wearing loud pink-and-fuchsia dresses, locking hands as they wove themselves into the dark again, followed by another group of child revelers who were flocking along the jetty past the sand dunes, some even waving up to me from below. I waved back with a familiar gesture of street fellowship and wiped the light spray that had moistened my face.

And suddenly I knew, as I touched the damp, grainy surface of the seawall, that I would always remember this night, that in years to come I would remember sitting here, swept with confused longing as I listened to the water lapping the giant boulders beneath the promenade and watched the children head toward the shore in a winding, lambent procession. I wanted to come back tomorrow night, and the night after, and the one after that as well, sensing that what made leaving so fiercely painful was the knowledge that there would never be another night like this, that I would never eat soggy cakes along the coast road in the evening, not this year or any other year, nor feel the baffling, sudden beauty of that moment when, if only for an instant, I had caught myself longing for a city I never knew I loved.

Exactly a year from now, I vowed, I would sit outside at night wherever I was, somewhere in Europe, or in America, and turn my face to Egypt, as Moslems do when they pray and face Mecca, and remember this very night, and how I had thought these things and made this vow. You're beginning to sound like Elsa and her silly seders, I said to myself, mimicking my father's humor.

On my way home I thought of what the others were doing. I wanted to walk in, find the smaller living room still lit, the Beethoven still playing, with Abdou still clearing the dining room, and, on closing the front door, suddenly hear someone say, "We were just waiting for you, we're thinking of going to the Royal." "But we've already seen that film," I would say. "What difference does it make. We'll see it again."

And before we had time to argue, we would all rush downstairs, where my father would be waiting in a car that was no longer really ours, and, feeling the slight chill of a late April night, would huddle together with the windows shut, bicker as usual about who got to sit where, rub our hands, turn the radio to a French broadcast, and then speed to the Corniche, thinking that all this was as it always was, that nothing ever really changed, that the people enjoying their first stroll on the Corniche after fasting, or the woman selling tickets at the Royal, or the man who would watch our car in the side alley outside the theater, or our neighbors across the hall, or the drizzle that was sure to greet us after the movie at midnight would never, ever know, nor ever guess, that this was our last night in Alexandria.

Gini Alhadeff

Gini Alhadeff (Egypt-USA, 1951–) was born in Alexandria, Egypt, and grew up in Cairo, Khartoum, Florence, and Tokyo. Her mother's family was from Livorno and her father's family from Rhodes. Alhadeff was raised as a Catholic and did not know that she was of Jewish descent until she was twenty and had moved to New York. *The Sun at Midday: Tales of a Mediterranean Family* (1997) is a memoir of her peripatetic, colorful, cosmopolitan family of Sephardic Jews who "considered ourselves primarily free to be anything we wished." An uncle was a survivor of Auschwitz and a cousin became a monsignor. Alhadeff is also the author of a novel, *Diary of a Djinn* (2003), about a thirty-something woman working in the fashion industry in Milan and New York in the 1980s and 1990s.

From *The Sun at Midday*

THE SEPHARDI MEDITERRANEAN from which I come is a world of many languages and no borders. My father's family speak Ladino among themselves; my mother's speak French. Most of them have a "foreign" accent in every language they speak, though they speak very fluently. Contained in this trace of an accent, in this shred of difference, is the nature of their identity: belonging everywhere, but not quite. In Tuscany, my father is *il signore cinese* and in Italy, though we are Italian by passport, our Arabic surname, often mistaken for Russian, makes us all foreigners. We were never more Italian, in fact, than when we were in Japan because there it meant nothing that our surname did not end in a vowel.

Language to us is not neutral: it is a place, an identity, and a filter. My father uses it to establish fleeting complicities with waiters, cabdrivers, doormen. He can do so in seven languages, including Greek, Arabic and Japanese, the only one he learned as an adult.

Our generation, that of my brothers and myself, has achieved a deeper level of camouflage: we too belong everywhere and nowhere, but this telltale racial characteristic has been obscured by the chameleon-skin of our new identities. When we left Japan, my father choreographed our reentry into the West: one brother was sent to England, became visibly, audibly English, married an Englishwoman and has two daughters who are anti-Tory and feminist, and would be hard to describe as anything but English. The other brother was sent to America, became ostensibly American, married an American, though he now lives in Italy, and has a son who considers himself more American than Italian. I was sent to Florence and became Italian, to England and became English, to New York and became a New Yorker, if not an American. I am the worst of the chameleons: I have swallowed several ethnic identities whole and no single one lords it over the others. They are all equal and fully developed. I never feel I am translating "myself." There is an "original me" in every language I speak, though this "original" is constantly rendered false by the presence of other, just as original, "originals." And I have to curb my tendency to imitate the accent, dialect, or inflection of the person I am speaking to, and of the country, city, or neighborhood I am in. I sometimes find it hard to distinguish between identity and mimicry. At this rate, it is easy to see that our origins will soon have become invisible.

I COME FROM two versions of the Mediterranean: my mother's family, well, who knows, it has been said that they were pirates who settled in Livorno. There is little evidence to support that, and the name Pinto is, after all, quite common. If this particular strain of Pintos have one thing they share it is lethargy, a quality hardly suited to piracy. Even so, my great-grandfather ended up making a tidy fortune as a cotton merchant in Alexandria. My grandfather, Silvio, vastly increased this fortune in between visits to the Sporting Club, afternoon naps, and secret assignations.

With the help of his partners—relatives, mostly, of which the youngest was my uncle Aldo—little was left of Pinto Cotton for President Nasser to nationalize. Years later in Milan, Aldo met and married a woman with whom he would, in the course of less than three decades, build a fashion empire, acquire an island in the Caribbean, and houses by the sea, in a forest, in a city, in Italy. Secretly, he dreams of golf and the protracted holiday of retirement.

In Alexandria, my maternal grandmother ran her considerable staff of cooks, parlor maids, gardeners and chauffeurs, and organized afternoon canasta parties for what, even at the time, was an enormous number of people. Our parents had been living in Nairobi while we remained in Alex until the start of the Suez Canal crisis in 1956.

MY FATHER'S FAMILY lived in Rhodes, which was then still an Italian colony, and only left when Mussolini's "racial laws" were passed in 1938. My grandfather was a merchant banker and owned a large portion of the island (which to this day has a street named after him), but still my father, thirteen, and the youngest of seven, was barred from attending school. The entire family, except for the eldest son, Jacques, then moved to Alexandria. Jacques was left in charge of the family business and of the family fortune (except for one building belonging to my grandmother that she had, by some premonition, refused to sign over to him). In the years that followed he became increasingly convinced that it was all rightfully his, and ignored my grandfather's repeated requests for funds.

"The world is like a cucumber," says an Arabic proverb my father likes to quote in the original, "sometimes you have it in your mouth and sometimes you have it up your . . ."

So my parents met in Alexandria, in their mid-teens. She was at the English Girls' School; he was at Victoria College. It was here that their "Englishness" was planted and nurtured. Five years after they met, they decided to get married, or rather, he asked her to marry him, despite the fact that her brother Aldo thought, with characteristic disloyalty towards his nearest and dearest, that my father was throwing himself away, and told him so.

They had a honeymoon by the sea, at Agami, and there the news reached them from Alex that Gino, my mother's brother, had crashed into a farm cart on his way home from a party and died. The photographs show that he was very good-looking in a Leslie Howard sort of way, and there were at least two dozen of his horse-jumping trophies in my grandparents' bedroom. His untimely disappearance conferred on him all perfections. He was barely twenty when he died, my grandmother barely forty-five, but she took to flattening her hair under a hair net and wearing black, grey and lilac. Whatever interest she'd had in society deserted her, which left my grandfather free to make love to an undisclosed number of Alexandrian wives—French, British, Italian. I don't want to make him sound more rakish than he was: behind a Victorian exterior, it was what everybody did, given a chance, and what with the climate, the languor and the natural incestuousness of colonial life, there was no lack of chances.

Neither family was very religious, my mother's even less so than my father's. It is one of the effects of Italy that even people who have been transplanted as often as Jews have tend to feel Italian before they feel Jewish. And to feel Italian is to feel a little Catholic, after all. Not long after my parents had had their first son, Giampiero, my father decided they should convert to Catholicism. They were in their early twenties then, and one of my father's six brothers, Nissim, who had gone to Rome to study medicine, had been taken by the Germans, first to Auschwitz, then to Buchenwald. For a time, before news reached Alexandria of his whereabouts, no one even knew if he was still alive. It undoubtedly contributed to my father's decision to convert. No member of his family followed the example, except for us, naturally, though we didn't have a choice. Many years later (and by then Nissim had become a prosperous obstetrician in Jamaica Estates, Queens), we learned that none of them approved in the least, no matter what his reasons might have been. But since both of my parents' families were always discreet to the point of being uncommunicative, and certainly as much as possible avoided discussing matters of love, money and religion, I had no idea I was of Jewish descent until I was almost twenty, and came to New York.

In fact, we were brought up as Catholics, which meant that we were baptized, confirmed, and sent to Catholic schools—in Tokyo, they were the only schools for foreigners. When my mother had announced that we were moving from Varese and that we would have to guess where to, we named every city we could think of and had practically given up, till I yelled, *"Not Tokyo?"* and she nodded. My father had been asked to start a branch of Olivetti, the company that made typewriters and calculators, in Japan. We were given *Il poliglotta inglese,* a very thick book with a Union Jack on the cover whose only appreciable result was that I learned to say *beh-ah-oo-tee-full.* Bribes were offered to make me get through *Little Women* in English, but to no avail: I arrived in Tokyo at the age of ten knowing little more than *shurrupp* and *bye-bye.*

At the Sacred Heart in Tokyo, whose gravel driveway the feet of boys were not allowed to touch, I wore a white veil and white gloves, sang, "Jesus wants me for a sunbeam," and kneeled in front of a statue of the Virgin Mary reciting, "Oh Mary, I give thee the lily of my heart, be thou its guardian forever," planting a paper lily in a box at her feet. I expect it was our purity we were entrusting to her, and in that sense the prayer differed from an Italian one of later years, "Oh Mary, you who have conceived without sinning, allow us to sin without conceiving." But as far as my father was concerned, being Catholic boiled down to attending Mass on Christmas Eve. Religion was never discussed at home, nor the subject of his conversion. But one family religion that did come with us from country to country was the Mediterranean one of superstition. It was as much a part of our life as the rules of good manners: no walking under ladders, no hats on beds, no open umbrellas in the house, no seating thirteen people at a dinner table, no passing the salt shaker from hand to hand, no pouring wine backhandedly, no crossed handshakes, no toasting with water, no advancing on a street that had been crossed by a black cat, no spilling wine without dabbing it behind the ears, no spilling salt without casting it behind one's shoulders, no lighting more than two cigarettes with one match, no breaking mirrors without throwing the fragments into flowing water, no departures or arrivals on Tuesdays and Fridays. If any of these commandments were unwittingly violated, one had to count to thirteen skipping the even numbers, spit and count backwards, skipping the even numbers, then spit again.

If superstitions took care of what one shouldn't do, proverbs governed the rest. There were sayings accumulated from so many different culture—Ladino Italian, French, Turkish, and Arabic—that it seemed there was one for every situation. "You go to sleep with babies, you wake up wet," that was a Spanish one. "Never too much zeal" was French. "I know my chickens" was Italian. "One day honey, one day onions" was Arabic. It was one of the favorite family games to translate these from the original into a language that would make them sound ridiculous, like this one from the Italian, "So much does the she-cat go to the bacon that she leaves her little paw."

WE LIVED IN Alexandria, Cairo and Khartoum, then Tokyo, London and New York. For a time, between Alex and Tokyo, we lived at my grandparents' house in a place called Buguggiate, near Varese in northern Italy. My elder brother, Giampi, was sickly and had been sent to Switzerland with a witchlike governess called Mademoiselle Pourchot who was obsessed with table manners and little else in the realm of human endeavor. My younger brother, Gianchi, and I went to an Italian school in the nearby town of Azzate, where for the first time, in grade school, we studied what was after all meant to be our mother tongue. (In fact, we had already learned Arabic and French, and though the first was soon forgotten for lack of practice, the second is what we spoke at home.) There, in the course of a religion class, the parish priest explained that there were other creeds beside Catholicism, the Moslem one, for instance.

I knew there was something fishy about my grandparents' religion: they never came to Mass with us. That was it, I thought, they must be Moslems. I told the priest very excitedly. He was not only impressed but horrified and stamped home with us to talk to my grandmother. He was told that they were Jewish, not Moslem, and that made it all better, apparently, though it is hard to see why, considering that Islam at least recognizes Christ as a prophet.

There was a defection on my mother's side of the family too: Pierre, a cousin of hers, rose to the rank of monsignor in the Catholic Church. Flying from grand wedding to grand funeral, he has earned himself the honorary title of "Pastor to the Rich and Famous." One faction of the family firmly maintains that he is a spy, and if by that they mean that he is curious, they are right.

Our spinster aunt Nelly preferred Molière and Corneille to the enigmas of theology. Her disheveled mane of bluish hair prompted us to call her Ben-Gurion. She traveled with us from Egypt to Italy, Japan and England, and died peacefully on a plane.

My father's only sister, Sarah, known since her Paris schooldays as *les eaux de Versailles* for her easy tears, decided not to have slipcovers made for her new white couches in Alexandria so that when Nasser confiscated the house and all its contents the couches would be quite filthy. Years later, in Varese, my grandmother, who took pride in her orchard, would say to her, "Aren't these tomatoes good?" and she invariably replied, *"Pas comme en Egypte"* (Not like in Egypt).

I have never gone to Andalusia, where both of my parents' families probably originated and remained until the start of the Inquisition, or to Izmir, where my father's mother was born, or to Rhodes (except once a quarter of a century ago), where Jacques's son still lives with his family, but I did return to Alexandria three times. The first time, ten years ago, I found our house on Abukir Road in Bulkeley unchanged except for the two new office buildings planted on the grounds where the gardens had been. Inside, it was as though my grandparents had moved out the day before. There were still many books on the shelves with my grandmother's name on them. They were probably books she did not feel were "serious" enough to take with her; my grandfather's considerable library is intact, at the house in Varese.

That house now belongs to my uncle Piero, an architect in Milan. It contains whatever furniture and objects my grandparents were able to take with them on the boat from Alex, and many albums of photographs, meticulously labeled and dated. There are images of the houses in Alex, Cairo and Khartoum, of the Sporting Club, of my grandfather with Khadriya Pasha, Farouk's brother-in-law, and other protagonists of these multiple tales.

Finally, Tuscany is where my mother and father and several of his brothers have ended up: the olive groves and vineyards remind them of Rhodes. Mentally, I consider it "home," especially because I live in New York, but it is only one of my "homes" . . .

STRADA IN CHIANTI. Olive trees. Rabbits, ducks. Two clouds, one incandescent white, one stormy grey, side by side drawing the shape of a plump baby between them in sky blue, releasing a steady spray of silvery rain on the upraised needled arms of pines and the silvery-leafed olive trees. Theater of flower pots: red hibiscus, pomegranate and geranium, lilac plumbago and lilac, green grapefruit and a lemon tree, a white umbrella, a *hazuk* to open and to shut and to move, as it's held down by two meteorites that fell from the heavens when my father left. *Hazuk* is Arabic for the Turkish *kazik,* which is the name of a torture perpetrated with a pole, and a *hazuk* is an awkward thing. That my father left, for instance, might be termed a *hazuk* if it didn't deserve a bigger term. He left and the chaste reign of the little caliph began. The caliph is a brindle-furred houndlet who sleeps on linen sheets—my mother's—and follows her from room to room.

A surrealist painter who drew slices of prosciutto like flags unfurled in the wind made individual portraits of my mother and father—stone-faced, in black cloaks with starched white pleated collars—that would frighten away marauders. They are kept hidden behind the door of what my mother calls "the silly book room" because it contains hundreds of silly books.

The "serious books" are in what used to be my father's study. It was there that he was taken ill one night with a virulent attack of cervical arthritis that made him collapse on one of the two black leather armchairs facing a portrait of Mao Tse-tung. He had to be covered in blankets, he was shivering so. Does the body signal rebellion before the brain even suspects the enormity of the revolution about to take place? Does shock force pretense to fall away like dead skin? Does the fear of death bring on the fear of not having lived? Does the intensity of illness make one yearn for intensity at large? And do we run away from those who have seen us grappling with our own mortality?

That dizziness was the first taste of the greater dizziness of meeting Cristina and seeing himself reflected in her mirror, her forgiving mirror. He saw finally who he might have been had he not been saddled with the ambitions and morals of the entire Sephardic race, his rabbinical grandfather, stolid father, saintly mother, Victorian upbringing, Anglo-Saxon bias, wife's socially superior family. And I do sympathize: what does our past—his and mine—have to do with our present?

Why should I care about a little island in the Aegean from which he was after all cast off? Why should I have the disadvantages of attachment and roots when I and he have not had their advantages? We have recovered from that past as from every subsequent transient past, from the need for it, God knows from any pride of nationality—what nationality? Greek, Italian, Spanish, Egyptian?—recovered from any religious certainty—he converted because the shame of being Jewish was stronger than any pride of being Jewish and because he did not want to be persecuted for something he did not believe in, as his brother was. He was baptized, took a Christian name, and I was brought up a Catholic because I was not brought up a Jew because as I saw it, and see it still, we considered ourselves primarily free to be anything we wished, so why not Italian, and because my mother freed herself from a past of which she knows nothing and cared nothing, long before us.

Now I see different religions as merely a question of aesthetics—music and architecture—on one hand, and method on the other: how do you become acquainted with the strangers in you? But the more I follow the traces of a "self" that reveals itself as I go, like a path I cannot see, the more I reject every ready-made identity that I or my family might be entitled to, and the very notion of being entitled to any traits that might constrain me from transforming myself into the next "self" that will be as much of an illusion and a delusion as every other.

I feel no connection to the victims in my family, to all they have suffered: I have no pride in their martyrdom—it is not mine. Any faults I have are precisely due to my not having suffered their martyrdoms. Any faults I no longer have are due to my own small martyrdoms, which I take no pride in either, as they made me understand nothing other than savoring the nothing in particular that fills moments. And what the Sephardic Jews suffered was on account of what they were and what they were determined to be, rather than what they weren't. I sympathize, but I wish to open my eyes every day on the possibility of becoming what I am not yet, and of no longer being what I was. As for their languages—Hebrew and Ladino—I don't understand them, don't speak them. I want no family, no religion, no country, no self I have to answer to, please, conform to, die for.

I want to have all the names and lives that every absence of a precedent in me can make room for. I want to belong to nothing other than the secret air that flows through me and bends and colors me. But the chameleon wears a uniform: I am Jewish by race; I was baptized and confirmed a Catholic; I have lived in different countries; I speak some languages; I make a living as a journalist.

Still, this body does not date back to the expulsion of the Jews in 1492, or whenever it was, before or after the Inquisition. It is forty-four years old. It was not conceived in Rhodes, but in Alexandria, by accident—I was born eleven months after my brother—of a father who escaped from Rhodes, from Alexandria, from Italy, from his family's religion, from his family. I resisted the temptation of following his example in escaping from everything and for some years experienced the strangeness of going against myself, of assuming not my identity but my family's—not knowing that there is no such thing.

This body has been in its own places, and bears the mark of those travels. There, it finally forgot what it learned *por boca de madre.* It is the only geography through which I see all others, my only witness and nothing but a vessel of what I still have no idea about.

AND YET, who am I trying to fool? I look at a picture of myself and think what Mediterranean features I have after all. A long oval face, long dark hair, brown eyes, a long nose that opens out at the end of the bridge in the shape of a bicycle seat, as my father's does; cabdrivers ask, are you Turkish, are you Indian, are you Spanish? I may have broken with my past but my body hasn't. A woman came up close to me, scrutinizing me as though my skin might yield a label, and asked, "What are you?" I replied, "I am Italian," as I always do, simplifying. "Ah, I knew it," she said triumphantly, "I thought I'd heard an accent," her own accent that of Chief Inspector Clouseau. She said this not thinking perhaps that English is by an overwhelming margin the province of those whose first language it is not.

An Italian friend corrects me, in Italian, on the pronunciation of my vowels, which he considers too "northern" Italian, as though this mouth and throat and tongue of mine, that might once have spoken Aramaic, could adapt endlessly to any pronunciation. That they do, nearly, is what calls attention to the faults: there is no language I speak that is not a mimicry. My accent in every language adapts to the inflections of the person I am talking to, as though the wave of sound from their mouth penetrated my ears and insinuated itself around my vocal cords in spontaneous deference—not mine, my body's. Jews are famous for their powers of adaptation, but famous too for wanting to remain among themselves and separate from those who are not them. I want neither, but my body fails me at times.

My brother's eldest daughter, Lucie, speaks North London English, which is not the Queen's, and I see her need not to use the constricted music of a constricted class—the upper. Some summers ago, I asked her, "Woy jew spake loik vat?" And she explained, in "proper" English, "If I were to speak the way I'm speaking now at school, everyone would take me for a snob. Besides my boyfriend would think it funny . . ." I don't know how she speaks now, but no doubt, if I am anything to go by, her accent will change many times, until it becomes like mine: imperceptibly "foreign" in every language.

ON BOTH SIDES of the family, an obstacle was dismissed with, *"Ce n'est pas la mer à boire"* (It's not like having to drink the sea), and a dry biscuit was a Christian-choker, *étouffe-chrétien.* If you worried, you were told not to twist your soul into a thread, in Italian, *non farti a un filo.* Something unremarkable was said to leave the weather it found, in Italian, *lascia it tempo che trova,* or glided on the rails of one's indifference (from Molière). Ornamental objects were called "dust-gatherers," in French *ramasse-poussières,* or *harabish* in Arabic, worthless things, and *halintranke (de puerta)* in Ladino, an odd contraption like the lock on a door. Long after we had left Egypt, the garbage was called *zebala;* a fool was a *homar,* a donkey; how-are-you's were countered with *hamdulellah,* God be praised; a bitch was a *sharmuta;* to be happy was to be *mapsut;* to be light-spirited was to be *hafif.* A show of obstinacy was met with, *"Quand tu as une idée dans la tête, tu ne l'as pas dans les pieds"* (When you have an idea in your head, you don't have it in your feet). And if one pretended not to have heard criticism, one was rebuked with, *"On ne répète pas la messe aux sourds"* (Mass will not be repeated for the deaf).

This book should be in several languages, all the ones spoken by the different members of my family; but I will translate for them as I go along. They translate in their head from one language to another—"switching," as an Alexandrian called it. Among themselves they can speak in a stream whose currents are a number of different languages: in their mouth those tongues become one. English, to record their speech, is as fictional as if a single language had been chosen to record dialogues in the tower of Babel.

I BORROWED A little here, a little there, to make a soul for the here and now.

In a furry grey cell at the Museum of Modern Art, sitting on furry steps, I interviewed a young woman for the post of assistant. Her name was Rachel. I was twenty-two. She wasn't sure she wanted the job. She needed to go to Vermont to get her head together, she said. I had been living in England and had never heard the expression, but I said, fine, we could talk again. We got up. She walked to the elevator. I could see her standing in profile. The doors of the elevator opened, and suddenly, she turned on her heels, walked back towards me, right up to me, her mouth at the height of my throat, and said, "Excuse me, but are you a Sephardic Jew?" I was conscious of a feverish sensation in the brain, as though messengers in sharp heels were running to and fro, tying loose ends of information together. I said "No," immediately, then "I don't know," then "Yes, maybe." She left. I sat down. What? Of course: they spoke that funny Spanish among themselves, didn't they? And the name wasn't Italian. It seems incredible that I didn't know but it was such an obvious thing, so enormous, I would have known it if it had been true so the fact I didn't excluded it from my realm of conjecture, from my thoughts altogether.

The alleged Princess Anastasia Romanov, in her nineties and living in Virginia somewhere, when asked by a reporter to say something that would prove beyond a doubt who she was, replied, "Could you say anything to prove who *you* are?" What one is is only a matter of memory, and if parents "forget," the secret stays secret. I don't think they did it intentionally, but I don't recall that they ever pronounced the words "Jewish" and "Sephardic," either separately or together; besides after the age of fifteen I saw them once or twice a year, and they spent every moment we had getting me to toe the line, stay in my frescoed prison like a good girl, not smoke, study hard. At the boarding school of Poggio Imperiale, I wasn't sitting beneath a portrait of our blessed foundress Maria Carolina of Saxony, wondering, Jewish or not Jewish, Sephardic or Ashkenazi. I was reciting, "Hail Mary, full of grace, the Lord is with thee . . . ," as I had been taught.

EVEN NOW, the closest I've come to a rabbi was a travel agent specializing in cheap fares; if I asked for a ticket to Milan, he would say, "Voy not Tel Aviv? I gechoo goot kreis." One could only fly Pan Am, never on Friday or Saturday, and one had to be careful to not even graze his sleeve, or he would scuttle sideways like a threatened porcupine. "Hi, Joe," stewardesses cajoled when he entered the VIP lounge with me a few steps behind. "You vont a grink?" he'd say. "Havvah grink!" Once, he got me a ticket that made me out to be a Mrs. Rosenberg who had been to New York and was on her way back to Manchester and I thought that if the plane fell, no one would know I was on it. There was one other rabbi, at one of two synagogues I've been in, where a cousin had his bar mitzvah. I was in the ladies' room, fiddling with my camera. When I emerged, the rabbi said, "You're not supposed to put lights on on the Sabbath." "What lights?" I asked. I wasn't even using a flash.

. . .

WALKING BACK FROM the park, I become curious about the cement building on Fifth Avenue and Sixty-fifth Street, called Temple Emanu-El. It is so tall, and placed so right against the street, that it is difficult to perceive it as anything but a blank endless wall. I look up, see the façade, the sign saying "Meditation and Prayer . . . entrance on 65th Street." I go and see what it is like inside: the same mammoth, dwarfing proportions as the Metropolitan Opera. Here too a giraffe could stand, stretch its neck. Gold, turquoise, crimson mosaics. Five different hues of marble. The American flag. Hundreds of polished, upholstered pews. What do I feel? Nothing. What am I thinking of? Of Jesus overturning the merchants' stalls inside the temple. I recite a Buddhist prayer. At home, I listen to Vespers of the Annunciation. I can't help the cocktail of infidelities.

IT IS COMFORTING to think that there is *someone* who can help: for a long time that was what religion meant to me. When I still believed that I began and ended where I could see and understand, and saw myself as finite, I was afraid of my own shadow. How could I, if I was only this physical body and this brain, know anything of any use in the face of fear?

Of course, I don't remember being baptized, but I was, in Alexandria, shortly after my birth at the Benito Mussolini Italian Hospital presided over by my great-uncle Carlo, an obstetrician, and I don't expect that any other member of my family on my mother's or my father's side attended, Jewish as they still were, and are.

In Azzate, my brother Gianchi and I, after a suitable course in catechism, received our First Communion: he wore a pale grey suit and a white sash around his arm, and I a bride's white dress and veil. There is a photograph of me in profile, my tongue eagerly stretched towards the first taste of Christ in a wafer. It glued itself against my palate, then and every subsequent time I took Communion, and had to be pried away by a labor of the tongue. Wearing the same outfits, we were confirmed at the church in Varese by a slap on the cheek from the Cardinal of Milan, Montini, who later became Pope Paul VI, so it was a privileged slap.

A CERTAIN GASTON PIHA on my grandmother Berthe's side took a trip around the world, and in India, wishing to gain admittance to a Buddhist temple, converted to Buddhism. Years went by, he was married and widowed. One day, he decided to remarry—a Frenchwoman and a Catholic. The parish priest of Santa Caterina in Alexandria asked him what religion he belonged to, and he replied, "I am a Buddhist!" The priest was puzzled. "What is this Buddhist religion?" Gaston explained that he had converted to Buddhism many years before, but that he was Jewish by birth. The priest was relieved. "Oh, an Israelite, now that's a more Christian religion!" and proceeded to convert him.

When he was almost a year old, my uncle Aldo came down with gastroenteritis: he had a nanny from Friuli named Elda who had allowed him to eat fresh dates. His temperature rose horribly. The doctor came twice a day. One evening it seemed Aldo would die, but he was revived by an injection. Still, his condition worsened again to such a degree that the doctor took my grandfather aside and told him to prepare his wife as the case was desperate. The cook Lucia, who was very pious, persuaded my grandmother to light a candle to the Madonna. A friend sent a rabbi, to whom my grandfather gave a small donation. Next came my great-grandparents' servant, Mohammed, who swore by his Moslem guru, Sidi 'el Morghani, a Berber like himself; to him also my grandfather gave a donation. When the doctor returned from dinner, he held Aldo's wrist for a few seconds, then exclaimed, "This is a miracle, he is out of danger." From then on, Aldo was known as the miracle boy, though no one could say to whom he owed the miracle.

My brother Giampi had his First Communion in Cairo and on that occasion was given a little wooden Madonna with a halo. He took her with him wherever he went. In Alexandria he kept her on a wooden cabinet, along with other cherished possessions. He noticed that every time the family doctor came the Madonna was spirited away so that he wouldn't see it and report it to our grandmother Rebecca, who was supposed to know nothing of our conversion.

She took Giampi to see the windows of the most elegant department store in Alexandria, called Hannaux. At Christmas there was a decorated tree and Rebecca commented to him, "See what the pagans have wrought!" Giampi was six and had already noticed that if we were in our flat in Cairo there would be a tree at Christmas, but if we were in Alexandria there wouldn't be.

IN TOKYO, on my first day of school at the Sacred Heart, a Belgian nun in a wheelchair, Mother Lemmon, was wheeled out of retirement to ask me a question in French, since I did not yet understand English. She had a short white stubble on her chin from occasional shaving, and the folds of her face were enveloped in the crinkly white blinders of her order. The black veil flowed down from the top of her head in a pyramid shape, and as I write this it occurs to me that all nuns have something of the sphinx: they are allowed to keep their private life a secret. Like all the sisters at Sacred Heart, she wore a pleated black habit, with a black rosary hanging from the belt and vanishing into a seam pocket. Her eyes were pale blue jellied over with cataracts. Her question was, *"Voulez-vous vous communier?"* and though I knew I was being asked whether I wanted to take Communion, I was struck by the awkwardness of her French. I replied I did not.

The reason they wished to pry into something that even the Church considers to be a matter between the individual and his God was that two separate lines had to be formed to walk to Mass every Friday. Those who took Communion sat in the front pews, and so filed into the chapel from a separate entrance—a form of spiritual segregation. The lines would form on either side of the long wood-paneled corridors of the hybrid neoclassical building that was our school. On the walls were large signs, black on white, at regular intervals, that ordered, SILENCE—we were not allowed to talk in the files, a rule we loved to break. The floor was of mottled marble, the kind that seems to have been spat by a giant who has been chewing multicolored rocks. A line five inches wide had been drawn in white marble.

For Mass, we wore white nylon gloves and a tulle veil that had an elastic sewn onto the underside of it, which, slipped over our heads and behind our ears, would hold it down. There was a time when I was cast into transports of devotion at Mass. I prayed with my eyes shut and hoped one nun or another would notice my fervor. What I was hoping to achieve I don't know, but there was enough admiring talk of martyrs for me to want to be one. I watched in envy as schoolmates broke an arm and had to have it in a plaster cast, or hurt an eye and wore a black patch over it. I saw their injuries as distinctions and as opportunities to demonstrate bravery. One girl, in an accident, had both of her legs broken. She was put in a cast that went from her waist to her ankles, like a mummy, and a handle was attached across her stomach so that she could be carried. This, I thought, must be heaven.

The only three-day retreat I attended at the school, sleeping in a grey cell, was distinguished by the readings we were entertained with at lunchtime. We were made to vow not to speak for three days. And so, to fill the void of our silence while we ate and make it easier for us to resist talking, a nun would read to us from the lives of saints. It was the life, or rather, death, of Saint Eulalia that impressed itself on my memory as I ate my chicken stew: ". . . tender sides were torn with iron hooks, lighted torches were applied to her breasts . . . instead of groans, nothing was heard from her mouth but thanksgivings. The fire, at length catching her hair, surrounded her head and face and the saint was stifled by the smoke and flame . . . a white dove was seen to come out of her mouth and to wing its way upwards when the holy martyr expired . . . pilgrims came to venerate her bones . . ." In retrospect, this was a Catholic lesson in equanimity: as the martyr is tortured and killed, you continue to swallow your little meal.

We were made to say prayers before and after every class in spite of the fact that the Christians were not a majority. Mass lasted about an hour, except on special feast days, when it lasted, it seemed to me, an eternity—a foretaste of the purgatory of boredom. When I was about eleven I was taught a song I couldn't stop singing for several months:

Jesus wants me for a sunbeam,
at home, at school, at play,
in every way I try to please Him,
at home, at school, at play.

A sunbeam, a sunbeam,
Jesus wants me for a sunbeam,
a sunbeam, a sunbeam,
I'll be a sunbeam for Him.

This went on until I discovered *The Tales of Hoffman* and started humming, "Oh Hoffman's made you a victim of his brutal desires, only your beauty he admires . . ."

MY ELDER BROTHER would dare Gianchi to have an orgasm sitting at the long black crystal table in the dining room—a remnant of the German embassy that had once been there—with all the guests around him and nothing but a distended little smile to indicate he had won the bet. Gianchi was keeper of the secret of eros. Our second house in Tokyo was a sprawling low brick building all on one floor, except for my brothers' room, which was up three steps. There, past the lion skin—my pants often got caught on one of the teeth in its shellacked, eternally roaring mouth—I found Gianchi, on the bed with a postcard-sized television on his stomach, watching samurai films, which is how he learned to say "*Narukodo,*" in a low pensive voice, which means "Indeed." Shoguns said it to gain time. I sat on the side of the bed, and tried to infiltrate his symbiosis with the television screen. How is it done? I asked. The man puts his thing in. What? Nooooo—how can it point upwards when it points downwards? *Boh.* I had seen one in Varese, years earlier, and it had looked to me like a toad: the head, the haunches, the delicate creased skin like the lid of a sleepy eye. Candido, our gardener in Varese, seemed to be coaxing it as though to stand on its hind legs and crane its neck. He had caught me in the cottage by the gate where my parents lived, separated by a little hill, a big chestnut tree, a bed of dahlias, from the main house where we lived with our grandparents. I was opening bottles in the bathroom, sniffing their contents, smoothing my mother's creams on my cheeks—Velva by Elizabeth Arden . . . The samurai skipped from a roof, across a pond, onto a hillock, and brandished the sword at his opponent. Okay, then what? Nothing. Nothing? Nothing. I saw sex, after that conference, as a union of immobilities. It was a book by Giorgio Bassani, *Behind the Door,* in which a boy looking through a keyhole sees a couple making love, that revealed to me that there was movement too. I knew what an orgasm was but I didn't know anyone else did, that it had a name, or that it had anything to do with what I thought of as "sex"—an amorous sea into which one could sink and stay with the right person, kiss, and kissing too I saw as a still conjunction. I was raised a Catholic. I learned to confess to "impure thoughts," felt filthy thinking them, waited for love to cast a benediction over my life and cut the ribbon of its beginning. *Narukodo.*

Just as my brothers and I were becoming unbearably ourselves, we were sent away to three different countries: Giampi to Britain, Gianchi to America, I to Italy. Our parents stayed in Japan. My father went to "the office"—that magical and secret container of everything sanctified as duty. My mother practiced *sumi-e* brushstrokes and he went on business trips to Nagoya, Osaka, Yokohama, Fukuoka—like women's names, they all ended in *a*. The separation was thought necessary "for us," but also for him—so he could continue his life as a young man, or rather resume it where he had left off, before we came into existence.

One sign of my father having gone to Victoria College in Alexandria, from the age of fifteen on, was that he only wore English shoes and because his right foot was deformed, he had them custom-made in London. All his shoes looked alike—brogues and half-brogues, black or brown. But he could differentiate between them: a finer, shinier leather for evening, suede and coarse reddish leather and a thicker sole for weekends, plain black for the daytime. The number of holes also indicated a range of codes from the elegant to the casual: the more holes there were the sportier the shoe.

The tacit puritanical dictum was that one should always appear to be wearing the same shoes, that one didn't spend either one's time or money on anything so frivolous. If I have followed any sartorial model, it is my father's rather than my mother's: uniformity that renders variety invisible to all but the wearer, who alone wallows in the pleasure of a new jacket, without having to withstand the scrutiny of others. The only "loud" thing he ever wore was a checked jacket, on weekends, in tones of yellow, orange, mustard, green. Argyle socks always accompanied this flamboyance.

The first sign of another woman in his life was a belt he wore one day: it was of woven fabric mounted on leather depicting ducks flying eagerly towards the buckle. On his customary grey worsted suit, made to order in Hong Kong or Torino, with the usual brogues, white shirt, three-quarter socks, the belt spoke volumes. Later signs of liberation from his imaginary status as a British subject: more and more pairs of American shoes; windbreakers in the place of the usual blue or camel cashmere coats; pajamas with short pants.

When my parents left a bathroom, the toothbrush was in the glass, the cap on the tube of toothpaste had been replaced. I never saw a pair of knickers on the floor, clothes on a chair. All evidence of daily life was quickly effaced. The only transgressions in their existence ruled by cleanliness and neatness were provided by the dogs: hair everywhere, sprinklings of urine on bedspreads and couches, drool.

FOR THEY ARE WASP-like Jews. They discussed their feet with a degree of pride not accorded to any of their other traits, physical or intellectual. They do what they do without any apparent concern for tactics, strategy, artifice—all thought to be supremely vulgar if *consciously* exercised. It was understood that one did not talk about clothes, possessions, money or even food, unless absolutely unavoidable. The only two areas that allowed them some freedom were their dogs, for outbursts of emotion, and their feet, for expressions of self-worth and, make no mistake about it, superiority.

Pretending to be talking about their feet, they could say just how much better they thought they were: No one has feet like these; and, it's not easy to have pretty feet; and, have you ever seen such fine, regular toes; and, were there ever toes that were less marked by the constriction of shoes? etc. They would lie on the bed, sometimes, during a siesta, and compare their feet. This was the only instance too where they openly competed and my mother did not yield. My father would say, "Don't look at my right foot"—for that one had been deformed by a bout of meningitis in childhood—"look at the perfection of my left foot." And my mother countered, "But look at mine, so delicate . . ." This invariably ended with him conceding that her feet looked better on her than his would. It was, I suspect, their talk of love. ("Believe it or not," my mother said when she read this, "there was talk of love too—he would hug me at night and say, 'Never, never leave me,' or 'What would I do if you died before me?' ")

As for expressing their feelings towards others, they never did so with the abandon and unmitigated partiality that they showed the dogs—whatever dogs happened to be around at any given time, a minimum of one to a maximum of three. They were hugged, kissed, stroked, petted, talked to in baby voices, for every time any one of us, including my mother and father, wasn't.

My parents discussed their dogs the way others discuss their children. "Larry is very shy, poor thing, he hasn't yet recovered from the initial trauma of being kept in a low kennel for such a long time. But I think you are beginning to trust me now, Larry, aren't you? You know that if it hadn't been for me, you might still be there," my father would say, repeatedly kissing the miniature wirehaired dachshund on the muzzle and pulling on its paws as he held it cradled against his chest. Myron, the basset hound, had only to look soulful, which he did very easily, for them to start speculating he might be nostalgic for his first home in Germany. He also liked, having observed the presence of a visitor, to enter a room demurely and pee on the man's leg, for he did this only to men; there was no question whose side my parents would be on: "Myron was disturbed by the arrival of a stranger in the house, poor thing . . ." Papaya, a dachshund who wrapped his paws around every new woman's legs and became so aroused that the strawberry tip of his penis would protrude as he rhythmically thrust his pelvis back and forth with a look of rapt abandon in his eyes, was said to be "the most intelligent son of a bitch."

There was Chianti, a model of chivalry and kindheartedness; Dindo the Dalmatian—also known as Bhopal, for the toxic clouds he emitted from the pink creases of his bottom. All slept on their bed, sat on sofas, ate at their table. They were discussed tenderly, in a low voice. Every morning they were fed squares of buttered toast sprinkled with salt, because Tuscan bread is unsalted, and since this is something my mother likes to do she assumes the dogs share her tastes. Every evening, they would line up by the little chest next to my father's side of the bed; it contained a tin labeled "Good Boy Choc Drops." My father distributed the flat round pastilles gingerly, like a priest dispensing Communion. The number of pastilles never varied, and each dog received the same amount, as my father firmly believed that our dogs could appreciate a climate of supreme justice, or at any rate be offended by the least sign of favoritism. Now that my father has left home, this last ritual has been abolished, also because it proved ruinous: the Dalmatian—considered an albino—died prematurely of hepatic cirrhosis.

My father's place in the matrimonial bed is now being warmed, though partially, by the new dachshund, Vasco, who lies splayed on the white cotton crochet bedspread at night, his black head resting on a candid white linen pillow case. It would be extreme to say that he is the new master of the house, but there is no question that he has at least mitigated my mother's grief at my father's departure.

He eats spaghetti, barks at animals on television, and digs up roots of plants in the garden. He takes it upon himself too to make guests welcome by lavishing attentions on them when they come down for breakfast in the morning, and greeting them, every time they reappear on the scene, as though he had not lived in their absence, with strangled squeals, sinuous writhing, feverish wagging. It is not my father's outstretched hand and enamored green eyes beneath bushy brows, but it will do.

All the dogs that died at Strada in Chianti are buried in the garden there, between the pines and the vineyard. There is a large rock to mark the spot and on it have been affixed terra-cotta plates for each departed dog—specially made in nearby Impruneta—with names and dates.

How important is the matter of race if dogs have been some of the most venerated members of our family? If we, my parents my brothers and I, are purebred Sephardic Jews, they, most certainly, are not. Vasco, my mother's best-loved dog, was originally named Marko and came from Germany; he is even a von Something, and my mother, before falling for him completely, referred to him as "the Deutsch mark." Vasco was also my father's nickname for her, because like the explorer, she has a sense of direction.

. . .

"As my father used to say," my father tells me on the telephone, "there are times when everything comes up in the shape of a horn." Between words, he whispers to a secretary, "Please leave a copy of this on my desk," and "Thank you." He says he is going to Japan to "see" about a "thing" that could be interesting. "Is Cristina going with you?" I ask. "No, no," he replies quickly to the suggestion that amusement might be on the horizon, "this is strictly business." "Have you spoken to my mother?" I ask. "Yes, call her in Paxos, it will make her happy. She is swimming and working. She is much better, I think," he replies as one speaking of a patient.

"The patient" is in fact a good name for my mother, as patience has distinguished her forty-five years of dedicated service to the institution of marriage. "Nora," my father would order as soon as she opened one eye in the morning, "take a piece of paper and write." (This proved prophetic eventually as in the after-him she has written several cookbooks.) He would dictate a list of guests to be invited to dinner, the menu, letters to be sent. "We should invite Fiore to dinner," he would say, "the poor thing, he is all alone." In Tokyo, there was an endless, stream of "poor things"—people stranded far from home, without family or friends, in a city that was then impenetrable to foreigners. "At the Meiji ice-cream billboard, turn left," guests were told. Formal dinner invitations were accompanied by a little mimeographed map of the area and arrows indicating the route to be taken.

"Poor things" have besieged our existence, since, in case you had not understood, it was my father who decided everything, except what we thought. "Poor things" encountered in Sydney, Osaka, Cape Town, appeared on our doorstep in Chianti, with their entire family. "Take them to Florence and show them the city," my father would tell the patient, "the poor things don't speak the language." The other poor thing, my mother, followed his orders to the letter.

Of course my mother was not patient at all, only obedient. She seethed serenely, inconspicuously, clandestinely, behind her own back, for almost five decades. The tension of resentment lurked beneath her every gesture. It was ascribed to the Pinto character. To be short-tempered, bossy, or willful was "very Pinto." To be unnaturally considerate, to have big hands, to make jokes, was "very Alhadeff," and to make these distinctions was also very Alhadeff. It was presumed that to be an Alhadeff was better than being anything else, certainly better than being a Pinto.

There is the not irrelevant question of size: the Pintos are small, the Alhadeffs are big. The Pintos believe that do-goodering should begin and end at home; the Alhadeffs see the world at large as their mission. The Pintos follow their instincts, the Alhadeffs their morals. I needn't tell you that the former appear somewhat selfish while the latter appear heroic. But the selfish are true to themselves while the heroic often are not and at some point in their existence find the pretense intolerable and cast the whole bloody lot off to become the other face of the coin. Coins enter into this story as one half of my father's family were bankers. The other half were rabbis. Preachiness regarding money matters was the traditional cause of dissension between my father and myself.

An example of the heroic and the selfish? The "poor thing" mentioned earlier would come to dinner; my mother would, against her will, carefully prepare it, or have it prepared by our housekeeper, Emiko-san, and my father would reap the benefit of a gesture that generously disposed of someone else's time.

I breathed all this in and it molded every cell in my body, put down every trace of every plan I blindly followed till I began to see that there were at least two people inside me, one of whom proceeds straight from a father who built those around him in his image and a mother who built herself and those around her in his; the other I discover now.

"This *damn* country" my mother would say of Japan when its ways, which weren't hers, tried her patience too far. She was the unalterable foreigner whose task it was to reject difference at the very moment when even he, for all his enthusiasm and sympathy for Japan, could no longer bear it.

Her version of an evening at the Kabuki: the Japanese "crying like calves" at the truculent plots being enacted, and all the while chewing dried fish. Of the strangled cries of the actors, so moving to others, she said, "One more of those and I leave." Leave they did. Very likely my father was relieved not to have to test the limits of his own endurance.

When she lost her temper and raised her voice, he would whisper infuriatingly to her, "*Don't* shout, you know they never shout here." This always made the tension escalate. It stirred up the fundamental problem: he treated her as a slightly inferior being who could not understand *certain* things because she was prosaic, and he, infinitely tolerant, had to be patient in his attempt to redeem her. But I suspect that even in being what he wished she wasn't she was exactly as he wished her to be—expressing what he was too high-minded to express.

At the much mythicized tea ceremony, my mother resented all that made it mythical—the slow twisting and turning of the bowl this way and that, the deliberate whisking of the liquid, three circles to the left, three circles to the right, the silence, the pauses, the livid suspense, and all to obtain a "bitter thick green stuff with that disgusting foam on top." Not to mention the "sticky, tasteless" bean-paste sweets served with it.

Hers is not a contemplative nature and she would never accept a connection between her meticulous crochet work—320 squares to every bedspread—the just as meticulous completion of two full books of crossword puzzles a week, and contemplation. Once when she was persuaded to try yoga, she assumed the required position, then said, "Now what?"

She has a horror of healthy things: hot broths, cereals, low salt and low sugar, vegetarianism. When people talk about Milan being polluted, she dismisses it as facetious. Short of one's being at death's door, she does not consider illnesses worth thinking about; she does not consider most ailments even illnesses. She believes that vitamins are rubbish and that there is nothing wrong with pesticides and chemicals in general. She venerates plastic: "Tupperware," plastic glasses and dishes, "for the garden," which are not disposable (that would be an advantage) but, she maintains, lighter to carry. She loves the dishwasher to the point that she'll juggle things around endlessly until everything fits, even though it would have taken less time to wash the nonfitting item by hand. Before setting out on a car journey, she plots the course carefully: she'll choose a dirt road any time over the speedway if it's shorter in kilometers, no matter how ugly, no matter the lack of urgency.

She does not like anything, or anyone, at the last minute. The only thing she likes to do on the spur of the moment is what she had planned to do, and if that's nothing, then nothing it is. She has no aptitude at all for making herself appear as interesting as she is: at a first, even second or third glance, very little is revealed of her exotic past. She likes to be thought perfectly normal as opposed to extraordinary or idiosyncratic. If she captures the fancy of others it is for lack of trying. There is an aristocratic streak in this willful combination of doing nothing to please and assuming one will anyway. That is, as far as the outside world is concerned. Till recently, it was something she could afford to do because my father was her entire universe, and frankly she did not need anyone else.

Ruth Knafo Setton

Ruth Knafo Setton (Morocco-USA, 1951–) is the author of the novel *The Road to Fez* (2001), based on the life of Suleika, a nineteenth-century Moroccan-Jewish martyr who chose to die rather than renounce her faith. Suleika's identity intrigued Setton, as she recounted in an interview: "Who was [she]? A girl so astoundingly beautiful that the Sultan of Morocco fell in love with her? A Jewess who converted to Islam for love? Ironically, during my twenty-year search to recapture the truth behind the myth, I ended up uncovering the myth behind the truth. I came to recognize that what I had before me was a shifting mirror Jewish identity, particularly the identity of a Jewish woman, in the imagination of Muslims in precolonial Morocco, European Romantics, and men (Jewish, Muslim, and Christian) . . . The more I explored, the more Suleikas I discovered: jagged slivers of a mirror that reflect a woman's life but do not encompass the whole. In *The Road to Fez* I attempted to re-create Suleika—fragment by fragment—and realized that in piecing together the puzzle of her life, I was writing my own story: that of a Moroccan-Jewish girl who stood on the border between Africa and Europe, Judaism and Islam, tradition and modernity, the world of women and that of men, the sacred and the profane." Setton is a writer-in-residence at the Berman Center for Jewish Studies at Lehigh University and on the faculty at Georgia College & State University. She is also the fiction editor of *Arts & Letters: A Journal of Contemporary Culture.* "Ten Ways to Recognize a Sephardic 'Jew-ess' " was published in *The Best Contemporary Jewish Writing 2002,* edited by Michael Lerner.

Ten Ways to Recognize a Sephardic "Jew-ess"

[1] NAME: Often unpronounceable, unmanageable, redolent of incense and cumin. A name that twists letters into spirals the way a djinn emerges from a lamp. Abitbol. Afriat. Bahboul. Buzaglo. Aflalo. Dweck. Ohayon. Ben'Attar. Bensussan. Chouraqui. The Spanish echoes too, of arches and Alhambra, dusty streets and brown hoods: Cabessa, Corcos, Mendes, Pinto. But the true names are weirdly resonant, heavy, harsh, satisfying: a name you can sink your teeth into, one that emerges from dirt and mud and roots: *Knafo.* A brilliantly colored cloak, *knaf* also refers to a honey-drenched, shredded phyllo-dough Middle Eastern sweet, the kind set a thousand on a large tray in Jaffa or Casablanca, that you eat with your fingers, swirling the flaking pastry and syrup and nut mixture on your tongue with burning Moroccan mint tea perfumed with a drop of orange-blossom water. *Knafo.* Say this name aloud, every which way you can imagine. Try being called Knaf-Knuf. Knasoo—singularly ugly aberration. Konfoo, Kanfa, Knee, or in a stroke of malevolent genius: Kohenfo. The mysterious letter *k.* To pronounce or not? Arabs whisper it like an *h.* Hanafo. It's a breath, a wing. *Knaf* in Hebrew is a "wing." Legend has it that Knafo means "under God's wing," even to be protected by God because we are literally under His wing. This was especially evident to Maklouf Knafo and his family on a Thursday morning in July 1790, in the Berber village of Oufran hidden in the Anti-Atlas Mountains of Morocco.

[2] FOOD: Feed this child. Wide-eyed and yearning. This child has never tasted a bagel! Her mother distrusts anything served in a gel. Gefilte fish? She whisks her child away from it quickly. Kugel? The dough is too heavy, sinks into the stomach. Lox and cream cheese? Mom clicks her tongue against the roof of her mouth. They don't know how to be subtle, she murmurs, wielding her knife and beginning to chop. Behind her henna'd hair—beautiful auburn waves flowing down her back—I see my American backyard. A swing set on which my little sister soars, lost in her recurring daydream of rescuing stray cats and dogs and bringing them to her

doll hospital. A sandbox in which my tiny naked brother sits and throws handfuls of sand back and forth. Mom chops, cuts, slices. I lean on my elbow and watch everyone at once. Even my dad far away at work sorting produce at the A&P, struggling to make sense of English syllables—coiled and Germanic—as opposed to fluid French, guttural Arabic.

I think about my own rescue fantasy. Every night in bed I return to our little backyard. The alley behind is flooded. Help! Help! someone screams. It's *I Love Lucy*! I race from my yard to save her. Bring my trusty canoe through the gate and paddle up the hill. I pull her into the boat. Her red hair gleams in the dark. She thanks me, and I set her safely in my backyard, and return to save Desi and little Ricky. It's a dangerous world, something I can't remember ever learning and yet something I must have always known. To open the front door is to enter danger. I prefer leaving from the back, where I can ease my way into the outside world, through the yard and the gate, down the alley and around the corner past Old Man Minnich's store and his display of comic books and penny candy in the window.

See, Mom says, and gestures toward the salads: oranges and black olives, the colors alone nearly sending me on another voyage; purple beets and celery; cooked peppers red, yellow, and green, drizzled with olive oil and seasoned with preserved lemon, chili peppers, and cumin. Flavors shouldn't be obvious, Mom says, mix the unexpected: chicken, eggs, and almonds baked in phyllo dough and sprinkled with confectioner's sugar; jam made from sweet baby eggplants and walnuts; tagines simmered with smen, saffron, and za'atar. And *ma fille,* remember the importance of cinnamon.

[3] The Knafo Wheel: My cousin handed it to me one night at a lecture in New York. A huge sheet of paper to revolve, separated into sections: a round graph. I look at the center: Maklouf Knafo. The one who burned to death along with the other forty-nine *nisrafim* (burnt ones) in Oufran. And the branches spread out from him. Knafos, Knafos, as far as the finger extends. Knafos in Mogador of course, because that's where his wife walked with her baby. I close my eyes and imagine her voyage. A young woman, her eight-day-old infant son (just circumcised by Maklouf that morning), walking down the mountain paths—rocky and steep. But the danger is not in the rocks and winding roads; it is in the robbers and brigands who populate these mountains. A young woman and her baby. I scan the Knafo wheel, turn it around and around, try to read between the black lines and words and letters, but find no name for this young woman.

A nameless woman making her way down the mountains to save her son. Nameless—except for her husband's name, Knafo. Is she under God's wing as she stumbles down the road? Sun burns on her head. The baby is hot, hungry, crying. How does she maintain her supply of milk? Everything she owns is on her back. The baby cradled in a blanket against her breasts. Her husband left behind. Her husband, Maklouf Knafo. She walks fast, head down, afraid to breathe, to smell smoke.

[4] Purple Palestinians: Now this goes back years: we all lived in a shabby apartment building on Valencia in the Mission in San Francisco—above a bar, across from a bar, next door to a bar. Stumbling over drunks and homeless—only back then we didn't call them homeless, we called them bums. And winos. And I was alone for the first time in my life, scared to death, but—and here's the great mixture I can't get a handle on: high on hippie life, memories of my strange isolated family haunting me, trying with my gut to be as American as you, and to that end, sitting in my third-floor apartment in the Mission, looking down at the barmaid, at least eighty, with enormous pale tits and iridescent blue eye-shadow, walking to the bar on the corner to start her shift, and I set pen to paper and begin the American novel—as interpreted by a Moroccan-Jewish immigrant girl. But I've been burned already, even though I'm barely twenty-one. The first story I sent out returns with a rejection note: You write well. Next time try writing about the real Jews.

I am frozen to my soul. Too afraid to inquire more deeply into what the editor means. So ashamed I tear the note into a thousand slivers, shred them with my fingers, and throw them down the toilet. There. It's gone.

And the pain? as my father would say. He's known for that final aside, the joke after the punch line that sends it spinning into another dimension. He is known for that, the ironic aside that makes people realize that no joke has an end. No story truly finishes.

And so I write about an old Polish-Jewish man as I stare outside and ignore Hassan from down the hall banging on my door and screaming: I'm going to rape you the way you raped Palestine! And Amar, his roommate, the head cabdriver (the one who gives them all purple Hafiz Cab T-shirts when they arrive in the city, and the one who cooks for me and gets high with me, and we listen to Procol Harum and wonder over "A Whiter Shade of Pale" together, and stare at each other, attracted though trying not to be) Amar, sweet Amar with the desert eyes and the tightest purple T-shirt of all, tells his friend: leave her alone. She's a girl, she can't rape anyone . . .

[5] EXOTIC: Erotique. I line my eyes with black kohl and wear large gold hoops, and long Gypsy skirts and low-cut hand-embroidered Rumanian blouses. Paint my toenails red and wear sandals that tie around my ankles. But my legs are always cold so I begin to wear leggings beneath my skirts—and don't realize it's the way Arab women dress until my mother tells me. I play up the exotic, pronounce words with a faint French accent, *le bagel, qu'est-ce que c'est?* Boys like me; you and your crazy name, one murmurs as he bites my ear. They see me and think of *Casablanca* and Ingrid Bergman and play it again Sam. My first real boyfriend is black. He tells me: I am from Afrikaaa. I tell him: So am I. He tells me: I am black first, a man second. I tell him: In Paris they call me *pieds noirs,* black feet. He tells me: Here, they call me nigger. I tell him: they called me *dhimmi,* or the lowest of the low. We outblack each other, and even in bed, scratch and lash and attack, until we lie back, exhausted and content. We're an odd couple: he listens to Jimi and (in secret) Sweet Baby James. I listen to James Brown and John Lee Hooker. I dance better than he does. Later, the best dancer I will ever see, a Moroccan soul–sex machine come to life, whom I watched move to James Brown for hours at a time in a Netanya club called Azazel (or Hell), died at twenty-one in Lebanon.

[6] MEMORY: The years in the sunless *mellahs* and *juderías* and *quartiers juifs* have bleached our skin until it's fashionably Mediterranean, only a shade or two darker than yours. Our nomadic history has given us a variety of languages, none of which is ours, but all of which we have learned to speak—with a bite. You can recognize us by the rage we carry in us, the rage of the colonized, those who are still not permitted to meet the master class eye to eye. The bitter eyes that now refuse to stay lowered, the angry tongue that can no longer be silenced, the poet's heart that in spite of everything, continues to dream and hope, the soul that cannot forget. There is no wind and the smell of burning flesh remains in the square, incapable of moving elsewhere and freeing us.

[7] INVISIBLE: Even within postcolonial, Third World, border-crossing, multicultural ethnic feminist identities, I am nowhere to be found. I dare you. Look for me. Born in Morocco, raised in America, in a small town—a Jew from Africa who probably scared my Pennsylvania-Dutch neigh-

bors as much as they scared me—a minority within a minority. Be invisible, my father told me. I tried—but my black feet peeked out from every disguise. And now when I take off my veil and let you see the scratched lines of henna crisscrossing my face, the embroidered scrolls and curlicues that lace my palms, you avert your eyes. By multicultural, I didn't mean you. Latina is hot now. Lesbian Latina even better. Caribbean, mon? Remote Indian provinces, hot as curry. Even Arab-American, hotter than you. Who you anyway? Afrikaan? Arab Jew? Oriental Jew? Tied in with Israel. Israel not hot.

[8] NOMAD: I believe she traveled north to Taroudant in the Grand Atlas, then wound her way down the rocky hills and ravines to the east and the breezes of the Atlantic Ocean, and north once more, following the coastline past Cap Guir and Tamanar to Mogador. Mountain air is thin and clear, but in the Anti-Atlas Mountains it is pale gray, tainted with smoke. Take a deep breath. The smoke doesn't escape. Locked in the square, over a hundred years later, it smells of death, the end of the oldest Jewish community in Morocco, with a hiss and crack.

[9] THE CHOICE: LIFE OR DEATH?: Take a deep breath and decide if it's going to be life or death, says Bou Halassa, the sheik who owns the Jews of Oufran. Think carefully, he says. The choice is simple: Die as Jews, or live as Muslims—under my protection. All you have to do is say the words: There is no God but Allah, and Mohammed is His Prophet.

The sun is shining. It is a July morning in 1790 in the Anti-Atlas Mountains. Bou Halassa is on horseback, surrounded by his men who are already at work building the funeral pyre. The fifty Jews, merchants all, are wearing black (the only color permitted them); they are barefoot (no shoes allowed for Jews); and they are standing on the ground because they are not permitted to ride a horse. The horse is considered too noble an animal to carry a lowly Jew. Bou has interrupted the *souk el'khemiss,* the Thursday morning market. Merchants selling carpets and leather, artisans with brass trays and iron kettles. Cattle, mules, donkeys, chickens.

The leader of the Jews, Rabbi Naphtali Afriat, tells them: We have no choice. To say the words and live a lie is another form of death. To die for God is to live forever as Jews. It's the only way to carry on our faith so that our children can be Jews. So that everything doesn't die this morning.

A young man on the edge of the group is torn. Only this morning, with his own hands, he circumcised his first son. Die—for what? for Bou Halassa's whim? Bou is a tyrant, a sadist, notorious in the mountains for his hatred of Jews. Even though Bou's men have swords and are now circling the Jews, we are fifty in number—maybe we can fight back? And if they overpower us, then what? If we walk into the flames, will he then turn on our women and children?

Afriat, his gold earring glinting in the sun, announces in his quavering voice: We have decided. We choose death—in the name of God. You do not frighten us, Bou Halassa. You will answer for your brutality to God, not to us.

The young man bolts—without a thought, without hesitation—slips from the crowd of Jews and Arabs—and runs to his small cottage. Then he does—what? I'd love to see this scene: how he convinces her to take the baby and leave without him. I can almost hear her: You've already come this far! They don't know you're gone! Come with us.You'll do more good to us alive than dead. Why should you die for this sadist? Come with us!

He walks his wife and baby to the town wall, the stone wall that enclosed Oufran. She is unwieldy; the blanket that supports her baby forces her to lean forward, while the bag Maklouf stuffed with bread and dates loads down her back. He helps push her up the wall, and for a moment is caught there, in the cobblestones, between death and life—his wife's hand pulling him up, the hand of "God" pulling him back. Beneath his feet, red and purple flowers sprout in crevices between the rocks.

[10] The question of home: The sun shines through Amar's window. The Moody Blues sing about nights in white satin. I lean over Amar's shoulder as he fries a mixture of eggs, potatoes, and meat on the stove. The violent Hassan has left San Francisco. Crazy, Amar tells me, tapping his temple and handing me a fat joint. I breathe in the harsh smoke and the pungent spices that smell like my mother's food. You have to create your own home wherever you go, he says. This sounds wise, heavy. But first you have to know what a home is, I say, and hand back the joint. With a deep sigh that echoes through me, I move to the window, sit on the edge, and lean out. The sun licks my cheeks with burning tongue. The old barmaid walks down the street. I yell to her. She squints up, sees me and waves, smiles an orange and yellow smile. Her blue-veined, speckled tits jiggle like blobs of cream cheese, like gefilte fish squashed in satin.

Ruth Behar

Ruth Behar (Cuba-USA, 1956–) teaches at the University of Michigan in Ann Arbor. Her mother was Ashkenazic and her father Sephardic, with possible roots in the Iberian town of Bejar. Behar's identity as a Sephardic author was formed both by her father's cultural legacy and by anthropological research she had done in Spain early on in her career. "My Sephardic side," she stated in an interview, "is mysterious, which is perhaps why I'm so attracted to it . . . There are so few such characters in American culture, particularly in literature and film; for years I've felt compelled to fill this vacuum—to offer the 'other' side of Isaac Bashevis Singer and Woody Allen." Mentored by Victor Perera, with whom Behar shared an interested in ethnography and politics, she wrote *Translated Woman: Crossing the Border with Esperanza's Story* (1993) and *The Vulnerable Observer: Anthropology That Breaks Your Heart* (1996). She is also devoted to fostering a dialogue between Cubans who currently live on the island and those who are in exile. One result of that effort is *Bridges to Cuba/Puentes a Cuba* (1995), an anthology of writings by second-generation Cubans both on the island and in the Diaspora. Behar produced and directed an autobiographical documentary film about her Sephardic-Cuban ancestry, *Adio Kerida: Goodbye Dear Love,* which was released in 2002. The short story "Never Marry a Man Who Doesn't Beat You," published here for the first time, is a witty and insightful look at relations between the sexes—with a Sephardic twist.

Never Marry a Man Who Doesn't Beat You

I'VE JUST MADE the mistake of looking at myself in the mirror in the downstairs bathroom. The mirror's mean-spirited, and I shouldn't look at myself in it until I've put on my makeup. Now I'm feeling even more depressed about turning forty last week. Do I run to the plastic surgeon or to the fertility clinic? I mean, can something be done to fix the roostery thing that's starting to form on my neck? Or should I forget my neck and try to have a second child? Either way, I'm running out of time. The universe feels stuck in fast forward, and I can't find the pause button.

It's ten o'clock. My husband's at work and my son is at school. I never see them in the morning; I sleep so soundly I don't hear them leave the house. In the kitchen, still in my pajamas, I perform my daily ritual: jamming slices of carrot, apple, and ginger down the hopper of my juice machine. I absolutely swear by the health benefits of this juice. I gulp it down, while the vitamins are fresh, quickly getting to the bottom of the concoction, which is grainy and a bit disgusting. The ginger's burst of heat nearly chokes me, but I love the fierce warmth it sends through my body.

I scrub the filter of my juice machine with an old toothbrush while moving my hips to the beat of El Médico de la Salsa, a real-life doctor in Cuba who gave up his medical career to be a salsa musician. I'm listening to the song *"A pagar allá,"* in which the Salsa Doctor mourns the loss of his girlfriend to a wealthy Italian tourist. The doctor vows to call his girlfriend collect and tell her he still loves her and that she should come back to him if she misses his hot embraces. The music is so loud I don't hear the phone ringing. Just as the answering machine is about to come on, I drop the filter and toothbrush in the sink and pick up the receiver with wet hands.

"May I speak with Fanny Maya?"

"If this is phone solicitation, please take me off your list immediately."

"Fanny, don't hang up, it's Nissim. Remember? Nissim Behar."

"I'm sorry! I didn't recognize your voice."

"Listen, I know we agreed to meet at noon today, but an emergency's come up. I'm at the hospital and I'm the only anesthesiologist available, so I'm going into surgery in a few minutes. Can I call you back in a couple of hours?"

I assure him my schedule is flexible and tell him to call me when he's ready. But as soon as he hangs up, just a second before I do, I get angry. Isn't he the one who wants to meet me? I'm the one giving up my precious time. Why, then, am I being so damn accommodating?

"Come on, Fanny, don't be so hard on yourself." I say these words aloud, as though the walls could hear me. I decide to treat myself to a long hot shower. I massage Ginger Burst Body Wash into my skin and use the sugarcane cleansing polish on my legs. I wash my face with an exfoliant apricot scrub I bought the day before, following my facial and face-lift massage. I steep my frizzy hair in a hydrating conditioner and rinse it out slowly. When I come out of the shower, I rub peach-mango moisturizer all over my body and use extra on my elbows and heels. Moisturize, moisturize—that's my new mantra. Moisture—that's what we lose as we get older. It's as if we start shriveling up in preparation for turning into dust.

For mature skin, I recently bought vitamin C drops, an orange-blossom cleanser, and a face-firming activator. In two minutes, I blew three hundred dollars. I also bought a rose essential oil, which is good for dispelling anxiety, impatience, and confusion. The aesthetician, whose own face gleams like a porcelain doll's, spoke in ominous tones as she wrapped up my precious products in purple tissue paper. "We've destroyed the ozone layer, so we have to protect our skin. The sun used to take years to damage our skin. Now it only takes a few minutes."

Even though I live in a place with far more clouds than sun, I diligently apply the activator, being careful not to touch the area above the lip, which still feels sensitive. The day before my facial, I had my darker mustache hairs burned off with electrolysis. Then I went to the salon to have my eyebrows shaped. I'm due soon for my monthly massage. I'd better check my calendar. And see when I've scheduled my manicure and pedicure. These days a complete staff of professionals works on maintaining every inch of my body. Years ago I would have been disdainful of any woman who gave this much attention to her outer self. It's the inner self that counts, isn't it?

My nose practically touches the mirror as my myopic eyes try to focus. I line my lids where the lashes sprout, the way the makeup artist at the M.A.C. counter showed me. My eyelashes have lost their curl. They're still long but they're flat, as if pressed with an iron. The makeup artist told me to use an eyelash curler and apply mascara. It really does improve my appearance. I'm grateful to the woman at the counter. Thank goodness women look out for one another.

I slip in my contacts and go upstairs to get dressed. In the good mirror in the upstairs bathroom—the one that's always kind to me—I revise my previous assessment. I may actually have become more beautiful with age. But I feel like a sunset, knowing this sudden, late-blossoming beauty of mine will be short-lived.

Despite some cellulite on my thighs and that roostery business on my neck, I swear I'm more attractive than ever. For the first time in my life, I notice men's eyes on me. It's true, I wear more provocative clothing than I did in my twenties. But it's not just that. I have a sassiness about me now.

The only eyes that don't seem to notice me anymore are my husband Peter's. We may have become one of those new statistics I've read about in the junk magazines at the gym—that rising tide of married couples in the United States who just don't have time or energy for sex. I'm not sure how it happened to me and Peter. We used to have a nice sex life. Nothing too kinky. Just sweet, slow, languorous pleasure. Sometimes our love-making would turn into something wilder and more uncontrollable when, at the height of our passion, I'd remember the time I was in a Spanish village and saw a mare being mounted by her stallion.

In a weird way I'm actually more physical now than as a young woman. I used to spend entire days reading and writing. In middle age, I've become a gym junkie, which is pretty amazing since I had always hated the gym. I exercise every day on the StairMaster, the treadmill, the elliptical, and the exercise bike, and I pay a physical trainer to watch me lift weights three times a week. It's worth it for the results I've gotten. I'm slimmer and stronger. I dance salsa on Mondays and Saturdays and tango on Tuesdays and Thursdays. And I'm planning to take up flamenco and belly dancing.

Years of teaching and public speaking have cured me of my adolescent shyness and wallflower tendencies. Even if I'm not proud of my books because they're never going to be best sellers, I've gotten decent recognition for being one of those professors who writes autobiographically. Fans of my work say I'm daring and brave, but I don't feel daring and brave. I feel I've been a coward my whole life. If I had the nerve, I'd quit my job as a professor of anthropology and write novels. But I've never been sure whether I *could* write a novel. I've always wanted to be a novelist, but I fear I lack imagination. I have trouble making things up. I can't pretend I'm other people. I'm bad at lying, and I think you need to be a good liar to write novels. So maybe I'll always dream of writing novels and never be able to do it. When I get into a certain mood, like I start feeling my life is about to end, I tell Peter that when I die, they should write on my tombstone, "She never wrote a novel." He looks at me sadly when I say that.

Anyway, what should I wear for my meeting with Nissim Behar? I'll start with a red bra and the Jockey black thong underwear, which doesn't irritate my tush. Let's see if I can squeeze into the contouring stockings without snagging or tearing them. Oh, success! With my thighs and ass tethered in the stockings, I can wear a tight pair of pants and nothing wiggles. I'm very tush-conscious; my body image was deformed early on by the Cuban male obsession with women's backsides. Today I'll go for my latest pair of overpriced stretchy black Italian pants and team them up with a red turtleneck that accentuates my bust just a little, but not too much.

Just under an hour left, according to the clock in the kitchen, the handpainted ceramic clock I bought in Spain ages ago. I couldn't decide between two different models. "Which do you like better? The one with more yellow or the one with more red?" I asked Peter. He said they were both nice and either was fine with him. He wouldn't express a preference, which infuriated me. I finally bought them both, and one hangs by the front door and the other hangs in the kitchen. They tick softly, in unison—Peter has seen to that. He was so bored waiting for me to make up my mind. He found a chair in the corner of the store and dozed off, which made me even more furious. But he was the one who packed the clocks in newspaper and cardboard so they wouldn't break on the trip back to Michigan.

That's the way our marriage is, the way it's always been. I'm torn about what to do and he's indifferent. While I get worked up about things, he falls asleep. I get furious, and he ties things up in bundles. The good thing about my marriage is it's low maintenance. It doesn't take a lot of time away from my writing and my travels, and it doesn't wear me out emotionally. We may lack passion, but passion is overrated. My parents had passion, and they were always yelling ugly at each other when I was growing up. Peter and I never do that. Neither of us smashes plates, neither slams doors. No Cuban Sephardic melodramas in our household.

The phone rings.

"Fanny?"

"Peter?"

"Yes, me. Who did you think it was?"

"Sorry. I was a little distracted. I'm in the middle of something."

"You do want me to take you to the airport tomorrow, don't you?"

"Why are you asking me? You know the answer to that question perfectly well."

I get around by car fine in town, but I can't drive on the highway. Everybody drives too fast, like they're trying to kill one another, and it gives me panic attacks. So Peter always takes me to the airport.

"I wanted to make sure you wanted me to take you. I need to let people at the office know that I'm going to be late."

Peter is the librarian of the Iberian, Latin American, and Caribbean collection at Michigan. It's handy having him work in the library. Anytime I need a book, he brings it home for me. I've gotten spoiled and never go to the library anymore. But it's too bad that Peter, like me, gave up his dream to write novels after we got married and had Zak.

"Why are you always bending to other people's demands?"

"Fannica, please, I'm not bending to anybody's demands."

"Don't call me Fannica! Only my parents can call me that."

Afterward I feel bad. I know I shouldn't get annoyed with him. He does so much for me. He makes vegetable soup, washes the clothes, changes the sheets. He takes our son to school and prints out my e-mail attachments. He balances my checkbook and does my taxes. He isn't jealous and doesn't ask much of me. I know he's utterly faithful to me. What more can I ask? I ought to be more affectionate. I ought to tell him I'm grateful for everything he does. But somehow the appropriate moment never arises.

The phone rings again. I hold my breath.

"Fanny? Hi, Nissim Behar. I have a forty-five-minute window, not a lot of time, but enough to get to know each other. What do you say we meet in half an hour? I'm in the mood for a cappuccino. Do you know where they make a good one?"

"Let's meet at Sweetwaters. On Washington Street," I say. There's no irritation in my voice when I speak to Nissim Behar. "Will we recognize each other?"

"Don't worry, I'll recognize you."

I look out the window and am rudely reminded it's a winter day in February. The snow on all the front lawns has hardened into a thick sludge. My ugly but warm boots with the thick rubber soles are standing by the door, but I put on my tango shoes from Buenos Aires. They are glossy black with red trim and three-inch 1940s heels. As long as I set each foot down carefully, I should be all right. Anyway, with my New York hawk-eye parking skills, I'll find a spot and not have to walk far.

Sure enough, when I turn onto Washington Street, I find a parking space right in front of Sweetwaters and slide into Nissim Behar's arms, the two of us reaching the door of the café simultaneously. Nissim recognizes me from my photograph on the back flap of my latest book. And I recognize Nissim because he's a homeboy. He looks just like my brother—unruly hair and brown eyes so deep they eat up the pupils. He's wearing jeans, a purple ski jacket, and hiking boots. He looks like he's been for a long walk in the woods, rather than in an operating room administering anesthesia. He exudes so much vigor I feel he could lift me in his arms and I'd be light as a feather. We can't decide whether to greet each other the Cuban way or the American way, so we opt for a mix, shaking hands, then hugging and directing kisses in the direction of each other's cheeks.

Nissim holds the door for me and I dry my shoes on the soggy welcome mat. The tile floor is slick, so I walk on my toes to keep from slipping. Nissim is already at the counter when he turns and notices me gingerly advancing in my 1940s heels. He rushes to my side, and with exaggerated gallantry takes me by the arm.

"You sure those are the most appropriate shoes for this weather? We're not in Cuba, you know."

"Actually, they're tango shoes," I tell him, laughing.

"Tango shoes, excuse me," he says, also laughing.

At the counter he announces, "I'm having a double cappuccino. Should we make that two?"

"I don't drink coffee anymore. I'll have a ginger lemon tea."

"Much better for you. Your doctor approves," he says, winking at me.

He has spectacular curly eyelashes. Pity they're being wasted on a man.

"Don't get the wrong idea," I tell him. "I'm not a health nut, just a ginger fanatic. I'm constantly consuming ginger to stay warm. I'm always cold here."

"Michigan may not be the best place for a nice Cuban Sephardic girl," he says, gazing into my eyes, giving me another opportunity to admire his curly eyelashes.

"It's not, but here I am," I say, trying to sound breezy.

We carry our drinks to a quiet table next to a big plant with floppy rabbit ears which looks fake but is actually real. Nissim pulls my chair out from the table and waits until I sit down before he sits down. It's been a long time since a man did that for me.

He takes a sip of his cappuccino and says, "I've been wanting to meet you for years. Ever since I read that poem of yours in *Tikkun* about the Jewish cemetery in Guanabacoa. What a poem! And I really like your book, *Anthropology That Makes You Weep.* I'm amazed you can get away with writing so personally and still call yourself an anthropologist. You make me very proud, Fanny, and, as far as I know, we're the only Sephardic Jews from Cuba living in Ann Arbor. That's why I knew we should meet."

"I can't believe we've both been here for years and never crossed paths."

"My mother kept telling me to call you, but you know how it is. When you're a man, the last person whose advice you want is your mother."

I smile as he says this, but I'm thinking about my ten-year-old son Zak and wondering whether he's going to feel the same way about me when he gets older.

"So you don't drink coffee. What vices do you have?" he says, taking another sip of his cappuccino. He relaxes in his chair and his knees brush against mine. This makes my heart skip a beat. I feel as if a wall of resistance, inside me, wants to crumble. I hope I'm not blushing.

"I like to dance. Tango and salsa," I tell him.

"That's a virtue, not a vice. I love to dance. I dance salsa."

He removes his jacket, as if just talking about dancing salsa heats him up. Not even a light sweater underneath. He's got on a short-sleeved, tie-dyed Ann Arbor Art Fair T-shirt. His arms are strong without being repulsively muscular. I'm sure he does yoga.

I hesitate before I say, "The thing is I don't dance with my husband. He doesn't like to dance."

Nissim looks at me with curiosity. "Who do you dance with then?"

"Whoever asks me."

"And your husband doesn't mind?"

"I go out alone, so it's not as if he actually sees me dancing with other men." I try to sound blasé about this arrangement, as though my dancing were a form of physical fitness and nothing else. But sometimes I think I dance to remember the embraces I've stopped receiving from my husband.

"I'm not sure I could handle that. You're a very attractive woman. If I were with you, I'd be afraid another man would take you into his arms and never let you go."

"He's American. Only Latino guys get jealous."

Nissim laughs and shakes his head. "He's probably just doing a good job of hiding it. Trust me. Men are men. And you're a beautiful woman."

I don't know how to reply. I can't believe he said that out loud: that I'm an attractive woman, a beautiful woman.

"Do you dance with your wife?"

"Actually, we're about to be divorced."

"I'm sorry to hear that." The truth is I'm not. I have a sudden image of myself skipping town with him on a white horse and landing on a velvet-sanded beach in Cuba.

"No need for condolences. Our marriage died a long time ago. It was a relief for both of us finally to admit we'd be happier apart. Now I'm seeing someone, a woman named Ann. She's a nurse-midwife at the hospital."

I can feel my white horse skidding on the icy Ann Arbor pavement. "Do you think you'll marry again?" I ask, in my most neutral voice.

"I'm in no rush, but I know Ann would like to. She has this obsession about being 'the other woman,' even though I've told her dozens of times she isn't. When I met her, my wife and I were already estranged."

"You dance salsa with her?"

"She's started taking lessons, but she's more into rock music. She's a Grateful Dead fan. But she'll be good at salsa—she's picking it up quickly. She's a certified Pilates instructor, so she's got incredible control of her body."

I can feel my thighs pressing miserably against the tight nylon weave of my contouring stockings. So this midwife—I can't get myself to call the woman by her name, even in my thoughts—is a Pilates instructor! Right away I imagine a cheerful slim blond woman in tiny shorts showing off her perfect thighs as she demonstrates the swan pose. Then I imagine the midwife in a starched white hospital uniform. Women in labor are screaming in pain, bodies breaking open, and she bubbles with enthusiasm, telling them, "Remember to breathe now."

As if he's read my mind, Nissim Behar says, "But I haven't made any commitment to Ann yet. She'd like for us to move to some place warm, like New Mexico, but first I need to be sure everything is going to be okay with my daughter."

I'm glad to hear Nissim Behar is giving priority to his daughter. From the way he talks about the midwife, I can tell she isn't right for him. It's appalling the way she's pressuring him to get married when he's not even done getting divorced. And wanting him to move to New Mexico with her, which would put miles of flatland and desert between him and his daughter. What a possessive and selfish woman! I feel an urge to save Nissim Behar. What a horror it would be if he fell into the clutches of this blond midwife.

"So I hear you do a lot of traveling?" he says, sounding curious yet concerned.

"I'm on the road a lot. I'll be in Providence next weekend, at Brown. And I go to Cuba all the time. Three, four times a year."

"I've never been back to Cuba. I'm not sure I want to go back."

He reminds me of my father and my brother and the other men in my family, all of whom have refused to go back to Cuba. I argue with them constantly. But I don't want to argue with Nissim.

"You have to be ready for Cuba. It can be very traumatic when you return for the first time," I say. I don't tell him that I cried every day on my first trip back as a student, before I knew Peter. I never understood why I'd shed so many tears, if it was the sorrow or the joy of returning. Later I learned from my Cuban-American girlfriends that all of them had cried too.

Our private corner of the café, I notice, has filled with people. At neighboring tables, there's a young woman intently reading her organic chemistry textbook, a group of wool-sweatered male professor types with graying beards deeply immersed in discussion, a composed mother accompanied by two small children drinking her afternoon chamomile tea, and one of those elderly but very fit couples you often see in Ann Arbor, carefully dissecting a slice of blueberry cheesecake.

Nissim leans closer to me. His skin smells clean, of antiseptic soap, but his clothes hint at something more exotic, maybe patchouli incense. Looking at me with a slight hint of worry, he says, "Does your son mind that you're away from home so often?"

"He's used to it. And I tell him that, with all the public speaking I'm doing, we'll be able to buy a new car soon. We're still driving around in a ten-year-old Honda Civic. He really wants us to get a new car."

"Personally, I think you'd look fantastic in a BMW. A sportscar, of course. Red to match your sweater. You'd wear sunglasses and a flowing silk scarf around your long neck."

He speaks with such assurance I feel like with him I could be that dream woman. Tears try to form in my eyes. How can he imagine me so glamorously? Clearly, he hasn't spotted the roostery thing on my neck.

"I realize it's not a very politically correct car for a professor."

I laugh when he says that and he laughs with me.

"It's so easy to talk to you," Nissim says. "I've had a wonderful time." He grins and pats my hand. "I'm glad I've finally had a chance to talk with the other Cuban Sephardic Jew in town."

The way he says that, so tenderly, I'm ready to go with him to the end of the world. But before I can think of anything romantic but not too heavy to say to him, he announces he's got to pick up his daughter and gathers his napkin and cappuccino cup.

"Maybe we'll see each other again some time," I say.

"That would be wonderful," he says. "Here's my beeper number. Call me."

He hands me his card, and I tuck it into my purse and pull out my lipstick and compact. In recent months I've taken to painting my lips compulsively, retouching them whenever I'm done eating or drinking. He watches me as I brush a layer of lipstick over my top lip and then my bottom lip.

"Nice color."

" 'Rebel.' That's what it's called," I tell him and we both laugh.

He puts out his arm and I take it. He walks me to the driver's side of the car, making sure I don't slip. He does the Cuban gentleman thing of walking on the outside to protect me from the dangers of the street, and I find I like it when he does it. He's just a bit taller than I am, so we walk shoulder to shoulder. This is a new experience. Lanky Peter towers over me when he stands up straight. As Nissim and I say goodbye, he gives me a light kiss that almost touches my lips.

More than mere pleasure, what I feel in that kiss is a connection I've never known before, deep in the historical marrow of my being. Deep, I want to say, in my Cuban Sephardicness, if there is such a thing (and, God knows, an anthropologist should abhor such essentialized constructions of identity). But what can I do? His kiss reminds me of how my Sephardic grandfather from Turkey used to kiss—always aiming for my cheek but landing a little too close to my lips—and that shocks and excites me. We agree that I'll call him the following week after I get back from Providence.

MY PRESENTATION AT BROWN is a huge success. I wear a black turtleneck with a cut-out that reveals a bit of cleavage and nestle my hair in a sunflower-yellow headband, in honor of Ochún, the miraculous Venus of Cuba. There's a large audience, and I'm amazed I sound so confident and intelligent. A few students even ask me to autograph their copies of *Anthropology That Makes You Weep.*

But I can't wait to hop on the train to Boston and go visit my friend Miriam Levy Cohen. She's a Cuban-Jewish psychologist who specializes in the mental health of women prisoners. Her red hair is cropped close to her scalp, she wears turquoise jewelry and large hoop earrings, and she's partial to short skirts and tall boots. She's had a lot more experience with men and sex than I have, which I attribute to her being Ashkenazi rather than Sephardic. (If my father is any example, if they could, Sephardic fathers would make their daughters wear veils.)

In the kitchen Miriam bustles about mixing feta cheese, tomatoes, and kalamata olives for a salad, pouring egg-lemon sauce over the halibut, and checking to see that the rice pilaf is cooked just right. She's a dedicated cook who likes to mother her friends. She always makes a Sephardic meal for me when I visit. She's even gone to the trouble to prepare baklava. I try to control my desire to dip into the tray of honey-drenched pastries, but Miriam tells me to go ahead and have some. She says it's better to eat what you want when you want it. Life is too short, she says, to be self-punishing.

As soon as we sit down together with a glass of wine, I blurt out my story about Nissim Behar.

"I feel like destiny has come to me," I tell her. "I mean, Nissim's the only other Cuban Jew in Ann Arbor. He's Sephardic too. And a doctor!"

"Yes, it's quite overdetermined," Miriam says with a professional detachment I imagine she uses with her patients.

"This is all so strange, Miriam. When I was young I couldn't bear to be around men from our community. Every time my mother would try to hook me up with a Cuban Jew, I'd roll my eyes and tell her no, thank you. I couldn't wait to get away. And now I'm drawn to this guy who looks like my brother. The interesting thing is he also ran away from home. That's why we both ended up in Ann Arbor, Michigan, of all places."

"Life takes us by surprise sometimes," she says, still being the psychologist.

She serves me more fish and rice and urges me to have another helping of salad. I'm already full, but everything is so delicious I keep eating. I promise myself to do a longer cardio workout as soon as I get home.

"Imagine," I say. "He envisions me in a red BMW. And he's concerned that I'm dancing salsa alone."

"This Nissim Behar has a serious crush on you," she finally says.

"Really? So I'm not imagining it?"

"No, you're not. And you know what, it would do you good to have a little affair." She pauses, sipping a little wine before offering her diagnosis. "Your marriage is too safe. It's become imprisoning to you."

"But Peter has always been so good to me. He's so good it's unreal. He doesn't even know how to flirt. He's not like Cuban men."

"Let me tell you something my mother always said." Miriam pauses again for emphasis and pours each of us another glass of wine. "My mother always said, 'Never marry a man who doesn't beat you.' "

"That's horrible! I can't believe your mother said that to you."

"It wasn't to be taken literally. What she meant was, beware of men who are saints. You'll stay with them, even if you're unhappy."

"So you're advising me to commit adultery? But it's not going to be easy. There's a midwife who's putting incredible pressure on poor Nissim to tie the knot before he's even divorced."

"It's a tough world out there," Miriam says, shaking her head. She's not speaking as a psychologist anymore. This she knows firsthand. Her fun-loving, flirtatious, salsa-dancing Cuban husband, whom she adores, has just abandoned her for another woman.

She stands up and gathers our plates and slowly stacks them in the sink. She freezes momentarily and looks as if she could cry. Her husband used to wash the dishes.

"You'd better show Nissim Behar just how much you care about him," she says, her voice breaking. "I'm telling you, that midwife will slit your throat to get the doctor."

I RETURN TO Ann Arbor determined to dive into my budding relationship with Nissim and not to worry about the consequences. Miriam is right. I've lived too cautiously. I haven't allowed myself to take enough risks, even to imagine a life that isn't mine. No wonder I haven't become the novelist I dream of being.

I dial Nissim Behar's pager number. In less than a minute he returns my call. After we discuss my trip, he tells me the divorce proceedings are going smoothly. Then he says, "I told Ann about our meeting—I don't like to keep things from her. She said she'd like to meet you."

What? I hadn't expected to have to meet the midwife. But I'm ready for anything, even the ultimate battle with my nemesis. "How about if we all have lunch the day after tomorrow?" I say.

They arrive in separate cars, Nissim and the midwife, but they walk into the Lebanese restaurant together. The midwife, just as I expected, is blond, slim, and cheerful. I can't help wondering how many babies have come into the world that day thanks to her efforts.

We sit in a booth, Nissim and the midwife facing me. The three of us go for the daily special of couscous and vegetables.

"Nissim tells me you were also born in Cuba," the midwife begins.

"Yes, I was," I reply, forcing a smile.

"And that you're also a Sephardic Jew?"

"That's right," I reply, trying not to show any sign of impatience.

"I just don't get how the Jews got to Cuba," she says, scrunching her brows. "Nissim has tried to explain it to me, but I still don't get it."

At that innocent request for information, I launch into an explanation of how the Sephardic Jews were expelled from Spain in 1492 and resettled in the countries of the Ottoman Empire, where they continued to speak Spanish throughout the centuries, writing the language down in Hebrew letters.

"Between the two world wars, they left Turkey, as did my grandparents and Nissim's, because of growing economic troubles and anti-Semitism, but they couldn't get into the United States because of the 1924 Immigration and Nationality Act, which imposed a quota system on Jewish immigrants, so they went to Cuba, which was trying to increase the white population to prevent black Cubans from taking over the island."

The midwife listens in obvious bewilderment. It's clear she doesn't understand a word.

"Jews got to Cuba because there was racisim on all sides. In Europe, in the United States, and on the island. That's the story of the Jews of Cuba," I conclude.

"Wow, I never realized it was so complicated," the midwife says, suppressing a yawn.

She glances coyly at Nissim, who turns away. Instead, he gazes straight into my eyes and says, "That was wonderful. You've clarified a lot of things for me."

I was worried I'd gotten a bit pedantic, but Nissim's compliment convinces me he really is in need of being saved. But why has he chosen this bimbo as his new partner?

The next day, I call him on his pager phone, and he says he'd rather meet in a private place, so I invite him to my house. Peter is at work and Zak is in school when Nissim arrives at two in the afternoon. I serve him apple tea in the glass cups embossed with a gold swirl that I brought back from Turkey and my own homemade flan de coco.

"You have so many unusual things in your house," he says admiringly, walking around from room to room with me, each of us with a glass teacup in hand. I tell him where everything is from, the blood-red rugs from Istanbul, the pottery from Oaxaca, the lithographs and wood sculptures from Cuba. He points to the handpainted ceramic clock in the kitchen. "And that's from Spain," I explain, not mentioning that my husband played a crucial role in getting it back to Michigan intact.

"It's wonderful," he says. "You've created a wonderful home."

He uses the word "wonderful" a lot, I notice.

In the living room I sit in the Turkish chair made of old kilims. He sits in the pink velvet loveseat I got in a Michigan antiques sale.

"This is the best flan de coco," he says.

"My mother's recipe. I'd make it more often, but my husband hates coconut."

I offer him another slice, but he tells me he's full. He gets up and takes another tour around the house, continuing to admire things as if he were in a museum. He points to a small wedding photograph in the dining room.

"Your husband?"

"Yes, that's Peter."

"Where's he from?"

"Iowa. But he learned Spanish and converted to Judaism in order to marry me."

"That's pretty impressive. He must really love you."

I don't know what to reply when Nissim says that. I think Peter still loves me. But we haven't said "I love you" to each other in a long time. Peter is reticent, and I get tired of being the only one who talks, so we mostly speak in abbreviated whispers, as though we were at the movies. I thought that was okay, that it meant everything was understood between us. But now I'm not sure anymore.

Nissim points to another photograph, larger and in an elaborate carved wooden frame. "Your son?"

"That's Zak, yes."

"Handsome fellow. A nice combination of you and your husband."

He checks his watch. "Gotta go. My daughter gets out of school in a few minutes. I've really enjoyed this. Thanks for the flan and the apple tea."

"Wait. Let me give you some flan to take home."

Nissim tries to refuse the flan, but I put everything that's left in a Tupperware container and hand it to him. At the door of my house, he gives me another one of those parting kisses dripping with history.

As I rinse out the Turkish glass teacups, I try to imagine what I would take with me if my marriage were to end. Would Peter turn mean and demand to keep all the things he carefully packed and carried home for me? I see him snatching the Spanish clocks out of my hands while he tells me he's looked after them more than I have. But then I doubt such meanness is in him; he's more likely not to ask for anything. So I imagine myself weeping at the door and saying goodbye for the last time, overwhelmed by the goodness and purity of his love. And if my marriage were to end, would I have to leave my house? The house I've worked so hard for? The house where I've written the books I wish I were more proud of, the house where I've raised my one and only son?

Yes, I would have to give up the house. Even though I pay the mortgage and the house is filled with my things, I would have to give up the house. Every inch of the house is saturated with my marriage. I couldn't live there with Nissim Behar. And I would have to give up other things too. Nissim doesn't approve of my loose-woman habits. My travels by myself to Cuba. Late nights reading and writing. The pleasure I get dancing salsa and tango with different men. He's accustomed to having everything arranged to fit his schedule. He's a doctor, after all. But I want to shower upon Nissim all the affection and attention I withhold from my husband. I want to learn how to give all of myself to someone. I want to know what it's like to love until it hurts.

At night my son has trouble falling asleep. One night he calls to me from his room.

"Mami, I can't sleep."

"Just think relaxing thoughts, honey, you'll fall asleep soon."

"I try, Mami, but I can't. I'm scared."

Zak comes to our bed and wedges himself between his awake mother and sleeping father. He has the same lanky build and baby-fine brown hair as Peter, but eyes dark and searching like mine.

"Mami, can you hold my hand?"

I take his hand.

"Maybe I should see a psychiatrist," he says. His flawless pronunciation of the word scares me a little.

"Do you want to?"

"Do you think I need to?"

"No, I think we just need to talk. We need to know why you're afraid."

His child's hand is ice-cold. I wonder in how many ways, without even knowing, I've damaged him already. He clings to me and falls asleep holding my hand, while I lie awake, listening to the steady breathing of my son and husband, not falling asleep until the late, late hours of the night.

Maybe if I had that second child, Zak wouldn't be so afraid. There's still time, isn't there?

Dearest child, I think as I drift off, dearest child of an uncertain mother who strives without reason for things that will never be hers.

IT'S MONDAY NIGHT, my salsa night, and I'm dressed all in black, top and pants both skin-tight, thanks to the generous Lycra content in the garments. And nothing wiggles.

"Okay, boys," I call out to Peter and Zak, who are sitting in front of the television watching *Star Trek* reruns and eating pizza. "I'm going dancing for a while."

Peter swallows and says, "Have a good time!"

"Sure you don't want to go? My student, Margaret, says she can babysit."

Zak stops eating and looks worried, but his father, as always, is quick to assuage his fears.

"Thanks, honey, but I'm tired," Peter says. "I'm going to bed early. I just read that sleep deprivation is the most common cause of wintertime colds."

"Peter, please, my God, you sound like an old lady! I wish you liked going out as much as I do."

"And I wish you were the Fanny who used to like staying home at night with a good book."

"Oh, God, I was such a bore back then! A dull little bookworm. I can't believe I had to turn forty to learn how much fun it is to go out dancing."

"I'm not holding you back."

He tries to say that in a sprightly way, but I recognize he's being stoical again about his disappointment, like I imagine his Iowa ancestors were when their corn harvest got soaked in the rain.

"That's true, you're not."

As I say that, I can't help wondering: Does he not hold me back because he loves me? Or because he doesn't love me enough?

Peter follows me to the front door and watches me as I squeeze into my black leather jacket, which is so tight I can't zip up the front. I'll freeze my ass off in this little bullfighter jacket, but I want to look good.

"Did you know that you lose most of your body heat through your head? Shouldn't you at least wear a hat?" he admonishes.

"Stop being Mr. Science! If I wear a hat, it'll mess up my hair."

I shouldn't be so mean. My mother tells me that if I don't watch out, one day Peter's going to get tired of being treated so badly. I take a last look at myself in the hall mirror, which thankfully is also one of my good mirrors, and apply more lipstick.

"I'll try to get back early," I say, though we both know I won't.

I stretch up on my tiptoes to kiss him goodbye—he really is a good head taller than I am when he stands up straight—but I worry I might smudge my lipstick, so I give him a quick peck on the cheek. Something's better than nothing, I figure.

Nissim's afternoon visits have become a weekly event. There's no physical contact between us, but our talk, I feel, is very erotic. While I sit in the Turkish chair and he lounges in the pink velvet loveseat, we talk about everything. My quiet house becomes inundated with our words, drunk with our words. Nissim recites sonnets by Pablo Neruda in a gorgeous Spanish. He remembers melancholy Sephardic songs like *"Por amar una donzeya"* and *"Adio kerida"* and sings them in Ladino. He once dreamed of being a poet, but felt the immigrant impulse to do something more useful and gave up poetry in college. He likes being an anesthesiologist, he says, because it gives him the power to numb people's pain. He can't bear to see anyone in pain, he says.

When I don't offer him Turkish apple tea, I offer him Cuban coffee, real Cuban coffee brought back from the island in my own suitcase. He asks me about Cuba, and I tell him there's no place like it in the world and that we are fortunate to have been born there.

"You've inspired me," I say to him one afternoon. "I haven't written poetry in years, but I wrote some poems for you." I hand him a few sheets of paper. Before he can sneak a glance at them, I say, "Read them when you're by yourself."

"Thank you, Fannica," he says. "Mind if I call you that?" He winks at me and I still marvel at his fabulous eyelashes.

"Not at all," I say. "That's what my parents call me." Why is it I don't mind him calling me by my childhood name, but I get so angry if Peter dares to utter it?

"You're such a loving person. Your husband is a lucky man." He gazes at me with admiration I don't feel I deserve.

"I'm not nice to my husband. I find it hard to be nice to him." I hope I'm not scaring him by saying this. I've felt for years that I'm a mean and terrible person because I snap so much at Peter.

"Why have you stayed together?"

"Habit. We were so young when we met. We were in the same freshman English class. He sat next to me for the entire semester. And didn't say a word. He was too shy to talk to me. I was moved by his humility, I suppose."

"You sat next to each other for an entire semester and he never said anything?"

"Not a word. But afterward, he went away to Russia for a semester abroad and wrote me a long letter telling me how attracted he was to me. He couldn't say it to my face." The letter came in a blue envelope encrusted with Russian stamps. For a long time I carried the letter with me everywhere, keeping it in my purse like a talisman. Eventually I misplaced it and never found it again.

"Poor guy."

"Then I found out he's an orphan. He lost his parents in a car accident when he was a child. I reached out to him like a man drowning. And he wouldn't let me go. I became his anchor. My family became his family. He's tried so hard to become as Cuban and as Jewish as it's possible for him to be."

"That's admirable, don't you think?"

"But the fact is, he'll never be Cuban—or Jewish, for that matter. I know I shouldn't be saying this. When Peter converted, the rabbi said that from that moment on he was a Jew like any other Jew. I guess I just don't believe anymore that you can change your identity just because you want to. Peter will always be a nice plain guy from Iowa. And I'm this woman carrying too many abandoned countries on my back. We're as different as night and day, and that's what's creating the gulf between us."

Tears well up in my eyes. I excuse myself and rush to the bathroom to get some tissues and redo my lipstick. I examine myself in the bad mirror and see a woman who wants to leave her husband, but cries at the thought of doing it. Remembering that rose oil is good for mental confusion, I dab a few drops on my wrists and behind my ears.

When I sit down again in the Turkish chair, Nissim says, "You and your husband were clearly drawn to each other at one time. Maybe you can still find that spark. Divorce isn't easy. There's no turning back for me, but that doesn't take away the sadness. I have times when I wish I could anesthesize myself."

I'm disappointed by Nissim's words. I mean, they're heartfelt, but I'm not making any progress toward an affair with him. But then he reaches for my hand and tugs at it affectionately. "I feel so comfortable with you. As if I've known you always."

That sounds hopeful and I start to feel myself melting in my Turkish chair.

"Here's something else for you. It's a book from Cuba. I want you to have it."

I hand him my autographed copy of Dulce María Loynaz's famous collection of prose poems, *Poemas sin nombre.*

"She's my favorite poet," I tell him. "She writes about the longings and regrets of women. A lot of people say she's the Cuban Emily Dickinson. I go to see her in Havana. She's ancient, ninety-two years old, and lives in a mansion on the verge of collapsing. I read my poems to her in Spanish and she listens. She tells me to keep writing."

Nissim leafs through the book, but doesn't pause to read any of the poems. He glances at his watch. I know he needs to leave soon, but I want him to be more excited about receiving the book.

"Smell it. I swear, the book smells like Cuba. It's out of print, so I had to go looking for it among the outdoor booksellers at the Plaza de Armas. They're right near the port, so all their books smell like the ocean."

He opens the book to the title page. "Are you sure you want to give this to me? It's dedicated to you."

"Keep it as long as you like. Forever, if you want," I say, hearing the melodrama, but what can I do? He brings out the drama queen in me.

That day I realize it was meant to be. Nissim was put in my path for a reason, so I could fall in love with the only other Cuban Jew in Ann Arbor. I'm convinced he feels the same toward me, since he never mentions the midwife anymore. Any day now I'll tell Peter it's over between us. It's a matter of figuring out how to say goodbye.

THE NEXT DAY it's bitterly cold and snowing. I'm on my way to class in the old Honda Civic, and suddenly I'm breathless. "Oh, my God, I'm going to faint, I'm going to black out, I'm going to lose control of the car. Help, help!" Those are the words I hear in my head. Such despair. I try to remember what I've read in the self-help anxiety books. Keep going, I tell myself. Stay focused. But my heart doesn't feel right. "Maybe this is finally it, the heart attack, maybe this is the end, I'll pass out here."

I pull over on Madison Street, around the corner from my house, and roll down my window. There's no place to park on the street, it's dangerous to stop there, but I can't help it, my heart is beating too fast and too loud. I turn on my emergency lights and close my eyes for what I think is a moment. When I open them, I see the police car.

The big cop has the build of a football player just starting to develop a beer belly. He gets out first and asks, "Are you okay? Are you having medical problems?"

He looks me over, running his tongue over chapped lips. My hands are clasping the steering wheel, even though I'm not going anywhere. That morning I took off my wedding ring to see what it would feel like not to wear it. I'm certain the cop notices the empty space on my finger.

"I was feeling sick, but I think it's just a case of nerves. The streets are so icy."

"Oh, a little anxiety attack, huh?" he says. "I know all about it. Sometimes when I have to go after somebody who's armed, my heart goes nuts, and I feel like I don't know if I'm going to make it."

The cop is trying to be understanding, but I'm scared of him.

"I'm fine," I say. "It's just a few blocks to the university. I'm really okay." But he won't let me go that easily.

"What's your name?"

I tell him my name and he tells me his and then his partner's, a thin young man with bloodshot eyes.

"What time's your class?"

"It's right now. At one o'clock."

He smiles and leans closer to my car.

"I'm feeling better, sir. I can make it now."

"We'll follow you, miss, just to make sure you get there okay."

I drive to class, the cops following. They wait until I park and get out of my car and then they get out of theirs. I thank them and shake their hands. And again the cop who did the talking says he asked his doctor if he needed anti-anxiety drugs, and the doctor said he didn't, that it was normal in dangerous situations to feel anxious, and he didn't need any medicine.

I thank them again, and the cop looks me up and down and says, "It's too bad we didn't meet under different circumstances."

I feel the big cop's hungry eyes on me as I walk off in my tight black pants and little bullfighter jacket, carrying schoolbooks in my arms. So this is what it would be like not to be married, for men to know you're available as a woman. It's like being naked in the cold. I want to go home and put on my wedding ring.

When I get back from teaching, I drop my purse and books and run upstairs in my wet boots. My wedding ring is where I left it, in the mother-of-pearl jewelry box from Turkey. I've just slipped it on when I hear Peter calling me from downstairs.

"Fanny? Are you home?"

"Yeah, I'm back," I yell out. Then he says something else. "What? I can't hear you. Can't you come up? I'll be there in a minute."

As I come down, Peter is at the foot of the stairs, gazing at the snowy tracks I've made on the wooden steps. I feel like a thief, the way I snuck upstairs to find the ring, but he doesn't ask for an explanation and I don't give him one.

"You still want me to photocopy those articles for you?" he says. Behind my husband's thick glasses, I see the genuine concern in his bashful pale eyes.

"It's good you remembered! I need those articles for my talk in Arizona."

"That's what I thought. Oh, and what would you like for dinner?" he asks. "Do you want the vegetarian Indian food tonight?"

"I'd love Indian food. We haven't had it in a while."

He's already doing so much for me, I know I shouldn't ask for anything else, but I hear myself saying in my sweetest voice, "Do you think you could vacuum later? There's a lot of dust suddenly."

"Sure, no problem," he says, smiling. "I'll vacuum the entire house tonight."

"Thanks. I appreciate it."

I'd give him a kiss, but he's already zipping up his knapsack.

As he hurries out the door, Peter turns back and sees me standing on the frozen porch watching him go.

"I'll be right back," he says, and I nod.

"Don't take too long," I say softly.

"I won't," he replies, and looks at me hesitantly, as if he's worried he won't please me. It's the expression I remember from years ago, when he sat next to me in our freshman English class and I was a determined young woman who intimidated him.

For the next few days I have panic attacks everywhere I go in Ann Arbor. Now it's not just on the highway. Driving only a few blocks from my house brings them on. But I force myself to get to my destinations. Don't stop, don't stop, I tell myself. The only place I feel safe is at home, in the home I'm trying to leave.

I decide that I have to know whether I can dance with Nissim Behar. If we can dance, that will be the ultimate proof that our being together is worth every sacrifice. Worth the loss of my kind and good husband. Worth the loss of my Victorian house filled with all the pretty things I have brought back from my travels.

I can't wait for our weekly meeting, so I call him on his pager phone. He calls me back right away, as he always does, and I tell him it's urgent. He says he'll stop by on his way to pick up his daughter from school.

While waiting for him to arrive, I practice my dance steps to the music of the Salsa Doctor. I doubt the Pilatisized midwife can dance as well as I can. Wide hips and a tushy with plenty of *masita* are assets when it comes to dancing salsa. Surely my own salsa doctor knows this.

"I'm in a bit of a rush" is the first thing Nissim says. "What's wrong?"

"Nothing's wrong," I say. "Come in."

He looks adorable in his doctor's clogs. His hair is pulled back into a ponytail and he's wearing a Grateful Dead T-shirt under an unzipped green fleece jacket. I want him to discover my new push-up bra under my red blouse.

The music is playing. I decide to take action. I remember Miriam's warning, that the midwife will slit my throat to get the doctor, and I plaster my breasts against his chest and wrap my arms around him.

"Do you want to dance?" I ask.

Nissim lets me hold him tight for a moment, then freezes, as if he's witnessed a murder. With doctorly precision, he disentangles himself from my embrace. "I can't do this," he says. "You're married."

"I'll leave my marriage. Today, if you want."

He shakes his head. "Look, let's sit down for a moment."

I turn off the music and we take our usual seats. "Fanny, what can I say? I'm flattered that you feel that way about me." He's on the edge of the pink loveseat, as close as he can get to me on the edge of the Turkish chair without us touching. "I'm attracted to you too. Physically. And intellectually. Especially, intellectually. But you're so intense, it's exhausting sometimes. Who am I, compared to you and all your accomplishments?"

The weight of that word, crushing my heart like a boulder. *Intellectually . . .*

"Ann and I are about to sign the papers for our house. Well, it's not really a house. It's in a subdivision. But it's fine as long as you don't think of it as a subdivision. It's actually very comfortable. Close to the school my daughter attends. And my ex is buying a condo nearby. So it's going to be fine. Just fine. Ann and I have plenty of things in common. Sure, I'm a Cuban Jew, but I'm also more than a Cuban Jew. I've begun to think that to survive on this planet we all have to be citizens of the world."

There's a chill in the room. I haven't prepared Turkish tea or Cuban coffee.

"The other thing I want to say is that I'm angry with your husband for not being better to you." He gives me a look of such pity that I want to slap him.

I can't stand it when other people criticize Peter. It's fine for me to register all his imperfections, but I've never been able to handle other people's criticisms of him, even coming from the mouth of the man I want as my lover.

I hear myself yelling at Nissim, the way I remember my parents yelling at each other. "What do you know about what he's like to me? You're wrong, you're so wrong! Peter's such a good person. You can't imagine how incredibly good he is to me."

"Then he's oppressing you with his goodness. But you know what?" Nissim is yelling now. "You'll cheat on him until you die, but you're never going to leave him!"

"Go away," I mutter, and surrender my bulging thighs to the Turkish chair. I have just found out what it's like to love until it hurts. Nissim slams the door.

AFTERNOONS I SIT in the Turkish chair, lost and alone, drying my tears as soon as Peter and Zak come in the door. And then I can't wait anymore. I call Nissim on his pager phone, and he returns the call as quickly as ever. He says he can come to my house or we can meet at Sweetwaters. Like the first time, he only has a forty-five-minute window.

My house is a mess, so I choose Sweetwaters. I've been indoors all day and I'm still in my bathrobe, but I quickly throw on a pair of old jeans and a baggy Che Guevara T-shirt from my old fat days that I usually only wear around the house. I'm so tired of winter, so tired of being cold. I put on my black down coat that's less tailored than a potato sack and sink my feet into the thick-soled boots I avoided when I first met Nissim.

I lock the front door, regretting I look so frumpy, but it's late and Nissim will be waiting for me. I plan to jump in the car and get there in three minutes flat, but when I'm outside I remember that Peter has taken the car to go to the dentist. I have no choice but to walk. Off I go, as fast as I can, but feeling as if my feet are stuck in mud.

The town feels too quiet. I don't see a soul until I hit Ashley Street. I have an urge to scream, to call for help, to pound randomly on closed doors and ask the people who live inside if they're as afraid to die as I am.

Entering Sweetwaters, sweat pouring from my brow, I find the midwife sitting by the door like she's on sentry duty.

"Are you here to see Nissim? I saw him come in," she says.

I'm completely confused, but she looks me over calmly. "Why don't you get your drink? I'll go tell Nissim you're here."

Not knowing what else to do, I order a large ginger-lemon tea and walk to the other side of the partition, where Nissim and I sat the first time we met. Nissim and the midwife are looking so miserable under the plant with the floppy rabbit ears that it makes me feel sorry about everything, sorry the midwife is spying on him, sorry to be the one ruining their stab at happiness, sorry I chose Sweetwaters rather than my house.

The midwife tries to ease the tension by asking me about my drink.

"What's that you're having? A Caribbean drink?"

"Ginger-lemon tea."

"Is this the kind of thing you grew up drinking in Cuba?"

"No, this is something you'd be more likely to have in Jamaica. They use ginger a lot there in their cooking, and they make these great ginger beers. I grew up drinking a lot of ginger ale, but that was after we came to this country."

From the familiar bewildered look she gives me, I can tell these nuances of Caribbean life are of no interest to the midwife. She'll continue to think of my ginger-lemon tea as some kind of strange Cuban drink, no matter what I say. For the midwife, Nissim and I are members of some bizarre Cuban Jewish sect that she's never going to understand, but ultimately it really doesn't matter, because she's going to keep the doctor. Her thighs are slim and she's blond and cheerful.

The midwife turns to Nissim and says, "Honestly, I wasn't trying to follow you. It's just that after you left the hospital today, something strange happened."

"We'll talk later. I have to go." He starts to get up, but the midwife keeps talking.

"Let me tell you what happened. A bird came to the window. It wanted to fly, but its wing was torn, so I brought it inside. The poor thing was shivering. One of the incubators for the premies wasn't being used, so I put the bird in there. And it revived. I made a little bed for it out of cotton balls. Do you think it's going to survive?"

"Yes, I think it will," Nissim says. "I'll check on it tomorrow morning."

He gives her an efficient kiss on the lips and says he has to pick up his daughter at school. His ex will be furious if he's even a minute late.

I finish my drink and instinctively open my purse and pull out my lipstick.

"Rebel lipstick to go with your rebel Che T-shirt?" Nissim says, with a hint of sarcasm, and I can no longer tell if he's joking with me or making fun of me. He says goodbye without kissing me, and I know it's for the last time. I can foresee the future, how we'll find ways to look the other way and cross the street if our paths cross again.

I'm sure the midwife will leave with Nissim, but she stays where she is, under the plant. And I also stay, to my own surprise.

"So how do you like being a midwife?" I ask her.

"Oh, I like it well enough, though, I tell you, it can be exhausting. You get these long drawn-out labors, where the baby is clinging to the womb and afraid to be born. The nice thing is I'm always in touch with the essence of our womanhood."

The midwife pauses. The cheerfulness drains from her pert features, and she looks at me with worried eyes.

"You know, I never cared about school or studying or books. Being around Nissim, I feel so dumb sometimes. But I've focused my energies on developing my feelings, on developing my intuition, becoming smart about what my heart has to tell me."

"That sounds like a wise thing to have done," I say, and I really mean it.

The midwife shakes her head. "I need to start working on my mind. I've let it go for too long. That's my problem. I've abandoned my mind."

IT'S THE END of April, and the trees are struggling to remember how to sprout leaves. Spring is coming. *Primavera.* Beautiful, the sound of that word in Spanish. The days are longer, the sky more blue than gray. It's still too cold for the lilacs to release their perfume, but they're blooming anyway. I've used up all of my expensive lotions and creams, but somehow

I'm not in a rush to replace them. Classes are over and I'm working on my novel again. Maybe this year I'll actually finish it.

One day a mysterious package arrives in the mail. It's addressed to me, but the sender's address is missing. I've read about exploding packages and I'm afraid to open it. So I ask Peter to open it for me.

"It's a book," he says. "Just a book. Nothing to worry about."

He hands it to me, not even glancing to see what it is, with that infinite trust he has in me.

Tears come to my eyes when I see the book. It's my autographed copy of Dulce María Loynaz's *Poemas sin nombre.* Peter notices my tears, but he doesn't say anything. I almost want to tell him what I've been through. How my heart has been in another country and how it's home again. I think he would listen and understand, but I'm not sure. Secrets aren't lies, are they? They're more like lost gloves and lost socks. You're sure you know where you left them, but then they're gone, vanishing without a trace.

There's no note. That's what bothers me the most, that there's no note. He sent the book back to me without a note. He must not have read it, I realize, because the book still smells of tired boats and drowned orchids and desires quivering to life, the way the ocean smells in Cuba.

Ammiel Alcalay

Ammiel Alcalay (USA, 1956–) was born in Boston to Yugoslavian immigrants. He is a cultural critic, translator, and writer who teaches at Queens College and the CUNY Graduate Center. He strongly advocates multicultural and cross-cultural approaches to both literature and politics. In contemporary Jewish literature Alcalay sees an oppressive Ashkenazic complacency that limits the reach of alternative—or, more accurately, parallel—voices, Sephardic and Mizrahi, in particular. He also targets Israeli culture for fostering a Eurocentric, homogeneous worldview, with Hebrew as its unifying force. For Alcalay, the only way for a healthy Jewish culture in the Middle East to survive is "to grow backward: to bring to bear all the power and richness it can muster from the past by losing the fear of reaching the point of freedom it takes to be traditional." His views on this subject are conveyed in his essay "The Quill's Embroidery: Untangling a Tradition." Alcalay is the author of the controversial work *After Jews and Arabs: Remaking Levantine Culture* (1993), as well as *Memories of Our Future: Selected Essays, 1982–1999* (1999), a volume in which Sephardic identity and culture are explored in depth. His book-length poem, *in warring fractions* (2002), is dedicated to the Bosnian town of Srebrenica. Alcalay is the editor of *Keys to the Garden: New Israeli Writing* (1996), an anthology of contemporary Middle Eastern Jewish writing. "The Quill's Embroidery: Untangling a Tradition" is excerpted from *Memories of Our Future.*

The Quill's Embroidery: Untangling a Tradition

In a gathering whose emissaries mirror both the more recent movement as well as the more venerable stasis of the Sephardic diaspora—among those formerly of Egypt, Baghdad, Tunis, Aleppo, and Algiers, and more recently of Paris, Montreal, Los Angeles, and Israel, as well as those remaining in the Balkans, the *shearith Israel* from Sofia and Belgrade—I find myself, if not the least exotic, certainly the least attached to a place that can stake claims to a tradition, a place that, at least in appearance, seems so vested that its natives naturally assume residence within the richly textured arabesque this tradition has always been presumed to emerge from. So it is, ironically, as an American, from a position of indigence that I would draw the margins these soundings intend to trace—margins that verge on nativity and estrangement, memory and forgetfulness: the writing and rewriting, the reading and rereading of the past.

Writing and reading, no matter where, have much to do with the unearthing, the grasp, and often the mastery of both presences and absences. Reading as both recovery and relapse; the ink of writing as life-blood, animator, nourishment—the book as fertile ground nurtured by ink.

In Shem Tov Ardutiel's *Battle of the Pen and the Scissors,* written in Spain in the fourteenth century, "on a day of frightening snow, a day of terrible ice," the writer's inkwell has frozen and his pen, in despair at not being able to perform, "to remember what is absent from memory, and stand guard that nothing be lost," recounts past service to his master:

> Have I not written for you excellent things. . . . When my udders were filled with ink I emptied them all on the scroll. Riches I swallowed, and I spewed them forth, and not a drop did I retain for myself. Naked I came forth from my inkwell and naked I shall

> return. . . . When the ice has been melted and dispersed. . . . Then with joy shall you draw the waterspout of the wall of salvation, and the scroll and its writing will be like an irrigated field.

In the Crimean port of Theodosia, not far, in mind, "from Smyrna and Baghdad," the Russian poet Osip Mandelstam wrote of a "bookish earth," and dreamed of a place that, within the inherited wisdom of its people, embodied an allegiance to words—sentenced to internal exile, Mandelstam placed the form of his vision and the memory of his biblical ancestry in a Mediterranean world in which Spain was central—sowing dormant seeds, he unearthed his own genealogy.

THE SPANISH EXPERIENCE, packaged most garishly since the Jewish Enlightenment as "the Golden Age" and exploited by many, often at cross-purposes, remains, like Sinai or the Exodus from Egypt, part of the Jews' collective memory. But like any common, central experience that looms large in a people's past, it too runs the risk of diffusion, dispersion, and finally inertia: this field can become muddy and these furrows turn to drainage ditches that empty out into a still-born swamp, final resting place for what is allowed to go unquestioned and uninterpreted. Paradoxically, the movement of memory too often reappears in the form of fixed, unchanging images: resilient, indelible, and iconic, their clarity is blinding. In his *Commentary on the Mishnah,* also known as *The Eight Chapters,* Maimonides wrote:

> One action may resemble another action, so that the two actions are thought to be identical even though they are not. For example, consider three dark places: the sun shines upon one of them, and it is illumined; the moon rises over the second place and it is illumined; a lamp is lit in the third place, and it is illumined. Light is found in each one of them, but the reason for the first light and its cause is the sun, the cause of the second is the moon, and the cause of the third is fire. . . . There is no notion common to all of them except through equivocation. Grasp this notion, for it is extraordinarily marvelous.

Untangling the strands of the past is not simply an act of recognition, of fitting events into fixed patterns, of just seeing the light; it begins, rather, by apprehending the source of light and follows with an active, incessant engagement in the process of naming and renaming: distilling the light into sun, moon, and fire.

Of all the Jewish pasts, since it is almost impossible to speak of a recent single Jewish past, that of Sephardic Jewry has been recorded, transmitted, and interpreted in a way most alien not only to itself but to the very nature and basis of the more ancient Jewish structures out of which it emerged and grew. Disenfranchised, the head and heart safely removed from the body politic, Sephardic Jewry remains an anomalous and enigmatic entity to the vision of Judaism predominant since the French Revolution, a vision largely shaped by opposition and dichotomy: body and spirit, internal and external, secular and religious. Within this scheme, the history of Sephardic Jewry, the life space of its creative power and the almost singular diversity of its experience have been reduced to a frantic shuttle between light and darkness (the light of the Golden Age, the darkness of the Expulsion from Spain and its aftermath), without ever identifying the source of light or the subtle and sundry tones of its recalcitrant shades. Abridged into isolation (its nucleus distorted—the before and after assigned to obscurity), the longer tale of Sephardic Jewry remains to be told.

This before and after ranges from southern Arabia, Egypt, the Fertile Crescent, Persia, Central Asia, and India to North Africa, Western Europe, and the New World; its cities of residence and accomplishment, among them Kairouan, Fez, Aleppo, Tiberias, Cairo, San'a, Istanbul, Safed, Livorno, Salonika, Amsterdam, and London remained intertwined and bound by a generous surplus of tongues—mainly Hebrew, Arabic, and Ladino but also Aramaic, Latin, Portuguese, Italian, Provencal, Catalan, Greek, Serbian, Berber, Bulgarian, Persian, Marathi, French, English, Dutch, and more than a few others with much remaining in parchment and newsprint, divan and prayerbook, question and commentary, document and fable.

Of 350 writers in a proposed anthology, only two were born, lived, and died in the same city: Sarah Coppia Sullam, a poet from Venice, and Haim Palaggi, a rabbi from Smyrna. The others moved, often frequently, sometimes by choice, sometimes of necessity, in a world much like that envisioned by Mandelstam: a world that embodied an allegiance to words, centered around the Mediterranean. Yet, we have become so accustomed, as the historian Elie Kedourie writes, to "statements cast in the universal mode purporting to apply to all Jews at all times and everywhere . . . to a universal and inescapable Jewish fate," that it has become an almost arduous task to envisage and accept a world in which passage was not exotic, a world in which autonomy—religious, linguistic, and cultural—was expressed and realized in contexts and under assumption radically different than ours can accommodate.

MORE THAN SOME of the labor in seeing and accepting this world has been undertaken by S. D. Goitein in his great work, *A Mediterranean Society*. In this reconstruction of the Mediterranean world from the tenth to the thirteenth centuries, based on thousands of personal letters and business documents written by Jews and preserved in the geniza of a synagogue in Cairo, he writes:

> I have counted so far about 360 occupations of Jews. . . . There was constant cooperation between the various religious groups to the point of partnerships in business and even in workshops. In order to assess correctly the admissibility of the Geniza records for general sociological research, we have to free ourselves entirely from familiar notions about European Jews. . . . During the "middle" Middle Ages, around 1050, the unity of the Mediterranean world was still a fact. This is all the more remarkable since the European shores of the Mediterranean, including Spain, as well as the African and Asian sides, were split up into many separate units, often at war with one another. However, despite the many frontiers and frequent wars, people and goods, books and ideas traveled freely from one side of the Mediterranean to the other.

Even more remarkable may be the fact that, to a great extent and against great odds, this unity persevered among Sephardic Jews through the end of the nineteenth and into the twentieth century. "People and goods, books and ideas" continued to travel freely: songs originating in Andalucía, Castille, and Aragón continued to be sung in Tlemcen, Sarajevo, Casablanca, and even the Bronx; poetic forms brought to Córdoba from Baghdad in the tenth century continued to be written and renovated in Livorno, Jerusalem, Bombay, and Brooklyn. Fully alive to the possibilities of each idiom they encountered, these writers made their cities books and lived in words, but never as a means of excluding themselves from the world they inhabited—refusing to use tradition as a barricade, they avidly pursued and confronted the new: from the eleventh to the thirteenth century writers like Yosef Ibn Zabara and Yehuda al-Harizi, among others, worked within the structure of framed tales that mingled philosophy with fancy, invective with praise, and the hermetic with the evident, much in the style of their successors, Chaucer and Boccaccio. The first poet to write sonnets in a language other than Italian was Immanuel of Rome, using the form in Hebrew over a hundred years earlier than the French or the English; forged in the cauldron of the Inquisition, little attention has been paid to the writing of *marranos, conversos,* and crypto-Jews as reactions to catastrophe, works created by those who were, as Shmuel Trigano writes in *The New Jewish Question,* "both the prototype and the anguished laboratory of modernity; the 'political animal' divided into a private, fantasizing persona, and the universal citizen, abstract and theoretical." Like their more glorified and well-known predecessors in Islamic Spain, Sephardic Jews writing during and after the Inquisition faced this new state of being polymorphously, in many guises and under many rubrics: as crypto-Jews or the offspring of conversos bearing secret messages, writers like Moses Almosnino, Francisco Delicado, and Fernando de Rojas gave birth to and sustained the picaresque; discarding their veils, others like Antonio Enríquez Gomez and Moses Zacuto made Amsterdam center stage for the production of Hebrew and Spanish drama when European theater was at its height; seeking the reasons for persecution in time rather than text, Solomon Ibn Verga and Yosof HaKohen revived and reinvented the art of the Jewish historian; others like Esperanza Malki and Esther Kyra appeared as foreign missionaries and diplomats in the Ottoman court or Renaissance figures, like the poets, musicians, and patrons of the arts in Venice, Deborah Ascarelli and Sarah Sullam; medical scholars like Amatus Lusitano and David de Pomis, haunted ruthlessly by the very superstition and ignorance they fought against, answered their inquisitors with examples from the unheeded valor of classical antiquity and the New Testament; by undermining and tempering the gentlemanly or spiritual exile of the world of courtly love or the pastoral with the fact of their own suffering and the cutting edge of their art, the humanists Solomon and Abraham Usque overcame the semantic and psychological shackles affixed to the paradox of expressing both shame and rage in the language of their oppressors. Often reduced to the status of a nonperson, skirting and straddling generic, linguistic, and geographic borders, the work of these and other Sephardic writers remain apt and cogent but neglected rejoinders to the dilemna faced by Jewish writers of the generation prior to Kafka's—these writers lived between three impossibilities: the impossibility of writing in German and the impossibility of writing any other way, to which one could even add another impossibility, that of writing per se.

ALTHOUGH AN AWARENESS of this tradition as a way of negotiating the obstacles presented by nativity and the hierarchy of dominant and subject languages still lingers, to a remarkable degree, among Sephardic writers (Elias Canetti, for instance, when asked why he chose to write in German, stressed his full identification with the Jewish and crypto-Jewish writers engendered by the machinery of the Inquisition), the inherent impossibilities of the dilemma have only been exacerbated by contemporary catastrophe, entangled allegiance, and rebirth. Quite far from Prague, on a journey beginning in Baghdad and ending in what he describes as "the lovely town of Ma'alot," in northern Israel, the Baghdad-born Israeli novelist Sami Michael has outlined precisely three impossible possibilities (only substituting Arabic for German) in his struggle to write along the margins, between countries and languages. Writing and possibility, however, and the subversion of impossibility, seem to me to comprise a longer, more circuitous tale, one that goes well beyond the borders of particular languages, books, and countries to question the more radical temper of language and the book itself.

IN AN ARGUMENT that takes place in Albert Memmi's novel *The Scorpion,* Alexandre Mordechai Benillouche desperately tries to convince his old uncle of the need to color code the commentaries surrounding his sacred texts; adamantly refusing, his uncle insists that:

> "All the commentaries are true at the same time, so there is no reason to use colors to differentiate them . . ."
>
> "But," Alexandre argues, "authors contradict each other."
>
> "The contradiction is within yourself," Uncle Makhlouf answers, "it comes from your not having a view of the whole."

> "Even so, a commentary hasn't the same value as the original text! A commentary on a commentary hasn't the same value as the commentary itself!"

This time Makhlouf answers categorically:

> ". . . only if you don't know how to reconcile the whole. . . . You ask, which is essential, which embroidery? A bad way of looking at things. . . . You end up wondering which is the text and which are the commentaries. You end up doubting the text. Bad. Pernicious. Remember: everything is the development of a single text. And shall I tell you something? Even that text is a commentary. . . . When you need to hear God's voice itself, you have the Text. After all, what is it, if not the permanent presence of the word of God? It's up to you to understand it, as best you can, as you need to. That's why the commentaries may seem different."

Poor and almost blind, a tireless weaver of silk, Uncle Makhlouf, although his text is specific and his presence may be our absence, effortlessly eclipses us: having skipped modernity altogether, he is already well on his way into the "postmodern." His sense of palimpsest, that beneath one text there is always another, strikes the bedrock of Jewish thought but without implying the presence of an Ur-language, as many considered Hebrew "man's" or, more precisely, Adam and Eve's first tongue. Commenting on Adam's naming of the beasts in Chapter 2 of Genesis, Maimonides writes: "Among the things you ought to know and have your attention aroused to is the dictum: *And the man gave names and so on.* It informs us that languages are conventional and not natural, as has sometimes been thought." Assuming language to be immanent rather than transcendent, "an aspect of the continuous divine creative force itself," as Susan Handelman writes in *The Slayers of Moses,* "the *Torah* is not an artifact of nature, a product of the universe; the universe, on the contrary, is a product of the *Torah.* One does not pass beyond the name as an arbitrary sign towards a non-verbal vision of the thing, but rather from *the thing to the word* which creates, characterizes and sustains it . . . Jews adhere to signs because reality innately is constituted as linguistic for them. . . ."

. . .

To put it another way, the world is comprehensible only through the context the text provides, through language. To go further: the dean of Sephardic commentators, Abraham Ibn Ezra, in a note on Chapter 4, verse 35 of Deuteronomy, wrote that: "The human element of speech is divine or partakes of divinity." Since one of the most important divine attributes is infinity, both text and talk, the letter and the voice retain fluidity and remain limitless. The same logic that not only safeguards but vehemently protests against the word becoming either flesh or spirit also upholds the equality of the exegete: adhering to signs, beginning and ending with the words it expounds, commentary emerges not as reduction or limitation but a way of reinscribing and expanding the parameters of memory and knowledge, perpetual source of possibility and recuperation. In a commentary on Jacob's death, Benjamin Artom, chief rabbi of the Spanish-Portuguese congregation of London in the 1870s, subtly shifts some of the metaphysical assumptions about immortality simply by examining the memorial act in another context, a specifically philological context:

> After his prophetic blessing was over, Jacob said, "I am to be gathered unto my people; bury me with my ancestors in the cave of Machpelah." Can there be any connection between those two expressions—to be gathered unto his people and to be buried with his ancestors? Are they dependent on one another or are they equivalent? Abraham, in accordance with the promise of the Lord, was gathered unto his people, yet his tomb was far from that of his father or his ancestors. To be gathered unto his people means to ascend to the region of immortality; it means to return to our ancestors—to our father, mother, wife, husband, children brothers—to all those to whom the link of life had bound us *upon the earth;* it means to return to the country where from we were sent in the moment of our birth, it means not to die but to live.

Yet, to return also means asking where to and, more often than not, in what language. In *Return to the Book,* Edmond Jabès writes:

> In the cemetary of Bagneaux, dèpartement de la Seine, rests my mother. In Old Cairo, in the cemetary of sand, my father. In Milano, in the dead marble city, my sister is buried. In Rome where the dark dug out the ground to receive him, my brother lies. Four

graves. Three countries. Does death know borders? One family. Two continents. Four cities. Three flags. One language: of nothingness. One pain. Four glances in one. Four lives. One scream.

LOCUTION AND LOCATION: the Tower of Babel combines two fables, that of utterance, articulate or not, and that of place, which have become almost synonymous with a modernity that finds itself caught, eager to catch up with an inherited wisdom that embodies an allegiance to words but unsure of the markers mapping the path. In the argument between Makhlouf and his cousin Alexandre, the young man clings to a hierarchy that sees commentary and further commentary as regressive, a reduction or diminution of the original text. Makhlouf, however, accepts any writing, whether centrally placed or scribbled along the margins, as inaugural for "writing," as Jacques Derrida notes, "is the anguish of the Hebraic *ruah,* experienced in solitude by human responsibility; experienced by Jeremiah subjected to God's dictation, or by Baruch transcribing Jeremiah's dictation. . . . It is the moment at which we must decide whether we will engrave what we hear. And whether engraving preserves or betrays speech."

THIS SENSE OF WRITING as "inaugural" opens both the doors and the floodgates—extending the itinerary and increasing the way stations along the route, it also allows the sojourner to become a possible inhabitant. When Moses admonishes the people of Israel to remember Egypt, both the sojourning and the slavery, perhaps he meant, as the much neglected scholar Abraham Shalom Yahuda implied in his great study on the Egyptian influence on the Pentateuch, inscribe your experience within the very fabric of the language, take the land and the cities and the people with you and make them live in your book—reinscribe Egypt in such a way that you remain responsible for what Shmuel Trigano has called "the Egypt within, the interior exile." Freed by the desert and the breaking of the tablets and graciously exempted by God from the disappointment of seeing the promised land become a monarchy modeled on the banished one, only a child of Egypt like Moses could so thoroughly accept the exterior Egypt, since it posed no threat to him, and eradicate it by permanently inscribing it within the palimpsest. Just as Hobbes called Moses the perfect law-giver, he is, in this sense, also the perfect writer for he never reaches his destination.

. . .

This way of acceptance, this manner in which the exterior is internalized without being disowned or renounced is a stance of utmost respect and recognition toward the other, as well as an acceptance of the otherness of one's self: a fertile path furrowed in the very humus of the "bookish earth" by the biblical and rabbinic tradition, Sephardic writers kept well within its course. Sojourning in Alexandria on his way from Spain to Palestine, in a poem dated from the twelfth century, Yehuda Halevi wrote:

> See the cities:
> Behold the unwalled
> villages held once
> by Israel and pay
> homage to Egypt.

This constant referral back to something always anterior but newly circumscribed within the text can be seen as the flip side of apocalypse, or what apocalypse has been taken to be, the tone of defiance and urgency announcing the coming of the end. This flip side seems to say, rather, that the beginning is always at hand and may refer to what Jacques Derrida has characterized as a nonquestion:

> The nonquestion of which we are speaking is not yet a dogma; and the act of faith in the book can precede, as we know, belief in the Bible. And can also survive it. The nonquestion of which we are speaking is the unpenetrated certainty that Being is a Grammar, and that the world is in all its parts a cryptogram to be constituted or reconstituted through poetic inscription or deciphering.

Much of the certainty of writing in the Sephardic tradition owes itself to the acceptance of this nonquestion, a nonquestion that is also an *un*question—something prior to the act of questioning, Dante's "truth beyond whose boundary no truth lies." There is nothing surprising, then, in seeing how the creative genius of this tradition manifested itself in grammar and codification, two of the great projects of Sephardic rabbis. All the great commentators, in addition to being physicians, poets, diplomats, judges, or astronomers, were first and foremost grammarians. If the world is seen as an act of divine speech, then the study of grammar includes all the disciplines that have become disparate and even conflicting in the Western tradition since all categories of thought must struggle for and find their place of expression in language. Instead of the sterile discipline usually associated with the study of grammar, the Sephardic grammarians practiced their art as if the world depended on it, for it actually does. Humans are both God's speakers and readers, grammar is not the "after-effect" of language but the genesis of meaning—to hear is to understand.

ALTHOUGH CULTIVATED BY the learned, the route of this nonquestion was never restricted to them, constantly reappearing in songs, proverbs, fables, and even novels. Disguised in the form of a popular Spanish love song and composed anonymously somewhere in the Mediterranean world, the following Ladino lyric is typical of what hearkens back to something half-remembered but never forgotten:

> If the sea were made of milk
> I'd make myself a fisherman
> and fish for all my sorrows
> with little words of love.
> (Si la mar era de leche
> Yo me haria un peshkador
> Peshkaria las mis dolores
> Con palavricas d'amor).

Here the sea is the mother tongue, speaking love's idiom, and milk the invisible ink, perhaps of Rabbi Eliezer who said:

> If the seas were of ink and all ponds planted with reeds, if the sky and the earth were all parchments and if all human beings practiced the art of writing—they would not exhaust the learning I have mastered, just as the Law itself would not be diminished any more than is the sea by the water removed by a paint brush dipped in it.

Surrounding the nonquestion, like commentaries strung along the margins of sacred texts, are the endless questions announcing what may be most unique about this tradition of writing: its complete and conscious renunciation of originality in the conventional sense. Here the writer can be distinguished not as engenderer of icons but eternal iconoclast, an iconoclast who does not simply destroy but, as Shmuel Trigano writes, "is a creator whose lips form the word that arises again instantaneously." Unwilling to simply settle for either spirit or letter, light or darkness, this tradition has found its medium through questioning the nonquestion. As Edmond Jabès has noted:

> Answers embody a certain form of power, whereas the question is a form of non-power. But a subversive kind, one . . . that will be upsetting. . . . Power does not like discussions. Power affirms, and has only friends or enemies. Whereas the question is in between.

In many times and places, in many idioms, the Sephardic writer has found tradition along the interstices, between the milk of the mother tongue and the invisible ink of a beginning always at hand. This tale of the "in-between" is even more varied than the fragments I have so far tried to recount, and though it must wait for another time, it remains poised for the telling.

Sami Shalom Chetrit

Sami Shalom Chetrit (Morocco-Israel, 1960–) is an Israeli poet, filmmaker, and political activist who was born in Qasr as-Suq, Morocco. He attended Hebrew University and Columbia University. He was the founding director of Kedma, an alternative school in Tel Aviv, and currently teaches at Hebrew University. He is the author of *Openings* (1988), *Freha Is a Beautiful Name* (1995), and *The Ashkenazi Revolution Is Dead* (1999). Shalom Chetrit's poetry questions the official versions of the lives of the founding Zionist generation. He has also written about the Palestinian intifadah and his experiences as an Israeli soldier in Lebanon. Sami Shalom Chetrit is the editor of *A Century of Hebrew Writing: An Anthology of Modern Hebrew Writing in the Middle East* (1998). He maintains the Web site *Kedma: A Middle Eastern Gate to Israel* (www.kedma.co.il). His poem "Who Is a Jew and What Kind of a Jew?," translated by Ammiel Alcalay, examines the abyss that divides East and West.

Who Is a Jew and What Kind of a Jew?

1. The story is told:

An American Jew dies and he leaves no children.
In his will, the following is written:
"I hereby decree that all my money and property
be given over to the State of Israel and my last
wish is that I be buried in the Land of Israel.
The undersigned, Isaac Cohen."
The attendants sent the deceased and his money,
according to his last request, to the Land of Israel,
to eternal rest. The clerks of Zion collected
his money and transferred the corpse, as a matter
of course, to the burial society of the Ashkenazi Jews.
They turned his papers upside-down but found no authorization
to determine whether or not he really was an Ashkenazi.
Because of their doubts they deferred, sending him
on to the eternal resting place for Sephardic Jews.
The Sephardi sages sat down to take the matter
under advisement and, in conclusion, their answer
was formulated like this: "The name Isaac Cohen could
be either here or there, and given that this is so,
if he is a Sephardic Jew, then we have been privileged
to fulfill a wonderful commandment; and if he is
an Ashkenazi Jew, then we will gladly bury him!"

2. Getting to Know a Friendly American Jew: Conversation (translated into Hebrew)

Tell me, you're from Israel?
Yes, I'm from there.
Oh, and where in Israel do you live?
Jerusalem. For the last few years I've lived there.

Oh, Jerusalem is such a beautiful city.
Yes, of course, a beautiful city.
And do you . . . you're from West . . . or East . . .
That's a tough question, depends on who's drawing the map.
You're funny, and do you, I mean, do you speak Hebrew?
Yes, of course.
I mean, that's your mother tongue?
Not really. My mother's tongue is Arabic, but now she speaks Hebrew fine.
Oh, *"Ze Yofi,"* I learned that in the kibbutz.
Not bad at all.
And you are, I mean, you're Israeli, right?
Yes, of course.
Your family is observant?
Pretty much.
Do they keep the Sabbath?
Me, no, depends actually . . .
Do you eat pork?
No, that, no.
Excuse me for prying, but I just have to ask you, are you Jewish or Arab?
I'm an Arab Jew.
You're funny.
No, I'm quite serious.
Arab Jew? I've never heard of that.
It's simple: Just the way you say you're an American Jew. Here, try to say "European Jews."
European Jews.
Now, say "Arab Jews."
You can't compare, European Jews is something else.
How come?
Because "Jew" just doesn't go with "Arab," it just doesn't go. It doesn't even sound right.
Depends on your ear.
Look, I've got nothing against Arabs. I even have friends who are Arabs, but how can you say "Arab Jew" when all the Arabs want is to destroy the Jews?
And how can you say "European Jew" when the Europeans have already destroyed the Jews?

3. When I Left

It was only when I left that I remembered
I hadn't wanted to get so involved,
I really only wanted to tell her
that my first babysitter in Morocco was a Muslim girl
and that I have a black-and-white photo of her in an old album
sitting on the mosaic tiles in the courtyard
and that when I was a new Moroccan stiletto immigrant
I tried in vain to recall a little boy's conversation
with his babysitter in Moroccan Arabic.
And whenever we brought her up, my mother would say:
How she loved you, she never left you for a second.

Appendix: The "Other" Jew

SALMAN RUSHDIE

SALMAN RUSHDIE (India-Great Britain-USA, 1947–) was born in Bombay to Muslim parents. He was educated in Bombay and in England, briefly considered becoming an actor, but then went to work as a copywriter for an advertising agency in London. His first novel, *Grimus,* was published in 1975, but it was with the publication in 1981 of the award-winning *Midnight's Children,* a novel about India's independence, that he began to receive international acclaim. In 1988, Rushdie published *The Satanic Verses,* which was deemed blasphemous against Islam by Iran's Ayatollah Khomeini. Khomeini issued a fatwa—in effect, a death sentence—against Rushdie in 1989, and Rushdie spent the next decade in hiding in Great Britain. Rushdie's other fiction includes *Shame* (1983), *Haroun and the Sea Stories* (1990), *East, West* (1994), *The Moor's Last Sigh* (1995), *The Ground Beneath Her Feet* (1999), and *Fury* (2001). His nonfiction works include *The Jaguar Smile* (1987) and *Imaginary Homelands: Essays and Criticism, 1981–1991* (1991).

Rushdie is honorary professor in the humanities at MIT and a fellow of the Royal Society of Literature. He was elected to the board of American PEN in 2002. Much of Rushdie fiction is phantasmagorical, allegorical satire that deals with the clash between the religious and secular worlds, with religious and political hypocrisy, and with the alienation of the individual in a corrupt society. In commenting on the fatwa Rushdie has said: "What is freedom of expression? Without the freedom to offend, it ceases to exist."

The following excerpt is from *The Moor's Last Sigh.* The saga of the Zogoiby family as narrated by the last surviving scion of a dynasty of intermarried Sephardic spice merchants from Cochin, India (who trace their ancestry back to the expulsion from Spain in 1492), it is also a biting satire on contemporary Indian history, politics, and culture.

From *The Moor's Last Sigh*

In August 1939 Aurora da Gama saw the cargo vessel *Marco Polo* still at anchor in Cochin harbour and flew into a rage at this sign that, in the interregnum between the deaths of her parents and her own arrival at full adulthood, her unbusinesslike uncle Aires was letting the reins of commerce slip through his indolent fingers. She directed her driver to "go like clappers" to C-50 (Pvt) Ltd Godown No. 1 at Ernakulam dock, and stormed into that cavernous storehouse; where she momentarily stalled, unnerved by the cool serenity of its light-shafted darkness, and by its blasphemous atmosphere of a gunny-sack cathedral, in which the scents of patchouli oil and cloves, of turmeric and fenugreek, of cumin and cardamom hung like the memory of music, while the narrow passages vanishing into the gloom between the high stacks of export-ready produce could have been roads to hell and back, or even to salvation.

(Great family trees from little 'corns: it is appropriate, is it not, that my personal story, the story of the creation of Moraes Zogoiby, should have its origins in a delayed pepper shipment?)

There were clergy in this temple too: shipping clerks bent over clipboards who went worrying and scurrying between the coolies loading their carts and the fearsomely emaciated trinity of comptrollers—Mr. Elaichipillai Kalonjee, Mr. V. S. Mirchandalchini and Mr. Karipattam Tejpattam—perching like an inquisition on high stools in pools of ominous lamplight and scratching with feathered nibs in gigantic ledgers which tilted towards them on desks with long, stork-stilty legs. Below these grand personages, at an everyday sort of desk with its own little lamp, sat the godown's duty manager, and it was upon him that Aurora descended, upon recovering her composure, to demand an explanation of the pepper shipment's delay.

"But what is Uncle thinking?" she cried, unreasonably, for how could so lowly a worm know the mind of the great Mr. Aires himself?" He wants family fortunes to drownofy or what?"

The sight at close quarters of the most beautiful of the da Gamas and the sole inheritrix of the family crores—it was common knowledge that while Mr. Aires and Mrs. Carmen were the incharges for the time being, the late Mr. Camoens had left them no more than an allowance, albeit a generous one—struck the duty manager like a spear in the heart, rendering him temporarily dumb. The young heiress leaned closer towards him, grabbed his chin between her thumb and forefinger, transfixed him with her fiercest glare, and fell head over heels in love. By the time the man had conquered his lightning-struck shyness and stammered out the news of the declaration of war between England and Germany, and of the skipper of the *Marco Polo*'s refusal to sail for England—"Possibility of attacks on merchant fleet, see"—Aurora had realised, with some anger at the treachery of her emotions, that on account of the ridiculous and inappropriate advent of passion she would have to defy class and convention by marrying this inarticulately handsome family employee at once. "It's like marrying the dratted driver," she scolded herself in blissful misery, and for a moment was so preoccupied by the sweet horror of her condition that she did not take in the name painted on the little block of wood on his desk.

"My God," she burst out when at last the white capitals insisted on being seen, "it isn't disgraceful enough that you haven't got a bean in your pocket or a tongue in your head, you had to be a Jew as well." And then, aside: "Face facts, Aurora. Thinkofy. You've fallen for a bloody godown Moses."

Pedantic white capitals corrected her (the object of her affections, thunderstruck, moon-struck, dry of mouth, thumping of heart, incipiently fiery of loin, was unable to do so, having been deprived anew of the power of speech by the burgeoning of feelings not usually encouraged in members of staff): Duty Manager Zogoiby's given name was not Moses but Abraham. If it is true that our names contain our fates, then seven capital letters confirmed that he was not to be a vanquisher of pharaohs, receiver of commandments or divider of waters; he would lead no people towards a promised land. Rather, he would offer up his son as a living sacrifice on the altar of a terrible love.

And "Zogoiby"?

"UNLUCKY." In Arabic, at least according to Cohen the chandler and Abraham's maternal family's lore. Not that anyone had even the most rudimentary knowledge of that faraway language. The very idea was alarming. "Just look at their writing," Abraham's mother Flory once remarked. "Even that is so violent, like knife-slashes and stab-wounds. Still and all: we also have come down from martial Jews. Maybe that's why we kept on this wrong-tongue Andalusian name."

(You ask: But if the name was his mother's, then how come the son . . . ? I answer: Control, please, your horses.)

"You are old enough to be her father." Abraham Zogoiby, born in the same year as deceased Mr. Camoens, stood stiffly outside the blue-tiled Cochin synagogue—*Tiles from Canton & No Two Are Identical,* said the little sampler on the ante-room wall—and, smelling strongly of spices and something else, faced his mother's wrath. Old Flory Zogoiby in a faded green calico frock sucked her gums and heard her son's stumbling confession of forbidden love. With her walking-stick she drew a line in the dust. On one side, the synagogue, Flory and history; on the other, Abraham, his rich girl, the universe, the future—all things unclean. Closing her eyes, shutting out Abrahamic odour and stammerings, she summoned up the past, using memories to forestall the moment at which she would have to disown her only child, because it was unheard-of for a Cochin Jew to marry outside the community; yes, her memory and behind and beneath it the longer memory of the tribe . . . the White Jews of India, Sephardim from Palestine, arrived in numbers (ten thousand approx.) in Year 72 of the Christian Era, fleeing from Roman persecution. Settling in Cranganore, they hired themselves out as soldiers to local princes. Once upon a time a battle between Cochin's ruler and his enemy the Zamorin of Calicut, the Lord of the Sea, had to be postponed because the Jewish soldiers would not fight on the Sabbath day.

O prosperous community! Verily, it flourishéd. And, in the year 379 CE, King Bhaskara Ravi Varman I granted to Joseph Rabban the little kingdom of the village of Anjuvannam near Cranganore. The copper plates upon which the gift was inscribed ended up at the tiled synagogue, in Flory's charge; because for many years, and in defiance of gender prejudices, she had held the honoured position of caretaker. They lay concealed in a chest under the altar, and she polished them from time to time with much enthusiasm and elbow-grease.

"A Christy wasn't bad enough, you had to pick the very worst of the bunch," Flory was muttering. But her gaze was still far away in the past, fixed upon Jewish cashews and areca-nuts and jack-fruit trees, upon the ancient waving fields of Jewish oilseed rape, the gathering of Jewish cardamoms, for had these not been the basis of the community's prosperity? "Now these come-latelies steal our business," she mumbled. "And proud of being bastards and all. Fitz-Vasco-da-Gamas! No better than a bunch of Moors."

If Abraham had not been knocked sideways by love, if the thunderbolt had been less recent, he would in all probability have held his tongue out of filial affection and the knowledge that Flory's prejudices could not be argued away. "I gave you a too-modern brought-up," she went on. "Christies and Moors, boy. Just hope on they never come for you."

But Abraham was in love, and hearing his beloved under attack he burst out with the observation that "in the first place if you look at things without cock-eyes you'd see that you also are a comelately Johnny," meaning that Black Jews had arrived in India long before the White, fleeing Jerusalem from Nebuchadnezzar's armies five hundred and eighty-seven years before the Christian Era, and even if you didn't care about them because they had intermarried with the locals and vanished long ago, there were, for example, the Jews who came from Babylon and Persia in 490 to 518 CE; and many centuries had passed since Jews started setting up shop in Cranganore and then in Cochin Town (a certain Joseph Azaar and his family moved there in 1344 as everybody knew), and even from Spain the Jews started arriving after their expulsion in 1492, including, in the first batch, the family of Solomon Castile . . .

Flory Zogoiby screamed at the mention of the name; screamed and shook her head from side to side.

"Solomon Solomon Castile Castile," thirty-six-year-old Abraham taunted his mother with childish vengefulness. "From whom descends at least this one *infant* of Castile. You want I should begat? All the way from Señor Leon Castile the swordsmith of Toledo who lost his head over some Spaini Princess Elephant-and-Castle, to my Daddyji who also must have been crazy, but the point is the Castiles got to Cochin twenty-two years before any Zogoiby, so *quod erat demonstrandum* . . . And in the second place Jews with Arab names and hidden secrets ought to watch who they're calling Moors."

Elderly men with rolled trouser-legs and women with greying buns emerged into the shady Jewish alley outside the Mattancherri synagogue and gave solemn witness to the quarrel. Above angry mother and retaliating son blue shutters flew open and there were heads at windows. In the adjoining cemetery Hebrew inscriptions waved on tombstones like half-mast flags at twilight. Fish and spices on the evening air. And Flory Zogoiby, at the mention of secrets of which she had never spoken, dissolved abruptly into stutters and jerks.

"A curse on all Moors," she rallied. "Who destroyed the Cranganore synagogue? Moors, who else. Local-manufacture made-in-India Othello-fellows. A plague on their houses and spouses." In 1524, ten years after Zogoibys arrived from Spain, there had been a Muslim-Jewish war in these parts. It was an old quarrel to revive, and Flory did so in the hope of turning her son's thoughts away from hidden matters. But oaths should not be lightly uttered, especially before witnesses. Flory's curse flew into the air like a startled chicken and hovered there a long while, as if uncertain of its intended destination. Her grandson Moraes Zogoiby would not be born for eighteen years; at which time the chicken came home to roost.

(And what did Muslims and Jews fight over in the *cinquecento*?—What else? The pepper trade.)

"Jews and Moors were the ones who went to war," old Flory grunted, goaded by misery into speaking a sentence too many, "and now your Christian Fitz-Vascos have gone and pinched the market from us both."

"You're a fine one to talk about bastards," cried Abraham Zogoiby who bore his mother's name. "Fitz she says," he addressed the gathering crowd: "I'll show her Fitz." Whereupon with furious intent he strode into the synagogue, with his mother scrambling after him, bursting into dry and shrieky tears.

ABOUT MY GRANDMOTHER Flory Zogoiby, Epifania da Gama's opposite number, her equal in years although closer to me by a generation: a decade before the century's turn Fearless Flory would haunt the boys' school playground, teasing adolescent males with swishings of skirts and sing-song sneers, and with a twig would scratch challenges into the earth—*step across this line.* (Line-drawing comes down to me from both sides of the family.) She would taunt them with nonsensical, terrifying incantations, "making like a witch":

> Obeah, jadoo, fo, fum,
> chicken entrails, kingdom come
> Ju-ju, voodoo, fee, fi,
> piddle cocktails, time to die.

When the boys came at her she attacked them with a ferocity that easily overcame their theoretical advantages of strength and size. Her gifts of war came down to her from some unknown ancestor; and though her adversaries grabbed her hair and called her jewess they never vanquished her. Sometimes she literally rubbed their noses in the dirt. On other occasions she stood back, scrawny arms folded in triumph across her chest, and allowed her stunned victims to back unsteadily away. "Next time pick on someone your own size," Flory added insult to injury by inverting the meaning of the phrase: "Us pint-size jewinas are too hot for you to handle." Yes, she was rubbing it in, but even this attempt to make metaphors of her victories, to represent herself as the champion of the small, of the Minority, of *girls,* failed to make her popular. Fast Flory, Flory-the-Roary: she acquired a Reputation.

The time came when nobody would cross the lines she went on drawing, with fearsome precision, across the gullies and open spaces of her childhood years. She grew moody and inward and sat on behind her dust-lines, besieged within her own fortifications. By her eighteenth birthday she had stopped fighting, having learned something about winning battles and losing wars.

The point I'm leading up to is that Christians had in Flory's view stolen more from her than ancestral spice fields. What they took was even then getting to be in short supply, and for a girl with a Reputation the supply was even shorter . . . in her twenty-fourth year Solomon Castile the synagogue caretaker had stepped across Miss Flory's lines to ask for her hand in marriage. The act was generally thought to be one of great charity, or stupidity, or both. Even in those days the numbers of the community were decreasing. Maybe four thousand persons living in the Mattancherri Jewtown, and by the time you excluded family members and the very young and the very old and the crazy and infirm, the youngsters of marriageable age were not spoiled for choice of partners. Old bachelors fanned themselves by the clocktower and walked by the harbour's edge hand in hand; toothless spinsters sat in doorways sewing clothes for non-existent babies. Matrimony inspired as much spiteful envy as celebration, and Flory's marriage to the caretaker was attributed by gossip to the ugliness of both parties. "As sin," the sharp tongues said. "Pity the kids, my *God.*"

(*Old enough to be her father,* Flory scolded Abraham; but Solomon Castile, born in the year of the Indian Uprising, had been twenty years her senior, *poor man probably wanted to get married while he was still capable,* the wagging tongues surmised . . . and there is one more fact about their wedding. It took place on the same day in 1900 as a much grander affair; no newspapers recorded the Castile-Zogoiby nuptials in their social-register columns, but there were many photographs of Mr. Francisco da Gama and his smiling Mangalorean bride.)

The vengefulness of the spouseless was finally satisfied: because after seven years and seven days of explosive wedlock, during which Flory gave birth to one child, a boy who would perversely grow up to be the most handsome young man of his dwindling generation, caretaker Castile at nightfall on his fiftieth birthday walked over to the water's edge, hopped into a rowingboat with half a dozen drunken Portuguese sailors, and ran away to sea. "He should have known better'n to marry Roary Flory," according to contented bachelor-spinster whispers, "but wise man's brain don't come automatic along with wise man's name." The broken marriage came to be known in Mattancherri as the Misjudgment of Solomon; but Flory blamed the Christian ships, the mercantile armada of the omnipotent west, for tempting her husband away in search of golden streets. And at the age of seven her son was obliged to give up his father's name; unlucky in fathers, he took his mother's unlucky Zogoiby for his own.

After Solomon's desertion, Flory took over as caretaker of blue ceramic tiles and Joseph Rabban's copper plates, claiming the post with a gleaming ferocity that silenced all rumbles of opposition to her appointment. Under her protection: not only little Abraham, but also the parchment Old Testament on whose ragged-edged leathery pages the Hebrew letters flowed, and the hollow golden crown presented (Christian Era 1805) by the Maharaja of Travancore. She instituted reforms. When the faithful came to worship she ordered them to remove their shoes. Objections were raised to this positively Moorish practice; Flory in response barked mirthless laughs.

"What devotion?" she snorted. "Caretaking you want from me, better you take some care too. Boots off! Chop chop! Protectee Chinee tiles."

No two are identical. The tiles from Canton, 12" x 12" approx., imported by Ezekiel Rabhi in the year 1100 CE, covered the floors, walls and ceiling of the little synagogue. Legends had begun to stick to them. Some said that if you explored for long enough you'd find your own story in one of the blue-and-white squares, because the pictures on the tiles could change, were changing, generation by generation, to tell the story of the Cochin Jews. Still others were convinced that the tiles were prophecies, the keys to whose meanings had been lost with the passing years.

Abraham as a boy crawled around the synagogue bum-in-air with his nose pressed against antique Chinese blue. He never told his mother that his father had reappeared in ceramic form on the synagogue floor a year after he decamped, in a little blue rowing-boat with blue-skinned foreign-looking types by his side, heading off towards an equally blue horizon. After this discovery, Abraham periodically received news of Solomon Castile through the good offices of the metamorphic tiles. He next saw his father in a cerulean scene of Dionysiac willow-pattern merrymaking amid slain dragons and grumbling volcanoes. Solomon was dancing in an open hexagonal pavilion with a carefree joy upon his blue-tile face which utterly transformed it from the dolorous countenance which Abraham remembered. If he is happy, the boy thought, then I'm glad he went. From his earliest days Abraham had instinctive knowledge of the paramountcy of happiness, and it was this same instinct which, years later, would allow the grown-up duty manager to seize the love offered with many blushes and sarcasms by Aurora da Gama in the chiaroscuro of the Ernakulam godown . . .

Over the years Abraham found his father wealthy and fat in one tile, seated upon cushions in the Position of Royal Ease and waited upon by eunuchs and dancing-girls; but only a few months later he was skinny and mendicant in another twelve-by-twelve scenario. Now Abraham understood that the former caretaker had left all restraints behind him, and was oscillating wildly through a life that had deliberately been allowed to go out of control. He was a Sindbad seeking his fortune in the oceanic happenstance of the earth. He was a heavenly body which had managed by an act of will to wrench itself free of its fixed orbit, and now wandered the galaxies accepting whatever destiny might provide. It seemed to Abraham that his father's breakaway from the gravity of the everyday had used up all his reserves of will-power, so that after that initial and radical act of transformation he was broken-ruddered, at the mercy of the winds and tides.

As Abraham Zogoiby neared adolescence, Solomon Castile began to appear in semi-pornographic tableaux whose appropriateness for a synagogue would have been the subject of much controversy had they come to anyone else's notice but Abraham's. These tiles cropped up in the dustiest and murkiest recesses of the building and Abraham preserved them by allowing mould to form and cobwebs to gather over their more reprehensible zones, in which his father disported himself with startling numbers of individuals of both sexes in a fashion which his wide-eyed son could only think of as educational. And yet in spite of the salacious gymnastics of these activities the ageing wanderer had regained his old lugubriousness of mien, so that, perhaps, all his journeys had done no more than wash him up at the last on the same shores of discontent whence he had first set forth. On the day Abraham Zogoiby's voice broke he was gripped by the notion that his father was about to return. He raced through the alleys of the Jewish quarter down to the waterfront where cantilevered Chinese fishing nets were spread out against the sky; but the fish he sought did not leap out of the waves. When he returned in despondency to the synagogue all the tiles depicting his father's odyssey had changed, and showed scenes both anonymous and banal. Abraham in a feverish rage spent hours crawling across the floor in search of magic. To no avail: for the second time in his life his unwise father Solomon Castile had vanished into the blue.

I NO LONGER REMEMBER when I first heard the family story which provided me with my nickname and my mother with the theme of her most famous series of paintings, the "Moor sequence" that reached its triumphant culmination in the unfinished, and subsequently stolen masterpiece, *The Moor's Last Sigh.* I seem to have known it all my life, this lurid saga from which, I should add, Mr. Vasco Miranda derived an early work of his own; but in spite of long familiarity I have grave doubts about the literal truth of the story, with its somewhat overwrought Bombay-talkie *masala* narrative, its almost desperate reaching back for a kind of authentification, for *evidence* . . . I believe, and others have since confirmed, that simpler explanations can be offered for the transaction between Abraham Zogoiby and his mother, most particularly for what he did or did not find in an old trunk underneath the altar; I will offer one such alternative version by and by. For the moment, I present the approved, and polished, family yarn; which, being so profound a part of my parents' pictures of themselves—and so significant a part of contemporary Indian art history—has, for those reasons if no other, a power and importance I will not attempt to deny.

We have reached a key moment in the tale. Let us return briefly to young Abraham on hands and knees, frantically searching the synagogue for the father who had just abandoned him again, calling out to him in a cracked voice swooping from bulbul to crow; until at length, overcoming an unspoken taboo, he ventured for the first time in his life behind & beneath the pale blue drape with golden hem that graced the high altar . . . Solomon Castile wasn't there; the teenager's flashlight fell, instead, upon an old box marked with a Z and fastened with a cheap padlock, which was soon picked; for schoolboys have skills which adults forget as surely as lessons learned by rote. And so, despairing of his absconded father, he found his mother's secrets out instead.

What was in the box?—Why, the only treasure of any value: viz., the past, and the future. Also, however, emeralds.

. . .

AND SO TO the day of crisis, when the adult Abraham Zogoiby charged into the synagogue—*I'll show her Fitz,* he cried—and dragged the trunk out from its hiding-place. His mother, pursuing him, saw her secrets coming out into the open and felt her legs give way. She sat down on blue tiles with a thump, while Abraham opened the box and drew out a silver dagger, which he stuck in his trouser-belt; then, breathing in short gasps, Flory watched him remove, and place upon his head, an ancient, tattered crown.

Not the nineteenth-century circlet of gold donated by Maharaja Travancore, but something altogether more ancient was the way I heard it. A dark green turban wound in cloth rendered illusory by age, so delicate that even the orange evening light filtering into the synagogue seemed too fierce; so provisional that it might almost have disintegrated beneath Flory Zogoiby's burning gaze . . .

And upon this phantasm of a turban, the family legend went, hung age-dulled chains of solid gold, and dangling off these chains were emeralds so large and green that they looked like toys. *It was four and a half centuries old, the last crown to fall from the head of the last prince of al-Andalus; nothing less than the crown of Granada, as worn by Abu Abdallah, last of the Nasrids, known as "Boabdil."*

"But how did it get there?" I used to ask my father. How indeed? This priceless headgear—this royal Moorish hat—how did it emerge from a toothless woman's box to sit upon the head of Abraham; future father, renegade Jew?

"It was," my father answered, "the uneasy jewellery of shame."

I continue, for the moment, without judging his version of events: When Abraham Zogoiby as a boy first discovered the hidden crown and dagger he replaced the treasures in their hiding-place, fastened the padlock tight and spent a night and a day fearing his mother's wrath. But once it became clear that his inquisitiveness had gone unnoticed his curiosity was reborn, and again he drew forth the little chest and again picked the lock. This time he found, wrapped in burlap in the turban-box, a small book made up of handwritten parchment pages crudely sewn together and bound in hide. It was written in Spanish, which the young Abraham did not understand, but he copied out a number of the names therein, and over the years that followed he unlocked their meanings, for instance by asking innocent questions of the crotchety and reclusive old chandler Moshe Cohen who was at that time the appointed head of the community and the keeper of its lore. Old Mr. Cohen was so astonished that any member of the younger generation should care about the old days that he had talked freely, pointing towards distant horizons while the handsome young man sat wide-eyed at his feet.

Thus Abraham learned that, in January 1492, while Christopher Columbus watched in wonderment and contempt, the Sultan Boabdil of Granada had surrendered the keys to the fortress-palace of the Alhambra, last and greatest of all the Moors' fortifications, to the all-conquering Catholic Kings Fernando and Isabella, giving up his principality without so much as a battle. He departed into exile with his mother and retainers, bringing to a close the centuries of Moorish Spain; and reining in his horse upon the Hill of Tears he turned to look for one last time upon his loss, upon the palace and the fertile plains and all the concluded glory of al-Andalus . . . at which sight the Sultan sighed, and hotly wept—whereupon his mother, the terrifying Ayxa the Virtuous, sneered at his grief. Having been forced to genuflect before an omnipotent queen, Boabdil was now obliged to suffer a further humiliation at the hands of an impotent (but formidable) dowager. *Well may you weep like a woman for what you could not defend like a man,* she taunted him: meaning of course the opposite. Meaning that she despised this blubbing male, her son, for yielding up what she would have fought for to the death, given the chance. She was Queen Isabella's equal and opposite; it was *reina Isabel's* good fortune to have come up against the mere cry-baby, Boabdil . . .

Suddenly, as the chandler spoke, Abraham curled upon a coil of rope felt all the mournful weight of Boabdil's coming-to-an-end, felt it as his own. Breath left his body with a whine, and the next breath was a gasp. The onset of asthma (more asthma! It's a wonder I can breathe at all!) was like an omen, a joining of lives across the centuries, or so Abraham fancied as he grew into his manhood and the illness gained in strength. *These wheezing sighs not only mine, but his. These eyes hot with his ancient grief. Boabdil, I too am thy mother's son.*

Was weeping such a weakness? he wondered. Was defending-to-the-death such a strength?

After Boabdil handed over the keys to the Alhambra, he diminished into the south. The Catholic Kings had allowed him an estate, but even this was sold out from under his feet by his most trusted courtier. Boabdil, the prince turned fool. He eventually died in battle, fighting under some other kingling's flag.

Jews too moved south in 1492. Ships bearing banished Jews into exile clogged the harbour at Cádiz, obliging the year's other voyager, Columbus, to sail from Palos de Moguer. Jews gave up the forging of Toledo steel; Castile's set sail for India. But not all Jews left at once. The Zogoibys, remember, were twenty-two years behind those old Castiles. What happened? Where did they hide?

"All will be told in good time, my son; all in own good time."

Abraham in his twenties learned secrecy from his mother, and to the annoyance of the small band of eligible women of his generation kept himself to himself, burrowing into the heart of the city and avoiding the Jewish quarter as much as possible, the synagogue most of all. He worked first for Moshe Cohen and then as a junior clerk for the da Gamas, and although he was a diligent worker and gained promotion early he wore the air of a man in waiting for something, and on account of his abstraction and beauty it became commonplace to say of him that he was a genius in the making, perhaps even the great poet that the Jews of Cochin had always yearned for but never managed to produce. Moshe Cohen's slightly too hairy niece Sara, a large-bodied girl waiting like an undiscovered sub-continent for Abraham's vessel to sail into her harbour, was the source of much of this speculative adulation. But the truth was that Abraham utterly lacked the artistic spark, his was a world of numbers, especially of numbers in action—his literature a balance-sheet, his music the fragile harmonies of manufacture and sale, his temple a scented warehouse. Of the crown and dagger in the wooden box he never spoke, so nobody knew that that was why he wore the look of a king in exile, and privily, in those years, he learned the secrets of his lineage, by teaching himself Spanish from books, and so deciphering what a twine-bound notebook had to say; until at last he stood crown-on-head in an orange evening and confronted his mother with his family's hidden shame.

OUTSIDE IN THE Mattancherri alley the enlarging crowd grew murmurous. Moshe Cohen, as community leader, took it upon himself to enter the synagogue, to mediate between the warring mother and son, for a synagogue was no place for such a quarrel; his daughter Sara followed him in, her heart slowly cracking beneath the weight of the knowledge that the great country of her love must remain virgin soil, that Abraham's treacherous infatuation with Aurora the infidel had condemned her for ever to the dreadful inferno of spinsterhood, the knitting of useless bootees and frockies, blue and pink, for the children who would never fill her womb.

"Going to run off with a Christian child, Abie," she said, her voice loud and harsh in the blue-tiled air, "and already you're dressing, up like a Christmas tree."

But Abraham was tormenting his mother with old papers bound up twixt twine and hide. "Who is the author?" he asked, and, as she remained silent, answered himself. "A woman." And, continuing with this catechism: "What was her name?—Not given.—What was she?—A Jew; who took shelter beneath the roof of the exiled Sultan; beneath his roof, and then between his sheets. Miscegenation," Abraham baldly stated, "occurred." And though it would have been easy enough to feel compassion for this pair, the dispossessed Spanish Arab and the ejected Spanish Jew—two powerless lovers making common cause against the power of the Catholic Kings—still it was the Moor alone for whom Abraham demanded pity. "His courtiers sold his lands, and his lover stole his crown." After years by his side, this anonymous ancestor crept away from crumbling Boabdil, and took ship for India, with a great treasure in her baggage, and a male child in her belly; from whom, after many begats, came Abraham himself. *My mother who insists on the purity of our race, what say you to your forefather the Moor?*

"The woman has no name," Sara interrupted him. "And yet you claim her tainted blood is yours. Have you no shame, to make your mummy weep? And all for a rich girl's love, Abraham, I swear. It stinks, and by the way, so do you."

From Flory Zogoiby came a thin assenting wail. But Abraham's argument was not complete. *Consider this stolen crown, wrapped in rags, locked in a box, for four hundred years and more. If it was stolen for simple gain, would it not have been sold off long ago?*

"Because of secret pride in the royal link, the crown was kept; because of secret shame, it was concealed. Mother, who is worse? My Aurora who does not hide the Vasco connection, but takes delight; or myself; born of the fat old Moor of Granada's last sighs in the arms of his thieving mistress—Boabdil's bastard Jew?"

"Evidence," Flory whispered in reply, a mortally wounded adversary pleading for the death-blow." Only supposition has been given; where are hard-fast facts?" Inexorable Abraham asked his penultimate question.

"Mother, what is our family name?"

When she heard this, Flory knew the coup-de-grâce was near. Dumbly, she shook her head. To Moshe Cohen, whose old friendship he would, that day, forsake for ever, Abraham threw down a challenge. "The Sultan Boabdil after his fall was known by one sobriquet, and she who took his crown and jewels in a dark irony took the nickname also. Boabdil the Misfortunate: that was it. Anyone here can say that in the Moor's own tongue?"

And the old chandler was obliged to complete the proof. *"El-zogoybi."*

Gently, Abraham set down the crown beside defeated Flory; resting his case.

"At least he fell for a pushy girl," Flory said emptily to the walls. "I had that much influence while he was still my son."

"Better you go now," said Sara to pepper-odorous Abraham. "Maybe when you marry you should take the girl's name, why not? Then we can forget you, and what difference between a bastard Moor and a bastard Portugee?"

"A bad mistake, Abie," old Moshe Cohen commented. "To make an enemy of your mother; for enemies are plentiful, but mothers are hard to find."

FLORY ZOGOIBY, alone in the aftermath of one catastrophic revelation was granted another. In the sunset's vermilion afterglow she saw the Cantonese tiles pass before her eyes one by one, for had she not been their servitor and their student, cleaning and buffing them these many years; had she not many times attempted to enter their myriad worlds, those universes contained within the uniformity of twelve-by-twelve and held captive on so-neatly-grouted walls? Flory who loved to draw lines was enthralled by the serried ranks of the tiles, but until this moment they had not spoken to her, she had found there neither missing husbands nor future admirers, neither prophecies of the future nor explanations of the past. Guidance, meaning, fortune, friendship, love had all been withheld. Now in her hour of anguish they unveiled a secret.

Scene after blue scene passed before her eyes. There were tumultuous marketplaces and crenellated fortress-palaces and fields under cultivation and thieves in jail, there were high, toothy mountains and great fish in the sea. Pleasure gardens were laid out in blue, and blue-bloody battles were grimly fought; blue horsemen pranced beneath lamplit windows and blue-masked ladies swooned in arbours. O, and intrigue of courtiers and dreams of peasants and pigtailed tallymen at their abacuses and poets in their cups. On the walls floor ceiling of the little synagogue, and now in Flory Zogoiby's mind's eye, marched the ceramic encyclopaedia of the material world that was also a bestiary, a travelogue, a synthesis and a song, and for the first time in all her years of caretaking Flory saw what was missing from the hyperabundant cavalcade. "Not so much what as who," she thought, and the tears dried in her eyes. "In the whole place, no trace." The orange light of evening fell on her like thunderous rain, washing away her blindness, opening her eyes. Eight hundred and thirty-nine years after the tiles came to Cochin, and at the beginning of a time of war and massacres, they delivered their message to a woman in pain.

What you see is what there is," Flory mumbled under her breath. "There is no world but the world." And then, a little louder: "There is no God. Hocus-pocus! Mumbo-jumbo! *There is no spiritual life.*"

IT ISN'T HARD to demolish Abraham's arguments. What's in a name? The da Gamas claimed descent from Vasco the explorer, but claiming isn't proving, and even about that ancestry I have my serious doubts. But as for this Moor-stuff this Granada-yada, this incredibly *loose* connection—a surname that sounds like a nickname, for Pete's sake!—it falls down even before you blow on it. Old leather-bound notebook? Gas! Never seen it. Not a trace. As for the emerald-laden crown, I don't buy that, either; it's a fairy tale of the sort we folks love to tell ourselves about ourselves, and, gents & gentesses, it does not wash. Abraham's had never been a wealthy family, and if you believe that a boxful of gems would have remained untouched for four centuries, then, busters and busterinas, you'll believe anything. Oh, but they were *hair-looms*? Well, roll my eyes and strike my brow! What a blank-blank joke! Who in the whole of India cares two paisa about heirlooms if he's given the choice between old stuff and money in the bank?

Aurora Zogoiby painted some famous pictures, and passed away in horrific circs. Reason requires that we put the rest down to the self-mythologising of the artist, to which, in this instance, my dear father lent more than just a hand . . . you want to know what was in the box? Listen: forget about jewelled turbans; but emeralds, yes. Sometimes more, sometimes less.—Not heirlooms, though.—What then?—Hot rocks, that's what. Yes! Stolen goods! Contraband items! Loot! You want family shame, I'll tell you its true name: my granny, Flory Zogoiby, was a crook. For many years she was a valued member of a successful gang of emerald smugglers; for who would ever look under the synagogue altar for boodle? She took her cut of the proceeds, kept it safe, and was not so foolish as to spend spend spend. Nobody ever suspected her; and the time came when her son Abraham came to claim his illegal inheritance . . . it's illegitimacy you want? Never mind about genetics; just follow the cash.

The above is my understanding of what lay behind the stories I was told; but there is also a confession I must make. In what follows you will find stranger tales by far than the one I have just attempted to debunk;

and let me assure you, let me say to-whom-it-may-concern, that of the truth of these further stories there can be no doubt whatsoever. So finally it is not for me to judge, but for you. And as for the yarn of the Moor: if I were forced to choose between logic and childhood memory, between head and heart, then sure; in spite of all the foregoing, I'd go along with the tale.

ABRAHAM ZOGOIBY WALKED out of Jewtown and towards St. Francis's Church, where Aurora da Gama was waiting for him by Vasco's tomb with his future in the palm of her hand. When he reached the waterfront he looked back for a moment; and thought he saw, silhouetted against the darkening sky, the impossible figure of a young girl capering upon the roof of a storehouse painted in gaudy horizontal stripes, can-canning her skirt and petticoat and uttering familiar sorceries as she challenged him to fight: *Step across this line.*

> "Obeah, jadoo, fo, fum,
> chicken entrails, kingdom come."

Tears filled his eyes; he pushed them away. She was gone.

Selected Further Readings

THIS BIBLIOGRAPHY is meant as guide for English-language readers to delve into the history and literature of the Sephardim. It is by no means exhaustive.

Alcalay, Ammiel. *After Jews and Arabs: Remaking Levantine Culture.* Minneapolis: University of Minnesota Press, 1993.

———, ed. *Keys to the Garden: New Israeli Writing.* San Francisco: City Lights Books, 1996.

———, *Memories of Our Future: Selected Essays, 1982–1999.* Introduction by Juan Goytisolo. San Francisco: City Lights, 1999.

Altabé, David F. *Spanish and Portuguese Jewry Before and After 1492.* Brooklyn, N.Y.: Sepher-Hermon Press, 1993.

Angel, Marc. *"La America": The Sephardic Experience in the United States.* Philadelphia: Jewish Publication Society, 1982.

———. *Voices in Exile: A Study in Sephardic Intellectual History.* Hoboken, N.J.: KTAV, in association with Sephardic House, 1991.

Armistead, Samuel G., and Mishael M. Caspi, with Murray Baumgarten, eds. *Jewish Culture in the Hispanic World.* Newark, Del.: Juan de la Cuesta, 2001.

Ashtor, Eliyahu, *The Jews in Muslim Spain.* 3 vols. Translated from the Hebrew by Aaron Klein and Jenny Machlowitz. Philadelphia: Jewish Publication Society, 1973–84.

Avni, Haim. *Spain, the Jews and Franco.* Translated from the Hebrew by Emanuel Shimoni. Philadelphia: Jewish Publication Society, 1982.

Baer, Yitzhak. *A History of the Jews in Christian Spain.* 2 vols. Translated from the Hebrew by Louis Schofman. Philadelphia: Jewish Publication Society, 1966.

Barnet, Richard D., ed. *The Sephardi Heritage: Essays on the History and Cultural Contribution of the Jews of Spain and Portugal.* New York: Ktav, 1971.

Beinart, Haim. *The Expulsion of the Jews from Spain.* Translated by Jeffrey M. Green. Oxford, Eng., and Portland, Ore.: Littman Library of Jewish Civilization, 2002.

———, ed. *Moreshet Sepharad = The Sephardi Legacy.* Jerusalem: Magnes Press, 1992.

Benardete, José Meier. *Hispanic Culture and the Character of the Sephardic Jews.* New York: Hispanic Institute in the United States, 1953.

Benbassa, Esther, with Aaron Rodrigue. *Sephardi Jewry: A History of the Judeo-*

Spanish Community, 14th–20th centuries. Berkeley: University of California Press, 2000.

Bunis, D. M. *Voices from Jewish Salonika. Selections from the Judezmo Satirical Series Tío Ezra i su mujer Benuta and Tío Bohor i su mujer Djamila by Moshe Cazes.* Jerusalem: Magnes, 1999.

Cohen, Martin A., with Abraham J. Peck, eds. *Sephardim in the Americas: Studies in Culture and History.* Tuscaloosa: University of Alabama Press, 1993.

Díaz Más, Paloma. *Sephardim: The Jews from Spain.* Translated by George K. Zucker. Chicago: University of Chicago Press, 1992.

Elazar, Daniel Judah. *The Other Jews: The Sephardim Today.* New York: Basic Books, 1989.

Faber, Eli. *A Time for Planting: The First Migration, 1654–1820.* Baltimore, Md.: Johns Hopkins University Press, 1992.

Friedenreich, Harriet Pass. *The Jews of Yugoslavia: A Quest for Community.* Philadelphia: Jewish Publication Society, 1979.

Gampel, Benjamin R., ed. *Crisis and Creativity in the Sephardic World, 1391–1648.* New York: Columbia University Press, 1997.

Gaon, Solomon, with M. Mitchell Serels, eds. *Del fuego: Sephardim and the Holocaust.* New York: Sepher-Hermon Press, 1995.

Gerber, Jane S. *The Jews of Spain: A History of the Sephardic Experience.* New York: Free Press, 1992.

Gitlitz, David M. *Secrecy and Deceit: The Religion of the Crypto-Jews.* Introduction by Ilan Stavans. Albuquerque, N.M. University of New Mexico Press, 2002.

Haboucha, Reginetta. *Types and Motifs of the Judeo-Spanish Folktales.* New York: Garland, 1992.

Kaplan, Gregory B. *The Evolution of Converso Literature: The Writings of the Converted Jews of Medieval Spain.* Gainesville, Fla.: University Press of Florida, 2002.

Kaplan, Yosef. *An Alternative Path to Modernity: The Sephardi Diaspora in Western Europe.* Leiden and Boston: Brill, 2000.

Kedourie, Elie, ed. *Spain and the Jews: The Sephardi Experience: 1492 and After.* London: Thames and Hudson, 1992.

Lazar, Moshe, ed. *Sepharad in My Heart: A Ladino Reader.* Lancaster, Calif.: Labyrinthos, 1999.

———, ed. *The Sephardic Tradition: Ladino and Spanish-Jewish Literature.* New York: W. W. Norton, 1971.

———, with Stephen Haliczer, eds. *The Jews of Spain and the Expulsion of 1492.* Lancaster, Calif.: Labyrinthos, 1997.

Leroy, Béatrice. *L'Aventure séfarade.* Paris: Flammarion, 1991.

Lévy, Isaac Jack, ed. *And the World Stood Silent: Sephardic Poetry of the Holocaust.* Urbana: University of Illinois Press, 1989.

Logghe, J., and M. Sagan. *Another Desert: Jewish Poetry of New Mexico.* Santa Fe, N.M. Sherman Asher, 1999.

Matza, Diane, ed. *Sephardic-American Voices: Two Hundred Years of a Literary Legacy.* Hanover, N.H.: Brandeis University Press, 1997.

Menocal, María Rosa. *The Ornament of the World: How Muslims, Jews, and Christians Created a Culture of Tolerance in Medieval Spain.* Foreword by Harold Bloom. Boston: Little, Brown, 2002.

———, with Raymond P. Scheindlin and Michael Sells. *The Literature of Al-Andalus.* New York and Cambridge: Cambridge University Press, 2000.

Nepaulsigh, Colbert I. *Apples of Gold in Filigrees of Silver: Jewish Writing in the Eye of the Spanish Inquisition.* New York: Holmes and Meier, 1995.

Netanyahu, Benzion. *The Origins of the Inquisition in 15th Century Spain.* New York: Random House, 1996.

———. *The Marranos of Spain: From the Late 14th to the Early 16th Century, According to Contemporary Sources.* 3rd ed. Ithaca, N.Y.: Cornell University Press, 1999.

Oelman, Timothy, ed. and trans. *Marrano Poets of the Seventeenth Century: An Anthology of the Poetry of João Pinto Delgado, Antonio Enríquez Gómez, and Miguel de Barrios.* Rutherford and London: Fairleigh Dickinson University Press, 1982.

Papo, I., with R. Ovidija, G. Camhy, and C. Nikoidiski. *Cuentos sobre los sefardíes de Sarajevo: A Collection of Sephardic Stories from Sarajevo.* Split, Yugoslovia: Lagos, 1994.

Perera, Victor. *The Cross and the Pear Tree: A Sephardic Journey.* New York: Alfred A. Knopf, 1995.

Raphael, Chaim. *The Road from Babylon: The Story of Sephardi and Oriental Jews.* New York: Harper & Row, 1985.

Raphael, David. *The Expulsion 1492 Chronicles.* North Hollywood, Calif.: Carmi House Press, 1991.

Rodrigue, Aaron, ed. *Ottoman and Turkish Jewry: Community and Leadership.* Bloomington, Ind.: Indiana University, 1992.

Roth, Cecil. *History of the Jews in Italy.* Philadelphia: Jewish Publication Society, 1946.

———. *History of the Marranos.* Philadelphia: Jewish Publication Society, 1932.

Sachar, Howard Morley. *Farewell España: The World of the Sephardim Remembered.* New York: Alfred A. Knopf, 1994.

Shaw, Stanford J. *The Jews of the Ottoman Empire and the Turkish Republic.* New York: New York University Press, 1991.

Stavans, Ilan. *The Inveterate Dreamer: Essays and Conversations on Jewish Culture.* Lincoln: University of Nebraska Press, 2001.

———, ed. *The Scroll and the Cross: 1,000 Years of Hispanic-Jewish Literature.* New York and London: Routledge, 2003.

———, ed. *Tropical Synagogues: Shorts Stories by Jewish-Latin American Writers.* New York: Holmes and Meier, 1994.

Stillman, Norman A. *The Jews of Arab Lands in Modern Times.* Philadelphia: Jewish Publication Society, 1991.

Stillman, Yedid K., with George K. Zucker, eds. *New Horizons in Sephardic Studies.* Albany: State University of New York Press, 1993.

———, with George K. Zucker, eds. *From Iberia to Diaspora: Studies in Sephardic History and Culture.* Leiden and Boston: Brill, 1999.

Zuccotti, Susan. *The Italians and the Holocaust: Persecution, Rescue, and Survival.* New York: Basic Books, 1987.

Acknowledgments

THIS ANTHOLOGY is the product of sheer serendipity. The original idea for it came to me on an autumn evening in early 1998 in Stanford from Doug Abrams, then an editor at the University of California Press. He stopped me in an amphitheater after a performance, introduced himself (we were unaquainted), and, without further ado, stated that it was my *mandate* to edit a collection of Sephardic gems. I smiled and moved on. Soon he and I became friends. I put some thought into the matter, but other endeavors forced me to let the idea go by unattended until Eric Zinner of New York University Press, in a chatty telephone conversation, revived it in 2003. Again, Zinner put it less as a matter of free choice than as a command. This time around, I obliged. My heartfelt gratitude to Abrams and Zinner for serving as conduits and for making me come to terms with my duty.

Thanks to my friend and editor Altie Karper at Schocken Books, a division of Random House, Inc., for embracing the project instantaneously. She and I became acquainted years ago regarding a compilation of Latin American folktales. Our conversation quickly moved to Jewish culture and soon after to Sephardic civilization. I'm thrilled that the journey was done with such warm and encouraging a companion at my side.

Over the last six years, I've held innumerable conversations with friends and colleagues about Sephardim in general and about Sephardic literature in particular. Those conversations were a learning tool, and the contents of this volume was shaped by them. To name all the friends and colleagues who have answered my queries and defined my path is impossible. Nevertheless, I wish to acknowledge the irreplaceable ones: Glenda Abramson, André Aciman, Jennifer M. Acker, Kathleen Alcalá, Ammiel Alcalay, Robert Alter, Harold Augenbraum, Rifat Bali, Karen Barkey, Ruth Behar, Daniel Belasco, Aviva Ben-Ur, Dwayne E. Carpenter, Martin A. Cohen, Morris Dickstein, Ariel Dorfman, Blake Eskin, Moris Farhi, Lawrence Fine, Ellen Frankel, David M. Gitlitz, Hillel Halkin, Hugo Hiriart, Steven G. Kellman, Sorrel Kerbel, Gloria Kirchheimer, José Kozer, Luis S. Krausz, Shulamit Magnus, Robert Mandel, Ronnie Margulies, Angelina Muñiz-Huberman, Brigitte Natanson, Alana Newhouse, Rosa Nissán, Achy Obejas, Victor Perera, Daniel Asa Rose, Jonathan Rosen, Carl Rosenberg, Ruth Knafo Setton, Anthony Rudolf, Stephen A. Sadow, Gabriel Sanders, Moacyr Scliar, Ken Schoen, Guita Schyfter, Gershom Shaked, Neal Sokol, Joseph Tovares, Ruth R. Wisse, A. B. Yehoshua, and James E. Young.

In the composition of headnotes I made substantial use of *Jewish Writers of the Twentieth Century,* edited by Sorrel Kerbel (London: Fitzroy Dearborn, 2003). The essay by Abraham Joshua Heschel discussed in the introduction is "The Eastern European Era in Jewish History," included in *Voices from the Yiddish: Essays, Memoirs, Diaries,* edited by Irving Howe and Eliezer Greenberg (Ann Arbor: University of Michigan Press, 1972: 67–86). I also made use of "The Slow Agony of Judeo-Spanish Literature," by Edouard Roditi (*World Literature Today* 60,2 [Spring 1986]: 244–46). Finally, thanks to Haya Hoffman at the Institute for the Translation of Hebrew Literature for her help in exploring Israeli fiction and sorting out permissions. I also benefited from the assistance of Margaret A. Groesbeck and Michael Kasper at Frost Library, Amherst College. Patrice Silverstein did a thorough copyediting job, curing me from some self-inflicted wounds—my appreciation.

I'm also grateful for permission to reprint the following material:

André Aciman: "The Last Seder," from *Out of Egypt: A Memoir,* by André Aciman. New York: Farrar, Straus and Giroux, 1994. © 1994 by André Aciman. Used by permission of Farrar, Straus and Giroux, LLC.

Grace Aguilar: "The Escape," from *Grace Aguilar: Selected Writings,* edited by Michael Galchinsky. Peterborough, Ont.: Broadview Literary Texts, 2003.

Ammiel Alcalay: "The Quill's Embroidery: Untangling a Tradition," from *Memories of the Future: Selected Essays, 1982–1999,* by Ammiel Alcalay. San Francisco: City Lights Books, 1999. Used by permission of the author.

Gina Alhadeff: from *The Sun at Midday: Tales of a Mediterranean Family,* by Gini Alhadeff. © 1997 by Gina Alhadeff. Used by permission of Pantheon Books, a division of Random House.

Giorgio Bassani: "A Plaque on Via Mazzini," from *Five Tales from Ferrara,* by Giorgio Bassani. Translated from the Italian by William Weaver. New York: Harcourt Brace Jovanovich, 1971. Used by permission of the publisher.

Ruth Behar: "Never Marry a Man Who Doesn't Beat You." Used by permission of the author.

Yehuda Burla: "Two Sisters," in *Jewish Frontier,* October 1964: 167–24. Used by permission of the editors of *Jewish Frontier.*

Elias Canetti: "Family Pride," "*Kako la Gallinica:* Wolves and Werewolves," "Purim; the Comet," and "The Magic Language: The Fire," from *The Tongue Set Free: Remembrance of a European Childhood.* Translated from the German by Joachim Neugroschel. Translation copyright © 1979 by Joachim Neugroschel. New York: Seabury Press, 1979. Used by permission of Farrar, Straus and Giroux, LLC.

Veza Canetti: "Yom Kippur, the Day of Atonment" from *The Tortoises,* by Veza Canetti. Translated from the German by Ian Mitchell. © 1999 by Elias Canetti Erne. Translation copyright © 2001 by Ian Mitchell. Reprinted by permission of New Directions.

Hélène Cixous: "Coming to Writing," from *"Coming to Writing" and Other Essays,* by Hélène Cixous. Translated from the French by Sarah Cornell, Deborah Jenson, Ann Liddle, and Susan Sellers. Edited by Deborah Jenson. Cambridge and London: Harvard University Press, 1991. Used by permission of the President and Fellows of Harvard College.

Albert Cohen: From *Book of My Mother,* by Albert Cohen. Translated from the French by Bella Cohen. London and Paris: Peter Owen and UNESCO Publishing, 1997. Used by permission of the publisher.

Moris Farhi: "A Tale of Two Cities," from *Young Turk,* by Moris Farhi. London: Saqi Books, 2004. © 2004 by Moris Farhi. Used by permission of Saqi Books.

Natalia Ginzburg: "He and I," from *The Little Virtues,* by Natalia Ginzburg. Translated from the Italian by Dick Davis. New York: Seaver Books, 1986. Used by permission of the publisher.

Edmond Jabès: From *The Book of Questions.* Translated from the French by Rosmarie Waldrop. Middletown, Conn.: Wesleyan University Press, 1976. Used by permission of the publisher.

Ruth Knafo Setton: "Ten Ways to Recognize a Sephardic 'Jew-ess,' " from *The Best Contemporary Jewish Writing 2002,* edited by Michael Lerner. San Francisco: Jossey-Bass, 2002. Used by permission of the author.

Danilo Kiš: From *Garden, Ashes,* by Danilo Kiš. Translated from the Serbo-Croatian by William J. Hannaher. English translation copyright © 1975 by Harcourt. Reprinted by permission of the publisher.

Emma Lazarus: "In the Jewish Synagogue of Newport," "The New Colossus," and "The Banner of the Jew," from *Emma Lazarus: Selected Poems and Other Writings,* edited by Gregory Eiselein. Peterborough, Ont.: Broadview Literary Texts, 2002.

Primo Levi: "Shemà," from *Primo Levi: Collected Poems,* by Primo Levi. Translated from the Italian by Ruth Feldman and Brian Swann. London and Boston: Faber and Faber, 1988. Used by permission of Farrar, Straus and Giroux, LLC. "Story of a Coin," from *Moments of Reprieve,* by Primo Levi. Translated from the Italian by Ruth Feldman. New York: Summit Books, 1986. Used by permission of Simon & Schuster Adult Publishing Group.

Albert Memmi: "Chosen Out of Many," from *The Pillar of Salt,* by Albert Memmi. Translated from the French by Edouard Roditi. © 1955 by Criterion Books, Inc. Reprinted by permission of Beacon Press, Boston.

Sami Michael: From *Refugue,* by Sami Michael. Translated from the Hebrew by Edward Grossman. Philadelphia: Jewish Publication Society, 1988. © 1988 by the Jewish Publication Society. Used by permission of the Jewish Publication Society.

Angelina Muñiz-Huberman: "The Most Precious Offering," from *Enclosed Garden,* by Angelina Muñiz-Huberman. Translated from the Spanish by Lois Parkinson Zamora. Pittsburgh: Latin American Review Press, 1988. Used by permission of the publisher.

Yehuda Haim Aaron ha-Cohen Perahia: "After the Catastrophe in Salonika," from *And the World Stood Silent: Sephardic Poetry of the Holocaust*, edited and translated by Isaac Jack Lévy. Urbana and Chicago: University of Illinois Press, 2002. Used by permission of the publisher.

Victor Perera: "Israel," from *The Cross and the Pear Tree: A Sephardic Journey*, by Victor Perera. New York: Alfred A. Knopf, 1995. Used by permission of the publisher.

Shlomo Reuven: "Yom Hachoa," from *And the World Stood Silent: Sephardic Poetry of the Holocaust*, edited and translated by Isaac Jack Lévy. Urbana and Chicago: University of Illinois Press, 2002. Used by permission of the publisher.

Edouard Roditi: "Experience of Death" from *Thrice Chosen*, by Edouard Roditi. Berkeley, Calif.: Tree Books, 1974.

Salman Rushdie: Fragment from *The Moor's Last Sight*, by Salman Rushdie. New York: Pantheon, 1995. © 1992 by Salman Rushdie. Used by permission of Pantheon, a division of Random House.

Sami Shalom Chetrit: "Who Is a Jew and What Kind of a Jew?," by Sami Shalom Chetrit. Translated by Ammiel Alcalay. From *Keys to the Garden: New Israeli Writing*, edited by Ammiel Alcalay. San Francisco: City Lights Books, 1996. Used by permission of the author.

A. B. Yehoshua: "Partners," from *Mr. Manni*, by A. B. Yehoshua. Translated from the Hebrew by Hillel Halkin. © 1992 by Doubleday, a division of Bantam Doubleday Dell. Used by permission of Doubleday, a division of Random House.

Every effort has been made to locate the copyright holder of the entries in this anthology. In the event of an error or omission, please notify the publisher.

Index of Themes

Jewish Holidays

Jews and Islam

The Holocaust

Spain and Portugal

A Note About the Editor

Ilan Stavans is the Lewis-Sebring Professor in Latin American and Latino Culture at Amherst College. His books include *The Hispanic Condition* (1995), *Art and Anger* (1996), *The Oxford Book of Jewish Stories* (1998), *Mutual Impressions* (1999), *The Essential Ilan Stavans* (2000), *On Borrowed Words* (2001), *Octavio Paz: A Meditation* (2002), *The Poetry of Pablo Neruda,* and *Spanglish: The Making of a New American Language* (both 2003). The Library of America published his three-volume edition of *Stories by Isaac Bashevis Singer* in 2004. Stavans is general editor of the *Jewish-Latin America* series at the University of New Mexico Press. His work has been translated into a dozen languages.